MAD
SHIP

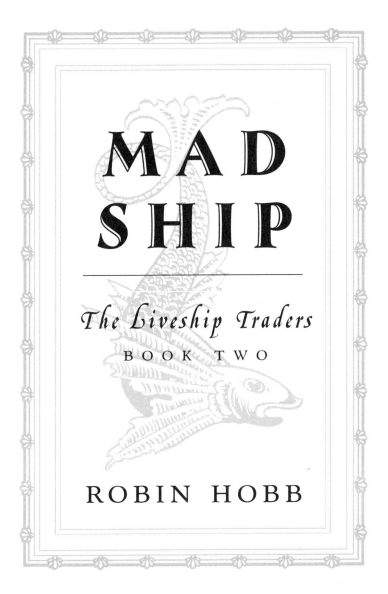

MAD SHIP

The Liveship Traders

BOOK TWO

ROBIN HOBB

BANTAM BOOKS

New York Toronto London Sydney Auckland

MAD SHIP

A Bantam Spectra Book/April 1999

SPECTRA and the portrayal of a boxed "s" are trademarks of Bantam Books,
a division of Random House, Inc.

Map illustration by James Sinclair

Book design by Laurie Jewell

Library of Congress Cataloging-in-Publication Data
Hobb, Robin.
Mad ship / Robin Hobb.
p.   cm. — (The liveship traders : bk. 2)
ISBN 0-553-10333-4
I. Title.   II. Series: Hobb, Robin. Liveship traders : bk. 2.
PS3558.O33636M33   1999
813'.54—dc21   98-51188
                                                          CIP

Published simultaneously in the United States and Canada

Bantam Books are published by Bantam Books, a division of Random House, Inc. Its trademark,
consisting of the words "Bantam Books" and the portrayal of a rooster, is Registered in U.S.
Patent and Trademark Office and in other countries. Marca Registrada. Bantam Books, 1540
Broadway, New York, New York 10036.

PRINTED IN THE UNITED STATES OF AMERICA
BVG   10 9 8 7 6 5 4 3 2 1

MAD
SHIP

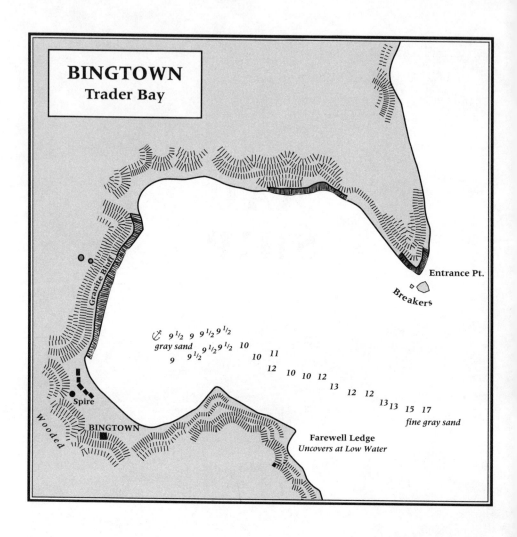

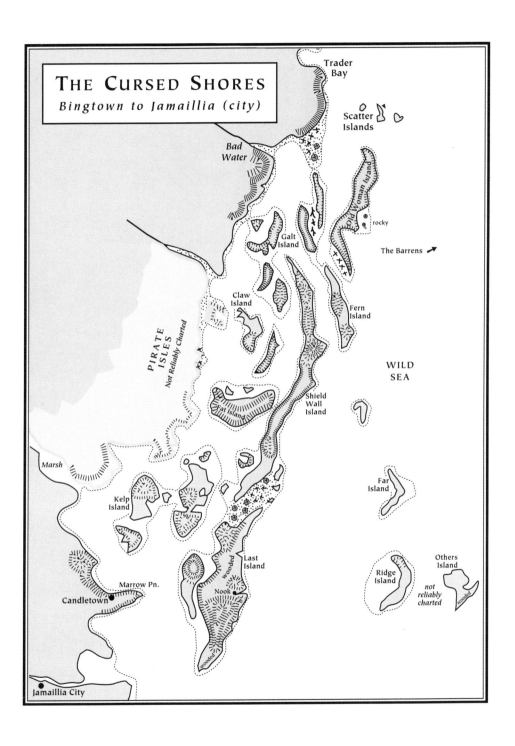

THE CURSED SHORES
Bingtown to Jamaillia (city)

Trader Bay

Scatter Islands

Bad Water

Old Woman Island

rocky

The Barrens

Galt Island

Claw Island

Fern Island

PIRATE ISLES
Not Reliably Charted

WILD SEA

Far Island

Shield Wall Island

Marsh

Kelp Island

Far Island

Last Island

Others Island

Ridge Island

not reliably charted

wooded

Marrow Pn.

Candletown

Nook

wooded

Jamaillia City

SPRING

A Recollection of Wings

BELOW THE SERPENTS, THE BEDS OF WEEDS SWAYED GENTLY IN THE CHANG-ing tide. The water was warm here, as warm as it had been in the south before they had migrated. Despite Maulkin's declaration that they would no longer follow the silvery provider, her tantalizing scent hung in the salt water. She was not far away; they trailed her still, but at a distance. Shreever considered confronting him about it, but decided against it. She eyed their leader anxiously. The injuries Maulkin had taken in his brief battle with the white serpent were healing slowly. The gouges disrupted the pattern of his scales. The golden false-eyes that ran the length of his body and proclaimed him a prophet were faded and dull.

Shreever, too, felt faded and dull.

They had come far in search of One Who Remembers. Maulkin had been so confident at the beginning of their journey. Now he seemed as confused as she and Sessurea were. The three of them were all that re-mained of the great tangle of sea serpents who had begun the migration. The others in their tangle had lost faith in their quest, and had fallen away from Maulkin. The last she had seen of them, they had been follow-ing a great dark provider, feeding mindlessly on the unresisting flesh it distributed to them. That had been many tides ago.

"Sometimes," Maulkin confided to Shreever quietly as they rested, "I lose my place in time. It seems to me that we have come this way before, done these things before, perhaps even shared these words before. Some-times I believe it so strongly that I think that today is actually a memory or a dream. I think, then, that perhaps we need do nothing, for whatever has happened to us will occur again. Or has, perhaps, already occurred." His voice was without strength or conviction.

She flanked him. They undulated gently in the current, finning no more than they must to maintain their position. Beneath them, Sessurea shook his mane suddenly, releasing a thin waft of toxins to alert them. "Look! Food!" he bugled.

Silver and shimmering, the school of fish came gliding toward them like a blessing. Behind the fish, shadowing them and feeding from the edges of the school, was another tangle of serpents. Three scarlets, a green and two blues they were. The hunters were not a large tangle but they appeared lively and healthy. Their gleaming hides and full flesh contrasted markedly with the slipping scales and sunken sides of Maulkin's tangle.

"Come," Maulkin bade them, and led them to join the others in their feeding. Shreever made a tiny sound of relief. There would be, at least, full bellies for them. Perhaps the others might even join Maulkin's tangle, once they realized he was a prophet.

Their prey were not separate fish, but a school, silver and glinting, baffling to the eye. They moved as one creature, yet it was a creature that could separate and stream around a clumsy hunter. The serpents of Maulkin's tangle were not clumsy hunters, and all three flowed gracefully after the fish. The other tangle trumpeted warnings at them, but Shreever saw no danger. With a lash of her tail, she drove herself into the school, her gaping jaws engulfing at least three fish. She distended her throat to swallow them.

Two scarlet serpents suddenly turned aside and struck Maulkin, battering him with their snouts as if he were a shark or other mutual enemy. The blue came after Shreever, jaws gaping. With a swift coiling she eluded him, changing direction to dart away. She saw the other scarlet try to wrap Sessurea. The scarlet's mane was distended, spewing poison as he trumpeted obscenities and threats. There was neither sense nor syntax to his curses, only fury.

She fled, shrilling her fear and confusion. Maulkin did not follow. He shook his great mane, releasing a cloud of toxins that near stunned the scarlets. They backed away, shaking their open jaws and pumping their gills as they strove to flush his poisons away.

"What is the matter with you?" Maulkin demanded of the strange tangle. He twisted himself through a spiral, his mane distending threateningly as he rebuked them. He summoned a faint gleam to his false-eyes. "Why do you attack us like soulless beasts fighting over food? This is not the way of our kind! Even if there were few, fish belong only to the one who catches them, not to those who see them first. Have you forgotten who you are, what you are? Have your minds been stolen completely?"

For a moment the other tangle hung motionless, save for the slight flicks of their tails stabilizing them. The school of fish fled, forgotten. Then, as if the very sanity of Maulkin's words had incensed them, they turned on him. All six converged, jaws wide to display their teeth, manes erect and streaming toxins, tails lashing. Shreever watched in horror as they wrapped him and bore him struggling down to the muck.

"Help me!" Sessurea trumpeted. "They'll smother him!"

His words broke her paralysis. Side by side, they arrowed down, to butt and lash at the tangle that held Maulkin captive. The other tangle savaged him with their teeth, as if he were prey. His blood mingled with his toxins in a choking cloud as he struggled. His false-eyes glimmered through the rising murk. Shreever cried out in horror at the mindless brutality of the attack. Yet, she found herself slashing at them with her teeth while Sessurea used his greater length to whip at them.

At an opportune moment, Sessurea wrapped Maulkin's lacerated body in his own and snatched him from the midst of the enraged tangle. He fled with Maulkin in his grasp, and Shreever was glad to break off the battle and follow him. The others did not pursue them. In their poisoned frenzy, the other tangle turned upon their comrades, roaring insults and challenges. Their cries were rote sounds, uttered without sense as they tore and lashed. Shreever did not look back.

Some time later, as Shreever smoothed healing slime from her own body onto Maulkin's lacerated flesh, he spoke to her. "They have forgotten. They have forgotten completely who and what they were. It has been too long, Shreever. They have lost every shred of memory and purpose." He winced as she nudged a flap of torn skin into place. She sealed a layer of mucus over it. "They are what we will become."

"Hush," Shreever told him gently. "Hush. Rest." She twined her long body more securely about him, anchored her tail against a rock to secure them from the current. Entangled with them, Sessurea already slept. Or perhaps he was merely silent and impassive, prey to the same discouragement that gnawed Shreever. She hoped not. She had barely enough courage left to shore up her own determination. Sessurea would have to rally himself.

Maulkin concerned her the most. Their encounter with the silver provider had changed him. The other providers that moved within both the Lack and the Plenty were merely sources of easy feeding. The silver one had been different. Her scent had wakened memories in all of them, and they had pursued her, certain that her fragrance must lead them to One Who Remembers. Instead, she had not even been one of their own kind. Still hoping, they had called to her, but she had not answered. To the white serpent who begged from her, she had given flesh. Maulkin had turned aside from her, proclaiming that she could not be One Who Remembers and they would follow her no longer. Yet, in the tides since then, her scent had always been present. She might be out of sight, but Shreever knew she was no more than a brief journey away. Maulkin still followed her, and they still followed him.

Maulkin gave a dull groan and shifted in her grip. "I fear it is the last time any of us will make this journey as anything more than beasts."

"What do you mean?" Sessurea demanded abruptly. He twisted awkwardly until his eyes met theirs. His own injuries were many, though none were serious. A deep score adjacent to one of his poison glands just behind his jaw hinge was the worst. If it had penetrated, his own toxins would have killed him. Sheer luck had kept their tangle intact.

"Search your memories," Maulkin commanded hollowly. "Search not just the tides and the days, but the seasons and the years, back decades upon decades. We have been here before, Sessurea. All the tangles have swarmed and migrated to these waters, not just once but scores of times. We have come here to seek those who remember, those few entrusted with the memories of all our kind. The promise was clear. We were to gather. Our history would be restored to us, and we would be led to a safe place for our transformation. There we would be reborn. Nevertheless, scores of times, we have been disappointed. Time upon time, we have swarmed, and waited. Each time, we eventually gave up our hopes, forgot our purpose, and finally we returned to the warm southern waters. Each time those of us who have a handful of memories have said, 'Perhaps we were mistaken. Perhaps this was not the time, the season, and the year for the renewal.' But it was. We were not wrong. Those who were to meet us failed. They did not come. Not then. Perhaps not this time, either."

Maulkin fell silent. Shreever continued to anchor him against the current. It was a strain. Even if there had been no current, there was no soothing mud to sink into here, only coarse sea grasses and tumbled stone and block. They should find a better place to rest. However, until Maulkin had healed, she did not wish to travel. Besides, where would they go? They had been up and down this current full of strange salts and she had lost her faith that Maulkin knew where he was leading them. Left to herself, where would she go? It was a question that was suddenly too heavy for her mind. She did not want to think.

She cleansed the lenses of her eyes and then looked down on her body tangled with theirs. The scarlet of her scales was bright and strong, but perhaps that was only in contrast to Maulkin's dull hide. His golden false-eyes had faded to dull browns. The suppurating slashes of his injuries marred them. He needed to feed and grow and then shed a skin. That would make him feel better. It would make them all feel better. She ventured the thought aloud. "We need to feed. All of us grow hungry and slack. My toxin sacs are nearly empty. Perhaps we should go south, where food is plentiful and the water is warm."

Maulkin twisted in her grip to regard her. His great eyes spun copper with concern. "You spend too much of your strength upon me, Shreever," he rebuked her. She could feel the effort it cost him to shake his mane free and erect. A second shake released a weak haze of toxin. It stung her and woke her, restoring her awareness. Sessurea leaned closer, wrapping them both in his greater length. He shared Maulkin's toxins, pumping his gills to absorb them.

"It will be all right," Sessurea tried to reassure her. "You are just weary. And hungry. We all are."

"Weary unto death," Maulkin confirmed tiredly. "And hungry almost to mindlessness. The demands of the body overpower the functioning of the mind. But listen to me, both of you. Listen and fix this in your minds and cling to it. If all else is forgotten, cherish this. We cannot go south again. If we leave these waters, it will be to end. As long as we can think, we must remain here and seek for One Who Remembers. I know it in my stomach. If we are not renewed this time, we shall not be renewed. We and all our kind will perish and be ever after unknown in sea or sky or upon the land." He spoke the strange words slowly and for an instant, Shreever almost recalled what they meant. Not just the Plenty and the Lack. The earth, the sky and the sea, the three parts of their sovereignty, once the three spheres of . . . something.

Maulkin shook his mane again. This time Shreever and Sessurea both opened their gills wide to his toxins and scalded his memories into themselves. Shreever looked down at the tumbled blocks of worked stone that littered the sea bottom, at the layered barnacles and sea grasses that were anchored to the Conqueror's Arch in an obscuring curtain. The black stone veined with silver peeped through only in small patches. The earth had shaken it down and the sea had swallowed it up. Once, lives ago, she had settled upon that arch, first flapping and then folding her massive wings back upon her shoulders. She had bugled to her mate of her joy in the morning's fresh rain, and a gleaming blue dragon had blared his reply. Once the Elderkind had greeted her arrival with scattered flowers and shouts of welcome. Once in this city under a bright blue sky . . .

It faded. It made no sense. The images wisped away like dreams upon awakening.

"Be strong," Maulkin exhorted them. "If we aren't fated to survive, then at least let us fight it to the end. Let it be fate that extinguishes us, not our own lack of heart. For the sake of our kind, let us be true to what we were." His ruff stood out full and venomous about his throat. Once more, he looked the visionary leader who had seized Shreever's loyalties so long ago. Her hearts swelled with love of him.

The world dimmed and she lifted her eyes to a great shadow moving overhead. "No, Maulkin," she trumpeted softly. "We are not destined to die, nor to forget. Look!"

A dark provider skimmed lazily along above them. As it swept over their heads, it cast forth food for them. The flesh sank slowly toward them, wafting down on the current. They were dead two-legs, one with chain still upon it. There would be no struggle for this meat. One needed only to accept it.

"Come," she urged Maulkin as Sessurea unwound from them and moved eagerly toward the meat. Gently she drew Maulkin up with her as she rose to accept the bounty of the provider.

CHAPTER ONE

The Mad Ship

THE BREEZE AGAINST HIS FACE AND CHEST WAS BRISK AND CHILL, YET SOME-thing in it hinted of spring soon to come. The air tasted of iodine; the tide must be out, exposing the kelp beds just off shore. Under his hull, the coarse sand was damp from the last heavy rain. The smoke of Amber's small fire tickled his nose. The figurehead turned his blind visage away from it then reached up to scratch his nose.

"It's a fine evening, don't you think?" she asked him conversationally. "The skies have cleared. There are still some clouds, but I can see the moon and some stars. I've gathered mussels and wrapped them in sea-weed. When the fire is stronger, I'll rake away some of the wood and cook them on the coals." Her voice paused hopefully.

Paragon did not reply.

"Would you like to taste some, when they're cooked? I know you have no need to eat, but you might find it an interesting experience."

He yawned, stretched, and crossed his arms on his chest. He was much better at this than she was. Thirty years hauled out on a beach had taught him true patience. He would outlast her. He wondered if she would get angry or sad tonight.

"What good does it do either of us for you to refuse to speak to me?" she asked reasonably. He could hear her patience starting to unravel. He did not bother to shrug.

"Paragon, you are a hopeless twit. Why won't you speak to me? Can't you see I'm the only one who can save you?"

Save me from what? he might have asked. If he'd been speaking to her.

He heard her get up and walk around his bow to stand in front of him. He casually turned his disfigured face away from her.

"Fine, then. Pretend to ignore me. I don't care if you answer me or not, but you have to listen to what I say. You are in danger, very real danger. I know you opposed me buying you from your family, but I made the offer anyway. They refused me."

Paragon permitted himself a small snort of disdain. Of course, they had. He was the Ludluck family's liveship. No matter how deep his disgrace, they would never sell him. They had kept him chained and anchored to this beach for some thirty years, but they'd never sell him! Not to Amber, not to New Traders. They wouldn't. He had known that all along.

Amber continued doggedly. "I spoke directly to Amis Ludluck. It wasn't easy to get to see her. When we did speak, she pretended to be shocked that I would make the offer. She insisted you were not for sale, at any price. She said the same things that you did, that no Bingtown Trader family would sell their liveship. That it simply wasn't done."

Paragon could not keep down the slow smile that gradually transfigured his face. They still cared. How could he have ever doubted that? In a way, he was almost grateful to Amber for making the ridiculous offer to buy him. Maybe now that Amis Ludluck had admitted to a stranger that he was still a part of her family, she'd be moved to visit him. Once Amis had visited him, it might lead to other things. Perhaps he would yet again sail the seas with a friendly hand on the wheel. His imagination went afar.

Amber's voice dragged him back ruthlessly. "She pretended to be distressed that there were even rumors of selling you. She said it insulted her family honor. Then she said—" Amber's voice suddenly went low, with fear or anger. "She said that she had hired some men to tow you away from Bingtown. That it might be better all around if you were out of sight and out of mind." Amber paused significantly.

Paragon felt something inside his wizardwood chest squeeze tight and hard.

"So I asked her who she had hired."

He lifted his hands quickly and stuffed his fingers in his ears. He wouldn't listen. She was going to play on his fears. So his family was going to move him. That didn't mean anything. It would be nice to be somewhere else. Maybe this time, when they hauled him out, they would block him up level. He was tired of always being at a list.

"She said it was none of my business." Amber raised her voice. "Then I asked her if they were Bingtown Traders. She just glared at me. So then I asked her where Mingsley was going to take you to have you dismantled."

Paragon began desperately to hum. Loudly. Amber went on talking. He couldn't hear her. He would not hear her. He plugged his ears more tightly and sang aloud, "A penny for a sweet-bun, a penny for a plum, a penny for the races, to see the ponies run. . . ."

"She threw me out!" Amber roared. "When I stood outside and shouted that I'd take it to the Bingtown Traders' Council, she set her dogs on me. They damn near caught me, too!"

"Swing me low, swing me high, swing me up into the sky," Paragon sang the childish rhyme desperately. She was wrong. She had to be wrong. His family was going to move him somewhere safe. That was all. It didn't really matter who they hired to do it. Once they had him in the water, he'd go willingly. He would show them how easy it could be to sail him. Yes. It would be a chance to prove himself to them. He could show them that he was sorry for all the things they had made him do.

She wasn't speaking anymore. He slowed his singing, then let it die away to a hum. Silence, save for his own voice. Cautiously he unstopped his ears. Nothing, save the brush of the waves, the wind nudging sand across the beach and the crackling of Amber's fire. A question occurred to him and he spoke it aloud before he remembered he was not speaking to her.

"When I get to my new place, will you still come to see me?"

"Paragon. You can't pretend this away. If they take you away from here, they'll chop you up for wizardwood."

The figurehead tried a different tack. "I don't care. It would be nice to be dead."

Amber's voice was low, defeated. "I'm not sure you'd be dead. I'm afraid they'll separate you from the ship. If that doesn't kill you, they'll probably transport you to Jamaillia, and sell you off as an oddity. Or give you as a gift to the Satrap in exchange for grants and favors. I don't know how you'd be treated there."

"Will it hurt?" Paragon asked.

"I don't know. I don't know enough about what you are. Did it . . . When they chopped your face, did that hurt?"

He turned his shattered visage away from her. He lifted his hands and walked his fingers over the splintered wood where his eyes had once been. "Yes." His brow furrowed. Then in the next breath he added, "I don't remember. There is a lot I can't remember, you know. My logbooks are gone."

"Sometimes not remembering is the easiest thing to do."

"You think I'm lying, don't you? You think I can remember, but I just won't admit it." He picked at it, hoping for a quarrel.

"Paragon. Yesterday we cannot change. We are talking about tomorrow."

"They're coming tomorrow?"

"I don't know! I was speaking figuratively." She came closer suddenly and reached up to put her hands flat against him. She wore gloves against the night's chill, but it was still a touch. He could feel the shapes of her hands as two patches of warmth against his planking. "I can't stand the thought of them taking you to cut you up. Even if it doesn't hurt, even if it doesn't kill you. I can't stand the thought of it."

"There's nothing you can do," he pointed out. He suddenly felt mature for voicing that thought. "There's nothing either of us can do."

"That is fatalistic twaddle," Amber declared angrily. "There's a lot we can do. If nothing else, I swear I will stand here and fight them."

"You wouldn't win," Paragon insisted. "It would be stupid to fight, knowing you couldn't win."

"That's as may be," Amber replied. "I hope it doesn't come to that. I don't want to wait for it to be that desperate. I want to act before they do. Paragon. We need help. We need someone who will speak to the Bingtown Traders' Council for us."

"Can't you?"

"You know I can't. Only an Old Trader can attend those meetings, let alone speak. We need someone who can go to them and convince them they should forbid the Ludlucks to do this."

"Who?"

Amber's voice was small. "I had hoped you knew someone who would speak for you."

Paragon was silent for a time. Then he laughed harshly. "No one will speak for me. This is a stupid effort, Amber. Think about it. Not even my own family cares for me. I know what they say about me. I am a killer. Moreover, it's true, isn't it? All hands lost. I rolled and drowned them all, and not just once. The Ludlucks are right, Amber. They should sell me to be chopped up." Despair washed over him, colder and deeper than any storm wave. "I'd like to be dead," he declared. "I'd just like to stop."

"You don't mean that," Amber said softly. He could hear in her voice that she knew he did.

"Would you do me a favor?" he asked suddenly.

"What?"

"Kill me before they can."

He heard the soft intake of her breath. "I . . . No. I couldn't."

"If you knew they were coming to chop me up, you could. I will tell you the only sure way. You have to set fire to me. Not just in one place, but many, to make sure they cannot put it out and save me. If you gathered dry wood, a little each day, and put it in piles in my hold . . ."

"Don't even speak of such things," Amber said faintly. Distractedly, she added, "I should put the mussels on to cook now." He heard her scratching at her fire, then the sizzle of wet seaweed steaming on hot coals. She was cooking the mussels alive. He considered pointing that out to her. He decided it would only upset her, not sway her to his cause. He waited until she had come back to him. She sat on the sand, leaning against his canted hull. Her hair was very fine. When it brushed against his planking, it snagged and clung to the wood.

"You don't make sense," he pointed out genially. "You vow you would stand and fight for me, knowing you would lose. But this simple, sure mercy you refuse me."

"Death by flames is scarcely mercy."

"No. Being chopped to pieces is much more pleasant, I'm sure," Paragon retorted sarcastically.

"You go so quickly from childish tantrums to cold logic," Amber said wonderingly. "Are you child or man? What are you?"

"Both, perhaps. But you change the subject. Come. Promise me."

"No," she pleaded.

He let out his breath in a sigh. She would do it. He could hear it in her voice. If there were no other way to save him, then she would do it. A strange trembling ran through him. It was a strange victory to have won. "And jars of oil," he added. "When they come, you may not have much time. Oil would make the wood burn fast and hot."

There followed a long silence. When she spoke again, her voice was altered. "They will try to move you in secret. Tell me how they would do it."

"Probably the same way I was put up here. They will wait for a high tide. Most likely, they would choose the highest tide of the month, at night. They will come with rollers, donkeys, men and small boats. It will not be a small undertaking, but knowledgeable men could get it done quickly."

Amber considered. "I shall have to move my things into you. I shall have to sleep aboard in order to guard you. Oh, Paragon," she cried out suddenly, "don't you have anyone who could speak up for you to the Bingtown Council?"

"Only you."

"I'll try. But I doubt they will give me a chance. I'm an outsider in Bingtown. They only listen to their own."

"You once told me you were respected in Bingtown."

"As an artisan and a merchant, they respect me. I am not an Old Trader. They would not have much patience with me if I began meddling in their affairs. Likely, I would suddenly find I had no customers. Or perhaps worse. The whole town is becoming more divided along Old Trader and newcomer lines. There is a rumor that the Bingtown Council has sent a delegation to the Satrap, with their original charter. They will demand he honor the word of Satrap Esclepius. The rumor is that they will demand he recall all the New Traders, and cancel all the land grants he has made them. They also demand that Satrap Cosgo live up to the old charter, and forbear from issuing any more land grants without the consent of the Bingtown Traders."

"A detailed rumor," Paragon observed.

"I have a keen ear for rumor and gossip. More than once, it has kept me alive."

A silence fell.

"I wish I knew when Althea was coming back." Amber's voice was wistful. "I could ask her to speak for us."

Paragon debated mentioning Brashen Trell. Brashen was his friend, Brashen would want to speak for him. Brashen was Old Trader. But even as he thought of that, he recalled that Brashen had been disinherited. Brashen was as much a disgrace to the Trell family as Paragon was to the Ludlucks. It would do no good to have Brashen speak out for him, even if he could get the Bingtown Traders' Council to hear him. It would be one black sheep speaking on behalf of another. No one would listen. He set his hand over the scar on his chest, concealing for an instant the crude, seven-pointed star branded into him. His fingers traveled over it thoughtfully. He sighed, then drew a deep breath.

"The mussels are done. I can smell them."

"Do you want to taste one?"

"Why not?" He should try new things while he still could. It might not be much longer before his chances to experience new things were gone forever.

CHAPTER TWO

The Pirate's Leg

"BACK IN THE MONASTERY, BERANDOL USED TO SAY THAT ONE WAY TO disperse fear and create decision was to consider the worst possible outcome of one's actions." After a moment Wintrow added, "Berandol said that if one considered the worst possible outcome and planned how to face it, then he could be decisive when it came time to act."

Vivacia glanced back over her shoulder at Wintrow. The boy had been leaning on the bow rail for the better part of the morning, staring out over the choppy water of the channel. The wind had pulled his black hair free of his queue. The ragged remnants of his brown garments looked more like a beggar's rags than a priest's robe. The sentient figurehead had been aware of him, but had chosen to share his silence and mood. There was little to say to each other that they did not both already know. Even now, the boy spoke only to put his own thoughts in order, not to ask any advice of her. She knew that, but still prompted him along. "And our worst fear is?"

Wintrow heaved a heavy sigh. "The pirate suffers from a fever that comes and goes. Each time it overpowers him, Kennit emerges from it weaker. The source is obviously the infection in his leg stump. Any animal bite is a dirty wound, but the sea serpent's bite seems unusually poisoned. The festering part must be cut away, and the sooner the better. He is too weak for such a surgery, but I see little prospect that he will grow stronger. So I tell myself I must act swiftly. I also know it is unlikely he will survive my cutting. If he dies, so must my father and I. That was the bargain I struck with him." He paused, and then went on, "I would die. That is not truly the worst outcome. The worst is that you must continue alone, a slave of these pirates."

He did not look at her but gazed out over the constantly moving waves as he added, "So you see why I have come to you. You have more right to a say in this than I do. I did not fully consider that when I struck my deal with Kennit. I wagered my death and my father's. In doing so, I unintentionally wagered your life as well. It was not mine to bet. You have, I believe, a great deal more to lose than I."

Vivacia nodded, but her own thought slid past Wintrow's and into one of her own. "He is not what I expected a pirate to be. Captain Kennit, I mean." Thoughtfully she added, "A slave, you just said. But I do not think he considers me his slave."

"Kennit is not what I thought a pirate would be, either. But despite his charm and intelligence, we must remember that he is one. Moreover, we must recall that if I fail, he will not be the one to command you. He would be dead. There is no telling who would then possess you. It might be Sorcor, his first mate. It might be Etta, his woman. Or perhaps Sa'Adar would once more attempt to claim you for himself and the freed slaves." Wintrow shook his head. "I cannot win. If the operation is successful, I must watch Kennit take you from me. Already he flatters and charms you with his words, and his crew works your decks. I have little say in anything that happens aboard you anymore. Whether Kennit lives or dies, I will soon have no power to protect you."

Vivacia shrugged one wizardwood shoulder. "And you did before?" she asked, somewhat coldly.

"I suppose not." The boy's voice was apologetic. "Yet, I had some idea of what to expect. Too much has happened too fast, to both of us. There has been too much death, and too many changes. I have had no time to mourn, no time to meditate. I scarce know who or what I am anymore."

They both fell silent, considering.

WINTROW FELT ADRIFT IN TIME. HIS LIFE, HIS REAL LIFE, WAS FAR AWAY, IN a peaceful monastery in a warm valley rich with orchards and fields. If he could step across the intervening days and distance, if he could wake up in his narrow bed in his cool cell, he was sure he could pick up the threads of that life. He hadn't changed, he insisted to himself. Not really. So he was missing a finger. He had learned to cope with that. And the slave tattoo on his face went no deeper than his skin. He had never truly been a slave; the tattoo had only been his father's cruel revenge for his attempt at escaping. He was still Wintrow. In a few quiet days, he could rediscover the peaceful priest inside him.

But not here. The recent swiftly shifting events in his life had left him with so many strong emotions, he could scarcely feel at all. Vivacia's feelings were as jumbled as his own, for her recent experiences had been as brutal. Kyle Haven had forced the young liveship into service as a slaver, prey to all the dark emotions of her miserable cargo. Wintrow, a blood member of her founding family, had not been able to comfort her. His own involuntary servitude on the ship had soured what should have been a natural bond between them. His alienation from her had only increased Vivacia's misery. Yet still they had hobbled along, like slaves shackled together.

In one stormy, bloody night, the slaves' uprising had freed her of Kyle Haven's captaincy and her role as a slaver. Of the original crew, Wintrow and his father were the sole survivors. As dawn lightened the sky, the crippled ship was overtaken by pirates. Captain Kennit and his crew had claimed Vivacia as a prize without striking a single blow. Then it was that Wintrow had struck his bargain with Kennit: he would try to save the pirate's life if Kennit would allow him and his father to live. Sa'Adar, a priest among the slaves and the leader of the uprising, had other ambitions. He wished not only to stand in judgment on Wintrow's father, Kyle, but also to demand Kennit turn the Vivacia over to the slaves as their rightful prize. No matter who prevailed, the future was uncertain for both Wintrow and the ship. Yet, the ship already seemed to favor the pirate.

Ahead of them, the Marietta cut a brisk path through the lace-edged waves. Vivacia followed eagerly in her wake. They were bound for some pirate stronghold; Wintrow knew no more than that. To the west, the horizon disappeared into the foggy coast of the Cursed Shores. The swift-running steaming rivers of that region dumped their warm and silty waters into this channel, which created near-permanent mists and fogs that cloaked an ever-changing shoreline of shoals and shallows. Sudden, violent storms were common in the winter months, and not unknown even in the kinder days of summer. The pirate islands were uncharted. What sense was there in charting a coast that changed almost daily? The conventional wisdom was to give it a wide berth and sail swiftly past it. Yet the Marietta surged forward confidently and Vivacia followed. Obviously, the pirates were very familiar with these channels and islands.

Wintrow turned his head and looked back over the Vivacia. In the rigging above, the pirate crew moved briskly and competently to Brig's bellowed commands. Wintrow had to admit he had never seen the Vivacia sailed with such skill. Pirates they might be, but they were also excellent sailors, moving with discipline and coordination, as smoothly as if they were living parts of the quickened ship.

But there were others on deck to spoil the image. Most of the slaves had survived the rebellion. Freed of their chains, they were still recovering the aspects of full humanity. The marks of manacles were yet on their flesh and the slave tattoos on their faces. Their clothes were ragged, and the bodies that showed through the rents were pale and bony. There were far too many of them for Vivacia's size. Although they now occupied the open decks as well as the holds below, they still had the crowded look of cattle being transported. They stood idly in small groups on the busy decks, moving only when the crew gestured them out of the way. Some of the healthier ones worked dispiritedly with rags and buckets, cleaning

Vivacia's decks and holds. Dissatisfaction showed on many faces. Wintrow wondered uneasily if they would act on it.

He wondered what he felt about them. Before their uprising, Wintrow had tended them belowdecks. His heart had rung with pity for them, then. True, he had had small comfort to offer them: the dubious relief of salt water and a washing rag seemed a false mercy now. He had tried to do a priest's duties for them, but there had simply been too many. Now whenever he looked at them, instead of recalling his compassion for them, he remembered the screams and the blood as they had killed all his shipmates. He could not name the emotion that now swept through him when he considered the former slaves. Compounded of fear and anger, disgust and sympathy, it wrenched his soul with shame at feeling it. It was not a worthy emotion for a priest of Sa to experience. So he chose his other option. He felt nothing.

Some of the sailors, perhaps, had deserved their violent deaths, as men judged such things. But what of Mild, who had befriended Wintrow, and the fiddler Findow and fun-loving Comfrey and the other good men? Surely, they had merited a kinder end. The *Vivacia* had not been a slaver when they signed aboard. They had remained aboard her when Kyle had decided to put her to that use. Sa'Adar, the slave priest freed in the rebellion, believed that all who had died had deserved it. He preached that by working as crew on a slaveship, they had become the enemies of all just men. Wintrow felt himself deeply divided on that. He clung to the comforting idea that Sa did not demand he judge others. He told himself that Sa reserved all judging for himself, for only the creator had the wisdom to be judge.

The slaves on board did not share Wintrow's opinion. Some looked at him and seemed to recall a soft-spoken voice in the darkness and hands with a cool damp rag. Others saw him as a sham, as the captain's son playing at mercy but doing little to free them until they had taken matters into their own hands. One and all, they avoided him. He could not fault them. He avoided them as well, choosing to spend most of his time on the foredeck near Vivacia. The pirate crew members came there only when the operation of the ship demanded it. Otherwise, they avoided it as superstitiously as the slaves did. The living, speaking figurehead frightened them. If their shunning of her bothered Vivacia, she gave no sign of it. For Wintrow's part, he was glad there was still one place aboard ship where he could be relatively alone. He leaned his head back against her railing and tried to find a thought that wasn't painful.

At home, it would almost be spring. The buds would be swelling in the monastery orchards. He wondered how Berandol was doing with his own studies, if his tutor ever missed him. He wondered with deep regret what he would be studying now if he were there. He looked down at his hands. Once they had transcribed manuscripts and shaped stained-glass windows. They had been a boy's hands, agile but still tender. Callus coated his palms now, and a finger was missing from one hand. They were the rough hands of a sailor. His finger would never wear a priest's ring.

Here it was a different kind of spring. The canvas snapped in the brisk chill wind. Migrating flocks of birds passed overhead with their haunting cries. The islands to either side of the channel had become even more lush, green and alive with shorebirds arguing about nesting space.

Something tugged at him.

"Your father calls for you," Vivacia said quietly.

Of course. He had sensed it through her. Their journey through the storm had affirmed and strengthened the bond of mind and spirit between the ship and himself. He did not resent it as he once had and he sensed that Vivacia did not cherish it as dearly as she once had. Perhaps in this, at least, their feelings were meeting in the middle. Since the storm, she had been kind to him, but no more than that. Like a preoccupied parent with a demanding child, he thought to himself.

"In some ways, we have exchanged roles since our journey began," she observed aloud.

He nodded, having neither spirit nor energy to deny the truth. Then he straightened his shoulders, ran a hand through his hair and set his jaw more firmly. He would not let his father see how uncertain he felt.

He kept his head up as he threaded his way across the deck, avoiding the knots of slaves and the working crewmen. No one met his eyes, no one challenged him. Foolish, he told himself, to believe they all watched his passage. They had won. Why should they care about the actions of one surviving crew member? At least he had come through it physically unscathed.

Vivacia bore the scars of the slave uprising. There were still blood-stains on the decks. The marks had not and would not yield to the sanding-stones the men used. The ship still smelled like a slaver, despite the near-continuous scrubbing Brig had ordered. The storm had taken a toll on her canvas as well; the hasty patching that the pirates had done showed plainly on her sails. In the aftercastle, doors had been forced when the slaves had hunted down the ship's officers. The gleaming woodwork was splintered and awry. She was not the tidy little vessel he had embarked upon from Bingtown. It suddenly shamed him to see his family ship this way, as if he had seen his sister whoring in a tavern. His heart went out to her and he wondered what it would have been like to have come aboard the ship of his own free will, as a boy perhaps, to serve under his grandfather's authority.

Then he set all such thoughts aside. He came to a battered door guarded by two sullen map-faces. He stepped past the former slaves as if he did not see them and knocked on Gantry's cabin door. At least, it had been the mate's while he was still alive. Now the stripped and looted room was his father's prison cell. He did not wait for a reply, but entered.

His father sat on the edge of the bare bunk. The stare he lifted to Wintrow's face was an uneven one. Blood filled the white of one eye in his swollen and discolored face. Kyle Haven's posture suggested pain and despair, but there was only acid sarcasm in his greeting. "Nice of you to recall me. I had supposed you were too busy groveling to your new masters."

Wintrow held back a sigh. "I came to see you earlier, but you were sleeping. I knew rest would heal you more than anything I could offer. How are your ribs?"

"Afire. My head throbs with every beat of my heart. And I'm hungry as well as thirsty." He made a slight motion with his chin toward the door. "Those two won't even let me out for some air."

"I left food and water here for you earlier. Didn't you . . . ?"

"Yes, I found it. A gill of water and two pieces of dry bread." There was suppressed fury in his father's voice.

"It was all I could get for you. There is a shortage of food and fresh water aboard. During the storm, much of the food was spoiled by saltwater. . . ."

"Gobbled down by the slaves, you mean." Kyle shook his head in disgust and then winced. "They didn't even have the sense to know they'd have to ration food. They kill the only men who can sail the ship in the midst of a storm, and then eat or destroy half the rations on board. They are no more fit to be in charge of themselves than a flock of chickens. I hope you are pleased with the freedom you dispensed to them. It's as like to be their deaths as their salvation."

"They freed themselves, Father," Wintrow said stubbornly.

"But you did nothing to stop them."

"Just as I did nothing to stop you from bringing them aboard in chains." Wintrow took a breath to go on, then stopped himself. No matter how he tried to justify what he had done, his father would never accept his reasons. Kyle's words nudged the bruises on Wintrow's conscience. Were the deaths of the crew his fault, because he had done nothing? If that was so, then was he also responsible for the deaths of the slaves before the uprising? The thought was too painful to consider.

In an altered tone he went on, "Do you want me to tend your injuries, or try to find food for you?"

"Did you find the medical supplies?"

Wintrow shook his head. "They're still missing. No one has admitted taking them. They may have been lost overboard during the storm."

"Well, without them, there is little you can do for me," his father pointed out cynically. "Food would be nice, however."

Wintrow refused to be irritated. "I'll see what I can do," he said softly.

"Of course you will," his father replied snidely. His voice lowered abruptly as he asked, "And what will you *do* about the pirate?"

"I don't know," Wintrow admitted honestly. He met his father's eyes squarely as he added, "I'm afraid. I know I have to try to heal him. But I don't know which is worse, the prospect of him surviving and us continuing as prisoners, or him dying and us with him, and the ship having to go on alone."

His father spat on the deck, an action so unlike him that it was as shocking as a blow. His eyes glittered like cold stones. "I despise you," he growled. "Your mother must have lain with a serpent, to bring forth something like you. It shames me to have folk name you my son. Look at you. Pirates have taken over your family ship, the livelihood of your mother and sister and little brother. Their very survival depends on you taking this ship back! But you don't even think of that. No. All you wonder is if you will kill or cure the pirate whose boot is on your neck. You have not given one thought to getting weapons for us, or persuading the ship to defy him as she defied me. All the time you wasted nursemaiding those slaves when they were in chains! Do you try to get any of them to help you now? No. You mouse along and help that damn pirate keep the ship he has stolen from us."

Wintrow shook his head, in wonder as much as sorrow. "You are not rational. What do you expect of me, Father? Am I supposed to single-handedly take this ship back from Kennit and his crew, subdue the slaves into being cargo again and then sail it on to Chalced?"

"You and this devil ship were able to overthrow me and my crew! Why don't you turn the ship against him as you turned her against me? Why can't you, just once, act in the best interests of your family?" His father stood up, his fists clenched as if he would attack Wintrow. Then he abruptly clutched at his ribs, gasping with pain. His face went from the red of anger to the white of shock, and he swayed. Wintrow started forward to catch him.

"Don't touch me!" Kyle snarled threateningly, staggering to the edge of the bunk. He eased himself back onto it. He sat glowering at his son.

What does he see when he looks at me, Wintrow wondered? He supposed he must be a disappointment to the tall, blond man. Small, dark and slight like his mother, Wintrow would never have his father's size or his physical strength. At fourteen, he was physically still more boy than man. But it wasn't just physically that he failed his father's ambitions. His spirit would never match his sire's.

Wintrow spoke softly. "I never turned the ship against you, sir. You did that yourself, with your treatment of her. There is no way I can reclaim her completely at this time. The very best I can hope to do is to keep us alive."

Kyle Haven shifted his gaze to the wall and stared at it stonily. "Go and get me some food." He barked out the order as if he still commanded the ship.

"I will try," Wintrow said coldly. He turned and left the room.

As he dragged the damaged door shut behind him, one of the map-faces spoke to him. The tattooed marks of his many masters crawled on the burly man's face, as he demanded, "Why do you take that from him?"

"What?" Wintrow asked in surprise.

"He treats you like a dog."

"He's my father." Wintrow tried to conceal his dismay that they had listened to their conversation. How much had they overheard?

"He's a horse's ass," the other guard observed coldly. He turned a challenging gaze on Wintrow. "Makes you the son of a horse's ass."

"Shut up!" the first guard snarled. "The boy isn't bad. If you can't remember who was kind to you when you were chained up, I can." His dark eyes came back to Wintrow. He tossed his head at the closed door. "You say the word, boy. I'll make him crawl for you."

"No." Wintrow spoke out clearly. "I don't want that. I don't want anyone to crawl for me." He felt he had to make it absolutely clear to the man. "Please. Don't hurt my father."

The map-face gave a shrug. "Suit yourself. I speak from experience, lad. It's the only way to deal with a man like that. He crawls for you or you crawl for him. It's all he knows."

"Perhaps," Wintrow conceded unwillingly. He started to walk away, then paused. "I don't know your name."

"Villia. You're Wintrow, right?"

"Yes. I'm Wintrow. I'm pleased to know your name, Villia." Wintrow looked at the other guard expectantly.

He frowned and looked uncomfortable. "Deccan," he said finally.

"Deccan," Wintrow repeated, fixing it in his mind. He deliberately met the man's eyes and nodded at him before he turned away. He could sense both amusement and approval from Villia. Such a minor way of standing up for himself, and yet he felt better for having done it. As he emerged onto the deck, blinking in the bright spring sunshine, Sa'Adar stepped into his path. The big priest still looked haggard from his confinement as a slave. The red kiss of the shackles had scarred his wrists and ankles.

"I've been looking for you," he announced. Two more map-faces flanked the priest like leashed pitdogs.

"Have you?" Wintrow resolved to continue as he had begun. He squared his shoulders and met the older man's eyes. "Did you post those two men outside my father's room?" he demanded.

The wandering priest was unruffled. "I did. The man must be confined until he can be judged and justice done to him." The priest looked down on Wintrow from his superior height and years. "Do you dispute that?"

"I?" Wintrow appeared to consider the question. "Why would it worry you if I did? Were I you, I would not worry about what Wintrow Vestrit thought. I would worry about what Captain Kennit might think of me taking such authority to myself."

"Kennit's a dying man," Sa'Adar said boldly. "Brig is the one who commands here. He seems to welcome my authority over the slaves. He gives out his orders through me. He has not challenged my posting of a guard on Captain Haven."

"Slaves? Surely they are all free folk now." Wintrow smiled as he spoke, and pretended not to notice how closely the map-faces were following the conversation. The other former slaves loitering on the deck were also eavesdropping. Some drew closer.

"You know what I mean!" Sa'Adar exclaimed in annoyance.

"Generally, a man says what he means. . . ." Wintrow let the observation hang a moment, then added smoothly, "You said you were seeking me earlier?"

"I was. Have you been to see Kennit today?"

"Why do you ask?" Wintrow countered quietly.

"Because I should like to know plainly what his intentions are." The priest had a trained voice and he now gave it a carrying quality. More than one tattooed face turned toward him as he spoke. "The tales told in Jamaillia City say that when Captain Kennit captures a slaveship, he kills the crew and gives the ship over to those who were slaves on it, so that they, too, can become pirates and carry on his crusade against slavery. Such was what we believed when we welcomed his aid in manning the ship that we had taken. We expected to keep it. We hoped it would be a tool for the new beginning each of us must make. Now Captain Kennit speaks as if he will keep it for himself. With all we have heard of him, we do not believe he is a man who would snatch from us the only thing of value we have. Therefore, we wish to ask him, plainly and fairly. To whom does he believe this ship belongs?"

Wintrow regarded him levelly. "If you wish to ask that question of Captain Kennit, then I encourage you to do so. Only he can give his opinion of the answer. If you ask it of me, you will hear, not my opinion, but the truth." He had deliberately spoken more softly than Sa'Adar so that those who wished to listen would have to draw near. Many had done so, including some of the pirate crewmen. They had a dangerous look to them.

Sa'Adar smiled sardonically. "Your truth is that the ship belongs to you, I suppose."

Wintrow shook his head, and returned the smile. "The ship belongs to herself. Vivacia is a free creature, with the right to determine her own life. Or would you, who have worn the heavy chains of slavery, presume to do to another what was done so cruelly to you?"

Ostensibly he addressed Sa'Adar. Wintrow did not look around to see how the question affected the others. Instead, he was silent, as if awaiting an answer. After a moment Sa'Adar gave a snort of disdainful laughter. "He cannot be serious," he told the throng. "By some sorcery, the figurehead can speak. It is an interesting bit of Bingtown trickery. But a ship is a ship, a thing, and not a person. And by rights, this ship is ours!"

Only a few slaves muttered assent, for no sooner was the question uttered than a pirate confronted him. "Are you talking mutiny?" the grizzled tar demanded. "'Cause if you are, you'll go over the side before you take another breath." The man smiled in a decidedly unfriendly way that bared the gaps in his teeth. To his left, a tall pirate laughed gutturally. He rolled his shoulders as if stretching, a subtle display of strength for Sa'Adar's map-faces. Both the tattooed men straightened, eyes narrowing.

Sa'Adar looked shocked. Obviously, he had not expected this. He stood straight and began indignantly, "Why should it be a concern of yours?"

The stocky pirate poked the tall priest in the chest. His jabbing finger stayed there as he pointed out, "Kennit's our captain. What he says, goes. Right?" When the priest did not answer, the man grinned. Sa'Adar stepped back from the pressure of his forefinger against his chest. As he turned to walk away, the pirate observed, "You'd do best not to talk against anything Kennit does. You don't like something, tell the captain to his face. He's a hard man, but fair. Don't wag your tongue behind his back. If you make trouble on this ship, it will only come down on you."

Without a backward glance, the pirates went back to their work. Attention shifted to Sa'Adar. He did not mask the angry glint in his eyes, but his voice sounded thin and childish when he said, "Be assured I will speak to Kennit about this. Be assured I will!"

Wintrow lowered his eyes to the deck. Perhaps his father was right. Perhaps there was a way he could regain his family ship from both slaves and pirates. In any conflict, there is opportunity for someone. His heart beat strangely faster as he walked away, and he wondered where such thoughts had bred in him.

VIVACIA WAS PREOCCUPIED. ALTHOUGH HER EYES STARED AHEAD OVER THE water to the stern of the *Marietta*, her real attention was turned inward. The man on the wheel had a steady hand; the crew that sprang to her rigging were true sailors one and all. The crew was cleansing filth from her decks and holds, and repairing woodwork and polishing metal. For the first time in many months, she had no qualms as to the abilities of her captain. She could let her mind be completely occupied with her own concerns, trusting that those who manned her knew their trade.

A quickened liveship, through her wizardwood bones, could be aware of all that happened aboard her. Much of it was mundane and scarcely worthy of attention. The mending of a line, the chopping of an onion in the galley, need not concern her. Those things could not change her course in life. Kennit could. In the captain's quarters, the enigmatic man slept restlessly. Vivacia could not see him, but she could feel him in a way humans had no words to describe. His fever was rising again. The woman who tended him was anxious. She did something with cool water and a cloth. Vivacia reached for details, but there was no bond there. She did not yet know them well enough.

Kennit was far more accessible to her than Etta. His fever dreams ran out of him carelessly, spilling into Vivacia like the blood that had been shed on her decks. She absorbed them but could make no sense of them. A little boy was tormented, torn between loyalty to a father who loved him but had no idea how to protect him, and a man who protected him from others but had no love at all in his heart. Over and over again, a serpent rose from the depths of his dreams to shear off his leg. The bite of its jaws was acid and ice. From the depths of his soul, he reached toward her, toward a deep sharing that he recalled only as a formless memory from a lost infancy.

"Hello, hello, what's this? Or who is this, perhaps I should say?"

The voice, Kennit's voice, came to her in a tiny whisper inside her mind. She shook her head, tousling her hair into the wind. The pirate did not speak to her. Even in her strongest communions with Althea and Wintrow, their thoughts had not come so clearly into her mind. "That is not Kennit," she murmured to herself. Of that, she was certain. Yet, it was certainly his voice. In his stateroom, the pirate captain drew a deep breath and expelled it, muttering denials and refusals as he did so. He groaned suddenly.

"No. Not Kennit," the tiny voice confirmed in amusement. "Nor are you the Vestrit you think yourself to be. Who *are* you?"

It was disconcerting to feel a mind groping after her reaction. Instinctively she recoiled from the contact. She was stronger far than he was. When she pulled away from him, he could not follow her. In doing so, she severed her tentative contact with Kennit as well. Frustration and agitation roiled through her. She clenched her fists at her side and took the next wave badly, smashing herself into it rather than through it. The helmsman cursed to himself and made a tiny correction. Vivacia licked the salt spray from her lips and shook her hair back from her face. Who and what was he? She held her thoughts still inside herself and tried to decide if she were more frightened or intrigued. She sensed an odd kinship with the being who had spoken to her. She had turned his aggressive prying aside easily, but she disliked that someone had even tried to invade her mind.

She decided she would not tolerate it. Whoever this intruder was, she would unmask him and confront him. Keeping her own guard up, she reached out tentatively toward the cabin where Kennit shifted in his sleep. She found the pirate easily. He still struggled through his fever dreams, hiding within a cupboard while some dream being stalked him, calling his name in a falsely sweet tone. The woman set a cool cloth on his brow, and draped another over the swollen stump of his leg. Vivacia almost felt the sudden easing it brought him. The ship reached out again, more boldly, but found no one else there.

"Where are you?" she demanded suddenly and angrily. Kennit jerked with a cry as the stalker in his dream echoed her words, and Etta bent over him, murmuring soothing words.

Vivacia's question went unanswered.

KENNIT SURFACED, GASPING HIS WAY INTO CONSCIOUSNESS. IT TOOK HIM A moment to recall his surroundings. Then a faint smile of pleasure stretched his fever-parched lips. His liveship. He was on board his liveship, in the captain's well-appointed chambers. A fine linen sheet draped his sweating body. Polished brass and wood gleamed throughout a chamber both cozy and refined. He could hear the water gurgling past as Vivacia cut through the channel. He could almost feel the awareness of his ship around him, protecting him. She was a second skin, shielding him from the world. He sighed in satisfaction, and then choked on the mucus in his dry throat.

"Etta!" he croaked to the whore. "Water."

"It's right here," she said soothingly.

It was true. Surprising as it was, she was standing right beside him, a cup of water ready in her hand. Her long fingers were cool on the back of his neck as she helped him raise himself to drink. Afterward, she deftly turned his pillow before she lowered his head again. With a cool cloth she patted the perspiration from his face and then wiped his hands with a moist cloth. He lay still and silent under her touch, limply grateful for the comfort she gave. He knew a moment of purest peace.

It did not last. His awareness of his swollen leg rose swiftly to recognition of pain. He tried to ignore it. It became a pulsing heat that rose in intensity with every breath he took. Beside his bed, his whore sat in a chair, sewing something. His eyes moved listlessly over her. She looked older than he recalled her. The lines were deeper by her mouth and in her brow. Her face looked thinner under the brush of her short black hair. It made her dark eyes even more immense.

"You look terrible," he rebuked her.

She set her sewing aside immediately and smiled as if he had complimented her. "It's hard for me to see you like this. When you are ill . . . I can't sleep, I can't eat. . . ."

Selfish woman. She'd fed his leg to a sea serpent, and now tried to make it out that it was her problem. Was he supposed to feel sorry for her? He pushed the thought aside. "Where's that boy? Wintrow?"

She stood right away. "Do you want him?"

Stupid question. "Of course I want him. He's supposed to make my leg better. Why hasn't he done so?"

She leaned over his bed and smiled down at him tenderly. He wanted to push her away but he had not the strength. "I think he wants to wait until we make port in Bull Creek. There are a number of things he wants to have on hand before he . . . heals you." She turned away from his sickbed abruptly, but not before he had seen the tears glinting in her eyes. Her wide shoulders were bowed and she no longer stood tall and proud. She did not expect him to survive. To know that so suddenly both scared and angered him. It was as if she had wished his death on him.

"Go find that boy!" he commanded her roughly, mostly to get her out of his sight. "Remind him. Remind him well that if I die, so does he and his father. Tell him that!"

"I'll have someone fetch him," she said in a quavering voice and started for the door.

"No. You go yourself, right now, and get him. Now."

She turned back and annoyed him by lightly touching his face. "If that's what you want," she said soothingly. "I'll go right now."

He did not watch her go but listened instead to the sound of her boots on the deck. She hurried, and when she went out, the door shut quietly but completely behind her. He heard her voice lifted to someone, irritably. "No. Go away. I won't have him bothered with such things right now." Then, in a lower, threatening voice, "Touch that door and I'll kill you right here." Whoever it was heeded her, for no knock came at the door.

He half closed his eyes and drifted on the tide of his pain. The fever razored bright edges and sharp colors to the world. The cozy room seemed to crowd closer around him, threatening to fall in on him. He pushed the sheet away and tried to find a breath of cooler air.

"So, Kennit. What will you do with your 'likely urchin' when he comes?"

The pirate squeezed his eyes tight shut. He tried to will the voice away.

"That's amusing. Do you think I cannot see you with your eyes closed?" The charm was relentless.

"Shut up. Leave me alone. I wish I had never had you made."

"Oh, now you have wounded my feelings! Such words to bandy about, after all we have endured together."

Kennit opened his eyes. He lifted his wrist and stared at the bracelet. The tiny wizardwood charm, carved in a likeness of his own saturnine face, looked up at him with a friendly grin. Leather thongs secured it firmly over his pulse point. His fever brought the face looming closer. He closed his eyes.

"Do you truly believe that boy can heal you? No. You could not be so foolish. Of course, you are desperate enough that you will insist he try. Do you know what amazes me? That you fear death so much that it makes you brave enough to face the surgeon's knife. Think of that swollen flesh, so tender you scarce can bear the brush of a sheet upon it. You will let him set a knife to that, a bright sharp blade, gleaming silver before the blood encarmines it. . . ."

"Charm." Kennit opened his eyes to slits. "Why do you torment me?"

The charm pursed his lips at him. "Because I can. I am probably the only one in the whole world who can torment the great Captain Kennit. The Liberator. The would-be King of the Pirate Isles." The little face snickered and added snidely, "Brave Serpent-Bait of the Inside Passage. Tell me. What do you want of the boy-priest? Do you desire him? He stirs in your fever dreams memories of what you were. Would you do as you were done by?"

"No. I was never . . ."

"What, never?" The wizardwood charm snickered cruelly. "Do you truly believe you can lie to me, bonded as we are? I know everything about you. Everything."

"I made you to help me, not to torment me! Why have you turned on me?"

"Because I hate what you are," the charm replied savagely. "I hate that I am becoming a part of you, aiding you in what you do."

Kennit drew a ragged breath. "What do you want from me?" he demanded. It was a cry of surrender, a plea for mercy or pity.

"Now there's a question you never thought of before this. What do I want from you?" The charm drew the question out, savoring it. "Maybe I want you to suffer. Maybe I enjoy tormenting you. Maybe . . ."

Footsteps sounded outside the door. Etta's boots and the light scuff of bare feet.

"Be kind to Etta," the charm demanded hastily. "And perhaps I will—"

As the door opened, the face fell silent. It was once more still and silent, a wooden bead on a bracelet on a sick man's wrist. Wintrow came in, followed by the whore. "Kennit, I've brought him," Etta announced as she shut the door behind them.

"Good. Leave us." If the damn charm thought it could force him into anything, it was wrong.

Etta looked stricken. "Kennit . . . do you think that's wise?"

"No. I think it is stupid. That's why I told you to do it, because I delight in stupidity." His voice was low as he flung the words at her. He watched the face at his wrist for some sort of reaction. It was motionless, but its tiny eyes glittered. Probably it plotted revenge. He didn't care. While he could breathe, he would not cower before a bit of wood.

"Get out," he repeated. "Leave the boy to me."

Her back was very straight as she marched out. She shut the door firmly behind her, not quite slamming it. The moment she was outside, Kennit dragged himself into a sitting position. "Come here," he told Wintrow. As the boy approached the bed, Kennit seized the corner of the sheet and flung it aside. It exposed his shortened leg in all its putrescent glory. "There it is," Kennit told him in disgust. "What can you do for me?"

The boy blanched at the sight of it. Kennit knew he steeled himself to approach the bedside and look more closely at his leg. He wrinkled his nose against the smell. Then he lifted his dark eyes to Kennit's and spoke simply and honestly. "I don't know. It's very bad." His glance darted back to Kennit's leg then met his eyes again. "Let's approach it this way. If we do not attempt to take off your leg, you will die. What have we to lose by trying?"

The pirate forced a stiff grin to his face. "I? Very little, it seems. You have still your own life and your father's on the scale."

Wintrow gave a short, mirthless laugh. "I well know that my life is forfeit if you die, with or without my efforts." He made a tiny motion with his head toward the door. "*She* would never suffer me to survive you."

"You fear the woman, do you?" Kennit permitted his grin to widen. "You should. So. What do you propose?" He tried to keep up his bravado with casual words.

The boy looked back at his leg. He furrowed his brow and pondered. The intensity of his concentration only made his youth more apparent.

Kennit glanced down once at his decaying stump. After that, he preferred to watch Wintrow's face. The pirate winced involuntarily as the boy extended his hands toward his leg. "I won't touch it," Wintrow promised. His voice was almost a whisper. "But I need to discover where the soundness stops and the foulness begins." He cupped his hands together, as if to capture something under them. He began at the injury and slowly moved his hands up towards Kennit's thigh. Wintrow's eyes were closed to slits and his head was cocked as if he listened intently to something. Kennit watched his moving hands. What did he sense? Warmth, or something subtler, like the slow working of poison? The boy's hands were weathered from hard work, but retained the languid grace of an artisan's.

"You have only nine fingers," Kennit observed. "What happened to the other one?"

"An accident," Wintrow told him distractedly, then bade him, "Hush."

Kennit scowled, but did as he was bid. He became aware of the boy's cupped hands moving above his flesh. Their ghostly pressure reawakened him to the pounding rhythm of the pain. Kennit clenched his teeth, swallowed against it and managed to push it from his mind once more.

Midway up Kennit's thigh, Wintrow's hands halted and hovered. The lines in his brow grew deeper. The boy's breathing deepened, steadied and his eyes closed completely. He appeared to sleep standing. Kennit studied his face. Long dark lashes curled against his cheeks. His cheeks and jaw had lost most of a child's roundness, but showed not even the downy beginning of a beard. Beside his nose was the small green sigil that denoted he had once belonged to the Satrap. Next to that was a larger tattoo, a crude rendering that Kennit recognized as the *Vivacia's* figurehead. Kennit's first reaction was annoyance that someone had so compromised the boy's beauty. Then he perceived that the very harshness of the tattoo contrasted with his innocence. Etta had been like that when he first discovered her, a coltish girl in a whorehouse parlor. . . .

"Captain Kennit? Sir?"

He opened his eyes. When had he closed them?

Wintrow was nodding gently to himself. "Here," he said as soon as the pirate looked at him. "If we cut here, I think we'll be in sound flesh."

The boy's hands indicated a spot frighteningly high on his thigh. Kennit took a breath. "In sound flesh, you say? Should not you cut below what is sound?"

"No. We must cut a bit into what is still healthy, for healthy flesh heals faster than poisoned." Wintrow paused and used both hands to push his straying hair back from his face. "I cannot say that any part of the leg is completely without poison. But I think if we cut there, we would have our best chance." The boy's face grew thoughtful. "First, I shall want to leech the lower leg, to draw off some of the swelling and foulness. Some of the monastery healers held with bleeding, and some with leeches. There is, of course, a place and a time for each of those things, but I believe that the thickened blood of infection is best drawn off by leeches."

Kennit fought to keep his composed expression. The boy's face was intense. He reminded Kennit of Sorcor attempting to plot strategy.

"Then we shall place a ligature here, a wide one that will slow the flow of blood. It must bind the flesh tightly without crushing it. Below it, I shall cut. I shall try to preserve a flap of skin to close over the wound. The tools I shall need are a sharp knife and a fine-toothed saw for the bone. The blade of the knife must be long enough to slice cleanly, without a sawing motion." The boy's fingers measured out the length. "For the stitching, some would use fine fish-gut thread, but at my monastery, it was said that the best stitches are made with hair from the man's own head, for the body knows its own. You, sir, have fine hair, long. Your curls are loose enough that the hair can be pulled straight. It will serve admirably."

Kennit wondered if the boy sought to unnerve him, or if he had completely forgotten that he was talking about Kennit's flesh and bone. "And for the pain?" he asked with false heartiness.

"Your own courage, sir, will have to serve you best." The boy's dark eyes met his squarely. "I shall not be quick, but I shall be careful. Brandy or rum, before we begin. Were it not so rare and expensive, I would say we should obtain the essence of the rind of a kwazi fruit. It numbs a wound wonderfully. Of course, it works only on fresh blood. It would only be effective after we had done the cutting." Wintrow shook his head thoughtfully. "Perhaps you should think well of what crewmen you shall want to hold you down. They should be large and strong men, with the judgment to ignore you if you demand to be released or threaten them."

Unwillingness washed over Kennit like a wave. He refused to consider the humiliation and indignity he must face. He thrust away the idea that this was inevitable. There had to be some other way, some alternative to vast pain and helplessness. How could he choose them, knowing that even if he endured it all, he might still die? How foolish he would look then!

". . . and each of those must be drawn out a little way, and closed off with a stitch or two." Wintrow paused as if waiting for his agreement. "I've never done this by myself," he admitted abruptly. "I want you to know that. I have seen it done twice. Once an infected leg was removed. Once it was a hopelessly smashed foot and ankle. Both times, I was there to help the healer, to pass tools and hold the bucket. . . ." His voice trailed off. He licked his lips and stared at Kennit, his eyes going wider and wider.

"What is it?" Kennit demanded.

"I'll have your life in my hands," he wondered aloud.

"And I have yours in mine," the pirate pointed out. "And your father's."

"That's not what I mean," Wintrow replied. His voice sounded like a dreamer's. "You are doubtless accustomed to such power. I have never even wished for it."

CHAPTER THREE

The Crowned Rooster

HER FOOTFALLS RANG HOLLOW IN THE CAVERNOUS CORRIDOR AS JANI Khuprus hastened down it. As she strode along, she trailed her fingers down the long strip of jidzin set into the wall. Her touch triggered a faint light that moved with her down the dark hall that carried her ever deeper into the Elderlings' labyrinthine palace. Twice she had to circle dark puddles of water on the stone floor. Each time, she routinely noted to herself the location. Whenever the spring rains returned, they had the same problem. The thick layer of soil on top and the questing roots that sought through it were beginning to win the long battle with the ancient buried structure. The quiet dripping of the water was a counter rhythm to her own hurrying feet.

There had been a quake last night, not a large one by Rain Wild standards, but stronger and longer than the usual gentle shivering of the earth. She resolved not to think about it as she hurried through the dimness. This structure had withstood the great disaster that had leveled most of the ancient city; surely, she could trust it to stand a bit longer. She came at last to an arched entryway closed with a massive metal door. She ran her hands over it lightly and the Crowned Rooster embossed on the surface shimmered into life. It never failed to impress her. She could well understand her ancestor discovering this and immediately making the Crowned Rooster his own heraldic device. The cock on the door was lifting a spurred foot threateningly and his wings were half-raised in menace. Every hackle feather on his extended neck shone. A gem set in his eye sparkled blackly. Elegance and arrogance combined in him. She set a hand firmly to his breast and pushed the door open. Darkness gaped at her.

Only familiarity guided her as she descended the shallow steps that led into the immense room. As she submerged herself in the vaster darkness of the Crowned Rooster Chamber, she scowled to herself. Reyn was not here after all. She had trotted all this way seeking her son for nothing.

She paused by the wall at the bottom of the steps, looking around blindly. She started when he spoke to her from the blackness.

"Have you ever tried to imagine to yourself how this chamber must have looked when it was new? Think of it, Mother. On a day like today, the spring sun would have shone down through the crystal dome to waken all the colors in the murals. What did they do here? From the deep gouges on the floor and the random ordering of the tables, I do not think the wizardwood logs were commonly stored here. No. I think they were brought here in haste, to shelter them from whatever disaster was burying the city. So. Prior to that time, what was the purpose of this huge room with its crystal dome and decorated walls? From the ancient pots of earth, we can surmise they grew plants in here. Was it merely a sheltered garden, where one could walk in comfort even in the stormiest weather? Or was it . . . ?"

"Reyn. Enough," his mother exclaimed in annoyance. Her questing fingers found the jidzin strip on the wall. She pressed on it firmly, and several decorative panels answered her dimly. She frowned to herself. In her girlhood, they had been much brighter; each petal of every flower had shone. Now they dimmed more with each passing day. She pushed aside her dismay at the thought of them dying. There was mild irritation in her voice as she demanded, "What are you doing down here in the dark? Why aren't you in the west corridor, supervising the workers? They have found another portal, concealed in a wall of the seventh chamber. Your intuition is needed there, to divine how to open it."

"How to destroy it, you mean," Reyn corrected her.

"Oh, Reyn," Jani wearily rebuked him. She was so tired of these discussions with her youngest son. Sometimes it seemed that he, who was most gifted at forcing the dwelling places of the Elderlings to give up their secrets, was also the most reluctant to employ his skills. "What would you have us do? Leave all buried and forgotten as we found it? Forsake the Rain Wilds and retreat to Bingtown to live with our kin there? That would be brief sanctuary."

She heard the light scuff of his feet as he circled the last great log of wizardwood that remained in the Crowned Rooster Chamber. He moved like a sleepwalker as he rounded the end of it. Her heart sank as she marked how he walked, his fingers trailing along the massive trunk as he did so. He was cloaked and hooded against the damp and chill of the chamber. "No," he said quietly. "I love the Rain Wilds as you do. I have no desire to live elsewhere. Neither do I think my people should continue to live in hiding and secrecy. Nor should we continue to plunder and destroy the ancient holdings of the Elderlings simply to pay for our own safety. I believe that instead we should restore and celebrate all we have discovered here. We should dig away the soil and ash that mask the city and reveal it once more to sunlight and moonlight. We should throw off the Satrap of Jamaillia as an overlord, deny his taxes and restrictions and trade freely wherever we wish." His voice died down as his mother glowered at him, but he was not silenced. "Let us display who we are without shame, and say we live where and as we do, not out of shame but by choice. That is what I think we should do."

Jani Khuprus sighed. "You are very young, Reyn," she said simply.

"If you mean stupid, say stupid," he suggested without malice.

"I do not mean stupid," she replied gently. "Young I said, and young I meant. The burden of the Cursed Shores does not fall as heavily upon you and me as it does the other Rain Wild Traders. In some ways, that makes our lot harder, not easier. We visit Bingtown and from behind our veils we look about and say, 'But I am not so very different from the folk who live here. In time they would accept me, and I could move freely among them.' Perhaps you forget just how hard it might be for Kys or Tillamon to stand unveiled before ignorant eyes."

At the mention of his sisters' names, Reyn cast his eyes down. No one could say why the disfigurement that was the normal lot of Rain Wild children should have fallen so heavily upon them and so lightly upon Reyn. Here, among their own kind, it was not so immense a burden. Why should one blanch at a neighbor's face that sported the same pebbled skin or dangling growths as his own? In contrast, the thought of his small half-sister Kys unveiled, even on a Bingtown street, was a daunting one. As clearly as if written on a scroll, Jani watched the thoughts unfurl across her son's visage. His brow wrinkled at the unfairness of it all.

Bitterness twisted his mouth when he spoke. "We are a wealthy folk. I am neither so young nor so stupid as not to know that we could buy acceptance. By all rights, we should be among the wealthiest in the world, were it not for the Satrap's foot on our neck and hands in our purse. Mark my words, Mother. Could we but throw off the burdens of his taxes and his restraints on our free trade, then we would not need to destroy the very discoveries that enrich us. We could restore and reveal this city, instead of stripping its treasures to sell elsewhere. Folk would come here, paying our ships to bring them up the river, and be glad to do it. They would look upon us and not turn aside their eyes, for folk can come to love whoever has wealth. We would have the leisure then to find the true keys to unlock the secrets that we now hammer and cut free. If we were truly a free folk, we could unearth the full wonder of this city. Sunlight would flood this chamber as it once did, and the Queen that lies trapped here—"

"Reyn," his mother spoke in a low voice. "Take your hand off the wizardwood log."

"It's not a log," he said as softly. "It's not a log and we both know it."

"And we both know that the words you now speak are not solely your own. Reyn. It little matters what we call it. What we both know is that you have spent far too much time in contact with it, studying the murals and contemplating the glyphs on the pillars. It sways your thoughts and makes you its own."

"No!" He denied it sharply. "That is not the truth of it, Mother. Yes, I have spent much time in this chamber, and studied the markings the Elderlings left here. I have studied, too, that which we tumbled from inside the other 'logs' that were once within the chamber." He shook his head, his coppery eyes flashing in the dimness. "Coffins. That was what you told me they were when I was young. But they are not. Cradles would be a truer name for them. Moreover, if knowing what I know now, I long to awaken and release the only one that is left, that does not mean I have fallen under her sway. It only means that I have come to see what would be right to do."

"What is right to do is to remain loyal to one's own," his mother retorted angrily. "Reyn, I tell you this plainly. You have spent so much time in the company of this wizardwood log that you do not know where your own thoughts leave off and its sly promptings begin. There is at least as much of a child's thwarted curiosity in your desire as there is righteousness. Look at your actions today. You know where you are needed. But where are you?"

"Here. With one who needs me most, for she has no other advocate!"

"She is most likely dead." His mother spoke bluntly. "Reyn. You tease your fancy with nursery tales. How long was that log there, even before we discovered this place? Whatever was within it has perished long ago, and left only the echoes of its longing for light and air. You know the properties of wizardwood. A log, broken free of its contents, becomes free to take on the memories and thoughts of those in daily contact with it. That does not mean the wood is alive. You put your hands on it, and you listen to the trapped memories of a dead creature from another time. That is all they are."

"If you are so sure of that, why do not we test your theory? Let us expose this log to light and air. If no dragon queen hatches from within it, then I shall concede I was wrong. I will no longer oppose it being cut into timber to build a great ship for the Khuprus family."

Jani Khuprus heaved a great sigh. Then she spoke softly. "It makes no difference, Reyn, whether you oppose it or not. You are my youngest son, not my eldest. When the time comes, you will not be the one to decide what is done with the last wizardwood log." At her son's downcast face, she felt she might have spoken too harshly. As stubborn as he was, he was also oddly sensitive. That came from his father, she thought, and feared. She tried to make him see her reasoning. "To do what you propose would divert workmen and time from the tasks they must do if we are to keep money flowing into our household. The log is too big. The entrance they used to bring it here collapsed long ago. It is too long to wend it down the corridors to get it outside. The only alternative would be for workmen to clear the forest above us and then dig away the soil. We would have to break away the crystal dome and hoist it out with tripods and pulleys. It would be a monumental task."

"If I am correct, it would be worth it."

"Would it? Let us pretend you are correct, and we have exposed this log to light and something has hatched from it. Then what? What assurances do you have that such a creature will feel kindly toward us, or regard us at all? You have read more of the scrolls and tablets of the Elderkind than any other man alive has. You yourself say that the dragons that shared their cities were arrogant and aggressive creatures, prone to take whatever they desired. Would you free such a creature to walk among us? Worse, what if it resented us, or even hated us, for what we unknowingly did to her kin in the other logs? Look at the size of that log, Reyn. It would be a formidable enemy you had loosed upon your own kind, simply to satisfy your curiosity."

"Curiosity!" Reyn sputtered. "It is not solely curiosity, Mother. I feel pity for the trapped creature. Yes, and I feel guilt for those others we so thoughtlessly destroyed over the years. Remorse and atonement can drive one as strongly as curiosity."

Jani knotted her fists. "Reyn. I am not going to discuss this any further with you. If you want to speak of it to me again, then you must do so in my sitting room, not in this damp cave with that . . . thing swaying your every thought. And that is final."

Reyn straightened slowly and crossed his arms on his chest. She could not see his face; she did not need to. She knew his mouth was set and his jaw clenched tight. Stubborn lad. Why did he have to be so stubborn?

She did not look at him as she made her peace offering. "Son, after you have helped the work crew in the west corridor, I thought we might sit down and plan your trip to Bingtown. Although I have promised the Vestrits that you will not turn Malta's head with presents, it is still fitting that you take gifts for her mother and grandmother. Those must be selected, as well as garments for your journey. We have not yet discussed how you will present yourself. You have always dressed so soberly. Yet, a man who goes courting should have plumage like a peacock. You must, of course, remain veiled. But how heavily veiled I will leave up to you."

Her gambit succeeded. His stance softened; she could sense his smile. "Veiled impenetrably, but not for the reason you think. I think Malta is a woman who enjoys mystery and intrigue. I think it is what first attracted her to me."

Jani began to walk slowly toward the chamber entrance. As she had hoped, Reyn trailed after her. "Her mother and grandmother seemed to think her very much a child still, but you refer to her as a woman."

"She is certainly a woman." Reyn's tone left no room for doubt. He took pride in his declaration. Jani found herself marveling at the change in her son. Never before had he expressed such an interest in a woman, though there had been no lack of them vying for his attention. Among the Rain Wild families, any of the Khuprus sons or daughters would be a good catch. Only once had they attempted to arrange a marriage on his behalf. His adamant refusal had been socially awkward. There had been a few alliance offers from Bingtown Trader families as well, but Reyn had disdained them. No, disdained was too strong a word for overtures he had scarcely acknowledged. Perhaps Malta Vestrit could save her son from this obsession of his. She smiled over her shoulder at Reyn as she led him from the room.

"I confess, I am intrigued by this woman-child Malta. Her family speaks of her one way, and you quite another. . . . I look forward to meeting her."

"I hope that shall happen soon. I plan to invite her and her kin to come for a visit, Mother. If that is all right with you, of course."

"You know I have no objections. The Vestrit family is well thought of among the Rain Wild Traders, despite their decision to forbear trading with us. With the alliance of our families in marriage, that will surely end. They have the liveship that is needed to trade up the Rain Wild River . . . and they will own it free of encumbrances once the wedding is celebrated. You and Malta have the prospect of prosperity before you."

"Prosperity." Reyn said the word with an overtone of amusement. "Malta and I have far better prospects than mere prosperity. Of that, Mother, I assure you."

They came to a divergence in the corridor. Jani paused there. "You will go to the west corridor and open the new door." Her tone stopped just short of making it a question.

"I will," Reyn replied, almost absently.

"Good. When you are finished there, come to me in my drawing room. I will have a selection of appropriate gifts from which you may choose. Shall I have the tailors come and bring their newest cloths with them?"

"Yes. Certainly." He frowned in distracted thought. "Mother, you promised I would not turn Malta's head with costly gifts. Am I permitted to bring the simple tokens that any young man may offer a maiden? Fruit and flowers and sweets?"

"I cannot see how they could object to such things as those."

"Good." He nodded to himself. "Could you have baskets prepared for me that I could offer each day of my visit?" He smiled to himself. "The baskets could be trimmed with ribbons and soft scarves in bright colors. And a bottle or two of excellent wine in each . . . I do not think that would be going too far."

His mother smiled wryly to herself. "You may wish to proceed cautiously, my son. Ronica Vestrit will tell you plainly enough if you overstep the boundaries she has set. I do not think you should hasten to cross wills with her."

Reyn was already walking away from her. He glanced back, a quick flash of copper eyes. "I shall not hasten to cross her, Mother. But neither shall I hasten to avoid it." He continued walking away from her as he spoke. "I'm going to marry Malta. The sooner they get used to me, the easier it will be for all of us."

Behind him, in the darkness, Jani folded her arms. Obviously, he had never met Ronica Vestrit. A glint of amusement came into her eyes as she wondered if her son's stubbornness would not find its equal in that of the Bingtown Trader.

Reyn paused. "Have you sent a bird to tell Sterb of my courtship?"

Jani nodded, pleased that he had asked. Reyn did not always get along with his stepfather. "He wishes you well. Little Kys says you must not marry until winter, when they return to Trehaug. And Mando says you owe him a bottle of Durjan brandy. Something about a bet you made, long ago, that your brothers would marry before you."

Reyn was already striding away. "A wager I am pleased to lose," he called back over his shoulder.

Jani smiled after him.

CHAPTER FOUR

Bonds

BRIG'S HANDS RESTED ON THE SPOKES OF VIVACIA'S WHEEL, CASUALLY COM-
petent. The pirate's face had the distant look of a man completely aware
of the ship as his larger body. Wintrow paused a moment to size him up
before approaching. He was a young man, no more than twenty-five. His
chestnut hair was confined under a yellow kerchief marked with the
Raven insignia. His eyes were gray, and the old slave tattoo on his face
had been over-needled with a dark blue raven that almost obscured it.
Despite his youth, Brig had a decisive air that made even older men jump
to his orders. Kennit had chosen well in putting him in charge of the
Vivacia until he recovered.

Wintrow took a deep breath. He approached the older man with
respect but dignity. He needed Brig to recognize him as a man. Wintrow
waited until the man's eyes swung to meet his own. Brig looked at him
silently. Wintrow spoke softly but clearly. "I need to ask you some questions."

"Do you?" Brig challenged. His eyes flicked away, up to his lookout
man.

"I do," Wintrow replied firmly. "Your captain's leg gets no better.
How much longer will it take us to get to Bull Creek?"

"Day and a half," Brig told him, after brief consideration. "Maybe
two." The expression on his face never seemed to change.

Wintrow nodded to himself. "I think we can wait that long. There are
supplies I'd like to have before I try to cut. I hope we can get them there.
In the meantime, I could keep him stronger if I had better supplies. When
the slaves rose up against the crew, they ransacked much of the ship. The
medical chest has been missing since then. It would be very useful to me
now."

"No one's owned up to taking it?"

Wintrow gave a small shrug. "I've asked but no one has answered.
Many of the freed slaves are reluctant to talk to me. I think Sa'Adar is
turning them against me." He hesitated. That sounded self-pitying. He

would not gain Brig's respect by whining. He went on more judiciously. "Maybe they do not realize what they have. Or in the confusion of the storm and the uprising, someone may have taken it, discarded it, and it may have gone overboard." Wintrow took a breath and got back to his intent. "There were things in it that could make your captain more comfortable."

Brig tossed him a brief glance. He looked unconcerned, but he suddenly bellowed, "Caj!"

Wintrow braced himself to be seized and hustled along. Instead, when the man appeared, Brig ordered, "Shake down everyone on board. The medical chest is missing. If someone has it, I want it found. At the very least, I want to know who touched it last. Do it."

"Aye," Caj replied, and hastened away.

When Wintrow did not leave, Brig sighed out through his nose. "Something else?" he demanded.

"My father is—"

"SHIP!" the lookout suddenly sang out. An instant later, he called out, "Chalcedean galley, but flying the flag of the Satrap's Patrol. They're coming up fast with oars and sail. They must have been laying back in that inlet."

"Damn," Brig spat. "He did it! The son of a whore brought in Chalcedean mercenaries. Clear the decks!" he suddenly roared. "Working crew only! Everyone else below and out of the way. Get some sail on!"

Wintrow was moving, sprinting toward the figurehead. He dodged men nimbly. The deck became as busy as a stirred ant-nest. Ahead of them, the *Marietta* was sheering off in one direction as *Vivacia* leaned another. Wintrow gained the foredeck and then clung to the bow railing. Behind him, he heard thin shouts as the Chalcedean ship hailed them. Brig did not bother to reply.

"I don't understand!" *Vivacia* called to him. "Why do Chalcedean war galleys fly the Satrap's colors?"

"I heard rumors of it in Jamaillia. Satrap Cosgo hired Chalcedeans to patrol the Inside Passage. They're supposed to clear out the pirates, but that doesn't explain why they'd pursue us. A moment!" He flung himself into the rigging, scrabbling up to where he had a better view of what was going on. The Chalcedean ship in pursuit was built for warfare, not trade. In addition to her sail, two banks of slaves plied her oars. She was long and lean and her decks swarmed with fighting men. The spring sunlight glinted on helms and swords. The Satrap's flag with the white spires of Jamaillia on a blue field looked incongruous above the galley's blood-red sail.

"He invites their warships into our waters?" *Vivacia* was incredulous. "Is he mad? The Chalcedeans are without honor. This is like putting the thief to guard your warehouse." She glanced fearfully over her shoulder. "Do they pursue us?"

"Yes," Wintrow said succinctly. His heart thundered within him. What should he hope? That they escaped cleanly, or that the Chalcedean patrol boat caught them? The pirates would not surrender the *Vivacia* without a battle. There would be more bloodshed. If the Chalcedeans prevailed, would they restore Vivacia to her legal owners? Perhaps. He suspected they would take the ship back to Jamaillia for the Satrap's decision. The slaves huddled belowdecks would be enslaved once more, and they knew it. They would fight. The slaves outnumbered the boarders that the Chalcedean vessel could be carrying, but they were unarmed and inexperienced. A great deal of bloodshed, he decided.

So. Should he urge Vivacia to flee, or dawdle? Before he could even voice his uncertainty, the decision was snatched from him.

The smaller, sleeker vessel, driven by oars as well as wind, was gaining on them. For the first time, Wintrow noted the cruel war ram at the bow of the galley. A flight of arrows rose from the Chalcedean's deck. Wintrow cried out a wordless warning to Vivacia. Some were aflame as they arced toward the ship. The first volley fell short, but they had made their intention plain.

In a display of both seamanship and daring, the *Marietta* suddenly heeled over, changing her course into a curve that would take her behind *Vivacia* and right across the Chalcedean ship's bow. Wintrow thought he glimpsed the pirate Sorcor on the deck, exhorting his men to greater efforts. The Raven flag blossomed suddenly, a taunting challenge to the Chalcedeans. For a moment, it gave Wintrow pause. What sort of a captain was this pirate Kennit to be able to command such loyalty in his men? Sorcor's plain intention was to draw the pursuit off his captain and to himself.

From Wintrow's perch, he saw the *Marietta* rock suddenly as her deckmounted catapults lofted a shower of ballast at the patrol vessel. Some of the stones fell short, sending white gouts of water leaping from the waves, but a satisfying amount of it rattled down onto the decks of the galley. It wrought havoc among the oarsmen. The steady beating of the oars suddenly looked like the wild scrabbling of a many-legged insect. The gap between the patrol vessel and *Vivacia* steadily and swiftly widened. The *Marietta* did not look as if she were staying to fight. Having worked her mischief, she was now piling on canvas and fleeing. As the galley regained the beat of its oars, it shot off in pursuit of her. Wintrow strained to see, but the helmsman was taking *Vivacia* into the lee of an island. His view was blocked. He suddenly understood the ruse. The *Vivacia* would be taken swiftly out of sight while the *Marietta* lured the pursuit well away.

He clambered down to drop lightly to the deck. "Well. That was interesting," he remarked wryly to Vivacia. But the ship was distracted.

"Kennit," she replied.

"What about him?" Wintrow asked.

"Boy!" The woman's sharp voice came from behind him. He turned to see Etta glaring at him. "The captain wants you. Now." She spoke peremptorily, but her eyes were not on him. Her gaze locked with Vivacia's. The figurehead's face grew suddenly impassive.

"Wintrow. Stand still," she ordered him softly.

Vivacia lifted her voice to speak to the pirate. "His name is Wintrow Vestrit," she pointed out to Etta with patrician disdain. "You will not call him 'boy.' " Vivacia shifted her eyes to Wintrow. She smiled at him benignly and politely observed, "I hear Captain Kennit calling for you. Would you go to him, please, Wintrow?"

"Immediately," he promised her and complied. As he walked away from them, he wondered what Vivacia had been demonstrating. He would not make the mistake of thinking that she had been defending him from Etta. No. That exchange had been about the struggle for dominance between the two females. In her own way, Vivacia had asserted that Wintrow was her territory and that she expected Etta to respect that. At the same time, it had pleased her to reveal to the woman that the ship was aware of what went on in the captain's stateroom. From the spasm of anger that had passed over Etta's features, he deduced she was not pleased by it.

He glanced back over his shoulder at them. Etta had not moved. He heard no voices, but they could have been speaking softly. He was struck again by the pirate woman's extraordinary appearance. Etta was tall, her long limbs spare of flesh. She wore her silk blouse and brocaded vest and trousers as casually as if they were simple cotton garments. Her sleek black hair was cut off short, not even reaching her shoulders. She offered neither roundness nor softness to suggest femininity. Her dark eyes were dangerous and feral. From what Wintrow had seen of her, she was savagely tempered and remorseless as a cat. Not one sign of tenderness had he seen in the woman. Nevertheless, all those traits contradicted themselves, combining to make her overwhelmingly female. Never before had Wintrow sensed such power in a woman. He wondered if Vivacia would win her battle of wills with Etta.

Kennit was indeed calling his name, not loudly, but with a panting intensity. Wintrow did not knock but entered immediately. The tall, lean pirate was supine on the bed, but there was nothing restful about his attitude. His hands gripped the linens, knuckles white, as if he were a woman in labor. His head was thrown back against the disheveled pillows. The bared muscles of his chest stood out strongly. His gaping mouth gulped air spasmodically; his chest heaved up and down with the effort. His dark hair and open shirt were soaked in sweat. The sharp tang of it filled the cabin.

"Wintrow?" Kennit gasped out yet again, as he reached the bedside.

"I'm here." Instinctively, he took one of the pirate's calloused hands in his own. Kennit gripped Wintrow's hand in so violent a clench it was all he could do to keep from crying out. Instead, he returned the grip, deliberately pinching down hard between the pirate's thumb and fingers. With his other hand, he wrapped Kennit's wrist. He tried to set his fingers to the pirate's pulse, but the man's bracelet was in the way. He contented himself with moving his hand to Kennit's forearm. Rhythmically he tightened and then loosened his grip in a slow, calming pattern while he maintained the pinch on Kennit's hand that was supposed to lessen pain. He dared to sit down on the edge of the bed, leaning over Kennit so that he could meet the tortured man's eyes. "Watch me," he told him. "Breathe with me. Like this." Wintrow took a slow steadying breath, held it for a count, and then slowly released it. Kennit made a faint effort to copy him. His breath was still too short and too brisk, but Wintrow nodded encouragingly at him. "That's right. That is right. Take control of your body. Pain is only the tool of your body. You can master it."

He held the pirate's gaze steady with his own. With every breath, he expelled soothing confidence and belief, so that Kennit might breathe it in. Wintrow centered himself within his own body, finding a core that touched his heart and both his lungs. He let the focus of his eyes soften, drawing Kennit's gaze deeper into his own so that he could share his calmness with the man. He tried to make his gaze draw Kennit's pain out and let it disperse in the air between them.

The simple exercises drew his mind back to his monastery. He tried to imbibe peace from those memories, to add their strength to what he was trying to accomplish. Instead, he suddenly felt a charlatan. What was he doing here? Mimicking what he had seen old Sa'Parte do with patients in pain? Was he trying to make Kennit believe he was truly a priest-healer, instead of a brown-robed acolyte? He did not have the complete training to do this simple pain alleviation, let alone remove a diseased leg. He tried to tell himself he was simply doing the best he could to help Kennit. He wondered if he were being honest with himself; perhaps he was only trying to save his own skin.

Kennit's grip on his hand slowly lessened. Some of the tension left his neck and his head lolled back onto his damp pillows. His breathing grew slower. It was the labored breathing of a man fighting exhaustion. Wintrow kept possession of his hand. Sa'Parte had spoken of a technique for lending strength to the suffering, but Wintrow's learning had not progressed that far. He had expected to be an artist for Sa, not a healer. Still, as he clasped Kennit's sweating hand between his own, he opened his heart to Sa and begged that the father of all would intervene. He prayed that his mercy would supply what Wintrow lacked in learning.

"I can't go on like this."

From another man, the words might have sounded pitiful or pleading. Kennit spoke them as a simple statement of fact. The pain was ebbing, or perhaps his ability to respond to it was exhausted. He closed his dark eyes and Wintrow felt suddenly isolated. Kennit spoke quietly but clearly. "Take the leg off. Today. As soon as possible. Now."

Wintrow shook his head, then spoke the denial aloud. "I can't. I don't have half of what I need. Brig said that Bull Creek is only a day or two away. We should wait."

Kennit's eyes snapped open. "I know that I can't wait," he said bluntly.

"If it's just the pain, then perhaps some rum . . ." Wintrow began, but Kennit's words over-rode his own.

"The pain is bad, yes. But it's my ship and my command that suffer the worst right now. They sent a boy to tell me of the patrol ship. All I did was try to stand. . . . I fell. Right in front of him, I collapsed. I should have been on the deck as soon as the lookout spotted that sail. We should have turned and cut the throats of every Chalcedean pig aboard that galley. Instead, we fled. I left Brig in command, and we fled. Sorcor had to fight my battle. In addition, all aboard know of it. Every slave on board this ship has a tongue. No matter where I leave them off, every one of them will wag the news that Captain Kennit fled the Satrap's patrol ship. I can't allow that." In an introspective voice, he observed, "I could drown them all."

Wintrow listened in silence. This was not the suave pirate who had courted his ship with extravagant words, nor the controlled captain. This was the man beneath that façade, exposed by pain and exhaustion. Wintrow realized his own vulnerability. Kennit would not tolerate the existence of anyone who had seen him as he truly was. Right now Kennit seemed unaware of how much he was revealing. Wintrow felt like the mouse pinioned by the snake's stare. As long as he kept still, he had a chance to remain undetected. The pirate's hand grew lax in his grip. Kennit turned his head on his pillow and his eyes began to sag shut.

Just as Wintrow began to hope he might escape, the door to the cabin opened. Etta entered. She took in the room at a glance. "What did you do to him?" she demanded as she crossed to Kennit's bedside. "Why is he so still?"

Wintrow lifted a finger to his lips to shush her. She scowled at that, but nodded. With a jerk of her head, she indicated the far corner of the room. She frowned at how slowly he obeyed her, but Wintrow took his time, easing the pirate's hand down gently on the quilt and then sliding slowly off the bed so that no movement might disturb Kennit.

It was all in vain. As Wintrow left his bedside, Kennit said, "You will cut off my leg today."

Etta gave a horrified gasp. Wintrow turned back slowly to the man. Kennit had not opened his eyes, but he lifted a long-fingered hand and pointed at him unerringly. "Gather what you have for tools and such, and get the job done. What we do not have, we must do without. I want to be finished with this. One way or another."

"Sir," Wintrow agreed. He changed course, moving hastily toward the door. As swiftly, Etta moved to block him. He found himself looking up into eyes as dark and merciless as a hawk's. He squared his shoulders for a confrontation. Instead, he saw something like relief in her face. "Let me know how I can help you," she said simply.

He bobbed a nod to her request, too shocked to reply, and slipped past her and out the door. A few steps down the companionway, he halted. He leaned suddenly against the wall and allowed the shaking to overtake his body. The bravado of his earlier bargain overwhelmed him. What had been bold words would soon become a bloody task. He had said he would set a knife to Kennit's flesh, would slice into his body and cut through his bone and separate his leg. Wintrow shook his head before the enormity of the situation could cow him. "There is no path but forward," he counseled himself, and hastened off to find Brig. As he went, he prayed the medicine chest had been found.

CAPTAIN FINNEY PUT DOWN HIS MUG, LICKED HIS LIPS AND GRINNED AT Brashen. "You're good at this. You know that?"

"I suppose," Brashen reluctantly acknowledged the compliment.

The smuggler laughed throatily. "But you don't want to be good at it, do you?"

Brashen shrugged again. Captain Finney mimicked his shrug, and then went off into hoarse laughter. Finney was a brawny, whiskery-faced man. His eyes were bright as a ferret's above his red-veined nose. He pawed his mug about on the ring-stained table, then evidently decided he had had enough beer this afternoon. Pushing the mug to one side, he reached for the cindin humidor instead. He twisted the filigreed glass stopper out of the dark wooden container. He turned it on its side and gave it a shake. Several fat sticks of the drug popped into view. He broke a generous chunk off one and then offered the humidor to Brashen.

Brashen shook his head mutely, then tapped his lower lip significantly. A little plug of the stuff was still burning pleasantly there. Rich, black, and tarry was the cindin that was sending tendrils of well-being throughout his bones. Brashen retained enough wit to know that no one was bribed and flattered unless the other party wanted something. He wondered hazily if he would have enough willpower to oppose Finney if necessary.

"Sure you won't have a fresh cut?"

"No. Thanks."

"No, you don't want to be good at this trade," Finney went on as if he had never interrupted himself. He leaned back heavily in his chair and took a long breath in through his open mouth to speed the cindin's effect. He sighed it out again.

For a moment, all was silent save for the slapping of the waves against the *Springeve*'s hull. The crew was ashore, filling water casks at a little spring Finney had shown them. Brashen knew that as mate he should be overseeing that operation, but the captain had invited him to his cabin. Brashen had feared Finney had a grievance with him. Instead, it had turned into drinking and cindin at midday, on his own watch. Shame on you, Brashen Trell, he thought to himself and smiled bitterly. What would Captain Vestrit think of you now? He lifted his own mug again.

"You want to go back to Bingtown, don't you?" Finney cocked his head and pointed a thick finger at Brashen. "If you had your wishes, that's what you'd do. Pick up where you left off. You was quality there. You try to deny it, but it's all over you. You weren't born to the waterfront."

"Don't suppose it matters what I was born to. I'm here now," Brashen pointed out with a laugh. The cindin was uncoiling inside him. He was grinning, matching the smile on Finney's face. He knew he should worry that Finney had figured out he was from Bingtown, but he thought he could deal with it.

"Exactly what I was about to tell you. See that? See? You're smart. Many men, they can't accept where they end up. They always go moping after the past, or mooning toward the future. But men like us—" He slapped the table resoundingly. "Men like us can grab what we're offered and make a go of it."

"So. You're going to offer me something?" Brashen hazarded slyly.

"Not exactly. It's what we can offer each other. Look at us. Look at what we do. I take the *Springeve* up and down this coast, in and out of lots of little towns. I buy stuff, I sell stuff, and I don't ask too many questions. I carry a good supply of fine trade goods, so I get the deals. I get fine quality stuff. You know that's true."

"That's true," Brashen agreed easily. Now was not the time to point out the pedigree of the goods they trafficked in. The *Springeve* and Finney traded throughout the pirate isles, buying up the best of the pirates' stolen goods and reselling them to a go-between in Candletown. From there, they were passed off as legitimate goods in other ports. Brashen didn't know much more than that and he didn't really care. He was mate on the *Springeve*. In exchange for that, and for acting as a bodyguard on occasion, he got his room, board, a few coins and some really good cindin. There wasn't much else a man needed.

"The best," Finney repeated. "Damn good stuff. And we take all the risks of getting it. Us. You and I. Then we take that stuff back to Candletown, and what do we get there?"

"Money?"

"A pittance. We bring in a fat pig and they throw us back the bones. But together, Brashen, you and I could do better for ourselves."

"How do you figure?" This was starting to make him nervous. Finney had an interest in the *Springeve*, but he didn't own it. Brashen didn't want any part of genuine piracy. He'd already done his share of that early in life. He'd had a gut full of it back then. No. This trading in stolen goods was as close as he wanted to get to it. He might not be the respectable first mate of the liveship *Vivacia* anymore—he wasn't even the hard-working second mate of a slaughter ship like *Reaper* anymore, but he hadn't sunk so low as piracy.

"You got that look to you, like I said. You are Trader born, ain't you? Probably a younger son or something, but you would have the connections in Bingtown, if you wanted to use them. We could take a good haul up there, you would hook us up, and we could trade some top-quality merchandise for some of that magical stuff that the Traders have. Them singing chimes and perfume gems and whatnot."

"No." Brashen heard too late how abrupt his reply was. Quickly he softened it. "It's a good idea, a brilliant idea, except for one thing. I don't have any connections." In a burst of generosity that was probably due to the cindin, he gifted Finney with the truth. "You're right, I'm Trader born. But I tangled those lines a long time ago, and my family cut me loose. I couldn't get a glass of water begging at my Da's door, let alone cut you a trade deal. The way my father feels about me, he wouldn't piss on me if I was on fire."

Finney guffawed and Brashen joined with a wry smile. He wondered why he spoke of such things at all, let alone why he made them a cause for levity. Better than being a crying drunk, he supposed. He watched Finney compose himself, laugh once more and then take another drink of his beer. He wondered if the older man still had a father of his own somewhere. Perhaps he had a wife and children, too. Brashen knew next to nothing about him. It was better so. If he had an ounce of sense, he'd get up now, say he had to check on the crew, and leave before he told Finney any more about himself. Instead he spat the soggy remains of the cindin into the bucket under the table and reached for the humidor. Finney grinned at him as Brashen broke another plug from the stick.

"Wouldn't have to be your own father. A man like you has chums, old friends, eh? Or you know someone with a bent for this, you've heard rumors about him. In any town, there are some that wouldn't mind adding

a few coins to their purses, quiet-like. We could go in there, once or twice
a year, with a load of our very best, held back from our usual buyers. Not a
lot, but of the finest quality. And that's what we would ask in return.
Confidentially. Only you and I would need to know."

Brashen nodded, more to himself than Finney. Yes. The man was
planning on going behind his partner's back, to make a bit more money
for himself. So much for honor among thieves. He was quietly offering to
cut Brashen in on the deal, if Brashen would help him find the sources. It
was a low trick. How could Finney look at him and believe he was that
sort of man?

How long could he pretend he was not? What was the point of it,
anymore?

"I'll think about it," Brashen told him.

"You do that," Finney grinned.

IN LATE AFTERNOON, WINTROW CROUCHED ON THE FOREDECK BESIDE KEN-
nit. "Ease him off the blanket," he directed the men who had borne him
there. "I want him to be lying on the planking of the deck, with as little
between him and the wizardwood as possible."

A short distance away, her arms crossed on her chest, Etta stood,
apparently impassive. She would not look toward Vivacia. Wintrow tried
not to stare at the pirate woman. He wondered if anyone else noticed her
clenched fists and tight jaw. She had battled his decision to do the cutting
here. She had wanted privacy and walls around this messy, painful business. Wintrow had brought her here, and showed her his own bloody
handprint on the deck. He had promised her that Vivacia could help
Kennit with the pain as she had helped him when his finger was cut off.
Etta had finally given in to his will. Neither he nor Vivacia were certain
how much help the ship could give, but as they still lacked the medicine
chest, anything she could do for Kennit would be helpful.

The ship was anchored in a nameless cove of an uncharted island.
Wintrow had gone to Brig, to ask once more about both where the medicine chest was and when they would get to Bull Creek. Both answers had
been disappointing. The medical supplies had not been found, and without the *Marietta* to guide him, Brig did not know how to get back to Bull
Creek. The answer had disheartened Wintrow but not shocked him.

Brig's temporary command of the *Vivacia* was a giant step up for
him. Only a few days ago, Brig had been a common seaman. He didn't
know how to navigate or read charts. He intended to find a safe place to
anchor up, and wait until either the *Marietta* found them or Kennit was
well enough to guide him. When Wintrow had asked incredulously if they
were completely lost, Brig had replied that a man could know where he
was, and still not know a safe course to somewhere else. The crisp anger in

the young sailor's voice had warned Wintrow to hold his tongue. There was no sense in letting the former slaves know of their situation. It presented too great an opportunity for Sa'Adar.

Even now, the wandering priest hovered at the edge of the group. He had not offered to be helpful and Wintrow had not asked him. Most often, wandering priests were judges and negotiators rather than healers or scholars. While Wintrow had always respected the learning and even the wisdom of that order, he had never been completely comfortable with the right of any man to judge another. It did not help right now to feel that scrutiny was being applied to him. Whenever he sensed Sa'Adar gaze at him, he felt a chill knowledge that the man found him unworthy. The older priest stood, arms crossed on his chest. Two map-faces flanked him; he spoke to them quietly. Wintrow pushed aside his awareness of them. If Sa'Adar would not help, Wintrow would not be distracted by him. He rose and walked to the bow of the ship. Vivacia looked back at him anxiously.

"I will do my best," she said before Wintrow could ask. "But keep in mind we have no blood bond with him; he is not kin to us. Nor has he been aboard long enough for me to be familiar with him." She lowered her eyes. "I will not be much help to you."

Wintrow leaned far down to touch his palm to hers. "Lend your strength to me, then, and that will do much," he consoled her.

Their hands met, confirming and increasing the strange bond between them. He did draw strength from her. As he acknowledged that, he saw an answering smile dawn on her face. It was not an expression of happiness, not even a sign that all was now right between them, but a sign of shared determination. Whatever else might threaten them, whatever doubts they harbored about one another, they still went into this together. Wintrow lifted his face to the sea wind and offered up a prayer that Sa might guide them. He turned back to his task. As he drew a deep breath, he could feel Vivacia with him.

Kennit lay limply on the deck. Even at this distance, Wintrow could smell the brandy. Etta had sat beside Kennit, and patiently coaxed him to drink far beyond his desire. The man had a good capacity for liquor. He was sodden but not senseless. Etta had also been the one to choose who would hold him down. To Wintrow's surprise, three of those she had chosen were former slaves. One was even an older map-face. They looked uneasy but determined as they stood amongst the gawking onlookers. That would be the first thing Wintrow would deal with. He spoke calmly but clearly.

"Only those who have been summoned should be here. The rest of you, disperse to give me room." He did not wait to see if they obeyed him. To watch them ignore his command would only be an additional humiliation for him. He was sure that if they did, Etta would intervene. He knelt down beside Kennit. It would be awkward to work with him lying flat on the deck, but Wintrow felt that whatever strength Vivacia could lend him would be worth it.

He looked over the paltry array of tools he had scavenged. They lay in a tidy row on a piece of clean canvas next to his patient. It was a motley assortment of makeshift equipment. The knives, freshly sharpened, had come from the cook's supplies. There were two saws from the carpenter's box. There were sail-making needles, large and coarse, and some sewing needles that belonged to Etta. Etta had provided him with neatly torn bandaging, both linen and silk. It was ridiculous that he had not been able to salvage better equipment. Almost every sailor aboard had had his own needles and tools. All the belongings of the slaughtered crewmen had disappeared. He was sure the slaves had claimed them when they took over the ship. That none of them had been surrendered to this need spoke deeply of how much the former slaves resented Kennit's claiming of the ship. Wintrow could understand their feelings, but it did not help his predicament. As he looked down on the crude tools, he knew he was doomed to fail. This would be little better than lopping the man's leg off with an axe.

He lifted his eyes and sought out Etta. "I must have better tools than these," he asserted quietly. "I dare not begin without them."

She had been musing, her gaze and thoughts afar. "I wish we had the kit from aboard the *Marietta*," she replied wistfully. For that unguarded moment, she looked almost young. She reached down to twine one of Kennit's black curls through her fingers. The sudden tenderness in her face as she looked on the drowsing man was startling.

"I wish we had *Vivacia*'s medicine chest," Wintrow replied as solemnly. "It was kept in the mate's cabin, before all this began. There was much in it that would be useful, both medicines and tools. It could have made this much easier for him. No one seems to know what became of it."

Etta's gaze darkened and her face hardened into a scowl. "No one?" she asked coldly. "Someone always knows something. You just have to ask the right way."

She stood abruptly. As she crossed the deck, she drew her knife from its hip sheath. Wintrow immediately discerned her target. Sa'Adar and his two guards had withdrawn but not left the foredeck. Too late, the wandering priest turned to acknowledge Etta's approach. His gaze of disdain became a goggle of shock as Etta casually ran the honed edge of her blade down his chest. He stumbled back with a shout, then looked down at the front of his ragged shirt hanging open. A thin line down his hairy chest became red and widened as the blood began to seep. His two burly guards looked down at Etta's knife held low and ready. Brig and another pirate had already closed ranks with her. For an instant, no one spoke or moved. Wintrow could almost hear Sa'Adar assessing his choices. The wound was a shallow scoring of his skin, very painful but not life-threatening. She could have gutted him where he stood. So. What did she want?

He chose wronged righteousness. "Why?" he demanded theatrically. He opened his arms wide to expose the slash down his chest. He half turned, so that he addressed the slaves still clustered amidships as well as Etta. "Why do you choose me to attack? What have I done, except come forward to offer my aid?"

"I want the ship's medicine chest," Etta responded. "I want it now."

"I don't have it!" Sa'Adar exclaimed angrily.

The woman moved faster than a clawing cat. Her knife licked out and a second line of blood bisected the first. Sa'Adar set his teeth and did not cry out or step back, but Wintrow saw the effort it cost him.

"Find it," Etta suggested. "You bragged that you organized the uprising that overthrew the captain. You go among the slaves, exhorting them that you are the true leader they should follow. If that is true, you should know which of your men plundered the mate's cabin. They took the chest. I want it. Now."

For a breath longer, the tableau held. Did some sort of a sign, a flicker of a glance, pass between Sa'Adar and his men? Wintrow could not be certain. Sa'Adar began talking, but to Wintrow his words seemed oddly staged. "You could have simply asked me, you know. I am a humble man, a priest of Sa. I seek nothing for myself, only the greater good of humanity. This chest you seek . . . what did it look like?" His querying eyes fell on Wintrow and his mouth stretched in a manufactured smile.

Wintrow forced himself to keep a neutral expression as he answered. "A wooden chest. So by so." Wintrow measured it in the air. "Locked. Vivacia's image was burned into the top of it. Within were medicines, doctoring tools, needles, bandaging. Anyone who opened it would know instantly what it was."

Sa'Adar turned to those gathered in the waist of the ship. "Did you hear, my people? Do any of you know of such a chest? If so, please bring it forth now. Not for my sake, of course, but for that of our benefactor, Captain Kennit. Let us show him we know how to be kind to those who are kind to us."

It was so transparent, Wintrow thought Etta would cut him down where he stood. Instead, an oddly patient look came over her face. By his knee, on the deck, Kennit spoke very softly. "She knows she can wait. She likes to take her time killing, and do it in privacy."

Wintrow's eyes snapped to the pirate, but he seemed to be nearly unconscious. His lashes lay long on his cheeks; his face was slack. A loose smile twitched over his mouth. Wintrow set two fingers lightly to Kennit's throat. His pulse still beat steady and strong there, but the man's skin was fevered. "Captain Kennit?" Wintrow asked softly.

"Is this it?" A woman's voice rang out. The freed slaves parted, and she came striding forward. Wintrow stood up. She carried the medicine chest. The lid had been splintered, but he recognized its worn wood. He did not move forward but let the woman bring it to Etta instead. Let this be her battle with Sa'Adar. He had enough bad blood with the man already.

She lowered her eyes to gaze down at the opened chest when it was placed before her feet. She did not even stoop to stir the disheveled contents. When she lifted her eyes back to Sa'Adar's face, she gave a small snort of contempt. "I do not enjoy games," she said very softly. "But if I am forced to play them, I always make sure I win." Her stare met his. Neither looked aside. The planes of her cheeks tightened, exposing her teeth in a snarling smile. "Now. Take your rabble off this deck. Get belowdecks and close the hatches. I neither wish to see you, nor hear you, nor even smell you while this is going on. If you are very wise, you will never draw my attention to you again. Do you understand?"

Wintrow watched as Sa'Adar made a very serious mistake. He drew himself up to his full height, not quite the match of Etta's. His voice was coolly amused. "Am I to understand that you, and not Brig, are in command here?"

It would have been a deft play, if there had been any rivalry between the two to exploit. Brig only threw his head back in a guffaw of laughter as Etta's knife danced in to add yet another stripe to Sa'Adar's chest. This time he cried out and staggered back a step. She had made the knife bite deeper. As the wandering priest clutched at his blood-slicked chest, she smiled darkly. "I think we understand that I am in command of *you*."

One of the map-faces started forward, his face dark with fury. Etta's knife moved in and out of him, and he went down, clutching at his belly. Vivacia gave a muffled cry at this new spillage of blood on her deck, an echo of the cries and gasps of the watching freed folk. Wintrow shared the deep shudder of horror that passed through the ship at this fresh violence, but he could not take his eyes away. Sa'Adar shrank back behind his other bodyguard, but that burly man was also cowering away from the woman with the knife. None of the others sprang forward to defend the priest. Instead, there was a subtle movement away from him as folk distanced themselves.

"Be clear on this!" Etta's voice rang out like a hammer on an anvil. She lifted the bloody knife and swept it in an arc that encompassed the whole ship and every staring face, tattooed or not. "I will tolerate no one who threatens the well-being and comfort of Captain Kennit. If you wish to avoid my wrath, then you will do nothing to inconvenience him." Her voice grew softer. "It is very simple, really. Now clear these decks."

This time the crowded folk on the deck disappeared like water swirling down a drain. In a matter of moments, the only people remaining abovedeck were the pirate crewmen and those few slaves Etta had chosen to hold Kennit down. Her chosen ones regarded her with an odd mixture of respect and horror. Wintrow suspected they had now completely changed allegiance and would follow her anywhere. It remained to be seen how formidable an enemy she had created in Sa'Adar.

As Etta came to Wintrow, their eyes met. The demonstration with Sa'Adar had been for his benefit as well. If Kennit died under his hands, Etta's vengeance would be furious if not swift. He drew a deep breath as she approached him, the medicine chest in her hands. He took it from her wordlessly, placed it on the deck and swiftly sorted through its contents. Some of it had been pilfered, but most of it was there. With a deep sigh of relief, he found kwazi rind preserved in brandy. The bottle was tiny. He reflected bitterly that his father had not seen fit to use it to ease his pain when his finger was amputated; then the thought intruded that if he had, Wintrow would not have it now to use on Kennit. He shrugged at the vagaries of fate and began methodically to set out his tools. He pushed aside his collection of kitchen knives, replacing them with the finer-edged blades in the chest. He selected a bone saw with a carved handle like a bow. Three needles he threaded with hair from Kennit's own head. When he lay them down on the canvas, the black hair spiraled into a lax curl. There was a leather strap with two rings on the end to cinch about the limb before he cut it.

That was all. He looked a moment longer at the row of tools. Then he glanced up at Etta. "I would like to offer prayers. A few moments of meditation might better prepare all of us for this."

"Just get on with it," she ordered him harshly. The line of her mouth was set flat, and the high planes of her cheeks were rigid.

"Hold him down," Wintrow replied. His own voice came out as harshly. He wondered if he were as pale as she was. A spark of anger burned inside him at her disdain. He tried to rekindle it as determination.

Etta knelt by Kennit's head but did not touch him. Two men took his good leg and pinned it to the deck. There was another man on each of his arms. Brig tried to hold Kennit's head, but his captain twisted free of his tentative grip. He lifted his head to glare wide-eyed at Wintrow. "Is it now?" he demanded, sounding both querulous and angry. "Is it now?"

"It's now," Wintrow told him. "Brace yourself." To Brig he said, "Hold his head, firmly. Put your palms on his forehead and pin him to the deck with your weight. The less he thrashes about, the better."

Of his own accord, Kennit lay his head back and closed his eyes. Wintrow lifted the blanket that had covered his stump. In the few hours since he had last seen it, it had become worse. Swelling stretched the skin tight and shiny. His flesh had a blue-gray cast to it.

Begin now, while he had courage still. He tried not to think that his own life depended on his success. As he gingerly worked the strap under the leg stump, he refused to think of Kennit's pain. He must focus on being swift and cutting him cleanly. His pain was irrelevant.

The last time Wintrow had seen a limb severed from a man, the room had been warm and cheery. Candles and incense burned as Sa'Parte had prepared for his task with prayer and chanting. The only prayer uttered here was Wintrow's silent one. It flowed in and out with his breath. *Sa, grant your mercy, lend me your strength. Mercy,* on an indrawn breath, *Strength* as he breathed out. It calmed his thundering heart. His mind was suddenly clearer, his vision keener. It took him a moment to realize Vivacia was with him, more intimately than ever before. Dimly, he could sense Kennit through her. Curiously, Wintrow explored that faint bond. It seemed as if she spoke to Kennit at a great distance, counseling him to courage and strength, promising that she would be there to help. Wintrow felt a moment of jealousy. He lost his concentration.

Mercy, strength, the ship prompted him. *Mercy, strength,* he breathed back at her. He threaded the leather strap through the rings and cinched it firmly about Kennit's thigh.

Kennit roared out his agony. Despite the men pinning his limbs, his back arched up off the deck. He flopped like a gaffed fish. Fluids broke through the crusted scabs on his stump and spattered on the deck. The foul odor poisoned the breeze. Etta threw herself across Kennit's chest with a cry and strove to hold him down. A moment of terrible silence fell when he ran out of breath.

"Cut him, damn you!" Etta shrieked at Wintrow. "Get it over with! Do it!"

Wintrow was frozen as he knelt, paralyzed by Kennit's agony. It inundated him like an icy wave, shocking and immersing him in its intensity. The force of the other man's experience flooded through his tenuous link with the ship and into Wintrow. He lost his identity in it. He could only stare dumbly at the whore, wondering why she was doing this to him.

Kennit drew in a ragged breath, and expelled it as a scream. Wintrow shattered like a cold glass filled with hot water. He was no one, he was nothing, and then he was Vivacia and abruptly Wintrow again. He fell forward, his palms flattening on the deck, soaking up his identity from the wood. A Vestrit, he was a Vestrit, moreover, he was Wintrow Vestrit, the boy who should have been a priest. . . .

With a shudder, Kennit suddenly lay senseless. In the stillness that followed, Wintrow grasped at his sense of himself, wrapped himself in it. Somewhere the prayer continued: *Mercy. Strength. Mercy. Strength.* It was Vivacia, setting the rhythm of his breath for him. He took control of himself. Etta was weeping and cursing at the same time. She sprawled on Kennit's chest, both restraining and embracing him. Wintrow ignored her. "Hold him," he said tightly. He chose a knife at random. He suddenly understood what he had to do. Speed. Speed was the essence. Pain such as this could kill a man. If he was lucky, he could finish cutting before Kennit recovered consciousness.

He set the shining blade to the swollen flesh and drew it across and down. Nothing had ever prepared him for that sensation. He had helped with butchering at slaughter time at the monastery. It was not a pleasant task, but it had to be done. Then he had cut through cold meat that was still, that was solid and stiff from a day's hanging. Kennit's flesh was alive. Its fevered softness gave way to the keen edge of the blade and closed up behind it. Blood welled up to hide his work. He had to grasp Kennit's leg below the spot where he cut. The flesh there was hot and his fingers sank into it far too easily. He tried to cut swiftly. The meat under the knife moved, muscles twitching and pulling back as Wintrow severed them. The blood poured forth in a constant crimson flood. In an instant, the handle of the knife was both sticky and slick. It puddled on the deck beneath Kennit's leg, then spread to soak into Wintrow's robe. He caught glimpses of tendon, glistening white bands that vanished as his knife divided them. It seemed forever before his blade met the bone and was defeated by it.

He flung the knife down, wiped his hands down his shirt and cried, "Saw!"

Someone thrust it toward him and he grabbed it. To insert it into the wound sickened him but he did it. He dragged it across the bone; it made a terrible sound, a wet grinding.

Kennit surged back to life, yelping like a dog. He pounded the back of his own head on the deck and his torso writhed despite the weight of those holding him down. Wintrow braced himself, expecting to be over-whelmed with the pirate's pain but Vivacia held it back. He had no time to wonder what it cost her to take that to herself. He did not even have time to be grateful. He bore down on the saw, working swiftly and vio-lently. Blood spattered the deck, his hands, and his chest. He tasted it. The bone gave way suddenly and before he could stop, he had sawed raggedly into flesh. He pulled the saw out of the clinging wound and threw it aside, then groped for a fresh knife. Somewhere Kennit barked, "Uh, uh, uh!" It was a sound beyond screaming. A splattering noise followed.

Wintrow smelled the sourness of vomit on the sea air. "Don't let him choke!" he said abruptly, but it was not Kennit who had puked but one of the men holding him. No time for that. "Hold him down, damn you!" Wintrow heard himself curse the man. With the knife in his hand, he cut down, stopping just short of severing the leg completely. He turned the blade at an angle, slicing himself a flap of skin from the stump before he made the final severing cut and rolled the rotten remains of the leg aside.

He looked down, sickened, at what he had wrought. This was not a neatly sliced piece of meat like a holiday roast. This was living flesh. Freed of their attachments, the bundled muscles sagged and contracted un-evenly. The bone glistened up at him like an accusing eye. Everywhere was the spreading blood. He knew with vast certainty that he had killed the man.

Do not think that, Vivacia warned him. Then, almost pleading, *Do not force him to believe that. For right now, linked as we all are, he must believe what we think. He has no choice.*

With blood-smeared hands, Wintrow found the small bottle that held the kwazi fruit rind. He had heard of its potency, but it seemed like a pitifully small amount to stop such vast pain. He unstoppered it. He tried to pour it sparingly, to save some against tomorrow's pain. The pieces of preserved rind clogged in the bottleneck. He shook it, and the pale green liquid splattered forth unevenly. Where it fell on Kennit's flesh, it brought a sudden silencing of the pain. He knew because through Vivacia he sensed it. Less than half of the extract was left in the bloody bottle when he capped it. He clenched his teeth and touched the flesh he had cut, patting the thick green liquid to spread it evenly. The cessation of pain was so sudden that it was like being stranded by a retreating wave. He had not realized how much of it was battering past Vivacia's shield until it stopped. He sensed, too, Vivacia's sudden relief.

He tried to remember all that he had seen Sa'Parte do when he had cut off the man's leg. He had tied the ends of some bleeding arteries, folding them back on themselves and closing them off. Wintrow tried. He was suddenly tired and confused; he could not remember how many the healing priest had sewn. All he wanted to do was get away from this gory mess he had created. He longed to flee, curl up in a ball somewhere and deny this. He forced himself to go on. He folded the slab of skin up over the raw end of Kennit's stump. He had to ask Etta to pull more hair from the pirate's head and thread the fine needles for him. Kennit lay abso-lutely still now, his breath puffing in and out of his lips. When the men started to ease up their holds, Wintrow rebuked them.

"Hold him fast still. If he stirs while I am stitching, he may tear all my work apart."

The flap did not fit neatly. Wintrow did the best he could, stretching the skin where he had to. He wrapped the stump with lint and bound it with silk. As fast as he hid it, the blood seeped through, smearing from his sticky hands, oozing out to blossom through the fabric. Wintrow lost count of how many layers he wrapped it in. When he was finally finished, he wiped his hands down the front of his robe yet again and then reached for the cinch. When he loosened it, the clean bandaging almost instantly reddened. Wintrow wanted to scream in horror and frustration. How could there be that much blood in a man? How could so much of it gush out of him, and yet leave him still clinging to life's thread? His own heart was thundering with fear as he wrapped it once again. Supporting the stump in his hands, he said dully, "I'm finished. We can move him now."

Etta lifted her head from Kennit's chest. Her face was white. Her eyes fell on the discarded leg. Heartbreak contorted her mouth for an instant. With a visible effort, she smoothed her features. Her eyes were still bright with brimming tears as she huskily ordered the men, "Fetch his litter."

It was an awkward trip. He had to be maneuvered down the short ladder to the main deck. Once they had crossed it, there were the narrow corridors of the officers' living quarters to navigate. Every time the wooden handles of the litter rapped against a wall and jostled Kennit, Etta snarled. As they moved him from his litter to the bed, his eyes opened momentarily and Kennit babbled wildly. "Please, please, I'll be good, I promise. I'll listen, and obey, I will." Etta scowled so blackly that every man lowered his eyes before her. Wintrow was sure the captain would never be questioned about his words. Once on his bed, Kennit closed his eyes and was as still as before. The other men left the cabin as swiftly as they could.

Wintrow lingered a moment longer. Etta scowled at him as he touched Kennit first at wrist and then throat. His pulse was light and flighty. Wintrow leaned close to him, and tried to breathe confidence into him. He set his sticky hands on Kennit's face with his fingertips touching the man's temples and prayed aloud to Sa to grant the man strength and health. Etta ignored him, folding a clean cloth and slipping it deftly under Kennit's bandaged stump.

"Now what?" she asked dully when Wintrow finished.

"Now we wait and we pray," the boy replied. "That is all we can do."

She made a small contemptuous sound and pointed at the door. Wintrow left.

HER DECK WAS A MESS. THE BLOOD SOAKING INTO IT MADE A HEAVY PLACE. Vivacia's eyes were half-closed against the brightness of the westering sun. She could feel Kennit breathing in the captain's cabin, and knew the slow leaking of his blood. The medicine had drowned his pain, but it remained for her a distant throbbing threat. Every beat brought it a minuscule step closer. Although she could not feel his agony yet, she sensed its immensity and dreaded its coming.

Wintrow moved on her foredeck, tidying up the mess. He damped a left-over piece of bandaging in his bucket of water. He wiped each knife as he put it away, cleaning the needles and the saw carefully. He stowed it all in the medicine chest, methodically returning it to order. He had washed his hands and forearms and wiped the blood from his face, but the front of his robe was stiff and soaked with it. He wiped clean the bottle of

kwazi-fruit essence and considered what was left. "Not much," he muttered to her. "Well, it matters little. I doubt that Kennit will live long
enough to require more. Just look at all this blood." He placed the bottle
back in the chest and then looked down at the piece of leg. Gritting his
teeth, he picked up the thing. Severed meat at both ends and a knee in
the middle, it balanced oddly light in his hands. He carried it to the side
of the ship. "This feels wrong," he said aloud to Vivacia, but he still threw
it over the side.

He staggered back with a low cry as the white serpent's head shot out
of the water to snatch the leg out of the air before it could even splash
into the sea. As swiftly as it had appeared, it was gone and the leg with it.

Wintrow darted back to the rail. He clung there, staring down into
the green depths, looking for some pale flicker of the creature. "How did
it know?" Wintrow demanded hoarsely. "It was waiting, it seized the leg
before it touched water. How could it have known?" Before she could
answer, he went on, "I thought that serpent was gone, driven away. What
does it want, why does it follow us?"

"It hears us, we two." Vivacia's voice was low, pitched for him alone.
She felt ashamed. People had started to come out of the hatches, back up
onto the deck, but no one ventured near the foredeck. The serpent had
come and gone so swiftly and noiselessly that no one else seemed to have
seen it. "I do not know how and I do not think it understands in full what
we think, but it understands enough. As to what it wants, why, exactly
what you just gave it. It wants to be fed, no more than that."

"Maybe I should fling myself to it. Save Etta the trouble of doing it
later." He spoke mockingly but she heard the despair under his words.

"You voice its thought, not your own. It reaches for you, clamoring for
food. It believes we owe it food. It does not scruple to suggest your own
flesh might satisfy it. Do not listen."

"How do you know what it thinks and wants?" Wintrow had abandoned his tasks and come to the rail, leaning over to speak to the figurehead. She glanced over her shoulder at him. The weariness on his face
aged him. She debated how much to tell him and then decided there was
no point in sheltering him. Eventually, he must know.

"He is family," she said simply. At Wintrow's astounded look, she
shrugged one bare shoulder at him. "That is how it feels to me. I get the
same sense of connection. Not as strong as you and I have now, but
undeniable."

"That makes no sense."

She shrugged at him again, and then changed the subject abruptly.
"You must stop believing that Kennit is certain to die."

"Why? Are you going to tell me that he is family also and can sense
my thoughts?"

There was an edge of bitterness in his voice. Jealousy? She tried not to be pleased about it, but could not resist prickling him more. "Your thoughts? No. He cannot sense your thoughts. It is I that he senses. He reaches toward me and I toward him. We are aware of each other. Tenuously, of course. I have not known him long enough to make it stronger. His blood soaking into my deck seals that bond in a way I cannot explain. Blood is memory. As your thoughts touch mine, so they also influence Kennit's. I try to keep your fears from intruding on him, but it is an effort."

"You are linked to him?" Wintrow asked slowly.

"You asked me to help him. You asked me to lend him strength. Did you think I could do that without bonding to him?" Vivacia felt indignant at his disapproval.

"I suppose I didn't think about that aspect of it," Wintrow replied reluctantly. "Do you sense him now?"

Vivacia thought about it. She found herself smiling softly. "Yes. I do. And more clearly than I did before." The smile faded from her face. "Perhaps that is because he is weakening. I think he no longer has the strength to hold himself separate from me." She brought her attention back swiftly to Wintrow. "Your conviction that he will die is like a curse upon him. Somehow, you must change your heart, and think only of him living. His body listens deeply to his mind. Lend it your strength."

"I will try," he said grudgingly. "But I can scarcely convince myself of something I know is a lie."

"Wintrow." She rebuked him.

"Very well." He set both hands to the forward rail. He lifted his eyes and fixed them on the horizon. The spring day was melting into twilight. The blue sky was darkening, its color changing gradually to meld with the darker blue of the sea. In moments, it was difficult to tell where the sea left off and the sky began. Slowly Wintrow withdrew into himself, calling his vision back from that far focus until his eyes closed of their own accord. His breathing was deep and even, almost peaceful. In curiosity she reached for the bond they shared, trying to read his thoughts and feelings without being intrusive.

It did not work. He was instantly aware of her. Yet, instead of being resentful of her invasion, he linked willingly with her. Inside him, she became aware of the steady flowing of his thoughts. "Sa is in all life, all life is in Sa." It was a simple affirmation and she realized instantly he had chosen words he absolutely believed. He no longer focused on the health of Kennit's body. Instead, he asserted that while Kennit lived, the life within him was of Sa and shared Sa's eternity. No end, his words promised her. Life did not end. After thought, she found she shared his conviction. No final blackness to fear, no sudden stopping of being. Changes and mutations, yes, but those things went on with every breath. Changes were the essence of life; one should not dread change.

She opened herself to Kennit, shared this insight with him. Life went on. The loss of a leg was not an ending, only a course adjustment. While life pulsed in a man's heart, all possibilities existed. Kennit did not need to fear. He could relax. It was going to be all right. He should rest now. Just rest. She felt the warmth of his expanding gratitude. The tensed muscles of his face and his back eased. Kennit took a deep breath and let it out slowly.

He did not draw another one.

CHAPTER FIVE

The Liveship Ophelia

ALTHEA'S WATCH WAS OVER; HER TIME WAS NOW HER OWN. SHE WAS TIRED, but pleasantly so. The spring afternoon had been almost balmy. It was rare for the season to be this kindly and Althea had enjoyed it. The *Ophelia* herself had been in an expansive mood all day. The liveship had made the sailors' tasks easy, moving northward toward home with a will. She was a ponderous old cog, now heavy with goods from a successful trading journey. The early evening wind was gentle rather than brisk, but *Ophelia*'s sails caught every breath of it. She slid effortlessly through the waves. Althea leaned on the forward rail, watching the beginning of the sunset off the port bow. Home was only a few days away.

"Mixed feelings?" Ophelia asked her with a throaty chuckle. The buxom figurehead gave her a knowing glance over her bared shoulder.

"You know you are right," Althea conceded. "About everything. Nothing in my life makes sense anymore." She began to tick her confusions off on her fingers. "Here I am, serving as first on a liveship merchant vessel, about the highest post a sailor can aspire to. Captain Tenira has promised me a ship's ticket out of this. It's all the proof I need that I am a competent sailor. With that credential, I can go home and press Kyle to keep his word, and give me back my ship. Yet, oddly enough, I feel guilty about it. You have made it so easy. I worked three times as hard when I was serving as ship's boy on the *Reaper*. It just doesn't seem right."

"I could make your tasks harder if you wish," Ophelia offered teasingly. "I could develop a list, or start taking on water or . . ."

"You wouldn't do that," Althea told her with certainty. "You're too proud of how well you sail. No. I do not wish my tasks to be harder. Nor do I regret my months aboard the *Reaper*. If nothing else, they proved to me that I could scramble. Serving aboard that hulk made me a better sailor, and showed me a side of sailing I had never seen before then. It wasn't a waste of time. It was time away from the *Vivacia*; that is where the rub is. Time lost forever." Althea's voice trailed away.

"Oh, my dear, that's so tragic." Ophelia's voice was full of solicitude.

A moment later, she went on sarcastically, "The only way it could be worse would be if you wasted still more time mooning about it. Althea. This is not like you. Look forward, not back. Correct your course and go on. You can't undo yesterday's journey."

"I know," Althea said with a rueful laugh. "I know that what I am doing now is the right thing to do. It just seems strange that it is so easy and pleasant. A beautiful ship, a lively crew, a good captain . . ."

"A very handsome first mate," Ophelia interjected.

"He is that," Althea admitted easily. "And I appreciate all Grag has done for me. I know he says he is enjoying the chance to read and relax, but it must be tedious to pretend he is ill so I can have the chance to fill his position. I have a lot of reasons to be grateful to him."

"Odd. You haven't shown him that gratitude." For the first time, a touch of chill crept into the ship's voice.

"Ophelia," Althea groaned. "Please, let's not get into that again. You don't want me to pretend feelings for Grag that I simply don't have, do you?"

"I simply can't understand why you don't have those feelings, that's all. Are you sure you do not deceive yourself? Look at my Grag. He is handsome, charming, witty, kind and a gentleman. Not to mention that he is born of a Bingtown Trader family and stands to inherit a sizable fortune. A fortune that includes a magnificent liveship, I might add. What more could you be looking for in a man?"

"He is all those things and more. I conceded that to you days ago. I find no faults with Grag Tenira. Or with his magnificent liveship." Althea smiled at the ship.

"Then the problem must be with you," Ophelia announced inexorably. "Why aren't you attracted to him?"

Althea bit her tongue for a moment. When she spoke, her voice was reasonable. "I am, Ophelia. In a way. Nevertheless, there are so many other things going on in my life that I cannot allow myself . . . I just do not have time to think about things like that. You know what I face when we get to Bingtown. I need to make amends with my mother, if that is possible. And there is another 'magnificent liveship' that occupies my thoughts. I have to persuade my mother to support me when I try to take the *Vivacia* back from Kyle. She heard him vow before Sa that if I could but prove myself a sailor, he would give me the ship. However rashly he spoke, I intend to make him keep that vow. I know it is going to be an ugly struggle to force him to surrender *Vivacia* to me. I need to keep my mind focused on that."

"Don't you think Grag could be a powerful ally in such a struggle?"

"Would you think it honorable of me to encourage his advances only to use him as a tool to get my ship back?" Althea's voice was cool now.

Ophelia laughed low. "Ah. He has made advances, then. I was beginning to worry about the boy. So. Tell me all about it." She quirked an eyebrow at Althea.

"Ship!" Althea warned her, but after a moment, she could not help joining her laughter. "Are you going to pretend to me that you don't already know everything that goes on aboard you?"

"Umm," Ophelia mused. "Perhaps I know most of what happens in the staterooms and belowdecks. But not all." She paused, then pried, "That was a very long silence inside his quarters yesterday. Did he try to kiss you yesterday?"

Althea sighed. "No. Of course not. Grag is far too well bred for that."

"I know. More's the pity." Ophelia shook her head. As if she had forgotten to whom she was speaking, she added, "The boy needs a bit more spark to him. Nice is fine, but there's a time when a man should be a bit of a rogue, to get what he wants." She cocked her head at Althea. "Like Brashen Trell, for instance."

Althea groaned. The ship had wormed his name out of her a week ago, and had given her no peace since then. If she was not demanding to know what was wrong with Grag, and why didn't Althea fancy him, then she was pestering her for the sordid details of her brief liaison with Brashen. Althea did not want to think about the man. Her feelings on that topic were too confusing. The more she decided she was finished with him, the more he intruded into her thoughts. She kept thinking of all the witty things she should have said at their last parting. He had been so rude when she had not kept a rendezvous she knew was unwise. The man had assumed too much, far too soon. He didn't deserve a moment of her thoughts, let alone dwelling on him. But despite her waking disdain for him, he intruded into her dreams. In her dreams, the poignancy of his gentle strength seemed a safe harbor worth seeking. In her dreams, she reminded herself, setting her teeth. In her waking hours, she knew he was no safe harbor, but a whirlpool of foolish impulses that would draw her to her doom.

She had been silent too long; Ophelia was watching her face with a knowing look. Abruptly Althea stood straight and put a small smile on her face. "I think I'll go and see Grag before I turn in. There are a few questions I need answered."

"Um," Ophelia purred, pleased. "Take your time asking them, my dear. The Tenira men think deeply before they act, but when they do act . . ." She lifted both her eyebrows at Althea. "You might not even remember Trell's name afterward," she suggested.

"Believe me. I'm already doing my best to forget it."

Althea was relieved to hurry away from her. Sometimes it was wonderful to spend part of the evening sitting and talking with the ship. The wizardwood figurehead incorporated many generations of Tenira sailors, but women had formed her first and deepest impressions. Ophelia retained a female perspective on life. It was not the fragile helplessness that now passed for femininity in Bingtown, but the independent determination that had distinguished the first women Traders. The advice she offered Althea was often startling to her, yet it frequently reinforced views Althea had privately held for years. Althea had not had many women friends. The tales Ophelia had shared with her had made her realize that her dilemmas were not as unique as she had believed. At the same time, Ophelia's brazen discussions of Althea's most intimate problems both delighted and horrified her. The ship seemed to accept Althea's independence. She encouraged Althea to follow her heart, but also held her responsible for the decisions she had made. It was heady to have such a friend.

She hesitated outside the door to Grag's cabin. She paused to straighten her clothing and hair. She had been relieved to abandon the boy's guise she had worn aboard the *Reaper*. On this ship, the crew knew her name. Althea Vestrit had to uphold the honor of her family. So although she dressed practically, in heavy cotton fabric, the trousers she wore were closer to being a split skirt. She had bound her hair back out of the way, but not tarred it into a queue. The laced-up blouse that she tucked carefully into her trousers even had a touch of embroidery on it.

She felt a pleasant anticipation at the thought of seeing Grag. She enjoyed sitting and talking with him. There was a gratifying little tension of awareness between them. Grag found her attractive and was undaunted by her competency. He seemed impressed by it. It was a new and flattering experience for Althea. She wished she could be certain that was all she felt. Despite her fling with Brashen—despite living aboard ship with men for years—in some areas she was very inexperienced. She was not sure if she was attracted to Grag for himself, or simply because he seemed to be fascinated with her. Surely, this was just a harmless flirtation between them. What more could it be, between two strangers flung together by chance?

She took a breath and knocked.

"Enter." Grag's voice was muffled.

She found him sitting up on his bunk, his face swathed in bandaging. There was a strong scent of cloves in the air. At the sight of her, a welcoming glint came into his blue eyes. As she shut the door behind her, he pulled the wrappings off his jaw and let them drop gratefully. The pretense of the bandages had left his hair tousled like a boy's. She grinned at him. "So. How's the toothache?"

"Convenient." He stretched, rolling his wide shoulders, then made a show of flinging himself back on his bunk. "I can't remember when I last had this much time to myself." He swung his legs up onto his bunk and crossed them at the ankle.

"You're not getting bored?"

"No. For any sailor, idle time is too much of a novelty. We always find a way to fill it." He fished around at the edge of his bunk and came up with a handful of ropework. He unrolled it on his lap to reveal a fancifully knotted mat. The intricate pattern had created a lacy effect from the stout twine he had used to create it. It was hard to believe such a delicate design came from his work-scarred fingers.

Althea touched the edge of it. "Beautiful." Her fingers traced the pattern of knotted twine. "My father could take an empty wine bottle, and some twine, and create this wonderful pattern of knots over the glass. It looked like flowers, or snowflakes. . . . He always promised he'd teach me how to do it, but we never found the time." The gaping sense of loss that she had believed she had mastered overwhelmed her again. She turned away from him abruptly and stared at the wall.

Grag was silent for a moment. Then he offered quietly, "I could teach you, if you wanted."

"Thanks, but it wouldn't be the same." She was surprised by the brusqueness in her own voice. She shook her head, embarrassed by the sudden tears that brimmed her eyes. She hoped he had not seen them. They made her vulnerable. Grag and his father had already done so much for her. She did not want them to see her as weak and needy, but as a strong person who would make the best of her opportunities. She drew in a long breath and squared her shoulders. "I'm all right now," she said in answer to his unspoken question. "Sometimes I miss him so badly. There's a part of me that can't accept that he's dead, that I'll never see him again."

"Althea . . . I know that perhaps this is a cruel question, but I've wondered. Why?"

"Why did he take the ship I'd worked on for so many years and will it to my sister instead?" She glanced over at Grag to see his quick nod. She shrugged. "He never told me. The closest he came to a reason was to say something about providing for my sister and her children. On good days, I tell myself that that meant he knew I could provide for myself and he was not afraid for me. On bad days, I wonder if he thought that I was selfish, if he feared that I would take *Vivacia* and care nothing for their welfare." She lifted her shoulders again.

She caught a glimpse of herself in Grag's shaving mirror. For an eerie instant, her father looked out at her. She had his wiry black hair and dark eyes, but not his size. She was small, like her mother. Nevertheless, the resemblance to her father was still strong, in the set of her jaw and the way her brows drew together when she was troubled. "My mother said that it was her idea and she talked him into it. She felt the estate had to be kept intact, the liveship inherited with the land holdings, so that the income from the one would go on supporting the other until all the debts were paid."

She rubbed at her brow. "I suppose that makes sense. When father decided that we would no longer trade up the Rain Wild River, he doomed us to a much lower income. The goods he brought back from the southlands were exotic, but nothing like the magic goods from the Rain Wilds. Our land holdings yielded well, but we could not compete with Chalced's slave-tended grain and fruit. Consequently, our debt for the ship is still substantial. Moreover, it is secured with our land holdings. If we fail to keep our promise to repay it, we could lose both ship and family land."

"And you are hostage for that debt as well." Grag pointed the fact out quietly. As a member of a Bingtown Trader family that owned a liveship, he was well aware of the standard terms for such a bargain. Liveships were rare and costly. Just as it took three generations for a liveship to quicken and come to cognizance, so it also took generations to pay for one. Only the Rain Wild Traders knew the source of the wizardwood lumber that made up the liveship hulls and figureheads. Only in a ship constructed of wizardwood could one safely negotiate the Rain Wild River and participate in the trade of their near-magical goods. Their value was such that families pledged their fortunes for them. "In blood or gold, the debt is owed," Grag added quietly. If the Vestrit family could not pay for the ship with coin, then a daughter or son of the family could be claimed.

Althea nodded slowly. Odd. She had known the terms of the bargain ever since she was old enough to be considered a woman, but somehow she had never applied it to herself. Her father had been a wonderful trader; he had always seen that there was money in the household to discharge their just debts. Now that her brother-in-law Kyle was in charge of the family's liveship and finances, who could say how things would go? Her sister's husband had never liked her. The last time they had been in the same room, in that final spectacular family argument, he had said it was her duty to marry well and stop being a burden on the family. Perhaps that was exactly what he had been hinting: that if she went willingly to a Rain Wild man, the family could enjoy a lessening of their debt.

Ever since she was a tiny child, her duties to her family's honor had been impressed upon her. A Bingtown Trader paid his debts and kept his word. No matter what their personal disagreements might be, when threatened by outsiders, the Traders closed ranks and endured. Those ties of kinship and duty included the Traders who had chosen to remain behind in the Rain Wilds and settle there. Distance and years might have separated them, but the Rain Wild Traders were still kin to the Bingtown Traders. Contracts with them were honored, and the duties of family were respected. She felt something inside her go hard and cold with purpose. If

Kyle failed in the Vestrit family obligations, it would be her duty to offer herself. Fecundity was the one treasure the Rain Wild folk lacked. She would have to go to the Rain Wilds, take a husband there and bear children to him. It was what her forebears had promised, so long ago. Not to do so would be unthinkable. Nevertheless, to be forced into it by Kyle's malice or ineptitude was intolerable.

"Althea? Are you all right?"

Grag's voice broke in on her thoughts and brought her back to herself. She realized she was glaring at a bulkhead. She gave a small shake and turned to face him. "I came to ask your advice, actually. I'm having a bit of trouble with one of the deckhands. I can't decide if I should take it personally or not."

The concerned look on Grag's face deepened. "Which one?"

"Feff." Althea shook her head in mock frustration. "One moment he listens and steps lively when I give an order. The next, he'll look me straight in the face and stand there with a silly grin on his face. I don't know if he's mocking me, or . . ."

"Ah!" Grag grinned. "Feff's deaf. In his left ear. Oh, he will not admit it to anyone. It happened when he fell from the mast about two years ago. He hit the deck hard, and for a day or so, we thought he wasn't going to live. Eventually, he came out of it. He's a bit slower about some things than he used to be, and I don't send him aloft unless I have to. He doesn't seem to have the balance he once did. He can't always hear what you say, especially if he's to the right of you. Sometimes if the wind is blowing strong, he can't hear at all. He doesn't mean to be insubordinate . . . that's what the silly smile is about. Other than that, he's a good man, and he's been with the ship a long time. It wouldn't be right to tie him up for that."

"Ah." Althea nodded to herself. "I wish someone had told me sooner," she said a bit crossly.

"It's one of those things Da and I don't even think about anymore. It's just how the ship is. No one meant to make your job harder."

"No, I didn't mean that," Althea replied hastily. "Everyone has gone out of their way to make my tasks easier. I know that. It's wonderful to be back on board a liveship again, and even more wonderful to discover that I actually can do this job. My father's will and my quarrel with Kyle and Brashen's concerns all made me wonder if I really was competent."

"Brashen's concerns?" Grag asked in a quietly leading voice.

Why had she said it? Where had her mind been? "Brashen Trell was my father's first mate on the *Vivacia*. After I signed aboard the *Reaper*, I found out he was part of her crew, too. When he discovered I was aboard as ship's boy . . . well. He had already made it plain to me back in Bingtown that he did not think I could cut it on my own."

"So. What did he do? Tell the captain?" Grag asked when the silence had lengthened.

"No. Nothing like that. He was just . . . watchful. That's the word, I suppose. I had a tough time on that ship. Knowing he was watching me scrabble just to keep up made me feel . . . humiliated."

"He had no right to do that to you," Grag observed in a low voice. Two sparks of anger burned deep in his eyes. "Your father took him on when no one else would. He owes your family. The least he could have done was protect you rather than mock your efforts."

"No. It wasn't like that, not at all." Suddenly she was defending Brashen. "He didn't mock me. Mostly he ignored me." When Grag's expression became even more indignant, she hastily clarified, "That was how I preferred it. I did not want special treatment. I wanted to make it on my own. And I did, eventually. What bothered me was that he was a witness to how hard I had to struggle. . . . I don't know why we're even talking about this."

Grag shrugged. "You brought it up, not I. There had always been a bit of speculation as to why your father took Brashen Trell on when his own family had given up on him. He'd been in enough trouble over the years that when his father threw him out, no one was really surprised."

"What kind of trouble?" Althea heard the avidity in her own question and toned it down. "I was just a girl when that happened, with little interest in Bingtown gossip. Years later, when he hired aboard the *Vivacia*, my father did not speak of it. He said a man deserves to be judged on who he is, not who he was."

Grag was nodding to himself. "It wasn't a noisy scandal. I know about it mostly because we schooled together. It started out in small ways. Pranks and silliness. As we got older, he was always the boy who would slip away when the master's back was turned. At first, it was just to avoid lessons, or go to the market and buy sweets. Later he was the boy who seemed to know more than the rest of us about things like girls and cindin and dice games. My father still says it was Trell's own fault his son went bad. Brashen always had too much money to spend and too much free time to amuse himself. No one drew a line with him. He'd get into mischief, like gambling more money than he had, or being drunk some-where public in the afternoon, and his father would drag him home and threaten him."

Grag shook his head. "He never carried out his threats. A day or so later, Brashen would be on the loose, doing the same things again. Trell always said he was going to cut off his credit, cane him or make him work off his debts. However, he never did. I heard his mother would always weep and faint when his father tried to punish him. He got away with everything that he did. Until one day Brashen came home and found the door closed to him. Just like that. Everyone, including Brashen, thought it was a bluff. We all expected the storm to blow over in a day or so. It didn't. A few days later, old man Trell made it known that he had officially recognized his younger son as his heir and disowned Brashen entirely. The only surprising thing about the whole affair was that Trell finally drew a line and stuck to it.

"For a time, Brashen was around town, staying wherever he could, but he soon wore out his welcome and ran out of money. He got a reputation for leading younger boys into trouble and wild ways." Grag grinned knowingly. "Both I and my younger brother were forbidden to associate with him. Soon no one wanted to be connected with him. Then he disappeared. No one knew what became of him." Grag made a wry face. "Not that anyone much cared. He left many debts behind him. By then folk knew he did not intend to pay them off. So he was gone. Most people felt Bingtown was a better place without him." Grag looked aside from her. "After he left, there was a rumor that a Three-Ships girl was carrying his child. The baby was stillborn; a mercy, I suppose. The girl was still ruined."

Althea felt faintly ill. She hated to hear Grag so disparage Brashen. She wanted to deny what he said of the man, but he obviously spoke with an insider's knowledge of the truth. Brashen had not been an ill-used, misjudged youth. He had been a spoiled eldest son without discipline or morals. Her father had taken him on years later and, under her father's control, he had become a decent man. Without her father, he had reverted. She had to admit to herself that was true. The drunkenness, the cindin. The whoring around, she added harshly to herself.

Ruthlessly she stripped the truth of her foolish embroideries. She had been pretending he had been infatuated with her when he bedded her. The truth was that she had been behaving like a slut and she'd found the partner she deserved. To prove it to herself, all she had to do was think about how they had parted. The moment he realized that she had come to her senses and was not going to allow him her body, he had turned against her. Shame flooded her. How could she have been so stupid and foolish? If he ever returned to Bingtown and spoke of what they had done, she would be ruined, just like the Three-Ships girl that he had left in his wake.

Grag was unaware of her discomfort. He had crouched down by a chest at the foot of his bed and was rummaging inside it. "I'm ravenous. Since I have this supposed toothache, Cook has only been bringing me soup and bread to sop in it. Would you care for some dried fruit? Jamaillian apricots or dates?"

"I've no appetite. Thank you."

Grag stopped his rummaging and swiveled to face her with a grin.

"Now that's the first time you've sounded like a proper Bingtown Trader's daughter since you came aboard. I don't know whether I'm relieved or disappointed."

Althea wasn't sure if she was flattered or insulted. "What do you mean?"

"Oh. Well." He brought the package of fruit out and sat down on his bunk with it. He patted the place beside him and she sat down. "There. You see," he exclaimed triumphantly. "Not only are we alone and un-chaperoned, behind a closed door, but you fearlessly sit down on my bed beside me. When I told you Brashen left a woman pregnant, you do not go pale or rebuke me for speaking of such things. You look thoughtful."

He shook his head, bemused. "You wear your hair sensibly on deck, I've seen you wipe your hands down your shirt front, and you went bare-foot and trousered the whole time you were pretending to be a ship's boy. Yet I can still remember a very feminine woman in my arms, perfumed like violets, and dancing as gracefully as . . . well, as gracefully as you scamper up the rigging. How do you do it, Althea?" He leaned back against the bulkhead, but the way he looked at her seemed to bring him closer to her. "How do you move so easily in both worlds? Where do you really belong?"

"Why must it be one or the other?" she countered. "You are both a capable seaman and the son of a Bingtown Trader. Why should not I have both sets of skills?"

He threw his head back and laughed. "There. That is not the answer one would expect from a Trader's daughter, either. At least, not one of our generation. A proper girl would be simpering over my compliment to her dancing, not asserting her ability to be a good sailor. You remind me of the tales Ophelia tells. According to her, there was a time when the women worked right alongside the men, in every trade, and sometimes excelled them."

"Anyone who knows the history of Bingtown knows that when our ancestors came to the Cursed Shores, each one had to scrabble for a living. You know that as well as I do." She felt a bit annoyed with him. Did he think she was improper?

"I know it," he admitted quietly. "But there are a lot of women in Bingtown who would no longer admit that."

"Mostly because it is no longer fashionable. Mostly because their fa-thers or brothers would be ashamed of them if they did."

"True. However, watching you, I have come to see that they are false, not just to history but to life. Althea. Of late, my parents have been urging me to seek a wife. I was born late in their lives; they'd like to see grandchildren before they are too old to enjoy them."

Althea listened in stunned silence. His sudden words shocked her. He could not be taking this conversation in that direction, could he?

"When I'm in Bingtown, my mother invites Trader daughters and their mothers over to endless teas. I've obediently attended the gatherings and balls. I've danced with a few women." Here he smiled at her warmly. "Several have seemed interested in me. Nevertheless, all the courtships I have begun have ended in disappointment. Always the same thing. My father looks at the woman I am seeing, and asks me, 'Will she be able to take care of herself and a household and children, while you are off sailing?' Then I look at her with that in mind, and no matter how lovely or witty or charming she is, she never seems strong enough."

"Maybe you are not giving the women a chance to prove themselves to you," Althea ventured.

Grag shook his head regretfully. "No. Two of them I asked directly. I reminded them that I expected to be someday the captain of the liveship *Ophelia*. How would it be, I asked, to know you must share me with a ship? A demanding and sometimes possessive ship, I added to be honest. I reminded them I would be gone months at a time. That I might not be home when my children were born, or when the roof sprang a leak or harvest season came around." He shrugged eloquently. "One and all, they told me that surely I could arrange to be home more after we were married. When I said I could not, they refused my suit. Genver went so far as to come aboard the *Ophelia*, and suggest that she could sail with me after we were married, if I could triple the size of the captain's room. But only until we had children. Then I would have to somehow arrange my life to be home more often than not."

"Did not you court anyone who was born into a liveship family? A girl who would understand what your ship meant to you?"

"I danced with one once," he said quietly.

The silence held. If he expected her to say something, Althea had no idea what. Grag moved very slowly, as if he were afraid she would startle. With one finger, he touched her hand where it rested on the bed. A small touch, but it sent a shiver up her arm even as dismay filled her heart. She liked Grag and found him attractive, but this was no time for either of them to act on that. Had she invited this? How should she deal with it? Was he going to try to kiss her? If he did, would she let him?

She suspected she would.

Grag came no closer. His voice went deeper and softer. His blue eyes were gentle and confiding. "In you, I see a strong woman. One who could sail with me, or capably manage things ashore while I was gone. I see someone who is not jealous of Ophelia." He paused and smiled ruefully. "If anything, I am a bit jealous of how quickly she has become fond of you. Althea, I cannot imagine a better choice for a wife than you."

Although she had been anticipating his words, they still stunned her. "But . . ." she began, but he lifted a warning finger.

"Hear me out. I have been giving much thought to this, and I see advantages for you, as well. It is scarcely a secret that the Vestrit fortunes have not prospered lately. The *Vivacia* is not yet paid for; that leaves you as ransom to the family's debt. It is also well known that the Rain Wild Traders would not consider taking a woman who is already married, or who has pledged marriage. Simply by considering my offer, you could put yourself out of their reach." He watched her face carefully. "We are a wealthy family. My wedding gift to your mother would be substantial, enough to secure her old age. You have made it clear you have no faith that Kyle will care for her."

Althea found it hard to speak. "I don't know what to say. We've talked as friends, and yes, we've flirted a bit, but I had no notion that your feelings ran strong enough to propose marriage."

Grag gave a small shrug. "I'm a cautious man, Althea. I see no sense in letting my feelings run ahead of me. In this stage of our relationship, I see planning rather than passion as what we must first share. We should be talking honestly with one another, to see if we share the same ambitions and goals." He was watching her face carefully. As if to give the lie to these words, he touched her hand again with one fingertip. "Do not think I don't feel an attraction toward you. You must know that I do. Nevertheless, I am not the sort of a man who would fling his heart where his head had not gone first."

He was so serious. Althea tried for a smile. "And I feared you were going to try to kiss me."

He returned her smile, shaking his head. "I am not an impulsive boy, nor a rough sailor. I would not kiss a woman who had not given me her permission to do so. Besides, there is no sense in taunting myself with what I cannot yet claim." He looked aside from her startled expression. "I hope I have not spoken too crudely. Despite the rough shipboard life you have shared, you are still a lady and a Trader's daughter."

There was no way to share with him the thought that had suddenly flashed through her mind. She knew, with vast certainty, that she would never desire to be kissed by a man who had first asked her permission. "Permission to come aboard," some impish part of her mind whispered, and she fought to keep from grinning. Perhaps, she suddenly thought, Brashen had already ruined her, but not in the social sense. After the sailor's matter-of-fact declarations of his desire, Grag's restrained and polite courtship seemed almost silly. She liked the man, truly she did. Yet, his careful negotiations left her unmoved. Abruptly, the situation was impossible. And as if Sa knew that there was no way Althea could rescue herself, fate suddenly intervened.

"All hands on deck!" someone roared in a voice that mixed both indignation and fear. Althea did not hesitate as she plunged out the door, nor did Grag even pause to put his toothache binding about his jaws. All hands meant all hands.

The crew of the *Ophelia* lined the bow railing, looking down. When she joined them, Althea was incredulous at the sight that met her eyes. A Chalcedean war galley, flying the Satrap's colors, was challenging *Ophelia*'s passage. The size comparison between the two ships might have been laughable were it not that the galley bristled with soldiers and their weaponry. The smaller, lighter galley confronting them was far more maneuverable than the cog. Such a vessel was often swifter than a sailing ship as well. In the light evening breeze, *Ophelia* could not avoid and outrun such a ship. The galley had run up to her on the windward side, taking advantage of the light breeze that pressed the ships together. They had no choice now; they would have to deal with the galley. The liveship's figurehead stared down at the Chalcedean's horse-prowed ship, still and shocked. Ophelia's arms were crossed stubbornly on her chest. Althea lifted her eyes to scan the horizon. The Chalcedean appeared to be operating alone. Captain Tenira shouted down, "What mean you by barring our way?"

"Throw down a line. In the name of your Satrap, we will board you!" declared a bearded man standing in the galley's bow. His blond hair was bound back in a long tail down his back, and battle trophies—finger bones bound with hanks of hair—decorated the front of his leather vest. Missing teeth gapped his threatening snarl.

"On what grounds?" Althea demanded of those around her, but Captain Tenira did not bother with such questions.

"No. You will not. You have no authority over us. Stand aside." The Trader captain stood firm, looking down on the galley. His voice was even and strong.

"In the name of the Satrap, throw down a line and submit to boarding." The Chalcedean smiled up at them, more teeth than affability. "Do not make us take you by force."

"Try," Captain Tenira suggested grimly.

The captain of the galley took a handful of documents from his mate. He waved the bundled tube of scrolls up at Tenira. A red ribbon bound them, weighted with a heavy seal of crimped metal. "We have authority. Right here. We shall bring our writs aboard to prove it. If you are an honest ship, you have nothing to fear. The Satrap has allied with Chalced to stop piracy in the Inside Passage. We are authorized by him to stop any suspicious ship and search for stolen goods and other signs of piratical activity." While the captain was speaking, several of his men had stepped forward with coils of line and grappling hooks.

"I'm an honest Bingtown Trader. You have no call to stop me, nor will I submit to search. Be out of our way!"

The grapples were already spinning, and as Captain Tenira finished speaking, three were launched toward the *Ophelia*. One fell short as the liveship sidled to one side. Another landed well on the deck but was immediately seized and thrown back by the *Ophelia*'s crew before it could be set in her wood.

Ophelia herself caught the third. In a sudden motion, she plucked it out of the air as it whirred past her. With a shout of anger, she gripped the line below the grapple and snatched up the rope. The man who had thrown it came with it, kicking and cursing in surprise. She disdainfully threw grapple, rope and sailor aside into the water. She set her fists to where a woman's hips would have been. "Don't try that again!" she warned them angrily. "Get out of our way or I'll run you down!"

From the galley came cries of amazement and fear. While many had undoubtedly heard of the liveships of Bingtown, few Chalcedean sailors would have ever seen one before, let alone seen one angered. Liveships seldom frequented the ports of Chalced; their trade routes were to the south. From the galley, a line was thrown to the Chalcedean sailor struggling in the water.

On board the *Ophelia*, Captain Tenira bellowed, "Ophelia, let me handle this!" while on the galley deck below them the Chalcedean captain angrily called for firepots to be prepared.

Ophelia paid no attention to her captain. At the mention of firepots, she had first gasped, then shrieked her wordless anger when she saw the smoking pots of tar brought out on his deck. For them to be readied so swiftly meant that the captain of the galley had had them prepared from the beginning. "In Sa's name, no!" Althea cried as she saw the pots readied for launching. Arrows were thrust headfirst into the small, fat pots; fuses of charred linen dangled. They would be lit before the arrows were released, and given time to ignite the contents of the pots. When the pots of grease and tar struck *Ophelia*, they would shatter, and the flames would leap up. *Ophelia* could not avoid them all, and every liveship was vulnerable to fire. It was not just for her rigging and decks that Althea feared, but for Ophelia herself. The only liveship that had ever died had perished in a fire.

The *Ophelia* was a trading cog, not built for fighting of any kind. Pirates seldom menaced liveships. It was well known that a liveship could out-maneuver and out-sail any ordinary ship of her kind. Althea doubted that anyone had ever challenged *Ophelia* for right of passage before, let alone demanded to board her. She carried no weaponry; her sailors had no experience in turning aside this kind of a threat. As Tenira shouted the orders that would veer *Ophelia* to one side, men raced to obey. "It won't be enough," Althea said in an undertone to Grag, at her side. "They'll set fire to us."

"Get oil from belowdecks. We'll throw firepots of our own!" Grag commanded angrily.

"And draw water for firefighting!" Althea shouted. "Grag. A spare spar, an oar, anything. Give Ophelia something to use to fight them! Look. She's not going to back down."

While her decks bustled with frantic activity, Ophelia again took matters into her own hands. Despite the man on the wheel, she leaned toward the galley, not away. She stretched forth both her arms, and as the Chalcedean firepots were kindled and the bows drawn, she slapped wildly at the galley like an infuriated schoolgirl, all the while shrieking insults. "You Chalcedean pigs! Do you think you can stop us in our own waters? You lying sons of whores! You are the true pirates, you slave-mongering vermin!" One of her windmilling slaps connected. Her great wooden hand struck the painted horse that was the galley's figurehead. Instantly her fingers closed on it. She thrust down on it savagely, a wild motion that pitched the decks of both ships. Sailors on both vessels cried out as they were flung off their feet. The smaller galley suffered the most. Ophelia released the bow abruptly so that the ship reared back up, a crazed rocking-horse of a vessel. The drawn bows went off, the tar pots flying wildly. One shattered and ignited the galley's own deck; two flew across Ophelia's decks to douse themselves in black smoke and steam on the other side of her.

One struck her on her starboard bow. Without hesitation, the ship slapped at the burning smear. She pulled back her hand and the tar on her hull flamed up again. She screamed as her fingers ignited suddenly.

"Smother the flames!" Althea yelled to her as crew members poured water down her hull in an effort to put out the fire on her bow. Ophelia was in too much panic to heed her. She bore down suddenly on the galley, her sheer will defying her rudder and with her flaming hands caught hold of the smaller boat. She shook it like a toy, then flung it contemptuously aside. She left most of the burning residue from her hands on the other ship. As she let go of it, she clasped her great hands together. Gritting her teeth savagely, she clenched her hands into fists, squeezing out the flames that had seared her. Then, like an affronted lady lifting her skirts and storming out of the room, she suddenly answered both helm and sails. She turned aside from the troubled galley, opening the water wide between her and the smaller vessel. She tossed her head as she sailed past it.

Flames roared, and black smoke billowed up in harmony with the cries of the sailors trapped on the burning ship. Some one or two had the wind and the will to shout threats after Ophelia, but the noise of the fire shushed their words into unintelligible cries. The Ophelia sailed on.

CHAPTER SIX

Satrap Cosgo

"I'M BORED AND MY HEAD ACHES. DISTRACT ME FROM MY PAIN. AMUSE ME."
The voice came from the divan behind her.

Serilla did not even put down her pen. "Magnadon Satrap, that is not
my duty," she pointed out quietly. "You summoned me here to advise you
on the Bingtown matter." She gestured at the opened scrolls and books
on the table. "As you can see, that is what I am prepared to do."

"Well, you can scarcely expect me to pay attention to your advice
while my head is throbbing so. I can hardly see for the pain."

Serilla set aside the texts she was perusing. She turned her attention
to the young man sprawled facedown on the divan. The Satrap was nearly
engulfed by silken cushions. She tried to keep the annoyance from her
voice. "I cannot promise that my advice will amuse you. However, if you
would care to join me here at the table, I can enlighten you as to the facts
of the Bingtown Traders' dispute."

The Satrap groaned. "Serilla, you delight in giving me headaches. If
you can't be more sympathetic, go away and send in Veri. Or that new
Companion from the Jade Island. What was her name? It reminded me of
a spice. Meg. Send in Meg."

"Gladly shall I obey you, Magnadon Cosgo." She did not bother to
hide her affront as she shoved the texts away and pushed back from the
table.

He rolled about in his pillows, then stretched a pale hand out toward
her. "No. I've changed my mind. I know that I must hear your wisdom
about Bingtown. All my advisors have told me the situation is crucial. But
how can I think when I am in such pain? Please. Rub my head for me,
Serilla. Just for a short time."

Serilla arose from her table, and put a determinedly pleasant expression on her face. She reminded herself that the Bingtown issue must be
resolved. It might even be resolved to her personal advantage.
"Magnadon Cosgo, I did not mean to be vexing. Do you have a headache?
Let me massage it away. Then we will speak about Bingtown. As you say,

the issue is crucial. And in my opinion, the Satrap's present position with them is untenable." She crossed the chamber and pushed a number of pillows to the floor. She seated herself on the end of the divan. Cosgo immediately crawled over and put his head in her lap. He closed his eyes and rubbed his cheek against her thigh like a lamb nuzzling for milk. She clenched her teeth.

"It is a curse. The headaches, the loose bowels, the flatulence. Some witch has put a curse on me. Why else should I be the victim of so much pain?" He moaned softly. He brought one hand up to rest on her thigh.

She set her fingers at the base of his skull and began to walk his tension points with her fingertips. There did seem to be some pain. "Perhaps some fresh air would ease you. Exercise is most efficacious for bowel problems. It is lovely in the grounds on the south side of the temple. If we took ourselves to the thyme gardens, the fragrance might ease your pain."

"It would be simpler to have a servant bring cuttings here. I do not care for bright days such as this. The light pains my eyes. How can you even suggest that I walk there myself when I am in such pain?" Almost idly, he lifted the hem of her robe. His fingers explored the smooth skin beneath. "And last time I was in the temple grounds, I stumbled on an uneven paving stone. I fell to my knees as if I was a slave. My hands went into the dirt. You know how I detest filth." He was petulant.

She set her hands to the muscles between his neck and shoulders and kneaded them deeply, making him wince with discomfort. "You were intoxicated, Magnadon," she recalled for him. "That was why you fell. The filth on your hands was your own vomit that they slipped in."

He twisted his head abruptly to stare up at her. "That makes it my fault, I suppose?" he asked sarcastically. "I thought the whole purpose of paving stones was to make the ground even and safe for walking. My poor gut was severely shocked by that fall. It was no wonder I could not keep my food down. Three healers agreed with me about that. But, I am sure that my well-educated Companion knows far better than the Magnadon Satrap Cosgo or his healers."

She stood abruptly, not caring that it unsettled him. She caught the wrist of his exploring hand and thrust it toward his own groin in disdain. "I am leaving. I am the Companion of your Heart. Nothing binds me to tolerate licentiousness from you."

Cosgo sat up. He clenched his hands on his knees. "You forget yourself! No one walks away from the Magnadon Satrap Cosgo. Come back. I shall say when you may leave."

Serilla drew herself up to her full height. She was easily a head taller than this pale, self-indulged young man. She looked him up and down, her green eyes flashing. "No. You forget yourself, Cosgo. You are not some Chalcedean so-called noble, with a harem of whores that scrabble to fondle and mouth you at your whim. You are the Satrap of Jamaillia. I am a Heart Companion, not some oiled and perfumed body tool. You say when I may leave, that is true. That does not mean I cannot leave when I find you disgusting." She spoke over her shoulder as she walked toward the door. "Send me word when you want to find out just how much trouble you can expect from Bingtown. That is my area of expertise. Find someone else to deal with your crotch."

"Serilla!" he protested frantically. "You cannot leave me in such pain! You know it is the pain that makes me forget myself. You cannot hold that against me."

She halted at the door. Her brow creased as she frowned at him. "I certainly can. And I do. Your father suffered extreme pain from his joints as he aged, yet he never treated me discourteously. Nor did he ever touch me uninvited."

"My father, my father," Cosgo whined. "That is all you ever say to me. That I am not as good as he was. It makes me sick to think of that shriveled old man touching you. How could your parents have given such a young girl to such an old man? It's disgusting."

She advanced several steps toward him, hands knotted into fists. "You are disgusting, for imagining such things! My parents did not 'give' me to your father. I came to Jamaillia City myself, on my own, determined to pursue my studies. He was impressed with my learning when he overheard me in the Library of the North Lands, reciting for my master. He invited me to be a Companion of his Heart, to advise him on those lands. I considered it well, for three days, before I consented and accepted his ring. I took the vow to remain at the Satrap's side and advise him. It had nothing to do with his couch. He was a fine man. He made it possible for me to study, and he always listened well to me when I counseled him. When we disagreed, he did not blame it on a headache." Her voice fell. "I still mourn him."

She opened the door and left the room. Outside, two stone-faced guards pretended they had not heard the squabble. She strode between them. She had not gone more than a dozen steps down the hall before she heard the door flung open. "Serilla! Come back!"

She ignored the imperious command.

"Please!" the Satrap's voice grated.

She kept walking, her sandals whispering over the marble floor.

"The Magnadon Satrap Cosgo courteously requests that Companion Serilla return to his chambers to advise him on the Bingtown matter." These words were bellowed after her down the hallway. She paused, then turned. The expression on her face was studiously polite. It was in her vows. She could not refuse him her company if he asked advice in her area of expertise. Her considered advice was all she had vowed to give him.

"I would be honored, Magnadon." She retraced her steps. He leaned in the doorway, his normally pale cheeks reddened. His dark hair was tousled over his bloodshot eyes. She had to admire the expressionless guards. She re-entered the chamber and did not flinch as he slammed the door behind her. Instead, she crossed the chamber and hauled the heavy drapes to one side. Afternoon sunlight spilled into the room. She went to the table, seated herself, and then leaned forward to blow out the lamp she had been using. The afternoon light was ample, once the drapes were opened. Cosgo came grudgingly to sit beside her. She had deliberately spread her elbows apart to keep him at a distance. He seated himself as close to her as he could without actually touching her. His dark eyes were reproachful.

She indicated the texts arranged on the table. "Here we have a copy of the original Bingtown Charter. This, the list of grievances they have submitted to us. This stack is made up of copies of new land grants you have issued in the Bingtown area." She turned to face him. "Considering their first point: I find that we have most definitely violated their original charter. All the new grants are in direct violation of the old agreement. You had no authority to issue new land grants to Bingtown lands without consulting the Traders first. That was clearly spelled out in their initial charter."

He scowled but said nothing. She ran her fingertip down the scroll. "They also protest the new tariffs that have been levied, as well as the increases in the old ones. Those, I think we can justify, though we may have to be more moderate in the percentages." She perused the Traders' list of grievances. "They complain also about the New Traders trafficking in slaves, and using slaves on their properties. And there is a final complaint about the financing of Chalcedean patrol boats and the stationing of patrol boats in Bingtown Harbor. These are areas in which I think we can negotiate compromises."

"Compromises," Cosgo muttered in disgust. "Am I not the Satrap? Why need I compromise at all?"

She set her chin in her hand and stared out over the gardens pensively. "Because you have violated the word of your ancestor. The Bingtown Traders are provincial in many ways. And conservative. They follow many of the old traditions. They keep their bargains to the written letter; a man's word does not die with him, it is the responsibility of his heirs to honor it. They expect others to do the same. The delegation was very angry when they arrived. They had had a long voyage in which to commiserate with one another. They reinforced one another's opinions until they were mutually convinced that their position was unassailable. And, of course, only those most angered by our recent actions would take the time to come so far to confront us. They were definitely our adversaries. Still, they might have been mollified on some of their complaints if you had agreed to meet with them personally." She turned back to face the Satrap.

He looked both grim and sulky. "I was ill that week. It was all I could do to meet with the Chalcedean trade delegation. You might also recall that there was an investiture of priests that I had to attend."

"You spent most of the week in a stupor, sampling the new pleasure drugs the Chalcedeans had brought you. Twice you promised me you would meet with the Bingtown delegation. Each time you kept them waiting for hours before sending word you were indisposed. You left me in a very uncomfortable position. They departed feeling snubbed and ignored. They were more convinced than ever of their own righteousness." She did not add that she agreed with them. It was her task to present the facts to him, not her feelings. At least, that was her present task. She hoped soon to take on more than that, if her plans prospered.

"Stiff-necked sons of outcasts and outlaws," he sneered. "I should do as my friend Duke Yadfin advised me. Put him in place as my appointed governor in Bingtown. Dissolve their silly, feuding Councils. Old Traders, New Traders . . . who can keep up with it all? A little Chalcedean discipline would do that rabble good."

Serilla could not help herself. She gaped at him. He scratched his nose negligently.

"You cannot be serious," she offered at last. She was even prepared to feign amusement at his tasteless jest. Put a Chalcedean noble in authority over Bingtown?

"Why not? Chalced is a good ally. Bingtown's base slandering of them has proven groundless. Bingtown is closer to Chalced than it is to Jamaillia. A governor from Chalced could better regulate the folk there, and as long as I still received my percentages and tariffs, what harm—"

"All of Bingtown would rise up in rebellion against you. There has already been talk of such a revolt. They would break with Jamaillia and govern themselves before they would tolerate a Chalcedean in power over them."

"Break with Jamaillia? They are nothing without Jamaillia. Bingtown is a backward trade town, a frontier settlement with no future save trade with my city. They would not dare break with Jamaillia."

"I fear you have greatly misjudged the temperament of the folk there. For too long, you have left them to fend for themselves. They begin to question why they should be taxed for protection and improvements they have not received for five years."

"Oh, I see. Since my father's death, you mean. You blame the discontent of this rabble on me, do you?"

"No. Not entirely." She kept her voice flat. "Before your father died, his mind had begun to wander. He was not as adept at detail work as he had been when a young man. He, too, had begun to neglect Bingtown. You have simply let the slide continue."

"All the more reason then to put a governor there. You see? By your own logic, my idea is a good one." He sat back, fanning himself content-edly.

She was silent until she could speak without shrieking. "It is not your idea, Magnadon. It is Duke Yadfin's plan to fleece you while you smile and smoke his pleasure herbs. Legally, you cannot appoint a governor for Bingtown, let alone one from Chalced. That is not the structure of the charter of their founding."

"Then do away with the stupid charter!" he roared at her. "Why do I owe them anything? They fled to the Cursed Shores, exiles, criminals and rebellious young lords. For years, they have lived as they pleased up there, enjoying all the benefits of Jamaillian citizenship without shouldering the burdens. . . ."

"They cede to you fifty percent of their profits, Magnadon. That is a higher rate than any other class of citizens pay. They argue, and well, that they receive few benefits, that they have paid for all improvements to their harbors and that the piracy in the Inside Passage is worse than it has been since . . ."

"Yet they resist my efforts to control the pirates. How can I protect them if they will not permit my patrol boats to shelter in their harbor?"

She sorted pages quickly. "Here. They propose that instead of your Chalcedean hirelings, they be allowed to keep those taxes and fund their own patrol vessels. Their argument is that as they are familiar with the tides and channels, that they could patrol their area more effectively. Their figures indicate they could do it less expensively."

"But would they do a good job?" Cosgo demanded.

Serilla sighed. "It is in their own best interests to do a good job." She leafed through several more sheets of thick paper. "I think this is one proposal you could have accepted easily, and gained much support from them in the process."

"Oh, very well." He shoved at her sorted papers in disgust. "I'll see them and agree to that one. But they have to . . ."

"Magnadon Cosgo, it is too late for that," she pointed out impa-tiently. "The delegation left here weeks ago. They went back to Bingtown."

"Then why are we worrying about any of this?" he demanded. He rose. "Come. Accompany me to the steam pools. I think it would ease my head."

Serilla didn't move. "You promised that you would consider their complaints and reply to each one. You promised you would send your decision to them soon." She weighed her chances, decided to risk all. "I would like to write up your decisions and take ship to Bingtown. The

sooner I carry your decisions to them, the sooner the crisis is resolved."
She shuffled papers yet again, aligning them with obsessive tidiness. "I
have drawn up a doctrine authorizing me to negotiate on your behalf. If
you wish, you could simply sign it. I could take ship tomorrow, and you
would not be bothered by any more of this discussion." She fought to keep
hope from her face and voice.

He leaned over the table to look at the document penned in her even
hand. Her heartbeat quickened. She longed to nudge the pen and ink
toward him, but resisted. That would be too obvious.

"This says I give my consent for you to make all decisions on my
behalf, as regards the Bingtown Charter controversy." He sounded outraged. "I do not give that sort of power to anyone!"

Her heart sank. It wasn't going to be as easy as she had hoped, but she
would not give up yet. "It is true that you have not given anyone that sort
of power in the past. Still, just a moment ago you spoke of appointing a
Chalcedean governor. That would be ceding a great deal more power than
this. This is but a temporary measure." She took a deep breath. She tried
to put concern into her voice. "There was a time when your health used
to be more robust. I know how these negotiations task you. I see no sense
why the entire Satrapy should endure the risk to your health. Bingtown is
my area of expertise. I should be very happy to serve you in this regard. I
feel it is my duty."

"Your duty? I wonder. Not your opportunity, then?"

He had always been slyer than he looked. She tried to appear baffled
by his words. "Magnadon, I have always considered my duty to the Satrapy to be my greatest opportunity in life. Now. As you can see, I have
left plenty of room at the bottom where we can write in some limitations.
A time limit seems called for, for example." She shrugged. "I simply saw
this as the swiftest, easiest way to solve this."

"You would go to Bingtown? Alone? The Companions of the Heart
do not leave the grounds of the palace. Not ever."

Freedom receded. She let nothing show on her face. "As I said, I
sought the swiftest, easiest way to resolve this without taxing your health.
I am completely informed on the history of the situation. I imagined you
would convey your wishes to me, and that in turn I would pass them on to
the Bingtown Traders. By honoring them with a visit from one of your
Heart Companions, you convince them of both your sincerity and your
regard for them. It would also present me with the opportunity to see first-
hand a city that has been at the heart of my studies for several years."
Fabled Bingtown. Frontier city of magic and opportunity. The only settlement that had ever survived the Cursed Shores, let alone prospered there.
How she longed to see it for herself. She said nothing of the Rain Wild
Traders, and their reputed cities far up the Rain Wild River. They were no
more than an elusive legend. To imply there was treasure he did not even

suspect would only excite his greed. She tried to refocus her thoughts. "Before your father died, he promised me that someday I would see that city for myself. This is also an opportunity for you to keep that promise." As soon as she uttered the words, she knew they were a mistake.

"He said he would let you go to Bingtown? Preposterous! Why would he promise you such a thing?" His eyes narrowed with sudden suspicion. "Or is that what you demanded in return for your favors? Did my father ever lie with you?"

A year ago, when he had first dared ask her that question, it had shocked her into silence. He had asked it so often since then that the silence was a reflex now. It was the only true power she had over him. He didn't know. He didn't know if his father had had what she refused him, and it gnawed at him.

She recalled the first time she had ever seen Cosgo. He had been fifteen, and she was nineteen. She was very young to be a Heart Companion. It was surprising that such an elderly Satrap would even take a new Companion. When she had been presented to Cosgo as his father's new advisor, the young man had looked from her to his father and back again. His glance had spoken his thoughts plainly. She had blushed, and the Satrap had slapped his son for his insolent gaze. Young Cosgo had taken that to mean that his base suspicions were true.

When his father died, Cosgo had dismissed all his father's Heart Companions. Ignoring all tradition, he had sent them off without the mercy of shelter and sustenance for their declining years. Most had been elderly women. Serilla alone he retained. She would have left then, if she could have. As long as she wore a Satrap's ring, she was bound to the Satrap's side. Cosgo was Satrap now. Her vows demanded that she stay and advise him as long as he desired it. Her advice was all he could require of her. From the beginning, he had made it plain he wished more. For his other Heart Companions, he had chosen women more educated in the flesh than in diplomacy. Not one of them refused him.

Traditionally, the Companions of the Heart were not a harem. They were supposed to be women with no other loyalties than to the Satrapy. They were supposed to be what Serilla was: blunt, out-spoken and ethically uncompromising. They were the Satrap's conscience. They were supposed to be demanding, not comforting. Sometimes Serilla wondered if she were the only Companion who remembered that.

Serilla suspected that if she ever did allow him into her bed, she would lose all power over him. As long as she represented a possession of his father's that he could not claim, he would want her. He would pretend to listen to her, and occasionally actually follow her advice in an attempt to please her. It was the last vestige of power left to her. She hoped she could use it as a lever to gain her freedom.

So now, she regarded him in cool silence. She waited.

"Oh, very well!" he suddenly exclaimed in disgust. "I will take you to Bingtown, then, if it means so much to you."

She teetered between elation and dismay. "You'll let me go, then?" she asked breathlessly.

A tiny frown creased his brow. Then he smiled at her. He had a tiny thin mustache that twitched just like a cat's whiskers. "No. That is not what I said. I said I'd take you there. You can accompany me, when I go."

"But you are the Satrap!" she faltered. "For two generations, no ruling Satrap has left Jamaillia City!"

"It is as you said. This will convince them of my sincerity when we negotiate. Besides. It is on my way to Chalced. I have been invited there numerous times. I had already decided to go. You shall accompany me there, after we have settled the rebellious rabble in Bingtown." His smile widened. "There is much you can learn in Chalced. I think it will be good for both of us."

CHAPTER SEVEN

A Bingtown Trader's Daughter

"SIT STILL."

"It hurts," Malta protested. She lifted a hand to touch the hair her mother was twining into gleaming coils. Her mother pushed her hand away.

"Most of being a woman hurts," Keffria told her daughter pragmatically. "This is what you wanted. Get used to it." She tugged at the weight of shining black hair in her hand, then deftly tucked a few stray strands into place.

"Please don't fill her head with nonsense like that," Ronica said irritably. "The last thing we need is her going about the house feeling martyred simply because she is a female." Malta's grandmother set down the handful of ribbons she had been sorting and paced a restless turn around the room. "I don't like this," she said suddenly.

"What? Getting Malta ready for her first beau?" There was bemused, maternal warmth in Keffria's voice.

Malta frowned to herself. Her mother had initially refused to accept Malta being treated as a woman. Only a few weeks ago, she had said her daughter was much too young to have men courting her. Did she now approve of the idea? Malta shifted her eyes to try to see her mother's face in the looking-glass, but Keffria's head was bent over her hairdressing task.

The chamber was light and airy, perfumed by hyacinths in small glass vases. Sunlight spilled into the room from the tall windows. It was a lovely afternoon in early spring, a day that should have brimmed with promise. Instead, Malta felt weighted with the listlessness of the two older women. There was no lighthearted chatter as they readied her to meet her first suitor. The house seemed stagnated in mourning, as if her grandfather's death last spring had visited a permanent desolation upon them.

On the table before Malta were small pots of paints and creams and perfumes. None of them were new. They were leftovers from her mother's rooms. It rankled Malta that they thought she deserved no better than that. Most were not even from the bazaar. They had been made at home, in the kitchen, rendered down like soup stock from berries, flowers, cream and tallow. Her mother and grandmother were so disappointingly old-fashioned about these things. How could they expect Bingtown society to respect them if they lived as meagerly as paupers?

They spoke over her head as if she were a baby incapable of understanding them.

"No, I've surrendered on that." Her grandmother sounded more irritable than resigned. "I don't like that we haven't heard anything from Kyle and the *Vivacia*. That is what worries me."

Keffria's voice was carefully neutral when she spoke of her husband and the family ship. "The spring winds can be fickle. No doubt, he will be home in a handful of days . . . if he chooses to stop in Bingtown. He may pass us and go directly to Chalced to sell his cargo while it is still in good condition."

"You mean while the slaves are still alive and marketable," Ronica observed relentlessly. She had always opposed using the family liveship as a slaver. She claimed to oppose slavery on principle, but that did not prevent her from keeping a slave in the house. Ronica had claimed it would be bad for the ship to be used as a slaver, that a liveship could not cope with the dark emotions of such a cargo. Vivacia had quickened only a short time before she set out on this voyage. Everyone said that liveships were very sensitive to the feelings of those who lived aboard them and young ships even more so. Malta had her doubts. She thought the whole thing about liveships was silly. As far as she could see, owning a liveship had brought her family only debt and trouble.

Look at her situation now. After she had begged for months to be allowed to dress and socialize as a young woman instead of a little girl, her family was finally giving in to her. And why? Not because they had seen how reasonable her request was. No. It was because some stupid contract said that if her grandmother could not keep up the payments on the family liveship debt, one of the family's children would have to be offered to the Rain Wilds in place of the gold.

The unfairness of the whole thing rose and choked her. Here she was, young, lovely, and fresh. Who would her first suitor be? A handsome young Trader like Cerwin Trell, a melancholy poet like Krion Trentor? No. Not for Malta Vestrit. No, she got some warty old Rain Wild Trader, a man so hideously deformed he had to wear a veil if he wished to come to Bingtown. Did her mother and grandmother even care about such things? Did they ever stop to think what it might mean to her to have such a man foisted upon her? Oh, no, not them. They were too busy worrying about the ship or what was happening to her precious brother Wintrow or where her Aunt Althea was. Malta counted for nothing. Here they were, helping her dress, doing her hair and still not paying attention to her. On what might be the most important afternoon of her life, they were arguing about slavery!

". . . doing the best he can for the family." Her mother spoke in a low even voice. "You have to admit that much. Kyle can be thoughtless of feelings. I admit that. He has injured mine more than once. Nevertheless, he is not an evil man, nor selfish. I have never known him to do anything that he did not believe was best for all of us."

Malta was a bit surprised to hear her mother defending her father. They had clashed badly right before her father sailed, and her mother had spoken little of him since then. Perhaps in her own dowdy, homebody way she still cared about her husband. Malta had always pitied her father; it was a shameful waste that so handsome and adventurous a sea-captain should be married to a mousy little woman with no interest in society or fashion. He deserved a wife who dressed well, one who orchestrated social gatherings in their home and attracted fit suitors for their daughter. Malta felt she deserved a mother like that also. A new thought filled her with sudden alarm.

"What are you planning to wear today?" she asked her mother.

"What I have on," her mother replied tersely. She added suddenly, "I will hear no more about that. Reyn is coming to visit you, not me." In a lower tone she added, almost reluctantly, "Your hair gleams like night itself. I doubt he will see anyone else but you."

Malta did not allow the rare compliment to distract her. The simple blue woolen robe her mother was wearing was at least three years old. It had been well cared for and did not look worn: merely sedate and boring. "Will you at least dress your hair and put on your jewelry?" she begged. Almost desperately, she added, "You always ask me to dress well and behave appropriately when I am about Trader business with you. Will not you and Grandmother do the same for me?"

She turned away from the mirror to confront them. They both looked surprised. "Reyn Khuprus may be a younger son, but he is still a member of one of the most wealthy and influential Rain Wild Trader families. You told me that yourself. Should not we dress as if we are receiving an honored guest, even if you are secretly hoping he will find me unappealing and simply go away?" In a lower voice she added, "Surely we owe ourselves at least that much self-respect."

"Oh, Malta," her mother sighed.

"I do believe the child is right," her grandmother said suddenly. The small dark woman, burdened in her widow's robes, suddenly straightened herself. "No. I know she is right. We have both been near-sighted in this. Whether or not we welcome Reyn's courtship of Malta is not the issue here. We have given permission for it. The Khuprus family now holds the note for the *Vivacia*. Our contract is now with them. Not only should we treat them with the same courtesy we did the Festrews, we should present the same face to them as well."

Ronica paced a quick turn about the room. She ticked off her concerns on her fingers. "We have prepared a fine table, and the rooms are newly freshened for spring. Rache can wait upon table; she does well at that. I wish Nana was still with us, but it was too good of an opportunity for her to ask her to let it go. Do you think I should send Rache to Davad Restart's, to beg the loan of other serving folk?"

"We could," Malta's mother began hesitantly.

"Oh, please, no!" Malta interjected. "Davad's servants are horrid, unmannered and impertinent. We are better off without them. I think we should present our household as it truly is, rather than make a false show with ill-trained servants. Which would you find more genteel? A household with limited means who chooses the best their budget allows, or a household that borrows lackadaisical help?"

It pleased Malta to see both her mother and her grandmother surprised. Her mother smiled proudly as she said, "The girl has sense. Malta, I am sure you have seen to the heart of it. It pleases me to hear you speak so."

Her grandmother's approval was more wary. She pursed her lips at Malta, and gave a brief nod. Malta looked at her mirror, turning her head to see how well her mother had succeeded with her hair. It would do. She glanced once more at her grandmother's reflection. The old woman was still perusing her. Malta decided it was hard for Ronica Vestrit to accept anyone else as clever. That was it. Her grandmother was jealous that Malta could think things through as clearly as she could. More clearly in fact. Her mother, however, had been proud of her. Her mother could be won over with her cleverness. Malta had never considered that before. A sudden inspiration came to her.

"Thank you, Mother. I love what you have done with my hair. Now let me fix yours for you. Come. Sit down." She rose gracefully and drew her startled mother to her seat before the mirror. She pulled the long pins from her mother's dark hair. It cascaded to her shoulders. "You dress your hair as if you were a dowdy old woman," she said artlessly. She did not need to point out that her grandmother wore hers in an identical fashion.

She leaned down to put her cheek beside her mother's, and met her eyes in the looking-glass. "Let me arrange it with some flowers, set off with your pearl pins. It *is* spring, you know, and time to celebrate the blossoming of life." Malta lifted the silver-handled brush and drew it through her mother's hair. She cocked her head to smile at her mother's reflection in the mirror. "If we cannot afford to buy new robes and gowns before Father returns, perhaps we could brighten some of our older ones with new embroidery. I am sure it would please him. Besides, it is time I learned your rosebud stitch. Perhaps, after Reyn's visit, you could teach me."

RONICA VESTRIT WAS SKEPTICAL OF HER GRANDDAUGHTER'S SUDDEN SWEETness. She felt diminished by her own pessimism, but dared not set it aside. She cursed the circumstances that had put her family's reputation and finances into the awkward hands of this giddy girl. Even more frightening was that those awkward hands were greedy and grasping, and that Malta's foolishness was fueled by cunning. If the girl had only applied her keen mind to doing what was genuinely best for her family and herself, she would have done the Vestrits proud. As it stood, she was a dangerous liability.

As Ronica silently withdrew from the room where Malta plaited her mother's hair into coils, she reflected sourly that if luck favored her, perhaps Reyn Khuprus would take Malta off their hands. It would be restful to have the conniving little wench out of the house; then Ronica imagined Malta as Jani Khuprus's daughter-in-law, and winced. No. Malta was a Vestrit problem. It was best to keep her at home until she had been taught to behave as befit her family. Sometimes Ronica thought the only way to do that would be with a strap.

She sought the relative peace of her own chambers. With the coming of spring, Ronica had had the room cleaned and freshened as she did every year. It had not helped. The memory of the odor of sickness lingered. The sunlight spilling in the tall windows seemed false. The clean linens on the bed looked glacially white and cold, not fresh and inviting. She went to her own dressing table and sat down. She looked at herself in the mirror. Malta was right. She had become a dowdy old woman. She had never considered herself beautiful, but when Ephron had been alive, she had maintained herself. Since he had died, she had forgotten. She had stopped being a woman at all. The lines in her face had deepened; the skin of her throat sagged. The few pots of cosmetics on the table were dusty. When she opened her jewelry chest, the contents seemed both familiar and foreign. How long had it been since she had last taken pains with her appearance? How long since she had cared at all how she looked?

She took a deep breath. "Ephron." That was all she said, simply speaking his name aloud. Part plea, part apology, part farewell. Then she reached up to release her hair. She shook it down to her shoulders, frowning at how it had thinned. She lifted her hands to her face, prodding the papery dryness of her skin, and trying to smooth away the lines that framed her mouth. She shook her head at herself and then lowered her head to blow the dust off the cosmetic pots. She opened the first one.

She was just finishing by applying perfume when Rache's hesitant tap came at her door. "Come in," Ronica called casually. Since Nana had left,

Rache was the sole remaining house servant in the formerly bustling household. When the slave-woman entered, Ronica instantly knew why she was there. Only a visit from Davad Restart put such a look of guarded hatred in the slave's eyes. Rache still blamed him for her son's death on board Davad's slave ship. Any mention of the Trader wakened that look in her; it was the only time when the young woman seemed truly alive. So although Ronica sighed and begged, "Please, no," she knew the man was already in the sitting room.

"I am sorry, ma'am," Rache said in a nearly toneless voice. "It is Trader Restart. He insisted he must see you."

"It's all right," Ronica replied with a deeper sigh. She rose from her dressing table. "I'll be down as soon as I'm dressed. No. Do not trouble to go and tell him that. If he cannot be bothered to send a runner ahead of a social call, then he can simply wait until I am ready. Help me with dressing, please."

She tried to make it a joke on Davad that the two of them could share, but Rache's mouth remained in a flat line. He had deposited Rache at the Vestrit household when Ephron was dying, ostensibly to help. Ronica suspected it had been to get rid of Rache and her murderous gaze. Technically, she supposed the woman still belonged to him, a slave under Jamaillian law. Bingtown did not recognize slavery. Here in Bingtown, she was genteelly referred to as an indentured servant. There were a great many "indentured servants" about Bingtown lately. Ronica treated her as she would any hired servant.

Ronica took her time choosing, finally selecting a dress of pale green linen. It had been so long since she had worn anything but a loose household robe. She felt oddly naked in it, even when the skirts were sashed about her waist and the over-blouse laced up from behind. She paused to look at herself again in the mirror. Well. She did not look lovely. She did not look young. However, she once more appeared as a matriarch of a Bingtown Family should present herself. She looked both groomed and dignified. She paused at her jewelry cask, to rope her throat recklessly with pearls and hang more from her ears. There. Now let the little minx insinuate she was a dowdy old woman.

She turned from the mirror to find Rache watching her with widened eyes. Ronica felt almost flattered by the serving woman's surprise. "I will see Davad now. Would you bring coffee and simple cakes from the kitchen, please? Nothing elaborate. I do not wish to encourage him to linger."

"Yes, ma'am." Rache sketched a curtsey and left silently.

Ronica's skirts whispered as she walked down the hall to the sitting room. The pearls were cool against her skin. Strange, how a change of garments and a bit of care for her appearance made her feel so different. Her deep mourning for Ephron was still there, as was her anger for all that had befallen her with his death. All winter she had done her best to cope with the blows as they fell. It had been staggering to find that her trust in her son-in-law had been misplaced. Kyle's greed had driven away Althea and his need for ruthless control had all but paralyzed Keffria. The discovery that his daughter Malta seemed set on growing up to be just like him had been unnerving. A few months back, Keffria had promised to take a hand with Malta and change her. Ronica snorted softly to herself. So far, the only changes were that Malta was becoming more deceptive daily.

At the entrance to the sitting room she paused, and put such thoughts out of her head. By an act of will she smoothed her brow and put a pleasant expression on her face. She straightened her back and shoulders, then opened the door and swept into the room with a "Good morning, Davad. Such a surprise to have you call on us like this."

His back was to her. He had taken a book from the shelf and was standing by the window to peruse it. With his wide rounded back encased tautly in a dark blue jacket, he reminded Ronica of a beetle. He closed the book and spoke as he turned. "Not surprising. Rude. Even as socially inept a blunderer as I know that I should have asked if you had time to see me. But I knew you would say no, and I had to . . . Ronica! You look amazing!"

His eyes swept up and down her, quite familiarly, bringing an unexpected blush to her face. A returning smile broke out on his ruddy round face.

"I had become accustomed to seeing you in such dreary clothes, I had forgotten how you truly looked. I remember that dress. It is quite old, isn't it? Didn't you wear it to one of the parties you gave to announce Keffria's wedding to Kyle? It takes years off your face. You must be quite proud to be able to squeeze yourself into it still."

Ronica shook her head at the old family friend. "Davad Restart. Only you can so completely ruin so many compliments in one brief speech." He stared at her, completely flummoxed. As was often the case, he was completely unaware of how tactless he was. She moved to a divan and seated herself. "Come and join me," she invited him. "I've asked Rache to bring coffee and cakes, but I warn you, I have only a brief moment or two to spare. We are receiving Reyn Khuprus this afternoon. He is coming to call on Malta for the first time, and I still have a great deal of preparation."

"I know," he admitted easily. "Bingtown gossip has been full of it. It's a bit unusual, isn't it, to allow a man to court her before she's even been presented as a woman? Not that she doesn't think she's ready, I'm sure. After her escapade last winter at the ball . . . well. I don't blame you for trying to marry her off quickly. The sooner that girl has a man to settle her down, the safer all of Bingtown will be." He paused and cleared his throat. For the first time, he looked a bit uncomfortable. "Actually, Ronica, that is why I'm here. To beg a very great favor from you, I'm afraid."

"You wish to ask a favor of me, and somehow it's connected to Reyn's visit?" Ronica was both puzzled and uneasy.

"Yes. It's simple. Invite me, too. Please."

She managed not to gape at him. She was saved from having to reply immediately by Rache's entry into the room with the coffee tray. Ronica dismissed her almost immediately; there was no sense in forcing Rache to serve coffee to a man that she hated. The small business of pouring coffee gave Ronica some time in which to think. Davad broke into her thoughts before she could begin her graciously worded refusal.

"I know it isn't proper, but I've thought of a way around that."

Ronica decided to be blunt. "Davad, I don't want to find a way around impropriety. The Khuprus family is socially powerful. I cannot afford to give anyone in Bingtown offense these days, let alone the son of such a family. You have not said why you wish to be here when we receive him. Traditionally, only the family of the girl is present when the young man first comes calling. To make him more at ease, you know."

"I know, I know. But seeing as how Ephron is dead and Malta's father is at sea, I thought you could present me as an old friend who was standing in . . . a sort of protector in the absence of your family men. . . ."

Davad's voice trailed off at the look on Ronica's face. She spoke in a low, controlled voice. "Davad. You well know that I have never required a man to be my protector. When the girls were small and Ephron was often at sea, I never asked his friends to settle business transactions for him, or deal with unpleasant realities in his absence. I coped. All Bingtown knows that. It is who I am. Now that I am truly alone, shall I quaver and faint and hide myself behind you? I think not. Reyn Khuprus comes today to meet the family of the girl he wishes to wed. He shall meet us as we truly are."

As Ronica paused to draw breath after this onslaught, Davad spoke hastily. "It's for me. For my benefit, I mean. I will be honest with you. There is no benefit to you, I admit that freely, and it might even cause you some embarrassment for me to be here. Sa knows, several families in Bingtown no longer receive me. I am well aware that I am a social embarrassment. At first, it was because I was inept. Well, I have never been good at the social things. Dorill was. She always took care of those things. After she died, many folk in Bingtown still treated me kindly, in memory of her, I think. But year after year, the number of Traders who hailed me as friend dwindled. I suppose I give offense without intention. Until now, of all the Bingtown Traders, you are the only one I dare call 'friend.' "

He paused and sighed heavily. "I have no one else to turn to in my isolation. I know I must rebuild my alliances. If I could form some trade connections with the Rain Wild Traders, I could do so. I know that many in Bingtown do not approve of my politics. They say I grovel to the New

Traders, that my dabbling in slavery is a disgrace, that I have betrayed the Bingtown Traders by negotiating for the New Traders. But you know that I only do so to survive. What else is there for me? Look at me! I have no one, nothing but my own wits to depend on. No wife to comfort me, no children to inherit my holdings. All I am trying to do is maintain enough property and income to keep me comfortable through my old age. After that, it all ends." He paused dramatically and then finished in a dwindling voice, "My line ends with me."

Ronica had closed her eyes halfway through this recitation. When Davad sighed yet again, she opened them. "Davad," she said in a warning voice. "Shame on you, trying such tricks on me. I refuse to pity you, any more than I pity myself. The pits we are in, we have dug ourselves. You know the roots of your problems; you just listed them yourself. If you want to regain the respect of the Bingtown Traders, leave off politicking for the New Traders. Stop 'dabbling' in the selling of humans. Go back to being who you were and your friends will return. Not quickly, for you have trodden firmly on too many toes. But eventually. You are Old Trader. As soon as you recall that to yourself, our compatriots will recall it as well."

"And in the meantime, I should genteelly starve?" Davad blustered. As if to fend off such a dire fate, he took a large bite of the spice cake in his hand.

"You will not starve," Ronica pointed out implacably. "As you have said, you have only yourself to support. You could live off your own holdings if you chose to apply yourself, even if you never negotiated another trade in your life. I venture to say that if you reduced your servants, you could supply most of your own wants from a kitchen garden, some chickens and a few cattle. You could revert to simplicity, as Keffria and I have been forced to do. As for your being alone in the world, well, as I recall, you have a grandniece. Approach her, if you want an heir. It might mend a great deal with that branch of your family."

"Oh, she hates me." Davad brushed the idea away with the cake crumbs that had fallen into his lap. "Some chance remark I made to her husband when he was courting her. She treats me as if I have the plague. It's beyond all mending." He took a drink of his coffee. "Besides. How can you criticize my 'dabbling' in slavery? Isn't that where Kyle and the *Vivacia* are right now, on a round of slave-trading?" At the darkening look on Ronica's face, he abruptly changed his tactics. "Please, Ronica. I won't linger. Just allow me to be here when he arrives, simply introduce me as a family friend. That's all I ask. Just help me to establish a nodding acquaintance. I'll do the rest for myself."

He looked at her appealingly. The perfumed oil on his hair had left a sheen on his brow. He was pathetic. He was an old friend of the family. He trafficked in slaves. He and Dorill had been wed a week after she and

Ephron had married; they had danced at one another's weddings. He was certain to say something unfortunate to Reyn. He had come to her as his last hope.

He was a disaster in the making.

She was still looking at him dumbly when Keffria came into the room. "Davad!" she exclaimed. She smiled stiffly. Her eyes were round with horror. "Such a surprise! I did not know you were here."

Davad rose hastily, nearly oversetting his coffee cup. He charged at Keffria, took her hand and beamingly exclaimed, "Well, I know it is not completely correct, but I simply could not resist. With Kyle away, I thought it only fitting that there be some man about your household to appraise this youngster who thinks to come courting our Malta!"

"Indeed," Keffria said faintly. She turned an accusing gaze on her mother.

Ronica steeled herself to the truth. In a quiet voice she spoke. "I've told Davad it is completely inappropriate. Later in the courtship, if both young people choose to continue it, we will offer a tea and invite family friends. That would be a more appropriate time for him to meet Reyn and his family."

"I suppose," Davad said heavily. "If that's the best you can offer your oldest, truest friend, Ronica Vestrit. I'll come back when I'm invited, then."

"It's too late for that," Keffria said faintly. "That's why I came to find Mother. Reyn and his family are already here."

Ronica rose swiftly. "His family! Here?"

"In the morning room. I know: I did not expect them either. I did not expect Reyn until late this afternoon; the ship had good sailing. Nevertheless, Jani Khuprus is here with him, and an older brother . . . Bendir. Awaiting outside is a train of servants bearing baskets of gifts and . . . Mother, I need your help. With such a reduced staff of our own, how are we to deal—"

"Quite simply," Davad interjected. Suddenly, his whole attitude had changed from petitioner to commander. "You still keep a boy for the garden and stable. Send him here to me. I'll jot down a note, he can carry it to my house, and in no time, my serving staff will arrive here. Discreetly, of course. I'll give very specific instructions that they are to behave as if they are your servants and this is their normal place of employment and . . ."

"And when the gossip spreads through Bingtown, as it must whenever servants are involved, we shall be a matter of much jest. No, Davad." It was Ronica's turn to sigh. "We'll take you up on your offer. We must. However, if we must borrow servants, then I shall not hesitate to admit that is so. Nor should your kindness in this matter be hidden for the sake of our pride." Belatedly recalling that her daughter's opinion might differ, Ronica turned to Keffria. "Do you agree?" she asked her bluntly.

She shook her head helplessly. "I suppose I must. Malta is not going to care for this one bit." The last she added almost to herself.

"Simply don't let her trouble her pretty little head about it." Davad was beaming now. Ronica longed to club him as he went on, "I am sure she is going to be too much interested in her suitor to pay much attention to an old family friend anyway. Now. Where's that paper, Ronica? I'll dash a note off and you can get your boy on his way."

Despite Ronica's misgivings, all was accomplished quickly and easily. Keffria returned to the guests, assuring them that her mother would appear shortly. The message was sent. Davad insisted on a last-minute peek in a mirror. Ronica was not sure if she was motivated by pity for him or for herself, but she persuaded him to blot the oil from his hair and forehead, and re-comb his hair in a more dignified styling. The way his hose sagged at the knees could not be helped, he told her, all his leggings did that, and as for the coat, it was new, and the cut of it was considered quite stylish. Ronica bit her tongue and did not point out the difference between stylish and becoming. Then, with a great deal of trepidation, she entered the morning room on Davad's arm.

She had heard that the courtship of a Rain Wild man was less restrained than that practiced in Bingtown. Before Keffria had consented to Reyn courting her daughter, they had been promised that the young man would not offer her expensive gifts that might turn a young girl's head. Ronica had been prepared for him to present Malta with a bouquet of flowers and perhaps some sweets. She had expected to be introduced to a shy young man, accompanied perhaps by his tutor or uncle.

The morning room had been transformed. The simple arrangements of spring flowers that she and Keffria had contrived from the garden had all but disappeared. Baskets, bowls and vases of exotic Rain Wild blooms blossomed in profusion throughout the room. The heady floral fragrance was thick as smoke. Platters and bowls of fruit, bottles of wine and trays of sweets and pastries had joined the carefully arranged repast on the table. Brightly colored songbirds twittered in a brass cage hung in an artificial tree constructed from bronze and cherry wood. A little spotted hunting cat, no more than a kitten, prowled hopefully beneath the cage. Servants, both veiled and open-faced, moved silently and industriously about the room, completing its metamorphosis. As Ronica entered, a young man whose veiled face proclaimed him a Rain Wild Trader struck up a plaintive melody on a lap-harp.

As if carried by the music, Jani Khuprus swept up to greet her. Her face veil was white lace shimmering with pearls. The loose hood that covered her hair was decorated with braided and coiled silken tassels in many shades of blue. She wore an extravagantly beribboned blouse and loose pantaloons that were gathered at her ankles with yet more ribbons. Fanciful embroidery almost obscured the white linen that backed it. Ronica had never seen a woman in such garb, but she knew instantly it would become the new style in Bingtown. As Jani greeted her in the transformed room, Ronica felt as if she had been magically transported to the Rain Wilds, and that she was the guest in Jani's home. Jani's smile was warm, and only one quick puzzled glance betrayed her curiosity about Davad. "I am so glad you have come down to join us," Jani welcomed her. With unnerving familiarity, she took both Ronica's hands in hers. She leaned closer to confide, "You must be quite proud of your daughter, Keffria. She has greeted us so warmly and so graciously! She is a credit to her upbringing. And Malta! Oh, I can see why my son was smitten so swiftly and so deeply. She is young, as you warned me, but already she is like an opening blossom. Any young man would fall prey to such eyes. No wonder he took such pains choosing what gifts to bring her. I confess, when the flowers are massed like this, they do appear a bit overwhelming, but surely you can forgive a young man's impetuosity in this."

"Especially as it's much too late to do anything else!" Davad replied while Ronica was still composing a response. He stepped forward to set his hand on top of Jani's and Ronica's clasp. "Welcome to the Vestrit home. I'm Davad Restart, a long-time friend of the family. We are so thrilled to have you here, and deeply honored by Reyn's courtship of our Malta. Don't they look charming together!"

His words were so different from anything that Ronica would have chosen to say that she nearly lost control of herself. Jani's eyes went from Davad's face to Ronica's before she gently but unmistakably removed her hands from his clasp. "I recall you well, Trader Restart." The tone of her voice was chill; evidently, her recollection of him was not a kindly one. The subtlety was lost on Davad.

"I am so pleased and honored that you do," he exclaimed jovially. He beamed a smile at Jani Khuprus. He obviously believed that things were going well.

Ronica knew she had to say something, but for the life of her, she could not find any significant words. She retreated into banality. "Such lovely flowers. Only the Rain Wild yields such extravagant colors and fragrances."

Jani shifted her body, very slightly, but it was enough that she now faced Ronica while her shoulder was toward Davad, excluding him. "I am so glad you like them. I had feared you would rebuke me for letting Reyn indulge himself in such plenty. I know we had agreed he must keep his gifts simple."

In actuality, Ronica felt that Jani had overstepped the bounds of her agreement. Before she could find a tactful way to let her know that Reyn must not do it again, Davad chimed for her. "Simple? What place has simplicity in a young man's passion? Were I a boy again and courting such a girl as Malta, I, too, would attempt to overwhelm her with gifts."

Ronica finally found her tongue. "But I am sure a young man like Reyn will want to be valued for himself, not his presents. Such a display is worthy of their first presentation to one another, but I am sure his courtship to follow will be more restrained." By addressing her words to Davad rather than Jani, Ronica hoped to avoid giving offense while still letting her position be known.

"Nonsense!" Davad insisted. "Look at them. Does she look to you as if she wishes him to be restrained?"

Malta was all but enthroned in flowers. She sat in an armed chair, holding a great bouquet on her lap. Pots and vases of blooms and greenery had been placed around her. A single red flower had been pinned to the shoulder of her demure white dress. Another had been fastened into her upswept hair. They complemented the warm tones of her skin, and made her black hair seem even glossier. Her eyes were downcast as she spoke softly to the young man that stood so attentively beside her. Yet every so often, she would glance up at him through her eyelashes. When she did, her mouth would curve in the tiniest of cat-smiles.

Reyn Khuprus was dressed all in blue. A discarded cloak of azure draped an adjacent chair. His traditional Rain Wild garb of loose trousers and a long-sleeved shirt effectively camouflaged any deformities from the casual eye. He had a lean waist that he had proudly sashed with a wide silk belt. It was a darker hue than his other clothes. Black boots peeped out from the loose cuffs of his trousers. The backs of his fine black gloves were studded with blue flame gems in a breath-taking display of casual wealth. His hood was plain, made from the same silk as his sash. His face veil was black lace, effectively obscuring his features. Although his face was invisible, one sensed his rapt attention in the cant of his head.

"Malta is very young," Ronica said. She spoke quickly, before anyone could say any more of the situation. "She does not have the wisdom to know when to go slowly. It is up to her mother and me to exercise that caution. Jani and I have agreed that, for their own sakes, these young people must not be allowed to be too impulsive."

"Well, I fail to see why," Davad contradicted her jovially. "What can come of this except good? Eventually, Malta must wed. Why stand in the path of young romance? Think of what may come of this: grandchildren for Jani, great-grandchildren for you, Ronica. And mutually profitable trade arrangements for all, I don't doubt."

It pained Ronica to hear Davad so laboriously drag the conversation in the direction he wished it to go. Over the years, she had come to know the man too well. This was why he was truly here. He was an old friend of the family; he genuinely cared for Malta and what became of her. But the greatest part of his heart had long ago been given over to trade and the profits therefrom. For good or ill, it was how Davad's mind worked. He had never hesitated to use his friendships to the good of his business deals, though he seldom risked a business profit for the sake of friendship.

All this passed through Ronica's mind in a fraction of a moment. She saw Davad clearly, as she had always known him to be. She had never evaluated what it meant to have such a friend. Differences in politics had not persuaded her to set him aside, even when many other Traders ceased dealing with him. He was not a truly evil man; he simply did not give much thought to what he did. Profits beckoned and he followed, into slave trading, into the questionable practices of the New Traders, even to making a profit from Malta's unsought courtship. He meant no harm by it; he never considered it in terms of right and wrong.

That did not make him harmless. Not in terms of what he could inadvertently do to the Vestrit family if he offended Jani Khuprus just now. The Khuprus family held the note on the liveship *Vivacia*. Ronica had reluctantly accepted Reyn's courtship of Malta in the certainty that he would soon realize how young and unsuitable she was. For Reyn to begin such a courtship and then break it off would give her an odd social advantage. The Vestrit family might be seen as the injured party; the Khuprus family would be expected to be more than civil in their business dealings. But if the Khuprus family broke off the courtship because the Vestrit family had undesirable political connections, the attitude of the other Traders toward her family might be substantially different. Ronica had already felt social pressure to cut off her association with Davad Restart. She would be in a financial quagmire if that were extended to trading pressure.

The wise thing to do would be to dump Davad Restart.

Loyalty forbade that. And pride. If the Vestrit family allowed itself to be governed by what others perceived as correct, they would lose all control of their destiny. Not that much control truly remained in their hands.

The silence had grown uncomfortable. Ronica felt a resigned fascination coupled with horror. What dreadful thing would Davad say next? He was completely unaware of how gauche he was being. He smiled brightly and began, "Speaking of trade alliances—"

Rescue came from an unexpected quarter. Keffria swept up to them. A very fine mist of perspiration on her brow was the only visible sign of the agitation she undoubtedly felt at seeing Davad stand so close to Jani Khuprus for so long. She touched his arm lightly and asked him quietly if he could assist her in the kitchen, just for a moment. The servants were having difficulty opening some of the old wines she had chosen; could he come and supervise that task?

Keffria had chosen well. Wine and the correct serving of it were one of Davad's favorite obsessions. He hastened away with Keffria following him, nodding as he spoke learnedly of the correct way to uncork a bottle to minimize agitation. Ronica sighed out in relief.

"I wonder that you even tolerate him being here," Jani observed quietly. Now that Davad had gone, she stood at Ronica's side. She spoke confidentially to her, beneath the music and conversation in the room. "The other day I heard him referred to as the Traitor Trader. He denies it, but all know he has been the go-between for the New Traders in many of their most tawdry dealings. It is even said that he is behind the New Traders who are making such ridiculous offers in the hope of buying the *Paragon*."

"Shockingly ridiculous offers," Ronica agreed in a low voice. "I think it is scandalous that the Ludluck family even allows them to be presented." She ventured a small smile as she presented this thought to Jani. To be sure her point was not missed, she added the old Trader adage, "After all, it takes two to strike a bargain."

"Indeed," Jani agreed coolly. "But isn't it cruel of Davad that he tempts the Ludlucks with such offers? He knows how straitened their circumstances are."

"Most Bingtown Traders are feeling the pinch these days. Including the Vestrits. So we form alliances with one another, ones that may strike others as strange. Davad, for instance, came by today to offer me the use of his servants, for he was well aware we had reduced our staff to a mere skeleton."

There. That was out in the open now. If Reyn's courtship were mistakenly based on a supposed wealth the Vestrit family no longer possessed, it would soon be terminated.

When Jani Khuprus replied, Ronica discovered she had misjudged the depth of the woman's graciousness. "I, too, was aware of your financial worries. It pleases me to see Reyn courting a young woman who understands the necessity of living within one's means. Thrift and discipline are virtues always, no matter what one's wealth. The servants we brought with us were meant not to embarrass you, but to assist in making this a carefree time for all." Sincerity rang in her voice.

Ronica answered it. "Davad can be a difficult friend. I could abandon him. However, I have never seen the virtue in that. I have never respected folk who cast out offspring or relatives that displeased them. It always seemed to me that the duty of family is to continue trying to correct, no matter how painful. Why should it be different with old family friends? Especially when, in many ways, we have become Davad's family. He lost his wife and sons to the Blood Plague, as you perhaps know."

Jani's reply caught Ronica off balance. "Then you did not force Althea out of your home for improper behavior?"

The shock of the question astounded Ronica. Was that the Bingtown rumor? Spread as far as the Rain Wilds? She was grateful for the servant that suddenly presented them with a tray of delicate cakes. Was it only last night she and Keffria had baked these? She took one and then was immediately confronted by another serving person offering a fluted glass of some Rain Wild liqueur. She accepted it with thanks and took a sip from it. "This is wonderful," she told Jani with genuine pleasure.

"As are the cakes," Jani replied. She looked aside, letting her gaze linger on Reyn and Malta. Whatever she had just said to him had made him laugh. The cant of Jani's head suggested she smiled also.

Ronica considered letting the topic drop, but then steeled herself. Best to snuff rumors as soon as they were heard. Sa alone knew how long that one had been circulating, but it had probably been about ever since last summer.

"I did not ask Althea to leave our home. In fact, she left against my will. The division of the inheritance from her father much distressed her. She had expected to inherit the *Vivacia*. She was hurt when she did not, and she disagreed with how Kyle chose to run the ship. There was a quarrel and she left." She found it hard, but she stared squarely at Jani's veil and added, "I do not know where she is now or what she is doing. If she came to the door this very moment, I would welcome her with all my heart."

Jani seemed to return her look. "It was an awkward question, perhaps. It is my way, to speak directly. I do not mean to give offense by it. It has always seemed to me that honest words leave the least room for misunderstanding."

"I share that sentiment." Ronica's eyes followed Jani's gaze as she turned to look at Reyn and Malta. Malta had lowered her face and turned her eyes aside. Her cheeks were pink with a blush, but her eyes were merry. The tilt of Reyn's head showed that he shared her amusement as he tried to see into her averted face.

"Within a family, there is no room for secrets," Jani added.

IT WAS WONDERFUL, FAR MORE WONDERFUL THAN MALTA HAD EVER IMAG-ined it would be. So this was what it was like to be treated properly. Her soul had starved for this her entire life, and now it was able to sate itself in sweet sensations. Flowers scented the air all around her, every type of dainty food and fine drink that she could imagine had been offered to her, and Reyn himself could not have been more attentive. She could think of nothing that could have improved the day, unless perhaps some of her friends could be present to be enviously impressed. She indulged herself in imagining that scene. Delo and Kitten and Carissa and Polia would be seated over there, and as each tray of food or drink was offered to Malta, she would take her pick of it, and then send the rest over to her friends.

Later, she would apologize warmly to them that she had had so little time for them. What a shame that Reyn had insisted on monopolizing her time! But, well, they knew how men were! She would smile at them knowingly. Then she would recount some of the compliments he had showered on her, or repeat some of his witticisms—

"May I ask what now brings such a smile to your face?" Reyn requested gently. He stood a respectful yet attentive distance from her chair. He had not accepted her offer of a seat. She lifted her eyes to his veiled face. Her pretty daydream soured. Who knew what sort of a visage smiled beneath that veil? A little quivering turned restlessly in her belly. She did not let her unease show on her face. Instead, she answered in a pleasantly modulated voice, "Why, I was but thinking how gay it might be if some of my friends were here to share all this with us." She gracefully gestured at the festive room.

"And I was thinking the opposite," he replied. He had a pleasant voice. It was cultured and richly masculine. His face veil stirred lightly with the wind of his breath.

"The opposite?" she wondered aloud as she raised an eyebrow to his words.

He did not move from where he stood, but pitched his voice for more intimacy. "I was thinking how pleasant it will be when I am deep enough in your trust to see you more privately."

All she had to go by was his posture and his voice. There was no raised brow or shy smile to accompany the words. She had spoken to men before, even flirted when her mother or grandmother was not present, but no man had ever been so frank with her. It was both heady and daunting. All the time she hesitated, she knew he studied her bared face. Try as she might, she could not keep all expression from it. How could one flirt and smile when one did not know if a man or a grotesque freak answered that smile? The thought put a tiny chill into her words. "Surely, we must first decide if this courtship is even to begin. Is not that what this first meeting is about: to see if we are suited to one another?"

He gave a small snort of amusement. "Mistress Malta, let us leave that sport to our mothers. That is their game. See how, even now, they circle one another like wrestlers, awaiting an opening, a tiny bit of imbalance in the other? They will strike the bargain that joins us, and I do not doubt that both families will benefit in every way."

He inclined his hooded head, very slightly, toward Jani Khuprus and Ronica Vestrit. Their facial expressions were carefully pleasant, but there was a poised alertness to them that suggested some verbal contest was in progress.

"That is my grandmother, not my mother," Malta pointed out. "And I do not understand why you speak of this meeting as a game. Surely, this is a serious moment. At least, it is for me. Do you find it trivial?"

"I will never find trivial any moment spent in your presence. Of that, you may be assured." He paused, then let his words pour forth. "From the moment that you opened the dream-box and we ventured together into your imaginings, I have known that nothing could turn me aside from this courtship. Your family sought to dampen my hopes with the notion that you were more child than woman. That I found laughable. That is the game I spoke of, the game that all families play when their offspring wish to wed. Obstacles will be invented, only to dissolve when the balance is weighted with enough gifts and trade advantages . . . but this talk is too blunt for us. It speaks of the pocket and not of the heart. It speaks not at all of my hunger for you." His words tumbled swiftly, unchecked. "Malta, I ache for you. I long to possess you, to share every secret of my heart with you. The sooner my mother surrenders to every demand of your family, the better. Tell your grandmother that. Tell her she may ask anything she wishes and I will be sure the Vestrits receive it, so long as I may find you soon in my arms."

Malta recoiled with a swift intake of breath. Her shock was not feigned, but Reyn mistook the source of it. He stepped back from her and inclined his head gravely. "Forgive me, I beg you." His voice went husky. "I am cursed with a tongue that speaks the words of my heart before my head can intervene. How crude I must seem to you, like an animal panting after you. I vow to you, that is not so. Ever since I saw you that evening outside the Traders' Concourse, I became aware that I had a soul as well as a mind. Before that, I was little more than an intelligent tool, serving my family as well as I could to advance their fortunes. When my brother or sisters spoke of passion and attractions, I could not grasp what they meant." He paused for breath, and gave a sort of laugh. "If you know aught of Rain Wild Folk, you will know that we usually find our hearts when we are young and wed soon after. By the customs of my folk, I have always been an odd fish. Some say I was ensorcelled young by my work, and would never know a true love for anyone human." A snort of disdain bespoke his disgust.

He shook his head, then went on, "Some whispered that I was a eunuch, incapable of a man's passions. Their words did not bother me. I knew I had a heart, but it slept within me and I saw no need for it to awaken. In the runes I traced and deciphered, in the strange mechanisms I dismantled, I thought I had enough to occupy all my thoughts. I was annoyed when my mother insisted I accompany her to Bingtown for that meeting. Annoyed! All that was swept aside in the first moment I dared speak to you. As jidzin is wakened to light by touch, so your voice woke my heart to longing. Wild, boyish hope drove me to leave the dream-box for you. I was sure you would not open it, sure that one such as yourself would discard my dream before I could even broach it to you. But you did not. You opened my soul and shared with me a vision of such enchant-

ment . . . you walked through my city and your presence awoke it to
life! I had always believed the cold and silent city was my heart. You can
guess what that meant to me."

Malta heard his impassioned words with only half an ear. Her
thoughts and heart were full of what he had already said. Anything that
she asked, he would see that his family conceded. Anything! Her mind
darted about like a startled fish. She should not ask so much that she
seemed greedy. That might make him rethink his passion for her. Nor
should she ask so little that she appeared foolish, or undervalued by her
family. No. There was a line to tread here, one to be carefully considered.
Instantly she seized on the one she considered wisest in the way of bargaining. Oh, if only her father were here, he would see to it that she used
Reyn's passion to her best advantage. In an instant, she realized that was
what she must do: delay the negotiations until her father returned.

"You are silent," Reyn observed in a chastened voice. "I have offended you."

She moved to seize the advantage. He must think his position uncertain, but not hopeless. She tried to put a timorous smile on her face. "I am
not accustomed . . . that is, no one has ever spoken to me of such . . ."
She let her voice trail away doubtfully. She took a breath as if composing
herself. "My heart is beating so. . . . Sometimes, when I am frightened, I
become quite . . . Do you suppose you could bring me a glass of wine?"
She lifted both hands and patted lightly at her cheeks, as if endeavoring
to restore herself. After the dream they had shared, could she make him
believe her spirit was so delicate as to be distressed at such frank speech?

She could. There was suppressed panic in the set of his shoulders as
he turned hastily from her. He snatched up a glass from the sideboard and
poured her wine so hastily that it threatened to leap from the glass. When
he brought it to her, she drew back slightly, as if fearing to take it from his
hand. He expelled a small sound of dismay, and she forced a tremulous
smile to her lips. As if she steeled herself to courage, she took the glass
from him and raised it to her lips to sip delicately from it. It was an
excellent vintage. She lowered the glass and sighed softly. "That is better.
Thank you so much."

"How can you thank me, when I am the one who caused you such
distress?"

She widened her eyes and looked up at him. "Oh, I am sure the fault
is with me," she said disingenuously. "How foolish I must appear to you,
that I begin to tremble at mere words. My mother warned me that there
was still a great deal that I did not know of what it is to be a woman. This,
I suppose, is part of it." She made a small gesture around at the room. "As
you can tell, we live a quiet life here. I suppose I have been more sheltered than I thought. I have well understood my family's need to live
simply, within our means. Nevertheless, it has kept me apart from many

experiences." With a tiny shrug, she confessed, "I know so little of the ways of young men." She folded her hands in her lap and looked down at them as she added meekly, "I must ask you to be patient while I learn, I fear." A final glance up at him through lowered lashes. "I hope you will not think me stupid and dull, nor be wearied with the need to teach me such things. I hope you do not give up on me as hopelessly simple. Almost, I wish I had had other suitors, that I could already know something of the ways of men and women." She gave a tiny shrug and a sigh as she looked back down. She held her breath for a moment, hoping the effort would redden her cheeks as with a blush. She whispered breathlessly, "I confess, I almost did not understand my own dream, that night I opened the box." She did not look up as she pleaded prettily, "Could you teach me what such things signify?"

She did not need to see his face. She didn't even need to look up at his stance. She knew she had conquered completely in the moment he replied, "I could think of nothing I should like better than to be your tutor in such things."

CHAPTER EIGHT

Immersions

"HE STOPPED!" VIVACIA WAS ASTONISHED.

"No!" Wintrow shrieked, his voice breaking to a boy's on the word.

He spun away from the railing and hurled himself from the foredeck to the main. He crossed it at a run, then raced down the companionway. Fear of death had been all that had kept the pirate clinging to life. When Wintrow and Vivacia had persuaded him not to fear it, Kennit had simply let go. At the door to the captain's quarters, Wintrow did not knock nor pause. Etta looked up in astonished anger at his mad entrance. She had been folding lint bandages. As Wintrow rushed to Kennit's bedside, she dropped them to the deck and tried to intercept him.

"Don't wake him!" she cautioned him. "He's finally resting."

"He's trying to be dead!" Wintrow contradicted her as he shouldered past her. At Kennit's bedside, he took the pirate's hand and called his name. There was no response. He tapped Kennit's cheek, then slapped it almost sharply. He pinched the man's cheek gently, then hard, trying to get a reaction. There was none. Kennit was not breathing.

He was dead.

KENNIT SETTLED INTO THE DARK, DRIFTING DOWN GENTLY LIKE A LEAF falling to the forest floor. He felt warm and comfortable. A thin silver thread of pain anchored him to his life. It attenuated as he fell. Soon it must fade to nothing and then he would be free of his body. It did not seem worth his attention. Nothing was worth his attention. He let go of himself and felt his consciousness expand. Never before had he comprehended how cramped a man's thoughts were when confined to a mere body. All those discordant worries and ideas jumbled together like a sailor's swag in his sea bag. Now they could spread out and disconnect. Each could assume its own importance.

Abruptly he felt a tug. An insistence he could not resist drew him into itself. Reluctantly he gave way to it, but once it possessed him, it did not seem to know what to do with him. He mingled with it confusedly. It was like being plunged into a kettle of simmering fish chowder. First one thing and then another bobbed to the surface, only to float away a moment later. He was a woman, combing out her long hair as she stared thoughtfully across the water. He was Ephron Vestrit, and by Sa, he would bring his cargo through intact and on time, storm or no. He was a ship, the cold water purring past his bow, shining fish flickering below and stars glittering above him. Deeper, higher and wider than all others, encompassing them all but thin as a coat of shellac, there was another awareness, one that spread wide her wings and soared through a summer sky. That one drew him more strongly than any of the others did and when it drifted away from him, he tried to follow it.

No, someone forbade him, gently but firmly. *No. I do not go there and neither shall you.* Something drew him back and held him together. He felt like a child, supported in a mother's arms, protected and cherished. She loved him. He settled into her embrace. She was the ship, the lovely, intelligent ship he had won. The stirring of that memory was like a breath on the ember of his being. He glowed brighter and almost became aware of who he had been. That was not what he desired. He rolled over and burrowed into her, merging with her, becoming her. Lovely, lovely ship, hull to the cupping water, sails in a caressing wind, I am you and you are I. When I am you, I am wondrous and wise. He sensed her amusement at his flattery, but flattery it was not. *In you, I could be perfect,* he told her. He sought to dissipate himself but she held him intact.

She spoke again, her words intended for someone else. *I have him. Here. You must take him and put him back. I do not know how.*

A boy's voice replied. It was uncertain and thin as smoke, coming from a great distance. Fear was making him jabber. *I don't know what you mean. How can you have him, how can I take him? Put him back how? Put him back where?* The pleading desperation in the young voice rang against something inside him. It woke echoes of another boy's voice, just as desperate, just as pleading. *Please. I can't do that. I don't know how, I don't want to, please, sir, please.* It was the hidden voice, the secret voice, the voice that must never be acknowledged. No one else must hear it, no one. He flung himself upon it, wrapped himself around it and stilled it. He absorbed it into himself to conceal it. The divergence that was the key to him was restored. A shiver of anger ran over him, that they had forced him to be himself again.

Like that, she said suddenly to the other one. *Like that. Find the pieces of him and put them back into one.* More softly, she added, *There are places where you almost match. Begin with those.*

What do you mean, he matches me? How could he match me?

I meant only that in some ways you resemble one another. You share more than you realize. Do not fear him. Take him. Restore him.

He clung to the ship's being more tightly than ever. He would not allow himself to be separated from her. Frantically, he strove to weave himself into her, twining his consciousness into hers as a single rope is woven from multiple strands. She did not repulse him, but neither did she welcome him in. Instead, he felt himself gathered back together, and offered in turn to an entity that was both of her and distinct from her.

Here. Take him. Put him back.

The connection between the two was amazingly complex. They loved one another and yet struggled not to be one another. Resentments burned like isolated brush fire in the landscape of their relationship. He could not discern where one left off and the other began, yet each clearly asserted ownership to a greatness of soul that could not be encompassed by a single creature. The outstretched wings of an ancient creature both sheltered and overshadowed them, yet they were unaware of it. Blind funny little creatures they were, fumbling in the midst of a love they feared to acknowledge. To win, all they had to do was surrender but they could not perceive that. The beauty of what they could have been together made him ache. It was a love he had been seeking all his life, a love to redeem and perfect him. That which he most desired, they feared and avoided.

Come back. Please. It was the boy's voice, pleading. *Kennit. Please choose to live.*

The name was a magic. It bound and defined him. The boy sensed that. *Kennit.* He repeated the name coaxingly. *Kennit, please. Kennit. Live.* At each touch of the word, he became more solid. Memories coagulated around the name, scabbing over the old wound of his life and sealing him into it.

Please, he begged. He groped for his tormentor's name. *Wintrow. Please let me go. Wintrow.* He sought to bind the boy as he had been bound, by the use of his name. Instead of bending Wintrow to his will, it only locked him into an awareness of the boy.

Kennit, the boy acknowledged him eagerly. *Kennit. Help me. Come back to yourself, become yourself again. Enter your life again.*

A curious thing happened then. In Wintrow's urgent welcome of his self-awareness and Kennit's sensing of the boy, they mingled. Memories churned and tumbled free of their owners. A boy wept silent tears the night before he was sent from his family to a monastery. A boy yammered in terror as he watched his father beaten unconscious while a man held him and laughed. A boy struggled and yelped in pain as a seven-pointed star was needled into his hip. A boy meditated, and saw shapes of dragons in the clouds and images of serpents in swirling water. A boy struggled with his tormentor, who throttled him into compliance. A boy sat long and still, transported by a book. A boy choked and gasped, resisting the tattooing of his face. A boy spent hours practicing the careful formation of letters. A boy held his hand to the deck and refused to cry out as his infected finger was cut from his hand. A boy grinned and sweated with joy as a tattoo was seared from his hip.

The ship had been right. There were many conjunctions, many places where they matched. The congruency could not be denied. They overlapped, they were one another, and then they separated again.

Kennit knew himself again. Wintrow cowered at the harshness that had been Kennit's early years. In the next instant, a wave of pity and compassion overwhelmed Kennit. It came from the boy. Wintrow reached out to him. Ignorantly, he sought to fix the parts that Kennit had deliberately broken away from himself. *This was you. You should keep it*, Wintrow kept insisting. *You cannot simply discard parts of yourself because they are painful. Acknowledge them and go on.*

The boy had no concept of what he was suggesting. That whimpering, crippled thing could never be a part of Kennit the Pirate. Kennit defended himself from it in the same fashion he always had. With anger and contempt he rebuffed Wintrow, severing that brief connection of empathy. In the moment before they parted, he became aware of the boy's sudden hurt at his act. For the first time in many years, he felt remorse burn him. Before he could truly consider it, he heard as from a great distance, a woman's voice calling his name.

"Kennit. Oh, my Kennit. Please, please, please, don't be gone. Kennit!"

Unavoidable pain defined the confines of his body. There was a weight on his chest and his leg ended in a sensation of wrongness. He drew in a deep breath through a throat that was raw with spirits and bile. As if pulling up an anchor by himself, he hauled his eyelids open. Light scorched his brain.

The whore clutched his left hand, weeping over it. Her wet face and disheveled hair, her shrill cries . . . it was really too distressing to tolerate. He tried to jerk his hand free of her grip, but he was too weak. "Etta. Do stop that. Please." His words came out in a hoarse croak.

"Oh, Kennit!" she cried out in sudden joy. "You aren't dead. Oh, my love."

"Water," he said to her, as much to be rid of her as for the sake of his thirst. She sprang to the task, hastening to the carafe on the sideboard across the room. He swallowed in a dry throat, then pushed vaguely at the weight on his chest. Hairy. Rough hair under his hand, and a sweaty face. He managed to lift his head a tiny bit and look down at his chest. It was Wintrow. From a chair next to the bed, the boy was collapsed forward onto Kennit. The boy's eyes were shut, his face was a dreadful pasty color, and tears streaked his cheeks. Wintrow wept for him. A sudden rush of feeling confused Kennit. The boy's head was on his chest, making breathing even more difficult. He wanted to push him away, but the warmth of his hair and skin under his hand awoke a foreign longing as well. It was as if he himself were embodied afresh in this lad. He could protect this boy as he had not been protected himself. He had the power to stave off the destructive forces that had once torn his own life apart.

After all, they were not that different. The ship had said so. To protect him would be like saving himself.

It was a curious feeling, that power. It offered to sate a deep hunger that had lived nameless inside him since he had been a boy himself. Before he could wonder further at it, Wintrow's eyes opened. The boy's gaze was dark and unguarded. He looked full into Kennit's face with an expression of bottomless woe that changed suddenly to wonder. The boy's hand rose to touch Kennit's cheek. "You're alive," he said in whispery awe. His voice wandered as if that of a fever victim but joy began to kindle in his eyes. "You were all in pieces. Just like a stained-glass window, all in pieces. So many parts to a man. I was amazed. You still came back." His eyes sagged shut on a sigh. "Thank you. Thank you. I didn't want to die."

The boy blinked his eyes and suddenly seemed more himself. He lifted his head from Kennit's chest and looked around groggily. "I must have fainted," he said to himself in a thin voice. "I went so deep in the trance . . . that's never happened to me before, but Berandol warned me. . . . I suppose I'm lucky that I found my way back at all." He leaned back abruptly into the chair he was perched on. "I suppose we're both lucky," he said woozily.

"My leg is wrong," Kennit told him. With the boy's head off his chest, it was easier to take breath and speak. He was now free to focus entirely on the strange sensation of his truncated body.

"It's numb. I treated it with kwazi-fruit rind, to take the pain away for a while. You should sleep while you can. The pain will be back. We don't have enough rind to keep it away forever."

"You're in my way," Etta said tartly.

Wintrow gave a guilty start. She stood beside him, holding a cup of water. The boy was not truly in her way; she could have simply brought it to the other side of the bed. Wintrow took her true meaning, however. "Beg pardon," he said hastily, and rose. He staggered two steps toward the door and then collapsed to the deck as bonelessly as a dropped rag. He lay where he had swooned.

Etta gave an exclamation of annoyance. "I'll call a crewman to take him away," she said. The sight of the unconscious boy on the deck distressed the pirate until she offered him the dripping cup.

Her long-fingered hand was cool on the back of his neck as she held up his head. His thirst was suddenly all-consuming. It was ship's water, neither cold nor fresh, tasting of the barrel it had been stored in. It was nectar. He drank it down. "More," he croaked when she took the cup away.

"Right away," she promised him.

His eyes followed her as she returned to the water ewer. He noted in passing the limp boy on the floor. A moment ago, there had been something about him, something urgent he wished Etta to do. It had been important, but now he could not recall it. Instead, he was starting to float, rising off the bed. The experience was both unnerving and pleasant. The cup of water came back. He drank it all. "I can fly," he observed to the woman. "Now that the pain is gone, I can fly. The pain was anchoring me down."

She smiled at him fondly. "You're light-headed. And perhaps a bit drunk still."

He nodded. He could not keep the foolish smile from his lips. A rush of gratitude suffused him. He had lived with the pain for so long and now it was gone. It was wonderful. His gratitude swelled to engulf his whole world.

The boy had done it.

He looked at Wintrow still sprawled on the floor. "He's such a good boy," he said affectionately. "We care so much about him, the ship and I." He was getting very sleepy but he managed to bring his eyes back to the woman's face. Her hand was touching his cheek. He reached up slowly and managed to capture it. "You'll take care of him for me, won't you?" His eyes moved across her face, from her mouth to her eyes. It was hard to make his eyes see her whole face at once. It was too much work to refocus them. "I can count on you for that, can't I?"

"Is that what you want?" she asked him reluctantly.

"More than anything," he declared passionately. "Be kind to him."

"If that is what you want, I will," she said, almost unwillingly.

"Good. Good." He squeezed her fingers gently. "I knew you would if I asked you. Now I can sleep." He closed his eyes.

WHEN WINTROW OPENED HIS EYES, THERE WAS A CUSHION UNDER HIS HEAD and a blanket thrown over him. He was on the deck of the captain's stateroom. He tried to find his place in time. He had a fragmented dream of a stained-glass window. A frightened boy had been hiding behind it. The window had broken. Somehow, Wintrow had reassembled the window. The boy had been grateful. No. No, in the dream, he had been the boy . . . no, he had pieced the man back together, while Berandol and Vivacia advised him from behind a curtain of water. There had been a serpent and a dragon, too. A seven-pointed star that hurt horribly. Then he had wakened, and Etta had been annoyed with him and then . . .

It was no good. He could not make it come together. The long day was broken into pieces that he could not reconcile. Some parts, he knew, were from his dreams. Others seemed relentlessly real. Had he actually cut off a man's leg earlier this afternoon? That seemed the most unlikely recollection of all. He closed his eyes and groped toward Vivacia. He was aware of her, as he always was whenever he reached toward her. A wordless communion was constant between them. He could feel that much of her, but she seemed distracted. Not disinterested in him so much as intrigued with something else. Perhaps she was as disoriented as he was. Well. It was not going to do any good to lie here.

He rolled his head and looked up at Kennit's bunk. The pirate's chest rose and fell reassuringly under his bedding. His color was terrible, but he was alive. At least that much of Wintrow's dream had been true.

He drew a deep breath, and got his arms under him. He pushed up carefully from the deck, fighting his way through a wall of vertigo. Never had a working trance so weakened him. He still was not quite sure what he had done, or if he had truly done anything at all. In his work trances at the monastery, he had learned how to engage completely with his art. Immersed in it, the various tasks of creation became a whole act. It seemed he had somehow applied that to healing Kennit, but he did not understand how. He could not remember composing himself for a work trance.

Once on his feet, he moved carefully toward the bed. Was this how it felt to be drunk, he wondered? Unsteady and dizzy, seeing colors as too bright, edges of objects sharply defined? It could not be. This was not pleasant. No one would willingly seek out these sensations. He halted at the edge of the bed. He dreaded checking the bandages on Kennit's leg, but he knew he should. He might still be bleeding. If he was, Wintrow had no idea what he would do. Despair, he decided. He reached gingerly for the edge of the blanket.

"Don't wake him, please."

Etta's voice was so gentle he almost did not recognize it. He turned his whole body to see her. She was seated in a chair in the corner of the room. There were hollows under her eyes that he had not noticed before. Dark blue fabric overlay her lap while she plied a busy needle. She looked up at him, bit off a thread, turned her work and began a new seam.

"I have to see if he's still bleeding." His words sounded thick and misshapen to his ears.

"He doesn't seem to be. However, if you disturb the bandages to check the wound, you might start blood flowing. Best to leave well enough alone."

"Has he awakened at all?" His mind was starting to clear itself.

"Briefly. Right after you . . . brought him back. I gave him water, lots of it. Then he dozed off again. He's slept ever since."

Wintrow rubbed at his eyes. "How long has that been?"

"Nearly all night," she told him placidly. "It will be dawn soon."

He could not fathom her kindly manner toward him. It was not that she looked at him warmly or smiled. Rather something was gone from her voice, an edge of jealousy or distrust that had always been there before now. Wintrow was glad that she didn't seem to hate him anymore, but he wasn't quite sure how to deal with it. "Well," he said inanely. "I suppose I should go back to sleep for a while then."

"Sleep where you were," she suggested. "It's clean and warm in here. You're close to Kennit in case he needs you."

"Thank you," he said awkwardly. He was not sure that he wanted to sleep on the deck here. His bed would be the deck no matter where he went on the ship, but the thought of having a stranger watching him while he slept was unnerving. What happened next was even stranger. She shook out the work on her lap, holding it up between them, her eyes going from him to her needlework and back again. It was a pair of trousers, and she was obviously eyeing him to see if they would fit. He felt like he should say something, but he did not know what. She folded it back into her lap without comment. She threaded her needle again and resumed her work.

He returned to his blanket on the floor, rather like a dog returning to its designated spot. He sat but could not bring himself to lie down. Instead, he shawled the blanket over his shoulders. He looked at Etta until she returned his gaze. "How did you become a pirate?" he abruptly asked her. He hadn't realized he was going to speak until the words popped out.

She took a breath, then spoke thoughtfully. There was no trace of regret in her voice. "I worked as a whore in a house in Divvytown. Kennit took a liking to me. One day I helped him kill some men who attacked him there. Afterwards, he took me out of the whorehouse and brought me here. At first, I was not sure why he had brought me to his ship, or what he expected of me. However, after a time, his thought became clear to me. I could be much more than a whore, if I chose to. He was giving me the chance."

He stared at her. Her words had shocked him. Not her admission that she had killed men for Kennit; he had expected that of this pirate. She had called herself a whore. That was a man's word, a shame-word flung at a woman. But she did not seem ashamed. She wielded the word like a sword, slicing away all his preconceptions of who she was. She had earned her living by her sex, and she did not seem to regret it. It roused a strange shivering of interest in him. She suddenly seemed a more powerful creature than she had just moments ago. "What were you before you were a whore?" Unaccustomed to speaking the word, he put too much emphasis on it. He had not meant it to sound that way, he had not meant to ask that question at all. Had Vivacia nudged him to it?

She frowned at him, thinking he rebuked her. Her eyes were straight and flat as she said, "I was a whore's daughter." A note of challenge crept into her voice as she asked in turn, "And what were you, before your father made you a slave on his ship?"

"I was a priest of Sa. At least, I was in training to be one."

She lifted one eyebrow. "Really? I'd rather be a whore."

Her words ended their conversation irrevocably. There was nothing he could say in reply. He did not feel offended. She had pointed up the vast gulf between them in a way that denied they could communicate at all, let alone offend one another. She went back to her sewing, her head bent over her work. Her face was carefully expressionless. Wintrow felt he had lost a chance. Moments ago, it had seemed that she had opened a door to him. Now the barrier was back, solid as ever. Why should he care, he asked himself, for the depth of his disappointment surprised him. Because she was a back door to influencing Kennit, because he might need her good will someday, the sly part of himself suggested. Wintrow pushed the thought aside. Because she, too, is a creation of Sa, he told himself firmly. I should reach out to befriend her for herself, not for any influence she has with Kennit. Nor because she is unlike any woman I have ever known at all and I cannot resist the puzzle of her.

He closed his eyes for a moment and tried to sweep aside all social artifice. When he spoke, his words were sincere. "Please. Can we try again? I'd like to be friends."

Etta looked up in surprise. Then her expression changed to a humorless smile. "In case I can save your life later? By intervening with Kennit?"

"No!" he protested.

"That's good. Because I have no influence over Kennit that way." Her voice dropped a note. "What there is between Kennit and me, I would not use that way."

Wintrow sensed an opening. "I would not ask you to. I just . . . it would be nice to talk to someone. Just to talk. So much has befallen me recently. My friends are all dead, my father despises me, the slaves I helped do not seem to recall what I did for them, I suspect Sa'Adar would like to do away with me. . . ." His voice trailed away as he realized how self-pitying he sounded. He took a breath, but what came out next sounded even whinier. "I'm more alone than I've ever been. And I have no idea of what will become of me next."

"Who ever does?" Etta asked him heartlessly.

"I used to," he said quietly. His thoughts turned inward as he spoke. "When I was at the monastery, life seemed to stretch out before me like a shining road. I knew I would continue my studies. I knew I excelled at my chosen work. I genuinely loved my life. I had no desire to change any of it. Then I was summoned home, my grandfather died, and my father forced me to serve aboard the ship. Since then, I have had no say in my life. Every time I tried to take control of it, I only bent it in a stranger direction."

She bit off her thread. "Sounds normal to me."

He shook his head sadly. "I do not know. Perhaps it is, for other folk. I only know it was not what I was accustomed to, nor what I expected. I keep trying to think of a way to get back to where I was and restore my life to what it is supposed to be, but—"

"You can't go back," she told him bluntly. Her voice was neither kind nor unkind. "That part of your life is over. Set it aside as something you have finished. Complete or no, it is done with you. No being gets to decide what his life is 'supposed to be.'" She lifted her eyes and her gaze stabbed him. "Be a man. Discover where you are now, and go on from there, making the best of things. Accept your life, and you might survive it. If you hold back from it, insisting this is not your life, not where you are meant to be, life will pass you by. You may not die from such foolishness, but you might as well be dead for all the good your life will do you or anyone else."

Wintrow was stunned. Heartless as her words were, they brimmed with wisdom. Almost reflexively, he sank into meditation breathing, as if this were a teaching direct from Sa's scrolls. He explored her idea, following it to its logical conclusions.

Yes, these thoughts were of Sa, and worthy. Accept. Begin anew. Find humility again. Pre-judging his life, that was what he had been doing. Always his greatest flaw, Berandol had warned him. There was opportunity for good here, if he just reached out toward it. Why had he been bent on returning to his monastery, as if Sa could only be found there? What had he just said to Etta? That the more he tried to take control of his life, the further he bent it. It was no wonder. He had been setting himself in opposition to Sa's will for him.

He suddenly grasped how the slaves must have felt when the shackles were loosed from their ankles and wrists. Her words had freed him. He could let go of his self-imposed goals. He would lift up his eyes and look around him and see where Sa's way beckoned him most clearly.

"Stop staring at me like that." There was both command and an edged uneasiness in Etta's voice. Wintrow immediately dropped his eyes.

"I was not . . . I mean, I did not intend to stare. Your words simply woke in me such thoughts. . . . Etta. Where were you taught such things?"

"Such things as what?" There was definite suspicion in her voice now.

"Such things as accepting life and making the best of it . . ." Spoken aloud, it seemed such a simple concept. Moments ago, those words had rung for him like great bells of truth. It was right, what they said: enlightenment was merely the truth at the correct time.

"In a brothel."

Even that revelation opened his mind to light. "Then Sa is truly there, as well, in all his wisdom and glory."

She smiled and it almost reached her eyes. "To judge from the number of men who grunt out her name as they finish, I would say Sa is definitely there."

Wintrow looked aside from her. The image was uncomfortably vivid. "It must be a hard way to make your living," he blurted out.

"Do you think so?" She laughed aloud, a brittle sound. "That's a surprise to me, to hear you say that. But you are still just a boy. Most men tell us they wish they could earn their bread on their backs. They think we have it easy, dealing in 'pleasure' all day."

Wintrow considered it for a moment. "I think it would be very hard, to be that intimate and vulnerable to a man one had no true feelings for."

For just an instant, her eyes went pensive and dark. "After a time, all feelings go away," she said in an almost-childish voice. "It's a relief when they do. Things get so much easier. Then it is no worse than any other dirty job. Unless you get a man who hurts you. Still, one can get hurt working anywhere: farmers are gored by their oxen, orchard workers fall from trees, fishermen lose fingers or drown. . . ."

Her voice trailed away. Her eyes went back to her stitching. Wintrow kept silent. After a time, a pale smile came to the edges of her mouth. "Kennit brought my feelings back. I hated him for it. That was the first thing he taught me to feel again: hate. I knew it was a dangerous thing. It is dangerous for a whore to feel anything. Knowing that he had made me feel emotions again just made me hate him even more."

Why, Wintrow wondered, but he did not say the word aloud. He did not need to.

"He came into the bagnio one day and looked around." Her voice was distant in reminiscence. "He was dressed very fine, and was very clean. A dark green broadcloth jacket with ivory buttons, and a spill of white lace down his chest and at his cuffs . . . He had never come to Bettel's bagnio before, but I knew who he was. Even then, most of Divvytown knew who Kennit was. He did not come to the brothel like most men did, with a friend or two, or his whole crew. He did not come drunk and boasting. He came alone, sober and purposeful. He looked at us, really looked at us, and then he chose me. 'She'll do,' he told Bettel. Then he ordered the room he wanted and the meal. He paid Bettel, right then, in front of everyone. Then he stepped up to me as if we were already alone. He leaned close to me. I thought he was going to kiss me. Some of the men do that. Instead, he sniffed the air near me. Then he ordered me to go wash myself. Oh, I was humiliated. You would not think a whore can feel humiliation, but we can. Nevertheless, I did what I was told. Then I went upstairs and did as I was told, but no more than that. I was in a fury, and was cold as ice to him. I expected him to slap me, refuse me, or complain to Bettel. Instead, it seemed to suit his wishes."

She paused. For a time, the silence rang in Wintrow's ears. He knew he did not want to hear any more about this, yet he avidly hoped she would say more. It was voyeurism, pure and simple, a keen curiosity to know in detail what went on between a man and a woman. He knew the physical mechanics; such knowledge had never been concealed from him. But knowing how such things are done does not convey the real knowledge of how it happens. He waited, looking at the deck by her feet. He dared not lift his eyes to see her face.

"Every time after that, it was the same. He came, he chose me, he told me to wash, and he used me. He made it so cold. The other men who came to the bagnio, they'd pretend a bit. They would flirt, and laugh with the girls. They would tell stories and see who listened the best. They acted as if we had some say. They made us compete for them. Some would even dance with the whores, or bring little gifts, sweets or perfumes for the ones they liked best. Not Kennit. Even when he began asking for me by my name, it was still just a transaction."

She shook out the trousers, turned them right side out, and began to sew on them again. She took a breath once, as if she would continue. Then she gave her head a minute shake and went on with her sewing. Wintrow could not think of anything to say. Despite his fascination with her story, he was suddenly horribly tired. He wished he could go back to sleep, but he knew that even stretched out on the floor, sleep would not come to him. Outside, the night paled. Soon it would be dawn. He felt a brief stirring of triumph. He had cut Kennit's leg off yesterday, and the pirate was still alive today. He had done it. He had saved the man's life.

Then he rebuked himself sharply. If the pirate still lived, it was only because his will had coincided with Sa's. To believe anything else was false pride. He glanced again at his patient. His chest still rose and fell. However, he had known that Kennit still lived before he looked. Vivacia knew, and through her, he knew. He did not want to consider that link, nor wonder how strong it was. It was bad enough that he was connected so to the ship. He did not want to share such a bond with the pirate.

Etta made a tiny sound, an intake of breath. Wintrow swung his attention back to her. She didn't look at him. She kept her eyes focused on her stitching. Yet, there was a quiet glow of pride about her. Plainly, there was something she had well considered and decided to say to him. When she spoke, he listened silently.

"I stopped hating Kennit when I realized what he was giving me, each time he came. Honesty. He preferred me, and he did not fear to show that. In front of everyone, he chose me, every time. He did not bait me to simper and flirt. I was what he wanted, and I was for sale, so he bought me. He was showing me that as long as I was a whore that was all we could ever share. An honest transaction."

An odd little smile crossed her face. "Sometimes, Bettel would offer him other women. She had many. Some were fancier women, far more beautiful than I am, some were women who knew exotic ways to please a man. Bettel sought to win his favor that way. She did that with the house patrons, to keep them loyal to her. She offered them variety, and tempted them to . . . acquire new preferences. I knew it did not please her to see Kennit always come to me. It made her feel less important, I suppose. Once, in front of everyone, she asked him, 'Why Etta? So lanky, so plain. So ordinary. I have courtesans trained in the finest houses in Chalced. Or, if you prefer innocence, I have sweet virginal things from the countryside. You could afford the best in my house. Why do you prefer my cheapest whore?' " The tiny smile reached Etta's eyes. "I think she thought to shame him, before the other patrons there. As if he could ever have cared what they thought. Instead, he said, 'I never confuse the cost of something with its value. Etta, go and wash yourself. I shall be upstairs.' After that, all the other whores called me Kennit's whore. They tried to make it a name that stung. But it never bothered me."

Obviously, Kennit was a deeper man than Wintrow had supposed him to be. Most sailors did not look beyond a whore's face and figure to make a choice. Kennit evidently had. On the other hand, perhaps the woman was deceiving herself. He glanced up at Etta's face and then away. Uneasiness swept through him. Whence had that thought sprung? For an instant, he had felt the sting of jealousy. Had it been from the ship herself? He felt the sudden need to speak with Vivacia.

He stood, his knees crackling. His lower back was stiff, his shoulders sore. When had he last slept in a real bed, slept until he had awakened naturally? Eventually, he must pay heed to the needs of his own body, or it would enforce its demands for rest and food. Soon, he promised himself. As soon as he felt safe, he would see to himself. "It's dawn," he said awkwardly. "I should check on the ship and on my father. I need to get some sleep for myself, also. Will you send for me if Kennit awakens?"

"If he needs you," Etta replied coolly. Perhaps that had been the point of her entire conversation: to make clear to Wintrow her prior claim upon Kennit. Did she see him as a threat somehow? Wintrow decided he did not know enough about women. She lifted her work to her mouth, and bit off a thread. Then she too, stood, shaking out the garment she had finished. "For you," she said abruptly, and thrust the trousers at him. He started toward her to take the gift from her hands, but she tossed it at him, forcing him to catch it awkwardly. One trouser leg slapped him lightly in the face.

"Thank you," he said uncertainly.

She didn't look at him, nor acknowledge his words. Instead she opened a clothes chest and rummaged through it. She came up with a shirt. "Here. This will do for you. It's one of his old ones." She fingered the fabric for a moment. "It's a very good weave. He knows quality, that one."

"I am sure he does," Wintrow replied. "He chose you, as you have told me." It was his first effort at gallantry. Somehow, it did not come out quite right. The comment hung crookedly between them. Etta stared at him, sorting the words to see if they held an insult. The heat of a blush rose to his cheeks; what had ever possessed him to say such a thing? Then she tossed the shirt at him and it opened wide, a white bird a-wing. It collapsed over his hands, heavy cloth, strong yet supple. It was a very good shirt, much too fine to dispose of so casually. Was there, he wondered, a message here, one that Etta scarcely knew that she conveyed? He draped the garments over his arm. "Thank you for the clothing," he said again, determined to be polite.

Her eyes leveled with his. "Kennit wants you to have them, I am sure," she said. Just as he began to feel grateful, she doused it with, "You will be looking after him. He demands cleanliness of those around him. You should take time today to wash yourself, including your hair."

"I'm not . . ." he began and then stopped. He was dirty. A moment's reflection made him realize he stank. He had cleansed his hands after he cut off Kennit's leg, but he had not washed his entire body for days. "I will," he amended humbly. Carrying the clothes, he left the captain's cabin.

The disarray and crowding on the captured ship almost seemed normal now. His eyes no longer snagged on every splintered door-jamb. He could look past bloodstains on the decks and walls. As he emerged onto the deck, he pressed his back to the wall to make room for a couple to pass him. They were both map-faces. The man was a bit simple, Wintrow recalled. Dedge was his name. He was one of the map-faces Etta had chosen to hold Kennit down. He always seemed to be with the younger, quicker Saylah. They scarcely noticed Wintrow as they brushed past him, so caught up were they in one another. That, too, had begun to happen. He should have expected it. After any disaster, that was always the first sign of returning hope. Men and women paired off and coupled. He looked after them curiously, wondering where they would find privacy. Idly, he wondered if they had been slaves long, if privacy were of any concern to them any more. He realized he was staring after them. With a twitch of annoyance at himself, he called to mind his errands. Confer with Vivacia. Check on his father. Eat. Bathe. Sleep. Check on Kennit. His life suddenly assumed a shape, with a schedule to his hours and purpose to his acts. He made his way forward.

The *Vivacia* still swung at anchor in the small cove. Had it truly been just one night since they had hidden here? A mist was dispersing in the morning sunlight. Soon the sun might have enough strength to warm the day. The figurehead stared out toward the wide channel as if keeping watch. Perhaps she was.

"I worry that the other ship will never find us." She spoke aloud in answer to his silent thought. "How will they know where to look?"

"I have the feeling that Kennit and Sorcor have sailed together for a long time. Such men have ways of doing things, ways they pass on to their crews. Besides, Kennit is still alive. Before long, he may feel well enough to guide us to Bull Creek himself." Wintrow spoke reassuringly, attempting to comfort the ship.

"Perhaps," Vivacia conceded grudgingly. "But I would feel better if we were underway already. He has survived the night, that is true. Nevertheless, he is far from strong, or cured. Yesterday, he died when he stopped struggling to live. Today, he struggles to cling to life. I do not like how his dreams twitch and dance. I would feel better if he were in the hands of a real healer."

Her words stung, just a bit. Wintrow knew he was not a trained healer, but she might have spoken some word of admiration at how well he had done so far. He glanced down at the deck where he had performed his crude surgery. Kennit's flowing blood had followed the contours of his supine body. The dark stain was an eerie outline of his injured leg and hip. It was not far from Wintrow's own bloody handprint. That mark had never been erased from the deck. Would Kennit's shadow stay as well? Uneasily, Wintrow scuffed at it with his bare foot.

It was like sweeping his fingers across a stringed instrument, save that the chord he awoke was not sound. Kennit's life suddenly sang with his own. Wintrow reeled with the force of the connection, then sat down hard on the deck. A moment later, he tried to describe it to himself. It had not been Kennit's memories, nor his thoughts or dreams. Instead, it had been an intense awareness of the pirate. The closest comparison he could summon was the way a perfume or scent could suddenly call up detailed memories, but a hundred times stronger. His sense of Kennit had almost driven him out of himself.

"Now you glimpse how it is for me," the ship said quietly. A moment later she added, "I did not think it could affect you that way."

"What was that?"

"The power of blood. Blood remembers. Blood recalls not days and nights and events. Blood recalls identity."

Wintrow was silent, trying to grasp the full import of what she was saying. He reached out a hand toward Kennit's spilled shadow on the deck. Then he pulled back his fingers. No amount of curiosity could draw him to experience that again. The potency of it had dizzied his soul and nearly displaced him from himself.

"And that is what you felt," the ship added to his thought. "You, who have blood of your own. At least you possess your own body, your own set of memories and your own identity. You can set Kennit aside and say, 'He is not I.' I have none of that. I am no more than wood impregnated with the memories of your family. The identity you call Vivacia is one I have cobbled together for myself. When Kennit's blood soaked into me, I was powerless to refuse it. Just like the night of the slave uprising, when man after man entered me, and I was powerless to deny any of them.

"The night all that blood was spilled . . . Imagine being drenched in identities, not once or twice, but dozens of times. They collapsed on my decks and died, but as their blood soaked into me, they made me the reservoir of who they had been. Slave or crew member, it made no differ-ence. They came to me. All that they were, they added to me. Sometimes, Wintrow, it is too much. I walk the spiral pathways of their blood, and I know who they were in detail. I cannot free myself from those ghosts. The only more powerful influences are those of you who possess me doubly: with your blood soaked into my planks and your minds linked to mine."

"I do not know what to say," Wintrow replied lamely.

"Do you think I do not already know that?" Vivacia replied bitterly.

A long silence fell between them. To Wintrow, it was as if the very planks of the deck emanated cold toward him. He crept away quietly, his new clothes bundled under his arm, but he took the knowledge with him that there was nowhere he could go that would free her from his presence. Accept life as it came. That was what Etta had said to him but a short time ago. Then, it had seemed brilliant. He tried to imagine accepting that their eternal fate was to be bound together. He shook his head to himself.

"If this be your will, O Sa, I know not how to endure it gladly," he said quietly. It was pain to feel Vivacia echo the same thought.

IT WAS HOURS LATER AND THE SUN WAS HIGH WHEN THE MARIETTA FOUND them. She had a long scorched area along her starboard railing. Deck-hands were already at work repairing it. An even plainer sign of both her encounter and her triumph was the string of severed heads that dangled from her bowsprit. The cry of the lookout had brought Wintrow out on deck. Now he stared in sick fascination as the ship drew nearer. He had seen carnage the night the slaves had risen and taken over the Vivacia. These trophies went beyond carnage into a planned savagery that he could not completely grasp.

The men and women that lined the railings alongside him lifted up a cheer at the bloody prizes. To them, the heads represented not only the Satrap who had condoned their slavery but Chalced, the most avaricious market for enslaved humanity. As the Marietta drew closer, Wintrow could see other signs of their battle with the patrol galley. Several of the pirates wore crude bandages. That didn't stop them from grinning and waving to their compatriots aboard Vivacia.

There was a tug at Wintrow's sleeve. "The woman says you're to come and wait on the captain," Dedge told him dourly. Wintrow looked at him carefully, fixing the man's face and his name in his memory. He tried to look past the lineage of his slavery and see the man beneath the sprawling tattoos. His eyes were sea-gray, his hair no more than a fringe above his ears. Despite his years, muscle showed through his rags. Etta had already marked him as her own; he wore a sash of silk about his waist. "The woman" he had called her, like a title, as if she were the only woman aboard the ship. Wintrow supposed that in a sense, she was. "I'll come right away," he responded to the man.

The Marietta was dropping anchor. Soon a gig would be lowered to bring Sorcor aboard to report to Kennit. Wintrow had no idea why Kennit had summoned him, but perhaps Kennit would allow him to be in the room when Sorcor reported. Earlier today, when he had checked on his father, Kyle had insisted Wintrow must gather as much knowledge of the pirates as he could. Wintrow tried to push the memory of that painful hour away.

Confinement and pain had made Kyle more of a tyrant than ever, and he seemed to believe Wintrow was his only remaining subject. In truth, the boy felt almost no loyalty to him at all, save for a residue of duty. His father's insistence that he must constantly spy and plot for a way to regain control of the ship struck him as laughable. But he had not laughed; he had merely let the man rant while he saw to his injuries and coaxed him to eat the dry bread and old water that were the only rations afforded him. It was easier to let his words flow past. Wintrow had nodded to them, but said little in reply. To try to explain their real situation aboard the Vivacia would only have angered Kyle. Wintrow had let him keep his far-fetched dream that they would somehow regain control of the ship. It seemed the easiest thing to do. Soon enough, they would reach Bull Creek, and then they both must confront what had befallen them. Wintrow would not battle his father to make him recognize reality; reality would do that itself.

He tapped at the door, then entered at Etta's soft response. Kennit was awake on the bunk. He turned his head to greet him with, "She won't help me sit up."

"She is right. You should not sit up, not yet," Wintrow replied. "You should lie still and rest completely. How do you feel?" He set his hand to the pirate's forehead.

Kennit rolled his head away from the touch. "Wretched. Oh, do not ask me what I feel. I am alive; what can it matter, what I feel? Sorcor is coming, fresh from triumph, and here I lie, mauled and stinking like a corpse. I will not be seen like this. Help me to sit up, at least."

"You must not," Wintrow warned him. "Your blood is quiescent just now. Lie still and let it remain so. To sit up will change the reservoirs of your organs, and may spill blood that then must find its way out through your wound. This I learned well at the monastery."

"This I learned well on the deck: a pirate captain who can no longer actively lead his crew is soon fish bait. I will be sitting up when Sorcor arrives here."

"Even if it kills you?" Wintrow asked quietly.

"Are you challenging my will in this?" Kennit demanded abruptly.

"No. Not your will. Your common sense. Why choose to die here, in your bed, for a certainty, simply to impress a man who impresses me as unfailing in his loyalty to you? I think you misjudge your crew. They will not turn on you over your need to rest."

"You're a puppy," Kennit declared in disdain. He rolled his head away from the boy, choosing to look at the wall. "What can you know of loyalty, or how a ship is run? I tell you, I will not be seen like this." There was an edge in his voice that Wintrow suddenly recognized.

"Why did you not say that your pain was back? The kwazi-rind essence can dull it again. You will think more clearly without agony distracting you. And you will be able to rest."

"You mean I will be more tractable if you drug me," Kennit snarled. "You simply seek to impose your will upon me." He lifted a shaking hand to his brow. "My head pounds with pain; how can that be due to my leg? Is it not more likely the result of some poison given me?" Even in his weariness, the pirate managed to summon up a look of sly amusement. Clearly, he supposed he had surprised Wintrow in a plot.

His words shocked Wintrow into momentary silence. How did one deal with such suspicion and distrust? In a cold, stiff voice he heard himself say, "I will force no medicines upon you, sir. If your pain becomes such that you desire release from it, summon me and I shall apply the kwazi rind. Until then, I shall not trouble you." He spoke over his shoulder as he turned to go. "If you sit up to see Sorcor, the flow of blood you cause will end both our lives. But I cannot argue with your stubbornness."

"Stop this," Etta hissed at both of them. "There is a simple solution, one that may please us all. Will you allow me to suggest it?"

Kennit rolled his head back to stare at her with dulled eyes. "It is?" he prompted.

"Do not receive Sorcor. Simply give him an order to sail for Bull Creek and we will follow him. He does not need to know how weak you are. By the time we arrive in Bull Creek, you may be stronger."

A spark of cunning lit in Kennit's eyes. "Bull Creek is too close," he declared. "Have him lead us back to Divvytown. That will give me more time to recover." He paused. "But Sorcor will surely wonder that I do not wish to hear his report. He will suspect something."

Etta folded her arms across her chest. "Say you are busy. With me." She gave him a small smile. "Send the boy to give the word to Brig, to pass to Sorcor. He will accept it."

"It might work," Kennit assented slowly. He flapped a slow hand at Wintrow. "Go now, right now. Tell Brig I am with Etta and do not wish to be disturbed. Pass on to him my orders that we are to head for Div-vytown." Kennit's eyes narrowed, but from slyness or weariness, Wintrow could not tell. "Suggest I may judge Brig's seamanship by how well he manages the ship between here and there. Imply this is a test of his skill, not a lapse on my part." His eyelids sagged further. "Wait a time, until we are under way. Then come back here. I will judge you by how well this task is done. Convince Brig and Sorcor, and perhaps I will trust you to numb my leg for me." Kennit's eyes closed completely. In a smaller voice he added, "Perhaps I shall let you live."

CHAPTER NINE

Bingtown

DEEP INSIDE *PARAGON*, AMBER TOSSED AND TURNED LIKE A BADLY DIGESTED biscuit in a sailor's gut. A dream he was not privy to tore at her sleep, rending her rest into a blanketed struggle with herself. Sometimes Paragon was tempted to reach for her thoughts and share her distress, but most nights he was simply grateful that her torment was not his.

She had come to live aboard him, to sleep inside him at night and guard him from those who might come to tow him away and destroy him. In her own way, she had complied with his request as well. She had stocked several of his holds, not with driftwood and cheap lamp oil, but with the hardwoods and finishing oils of her trade. The fiction between them was that she stored them there so that she could sit beneath his bow of an evening and carve. They both knew that it would take but a moment to kindle the dry wood with the oil and fill him with flame. She would not let him be taken alive.

Sometimes he almost felt sorry for her. It was not easy for her to live inside the tilted quarters of the captain's room. With much muttering, she had cleared Brashen's abandoned possessions from the chambers. Paragon had noticed that she had handled them thoughtfully before she carefully stowed them belowdecks. Now she had taken over those quarters and slept in his hammock at night. She cooked out on the beach when the evenings were fine, and ate cold food at other times. Each day when she trudged off to her shop at daybreak, she took a water bucket with her. Every evening she returned laden with the brimming bucket and whatever she had brought from the market for her dinner. Then she would bustle about inside him, singing nonsense songs to herself. If the evening was fine, she kindled a cook fire and talked to him while she prepared her simple meal. In a way, it was pleasant to have company on a daily basis. In another way, it chafed him. He had grown accustomed to his solitude. Even in the midst of a companionable talk, he would know that their arrangement was temporary. All humans did was temporary. How else could it be, with creatures who died? Even if she stayed with him the rest of her life, she would still eventually be gone. Once he had grasped that thought, he could not be rid of it. To know that his days with Amber must, eventually, come to an end gave him a feeling of waiting. He hated waiting. Better to be done with it, and have her gone than to spend all his time with her waiting for the day she would leave him. Often it made him cross and short-spoken with her.

But not tonight. Tonight they had had a merry evening together. She had insisted on teaching him a silly song, and then they had sung it together, first as a duet for two voices and then as a round. He had discovered he liked singing. She had taught him other things as well. Not weaving a hammock: that he had learned from Brashen. He did not think she knew such sailorly skills. However, she had given him softwood and an oversize blade that he might try his hand at her trade. Sometimes she played another game with him, one that was somewhat unsettling. With a long light pole, she would reach up to tap him gently. The game was that he must bat the pole aside. She praised him most when he could deflect the tip before it actually touched him. He was getting good at the game. If he concentrated, he could almost feel the pole by the slight movement of air that it caused. Another fiction between them was that this was just a game. He recognized it for what it was: a drill in skills that might help him protect himself, if it came to a direct attack. How long could he protect himself? He smiled grimly into the darkness. Long enough for Amber to be able to kindle fires inside him.

He wondered if that was what brought her bad dreams. Perhaps she dreamed that she had set fire to him and had not had time to escape. Perhaps she dreamed that she was burning inside his hull, the flesh crisping away from her bones as she screamed. No. This was more of a whimpering and pleading she made in her sleep, not the scream that could wake her. Sometimes, when the nightmares were upon her, it took her a long time to struggle back to wakefulness. Then, smelling of fear sweat, she would come out onto the deck to take in great gasps of cool night air. Sometimes when she sat down on his sloping deck with her back to the cabin, he could feel the trembling of her slender body.

That thought made him lift his voice. "Amber? Amber, wake up! It's only a dream."

He felt her shift restlessly and heard her incoherent reply. It sounded as if she called to him from a vast distance.

"Amber!" he called back.

She thrashed violently, more like a fish caught in a net than a woman sleeping in a hammock, then she was suddenly still. Three breaths later, he felt her bare feet hit the floor. She padded toward the hooks where she kept her garments. A moment later she was moving across his canted deck. Light as a bird, she dropped over his side to land on the sand. A moment later she leaned against his planking. Her voice was hoarse. "Thank you for waking me. I think."

"You wished to remain in your nightmare?" He was puzzled. "I understood such experiences were unpleasant, almost as unpleasant as living through the reality."

"They are. Extremely unpleasant. But sometimes, when such a dream comes repeatedly, it is because I am meant to experience it and heed it. After a time, such dreams can come to make sense. Sometimes."

"What did you dream?" Paragon asked unwillingly.

She laughed unevenly. "The same one. Serpents and dragons. The nine-fingered slave boy. Moreover, I hear your voice, calling warnings and threats. But you are not you. You are . . . someone else. And there is something . . . I don't know. It all tatters away like cobwebs in the wind. The more I grasp after it, the worse I rend it."

"Serpents and dragons." Paragon spoke the dread words unwillingly. He tried to laugh skeptically. "I've taken the measure of serpents in my day. I do not think much of them. However, there are no such things as dragons. I think your dream is only a nasty dream, Amber. Set it aside and tell me a story to clear our minds."

"I think not," Amber replied unsteadily. Her dream had shaken her more than Paragon had thought. "For if I tried to tell stories tonight, I would tell you of the dragons I have seen, flying overhead against the blue sky. It was not so many years ago, and not so far to the north of here. I will tell you this, Paragon. Were you to tie up in a Six Duchies harbor, and tell the folk there that there were no such things as dragons, they would scoff at you for foolish beliefs." She leaned her head back against him and added, "First, though, they would have to get used to the idea that there was truly such a thing as a liveship. Until I saw one and heard him speak, I had believed liveships were only a wild tale concocted to enhance the reputation of the Bingtown Traders."

"Did you truly find us that strange?" Paragon demanded.

He felt her turn her head to gaze up at him. "One of the strangest things about you, my dear, is that you have no idea how wondrous you are."

"Really?" He fished for another compliment.

"You are fully as marvelous as the dragons I saw."

She had expected the comparison to please him. He sensed that, but instead it made him uneasy. Was she fishing for secrets? She'd get none from him.

She seemed unaware of his displeasure as she mused, "I think there is in the heart of a man a place made for wonder. It sleeps inside, awaiting fulfillment. All one's life, one gathers treasures to fill it. Sometimes they are tiny glistening jewels: a flower blooming in the shelter of a fallen tree, the arch of a small child's brow combined with the curve of her cheek. Sometimes, however, a trove falls into your hands all at once, as if some greedy pirate's chest spilled before an unsuspecting beholder. Such were the dragons on the wing. They were every gem color I know, and every possible shape one could imagine. Some were dragons such as I knew from childhood tales, but others had shapes whimsical and still others were terrifying in their strangeness. There were proper dragons, some with long serpentine tails, some four-legged, some two, red and green and gold and sable. Flying amongst them were winged stags, a formidable boar who swept his tusks from side to side as he flew, and one like a great winged serpent and even a great striped cat, with striped wings. . . ." Her voice died away, subsiding in awe.

"They weren't real dragons, then," Paragon observed snidely.

"I tell you, I saw them," she insisted.

"You saw something. Or some things, some of which had stolen the shapes of dragons. Nevertheless, they were not real dragons. As well to say that you saw green, blue, and purple horses, some of which had six legs and some shaped like cats. Such things would not be horses at all. Whatever it was you saw, they were not dragons."

"Well . . . but . . ."

It pleased him to hear her flounder for words, she who was usually so glib. He didn't help her.

"Some were dragons," she finally defended herself. "Some were shaped and colored just as the dragons I have seen in ancient scrolls and tapestries."

"Some of your flying things were shaped like dragons and some like cats. As well to say that flying cats are real, and sometimes they are shaped like dragons."

She was silent for a long time. When she spoke, he knew she had been thinking and that her chain of thought had dragged her back to his personal history. "Why," she asked in a deceptively courteous tone, "is it so essential to your happiness that there be no such thing as dragons? Why are you so intent on crushing the wonder I felt at the sight of those creatures winging?"

"It isn't. I don't. I simply believe that one should say what one means. I don't care that you wondered at them. I just don't think you should call such things dragons."

"Why? If there are no such things as dragons, what does it matter what I call the creatures I saw? Why should not I name them dragons if that name pleases me?"

"Because," he declared, suddenly nettled beyond all reason. "Because if there were any such thing as dragons still, it would demean them to be grouped with such grotesques."

Suddenly, she sat up straight. He felt her shift away from him. He could almost feel her prying stare trying to pierce the darkness and see what little the hatchet had left of his face. "You know something," she accused him. "You know something about dragons, and you know something about my dream and what it means. Don't you?"

"I don't even know what you dreamed," he stated. He tried to make his voice reasonable, but it climbed up the scale and cracked. It always chose the worst times to do that. "And I've never seen any dragons."

"Not even in your dreams?" Her soft question was as insidious as drifting fog.

"Don't touch me," he warned her suddenly.

"I wasn't going to," she said, but he did not believe her. If she touched him, skin to wood, and reached hard enough, she would know if he were lying. That was not fair. He couldn't do that to her.

"Do you ever dream of dragons?" she asked him. It was a direct question, asked in a casual voice. He did not fall for it.

"No," he replied succinctly.

"Are you sure? I thought you had spoken to me about such dreams, once . . . ."

He shrugged, an elaborate charade. "Well, perhaps I did. I don't recall. Maybe I did dream such a dream, but it wasn't important to me. Not all dreams are important, you know. In fact, I wonder if any dreams are important or significant."

"Mine are," said Amber defeatedly. "I know they are. That is why it is so distressing when I cannot grasp what they mean. Oh, Paragon, I fear I've made an error. I pray it is not a grievous one."

He smiled in the darkness. "Well, how grievous an error can a bead maker commit? I am sure you are troubling yourself over nothing. Dragons and sea serpents indeed. What do such fantastic creatures have to do with you and me?"

"*Sea* serpents!" Amber suddenly exclaimed. "Ah!" For a long time, she was silent. Then he almost felt the warmth of her smile wash against him. "Sea serpents," she affirmed to herself softly. "Thank you, Paragon. Thank you for that much."

"IT'S NOT YOUR WATCH." OPHELIA SPOKE THE WORDS QUIETLY.

"I know that as well as you do. I couldn't sleep," Althea replied. She looked out past the figurehead. The waves were gentle swells. The soft spring wind pushed her light cloak against her body.

"I know that as well as you do," Ophelia countered. "You've been tossing in your bunk for two hours now. Why? Are you excited about docking in Bingtown tomorrow?"

"Yes. But not in a glad way. I fear all I must face tomorrow. My sister, my mother. Kyle, perhaps, if *Vivacia* is there. Oh, Ophelia, I even dread facing my ship when the time comes. How can I look at her and explain how and why I let her go?"

"You know you will not have to. Just put your hand to her planking and she will feel it all, as surely as I do."

Althea slid her hands lovingly along the polished railing. "It is such a wonder to me, the understanding that has developed between us. It is another reason I dread docking in Bingtown tomorrow. I have felt so safe aboard you. I hate to leave you."

A light footfall on the deck behind her turned her head. It was Grag. He moved across the moonlit deck, his bare feet falling softly. He wore only his trousers. His hair was tousled and boyish. Obviously, he was recently awakened, yet there was still a tigerish grace to his gait as he crossed the deck. A slow smile crept across Althea's face. Very softly, Ophelia answered her thought. "Men have no concept of their own beauty."

Grag grinned as he approached. "I tapped at your door. When I didn't find you there, I knew right away where to look."

"Oh?" Ophelia broke in archly. "Are you in the habit of tapping at Althea's door at this hour? With no shirt on?"

"Only when my father wakes me up and asks me to," Grag replied easily. "He said he wanted to have a quiet talk with both of us."

"I was not to be included in this 'quiet talk?' " Ophelia demanded, already offended.

"I assume you were, since he asked me to wake Althea and bid her to come here. I thought you might even have suggested it."

"No. It's my idea." Captain Tenira stepped quietly into their circle. A coal glowed in the bowl of his short-stemmed pipe and fragrant smoke drifted with him. "Call me a fearful old man if you will, but there are some precautions I'd like to take before we dock in Bingtown. And they involve Althea." His serious tone quenched their banter.

"What did you have in mind?" Althea asked.

"I've been thinking about our encounter with that Chalcedean galley. They were flying the Satrap's banner. Things have been changing in Bingtown for the last few years. I don't know how much favor and influence that captain may have there, or whether he would send a complaint there about our response." Captain Tenira gave a disgusted snort. "When he finally got under way again, he may even have fled there. So. Depending on how much influence he has there . . . and on how badly the Satrap currently grovels to Chalced . . . we may have an unpleasant welcome awaiting us."

A little silence fell over the group. It was obvious to Althea that Grag had given this no more thought than she had. It was not that she had dismissed the incident as trivial: never that! Ophelia's beautiful, slender-fingered hands were scorched. No matter how many times the figurehead assured her that she did not feel pain, at least not as humans did, Althea still winced at every glimpse of her blackened hands. Althea had looked forward to reaching Bingtown, and expected that the other Old Traders would share her deep anger and affront at the attack. Never had she paused to think that others there might think the Chalcedean galley and her crew had been wronged.

Captain Tenira gave them time to mull this before he spoke again. "As I said, I might simply be a fearful old man. What, I asked myself, is the worst they can do to me? Well, I answered, they could seize my ship when I tied up at the tax dock. Why, they might even take custody of my first mate and me. Then who would go to my family, to tell what had befallen us? Who would witness to the Bingtown Trader Council and demand their aid? I have many good hands, good sailors one and all, but," he shook his head, "good speakers they are not, nor are they Bingtown Traders."

Althea grasped it instantly. "You want me to go?"

"If you would."

"Of course. Without hesitation. I wonder that you think you need to ask this."

"Of that, I had no doubt. But there is more, I'm afraid," Captain Tenira said quietly. "The more I dwell on what may have changed in Bingtown, the less confidence I have of our welcome. To be safe, to be sure, I think it would be best if you resumed your boy's guise. That way, you could more easily slip away from the ship. If you had to."

"Do you really believe it is likely to come to that?" Grag asked incredulously.

Captain Tenira sighed. "Son, we carry a spare mast belowdecks. Why? Not because we are likely to need it but because someday we may. That is how I prefer to think of this as well."

"I would feel as if I were sending her to face danger alone," Grag objected suddenly.

His father eyed him levelly. "If it comes to this, we may actually be helping her to slip away from danger before the trap can close on her as well. It would be more advantageous to them to hold hostages from two Bingtown Trader families than one."

"Them? Who are 'them?'" Ophelia suddenly demanded. "And why should any Bingtown Trader have to fear anyone in Bingtown, save another Trader? Bingtown is our town. The Satrap Esclepius deeded it to us many years ago."

"And Satrap Cosgo has been whittling away at that deed ever since he inherited the Mantle of Righteousness." Captain Tenira closed his mouth suddenly, as if biting back bitter words. In a milder voice he went on, "Others have come to power in Bingtown. At first, we paid little heed to the tariff collectors. Even when they demanded a tax dock where each ship must first tie up, we conceded it as sensible. When they demanded the right to inspect cargoes for themselves rather than take the captain's word on what he carried, we laughed and agreed. It was our town. Their suspicions were offensive, but in much the same way that rude children are offensive. We did not count on this wave of so-called New Traders, who would ally with the Satrap's tax collectors to gain power. Nor did any of us ever believe that any Satrap would accept Chalced's grubby hand in friendship, let alone permit Chalcedean galleys in our waters under the guise of law and protection." He shook his head to himself. "These are the things I have been contemplating tonight, and that is why I have decided to err on the side of caution."

"It seems wise—" Althea began but Ophelia broke in, "You said they might seize me. I shall not allow it. I did not permit those Chalcedean swine to board me and I shall not permit—"

"Yes, you shall." Captain Tenira's grave voice stopped her defiance cold. "Just as Grag and I shall permit them to detain us, if they attempt it. I have thought this through, my dear, to the bitter dregs. It is time Bingtown awakened. We have been slumbering and letting others chip and nibble away at what is ours. A few days ago, Chalcedean pirates masquerading as the Satrap's patrol attacked us. A day or so from now, brigands and kidnappers masquerading as lawful tariff collectors may hold us. We shall let them seize us and detain us. Not because we recognize their right to do so, nor because we cannot defy them, but only to show the rest of Bingtown the powers these little upstarts have claimed. The danger must be recognized, while it is still easy to destroy. Therefore, I beg you, if they attempt to seize you, even to put armed guards aboard you, I think we should permit it. They cannot hold us long, once Bingtown is roused. Let Ophelia become a rallying point for Bingtown Trader pride."

Ophelia allowed the silence to hang for a moment. "I suppose I shall allow it," she finally conceded. "Only because you ask it of me."

"That's my good girl," Tenira praised her warmly. "Never fear. Grag and I will see that you take no harm."

Ophelia rolled her shoulders. "I shall see that you take no harm," she suggested.

Her captain smiled wanly. "Well. That is certainly a great relief to me." His glance went from Grag to Althea and then to the moonlit night above them. "I am suddenly weary," he announced. He looked only at Althea. "Will you take my watch for me? You seem wide awake."

"Pleased to do so, sir. You've given me a great deal to mull over."

"Thank you. Carry on, then, Althea. Good night, Grag."

"Good night, sir," his son replied.

Just before the captain was out of earshot, Ophelia observed, "How sweet! He found a way to leave you two alone in the moonlight."

"Pity you can't do the same," Grag replied without rancor.

"Leave you unchaperoned? Shame upon you, for even suggesting such a thing."

He made no reply to that, but only went to the port side to lean on the railing. With a wink and a toss of her great head, Ophelia urged Althea to join him there. Althea sighed ruefully, then followed the ship's suggestion.

"You haven't said much to me, these last few days," Grag remarked quietly to the night sea.

"My work has kept me busy. When your father gives me a ship's ticket, I want to have truly earned it."

"You already have. No one on board this vessel would ever dispute your ability. However, I do not think you have truly been that busy. I think our last conversation made you uncomfortable."

She did not deny it. Instead, she noted, "You speak very directly, don't you? I like that."

"Simple questions usually get simple answers. A man likes to know where he stands."

"That's reasonable. A woman needs some time to think." Althea tried to keep her tone light but not flippant.

He did not meet her eyes as he pressed her. "Most women don't need time to think about whether or not they could love someone." Was there a trace of hurt in his voice?

"I didn't think that was what you had asked me," Althea replied honestly. "I thought the topic under discussion was a possible marriage between us. If you are asking whether I could come to care for you, then I believe the answer is an easy 'yes.' You are thoughtful, courteous and kind." Althea glanced toward Ophelia. The figurehead was intently motionless, staring over the water. Althea pitched her voice just a trifle louder. "Not to mention that you are very handsome and likely to inherit a beautiful ship."

As she had hoped, they both laughed, and suddenly the atmosphere eased. Grag reached casually to cover her hand with his. She did not move away but added in a lower voice, "Marriage is not about love alone. Especially not a marriage between two Bingtown Trader families. For that is what it would be, not a simple joining of you and me, but an alliance of our families. I have to think of many things. If I married you, and went to sea with you, what would become of my own ship? All I have done in the last year, Grag, I have done with an eye to recovering her. Would marrying you mean giving up *Vivacia?*" She faced him and he looked down on her with shadowed eyes. "Would you give up the *Ophelia* to marry me and live with me aboard the *Vivacia* while I captained her?"

The shock on his face made it evident he had never considered such a question.

"And that is but the first of my considerations. I must ask myself, what would I bring to our partnership, other than my family's debts? I inherited nothing from my father, Grag. Nothing except the sailing skills he taught me. I am sure my family would give me some sort of a dowry for the sake of respectability. But it would not be what you could usually expect to accompany a Trader's daughter." Althea shook her head. "You could get more marrying a Three Ship's girl. They'd pay richly for the family connection."

He lifted his hand from hers. There was almost a chill in his voice as he asked, "Did you think that was why I made my proposal? To see how good an offer your family would make?"

"No. Nevertheless, it is something I must consider, if only for the sake of my pride. You were the one who suggested that perhaps planning should come ahead of passion. So I consider the situation from every angle. Look at it coldly, Grag. To marry you, I must not only give up my ship, but also see her in the hands of a man I despise. To marry me, you must give up other partners who might create lucrative alliances for your family. If you consider these aspects, it does not look promising for us."

Grag took in a slow breath. "I suppose you are right and—"

"Just kiss her, you great booby!" Ophelia hissed loudly.

Althea burst into a laugh that was cut off by Grag's mouth on hers. The kiss was startling, but her body's response to it was shocking. Heat washed through her and she turned toward him, lifting one hand to his shoulder. She expected him to embrace her and continue the kiss. Before she could wonder how far she would allow him to continue, he lifted his mouth from hers and drew back a little. He would not. This was Grag, not Brashen, she reminded herself. He was ruled by his head, not his passions. She denied the disappointment in the comparison. In the moment that he lifted his mouth from hers, she convinced herself that if he had not broken the kiss, she would have. Grag Tenira was to be taken seriously. He was not an anonymous fling in a distant seaport. How she conducted herself with him would affect the rest of her life in Bingtown. Caution was the better path.

She took a breath. "Well!" she said, in a tone intended to convey surprise without affront.

"Sorry," he muttered and looked aside with a half-grin that did not look repentant at all. "Ophelia's been bossing me around since I was eight years old."

"That did sound like a direct order," Althea agreed affably. She turned back to look out over the water. After a moment, his hand covered hers on the railing.

"There would be difficulties to surmount," he said judiciously. "That is true of any undertaking. Althea, I ask only that you consider my offer. I could scarcely ask you for an answer now. You have not discussed it with your family; I have not broached the subject with my parents. We do not even know what sort of a storm we shall encounter when we tie up in Bingtown. I'd just like you to consider my offer. That's all."

"That I will," she replied. The night was easy around them, and the clasp of his callused hand was warm.

SHE DID NOT KNOW WHAT CAPTAIN TENIRA OR GRAG SAID TO THE CREW, but no one evinced any surprise when she appeared on deck in her boy's togs. *Ophelia* entered Bingtown Harbor on a crisp breeze that made the hands work lively. If any of the crew recognized Althea as Athel from Candletown, no one was foolish enough to admit it. Instead, they accepted her toiling beside them with only a bit of good-natured teasing. *Ophelia* sailed with a will. The seasoned ship knew her business and cooperated with her crew, calling out suggestions to the man on the wheel. This was not operating a contraption of planks and canvas and lines to a place beside a dock, but the guiding of a cognizant creature into her home.

The *Ophelia*'s boats were put out to assist her to her berth at the tax dock. Althea took a spot on a bench and an oar; Captain Tenira had decided it was the best way to distance her from the ship and give her a chance to slip away if she needed it. After all their preparations, it was almost a disappointment to see the harbor traffic so ordinary. No one seemed to take any unusual notice of the *Ophelia*. As Althea's eyes roved over the busy trading port, she felt a sudden rush of emotion far stronger than any homesickness. She had been on longer voyages with her father, and traveled farther than on this last trip. Nevertheless, she felt as if she saw Bingtown for the first time in years.

Bingtown was cupped in a sparkling blue bay. Rolling hills in the bright greens of spring backed the lively merchant town. Even before they docked, she could smell the smoke and cooking and cattle. The shrill cries of the hawkers in the market floated out over the water. The streets bustled with traffic, and the waters of the harbor were no less busy. Small craft plied back and forth between the shore and anchored ships. Little fishing vessels threaded their way through the tall-masted merchant ships to bring their catch to market. It was a symphony of sight and sound and smell, and its theme was Bingtown.

A discordant note jarred the harmony as the departure of a ship slowly disclosed a Chalcedean galley tied up at the tax dock. The Satrap's banner hung flaccid from the single mast. Althea knew at a glance it was not the same galley that had accosted them; this one sported a fanged cat's face upon the figurehead, and showed no signs of fire damage. Her frown only deepened. How many of the galleys were in Bingtown waters? Why had it been allowed into the harbor at all?

She kept her thoughts to herself and performed her share of the docking tasks as if she were no more than a ship's boy. When Captain Tenira barked at her to bring his sea bag and follow snappy, she did not flinch at the unusual order. She sensed he wanted her to witness his meeting with the Satrap's tax minister. She shouldered the small canvas bag and followed meekly at his heels. Grag, as first mate, stayed aboard to supervise the ship.

Tenira strode into the tax minister's office. A clerk greeted them and brusquely demanded the manifest of the ship's cargo. Althea kept her eyes averted, even when Tenira slammed his fist on the counter and demanded to speak with the tariff minister.

The clerk gave a startled squeak, then got his face and voice under control. "I am in charge here today, sir. Your manifest, please."

Tenira tossed the bundled documents to the counter with a fine disdain. "There's my ship's manifest. Stick your nose in it, boy, and figure out what I owe. But get me someone down here who can talk of more than coppers and cargo. I've a complaint."

The door to an inner room opened and a robed man emerged. His shaven pate and topknot proclaimed his status as the Satrap's minister. He was a well-fleshed man. His robe was embroidered on sleeves, breast and hems. His pale hands nestled together before him. "Why are you abusing my assistant?" he demanded.

"Why is a Chalcedean war galley tied up to a Bingtown dock? Why did a similar galley accost my ship, supposedly in the Satrap's name? Since when have the enemies of Jamaillia been allowed safe harbor in Bingtown?" Tenira punctuated each query with a thud of his fist on the counter.

The minister was unruffled. "The Chalcedean privateers are agents of the Satrap. They have been allowed to dock here since the Satrap appointed them guardians of the Inside Passage. The galleys both reported here formally, presenting their letters of merit. Their sole purpose is to control piracy. They will attack pirates, on their ships and in their outlaw settlements. They will also combat the smuggling that supports the pirates; if those miscreants had no markets for their stolen goods, their trade would soon cease." The tariff minister paused to straighten a fold of his sleeve. In a bored tone, he resumed, "It is true there were some complaints from a few Bingtown residents about the Chalcedean presence, but the tariff dock is the property of the Satrap. No one save he can forbid the Chalcedeans to tie up here. And he has given his express permission that they may." The minister gave a small snort of contempt. "I do not think the captain of a trading ship can over-ride the Satrap's word."

"This dock may belong to the Satrap, but the waters that surround it are Bingtown Harbor, given by charter to the Bingtown Traders. By tradition and by law, we allow no Chalcedean galleys in our waters."

The minister looked past Tenira. In a bored voice he replied, "Traditions change, and laws do also. Bingtown is no longer a provincial back-water, Captain Tenira. It is a rapidly growing trade center. It is to Bingtown's benefit that the Satrap combats the pirates that infest the waterways. Bingtown should normalize trade with Chalced. Jamaillia sees no reason to consider Chalced an enemy. Why should Bingtown?"

"Jamaillia does not share a disputed boundary with Chalced. Jamaillian farms and settlements have not been raided and burned. Bingtown's hostility toward Chalced is well-founded on history, not suspicion. Those ships have no right to be in our harbor. I wonder that the Bingtown Traders Council has not challenged this."

"This is neither the place nor the time to discuss Bingtown's internal politics," the minister suddenly declared. "My function here is to serve the Satrap by collecting his rightful tariffs. Corum. Are not you finished with those figures yet? When I accepted you for employment here, I understood from your uncle that you were swift with numbers. What is the delay?"

Althea almost felt sorry for the clerk. He was obviously accustomed to being the subject of the minister's displeasure, however, for he only smiled obsequiously and clattered his tally sticks a bit faster. "Seven and two," he muttered, apparently for the benefit of those watching him. "Docking fee and security fee . . . and patrol fee brings it to . . . And the surcharge on non-Jamaillian woven goods." He jotted a number onto the tablet, but before Althea could decipher it, the minister snatched it away. He ran a long-fingered nail down it with a disapproving glare. "This is not right!" he hissed.

"I certainly hope not!" Captain Tenira agreed vehemently. He was taller than the minister and looked over his shoulder easily. "That is twice what I paid for 'fees' last time, and the percentage on non-Jamaillian woven goods is . . ."

"Tariffs have gone up," the minister interrupted him. "There is also a new surcharge on non-Jamaillian worked-metal goods. I believe your tin-ware falls into that category. Refigure this immediately, accurately!" He slapped the tablet back down before the clerk, who only bowed his head and nodded repeatedly to the criticism.

"Rinstin is a Jamaillian town!" Tomie Tenira declared indignantly.

"Rinstin, like Bingtown, acknowledges Jamaillia's rule, but it is not in Jamaillia and is therefore not a Jamaillian town. You will pay the surcharge."

"That I shall not!" Tenira exclaimed.

Althea suppressed a small gasp. She had expected Tenira to bargain over the tariffs that were due. Bargaining was the fabric of Bingtown society. No one ever paid what was first asked. He should have offered a generous bribe to the minister in the form of a lavish meal in a nearby establishment, or a selection from the more choice goods on board the *Ophelia*. Althea had never heard a Bingtown Trader simply refuse to pay.

The minister narrowed his eyes at Tenira. Then he gave a disdainful shrug. "As you will, sir. It is all one to me. Your ship will remain at this dock, her cargo on board until the proper fees are paid." He raised his voice suddenly. "Guards! Enter, please! I may require your assistance here!"

Tenira did not even look toward the two burly men who stepped inside the door. His whole attention was riveted on the minister. "There is nothing proper about these fees." He poked at the tablet the scribe was still trying to complete. "What is this for 'patrol' and this for 'security?' "

The minister gave a long-suffering sigh. "How do you expect the Satrap to reimburse those he has hired to protect you?"

Althea had suspected that Tenira's outrage might be some sort of a bargaining ploy. Color rose so high in his face that she no longer doubted the sincerity of his anger as he asked, "You mean those Chalcedean scum, don't you? May Sa close my ears before I hear such idiocy! I won't pay for those pirates to anchor in Bingtown harbor."

The guards were suddenly standing very close, right at Tomie Tenira's elbows. Althea in her role of ship's boy strove to look tough and follow her captain's lead. If Tenira threw a punch, she would be expected to jump in. Any ship's boy worth his scrap would do so, but it was a daunting prospect. She had never been in a real brawl before, other than that one brief dust-up with Brashen. She set her jaw and chose the younger of the two men as her mark.

It didn't come to that. Tenira suddenly dropped his voice and growled, "I'll be presenting this to the Traders Council."

"As you see fit, sir, I'm sure," the minister purred. Althea thought him a fool. A wiser man would have known better than to bait Tomie Tenira. She half expected the captain to strike him. Instead, he smiled a very narrow smile.

"As I see fit," he rejoined smoothly. With a curt gesture to Althea to follow him, they left the tariff office. He spoke not a word to her until they were back aboard the ship. Then he sent her to "Fetch the mate, and smartly now. Have him come to my cabin." Althea obeyed him promptly.

When they were sequestered in the captain's cabin, Tenira himself poured three jots of rum for them. He didn't pause to consider propriety, nor did Althea as she drank it off. The scene in the tariff office had chilled her worse than a cold night on deck. "It's bad," was Tenira's first greeting to his son. "Worse than I'd feared. Not only are the Chalcedeans tied up here, but the Traders Council hasn't even challenged it. Worse, the damn Satrap has tacked more duties and taxes on to our trade to pay them to be here!"

"You didn't pay them?" Grag asked incredulously.

"Of course not!" Tenira snorted. "Someone around here has to start standing up to this nonsense. It may be a bit rocky to be the first one, but

I'll wager once we've set the example, others will follow. The minister says he's going to detain us here. Fine. While we're tied up here, we take up this much dock space. A few more like us, and he won't be able to process ships or tariffs. Grag, you'll have a quiet word with Ophelia. Sa help us all, but I plan to give her free rein and let her be as unpleasant and bitchy as only she knows how. Let the dock workers and passers-by deal with that."

Althea found herself grinning. The small room was as charged as if a storm were brewing. It was a storm, she told herself, and one her father had seen gathering for years. Still, it humbled her to watch an old captain like Tenira announce that he would call the first bolt down on himself. "What do you want me to do?" she asked.

"Go home. Take word to your mother of all you saw and heard. I didn't see the *Vivacia* in the harbor, but if she is in, I ask you to set aside your differences with your brother-in-law and try to make him see why we must all be together in our defiance. I'll be heading home myself in a bit. Grag, I'll be trusting the ship to you. At the first whiff of any sign of trouble, send Calco to me with a message. Althea?"

Althea weighed his words, then nodded slowly. As much as she hated the idea of a truce with Kyle, Captain Tenira was right. It was no time for the Bingtown Traders to be divided on anything.

The smile the Teniras gave her was worth it. "I suspected I could count on you, lass," Captain Tenira said fondly.

Grag grinned at her. "And I knew I could."

CHAPTER TEN

Homecoming

THE VESTRIT MANSION, LIKE THE HOMES OF THE OTHER BINGTOWN TRAD-ers, was set in the cool and forested foothills that surrounded Bingtown itself. It was a brief carriage ride from the docks, or a comfortable walk on a pleasant day. Along the way, one could glimpse other elegant Trader homes set well back from the main road. She passed flowering hedges and drives lined with trees extravagantly green with spring growth. Ivy sprawled in a mantle over the Oswells' stone wall. Crisp yellow daffodils were showing their first blooms in clumps by their gate. The spring day was rich with birdcalls and the dappling shade of newly leafed trees and the scents of early flowers.

Never before had it seemed to be such a long walk.

Althea marched on as if going to her death.

She still wore her ship's-boy garb; it had seemed wisest to them all that she retain her disguise as she left the docks. She wondered how her mother and sister would react to it. Kyle was not home. Relief at that almost balanced her disappointment that *Vivacia* was not in the harbor. At least she did not have to worry about his extreme distaste. It was not quite a year since she had quarreled with her brother-in-law and then stormed out of their family home. She had learned so much since then that it seemed like a decade. She wanted to have her family recognize how she had grown. Instead, she feared they would see only her clothes and her oiled plait of hair and judge it all a childish masquerade of defiance. Her mother had always said she was headstrong; for years, her sister Keffria had believed her capable of disgracing the family name simply for her own pleasure. How could she go back to them now, dressed this way, and make them believe she had matured and was worthy to claim the captaincy of the family liveship? How would they greet her return? With anger or cold disdain?

She shook her head furiously to clear it of such thoughts and turned up the long driveway to her home. She noted with annoyance that the rhododendrons by the gate had not been pinched back. Last spring's leggy growth now sported this spring's swelling buds. When they were properly cut back, they would lose a whole year of flowers. She felt a tinge of worry. Col, the groundskeeper, had always been most particular about those bushes. Had something happened to him?

Her whole journey up the drive spoke to her of the garden's neglect. The herbaceous borders swelled and straggled out of their beds. Bright green leaf buds were unfurling on rose bushes that still bore the winter-blackened stalks of last year's growth. A wisteria had fallen off its trellis and now valiantly opened its leaves where it sprawled. Winter winds had banked last autumn's fallen leaves wherever they wished; branches broken by storms still littered the grounds.

She almost expected to find the house abandoned to match the neglected grounds. Instead, the windows were flung open to the spring day and sprightly music of harp and flute cascaded out to greet her. A few gigs drawn up before the front door told her that a gathering was in progress. It was a merry one, judging by the sudden trill of laughter that mingled for a moment with the music. Althea diverted her steps to the back entrance, wondering more with every step she took. Her family had hosted no gatherings since her father fell ill. Did this party mean that her mother had ended her mourning period already? That did not seem like her. Nor could Althea imagine her mother allowing the grounds to be neglected while spending coin on parties. None of this made sense. Foreboding nibbled at her.

The kitchen door stood open and the tantalizing smell of freshly baked bread and savory meat wafted out to mingle in the spring sunshine. Althea's stomach grumbled appreciatively at the thought of shore-side food: risen bread and fresh meat and vegetables. She abruptly decided that she was glad to be home, no matter what reception she might get. She stepped into the kitchen and looked around.

She did not recognize the woman rolling out dough on the tabletop, nor the boy turning the spit at the cook-fire. That was not unusual. Servants came and went in the Vestrit household. Trader families regularly "stole" the best cooks, nannies and stewards from one another, coaxing them to change households with offers of better pay and larger quarters.

A serving girl came into the kitchen with an empty tray. She clattered it down and rounded on Althea. "What do you want here?" Her voice was both chill and bored.

For once, Althea's mind was faster than her mouth. She made a sketchy bow. "I've a message from Captain Tenira of the liveship *Ophelia* for Trader Ronica Vestrit. It's important. He asked me to deliver it to her in private." There. That would get her some time alone with her mother. If there were guests in the house, she didn't want to be seen by them while she was still dressed as a boy.

The serving girl looked troubled. "She is with guests just now, very important ones. It is a farewell gathering. It would be awkward to call her away." She bit her lower lip. "Can the message wait a bit longer? Perhaps while you ate something?" The maid smiled as she offered this little bribe.

Althea found herself nodding. The smell of the newly cooked food was making her mouth water. Why not eat here in the kitchen, and face her mother and sister with a full stomach? "The message can wait a bit, I suppose. Mind if I wash my hands first?" Althea nodded toward the kitchen pump.

"There's a pump and trough in the yard," the cook pointed out, a sharp reminder of Althea's supposed status. Althea grinned to herself, then went outside to wash. By the time she returned, a plate was ready for her. They had not given her choice cuts; rather it was the crispy outside end of the pork roast, and the heels of the fresh cooked bread. There was a slab of yellow cheese with it and a dollop of fresh churned butter for the bread and a spoonful of cherry preserves. It was served to her on a chipped plate with a stained napkin. The niceties of cutlery were supposed unknown to a ship's boy, so she made do with her fingers as she perched on a tall stool in the corner of the kitchen.

At first, she ate ravenously, with little thought for anything other than the food before her. The crust of the roast seemed far richer in flavor than the best cut she had ever enjoyed. That crispy fat crunched between her teeth. The new butter melted on the still warm bread. She scooped up the tart cherry preserves with folded bits of it.

As her hunger was sated, she became more aware of the kitchen bustle around her. She looked around the once-familiar room with new eyes. As a child, this room had seemed immense and fascinating, a place she had never been allowed to explore freely. Because she had gone to sea with her father before she had outgrown that curiosity, the kitchen had always retained an aura of the forbidden for her. Now she saw it for what it was, a large, busy work area where servants came and went in haste while a cook reigned supreme. As every servant came in, he or she inevitably gave a brief report on the gathering. They spoke familiarly and sometimes with contempt of the folk they served.

"I'll need another platter of the sausage rolls. Trader Loud-Shirt seems to think we baked them for him alone."

"That's better than doing what that Orpel girl is doing. Look at this plate. Heaped with food we worked all morning to prepare, she's scarcely nibbled it and then pushed it aside. I suppose she hopes a man will notice her dainty appetite and think she's an easy keeper."

"How's the empress's second choice faring?" the cook asked curiously.

A serving man mimed the tipping of a wineglass. "Oh, he drowns his troubles and scowls at his rival and moons at the little empress. Then he does it all over again. All very genteelly, of course. The man should be on a stage."

"No, no, she's the one who should be on a stage. One moment she's simpering at Reyn's veil, but when she dances with him, she looks past his shoulder and flutters her lashes at young Trell." The serving maid who observed this added with a snort of disgust, "She has them both stepping to her tune, but I'll wager she cares not a whit for either of them, but only for what measures she can make them tread."

For a brief time, Althea listened with amusement. Then her ears and cheeks began to burn as she realized that this was how the servants had always spoken of her family. She ducked her head, kept her eyes on her plate, and slowly began to piece the gossip into a bizarre image of the current state of the Vestrit family fortunes.

Her mother was entertaining Rain Wild guests. That was unusual enough, given that her father had severed their trading connections there years ago. A Rain Wild suitor was courting a Trader woman. The servants did not think much of her. "She'd smile at him more if he replaced his veil with a mirror," one servant sniggeringly observed. Another added, "I don't know who's going to be more surprised on their wedding night: her when he takes off his veil and shows his warts, or him when she shows her snake's nature behind that pretty face." Althea knit her brow trying to think what woman was a close enough friend to the Vestrit family that her mother would host a gathering in her honor. Perhaps one of Keffria's friends had a daughter of marriageable age.

A kitchen maid tugged her empty plate from her lax hands and offered her a bowl with two sugar dumplings in it. "Here. You may as well have these; we made far too many. There are three platters left and the guests are already starting to leave. No sense a young man like you going hungry here." She smiled warmly and Althea turned her eyes aside in what she hoped was a convincing display of boyish shyness.

"Can I take my message to Ronica Vestrit soon?" she asked.

"Oh, soon enough, I imagine. Soon enough."

The sweet gooey pastries were messy to eat but delicious. Althea finished them, returned her bowl and used her sticky hands as an excuse to go back to the yard pump. A grape arbor screened the kitchen yard from the main entrance, but the new leaves were still tiny. Althea could watch the departing carriages through the twining branches. She recognized Cerwin Trell and his little sister as they left. The Shuyev family had also come. There were several other Trader families that Althea recognized more by crest than by face. It made her realize how long it had been since she had truly belonged to their social circle. Gradually the number of carriages dwindled. Davad Restart was one of the last to depart. Shortly after that, a team of white horses arrived drawing a Rain Wild coach. The windows were heavily curtained and the crest on the door was an unfamiliar one. It looked something like a chicken with a hat. An open wagon was drawn up behind it and a train of servants began carrying luggage and trunks from the house to that conveyance. So. The Rain Wild Traders had been houseguests at the Vestrit home. Increasingly mysterious, Althea thought to herself. Crane her neck as she might, she got no more than a glimpse of the departing family. Rain Wilders were always veiled by day and this group was no exception. Althea had no idea who they were or why they were staying at the Vestrit home. It made her uneasy. Had Kyle chosen to renew their trading connections there? Had her mother and sister supported such an idea?

Had Kyle taken *Vivacia* up the Rain River?

She clenched her fists at the idea. When the kitchen maid tugged at her sleeve, she spun on her, startling the poor girl. "Beg pardon," Althea apologized immediately.

The maid looked at her strangely. "Mistress Vestrit will see you now."

Althea suffered herself to be led back into her own home and down the familiar hallway to the morning room. Everywhere were the festive signs of guests and lively company. Vases of flowers filled every alcove and perfume lingered in the air. When she had left, this had been a house of mourning and family contention. Now the household seemed to have forgotten those difficult days and her with them. It did not seem fair that while she had toiled through hardship, her sister and mother had indulged in social celebration. By the time they reached the morning room, the simmering confusion inside her was so great she guarded against it breaking forth as anger.

The maid tapped at the door of the chamber. When she heard Ronica's murmured assent, she stepped aside, whispering to Althea, "Go in."

Althea bobbed a bow, then entered the room. She shut the door quietly behind herself. Her mother was sitting on a cushioned divan. A low table with a glass of wine upon it was close to hand. She wore a simple day-gown of creamy linen. Her hair was coiled and perfumed, and a silver chain graced her throat, but the face she lifted to meet Althea's gaze was taut with weariness. Althea forced herself to meet her mother's widening eyes with a direct look. "I've come home," she said quietly.

"Althea," her mother gasped. She lifted a hand to her heart, and then put both hands over her mouth and breathed in through them. She had gone so pale that the lines in her face stood out as if etched. She dragged in a shuddering breath. "Do you know how many nights I have wondered how you died? Wondered where your body lay, if it was covered in a decent grave or if carrion birds picked at your flesh?"

The flood of angry words caught Althea off-guard. "I tried to send you word." She heard herself lying like a child caught in a misdeed.

Her mother had found the strength to rise and now she advanced on Althea, her index finger leveled like a pike. "No, you did not!" she contradicted her bitterly. "You never even thought of it until just now." She halted suddenly in her tracks. She shook her head. "You are so like your father, I can even hear him lying with your tongue. Oh, Althea. Oh, my little girl." Then her mother suddenly embraced her, as she had not in years. Althea stood still in the circle of her pinning arms, completely bewildered. A moment later she was horrified when a sob wracked her mother's body. Her mother clung to her and wept hopelessly against her shoulder.

"I'm sorry," Althea said uncomfortably. Then she added, "It's going to be all right now." A few moments later she tried, "What's wrong?"

For a time, her mother did not reply. Then she drew a deep, rattling breath. Ronica stepped back from her daughter and rubbed her sleeve across her eyes like a child. It smeared the careful paint on her lashes and eyelids, marking the fabric of her sleeve. Her mother took no notice of that. She walked unsteadily back to her divan and sat down. She took a long drink of her wine, then set it down and tried to smile. The smeared paint on her face made it ghastly. "Everything," she said quietly. "Everything that could be wrong, is. Save for one thing. You are home and alive." The honest relief on her mother's face was more searing than her anger had been.

It was hard to cross the room and seat herself on the end of the divan. Harder still to say calmly and rationally, "Tell me about it." For so many months, Althea had looked forward to coming home, to telling her story, to forcing her family to finally, finally listen to her view. Now she was here, and she knew with the unerring truth of Sa's own revelation that duty demanded she listen first to all her mother would say.

For a moment, Ronica just looked at her. Then the words began to spill out. It was a disordered tale of one disaster after another. The *Vivacia* was late coming home. She should have been back by now. Kyle might have taken her straight on to Chalced to sell the slaves, but surely he would have sent word by another ship if he intended to do so. Wouldn't he? He knew how poor the family finances were; surely, he would have sent word so that Keffria would have *something* to tell their creditors. Malta had been into one kind of mischief after another. She didn't even know where to begin that tale, but the end of it was that a Rain Wild Trader was now courting Malta. As his family held the paper on the *Vivacia*, courtesy and politics dictated that the Vestrits at least entertain his suit, although Sa knew Malta was not truly a woman and old enough to be courted.

Moreover, Davad Restart had leapt into the midst of that tangle, and had made one gaffe after another all week in his determination to wring a profit from the courtship. Just because the man was totally tactless did not mean he was without tactics. It had taken all her ingenuity to keep him diverted and to keep Reyn's family from taking offense. Keffria was insisting on trying to manage the family businesses. That was her right, true, but she wasn't giving them the attention they needed. Instead she was all caught up in the flowers and the frills of this courtship, and never mind that the grain fields were only half-plowed and the planting moon was only a week away. A late frost had taken at least half the blooms from the apple orchards. The roof in the second bedroom in the east wing had begun to leak, and there was no money to have it seen to right now, but if it were not repaired soon, that entire ceiling would give way and . . .

"Mother," Althea said gently, and then, "Mother! A moment! My head is reeling with all this!"

"Mine, also, and for far longer than yours," her mother pointed out wearily.

"I don't understand this." Althea tried to speak calmly although she wanted to shout. "Kyle is using *Vivacia* as a slave ship? And Malta is being practically sold off to the Rain Wild Traders to pay our family debts? How can Keffria allow that, let alone you? Even if the *Vivacia* has not yet returned, how can our finances be so bad? Didn't the shore-side properties used to pay their own way?"

Her mother made small patting motions at her with her hands. "Calm down. I suppose this is a shock to you. I have seen the gradual slide, but you return to see us at the bottom of our fortunes." Her mother pressed her hands to her temples for a moment. She looked at Althea absently. "How are we to get you out of those clothes and properly attired without the servants asking questions?" she mused in an aside to herself. Then she drew a breath. "Just to explain all this to you wearies me so. It is like detailing the slow death of something you loved. Allow me to skip details and say just this instead: the use of slaves for field and orchard crops in Chalced and even in Bingtown lands has driven prices down. We have always hired workers for our fields; for years, the same men and women have plowed, planted and harvested for us. Now what are we to tell them? It would be more profitable to let the fields lie fallow or graze goats on them, but how can we do that to our farmers? So, we struggle on. Or rather, at my behest, Keffria does. She gives some heed to my counsel. Kyle, as you know, controls the ship. That was my error; I can not bear to look you in the face over it. But Sa help me, Althea! I fear he is right. If the *Vivacia* succeeds as a slaver, she may yet save us all. Slaves, it seems, are the only way to prosper. Slaves as cargo, slaves in the grain fields . . ."

Althea looked at her mother incredulously. "I cannot believe I am hearing those words from you."

"I know it is wrong, Althea. I know. But what are our alternatives? Let little Malta unknowingly flirt herself into a marriage she isn't ready for, simply for the sake of the family fortune? Surrender *Vivacia* back to the Rain Wilds in forfeiture of the debt, and live in poverty? Or perhaps we could just flee our creditors, leave Bingtown, and go Sa knows where . . ."

"Have you truly considered such things?" Althea asked in a low voice.

"I have," her mother replied wearily. "Althea, if we do not take action on our own, then others will decide our fate. Our creditors will strip us of all we own, and then we might look back and say, well, if we had allowed Malta to wed Reyn, at least she would have been spared living in poverty. At least the ship would have been ours."

" 'The ship would have been ours'? How?"

"I told you. The Khuprus family has bought the note on *Vivacia*. They have as much as said that forgiving the debt would be Reyn's wedding gift to the family."

"That's crazy." Althea uttered the words flatly. "No one gives wedding gifts like that. Not even Rain Wild Traders."

Ronica Vestrit took a deep breath. Changing the subject, she announced, "We have to sneak you up to your room and get you into some proper clothes. Though you look skinny as a rail. I wonder if anything you left here would still fit you."

"I can't resume being Althea Vestrit just yet. I bring a message for you from Captain Tenira of the liveship *Ophelia*."

"That is true? I thought it was only a ruse to get in to see me."

"It's true. I've been serving aboard the *Ophelia*. When we have more time, I'll tell you all about that. But for now, I want to give you his message, and then take your reply back to him. Mother, the *Ophelia* has been seized at the tariff docks. Captain Tenira has refused to pay the outrageous fees they have demanded, especially all the ones they have tacked on to support those Chalcedean pigs tied up in the harbor."

"Tied-up Chalcedean pigs?" Her mother looked confused.

"Surely you know what I mean. The Satrap has authorized Chalcedean galleys to act as patrol vessels throughout the Inside Passage. One of them actually attempted to halt us and board us on our way here. They are no more than pirates, and worse than the ones they are supposed to control. I cannot understand why they are tolerated in Bingtown harbor, let alone that anyone would stomach the extra fees demanded of us!"

"Oh. The galleys. There has been quite a stir about them lately, but I think Tenira is the first to refuse the fees. Fair or not, the Traders pay them. The alternative is no trade at all, as Tenira is finding out."

"Mother, that is ridiculous! This is our town. Why aren't we standing up to the Satrap and his lackeys? The Satrap no longer abides by his word to us; why should we continue to let him leech away our honest profits?"

"Althea . . . I have no energy left to consider such things. I don't doubt you are right, but what can I do about it? I have my family to preserve. Bingtown will have to look after itself."

"Mother, we cannot think that way! Grag and I have discussed this a great deal. Bingtown has to stand united before the New Traders and the Satrap and all of Jamaillia if need be. The more we concede to them, the more they take. The slaves that the New Traders have brought in are at the bottom of our family problems right now. We need to force them to observe our old law forbidding slavery. We need to tell the New Traders that we will not recognize their new charters. We need to tell the Satrap that we will pay no more taxes until he lives up to the letter of our original charter. No. We need to go further than that. We need to tell him that a fifty percent tax on our goods and his limits on where we may sell our goods are things of the past. We have already let it go on too long. Now we need to stand united and make it stop."

"There are some Traders who speak as you do," her mother said slowly. "And I reply to them as I do to you: my family first. Besides. What can I do?"

"Just say you will stand united with those Traders who refuse the tariffs. That is all I am asking."

"Then you must ask your sister. She has the vote now, not I. On your father's death, she inherited. She is the Bingtown Trader now, and the council vote is hers to wield."

"What do you think she will say?" Althea asked after a long silence. It had taken her a time to grasp the full significance of what her mother had said.

"I don't know. She does not go to many of the Trader meetings. She is, she says, too busy and she also says she does not want to vote on things that she has not had time to study."

"Have you spoken to her? Told her how crucial those votes can be?"

"It is only one vote," Ronica said almost stubbornly.

Althea thought she heard a trace of guilt in her mother's voice. She pressed her. "Let me go back to Trader Tenira and say this at least. That you will speak to Keffria, and counsel her both to attend the next Trader meeting, and to vote in Tenira's support. He intends to be there and to demand that the Council officially side with him."

"I suppose I can do that much. Althea, you need not carry this message back yourself. If he is openly defiant of the tariff minister, then he could precipitate some sort of . . . of action down there. Let me have Rache fetch a runner to carry your word. There is no need for you to be in the middle of this."

"Mother. I wish to be in the middle of this. Also, I want them to know I stand firmly with them. I feel I must go."

"But not right now! Althea, you have only just come home. Surely you can stop to eat and bathe and change into proper clothes." Her mother looked aghast.

"That I cannot. I am safer on the docks in these clothes. The guards at the tariff dock will not blink an eye at the errands of a ship's boy. Let me return for now, and . . . there is one other person I must go and see. But right after that, I shall return. I promise that by tomorrow morning, I shall be safely under your roof and attired as befits a Trader's daughter."

"You'll be out all night? Alone?"

"Would you rather I was with someone?" Althea asked mischievously. She disarmed her words with a quick grin. "Mother, I have been 'out all night' for almost a year now. No harm has come to me. At least, nothing permanent . . . but I promise I shall tell you all when I return."

"I see I cannot stop you," Ronica said resignedly. "Well. For the sake of your father's name, please do not let anyone recognize you! The family fortune is shaky enough as it is. Be discreet in whatever it is that you must do. And ask Captain Tenira to be discreet as well. You served aboard his ship, you said?"

"Yes. I did. Moreover, I said I would tell you all when I return. The sooner I leave, the sooner I'm back." Althea turned toward the door. Then she halted. "Would you please tell my sister I'm back? And that I wish to speak to her of serious things?"

"I will. Do you mean that you will try to, well, not make amends, or apologize, but make a truce with Kyle and your sister?"

Althea closed her eyes tight and then opened them. She spoke quietly. "Mother, I intend to take my ship back. I will try to make you both see that I am ready to do so and that I not only have the most right to her, but that I can do the most good for the family with her. But I do not want to say any more just yet, to you or to Keffria. Please do not tell her that. Say, if you would, only that I wish to speak to her of serious things."

"Very serious things." Her mother shook her head to herself. The lines on her brow and around her mouth seemed to deepen. She drank more wine, without relish or pleasure. "Go carefully, Althea, and return swiftly. I do not know if your coming home brings us salvation or disaster. I only know I am glad to know you are alive."

Althea nodded abruptly and slipped quietly out of the room. She did not go back the way she had come, but went out the front door. She acknowledged a serving man who was sweeping scattered flower petals from the steps. The massed hyacinths by the steps gave off a rising tide of perfume. As she hurried down the drive toward Bingtown, she almost wished she were simply Athel, a ship's boy. It was a beautiful spring day, her first day on shore in her homeport in almost a year. She wished she could take some simple gladness in it.

As she hurried down the winding roads back to Bingtown proper, she began to notice that the Vestrit estate was not the only one that showed signs of disrepair. Several other great homes that she passed showed the neglect of a pinched purse. Trees had gone unpruned and winter-wind damage unrepaired. When she passed through the busier streets of Bingtown's market district, it seemed to her that she saw many unfamiliar folk. It was not just that she did not recognize their faces; she had been so often away from Bingtown in the last ten years that she no longer expected to know many friends and neighbors. These strangers spoke with the accents of Jamaillia and dressed as if they were from Chalced. The men all seemed to be young, in their twenties or early thirties. They wore wide-bladed swords in filigreed sheaths, and hung their pouches at their belts as if to brag of their wealth. The rich skirts of the women who trailed after them were slashed to reveal filmy underskirts. Their vividly colored cosmetics obscured rather than enhanced their faces. The men tended to speak more loudly than was necessary, as if to draw as much attention to themselves as possible. More often than not, the tone of their words was arrogant and self-important. Their women moved like nervous fillies, tossing their heads and gesturing broadly when they spoke. Their perfumes were strong, their bangled earrings large. They made the courtesans of Bingtown seem like drab pigeons in contrast to their peacock strutting.

There was a second class of unfamiliar folk on the street. They bore the tattoos of slavery beside their noses. Their furtive demeanor said they wished nothing so much as to be unnoticed. The number of menial servants in Bingtown had multiplied. They carried packages and held horses. One young boy followed two girls little older than himself, endeavoring to hold a parasol over both of them to shield them from the gentle spring sunlight. When the younger of the girls cuffed him and rebuked him sharply for not holding the sunshade steady, Althea repressed an urge to slap her. The boy was far too young to cower so deferentially. He walked barefoot on the cold cobblestones.

"It could break your heart, if you let it. But those two have been schooled not to have hearts at all."

Althea started at the low voice so close to her ear. She spun to find Amber a step behind her. Their eyes met and Amber raised one knowing eyebrow. In a haughty tone, she offered, "I'll give you a copper, sailor-boy, if you'll carry this wood for me."

"Pleased to oblige," Althea replied and bobbed her head in a sailor's bow. She took the large chunk of ruddy wood from Amber's arms, and instantly found it much heavier than she had supposed. As she hefted it to a more secure grip, she caught the merriment in her friend's topaz eyes. She fell into step a deferential two paces behind Amber, and followed her through the Market to Rain Wild Street.

Things had changed here as well. There had always been a few shops that kept night guards, and one or two that even employed guards by day. Now nearly every shop boasted a surly doorman with a short sword or a long knife at his hip. Doors did not stand invitingly open, nor was merchandise displayed on racks and tables outside the shops. The intricate and near-magical goods imported to Bingtown from the Rain Wilds were now visible only through the barred windows. Althea missed the waft of perfumes and the ringing of wind chimes and the savor of rare spices on the breeze. The shops and street were as busy as ever, but in both merchants and buyers there was a guarded wariness very unpleasant to behold. Even Amber's shop had a guard outside the latched door. The young woman at her door wore a leather doublet and nonchalantly juggled two truncheons and a sap as she waited for her mistress to open up. She had long blonde hair caught back in a tail. She gave Althea a toothy smile. Althea edged past her uncomfortably. A large cat might so appraise a fat rodent.

"Wait outside, Jek. I'm not ready to open the store yet," Amber told her succinctly.

"Whatever your pleasure, mistress," Jek replied. Her tongue put a strange foreign twist on the words. She shot Althea one speculative glance as she carefully backed out the door and closed it behind her.

"Where did you find her?" Althea asked incredulously.

"She's an old friend. She is going to be disappointed when she discovers you're a woman. And she will. Nothing escapes Jek. Not that there is any danger of her betraying your secret. She is as close-mouthed as can be. Sees all, tells nothing. The perfect servant."

"It's funny. I never imagined you having servants of any kind."

"It's my preference not to, but I'm afraid a guard for the shop became necessary. I decided to live elsewhere, and with the increase of burglary in Bingtown, I had to hire someone to watch my shop at night. Jek needed a place to live; the arrangement works wonderfully." She took the chunk of wood from Althea's arms and set it aside. Then, to Althea's surprise, she seized her by both shoulders and held her at arm's length. "You do make a fetching youth. I can scarcely blame Jek for eyeing you." She gave her a warm hug. As she released her, she added, "I am so glad to see you return unscathed. I have thought of you often and wondered how you fared. Come into the back. I'll make some tea and we can talk."

As Amber spoke, she was leading the way. The back room was the cluttered cave Althea remembered. There were workbenches with scattered tools and partly finished beads. Clothes hung on hooks or were layered neatly into trunks. There was a bed in one corner and an unmade pallet in another. A small fire burned in the hearth.

"I'd love tea, but I haven't time just now. At least, not yet. I've a message to deliver first. However, as soon as I've done it, I'll come right back here. I intended to do so, even before you spotted me on the street."

"It is very important to me that you do so," Amber replied so seriously that Althea stared at her. In answer to that look, Amber added, "It's not something I can explain quickly."

Althea's curiosity was piqued, but her own concerns pushed it aside. "I need to speak to you privately as well. It's a delicate matter. Perhaps I have no right to interfere, but she is—" She hesitated. "Perhaps now is actually the best time, even though I haven't spoken to Captain Tenira about this yet." Althea paused, then plunged ahead. "I've been serving on the liveship *Ophelia*. She's been hurt, and I hope you can help her. A Chalcedean galley challenged us as we made our way back to Bingtown. Ophelia burned her hands fending them off. She says there is no pain, but she seems always to keep her hands clasped or otherwise hidden from view. I do not know how bad the damage is, or if a woodworker like yourself could do anything to repair scorched wood, but . . ."

"Challenged by a galley? And attacked?" Amber was horrified. "In the Inside Passage waters?" She exhaled in a rush. She stared past Althea, as if looking into a different time and place. Her voice went strange. "Fate rushes down upon us! The time drags and the days plod past, lulling us into thinking that the doom we fear will always so delay. Then, abruptly, the dark days we have all predicted are upon us, and the time when we could have turned dire fate aside has passed. How old must I be before I learn? There is no time; there is never any time. Tomorrow may never come, but todays are linked inexorably in a chain, and now is always the only time we have to divert disaster."

Althea felt a sudden sense of vindication. This was the reaction she had hoped to get from her mother. Strange that it was a newcomer, and not even a Bingtown Trader who instantly grasped the full significance of her news. Amber had completely forgotten her earlier offer of tea. Instead she flung open a chest in the corner of the room and began to haul garments from it in frenzy. "Give me just a few moments and I shall be fit to accompany you. However, let us not waste an instant. Begin with the day you left here, and talk to me. Tell me everything of your travels, even those things you consider unimportant." She turned to a small table and opened a box on it. She made a brisk check of its contents of pots and brushes, then tucked it under her arm.

Althea had to laugh. "Amber, that would take hours—no, days—to do."

"Which is why we must begin now. Come. Start while I change." Amber bundled up an armful of cloth and disappeared behind a wooden screen in the corner. Althea launched into an account of her experiences aboard the *Reaper*. She had barely got past her first miserable months and Brashen's discovery of her before Amber emerged from behind the screen. But it was not Amber who stood before her. Instead, it was a smudge-faced slave girl. A tattoo sprawled across one wind-reddened cheek. A crusty sore encompassed half her upper lip and her left nostril. Her dirty hair was pulling free from a scruffy braid. Her shirt was rough cotton and her bare feet peeked out from under her patched skirts. A dirty bandage bound one of her ankles. Rough canvas work gloves had replaced the lacy ones Amber habitually wore. She spread a dirty canvas tote on the table and began to load it with woodworking tools.

"You amaze me. How did you learn to do that?" Althea demanded, grinning.

"I've told you. I have played many roles in my life. This one disguise has proved very useful of late. Slaves are invisible. I can go almost anywhere in this guise and be ignored. Even the men who would not hesitate to force themselves on a slave are put off by a bit of dirt and a few well-placed scabs."

"Have the streets of Bingtown become that dangerous for a woman alone?"

Amber shot her a look that was almost pitying. "You see what is happening and yet you do not see. Slaves are not women, Althea. Nor men. They are merchandise, goods and property. Things. Why should a slave-owner care if one of his goods is raped? If she bears a child, he has another slave. If she does not, well, what is the harm done? That boy you were staring at . . . it costs his master nothing if he weeps himself to sleep every night. The bruises he is given cost his owner nothing. If he becomes sullen and intractable from poor treatment, he will simply be sold off to someone who treats him even worse. The bottom rungs of the ladder become very slippery, once slavery is accepted. If a human's life can be measured in counted coins, then that worth can be diminished, a copper at a time, until no value is left. When an old woman is worth less than the food she eats . . . well." Amber sighed suddenly.

As abruptly, she straightened herself. "No time for that." She ducked to peer at herself in a mirror on the table, then snatched up a ragged scarf and tied it about her head and over her ears. The tool tote was concealed inside a market basket. She tucked her earrings up out of sight. "There. Let's go. We'll slip out the back way. On the street, take my arm, lean close and leer at me like a nasty sailor. That way we can talk as we go."

Althea was amazed at how well the ruse worked. Those folk who took any notice of them at all turned aside in disgust. Althea continued the tale of her journey. Once or twice, Amber made small sounds as if she would interrupt, but when Althea paused she would insist, "No, go on. When you are finished, that is the time for questions." Never had anyone listened to her so intently, absorbing her words as a sponge soaks in water.

When they approached the tariff docks, Amber pulled Althea aside for a moment. "How will you introduce me to the ship?" she asked.

"I'll have you follow me aboard. I haven't discussed this with Captain Tenira yet." Althea frowned to herself as she suddenly realized how awkward all this could be. "You'll have to meet Captain Tenira and Grag before I take you forward to meet Ophelia. I honestly don't know how friendly they will be, to you or to the idea of someone not of Bingtown working on their ship."

"Trust me to handle them. I can be charming when it is required. Now, forward."

Althea was unchallenged at the ship's ramp. She gave a furtive look around and then made a show of beckoning Amber forward. The two tariff guards on the dock spotted her immediately. One made a grimace of distaste while the other brayed out a knowing laugh. Neither one interfered as the ship's boy smuggled his doxie aboard.

The seaman on watch aboard the *Ophelia* raised an incredulous eyebrow, but at a sign from Althea, he bit his tongue. He escorted them to the door of Captain Tenira's cabin and stood by while Althea tapped.

"Enter," Tenira called. Althea jerked her head at Amber and she followed her in. The captain had been busy with a pen and parchment at his table while Grag stood looking out the windows. "What's this?" Captain Tenira demanded incredulously while Grag's mouth twisted in distaste.

"I am not what I look, sir," Amber replied before Althea could utter a word. Her voice was so genteelly modulated, her accent so pure, that no one could have doubted her. "Please excuse that I come disguised. It seemed prudent. I've been a friend of Althea's for some time. She knows I can be trusted. She has told me of your encounter on your way here. I am here not just to lend my support to your defiance of the tariffs, but to see if I can repair the damage that was done to Ophelia's hands."

In one breath, she had smoothly stated everything that Althea would have stumbled over expressing. Then she stood quietly, hands clasped demurely in front of her, her spine straight, her eyes meeting theirs unashamedly. The two men exchanged a glance. The first words out of Captain Tenira's mouth shocked Althea.

"Do you really think you can do something for Ophelia's hands? It pains me to see her ashamed of their appearance."

There was a depth of emotion in the man's voice when he spoke of his ship that touched Althea's soul.

"I don't know," Amber replied honestly. "I know little of wizardwood. My small experience of it tells me that it is exceedingly fine-grained. The very density of it may have preserved her from taking deep harm. But I will know only when I look at her hands, and perhaps not even then."

"Then let us go forward and look," Tenira immediately declared. He gave an almost apologetic look at Althea. "I know you bear tidings for me from your mother. Do not think I under-value them. But *Ophelia* is my ship."

"She must come first," Althea agreed. "It was in my mind also, when I asked my friend Amber to accompany me."

"That is so like you," Grag observed warmly. He was so bold as to touch Althea's hand. He sketched a bow toward Amber. "Anyone that Althea calls friend, I am honored to know. It is the only credential you need with me."

"My son recalls me to my manners. Forgive me, lady. I am Captain and

Bingtown Trader Tomie Tenira of the liveship *Ophelia*. This is my son, Grag
Tenira."

Althea realized sharply that she did not know Amber's family name.
But before she could stumble through that introduction, Amber spoke. "I
am Amber the bead-maker, an artisan of Rain Wild Street. I look forward
to meeting your ship."

With no more ado, Captain Tenira led the way. Ophelia was obviously simmering with curiosity. She looked Amber up and down with a
scandalized restraint that brought a grin to Althea's face despite herself.
As soon as Amber's presence was explained, the ship showed no hesitation at turning to her and presenting her scorched hands for inspection.
"Do you think you can do anything for me?" she asked gravely.

It was the first time Althea had had a clear look at the damage. The
tarry fireballs had clung to her fingers as they burned her. It had licked up
the inside of Ophelia's left wrist. Her patrician hands looked like those of
a scrub maid.

Amber took one of the ship's large hands in both her own. She ran
her gloved fingertips over the scorched surface lightly, then rubbed at it
more firmly. "Tell me if I hurt you," she added belatedly. Her brow was
furrowed with concentration. "A most peculiar wood," she added to herself. She opened the tote of tools and selected one. She scraped lightly at
one blackened fingertip. Ophelia gave a sharp intake of breath.

"That hurts?" Amber asked immediately.

"Not as humans hurt. It feels . . . wrong. Damaging."

"I think there is sound wood just below the scorched surface. Working
with my tools, I could remove what is blackened. I might have to reshape
your hands a bit; you would end up with slimmer fingers than you have
now. I could keep a good proportion, I believe, unless the damage goes
much deeper than I think. However, you would have to endure that sense
of damage, unflinching, while I did my work. I do not know how long it
would take."

"What do you think, Tomie?" the ship demanded of her captain.

"I think we have little to lose by trying," he said gently. "If the
sensation becomes unbearable, then Mistress Amber will stop, I am sure."

Ophelia smiled nervously. Then a wondering look came into her eyes.
"If your work on my hands is successful, then perhaps something could be
done about my hair as well." She lifted a hand to touch the long loose
curls of her mane. "This style is so dated. I have often thought that if I
could contrive ringlets around my face and . . ."

"Oh, Ophelia." Tomie groaned as the others laughed.

Amber had kept possession of one of Ophelia's hands. Her head was
still bent over it, examining the damage. "I may have great difficulty in
matching the stain. Never have I seen stain that mimics so well the color
of flesh without obscuring the grain of the wood. Someone told me that a

liveship creates its own colors as it awakens." She met Ophelia's eyes without self-consciousness as she asked, "Will that happen again, if I have to plane so deep that I expose uncolored wood?"

"I do not know," Ophelia replied quietly.

"This will not be the work of an afternoon," Amber said decidedly. "Captain, you will have to give your watch permission to let me come and go. I shall keep this same guise. Is that acceptable?"

"I suppose so," the captain conceded grudgingly. "Though it may be hard to explain to other Traders why such delicate work is entrusted to a slave, or why I use a slave's labor at all. I oppose all slavery, you know."

"As do I," Amber replied gravely. "As do many, many folk in this town."

"Do they?" Tomie replied bitterly. "If there is any great public outcry about it, it has escaped me."

Amber lightly tapped her fake tattoo. "Were you to put on rags and one of these and stroll about Bingtown, you would hear the voices of those who oppose slavery most bitterly. In your efforts to waken Bingtown to its senses, do not ignore that pool of allies." She selected a small block plane from her tote of tools and began to adjust the blade on it. "If one were interested in, say, the inner workings of the household of the tariff minister, willing spies might easily be found among that pool. I believe the scribe who composes his correspondence to the Satrap is a slave, also."

A little shiver walked up Althea's spine. How did Amber come to know such things, and why had she troubled to find them out?

"You speak as if you were knowledgeable about such things," Captain Tenira pointed out gravely.

"Oh, I have known my share of intrigues and plotting. I find it all distasteful. And necessary. Just as pain is occasionally necessary." She set the block to Ophelia's palm. "Hold steady," she warned her in a low voice. "I'm going to take off the worst of the damage."

There was a tiny silence followed by a dreadful scraping noise. Charred wood powdered away. The smell reminded Althea of scorched hair. Ophelia made a tiny noise then lifted her eyes to stare out over the water. Her jaw was set.

Captain Tenira's face was almost expressionless as he watched Amber work. As if inquiring about the weather, he asked Althea, "Did you deliver my message to your mother?"

"I did." Althea pushed aside an emotion that was close to shame. "I'm sorry. I do not bring much that is of great comfort. My mother said she would speak to my sister Keffria. She is legally the Trader of the family now. Mother will urge her to attend the next Council meeting, and to vote in support of your actions."

"I see," Tenira replied. His voice was carefully empty.

"I wish my father were still alive," Althea added miserably.

"I could wish that you were Trader for the Vestrits. Truly, you should have inherited your family's ship."

Althea revealed her deepest wound. "I do not know if Keffria can stand beside you at all." A stunned silence followed her words. She kept her voice even as she added, "I do not know how she can side with you, and still support her husband. The increased tariffs are based on the Satrap protecting trade from pirates, but we all know it is the slave trade he cares most about. He never bothered about the pirates until they began attacking slavers. So, if the issue comes down to slavery, and she must take a stance . . . She . . . Kyle is trading in slaves. Using *Vivacia* as a slave ship. I do not think she would oppose her husband in this. Even if she does not agree with him, she has never had the will to set herself against him in anything."

Then, "No-o-o," Ophelia gasped. "Oh, how could they do such a thing! Vivacia is so young. How will she withstand all that? What was your mother thinking to allow this to happen? How could they have done that to their own family's ship?"

Grag and Captain Tenira were both silent. A stony look of condemnation settled over the captain's face while Grag looked stricken. The question hung in the air, an accusation.

"I don't know," Althea replied miserably. "I don't know."

Judgment

"WHERE COULD SHE BE? WHAT COULD SHE BE DOING?" KEFFRIA WORRIED.

"I don't know." Her mother replied testily.

Keffria looked down into the cup of tea she held. She forced her tongue to be still. She had nearly asked her mother if she was certain she had really seen Althea earlier. The last week had been so exhausting, she could have forgiven her mother for imagining the whole thing. That would be easier to forgive than her younger sister turning up and then abruptly vanishing again. It didn't help her temper that her mother seemed simply to accept Althea's outrageous behavior.

Her mother relented and added, "She told me she would be back before morning. The sun has scarcely gone down."

"Does it not seem odd to you that a young, unmarried woman of a good family should be out and about on her own at night, let alone on her first night home after she has been missing for nearly a year?"

"No doubt that is so. It seems very like Althea to me, however. I've come to accept that I can't change her."

"No such leeway is allowed to me!" Malta interjected pointedly. "I am scarcely allowed to walk around Bingtown by myself by day."

"That's true," Ronica Vestrit replied affably. Her needles ticked rhythmically against each other as she worked. She ignored Malta's noisy exhalation of frustration.

They had dined early and were now sitting together in the study. No one had said that they kept vigil for Althea's return. No one needed to. Her mother knit as if she were in some sort of race. Keffria had no such concentration. She stubbornly poked her needle through her embroidery and dragged another stitch into place. She would not let her sister upset her; she would not let the small peace she had found be stolen from her.

Malta did not even pretend to be constructively occupied. She had poked at their simple meal discontentedly and commented that she already missed Davad's servants. Now she strolled about the room, trailing her fingers on the desk-top, picking up the smaller mementos of her grandfather's sailing years, handling them and then putting them down. Her restlessness was an irritant to Keffria's raw nerves. Keffria was glad Selden was abed, exhausted after the long week of company. Malta had thrived on it. Ever since the last carriage had pulled away down the drive, the girl had had a desolate look to her. She reminded Keffria of some sea-creature stranded by a retreating tide.

"I'm bored," Malta announced, echoing her mother's thought. "I wish the Rain Wild Traders were still here. They don't sit about in the evening and do quiet work."

"When they are at home, I am sure they do," Keffria countered firmly. "No one has parties and games and music every night, Malta. You must not make that the basis for your relationship with Reyn."

"Well, if he marries me and we have a home of our own, it will not be dull every night, I can tell you that. We shall have friends over to visit, and bring in musicians. Or we will go out to visit other friends. Delo and I have decided that when we are married women and free to do as we please, we shall often have . . ."

"If you marry Reyn, you will live in the Rain Wilds, not in Bingtown," Ronica pointed out quietly. "You will have to make friends there, and learn to live as they do."

"Why do you have to be so dismal?" Malta demanded sharply. "No matter what I say, you always say something to make it not so. I think you just want me to be unhappy forever!"

"The fault is not in what I say, but in the silly fancies you spin to start. . . ."

"Mother. Please. I shall go mad if you two begin to bicker and snip tonight."

A heavy silence followed. "I'm sorry. I do not wish Malta to be unhappy. I want her to wake up and see that she must choose to be happy within the framework of her life. These wild fancies of endless parties and entertainment are not . . ."

"No wonder Aunt Althea ran away!" Malta's cry cut off her grandmother's words. "All you can see ahead for anyone is boredom and toil. Well, my life is not going to be like that! Reyn has told me many exciting things about the Rain Wilds. When we go to visit his family, he is going to show me the ancient city of the Elder race, where flame jewels come from, and jidzin and other wonderful things. He has told me that there are places where you can go, and at a touch of your hand, you can light the chambers as they were of old. He says that sometimes he has even glimpsed the ghosts of the Elder folk coming and going on their errands. Not all can do that, only the very sensitive, but he says perhaps I have that skill. Very sensitive folk often do. Those most gifted can sometimes hear their music echoing still. He will dress me as befits a woman of the Khuprus family. I will not have to dust furniture or polish silver or cook food; there will be servants to do that. Reyn says . . . Mother, why are you smiling at me like that? Are you making fun of me?" Malta demanded indignantly.

"No. It's not that at all. I was thinking that it sounds to me as if you like this young man very much." Keffria gave her head a small shake. "I remember all the grand plans that your father and I made for our life together. Those dreams do not always come true, but the spinning of them is very sweet."

"It sounds to me as if she likes the prospect of all he will bring her," Ronica corrected softly. More gently, she added, "But there is nothing wrong with that, either. Young people who share the same dreams often make very good partners."

Malta came back to poke at the fire in the grate. "Don't talk as if it were all agreed upon, because it isn't," she said petulantly. "There are a lot of bad things about him. Not just his veil and gloves; who can even imagine what he really looks like? He also goes on and on about politics. One minute he is talking of parties and friends; the next he speaks of war with Jamaillia and how we must stand firm no matter how difficult life becomes. He talks as if that would be some big adventure! Moreover, he says slavery is evil, although I told him that Papa thinks it might be good for Bingtown and that Papa is rebuilding our fortune by selling slaves. He dared to say that Papa would have to change his ways and see that slavery is wrong and bad for our economy, too, and trade up the Rain Wild River instead!

"And he talks about having children as if I am to have a baby the day after we are wed! When I said we must have a house in Bingtown as well as in the Rain Wilds so we can visit often and see my friends, he laughed! He says that once I see the wonders of his city, I will forget all about Bingtown, and that we will not have our own house, but only a set of rooms in the great house the Khuprus family shares. So. I am not at all certain that I will choose Reyn."

"It sounds as if you two talked a great deal about your future together," Ronica ventured.

"*He* speaks as if it is all assured! When I tell him it is not, he smiles and asks why I love to torture him so. Are all men so obtuse?"

"Every one of them that I've ever known," Ronica assured her complacently. Then, more seriously, she added, "But if you have decided to deny his suit, then you must tell us so. The sooner the courtship is broken off, the least discomfort to both families."

"Oh . . . I haven't decided. Not really. It may take me a while."

The room fell silent as Malta considered her prospects and the two older women privately contemplated what her choices might mean to them.

"I wish I knew where Althea was," Keffria heard herself say again. Her mother sighed.

ALTHEA SET HER MUG DOWN. THERE WAS VERY LITTLE LEFT OF THE ROAST fowl on the table before them. Across the table from her, Amber set her knife and fork carefully across her plate. Jek leaned back in her chair and picked at something caught in her teeth. She caught Althea watching her and grinned. "You don't have any big brothers at home, do you?" she teased. "Eyes such as yours are wasted on a woman."

"Jek," Amber rebuked her amusedly. "You are making Althea uncomfortable. Why don't you go stroll about Bingtown for a bit? We have some serious talking to do."

Jek pushed up from the table with a grunt. She rolled her shoulders and Althea heard the crackling of muscle. "Take my advice. Do some serious drinking instead. Serious talking is no way to spend your first evening back in your home town." When she grinned, her teeth were white as a carnivore's.

"Who knows? It may come to that as well," Amber conceded affably. She watched Jek tug on her boots and then find a light cloak. As soon as the door closed behind her, Amber leaned forward on her elbows. She pointed a long finger at Althea. "Continue from where you left off. And this time, don't bother to gloss over the parts where you feel you behaved badly. I'm not asking this of you so I can judge you."

"Why are you asking this of me?" Althea asked. To herself, she wondered why she was granting this to Amber. She still knew relatively little about the woman. Why was she favoring her with a detailed account of her travels and experiences since the last time she had seen her?

"Ah. Well. I suppose that is a fair trade, considering all I've asked you." Amber took a breath as if putting her words in order. "I cannot leave Bingtown. I must do things here. But the timing of those tasks is dependent on events that are happening elsewhere. In Jamaillia and the Inside Passage, for instance. So I ask you to tell me what changes you have seen in those places."

"That tells me nothing at all," Althea pointed out quietly.

"I suppose it doesn't. Let me be blunt then. I am dedicated to bringing about certain changes. I wish to see an end to slavery, not just in Bingtown, but in all of Jamaillia and Chalced as well. I wish to see Bingtown shake off Jamaillian rule. And I wish, most of all, to solve the riddle of the dragon and the serpent." She smiled significantly at Althea as she said this. She tapped first the dragon earring she wore in her left ear and then the serpent that swung from her right. She raised an eyebrow at Althea and waited in anticipation for her response.

"The dragon and the serpent?" Althea queried, baffled.

Amber's face changed. A terrible dread washed over it, followed by a look of weariness. She leaned back in her chair. She spoke quietly. "When I finally said that to you, you were supposed to leap to your feet and look startled. Or perhaps shout, 'Aha!' or shake your head in wonderment and then explain it all to me. The last thing I ever imagined you doing was sitting there being politely puzzled."

Althea shrugged. "Sorry."

"The words have no significance to you at all? The dragon and the serpent?" There was a desperate note in Amber's voice.

Althea shrugged again.

"Think hard," Amber begged. "Please. I have been so certain that you were the one. Certain dreams have shaken that conviction from time to time, but when I saw you again on the street, surety leapt up in me once more. You are the one. You have to know. Think. The dragon and the serpent." She leaned forward on the table and fixed Althea with a pleading stare.

Althea took a deep breath. "Dragon and serpent. All right. On one island in the Barrens, I saw a rock formation that is called the Dragon. And our ship was attacked by a sea serpent on the way home."

"You mentioned nothing of a dragon when you told me about your time on the Barrens!"

"It didn't seem significant."

"Tell me now." Amber's eyes burned with a cat-like intensity.

Althea leaned forward and replenished her mug from the earthenware pitcher of beer on the table. "There's not much to tell. We camped in the lee of it when we were working the slaughter. It is just a big rock that sticks out of the earth. When the light hits it right, it looks like a dead dragon. One of the older hands spun a yarn that it was really a slain dragon and that if I climbed up there, I'd find an arrow in its chest still."

"Did you?"

Althea grinned sheepishly. "I was curious. I climbed up on its chest one night. Reller had told the truth. Its forelegs were clutching at an arrow sticking out of its chest."

"Then it wasn't just an accidental formation of stone? It truly had forelegs?"

Althea pursed her lips. "Or maybe some sailors with a bit of time on their hands had 'enhanced' it a bit. That was my opinion. Reller's claim was that that thing had been sprawled there for ages and ages. But the arrow shaft didn't look weathered or splintered. It was as nice a piece of wizardwood as I've ever seen. The only surprising thing to me was that no one had ever taken it. But sailors are a superstitious lot, and wizardwood has a dangerous reputation."

Amber sat as if transfixed.

"The serpent—" Althea began, but "Hush!" Amber ordered her. "I need to think a moment. A wizardwood arrow. Is that what all this has been about? A wizardwood arrow? Shot by whom, and when? Why?"

Althea had no answers to any of that. She lifted her mug and took a long drink. When she set it down, Amber was smiling at her. "Go back to your tale, and finish it for me. Put in the serpent when you come to him, and tell me as much about him as you can. I promise to be a good listener." Amber tipped a small measure of golden brandy into her own glass and leaned back expectantly.

Jek was right. The beer pitcher had been emptied twice and Amber's bottle of brandy was seriously lightened before the tale was told. Amber went over Althea's account of the serpent attacking the ship several times. She seemed interested in how its spittle had eaten through cloth and flesh, and nodded to herself at Brashen's assertion that it was not a mere predatory attack, but a thinking creature bound on vengeance. Nevertheless, Althea sensed that nothing in that part of her tale rang Amber's interest as the wizardwood arrow had. At last, even Amber's questions seemed to run out. The flames in the grate had burned low. Althea returned from a trip to the back-house to find Amber spilling the last of the brandy into two small glasses. Carved wooden holders, obviously the work of Amber's hands, twined ivy leaves around the glasses.

"Let us drink," Amber proposed. "To all that is right with the world. To friendship, and good brandy."

Althea lifted her glass but could not think of anything to add to the toast.

"The *Vivacia?*" Amber suggested.

"I wish her well, but until her decks are under my feet again, she is tangled with all that is most wrong in my world."

"To Grag Tenira?" Amber proposed facetiously.

"That is also too complicated."

Amber grinned broadly. "To Brashen Trell!"

Althea groaned and shook her head, but Amber raised her glass anyway. "Here's to irresponsible men who give in to their passions." She drained off her brandy. "So women can claim it was none of their doing."

This last she uttered just as Althea had given in and was tossing her brandy down. She choked and sputtered. "Amber, that's not fair. He took advantage of me."

"Did he?"

"I told you," Althea replied stubbornly. Actually, she had told Amber very little, other than to admit with a shrug that it had happened. At the time, Amber had let it pass with but a raised eyebrow. Now she met

Althea's glare with a steady gaze and a small knowing smile. Althea took a breath. "I had been drinking, and drugged beer at that, and I'd taken a good blow to the head. Then he gave me some of his cindin. And I was cold and wet and exhausted."

"All of that was true of Brashen as well. I'm not finding fault, Althea. I don't think either of you needs to make excuses for what happened. I think you shared what you each needed most. Warmth. Friendship. Release. Acknowledgment."

"Acknowledgment?"

"Ah, so you agree to the first three without question?"

Althea didn't answer the question. "Talking to you is a balancing act," she complained. Then, "Acknowledgment of what?" she demanded.

"Of who you are. What you are." Amber's voice was soft, almost gentle.

"So you think I'm a slut, too." The effort at putting humor in her voice fell flat.

Amber considered her for a moment. She tipped back on her chair, balancing it on two legs. "I think you know what you are. You don't need my opinion. All you have to do is look at your daydreams. Have you ever fancied yourself settled down, a wife and mother? Ever wondered what it will be like to carry a babe within you? Do you dream of taking care of your wee ones while awaiting your husband's return from sea?"

"Only in my worst nightmares," Althea heard herself admit with a laugh.

"So. If you never truly expect yourself to be a settled wife, do you expect that you will live all your life knowing nothing of men?"

"I hadn't given much thought to it." She pulled her beer mug closer.

Amber snorted. "There is a part of you that thinks of little else, did you but care to admit it. You simply don't want to accept the responsibility for it. You'd like to pretend it is just something that happens to you, something a man tricked you into doing." She returned her chair to the floor with a thump. "Come on," she invited Althea. "The tide is rising and I've an appointment." She gave a small belch. "Walk with me."

Althea rose. She could not decide if Amber's words had offended or amused her. "Where are we going?" she asked as she accepted a ragged coat.

"The beach. I want you to meet a friend of mine. Paragon."

"Paragon? The ship? I know Paragon well!"

Amber smiled. "I know you do. He spoke of you one night. It was a slip of his tongue and I gave no sign of recognizing your name. However, even if he hadn't, I would have known. You left signs of your stay aboard him. They were mixed in with Brashen's things."

"Like what?" Althea demanded suspiciously.

"A little hair comb I had seen you wearing the first time I noticed you. It was left perched on a window ledge, as if you had stood there to fix your hair and then forgotten it."

"Ah. But what have you to do with the *Paragon?*"

Amber measured her reaction as she said, "I told you. He's my friend." More cautiously, she added, "I'm in the process of buying him."

"You can't!" Althea declared, outraged. "The Ludlucks cannot sell their liveship, no matter how he has disgraced himself!"

"Is there a law against it, then?" Amber's voice was inquisitive, nothing more.

"No. There has never been any need to make such a law. It is the tradition of Bingtown."

"Many of Bingtown's most venerated traditions are giving way before the onslaught of the New Traders. It is not publicly noised about, but anyone in Bingtown who cares about such things knows that the *Paragon* is up for sale. And that bids from New Traders are being considered."

Althea was silent for a time. Amber put on a cloak and drew a hood well up over her pale hair. When Althea spoke, her voice was low. "If the Ludluck family is forced to sell *Paragon*, they will sell him to other Old Traders. Not a newcomer like you."

"I wondered if you would point that out," Amber replied in a conversationally even voice. She lifted the bar on the back door and opened it. "Coming?"

"I don't know." Althea preceded her out the door, then stood in the dark alley as Amber locked up. The last few minutes of conversation with Amber had taken a decidedly uncomfortable turn. Most unsettling was the feeling she had that Amber had deliberately engineered this small confrontation. Was she trying to test their friendship? Or was there some larger agenda behind her needling? She chose her words carefully.

"I don't think you are less, or not as good as I am, simply because I am Trader born and you are not. Some things are the sole province of the Bingtown Traders, and we guard those things jealously. Our liveships are very special. We feel the need to protect them. It would be hard to make an outsider understand all that our liveships are to us."

"It is always difficult to explain that which you don't understand yourself," Amber retorted quietly. "Althea, this idea has to break through, not just to you but to all the Bingtown Traders. To survive, you will have to change. You will have to decide what things are most important to you, and preserve those things. You must accept the allies who share those values, and not be so suspicious of them. Above all, you must relinquish your claims to things that don't belong to you. Things that don't belong even to the Rain Wild Traders, but are the rightful heritage of all."

"What do you know about the Rain Wild Traders?" Althea demanded. She peered at Amber in the dimness of the alley.

"Precious little. Your close-mouthed Bingtown traditions have seen to that. I suspect they plunder the cities of the Elderlings of their treasures, and claim that ancient magic as their own. Bingtown and the Bingtown Traders act as a shield to conceal a people unknown to the rest of the world. Those people delve deep into secrets they cannot grasp. They dismantle the hard-won knowledge of another folk and time, and market it as amusing trinkets. I suspect they destroy as much as they pilfer. Come on."

Althea took a deep breath to reply, then clamped her jaws firmly. She followed Amber.

A brief silence fell. Then Amber laughed. "You see. You will not even tell me if my deductions are correct."

"Those things are Bingtown Trader business. One doesn't discuss it with outsiders." Althea heard the coldness in her own voice but could not repent it.

For a time, they walked in false companionship. The revelry of the Night Market reached them as distantly as a memory of better times. The wind off the water was cold. In these hours before dawn, spring was forgotten. The world returned to the dark and chill of winter. Althea touched the bottom of despair. She had not realized how much she had valued her friendship with Amber until it was threatened.

Amber took her arm suddenly. The contact made the intensity of her voice more compelling. "Bingtown cannot stand alone," she said. "Jamaillia is corrupted. The Satrap will cede you to Chalced, or sell you to New Traders without even a moment of consideration. He doesn't care, Althea. Not about his honor, or his ancestor's pledge or the people of Bingtown. He doesn't even care about the citizens of Jamaillia. He is so engrossed in himself, he cannot perceive anything except as it relates to him." Amber shook her head, and Althea thought she sensed a deep sadness. "He comes to power too young, and unschooled. He had great promise and much talent. His father took joy in his potential, and he charmed his teachers. No one wished to daunt that inquisitive spirit; he was allowed complete freedom in his explorations. No discipline was imposed on him. For a time, it was like watching an extravagant blossom unfold."

Amber paused as if remembering a better time. She went on with a sigh, "But nothing thrives without limits. At first, the court was amused when he discovered the pleasures of the flesh and indulged in them. Characteristically, he set out to explore them all. Everyone supposed it was but a stage of his growth. It wasn't. It was the end of his growth. Mired in pleasure, lost in all but the titillation of his own senses, he became ever more self-centered. Ambitious people saw it as a path to the future Satrap's favor; they began to supply his desire. The unscrupulous saw it as a pathway to power. They taught him exotic new pleasures, ones they alone could supply. When his father died abruptly and he was cat-apulted into power, the strings of the puppet were already fixed. Since then, they have only become more confining." Amber gave a mirthless laugh. "It is bitter. The young man who was never restricted by the walls of discipline is now choking on the leashes of his addictions. His enemies will rob his folk and enslave his lands, and he will smile as the dream herbs smolder in his chambers."

"You seem well versed in this history."

"I am."

The brusqueness of her answer cut off Althea's next question. She found a different one. "Why are you telling me all this?" she asked in a low voice.

"To wake you up. Appeals to the Satrap's honor, and reminders of ancient promises, will not produce results. The diseases of power have eaten too deeply into the Satrap and the influential families of Jamaillia. They are too busy saving themselves and gathering what scraps of power they can to be interested in Bingtown's plight. If Bingtown wishes to continue as it has, then it must find its own allies. Not just those of the newcomers who share Bingtown's ideals, but the slaves brought here against their will, and . . . any others who share Bingtown's enemies. The Rain Wild Traders must also step out from the shadows, not only to assert their rights but also to take responsibility for what they do."

Althea halted suddenly in the street. Amber took another step, then stopped and looked back at her.

"I need to go home, to my family," Althea said quietly. "All of what you say speaks to me, not only of Bingtown, but of my family's predica-ment."

Amber released her arm. "If I have made you see that those two things are connected, I have not wasted my time this evening. Another time, you will come to Paragon with me. And you will help me convince him that he must support my efforts to buy him."

"First I will have to convince myself of that," Althea cautioned her. She took satisfaction in knowing that Paragon had had the good sense to resist Amber's efforts. As much as she liked her, there had to be a better buyer for the *Paragon* than she. Althea added that to her list of concerns. She would discuss it with Grag and his father when next she saw them.

"You will be convinced, if you open your ears and eyes. Go carefully, Althea, and reach home safely. Visit me when you can. Until then, be aware. Consider all that troubles Bingtown. Notice all that seems wrong to you, even that which does not seem to involve you. You will reach the same conclusions I have."

Althea nodded at her. She didn't speak. It saved her from having to say she would reach her own conclusions. What was best for her family would come first.

"ARE WE GOING TO SIT UP ALL NIGHT?" MALTA FINALLY ASKED.

Keffria's reply was surprisingly mild. "I'm going to stay up until Althea gets home. I know you must be tired, dear. It's been quite a week for you. You can go to bed if you wish."

"I thought you told me that Grandmother would start treating me more like an adult if I acted like one." She kept an eye on her grandmother as she said this, and saw the small flicker of her eyes that said her barb had struck. It was time the old woman realized that she and her mother did talk together about such things. "I think if you are both going to stay up and talk to Aunt Althea when she gets home, I should, too."

"As you wish," her mother said wearily. She picked up the needlework she had set aside and looked at it.

Malta leaned back in her chair. She had curled her legs up and tucked her feet under her. Her back ached and her head pounded. She still smiled. It had been quite a week for her. She reached up and began to take her hair down. As she plucked the pins out and it cascaded darkly about her shoulders, she wondered what Reyn would think if he could see her like this. She imagined him sitting across from her, watching her hair slowly come down. He would tilt his head and his veil would move slightly when he sighed. He would toy with the fingertips of his gloves. He had confided to her that he found them more annoying than the veil. "To touch something, skin to surface, can tell one so much. A shared touch, skin to skin, can speak the words our mouths are not free to say." He had held his hand out, as if inviting her to touch his gloved fingers, but she had not moved. "You could remove your gloves," she had told him. "I would not be afraid."

He had laughed lightly, his veil puffing out with his amusement. "I think there is not much you would fear, my little hunting cat. But that would not make it proper. I have promised my mother that this courtship will be proper."

"Did you?" She had leaned forward, dropping her voice to a breathy whisper. "Do you tell me that to make me feel safe? Or to discourage me from attempting any impropriety?" She had let a tiny smile curl her mouth and lifted one brow. It was an expression often practiced in her mirror.

A slight movement of the lace over his face told her she had scored. That quick little intake of breath said he was both shocked and delighted at her boldness. But even better, past his shoulder, she glimpsed the dark scowl on Cerwin Trell's face. She had given a throaty little trill of laughter, contriving that her whole attention seemed focused on Reyn as she watched for Cerwin's reaction. Cerwin had snatched up a bottle of wine from a passing servant's tray and refilled his own glass. He was far too well bred to slam the bottle down on the table at his elbow, but it had made an audible thud. Delo had leaned over to rebuke him, but he had brushed his sister's remark away. What had he thought then? That he had been too timid in his suit? That he had missed his opportunity to have such a rare creature as Malta Haven smile at him like that?

Malta certainly hoped so. She thought of the simmering tension between the two men and a shiver ran over her. She was so glad she had been able to talk her mother into the farewell party before Reyn left. She had begged a chance to introduce her friends to him, saying she needed to see for herself if they could accept her Rain Wild suitor. It had been more successful than she had ever dared dream. One and all, the girls had been eaten up with jealousy to see her pampered so.

She had found a moment to slip aside with Delo and show her all the "small trinkets" that Reyn had managed to slip in with her approved gifts. The dragonfly perched motionless upon the flowers sent to her bed-chamber had been artfully fashioned from precious metals and tiny gems. A tiny perfect deep blue flame gem had been inside a bottle of scent. A little basket of candied violets had been lined with what at first glance appeared to be a handkerchief. Shaken out, the fine sheer fabric was large enough to drape her bed. An unsigned note in its folds told her that Rain Wild women used such cloth to fashion their night garments for their bridal trousseau. An apple in a basket of fruit proved to be a clever deception. At a touch, it unfolded to present a string of water-opals and a tiny packet of silver-gray powder. The note with that directed her to place the powder in the dream-box ten days after his departure. When Delo had asked her what the dream-box did, Malta told her it sent her dreams that she and Reyn could share. Asked what sort of dreams, Malta had turned aside and managed a blush. "It would not be proper to speak of them," she had whispered breathily.

No sooner had they returned to the festivities than Delo excused herself. A short time later Malta saw her in excited conversation with Kitten. The gossip had spread swiftly as a rising tide after that. Malta had seen it engulf Cerwin. She had refused to meet his eyes today, save for one glance. He had not hesitated to let her see the heartbreak in his gaze. She had sent him a stricken look of appeal. After that, she had feigned ignoring him. Enrapt in Reyn's conversation, she had left it to her mother to make her farewells to the departing guests.

It was so delicious to wonder what Cerwin would do next.

She was broken from her musings by the soft working of the kitchen door. Her mother and grandmother exchanged a glance. "I left it unlatched for her," Grandma Vestrit said quietly. They both got to their feet, but before they could move, a man entered the room. Keffria gave a gasp and stepped back in horror.

"I'm home," Althea announced. She took off the ragged coat she was wearing and smiled at them all. Her hair was disgusting, bound flat to her head and then swinging behind her in a boy's plait. The skin of her face was red and wind-chapped. She strode into the room and held her hands out to the fire as if she were perfectly at home here. She smelled of tar, oakum and beer.

"God of Fishes!" Keffria said, startling them all with the coarseness of the oath. She shook her head as she stared in dismay at her sister. "Althea. How can you do this to us? How can you do this to yourself? Have you no pride, no care at all for your family name?" She sat down heavily in her chair.

"Don't worry about it. No one who saw me recognized me," Althea retorted. She moved around the room like a stray dog sniffing. "You've moved Father's desk," she accused them all.

"The light is better by the window," Grandmother said mildly. "The older I get, the harder it is to see fine lettering. It takes me four or five efforts to thread a needle now."

Althea started to speak, then stopped. Her features changed slightly. "I am sorry to hear that," she said sincerely. She shook her head. "It must be hard, to lose things you have always taken for granted."

Malta was trying to watch them all at once. She saw her mother fold her lips tightly and guessed she was angered at how her complaint had been ignored. In contrast, Grandmother met Althea's eyes without anger, only a grave sadness. Malta ventured a move. "You can't know that no one recognized you. All you know is that no one showed that they had recognized you. Perhaps they were too ashamed for you to react."

For an instant, Althea looked shocked that Malta had spoken at all. She narrowed her eyes. "I think you should remember your manners when you speak to your elders, Malta. When I was your age, I was not encouraged to speak out of turn when adults were conversing."

It was like a spark to well-laid tinder. Malta's mother surged to her feet and stepped between them. "When you were Malta's age, as I recall clearly, you were a barefoot hoyden climbing around in the ship's rigging and conversing freely with all kinds of people. And sometimes doing more than conversing."

Althea's face paled, making the smudges on it stand out more clearly. Malta smelled a secret there. Her mother knew something about Aunt Althea, something dirty. Secrets were power.

"Stop it." Grandmother spoke in a low voice. "You two have been apart for almost a year, and the first time you are in a room together, all you do is spit at each other like cats. I haven't stayed up all night to listen to you squabble. Sit down, all of you, and keep silent for a moment. I intend that you should listen to me."

Her mother returned slowly to her chair and her grandmother sat down with a sigh. As if to pique her sister, Althea sank down to sit on the hearthstones. She crossed her legs like a tailor; for a woman in trousers to sit like that struck Malta as obscene. She caught Malta staring at her and smiled back. Malta caught her mother's eye and gave a small shake of her head. Keffria gave a small sigh. Grandmother ignored it all.

"Instead of criticizing each other, we all need to look at our family's situation and do what we can to improve it," Grandmother began.

"Aren't you even going to ask her where she's been all this time and what she has been doing? We were worried to death about her! Now she comes dragging in, dirty and dressed like a man, and—"

"My niece is dressed like a woman, and is evidently being used as a lure to attract Rain Wild money. Why don't we talk about family pride and the morality of that first?" Althea demanded tartly.

Grandmother stood up and walked between them. "I said it was my turn to speak. I am trying to talk about what is most important first, before we bog down in bickering. We all have questions. Those questions will keep until we have determined if we can act as a family. If we cannot, then there is no point to asking the questions."

"If Althea had been here, as she should have been, she would know what we face," Keffria put in quietly. "But, I am sorry to interrupt. I will hear you out, Mother."

"Thank you. I will be brief. Some of this, Althea, I told you about earlier today, but not in detail. I think all of us need to consider our family's situation, rather than our own individual concerns. We need to set aside our differences. Or at least conceal them. We must decide where this family stands, and then we must show that image to Bingtown. We can show no trace of dissent. We could not weather the slightest breath of scandal."

Grandmother turned slightly so that her words were addressed more to Aunt Althea. "Althea, we are beset by our creditors. Our reputation is the only thing that keeps them at bay. Right now, they still believe that we will eventually pay them off, interest and all. Keffria and I—and Malta, I should add—have made many sacrifices to maintain an image of stability. We are living very simply. I have let go the servants, save for Rache. We have been doing for ourselves. We are not the only Bingtown Traders who have had to make this compromise, though few find themselves as straitened as we are. In some ways, it makes our situation worse. Many of our creditors are pinched; some who would have extended us understanding cannot afford to do so, for the sake of their own families."

Grandmother went on and on. It was too familiar a litany to Malta.

She had to fight to keep her eyes open. The only interesting thing was watching Aunt Althea as it was explained to her. Guilt and shame flickered across her face from time to time. Odd. Grandmother was not telling her that part of this was her fault, that if she had stayed at home properly she could have helped her family, but Althea still reacted as if the accusations had been spoken. When Grandmother spoke of how the Khuprus family had bought the note on the *Vivacia* and told her that there was no gracious way for little Malta to refuse the courtship, Althea even shot her a look of sympathy. Malta looked properly martyred in response.

Grandmother finished with, "I am sure you have noted the changes in the house and grounds. Now you know they were necessary sacrifices, not neglect. Althea, this is what I ask you to do. Stay home. Dress properly, behave sedately. If Keffria concurs, you might be helpful in managing some of the properties that demand a more active overseeing. Or, if you feel you need more . . . freedom, you could take over the little farm from my dowry. Ingleby is a quiet place, but cozy. It could benefit from someone taking an interest in it. You might find it satisfying to make a project of it, and see what you could—"

"Mother. That is not why I came home." Althea sounded almost sad. "I don't want a toy or a project. Nor do I wish to shame my family. I have come home to assist, but it will be in what I do best." Althea looked past Grandmother and locked eyes with her sister. "Keffria, you know the *Vivacia* should have been mine. You have always known that. I come home to claim her, to rescue her from being abused as a slaveship, and use her to create income for the family."

Malta leaped to her feet. "My father owns that ship. He will never allow you to take it from him."

Althea caught her breath. Anger blazed in her eyes. For an instant, she clenched her jaws. Then she turned aside from Malta to address only Keffria. She spoke in an even voice. "My sister, you 'own' the ship. What becomes of it is solely up to you. Bingtown is not Chalced, to steal a woman's wealth and give it to her husband. Moreover, you all heard Kyle vow before Sa that if I could but show him a ship's ticket saying I am a worthy sailor, he would give the ship to me. I have that ticket, stamped with the likeness of the liveship *Ophelia*. Both her master and her mate will speak out as to my worthiness to command. I have been away nearly a year. In that time, this has been my only thought: not to shame my family, but to prove myself worthy of that which should have been mine without question." Althea's voice took on a note of appeal as she added, "Keffria, don't you see? I have made it easy for you. Give me the ship. Kyle would be keeping his oath before Sa; you would be doing what you know is right. I give you my word, but I will commit it to writing if you wish: the profits from every voyage will go back into your estate, save enough for me to refit and sail again."

Malta felt sickened at her mother's expression. She was being swayed by Althea's words. But before she could intervene, Althea thwarted herself.

"How could this be hard for you?" she demanded rhetorically. "Kyle may object, but all you have to do is stand up to him. You should have stood up to him a long time ago. This is family business, Vestrit business, Bingtown Trader business. It has nothing to do with him."

"He is my husband!" Keffria cried out, affronted. "He has his faults, and I am sometimes angry at him. But he is not a pet, nor a piece of furniture. He is a part of my family. He is a part of this family. For good or ill, that bond exists, Althea. I am sick at how he is dismissed by you and Mother. He is my husband and the father of my children, and he truly believes he is doing what is right. If you cannot have any respect for him, could you not at least respect my feelings for him?"

"As he has respected mine?" Althea asked sarcastically.

"Stop it," Grandmother broke in, her voice low. "This is what I fear, more than anything. That we cannot set aside our own differences long enough to preserve our family fortune."

For a moment longer, the two daughters glowered at one another. Malta bit her tongue. She longed to leap up and say that Althea should just leave. What was she, anyway? A husbandless, childless woman, a dead branch on this family's tree. She had no interest in the family's fortune, save what riches it could bring to her. Malta and Selden were the ones most sharply affected by the mess that her grandparents' mismanagement had caused. It seemed so logical to her: why could they not see it? Her father was the only strong man that remained to them. His children would profit most or suffer greatest from how the fortune was handled. He should be the one to make all the decisions. Oh, if only he were here.

But he was not. All Malta could do was to be his eyes and ears for him. When he came back, he would know all. She would not let him walk about vulnerable to the treachery of these power-hungry women.

Her grandmother had risen. She stood between her quarreling daughters. Slowly and silently, she extended a hand to each of them. Neither daughter was eager; each reluctantly took her hand. "This is what I ask of you," she said quietly. "For now. Let our quarrels remain within our walls. Outwardly, let us act as one. Althea, Keffria, no action can be taken as regards the *Vivacia* until she returns to port. Let us, until then, do what we have not done for years. Let us live as a family in one house, putting all our efforts to our mutual good." She looked from one daughter to another. "You are not so different from one another as you believe. I think that once you have seen what your united strength can do, you will have no wish to oppose each other. You have taken opposite positions, but there are many possible compromises. Once you have come to know one another again, you may be more open to them."

The power her grandmother exerted over her daughters was almost palpable. A silence filled the room. Malta could almost feel them struggle to refuse. Neither would look at each other or their mother. Nevertheless, as the silence lengthened, first Althea and then Keffria lifted her eyes to the other. Malta clenched her hands into fists as their eyes met and something passed between them. What was it? A memory of long ago accord? An acknowledgment of duty to their family? Whatever it was, it bridged the gulf between them. There were no smiles, but the stubbornness faded from their mouths and eyes. Keffria lifted a traitorous hand toward her sister. Althea reached in surrender to take it. Grandmother heaved a vast sigh of relief. They closed the circle of family.

No one save Malta marked that she was excluded from it.

Coldness burned inside her as Ronica promised them, "You will not be sorry you tried. I promise you that."

Malta showed her bitter smile only to the dying fire. She had promises of her own to keep.

CHAPTER TWELVE

Portrait of Vivacia

BRASHEN LOUNGED AGAINST THE WALL IN THE CAPTAIN'S CABIN, ATTEMPT-ing to look both threatening and unconcerned. It was not an easy pose, keeping both his affable smile and his heavy truncheon equally in evidence. Then again, very little about this job had turned out to be as simple and easy as he had expected it to be.

A stream of servants bearing wares flowed through the cabin. They were rapidly transforming Finney's untidy domain into a showplace for the merchant's goods. The chart table already had been spread with a length of lush velvet the color of a blue midnight. Arranged against this backdrop and securely stitched to it to prevent theft were an assortment of earrings, necklaces, bracelets and baubles in a variety that indicated their many sources. The gaudy vied with the sophisticated. Every kind of precious stone or metal seemed to be represented. Finney sat at his ease, contemplating this trove. His thick fingers grasped the delicately fluted stem of a wine glass. The merchant-trader, a Durjan named Sincure Faldin, stood respectfully at his shoulder. He called Finney's attention to each piece of jewelry in turn.

As he gestured at a simple but elegant pearl necklace with matching earrings, he attested, "These, now, these were the property of a noble-man's daughter. Note the twisting of the gold links between each pearl, as well as their warm luminescence. It is well known that pearls bloom best on those of a passionate nature, and this woman . . . ah, what can I say of her, save that once she beheld her captors, she had no wish to be ransomed back to her wealthy family. Such pearls, it is said, if given to a cold woman will allow her hidden passions to surface, while if given to a warm-natured woman, well, a man does so at the risk of his own complete exhaustion."

The trader quirked his eyebrows and grinned broadly. Finney laughed aloud in delight.

The trader had a knack for tales. To hear him tell it, every piece on the table had a history at once romantic and fascinating. Never before had Brashen seen stolen goods so elaborately displayed. Resolutely alert, the mate drew his attention away from the brightly attired Sincure Faldin to keep an eye on his sons who were still bringing aboard and displaying other wares. The whole family seemed to share the father's flair for showmanship. Each of the three boys was dressed as opulently as his father, in garments fashioned from the same fabrics that one boy was now arranging in a rainbow of swaths unrolled from fat bolts of cloth. An older son had opened the doors of an elaborately carved cabinet he had carried aboard, to display several racks of tiny stoppered bottles. Brashen did not know if they were samples of liquors and wine or oils and perfumes. The third son had spread a white cloth over Captain Finney's bunk and was setting out a hodge-podge of weaponry, table cutlery, books, scrolls and other items. Even this was not done randomly. The knives were arranged in a fan of blades and hilts, the scrolls and books fixed open to illustrations, and every other item displayed in a way calculated to invite the eye and intrigue the buyer.

This third boy was the one Brashen watched most closely. He doubted they were anything other than diligent and enthusiastic merchants, but he had resolved to be more suspicious since the unfortunate incident ten days ago. It had taken the ship's boy the better part of a day to holystone that rogue's bloodstain from the *Springeve's* deck. Brashen was still unable to decide how he felt about what he had done. The man had forced him to act; he could not have simply stood by and let him rob the ship, could he? Yet, Brashen could not shake the uneasy notion that he should never have taken this berth. If he had not been here, he would not have had to shed blood.

Where would he have been? He had not known where this job was leading. Nominally, he had been hired on simply as the first mate. The *Springeve* was a lively little ship, shallow draft and skittish in high winds, but wonderful for negotiating the waterways to the lagoon towns and river settlements she frequented. Nominally, the *Springeve* was a tramp freighter and trader, hauling and bargaining whatever goods came her way.

The reality was grimmer. Brashen was whatever Captain Finney told him he was: mate, bodyguard, translator or longshoreman. As for Finney himself, Brashen still could not fathom the man. He wasn't sure if Finney had decided to trust him, or was testing him. The man's disarming frankness was a guise used to gull the mostly disreputable merchants who traded with him. The stout man could never have survived all his years in this trade if he were actually as trusting and open as he appeared to be. He was a capable man on board his ship, and adept at charming people. However, Brashen suspected that he was capable of near anything for self-survival. At some time, a knife had left a long mark across his belly; the ridged scar was at odds with the man's seemingly affable nature. Ever since Brashen had seen it, he had found himself watching his captain as closely as he did those whom came aboard to trade.

Now he watched Finney lean forward casually to tap, in swift succession, twelve different pieces of jewelry. "These I wish included in our trade. Take the others away. I have no interest in street vendors' wares." The captain never lost his easy smile, but the swiftly tapping finger had unerringly chosen what Brashen also considered the better pieces in Faldin's collection. Faldin smiled back at him, but Brashen's eyes caught a flash of unease on the merchant's face. Brashen's face remained neutral. Repeatedly, he had seen Finney do this. The man would be as soft and easy as a fat purring cat, but when it came to the bargaining, this Faldin would be lucky to walk off with the shirt still on his back. Brashen himself did not see the advantage to such a tactic. When he had worked for Ephron Vestrit, his captain had told him, "Always leave enough meat on the bones that the other man is also satisfied. Otherwise, you'll soon have no one willing to trade with you." Then again, Captain Vestrit had not been trading with pirates and those who disposed of stolen goods for pirates. The rules were bound to be different.

Since they had left Candletown, the *Springeve* had made a very leisurely trip up the coast of the Cursed Shores. The little craft had nosed up sluggish rivers and tacked into lagoons that were on no charts Brashen had ever seen. The whole section of "coast" known as the Pirate Isles was constantly in flux. Some claimed that the multitude of rivers and streams that dumped into the Inside Passage around the Pirate Isles were actually one great river, eternally shifting in its many-channeled bed. Brashen didn't much care if the steaming waters that emptied out into the channel were from one river or many. The facts were that although the warm water mellowed the climate of the Pirate Isles, it also stank, fouled boat bottoms at a prodigious rate, weakened ropes and lines and created billowing fogs in every season of the year.

Other ships did not willingly linger there. The air was humid, and what "fresh" water they took on turned green almost overnight. If the *Springeve* anchored close to shore, insects swarmed to feast on the crew. Strange lights danced often on these waters and sound traveled deceptively. Islands and channels shifted and disappeared as the wandering rivers dumped their silt and sand only to have a storm, rain flood or tide gulp away in a single night all that had been deposited during a month.

Brashen had only hazy memories of this area from the days when he had unwillingly sailed as a pirate. As a ship's boy, he had been little better than a slave. Weasel, they had called him when he crewed aboard the *Hope*. He had paid little attention to anything save scrabbling fast to stay ahead of a rope's end. He recalled the villages as tiny clusters of decaying huts. The only residents had been desperate men who had nowhere else to go. They had not been swaggering pirates, but little more than castaways who lived off whatever trade the true pirates brought to their tiny settlements.

Brashen winced at those memories. Now he had come full circle and could only marvel at how a few clusters of outlaw settlements had apparently grown into a network of towns. When he had been mate on the *Vivacia*, Brashen had listened skeptically to tales of permanent pirate settlements built on pilings or far up the brackish rivers and lagoons. Since he had begun sailing on the *Springeve*, he had gradually formed a different picture of these shifting islands and the bustling settlements that clung to their unreliable shores. Some were still little more than places where two ships might stop to trade goods, but others boasted houses with paint on their boards, and little shops along their muddy streets. The slave trade had swelled the population, and widened its variety. Artisans and educated slaves who had escaped Jamaillian owners rubbed elbows with criminals who had fled the Satrap's justice. Some residents had families. Women and children now formed a minor part of the population. Many of the escaped slaves were obviously trying to re-establish the lives stolen from them. They added a note of desperate civilization to the renegade towns.

Captain Finney seemed to rely solely on his memory to navigate the treacherous channels, tides and currents that brought them to each hamlet. Unerringly he guided the *Springeve* from town to town. Brashen suspected that he had private charts he consulted, but so far, he had not seen fit to give his mate so much as a glimpse of them. Such a lack of trust, Brashen reflected, as he watched the merchant's sons through narrowed eyes, almost demanded treachery in return. At least, he suspected that Finney would see the careful inking of shorelines and soundings that Brashen had marked onto the canvas scraps under his bunk as treachery. A good part of Finney's value as captain depended on his arcane knowledge of the Pirate Isles. He would see Brashen's careful hoard as a theft of his hard-won knowledge. Brashen saw it as the only long-term benefit he might carry away from this voyage. Money and cindin were all very well, but they were too soon gone. If fortune forced him into this trade, he would not sail as a mate forever.

"Hey. Brash. Over here. What do you think of this?"

He glanced away from the boys to the new selection of merchandise Finney was considering. Finney was holding up an illustrated scroll. Brashen recognized it as a copy of the Contradictions of Sa. The qualities of the parchment made him suspect it was a good one. Too familiar a knowledge of such things might indicate to Finney that he was not illiterate. He gave a shrug. "Lots of pretty colors and fancy birds."

"What do you think it's worth?"

Brashen shrugged. "To whom?"

Finney narrowed his eyes. "In a Bingtown shop, say."

"I've seen them there. Never wanted to buy one, myself."

Sincure Faldin rolled his eyes at the sailor's ignorance.

"I might take it." Finney began to rummage through the rest of the goods. "Set it aside for now. What is this?" There was a trace of amused annoyance in Finney's voice. "It's broken. You know I trade only in the finest merchandise. Take it away."

"Only the frame is damaged, no doubt in the haste of, er, salvaging it. The canvas is intact and quite valuable, I am told. It appears to be the work of a noted Bingtown artist. But that is not the only thing that makes it exceedingly valuable." His voice hinted of a great secret to share.

Finney pretended disinterest. "Oh, very well, I shall look at it. A ship. Now that's original. A ship under sail on a pretty day. Take it away, Sincure Faldin."

The merchant continued to hold the painting proudly. "I think you shall regret it if you let this get by you, Captain Finney. It was painted by Pappas. I am told he accepts few commissions, and that all of his canvases go dearly. However, as I told you, this is even more unique. It is a portrait of a liveship. It was taken from a liveship."

Brashen felt an odd little sideways wrench in his gut. Althea had commissioned a portrait of *Vivacia* from Pappas. He didn't want to look. He had to. Foolish not to, it could not be what he feared. No pirate vessel could ever overtake the *Vivacia*.

It was.

Brashen stared, sickened, at the familiar painting. It had hung in Althea Vestrit's stateroom on the *Vivacia*. The lovely rosewood frame was splintered where someone had hastily pried it free from the wall instead of unfastening it. *Vivacia* as she had been before she was quickened was the subject. In the painting, the figurehead's features were still, her hair yellow. Her graceful hull cut through the painted waves. The artist's skill was such that Brashen could almost see the clouds scudding across the sky. The last time he had seen that painting, it had still been securely fastened to a bulkhead. Had Althea left it there when she left the ship? Had it been taken from the ship by pirates, or somehow stolen from the Vestrit family home? The second possibility did not make sense. No thief would steal such a thing in Bingtown and then bring it to the Pirate Isles to sell it. The best prices for art were in Chalced and Jamaillia. Logic told him that the painting had been taken off the *Vivacia*. Yet, he could not believe pirates could have overtaken the sprightly little liveship. Even before she had quickened, Ephron Vestrit had been able to show her heels to anything that even considered pursuing her. Quickened and willing, nothing should have been able to catch her.

"You know the ship, Brash?" Finney asked in a soft, friendly voice.

The captain had caught him staring at the painting. He tried to make his look of dismay seem one of puzzlement. He knit his brows deeper.

"Pappas. I was looking at that name, thinking I knew it. Pappas, Pappas . . . naw. Pappay. That was the fellow's name. Terrible cheat at cards, but a good hand aloft." He gave Finney a shrug and a half-hearted grin. He wondered if he had fooled him.

"It's a liveship, out of Bingtown. Surely, you know her. Liveships are not that common." Finney pressed.

Brashen took a step closer, peered at the painting, then shrugged. "They're not that common, true. But they tie up at a different dock from the common ships. They keep to themselves, and idlers aren't too welcome there. Traders can be a snooty lot."

"I thought you were Trader born." Now both of them were looking at him.

He spat out a laugh. "Even Traders have poor relatives. My third cousin is the real Trader. I'm just a shirt-tail relative, and not a welcome sight on the family's doorstep. Sorry. What's her name plate say?"

"*Vivacia*," Finney said. "I thought that was a ship you'd served on. Didn't you say as much to the agent back in Candletown?"

Brashen cursed his cindin-fogged memories of that meeting. He shook his head thoughtfully. "No. I told him I was mate on the *Vicious Vixen*. She was out of a Six Duchies harbor, not Bingtown. Not a bad vessel, if you like living with a bunch of barbarians who think fish-head stew is a real treat. I didn't."

Finney and Faldin both chuckled dutifully. It wasn't much of a jest but it was enough to turn the topic. Faldin flourished the painting a final time; Finney dismissed it with a headshake. Faldin made a great show of carefully re-wrapping the painting, as if to emphasize the value that Finney was missing. Finney was already poking through the rest of the scrolls. Brashen tried to resume his watchful air, but he felt sick. The splintered frame indicated the painting had been taken hastily. Had she been sinking as the framed painting was torn off the wall? One of Faldin's boys, passing near him, shot him a fearful glance. Brashen realized he was glaring at no one, and rearranged his face.

Some of the men he had worked with aboard the *Vivacia* had been his comrades for years. Their faces rose in his memory: Grig, who could splice line faster than most men could lie, and Comfrey the prankster, and half a dozen others with whom he had shared the forecastle. The ship's boy, Mild, had had the makings of a top-notch sailor, if his love for mischief hadn't killed him first. He hoped they had had the good sense to turn pirate when they were offered that option. His need to ask the merchant what he knew of the liveship burned inside him. Was there a way to be curious without betraying himself? Brashen suddenly didn't care.

"Where did you get the picture of the liveship, anyway?" he asked.

The other two men turned to stare at him.

"Why do you care?" Captain Finney asked. His voice was not casual.

Sincure Faldin broke in, obviously still hoping to dispose of the painting. "The painting comes from the ship herself. Rarely is a liveship ever captured: this authentic memento of such an event is among the rarest of the rare." As he re-pitched the desirability of the painting, he had snatched it up and was once more freeing it of its shroud.

Brashen shifted the small plug of cindin in his lip. "Don't believe it, then," he said gruffly. He met Finney's eyes. "That's what was bothering me. If a man has a picture of a ship aboard, it is likely a picture of his own ship. But liveships don't get caught. Everyone knows that. It's a fake." He shifted his gaze, as if by chance, to the merchant. "Oh, I'm not calling you a liar," he added hastily at the look of outrage on Faldin's face. "I'm just saying whoever sold it to you was probably gulling you." He smiled at the man, knowing well that insinuating that a man didn't know what he was talking about was the best way to get him to share all he knew.

It worked. The trader's outrage faded to a look that was coldly smug. "I don't think so. Yet, I can understand why you might believe that was so. The taking of a liveship is not an ordinary feat. An ordinary man did not accomplish it. Captain Kennit did. If you know his name at all, you will not be surprised by it."

Captain Finney gave a snort of contempt. "That horse's ass? Is he still alive? I would have bet gold that someone would have spilled his guts by now. He isn't still spouting that nonsense about becoming the King of the Pirates, is he?"

For the first time, Brashen suspected Sincure Faldin's affront was genuine. The portly merchant drew himself up and took in a breath. His gaudy shirt filled like a sail bellying with wind. "You speak of a man who is all but engaged to my daughter. I have the highest regard for Captain Kennit, and am honored that he gives me the exclusive privilege of selling his goods. I will hear no disparagement of him."

Finney rolled his eyes at Brashen. "Then you won't hear anything from me about him. The man is insane, Sincure. He's a top-notch captain, and he runs a tight ship. I won't fault him there. Last year there was all that wild talk about him saying he was destined to be King of the Pirate Isles. Rumor was that he'd gone to the Others Island, and got an oracle to say it was so. Well, you know how much we all want a king. Faugh! Then the next thing I hear about him, he's running down slave-ships just for the sake of freeing the cargo. Not that I don't feel for those poor clods chained up in Chalcedean holds. I do. I feel for myself, too, when that damn Kennit stirred up enough dust that the boy Satrap thought he needed to send patrols out after pirates. The kid doesn't even have the sense to keep it a Jamaillian problem, no; he invites in Chalcedean privateers, supposed to clean us out of here. But all they're really doing is picking off the best cargoes for themselves and leaving us to take the blame." Finney shook his head. "King of the Pirate Isles. Sure.

That's just about exactly what we'd expected we would get from a king. More dung raining down on us."

Sincure Faldin crossed his arms stubbornly. "No, no, my dear friend. Far be it from me to disagree with a customer, but you are not seeing the larger picture. Kennit has done great good for us all. The slaves he has freed have joined us, supplying our towns with artisans and craftsmen, not to mention fertile women. Who used to flee to us? Murderers and rapists, thieves and cut-throats. Those few honest men who ended up among us have had to do as you and I have done: devise a way to make an honest living in the midst of disorder. Kennit has changed all that. He swells our towns with folk who ask no more than a chance to live free again. He will make of us a nation rather than a collection of bickering outposts for renegades and refugees. Yes, he stirred the Satrap's wrath. Those among us so blind as to think we still owed loyalty to a drug-lulled boy who is ruled by his women and advisors now see him for what he truly is. His actions have shattered that sentimental fealty. All of us are coming to realize that we owe no loyalty at all to Jamaillia, that our concerns should be only for ourselves."

A grudging agreement spread over Finney's face. "I don't say he's all bad. But we don't need a king. We've done fine running things ourselves."

Brashen dredged up a fragment of half-forgotten gossip. "Kennit. Isn't he the one who kills everyone aboard a ship when he takes it?"

"Not always!" Faldin objected. "Only on slaveships does he kill the whole crew. But there is a rumor he has spared some of the liveship's crew, although she was a slaver. The ship was joyous at being rescued. Now she dotes on Captain Kennit."

"A liveship was being used as a slaver, and when she was captured, she abandoned her loyalty to her family?" Brashen shook his head, amused and disdainful. He spoke to his captain. "I may not know this particular ship, but I know enough of liveships to tell you those two things cannot be true."

"But they are!" Faldin looked from one man to the other. "You do not have to believe me," he added in a superior voice. "You are only a day or so from Divvytown. Go there, if you doubt me. The liveship has been there the better part of a month, undergoing repairs. Speak to the slaves, now free folk, delivered by Kennit from her holds. I have not spoken to the ship myself, but those bold enough to do so say that she speaks well of her new captain."

Brashen's heart was thundering in his chest. He felt as if he could not get quite enough air. It couldn't be true. Everything he knew about *Vivacia* and liveships told him it could not be true. Every scrap of evidence that Sincure Faldin offered him told him that it was. He managed a shrug and then coughed in an attempt to ease the tightness in his throat. "Up to the captain," he managed to say. He made a great show of shifting the cindin in his mouth. He spoke around the plug. "He makes those decisions. Me?" He shifted the truncheon in his hands. "I do other things." He grinned at them both, a setting of his teeth.

"If you came to Divvytown, I could show you a much fuller selection of merchandise." Sincure Faldin had suddenly reverted to being a merchant. His smile returned as he made his spiel. "My warehouse is there. Kennit's most recent voyage has stocked it well for me, though there is little else that is actually from the liveship. Slaves were the major cargo. Those he has freed. He has chosen to keep the choice appointments of the officers' quarters intact and otherwise restore the ship. He has not felt well enough yet to welcome visitors, but I am told that the captain's quarters are very fine, all polished wood and shining brass."

Captain Finney made a nondescript noise. Brashen kept very still. The glint of interest had kindled in his captain's eyes. There was the prospect of seeing a captured liveship, perhaps even speaking to her. Given that sort of proof, and Faldin's assurance that the painting was the only trophy of its taking, he'd probably buy the portrait. Rarity always brought coin. Finney cleared his throat. "Well. Set the picture aside. I have got a bit of space in the hold to fill. Sounds like Divvytown might be the place to do it. If I see this liveship and your tale proves true, I'll buy the picture. Now. Let's back to business. Have you got any tapestries like those you sold me last year?"

HAMMERS RANG ABOVE A CHORUS OF SAWS BURRING. THE SMELL OF HARD-wood sawdust and fresh varnish filled the ship's companionways. The slaves that had crowded the decks and holds of the *Vivacia* had been replaced with gangs of carpenters and shipwrights. Wintrow stepped around a man applying varnish to a repaired doorframe, then dodged an apprentice bearing blocks of beeswax. With amazing swiftness, the *Vivacia* was being restored. The damage she had taken in the slave uprising had nearly been eradicated. Her holds were being cleaned, not just scrubbed but freshened by the careful burning of aromatic herbs. Soon only the stains of spilled blood would remain on her decks. Despite scrubbing, sanding or soaking, the wizardwood refused to forget.

Sorcor was very much in evidence, striding about the ship energeti-cally supervising everyone. His voice carried well and men jumped to obey his orders. Less obvious but no less commanding was Etta. She did not announce her presence with a bellowed command, but her quiet comments served just as well. Deckhands beamed at a word of praise from her. Wintrow had been watching her surreptitiously. He had expected that she would be waspish in her direction, sharply sarcastic. He had felt the razor edge of her tongue so often that he assumed it was her common demeanor. Instead, he discovered that she had a great talent for both charm and persuasion. He also detected the careful line she walked to get tasks accomplished to her satisfaction without interfering with Sorcor's authority. When the mate and the captain's woman were in proximity, they displayed both camaraderie and rivalry. It intrigued and puzzled Wintrow. Both their bond and their dispute was Kennit.

How could one man command such loyalty from such diverse people? At the monastery, one oft-repeated old saying was "Sa's hand can fit around any tool." It was usually uttered when an unlikely novice suddenly bloomed with talent. After all, Sa had a purpose for all things. It was the limit of humanity that those reasons could not always be perceived. Maybe Kennit truly was a tool of Sa, and was aware of his destiny. Wintrow supposed that stranger things had happened. He simply could not recall any.

Wintrow rapped once at a freshly restored door, then worked the latch and entered. Despite the sunshine slanting in through the porthole, the chamber seemed dark and close. "You should open the window and let in some fresh air," he observed aloud. He set down the tray he was carrying.

"Shut the door," his father replied gruffly. He unfolded his legs, stretched, and then stood. The rumpled bed behind him retained the imprint of his body. "What did you bring me this time? Sawdust cakes full of weevils?" He glared at the door that still stood open. In one angry stride he crossed the small room and slammed it shut.

"Turnip and onion soup and wheatcakes," Wintrow replied evenly. "The same food that everyone else got today."

Kyle Haven grunted in reply. He lifted the bowl of soup, poked it with a finger. "It's cold," he complained, and then drank it where he stood. His whiskery throat moved as he swallowed. Wintrow wondered when he had last shaved. When he lowered the bowl, he wiped his mouth on the back of his hand. He caught his son staring and glared back. "Well? What sort of manners do you expect of a man kept like a dog in a kennel?"

"There are no longer any guards on the door. I asked some days ago if you might be allowed out on deck. Kennit said you could, so long as I was with you and took responsibility for you. It is your own decision to remain in this room as if it were a cell."

"I wish there were a mirror in here, so I could see if I look as stupid as you think I am," his father retorted sourly. He snatched up a wheatcake and wiped out the bowl with it before he bit into it. "You'd like that, wouldn't you?" he muttered around a mouthful of food. "You could trot along beside me on deck, and be oh-so-surprised and horrified when some sneaking bastard put a knife in my ribs. Then you would be rid of me for good and all. Don't think that I don't know that's what you want. That's

what this has all been about. Not that you have the guts to do it yourself.
Oh, no, not the boy in the skirts. He prays to Sa, rolls his big brown eyes,
and sets it up for others to do his dirty work. What's this?"

"Alde tea. And if I wanted so badly to be rid of you, I'd have poisoned
it." Wintrow heard with a shock the heartless sarcasm in his own voice.

His father halted with the mug halfway to his lips. He gave a hoarse
bark of laughter. "No, you wouldn't. Not you. You'd get someone else to
poison it, and then you would give it to me, so you could pretend none of
it was your doing. Not my fault, you could whine, and when you crawled
back to your mother, she would believe you and let you go back to your
monastery."

Wintrow pinched his lips together. *I am living with a madman*, he
reminded himself. *Conversing with him is not going to bring him to his senses.
His mind has turned. Only almighty Sa can cure him and only in his own time.*
He found a modicum of patience within himself. He tried to believe it
was not a show of defiance when he crossed the small room and opened
the window.

"Shut that," his father growled. "Do you think I want to smell that
scummy little town out there?"

"It smells no worse than the stench of your own body that fills this
room," Wintrow countered. He walked two steps away from the open
window. At his feet was his own pallet, seldom slept in, and the small
bundle of clothes he could call his own. Nominally, he shared this small
room with his father. The reality was that he slept most nights on the
foredeck near Vivacia. The proximity made him uncomfortably aware of
her thoughts, and through her, the presence of Kennit's dreams. Still, that
was preferable to his father's irascible and critical company.

"Is he going to ransom us?" Kyle Haven demanded suddenly. "He
could get a good price for us. Your mother probably could scrape up a bit,
and the Bingtown Traders would come through with more, to get a liveship back. Does he know that? That he could get a good price for us? You
should tell him that. Has he sent a ransom note yet?"

Wintrow sighed. Not this conversation again. He cut swiftly to the
meat of it, hoping for a mercifully quick end. "He doesn't want to ransom
the ship, Father. He intends to keep it. That means I have to stay with it.
I don't know what he plans to do with you. I've asked him, but he doesn't
answer. I don't want to make him angry."

"Why? You never feared to make me angry!"

Wintrow sighed. "Because he is an unpredictable man. If I push him,
he may take . . . rash action. To demonstrate his power. I think it is
wiser to wait for him to see he has nothing to gain from holding you. As
he heals, he seems more reasonable. In time—"

"In time I shall be little more than a living corpse, shut up in here,
taunted and mocked and despised by all on this ship. He seeks to break

me with darkness and poor food and no company save that of my idiot son!"

His father had finished eating. Without a word, Wintrow picked up the tray and turned to go. "That's right, run away! Hide from the truth." When Wintrow made no reply as he opened the door, his father bellowed after him, "Make sure you take the chamberpot and empty it! It stinks."

"Do it yourself." Wintrow's voice came out flat and ugly. "No one will stop you."

He shut the door behind himself. His grip on the tray was so tight his knuckles were white. His molars hurt where his teeth were clenched together. "Why?" he asked aloud of no one. More quietly, he added to himself, "How could that man be my father? I feel no bond to him at all."

He felt a faint tremor of sympathy from the ship.

Just before he reached the galley door, Sa'Adar caught up with him. Wintrow had been aware of him following him since he left his father's room, but he had hoped to elude him. The priest became more frightening with every passing day. He had all but disappeared for a time, after Etta had marked him with her knife. Like some parasitic creature, he had burrowed deep into the holds of the ship, to work his poison silently among the freed men and women. There were fewer discontents as the days passed. Kennit and his crew treated them even-handedly. They were fed as well as any crew member, and the same level of effort was expected from them in caring for the ship.

When they reached Divvytown, it was announced to the former slaves that any who wished to disembark might take their freedom and go. Captain Kennit wished them well and hoped they would enjoy their new lives. Those who desired could request to stay aboard as crew, but they would have to prove themselves worthy and loyal sailors to Kennit. Wintrow had seen the wisdom in that; Kennit had effectively pulled Sa'Adar's teeth. Any slave who truly desired a life of piracy and had the skill to compete could claim one. The others had their freedom. Not many had taken the road to piracy.

The taller, older man stepped abruptly around Wintrow. Sa'Adar stood before him, blocking his passage. Wintrow glanced past him. He was alone. He wondered if his map-face guards had forsaken him to regain lives of their own. Wintrow had to turn his eyes up to look at Sa'Adar. The man's face was graven with discontent and fanaticism. His unkempt hair spilled onto his forehead; his clothes had not been washed in days. His eyes burned as he accused, "I saw you leave your father's room."

Wintrow spoke civilly and ignored the question. "I'm surprised you are still aboard. I am sure there is much work for a priest of Sa in a place like Divvytown. The freed slaves would surely appreciate your assistance in beginning new lives there."

Sa'Adar narrowed his dark eyes at Wintrow. "You mock me. You mock my priesthood, and in doing so you mock yourself and Sa." His hand snaked out to seize Wintrow's shoulder. The boy still gripped his father's breakfast tray. He clutched it tightly to keep from spilling the crockery on the deck, but he stood his ground. "You forsake your priesthood and Sa in what you do here. This is a ship built of death, speaking with death's tongue. A follower of the Life God should not be servant to it. But it is not too late for you, lad. Recall who you are. Align yourself once more with life and right. You know this ship belongs by right to those who seized it for themselves. This vessel of cruelty and bondage could become a ship of freedom and righteousness."

"Let me go," Wintrow said quietly. He tried to squirm out of the madman's grip.

"This is my last warning to you." Sa'Adar came very close to him, his breath hot and rancid in Wintrow's face. "It is your last chance to redeem yourself from your past errors and put your feet on the true path to glory. Your father must be delivered to judgment. If you are the instrument of that, your own part in the transgressions can be forgiven. I myself will judge it is so. Then this ship must be surrendered to those who rightfully claim her. Make Kennit see that. He is a sick man. He cannot withstand us. We rose and unseated one despot. Does he believe we cannot do it again?"

"I believe that if I spoke such words to him, it would be death for you. Death for myself as well. Sa'Adar. Be content with what he has given you: a new chance at life. Seize it and go on." Wintrow tried to writhe away, but the man only tightened his grip. He bared his teeth in a snarl. Wintrow felt his self-control slipping. "Now get your hands off me and let me go." Suddenly, vividly, he was recalling this man in the hold of the *Vivacia*. Freed of his chains, his first act had been to take Gantry's life. Gantry had been a good man, in his way. A better man than Sa'Adar had ever shown himself to Wintrow.

"I warn you—" the erstwhile priest of Sa began, but Wintrow's pent grief and banked anger suddenly overwhelmed him. He shoved the wooden tray hard into the man's gut. Taken by surprise, Sa'Adar staggered back, gasping for air. A part of Wintrow knew it was enough. He could have walked away. He was shocked when he dropped the tray, to drive two more blows into the man's chest. In detachment, he saw his right, and then his left fist connect. They were body punches, connecting with satisfyingly solid sounds. Even so, Wintrow was amazed to see the taller man give ground, stumbling back against the wall and sliding partially down it. It shocked him to discover his own physical strength. Worse, it felt good to knock the man down. He gritted his teeth, resisting the impulse to kick him.

"Leave me alone," he warned Sa'Adar in a low growl. "Don't talk to me again or I'll kill you."

The shaken man coughed as he clambered up the wall. Puffing, he pointed a finger at Wintrow. "See what you've become! It's the voice of this unnatural ship, using you as mouthpiece! Break free, boy, before you are damned forever!"

Wintrow turned on his heel and strode away. He left the tray and crockery where it had fallen. It was the first time in his life he had fled from the truth.

KENNIT SHIFTED IN HIS BEDDING. HE WAS DAMNABLY TIRED OF BEING CON-fined to his bunk, but both Wintrow and Etta had convinced him that he must endure it a bit longer. He frowned at himself in a bedside mirror, then set his razor aside. His freshly trimmed mustache and beard improved his appearance, but the swarthiness of his skin had turned sallow and the flesh had fallen away from his cheeks. He practiced his hard stare at the mirror. "I look cadaverous," he said aloud to the empty room. Even his voice sounded hollow. He set the mirror aside with a sharp clack. The action focused his attention on his hands. Veins and tendons stood out on their backs in sharp relief. When he turned them over, the palms looked soft as tallow. He made a fist and gave a snort of disdain at the result. It looked like a knot tied in a piece of old string. The wizardwood talisman, once strapped tightly to his pulse point, now dangled about his wrist. The silvery wood had gone gray and checked as if it, too, suffered from his lack of vitality. Kennit's lips tightened in a bare smile. Good. It should have brought him luck and instead it had served him this. Let the charm share his fate. He tapped at it with his fingernail. "Nothing to say?" he jeered at it. It was impassive.

Kennit snatched up the mirror again and peered into it. His leg was healing; they all told him he would live. What was the good of that if he could no longer command respect from his crew? He had become a withered scarecrow of a man. His haggard reflection reminded himself of a street beggar in Divvytown.

He slammed the mirror down again on the bedside table, half daring himself to break it. The ornate frame and heavy glass defied him. He flung the covers back from his legs and glared down at his stump. It lay on the creamy linen like a badly stuffed sausage, slightly withered at the end. He poked it savagely with a finger. The pain had receded substantially, leaving behind an obnoxious sensation between a tingle and an itch. He lifted it from the bed. It looked ridiculous, a seal's flipper, not a man's leg. Total despair washed over him. He imagined drawing cold salt water into his mouth and nose, pulling icy death into him, refusing to choke or splutter. It would be quick.

The passion of his despair retreated abruptly, stranding him in help-lessness. He did not even have the wherewithal to take his own life. Long before he managed to drag himself to the ship's railing, Etta would clutch at him, whining and imploring and bearing him back to this bed. Perhaps that had always been her aim in maiming him. Yes. She had chopped off his leg and fed it to the sea serpent so that she could finally master him. She intended to keep him here as her pet while she secretly undermined his command and became the true captain of the ship. Teeth clenched, fists knotted, the anger that rushed through him was intoxicating in its fierceness. He tried to feed on it, imagining in detail how she had probably planned it for months. Her eventual goal was to keep the liveship for herself, of course. Sorcor was probably involved in it as well. He would have to be very careful to conceal from them that he suspected. If they knew, they'd—

Ridiculous. It was ridiculous and silly, the product of his long convalescence. Such thoughts were unworthy of him. If he must put such intensity of feeling into something, then let him put it into regaining his health. Etta might be lacking in many things, including breeding and courtesy, but she was certainly not plotting against him. If he was tired of his bed, he should tell them so. It was a fine spring day. He could be assisted to the foredeck. She would love to see his face again. It had been so long since they had talked.

Kennit had dim, resentful memories of his mother's gentle hands carefully unfolding his chubby fingers from some forbidden object he had managed to possess. So had she spoken to him then, softly and reasonably as she took the gleaming wood and shining metal of the knife away. He recalled he had not succumbed to her gentleness but had screamed his displeasure. He felt the same defiance now. He did not want to be reasonable, he did not want to be consoled with something else. He wanted his fury to be justified and proven.

But Vivacia was inside him, weaving herself through his being. He was too weakened to resist her as she took his angry suspicions and set them out of his reach. He was left with a sourceless dissatisfaction that made his head ache. He blinked the sting of tears from his eyes. Weepy, like a woman, he jeered at himself.

Someone tapped at his door. He took his hands away from his face. He flipped the blankets back over the remains of his legs. A moment, to compose himself. He cleared his throat. "Enter."

He had expected Etta. Instead, it was the boy. He stood uncertainly in the door. The dim companionway framed him and the light from the stern windows fell on his face. His tattoo was hidden in shadow. His face was unflawed and open. "Captain Kennit?" he queried in a low voice. "Did I wake you?"

"Not at all. Come in." He could not say why the sight of Wintrow was like balm to his spirit. Perhaps it had to do with the ship's feelings. The boy's appearance had improved since he had been in Kennit's care.

He smiled at the youth as he approached the bed, and had the pleasure of seeing the boy shyly return it. His coarse black hair was sleeked back from his face and bound into the traditional seaman's queue. The clothing Etta had sewn suited him well. The loose white shirt, a bit large for him, was tucked into his dark blue trousers. He was small for his age, a lean and supple youth. Wind and sun had weathered the boy's face. The warm color of his skin, his white teeth and dark eyes, the dark trousers merging into the darkness of the corridor behind him: it was all a chance composition of perfect light and shadow. Even the hesitant, questioning look on his face was perfect as he emerged from dimness into the muted light of the chamber.

Another step carried Wintrow further into the room. The tattoo on his face was suddenly not only visible; it was an indelible flaw, a stain on the boy's innocence. The pirate could see the torment in the boy's eyes, and sensed a misery in him. Kennit knew a moment of rage. "Why?" he demanded suddenly. "Why were you marked like that? What possible excuse did he have?"

The boy's hand flew to his cheek. A flickering show of emotions rushed across his face: shame, anger, confusion, and then impassivity. His voice was even and low. "I suppose he thought it would teach me something. Perhaps it was his revenge because I had not been the son he wished me to be. Perhaps it was his way of repairing that. He made me a slave instead of his son. Or . . . it could have been something else. He was, I think, jealous of my bond with the ship. When he marked my face with hers, it was his way of saying we were welcome to one another, because we had rejected him. Maybe."

It was enlightening to watch Wintrow's face as he spoke. The careful words could not completely disguise the pain. The boy's floundering attempts at an explanation revealed that it was a question he had agonized over often. Kennit suspected that none of the possible answers satisfied him. It was obvious his father had never bothered to explain it. The boy advanced to his bedside. "I need to look at your stump now," he said. Blunt, this boy was. He didn't call it a leg, or an injury. It was a stump and that was what he called it. He didn't mince his way past Kennit's feelings. That integrity was oddly comforting. The boy would not lie to him.

"You say you had rejected your father. Is that how you still feel about him?" Kennit could not say why the boy's answer would be so important to him.

A shadow crossed the boy's face. For a moment, Kennit thought Wintrow would lie to him. But the hopelessness of truth was in his voice when he spoke. "He is my father." The words were almost a cry of protest. "I owe him the duty of a son. Sa commands us to respect our parents and exult over any goodness we find in them. But in truth, I wish—" His voice dropped lower as if to speak the thought shamed him. "I wish he were out of my life. Not dead, no, I don't wish that," he added hastily as he met Kennit's intent stare. "I just wish he were somewhere else. Somewhere safe but," his voice faltered guiltily, "where I just didn't have to deal with him anymore," he finished in a near whisper. "Where I didn't have to feel diminished each time he looked at me."

"I can arrange that," Kennit answered him easily. The stricken look on the boy's face plainly wondered what wish he had just been granted. He started to speak, then apparently decided that keeping silent was safer.

"Does the tattoo bother you?" he heard himself ask as Wintrow turned the blankets back. The boy-priest bent over Kennit's leg, his hands hovering above the stump. Kennit could almost feel a tickling ghost-touch on his flesh.

"A moment," Wintrow requested quietly. "Let me try this."

Kennit waited expectantly for him to do something. Instead, Wintrow became absolutely still. He held his hands fractionally above Kennit's stump, so close he could feel the warmth of the boy's palms. The gaze of his eyes was focused on the backs of his own hands. The tip of his tongue crept out of his mouth and he bit it in his concentration. His breath moved in and out of him so silently, it was as if he did not breathe at all. The pupils of his eyes grew large, almost erasing the color. His hands trembled slightly as in vast effort.

After a few moments, the boy drew a sharp breath in. He lifted his eyes to give Kennit a dazed glance and shrugged in disappointment. He sighed. "I suppose I'm doing it wrong. You should have felt something." He frowned to himself, then remembered Kennit's question about his tattoo. He answered as if they were discussing the weather. "When I think of it. I wish it were not there. However, it is there, and will be there the rest of my life. The sooner I accept it as part of my face, the wiser I will be."

"Wiser how?" Kennit pressed him.

Wintrow smiled, thinly at first, but as he spoke it grew more genuine. "It was said often at my monastery, 'The wise man takes the shortest path to peace with himself.' Acceptance of what is, that is the shortest path." As he spoke the final words, his hands came to rest on Kennit's stump in a light but firm grip. "Does this hurt?"

Warmth started at the boy's hands and shot out from them. A jolt of heat went up Kennit's spine. The pirate was struck dumb. Wintrow's words seemed to echo through his bones. *Acceptance of what is. That is the shortest path to peace with yourself. This is wisdom. Does it hurt? Does wisdom hurt? Does peace hurt? Does acceptance hurt?* His skin tightened and tingled all over his body. Kennit gasped for breath. He could not answer. He was suffused with the boy's simple faith. It rushed through him, warm and reassuring. Of course, he was right. Acceptance. He could not doubt or deny it. What had he been thinking? Whence the weakness that had made him falter? His earlier thoughts of drowning himself were suddenly abhorrent, the self-pitying whining of a weakling. He was meant to go on, he was destined to go on. His luck had not failed him when the serpent took his leg. His luck had sustained him; his leg was all it had taken.

Wintrow took his hands away. "Are you all right?" he asked worriedly. The words seemed unnaturally loud to Kennit's renewed senses.

"You've healed me," he said in a hoarse whisper. "I'm healed." He dragged himself to a sitting position. He looked down at his leg, almost expecting to find it restored. It was not, it was a stump, and there was still a pang of loss at beholding it. But that was all. The shape of his body had changed. Once he had been young and beardless, and now he was not. Once he had walked upon two legs; now he would learn to get about on one. That was all. A change. To be accepted.

Quick as a cat's pounce, he seized the boy by his shoulders and jerked him near. Wintrow cried out and braced his hands on the bunk to keep from falling. Kennit captured the boy's head between his hands. For an instant, Wintrow struggled. Then his eyes locked with Kennit's. He stared, his gaze going wider and wider. Kennit smiled at him. He smoothed one long thumb across the boy's tattoo. "Wipe it away," he commanded him. "On your face, it goes no deeper than your skin. You do not need to bear it on your soul." For five breaths more Kennit held him, until he saw a sort of wonder cross Wintrow's features. Kennit placed a kiss on his brow, then released him. As Wintrow drew back, Kennit sat all the way up. He swung his leg off the bed.

"I'm tired of lying here. I need to be up and about. Look at me. I'm wasted to a shadow of myself. I need wind in my face, and plenty of food and drink. I need to command on my own deck again. Most of all, I need to discover what I can and cannot do. Sorcor made me a crutch. Is it still about?"

Wintrow had staggered back from the bedside. He looked shocked at the change in the man. "I . . . I believe it is," he stuttered.

"Good. Lay out some clothes for me and help me dress. No. Lay out clothes for me and leave me to dress myself while you go to the galley. Bring me back a proper meal. If Etta is about, send her to me. She can fetch me bathing water. Be quick, now. The day is half spent as it is."

It brought him great satisfaction to see Wintrow hasten to obey his commands. The boy knew how to take an order; now, that was a useful thing in a pretty lad, and no mistake. He did not know his way about Kennit's possessions. Etta was better at matching up his clothes, but what Wintrow had set out was serviceable enough. There would be plenty of time to educate his eye for dress.

When Wintrow had bowed his way out of the room, Kennit turned his attention to educating himself. His shirt was not too difficult, but it displeased him to see how his chest and arms had dwindled. He refused to dwell on it. The trousers were more of a challenge. Even standing on his leg and leaning on the bed, it was awkward. The fabric hung up on his stump and rubbed against the new skin unpleasantly. He told himself he would soon build a callus. The empty pant leg flapped in a ghastly way; Etta would have to pin that for him, or better yet, sew it. The leg was gone. There was little sense in pretending otherwise.

He grinned wryly as he struggled with a single stocking and boot. Why should half as much work take twice as long? His body kept overbalancing and teetering on the edge of the bed. He was just finishing when Etta entered the room. She gave a start at the sight of him sitting jauntily on the edge of the bed. Her gaze turned reproachful. "I would have helped you with all that." She set a basin and a jug of hot water down on the stand by his bed. The scarlet blouse she wore picked up the red of her lips. Her skirts were black silk and shifted with her hips, rustling invitingly when she walked.

"I didn't need help," he retorted. "Save with this pant leg. You should have sewn them up for me. I intend to be out of bed today. Where is my razor? Do you know where my crutch is?"

"I think you are rushing yourself," she complained. She frowned at him. "Only the night before last, you still had a touch of fever. You probably feel better, Kennit, but you are far from healthy. Your bed is the place where you belong, for a time yet." She came to the bed and began to fuss with his pillows, as if she would make him lie down again. How dare she? Had she completely forgotten who he was and what she was?

"My bed is my place?" His hand shot out, to trap her wrist. Before she could react, he jerked her close to him, his other hand seizing her jaw. He turned her face to meet his eyes. "Don't ever tell me what I am healthy enough to do!" he reminded her severely. The closeness of her, her quick breath against his face and her wide eyes, suddenly stirred him. She took in a quick fearful breath and triumph coursed through him. This was right. Before he could take command on his deck again, he'd have to take command in his own chamber. This woman must not be allowed to think she was in charge. He hooked one arm about her waist and pulled her close. With his free hand, he seized the front of her skirt and hiked it up. She gasped as he pulled her against him. "My bed is where you belong, wench," he told her in a voice suddenly gone husky.

"If you say so," she murmured submissively. Her eyes were black and huge. Her breath was coming very fast. He could almost hear the rapid beating of her heart. There was no resistance left in her as he yarded her onto the bunk and pushed her down.

THE SUN WAS JUST GOING DOWN AS THE SPRINGEVE SAILED INTO DIV-vytown's so-called harbor. Brashen looked at the sprawling settlement with amazement. When he had been here last, years ago, there had been a few huts, a wharf and some shacks that passed for taverns. Now candle-light shone through dozens of windows, and the brackish anchorage boasted a small forest of masts. Even the smells of squalor that hung in the air had become thicker. If all the scattered pirate settlements he had seen were gathered into one place, they would equal or possibly exceed the population of Bingtown. They were growing, too. If they were mus-tered under one leader, they would be a force to reckon with. Brashen wondered if that was the potential this Kennit, would-be King of the Pirates, also saw. If he gained such power, what would he do with it? Captain Finney had seemed to think him mostly a braggart; Brashen fervently hoped it was so.

Then, as they passed slowly down the long line of anchored vessels, Brashen saw a familiar profile limned against the setting sun. His heart turned over in his chest then sank inside him. The *Vivacia* rocked at anchor there. At her masthead, the Raven flag fluttered fitfully in the evening breeze. Brashen tried to convince himself that it was only a ship similarly outfitted and with a similar figurehead. Abruptly Vivacia gave her head a shake, then reached up to smooth her hair. It was a liveship all right, and she was unmistakably Vivacia. This Kennit had captured her. If the rumors were true, that meant that every one of her crewmen had been slaughtered. He squinted at the silhouetted ship, trying to make out more detail. A skeleton crew moved leisurely about on her decks. He did not recognize anyone; would he have recognized any of them, in this light, at this distance? He did not know. Then he spotted a small slender figure coming onto the foredeck. The figurehead turned to exchange greetings. He knit his brow. The way the sailor moved seemed familiar. Althea! No, he told himself. It could not be. He had last seen Althea in Candletown. She had declared she would find work on a Bingtown-bound ship. *Vivacia* had not been in the harbor. She could not be on the ship. It was impossi-ble. Save that he was familiar with the strange ways of winds, tides and ships, and how unlikely paths always seemed to cross in the strangest ways.

He watched the slender figure come to the bow rail and lean on it. He stared, hoping for some gesture, some sign that would let him know it was or was not Althea. He got none. Instead, the longer he watched the more convinced he became that it was she. So did Althea cock her head when she listened to the ship. Thus did she lift her face to the wind. Who else would converse so familiarly with the figurehead? By what chance, he knew not, but the figure on the foredeck was Althea.

Brashen's emotions churned. What should he do? He was one man alone. He had no way to make his presence known to her or the ship. Anything he tried now would likely just get him killed, and no one in Bingtown would ever know what had become of any of them. His dull fingernails bit right through his callused palms. He closed his eyes tightly and tried to think what, if anything, he could do.

Captain Finney spoke softly from close behind him. "Sure you don't know her?"

Brashen managed a shrug. His voice was too tight. "I could have seen her before . . . I don't know. I was just marveling. A liveship, taken by a pirate. That's a first."

"No, it ain't." Finney spat over the side. "Legend says that Igrot the Bold took a liveship and used it for years. That's how he managed to take the Satrap's treasure ship. Fleet as it was, it couldn't outrun a liveship. After that, Igrot lived like a gentleman. The best of everything for himself, women, wine, servants, clothes. Lived very elegant, they say. He had an estate in Chalced and a palace in the Jade Islands. It has been said that when Igrot knew he was dying, he hid his treasure and scuttled his liveship. If he couldn't take the damn thing with him, he was going to be sure no one else got it."

"I've never heard that before."

"Probably not. It's not a commonly told tale. They say he kept it painted and made it keep still so no one would know what he had."

Brashen shrugged stiffly. "Sounds to me like he had a regular ship, but just lied about it to make people think it was a liveship. Maybe," he added in a more conciliatory tone. He glanced about the deck to be sure they were alone, then shifted the conversation abruptly. "Cap. Remember what we talked about, months ago? About how maybe you'd like to make a little side run into Bingtown if I knew of anyone who could make you a good price on some choice bits?"

Finney gave a short, guarded nod.

"Well, I've just been thinking. If you were to buy that portrait from Faldin, well, the place it would sell best is Bingtown. That's where folk would know what it was and how much it was worth." He crossed his arms and leaned back against the railing. He tried to look like a man well pleased with himself.

"And that's also where a man could get into the hottest water, selling such a thing," Finney pointed out suspiciously.

Brashen affected a casualness he did not feel. "Not if you knew the right people and pitched it the right way. Now, if you came to town, and I hooked you up with the right go-between, why, you could make it seem like you were doing a good deed. Just bringing the portrait home, with a sad tale of what you knew. Leave it to the go-between that such a kind-hearted trader captain deserved a hefty reward for such a turn."

Finney moved a quid of cindin in his lip. "Maybe. But the trip wouldn't be worth it just to unload one piece."

"Of course not! I'm just betting that would be the plum piece of the deal. It might bring you a lot more than you'd imagine."

"Maybe a lot more trouble than I'd imagined, too." Finney scowled into the sunset. After a time, he asked, "What else do you suppose might go there?"

Brashen shrugged. "Anything Bingtown can't make for itself or get from further north. Think spices, teas . . . Jamaillian spirits and wines. Exotic stuff from the southlands, or good Jamaillian antiques. That sort of thing."

"You know of someone who would be the go-between?"

Brashen tilted his head. "I've thought of a likely candidate." He gave a brief chuckle. "If all else failed, I suppose I could try doing it myself."

Finney wordlessly held out his hand. Brashen took it and in the clasp the deal was sealed. He felt a deep sense of relief. He had a way to carry word back to Bingtown. Surely Ronica Vestrit would have the where-withal to rescue both her daughter and her ship from these pirates. He glanced back at the *Vivacia* and Althea apologetically. This flimsy plan was the best rescue effort he could offer. He prayed Althea and the ship would both be well until then.

He swore suddenly and vehemently.

"What's the matter?" Finney demanded.

"Nothing. Just got a splinter under my nail. I'll put the boys to sand-ing this railing tomorrow." He turned away from his captain and made a pretense of examining his hand.

In the distance, the slim silhouette urinated off the side of the *Vivacia.*

SUMMER

CHAPTER THIRTEEN

Interlude

IT WAS NOT A TRUE TANGLE, SHREEVER REFLECTED TO HERSELF. A TRUE tangle gathered itself to follow a respected leader. These were stray serpents whom they had picked up one or two at a time as the provider moved north and the tangle followed it. The serpents that swam alongside them now shared no camaraderie with Maulkin's tangle. They were simply following the same food source. Still, there was comfort in the company of other serpents. Some of them seemed almost lucid at times. Others were ghost-like in their silence and blank stares. The worst ones were little better than animals, likely to turn venom or fangs on anyone who came too close to food they had claimed. Shreever, Maulkin and Sessurea had learned to ignore those who had reverted to such a bestial level. In truth, their presence was not the hardest to bear. The heart-wringing ones were those who were pathetically close to recalling who they were and what they had been.

The three original serpents of Maulkin's tangle had fallen almost as silent as the newcomers. It was difficult to find topics that did not lead all of them deeper into despair. Shreever could dimly recall earlier times of physical starvation. Too long a fast could make anyone's thoughts become scattered and unfocused. She had her small rituals to keep herself sane. Daily she reminded herself of their purpose. They had come north when Maulkin had known the time was right. She Who Remembers should have greeted them. That one should have renewed all their memories, and should have led them through the next step.

"But what would that be?" she muttered softly to herself.

"Eh?" Sessurea asked sleepily.

The three were anchored together in the midst of a grove of slumbering serpents. There were about a dozen of the other serpents. Only at night did they seem to recall any vestige of civilized ways, and link their coils in slumber as if they were a true tangle. Shreever gripped her thought tightly. "After we find One Who Remembers, and our memories are restored. What happens then?"

Sessurea heaved a sleepy sigh. "If I knew the answer to that, perhaps we would not need to find a memory keeper."

Between them, Maulkin did not even stir. The prophet seemed to dwindle every day. She and Sessurea had become more aggressive in holding on to the food the provider distributed to them. Maulkin refused to forsake the old ways. Even after he had grasped a limp body tumbling through the Plenty, if one of the soulless ones seized it, he would let it go. He would relinquish his rightful claim to food rather than fight for it like an animal. The once bright false-eyes that ran the length of his body were now little more than dappling in his color. Sometimes, he would allow Shreever to bring him food, but as often he turned away from it. She had not had the courage to ask him if he, too, were close to abandoning their quest.

There was a sudden shifting in the forest of sleeping serpents. With dreamlike slowness, a slender, verdantly green serpent wriggled free of the slumbering tangle and languorously rose up to the Lack. Shreever and Sessurea exchanged glances that were at once puzzled and too weary to be curious. The actions of the soulless ones made no sense; there was no future in speculating about his action. Shreever lidded her eyes.

Then, from high above them, came the curiously pure notes of a voice raised in song. For a time, Shreever listened in awe. Each note was true, each word perfectly enunciated. It was not the random piping and roaring any lighthearted serpent might indulge in, but the glorious exultation of one called to sing. She unlidded her eyes.

"Song of Simplicity," Maulkin breathed hoarsely. Sessurea's eyes spun slowly in agreement. Gently the three worked themselves free, to undulate to the top of the Plenty, and then lift their heads out into the Lack.

There, under the light of a full round moon, the green serpent flung back his head and sang. His heavy mane hung lax about his throat. His maw gaped wide in full, carrying voice. Clear and sweet, the words emerged from one who had been mute. Verse after verse he sang of the elegant words of the ancient song of beginnings. In the old days, listeners would have joined in the refrain, to celebrate together the days of warmer Plenty and migrating fish. Now they were voiceless, listening to this blessing, but fearing to join in lest they break it.

The singer was beautiful in his intensity and concentration. His head swayed slowly as he sang, his throat distending and then stretching as he pumped out the deep, rich notes. Shreever did not look at his eyes. They were wide and empty of intent even as he gave voice to this most sacred of songs. Beside her, Maulkin bowed his head. Emotion rippled through him, bringing a brief gleam to his false-eyes. Very slowly, his mane began to stand out about his throat. His venom, once so plentiful and toxic, now barely brimmed to the tips. A single drop fell to sting ecstatically on

Shreever's skin. For a long moment, the night was clear, bright and warm with promise.

"Save your strength," Sessurea advised him sadly. "His music is beautiful, but there is no heart behind it. We cannot revive him. To try would only weaken you."

"My strength is not my own to hoard," Maulkin observed. More sourly, he added, "Sometimes I fear there is nothing to save it for." Despite his words, he did not move toward the green serpent. Instead, the three remained as they were, sharing in his enraptured song but oddly divorced from it. It was as if the words reached them from a distant past, a time they could never revisit.

His gaze fixed on the moon, head swaying gracefully to his song, the green serpent repeated the final refrain the prescribed three times. As he held a last pure note, Shreever became aware that some of the other serpents had joined them. Most gazed randomly about as if they expected a food source. The provider had moved on through the night as it always did. Its bulk did not distort the horizon. Tomorrow they would all follow its scent through the Plenty. It was easy to catch up with it.

Without the provider to focus on, their eyes turned to the green serpent. He remained poised as he had been, his gaze fixed on the moon. The last of his breath flowed from his throat in that single sustained note. It ended. A silence that seemed the only correct continuation of the song engulfed them all. In that moment, Shreever became aware of a very slight difference in the group. Some of the other serpents looked puzzled as if they struggled to recall something. All kept the stillness and silence.

All save Maulkin. With a suddenness that belied his dimmed coat and shrunken girth, the great serpent flashed across the distance between himself and the green. His faded false-eyes gleamed gold briefly and his eyes spun copper as he wrapped the green. Maulkin smeared the other serpent with what little toxin he had been able to produce, then bore him down in his embrace.

Shreever heard the creature's outraged shriek. There was nothing of intelligence in that cry. It was the fury of a cornered animal given vent. She and Sessurea dove down, following the struggling pair to the mucky bottom. As they thrashed together, silt clouded and then choked the Plenty. "He'll smother!" Shreever cried out in alarm.

"Unless that green shreds him to pieces first," Sessurea replied grimly. Both of their manes began to swell with toxins as they lashed downward in pursuit. Behind them, Shreever was dimly aware of the other serpents coiling and tangling in confusion. Maulkin's actions had alarmed them; there was no telling how they would react. It was possible, she thought coldly, that they would all turn upon the three. If they did, Maulkin's tangle had small chance of survival.

She flanked Sessurea as he plunged into the silt-laden darkness. Almost instantly, she was choking. It was a terrible sensation. Every instinct she possessed urged her to flee to cleaner water. However, she was not an animal to be controlled by her instincts. She forced herself down and deeper until she felt the vibration of the struggle and could wrap the combatants. She was so choked she could not smell who was who. She had lidded her eyes twice against the gritty silt. She released the puny cloud of toxin she could muster; she hoped it would not stun or weaken Sessurea. Then she lapped a coil of herself about the struggling bodies and devoted all her strength to pulling them up to clear water where they could all breathe.

She felt she swam through a school of tiny glowing fish. Specks and streaks of colors taunted her vision. Someone beside herself had released venom. It scorched and seared her, burning visions into her mind. Surely, it was the floor of the Plenty itself that she strove to lift. She longed to let go of her burden and shoot up to where she could breathe. Doggedly she struggled on.

Suddenly her gaping gills sensed cleaner water. Cautiously she unlidded her eyes. She opened her mouth wide, flushing out her gills. The act made her more susceptible to the mixed poisons in the water. She tasted the faint echo of Maulkin's once-powerful toxins, and the less-disciplined acids of Sessurea. The green had released toxins, too. They were thick and strong, but formulated mostly for the stunning of fish. Unpleasant as they were, they did not confound her. Her gaze met Sessurea's whirling glance. He gave a final shake of his mane, and the feebly struggling green grew limp.

Maulkin managed to lift his head. "Gently, gently," he cautioned them. "As we fought, he spoke to me. It was just curses at first, but then he demanded by what right I attacked him. I think he might still be awakened."

Shreever did not have the strength to reply. It took all her will to maintain her grip on the others as she and Sessurea strove to traverse the clouded bottom. Sessurea spotted an upthrust of stone. It was awkward to maneuver them there and even harder to find secure grips that would hold them all. Maulkin was no more helpful than a thick strand of kelp. The green was senseless still. Once they had settled, Shreever could think of nothing but rest. She dared not relax, however. They still cradled a stranger in their midst, one who might awaken violently. Several of the other serpents had discovered them, also. They hung back at a distance, eyeing them curiously. Or hungrily, perhaps. With a shudder of revulsion, she wondered if that was their interest. If they had seen Maulkin's tangle devouring the green, would they have pressed in to steal a portion? So she feared. She watched them warily.

Maulkin was exhausted. The terrible dun color of his hide betrayed that. But he did not give up. He massaged the green serpent with his coils, anointing him with the small drops of toxin he could muster. "Who are you?" he kept demanding of the lax green serpent. "You were a minstrel once, and an excellent one. Once you had a memory that could hold thousands of melodies and the words of those songs. Reach for it. Tell me your name. Just your name."

She wanted to tell him to stop wasting his strength, but could not summon the energy to do so. It was obviously futile. It did not seem to her that the green serpent was even conscious. She wondered how long Maulkin would insist on trying. Did any of them have the reserves to do this now and still catch up with the provider tomorrow? Maulkin's actions might have cost them their last chance at survival.

"Tellur," the green muttered. His gills fluttered a moment. "My name is Tellur." A rippling shudder ran the length of his body. He suddenly twined his body about Maulkin's and held tight as if a strong current threatened to sweep him away. "Tellur!" he cried out. "Tellur. Tellur. I am Tellur." He lidded his eyes and lowered his head. "Tellur," he muttered quietly. He was exhausted. Shreever tried to feel some sense of triumph. Maulkin had reawakened this one. But for how long? Would he help them in their quest, or simply become one more drain on their resources?

The watching ring of serpents had drawn closer. Shreever felt Sessurea shift wearily and knew that he prepared himself for battle. She lifted her own head and tried to shake out her mane. Precious little venom answered. She attempted a baleful glare at the surrounding serpents. They were not impressed. A massive cobalt, the largest of the other serpents, drew closer. He was easily a third longer than Sessurea, and twice his bulk. His maw gaped wide, tasting the water for toxins. He suddenly threw back his head and brought his own mane to a full bristle. "Kelaro!" he bellowed. "I am Kelaro!" His jaws worked hungrily, gulping in the diluted toxins and pumping them over his gills. "I remember," he proclaimed. "I am Kelaro!" At his bellow, some of the others retreated like startled fish. Others ignored his outburst. He turned his head to regard a much-scarred red in the group. "And you are Sylic. My friend Sylic. Once we were part of Xecres' tangle. Xecres. What became of Xecres? Where is the rest of our tangle?" He advanced almost angrily on the scarred scarlet serpent who continued to regard him with wide empty eyes. "Sylic. Where is Xecres?"

Sylic's blank stare roused his fury. The great blue suddenly wrapped his companion, squeezing him as if he were a whale to be drowned and devoured. His own ruff stood out full and poisonous. Toxins trailed in a cloud about them as they struggled. "Where is Xecres, Sylic?" he demanded. When the scarlet serpent only struggled the harder, he squeezed him tighter. "Sylic! Say your own name. Say, 'I am Sylic!' Say it now!"

"He's going to kill him," Sessurea warned them in a low, horrified voice.

"Stay out of it," Maulkin rumbled low. "Let it happen, Sessurea. For if he cannot awaken Sylic, then he is better off dead. We all are."

The resignation in his voice was chilling. Shreever turned her head to look at him but Maulkin avoided her stare. He looked instead at the slumbering green in the midst of their tangle. She heard a new voice behind them, shrill and breathless.

"Sylic," it conceded. "My name is Sylic." The red struggled feebly. Kelaro loosed his coils but did not release him.

"What has become of Xecres?"

"I don't know." The edges of Sylic's words were blurred, as if speech were an effort. His statements came slowly, as if he struggled to link words with thoughts. "He forgot himself. One morning we awoke to find him gone. He abandoned his tangle. Soon after, the others began to forget themselves." He shook his head angrily, a cloud of toxins spilling from his own ragged mane. "I am Sylic!" he repeated bitterly. "Sylic the friendless. Sylic of no tangle."

"Sylic of Maulkin's tangle. Kelaro of Maulkin's tangle. If you wish."

Maulkin's voice had regained some of its lost timbre. His false-eyes even gleamed gold briefly. Kelaro and Sylic regarded him in silence briefly. Then Kelaro advanced on them, Sylic still casually wrapped in his grasp. His eyes were huge and baleful. They spun blackly with hints of silver in their depths as he regarded the battered tangle he had been invited to join. Then he gravely bowed his great maned head.

"Maulkin." He acknowledged him. He lapped a coil of himself about their anchoring rock and drew his friend in close to them. Carefully, lest he give offense, he intertwined with Sessurea, Shreever and Maulkin. "Kelaro of Maulkin's tangle greets you all."

"Sylic of Maulkin's tangle," echoed the battered scarlet serpent.

As they wearily settled themselves for rest, Sessurea observed, "We cannot sleep too long if we intend to catch up with the provider."

"We can sleep until we are ready to travel," Maulkin corrected him. "We are finished with providers. From now on, we hunt as befits serpents. A strong tangle need depend on no one's largesse. When we do not hunt food, we hunt for One Who Remembers. We have been given a final chance. We must not squander it."

CHAPTER FOURTEEN

Serilla's Choice

THE RICHLY APPOINTED CHAMBER WAS CLOSE AND STUFFY WITH SMOKE. Serilla's head reeled with it while her stomach protested the constant swaying of the deck. Every joint in her body ached from the unending motion. She had never been a good sailor, not even when she was a girl. The intervening years in the Satrap's palace had not improved her stomach for travel. She wished they had taken a smaller, more sea-worthy vessel. The Satrap had insisted on an immense, full-bellied ship for himself and his entourage. Half of the delay in their departure had been the revamping of the ship's interior to allow for these spacious quarters. Serilla had heard some arguments from the shipwrights doing the work. It had had something to do with ballast and stability. Serilla had not understood the basis for their concerns, but she now suspected that the ship's wallowing gait was the result of Cosgo's insistence on his own plans. She reminded herself yet again that every tedious lurch carried her one wave closer to Bingtown.

It was hard to recall that she had spent days looking forward with eagerness to this voyage. She had packed and re-packed garments, choosing and discarding and choosing again. She did not want to look dowdy, nor suggestive. She did not want to look young, nor old. She had agonized over what attire would make her appear scholarly but still attractive. She had settled on simple robes, modestly cut, but elaborately embroidered by her own hand. She had no jewelry to adorn herself. By tradition, a Heart Companion possessed and wore only the jewelry the Satrap had given her. The old Satrap had always given her books and scrolls instead of jewels. Cosgo had never given her anything, though he decorated the Heart Companions he had chosen for himself with jewels as if they were cakes to be sprinkled with sparkling sugar. She tried not to care that she must appear before the Bingtown Traders unadorned. She was not going to Bingtown to impress them with her jewelry. She was going there to see, at last, the land and the folk she had studied for more than half her life. She had not known such anticipation since the old Satrap had first noticed

her and invited her to become his Companion. She prayed that this visit
to Bingtown would be a similar beginning.

At the present moment, it was difficult to cling to such dreams. Never
had she felt her life so sordid and tawdry as now. In Jamaillia, she had
always been able to insulate herself from the more debased practices of the
Satrap's court. When the young Satrap had begun to let the feasts degen-
erate into celebrations of gluttony and lewdness, she had simply stopped
attending them. On board the ship, there was nowhere to flee his ex-
cesses. If she wished to eat, she must eat with the Satrap. To leave this
chamber and walk in the fresh air on the open deck was to invite the
coarse attention of the Chalcedean crew. There was no relief there, even
if she had had Cosgo's leave to depart the room.

Satrap Cosgo and Companion Kekki sprawled on the large divan of
the chamber. They were both nearly insensible from pleasure herbs and
smoke. Kekki had whined that they were the only way to keep her mind
from her queasiness, and loudly lamented that never before this had she
been so seasick. Serilla had been too tactful to ask if she might be pregnant. It was not unheard of for a Satrap to impregnate one of his Heart
Companions, but it was still seen as tasteless. Children of such unions
were turned over to the servants of Sa as soon as they were born, to be
raised as priests. They were never told of their parentage. Only with his
lawful spouse could the Satrap conceive an heir. Cosgo had not yet taken
a wife. Serilla doubted that he would until his nobles forced it on him.

If he lived that long. She glanced at him, sprawled half atop Kekki
and breathing hoarsely. Another Companion, also stupefied, lolled across
the pillows at his feet. Her head was flung back, her dark hair scattered
across the cushions. Her slitted eyes showed slices of white. Periodically,
her fingers spasmed. To look at her made Serilla queasy.

The entire voyage so far had been a series of feasts and entertainment,
followed by Cosgo's extended periods of nausea and stupor brought on by
too much wine and soporifics. Then he would demand his healers, who
would dose and drug him in a different direction, until he felt well enough
to prescribe his own pleasures again. The other nobles on board were as
self-indulgent, save a few who often claimed seasickness as an excuse to
remain in their quarters.

Several Chalcedean nobles journeyed north with him. Their ships
traveled in company with the Satrap's flagship. They often joined him for
dinner. The women they brought with them were like dangerous pets as
they vied for attention from those they deemed most powerful. They
horrified Serilla. The only more terrifying aspects of those dinners were
the political discussions that followed. The Chalcedean nobles urged
Cosgo to make an example of Bingtown, to tolerate none of the Traders'
rebellious talk, to take a firm hand and quash them. They were building in
the Satrap a sense both of self-righteousness and anger that Serilla

deemed unjustified. She no longer attempted to make her own voice heard. The Chalcedeans only shouted her down with their laughter, or made mock of her. Last night Cosgo had bid her to be silent as befit her. The thought of his public insult to her still stirred the flames of anger in her heart.

The Chalcedean who captained his ship accepted the rare wines that Satrap Cosgo offered him, but disdained the young ruler's company. He pleaded the responsibility of his command, but Serilla saw the veiled contempt in the older man's eyes. The more Cosgo tried to impress him, the more the captain ignored him. Cosgo's attempts to mimic the Chalcedean's swagger and aggression were humiliating to watch. It pained Serilla to see Companions like Kekki encourage him in it, as if his juvenile pushiness were manly. Cosgo now took umbrage at everything that was not precisely as he ordered it. His behavior reminded Serilla of a spoiled child. Nothing pleased him. Cosgo had brought jesters and musicians with him, but their routines had grown stale. The Satrap grew ever more peckish with boredom. The slightest challenge to his will propelled him into cursing, stamping tantrums.

Serilla sighed. She wandered the room, then paused to toy with the tasseled edge of the embroidered tablecloth. Wearily she moved some of the sticky dishes out of the way. She sat down at the table and waited. She longed to return to the small closet that was her own chamber, but as Cosgo had summoned her on the pretext of seeking her advice, she could not leave until he dismissed her. If she woke him to ask his permission, he would surely refuse it.

She had tried to dissuade him from this journey. He had suspected her of wanting to travel alone. That was true; she would far rather be traveling to Bingtown alone, empowered to make decisions for a land she knew much better than he did. However, he was too jealous of his power to allow that. He, the reigning Satrap, would descend upon Bingtown in all his power and glory and cow them with his might. The Bingtown Traders would be brought to heel, and reminded that he ruled them all by the grace of Sa. They had no right to dispute that.

She had been confident that the Council of Nobles would dissuade him and had been sick with astonishment when they had supported the journey. His Chalcedean allies had encouraged him as well. There had been many nights of drinking with them before the preparation for the journey began. She had heard of their bragging and promises. They would support him. Let him show those Bingtown upstarts who ruled Jamaillia. His Chalcedean friends would back him up. He need not fear those festering rebels. If they dared to lift a hand against their rightful rulers, Duke Yadfin and his mercenaries would give them fresh reason to call their land the Cursed Shores. Even now, Serilla shook her head to herself when she thought of it. Could not Cosgo see that he could be used as bait in a trap?

If the Chalcedeans could provoke the Old Traders to kill him, they would have complete license to plunder and destroy all of Bingtown.

The wallowing mother ship carried, in addition to the Satrap, a selection of his Companions, a full complement of servants and six nobles he had ordered to attend him, with their smaller entourages. A lesser vessel, full of hopeful younger sons from noble houses, accompanied the Satrap's ship. These he had lured into the adventure with the prospect that, if their families invested in his expedition, their sons might be given grants of land in Bingtown. In vain had Serilla remonstrated with him about that. To arrive with these would-be settlers would insult the Traders. It was a plain sign that the Satrap had never taken their complaints about the New Traders seriously. He ignored her.

To make matters worse, ranging ahead of the sailing ships and flanking them were seven large galleys, fully armed with well-equipped Chalcedean mercenaries. Their announced purpose was to escort safely the Satrap's vessel through the pirate-infested waters of the Inside Passage. Only when they were underway did Serilla discover that they would provide a further show of the Satrap's power enroute. They intended to raid and pillage any pirate settlements the ranging galleys discovered on the journey north. Whatever wealth and slaves they carried off from these raids would be transported to Chalced in the young nobles' ship, to help offset the cost of the diplomatic mission. The younger sons would participate in the raids, to prove themselves worthy of favor.

The Satrap had been especially proud of this bit of accounting. Over and over, Serilla had had to listen to him enumerate the advantages. "One, Bingtown will be forced to admit that my patrol ships have discouraged the pirates. The slaves we take will be proof of that. Two, Bingtown will be impressed with the might of my allies, and hence will be less prone to oppose my will. Three, we will be reimbursing the treasury for the cost of this little expedition. Fourth, it will make of me a living legend. What other Satrap has ever gone forth like this, to take matters into his own hands and straighten things out? What other Satrap has ever been so bold?"

Serilla could not decide which danger was greater: that the Chalcedeans would take him to Chalced, hold him as a hostage and make him a puppet ruler, or that the nobility of Jamaillia would seize every scrap of power they could while the boy Satrap was gone. Probably both, she decided bitterly. There were times, like tonight, when she wondered if she would ever see Bingtown at all. They were completely in the power of the Chalcedean mercenaries operating the ships. There was nothing to stop them from taking Cosgo directly to Chalced. She hoped they would believe it was to their advantage to take him to Bingtown first. If they did, she swore that somehow she would escape there. Somehow.

Only two of his old advisors had tried to dissuade the Satrap Cosgo from this trip. The others had all nodded affably, admitting that it was an unheard-of journey for a reigning Satrap, but encouraging him to do as he thought best. None had offered to attend him. They had loaded him with gifts for traveling and all but nudged him onto the ship. Those he had ordered to accompany him had gone reluctantly. Still Cosgo had been unable to see the danger signs of a conspiracy to be rid of him. Two days ago, she had dared speak of her concerns to him. He had first mocked her, and then become angry. "You are playing on my fears! Well you know how my nerves trouble me! You seek to upset me, to ruin my health and digestion with your wild talk. Be silent! Go to your cabin and remain there until I summon you."

Her cheeks burned when she recalled how she had been forced to obey him. Two grinning Chalcedean seamen had escorted her there. Neither one had touched her, but they had discussed her body freely, in word and gesture, as they took her there. She had set the flimsy door catch as soon as she was inside and then put her clothing chest against the door. He had let a full day pass before he called her. When Cosgo did summon her back to his side, the first thing he asked her was if she had learned her lesson. Fists on his hips, he had stood grinning, awaiting her reply. Never would he have dared speak so to her if they had been in Jamaillia still. She had stood before him, eyes downcast, and muttered that she had. It had seemed the wiser course, but inside she had been seething.

She had learned her lesson. She had learned that he had left civilized ways behind him. Before, he had been a man toying with dissipation. Now he embraced degeneracy. She decided to take her freedom as soon as she could. She owed this swine nothing. Only her loyalty to the Satrapy troubled her conscience. She had silenced it by convincing herself that there was little she, a woman alone, could do to stop its decay.

Ever since then, the Satrap had watched her like a cat, waiting for her to challenge him. She had been careful to avoid that, yet would not appear too subservient either. She had set her jaw and been both deferential and courteous, while contriving to avoid him as much as possible. When he had summoned her tonight, she had feared a clash of wills. She had blessed Kekki's rabid jealousy. The instant Serilla had been admitted to the Satrap's chamber, the other Companion had done all in her power to occupy Satrap Cosgo completely. She had succeeded very well. Cosgo was unconscious.

Kekki had no shame. She had become a Companion on the strength of her knowledge of Chalcedean language and customs. It was now apparent to Serilla that she had embraced their culture as well. In Chalced, a woman enjoyed power only through whatever man she could captivate. Tonight, Kekki had shown she would go to any limit to keep Cosgo's attention. A shame, Serilla thought, that Kekki's path was the swiftest way to lose Cosgo's fascination with her. She would soon be discarded. Serilla only hoped Kekki's blandishments could keep him entertained until they reached Bingtown.

Serilla was still staring at them when the Satrap opened one drug-reddened eye. She did not avert her glance. She doubted he was even aware of her presence.

It was a mistake.

"Come here," he ordered her.

She crossed the thickly carpeted deck, picking her way past abandoned garments and discarded dishes. She stood an arm's length from his couch. "You summoned me for consultation, Magnadon?" she asked him formally.

"Come here!" he repeated petulantly. His forefinger stabbed at a spot adjacent to his couch.

She could not take those final steps. Her pride simply would not allow it. "Why?" she demanded of him.

"Because I am the Satrap and I command it!" he spat out. He was abruptly furious. "You need no more reason than that." He sat up suddenly, shoving Kekki aside. She moaned dismally, but rolled away from him.

"I am not a servant," Serilla pointed out. "I am a Companion of the Heart." She drew herself up straight and recited. " 'lest his head be turned by flattering women, lest his vanity be stroked by those who seek only to gain, let him choose for himself Companions, to sit beside him. Let them not be above him, let them not be below him, but let them speak their wisdom openly, advising the Satrap only in each one's specific area of erudition. Let him have no favorites amongst them. Let him not choose them based on comeliness or amiability. Let his Companion not praise him, let her not defer to his opinion, let her not be fearful of disagreeing with him, for any of these things may compromise the honesty of her counsel. Let her . . .' "

"Let her shut up!" Cosgo shouted out and then laughed uproariously at his own wit.

Serilla fell silent, but not at his command. She did not move from where she stood.

For a moment, he surveyed her silently. An odd spark of amusement lit his eyes. "You foolish woman. You are so full of yourself, so certain that a mouthful of words can protect you. Companion of my Heart." He sneered the words. "A title for a woman who fears to be a woman." He leaned back against Kekki's body as if she were a cushion. "I could cure you of that. I could give you to the sailors. Have you thought of that? The captain is Chalcedean. He would think nothing of me discarding a woman who had displeased me." He paused. "Perhaps he would use you first. Before he passed you on."

Serilla's mouth went dry. Her tongue stuck to the roof of it. He could, she realized dully. He had become capable of it. It would be months before he returned to Jamaillia. Who would demand an accounting of what had become of her? No one. None of the nobles on board would oppose him. If they had had that strength of will, they would not be aboard. Some might even feel she had brought it upon herself.

She had no alternative. Once she capitulated to him, his debasement of her would know no bounds. If she showed fear of this threat, he would continue to use it. She suddenly saw that clearly. Her only hope was to challenge him. "Do it," she said coolly. She stood up straighter and crossed her arms on her chest. She could feel her heart hammering inside her. He could do it. He might do it. If he did, she would not survive it. The crew was large and rough. Some of the female servants had already appeared with bruised faces and unsteady gaits. No rumors had reached her ears, but she did not need rumors to have suspicions. Chalcedeans saw women as little more than cattle.

She prayed he would back down.

"I will." He lurched to his feet. He took two unsteady steps toward the door.

Her traitorous legs began to tremble. She clenched her jaws to keep her lips from quivering. She had made her move and lost the game. *Sa, help me*, she prayed. She wanted to wail with fear. She feared she would faint. She blinked rapidly, trying to drive away the shadows at the corners of her vision. It was a bluff. He would stop. He wouldn't dare follow through on this.

The Satrap halted. He swayed, but she could not tell if it was indecision or instability. "Are you sure this is what you want?" There was a leering taunt to the words. He cocked his head at her. "You would rather go to them than attempt to please me? I'll give you a moment to decide which you want."

She felt dizzy and sick. It was the cruelest thing he could have done, to offer her this last chance. She felt her strength ebbing away from her. She wanted to fling herself to her knees and beg his mercy. Only her conviction that he had no concept of mercy held her still and upright. She swallowed. She could not reply. She clung to her silence and hoped it would pass for refusal.

"Very well. Remember, Serilla, you chose this. You could have had me."

He opened the door. There was a sailor outside it. There was always a sailor outside it. Serilla had always suspected he was as much gaoler as sentry. Cosgo leaned on the doorjamb and patted the man affably on the shoulder. "Run a message to your captain, my good man. Tell him that I offer him one of my women. The green-eyed one." He pivoted unsteadily to leer at her. "Warn him that she is bad-tempered and unwilling. Tell him I have found her a sweet mount, all the same." His eyes walked up and down her body. A cruel smile curved his mouth. "Have him send someone to claim her."

CHAPTER FIFTEEN

Tidings

ALTHEA ABRUPTLY HEAVED A SIGH. SHE PUSHED BACK FROM THE TABLE, causing Malta's pen to leave a squiggle on the paper. She stood up and rubbed her eyes. Malta watched her aunt walk away from the table and the scattered papers and tally sticks on it. "I have to go out," she announced.

Ronica Vestrit had just entered the room with a basket of cut flowers on her arm and a pitcher of water in her free hand. "I know what you mean," she conceded as she set her burdens down on a side table. She filled a waiting vase with water and began to put the flowers into it. She had a mixed bouquet of daisies, baby's breath, roses and fern fronds. She scowled at the flowers as she arranged them, as if everything were their fault. "The accounting of our debts is hardly cheery work. Even I need to get away from it after a few hours." She paused, then added hopefully, "The flowerbeds by the front door need attention if you're in the mood for outdoor work."

Althea shook her head impatiently. "No," she said. She softened her tone and added, "I'm going to go down into town for a bit. Stretch my legs, see some friends. I'll be back before dinner." With a sideways glance at her mother's frown, she added, "I'll see to the walkway then. I promise."

Her mother folded her lips but said no more. Malta let Althea get almost to the door before she asked curiously, "Are you going to go see that bead-maker again?" She made a pretense of rubbing her eyes as she set aside her own pen.

"I might," Althea said evenly. Malta heard the restrained annoyance in her voice.

Ronica made a small sound as if deciding whether to speak. Aunt Althea turned back to her wearily. "What?"

Ronica gave a small shrug, her hands still busy with the flowers. "Nothing. I just wish you would not spend so much time with her, so openly. She is not Bingtown, you know. And some say she is no better than the New Traders."

"She is my friend," Althea said flatly.

"The talk about town is that she has been squatting in the Ludlucks' liveship. That poor ship has never been right, and she has so unhinged him by living there that when the Ludlucks sent men to move her out of their rightful property, the ship had a fit. He said he'd rip their arms off if they tried to come aboard. You can imagine how distressing that was to Trader Ludluck. Amis has tried for years to keep her family name clean of scandal. Now it has been stirred again, and with it all the old tales of how Paragon went mad and killed everyone aboard him. It is entirely that woman's fault. She should not be meddling in Trader business."

"Mother." Althea's patience sounded strained. "There is a great deal more to that story than you have heard. If you wish, I'll tell you all I know. But later. When only adults are around."

Malta knew that little sling was intended for her. She rose to it like a shark to chum. "The bead-maker has an odd reputation about town. Oh, everyone says she is a wonderful artist. However, as we all know, artists can be strange. She lives with a woman who dresses and acts like a man. Did you know that?"

"Jek is from the Six Duchies or one of those barbarian lands. That is just how women behave up there. Grow up, Malta, and stop listening to dirty little whispers," Althea suggested brusquely.

Malta drew herself up to her full height. "Usually, I ignore such gossip. Until I hear our own family name dragged into it. I know it is scarcely ladylike to discuss such things, but I feel you should know that some people say that you visit the bead-maker for the same reason. To sleep with her."

During the ensuing shocked silence, Malta added a spoonful of honey to her tea. As she stirred it, the sound of the spoon against the cup seemed almost merry.

"If you mean fuck, say fuck," Althea suggested. She enunciated the crudity deliberately. Her voice was cold with fury. "If you are going to be coarse, why be circumspect with the language?"

"Althea!" Ronica finally emerged from her scandalized silence. "You will not say such things in our home!"

"It was already said. I but clarified the topic." Althea bit off each word as she glowered at Malta.

"You can scarcely blame people for talking," Malta went on after she had sipped her tea. She made her voice casually conversational. "After all, you were gone almost a year, and then came home dressed like a boy. You are well past marrying age, but show no interest in men. Instead, you swagger about town acting as if you were a man yourself. People are bound to speculate that you are . . . strange."

"Malta, that is both unkind and untrue," Ronica said firmly. There were high spots of color on the tops of her cheeks. "Althea is not too old to be considered marriageable. You well know that Grag Tenira has expressed more than a passing interest in Althea of late."

"Oh, him. We all well know that the Teniras have expressed an even greater interest in the ability of the Vestrits to sway the Bingtown Council. Ever since they began that futile show of defiance down at the Satrap's tariff dock, they have been trying to recruit others to their cause—"

"It is scarcely futile. The principle of Bingtown's authority is at stake, not that I expect you to understand that. The Teniras defy the Satrap's tariffs because the tariffs are both unlawful and unjust. However, I doubt you have the wits to grasp that, and I have no desire to spend the afternoon listening to children prattle of matters they do not understand. Mother. Good afternoon."

Her head up, her face tight with anger, Althea swept out the door.

Malta listened to her footsteps fade down the hall. She pushed disconsolately at the paper in front of her. As it moved across the desk, it broke the silence in the room.

"Why did you do that?" her grandmother asked her quietly. There was no real anger in her voice. Rather it was a flat curiosity.

"I did nothing," Malta protested. Before Ronica could dispute that, she asked, "Why can Althea abruptly announce she is tired of our work and take herself off to town? If I attempted that—"

"Althea is older than you. She is more mature. She is accustomed to making her own decisions. She has kept her part of the bargain we struck. She has lived quietly and respectfully, she has not . . ."

"If she had not, then why are there rumors?"

"I have heard no rumors." Her grandmother picked up the now-empty basket and pitcher. She centered the fresh vase of flowers on the table. "I think I've had enough of you for now," she said. "Good afternoon, Malta." As before, there was no anger in her voice, only a strange flatness, and a sort of hopelessness. On her face, she wore a look of distaste. She turned and walked away from Malta without another word.

When she was around the corner but not quite out of earshot, Malta spoke aloud to herself. "She hates me. That old woman hates me. Oh, I hope Father gets back soon. He will quickly put things right around here."

Ronica Vestrit's steps did not even falter. Malta slumped back in her chair. She pushed away the too-sweet tea. Everything here was so dull since Reyn had left. She could not even provoke her relatives into quarreling. The boredom was driving her mad. Lately she found herself nettling those around her simply to stir them up. She missed the excitement and importance of Reyn's visit. The flowers were long faded, the sweets eaten up. Save for her secret hoard of smuggled trinkets from him, it was as if he had never come calling at all. What good was a beau who lived far away?

She felt she had once more fallen into a pit of ordinariness. Each day was filled with work and chores. Her grandmother would constantly nag at her to live up to family expectations, while letting Aunt Althea do whatever she wanted. It all came to the same thing. Do what her mother and grandmother wanted her to do. Be a little puppet on their strings. That was what Reyn wanted from her, also. She recognized that even if he did not. He was attracted to her not just for her beauty and charm, but because she was young. He thought he could control all her actions and even her thoughts. He would find out he was wrong about that. They would all find out they were wrong.

She got up from the table where she had been reconciling the accounts and drifted over to the window. It looked out on gardens gone untidy and wild. Althea and her grandmother pecked at keeping them up, but it took a real gardener and at least a dozen assistants to keep the grounds properly. By the end of summer, the gardens would be completely unkempt if things went on as they were. That would not happen, of course. Her father would be home long before then, with a pocketful of money. He would put things right. There would be servants again, and good food and wine. He would be home any day now, she was sure of it.

She clenched her teeth as she thought of the conversation at the dinner table last night. Mother had worried aloud that the ship was so late in returning. Aunt Althea had added that there was no word of *Vivacia* down at the docks. None of the ships arriving in Bingtown reported seeing her. Mother had said that perhaps Kyle had chosen to bypass Bingtown and take his cargo straight to Chalced. "None of the ships arriving from that direction have seen her either," Althea had reported darkly. "I wonder if he ever intended to return to Bingtown. Perhaps from Jamaillia, he simply sailed south."

She had said the words cautiously, feigning that she didn't intend to offend anyone. Mother had quietly but fiercely said, "Kyle would not do that." After that, Aunt Althea had kept silent. She had killed all the talk at the table.

Malta cast about for any amusement. Perhaps she would use the dream-box tonight. The excitement of the forbidden shared dream beckoned her. In their last dream, they had shared a kiss. Would another dream stop there? Would she want it to continue? Malta shivered. Reyn had told her to wait ten days after he left and then use it. He would be home by then and settled back in. Malta had not done so. He had been too confident that she would do as he bid her. As much as she longed to use the box, she would not. Let him wait and wonder why she did not use the powder. Let him discover she was not his puppet. That was a lesson that Cerwin had learned well.

She smiled slightly to herself. In the cuff of her sleeve was his latest note to her. It implored her to meet with him, at any time or any place she could manage. He promised his intentions were purely honorable. He would bring his sister Delo along, so her reputation would not be compromised. The thought of her being given to that Rain Wilder was driving him mad. He had known for ever so long that she was destined to be his. Please, please, please, if she had any feelings for him at all, she must meet with him so that they might discuss what could be done to forestall this tragedy.

She had the note memorized. It was a lovely composition of black pen strokes on thick creamy paper. Delo had delivered it yesterday when she came to call. The wax seal, imprinted with the Trell willow, had still been intact. Nevertheless, Delo's wide eyes and conspiratorial manner had betrayed that she was fully aware of the contents. When they were alone, Delo had confided that she had never seen her brother so distraught. Ever since he had seen Malta dancing in Reyn's arms, he had been unable to sleep. He only picked at his food. He had even given up gaming with the other young men. Instead, he burned the long evenings into the early morning hours sitting alone by the study fire. His father was becoming very impatient with him. He had accused Cerwin of being lazy, and declared that he did not disinherit his eldest son simply so that the younger boy could become as idle as the first. Delo was at her wit's end. Surely, Malta could do something to give her brother some tiny ray of hope.

Malta replayed the scene in her mind. She had stared off into the distance. A tiny tear had come into her eye and run down her cheek. She had told Delo she feared there was little she could do. Her grandmother had seen to that. She was no more now than a shiny bauble to be sold off to the highest bidder. She would do her best to stave off everything until her father returned home. She was certain he would rather see her in the arms of a man she cared for than one who was simply the wealthiest. Then she had given Delo a message to carry back. She dared not entrust it to paper, but would have to rely on her best friend's honor. Malta would meet him at midnight at the gazebo just past the ivy-covered oak at the bottom of the rose garden.

That was tonight. She still had not decided if she would keep that tryst or not. A summer night spent outside under the oak tree would not hurt Cerwin a bit. Nor Delo. She could always plead later that she had been unable to escape the scrutiny of her guardians. It might heighten Cerwin's sense of urgency.

"THE WORST PART IS THAT SHE HAS SPIRIT AND INTELLIGENCE. I LOOK AT her and think, 'there, but for my father's interference, go I.' If he had not taken me to sea, if I had been forced to stay at home and be suffocated under what was 'proper and correct for a girl to do,' I might have rebelled in the same way. I think my mother and sister are wrong to allow her to dress and behave as if she was a woman grown, but she is certainly not a child either. She has set herself up in opposition to all of us, and will not open her eyes to see that we are one family and must act together. She is so busy defending her notion of her father's perfection that she cannot even see our other problems. As for Selden, he has almost disappeared. He mouses about the house, and scarcely speaks above a whisper except when he is whining. Then they give him sweets and tell him to run and play, they are busy. Malta is supposed to help him with his lessons, but all she does is make him cry. I don't have time to do anything with him, even if I knew what it was a boy that age needs." Althea shook her head in exasperation and hissed out a sigh.

She lifted her eyes from the tea she had been methodically stirring as she talked and met Grag's eyes. He smiled at her. They were sitting at a small table outside a Bingtown bakery. Here, in plain view, they did not need to fear the gossip-mongers who might otherwise be intrigued at their meeting unchaperoned. Althea had run into Grag in the street on her way to Amber's shop. He had convinced her to pause long enough to have some refreshment with him. When he had asked her what had upset her enough to send her out of the house without a hat, she had unloaded the morning's tale on him. Now she felt a bit shamed.

"I'm sorry. You invite me to tea and all I do is whine about my niece. It can't be pleasant for you to listen to such things. Nor should I be speaking so of my family. But that Malta! I know she goes into my room when I am not home. I know she goes through my things. But . . ." Belatedly, Althea stopped her tongue. "I shouldn't let the little minx get to me. I see now why mother and my sister agreed to this early courtship. It might be our only chance to be rid of her."

"Althea!" Grag rebuked her with a grin. "I am sure they would not do that."

"No. They actually have the best interests of all in mind. My mother has told me, plainly, that she expects Reyn will drop the courtship when he gets to know Malta better." Althea gave a sigh. "If it were up to me, I'd hurry it along before he gets wise."

Grag lifted a finger from the tabletop and boldly touched the back of her hand. "No you wouldn't," he assured them both. "You haven't got that kind of meanness in you."

"Are you sure of that?" she teased him gently.

He widened his blue eyes in mock alarm.

"Oh, let us speak of something else. Anything would be a more pleasant topic. Tell me how your battle has been going. Has the Council agreed to hear you?"

"The Bingtown Council has been a more stubborn opponent than the

Satrap's officials. But, yes, they have finally agreed to hear us. Tomorrow night, in fact."

"I'll be there," Althea promised him. "I'll lend what support I can. And I'll do my best to get my mother and sister there, also."

"I'm not sure that it will do us any good, but I'll be glad to get a hearing. I have no idea what Father will decide to do." Grag shook his head. "He has refused all compromises so far. He won't pay; he won't promise to pay later. There we sit, a full cargo, merchants waiting for it, but the tariff dock won't release us, Father won't pay, and no other Bingtown Trader will back us. It's hurting us, Althea, hurting us badly. If it goes on much longer, it may break us." He stopped abruptly, shaking his head. "You don't need any more worries and bad news. You have enough of your own. But, you know, there is some good news. Your friend Amber finished with Ophelia's hands, and the results are magnificent. It has been difficult for Ophelia. Although she says she does not feel pain as we do, I feel it as discomfort and loss when . . ." Grag's voice trailed away. Althea did not press him. She understood that speaking of what he shared with his liveship could be too self-revealing.

The dull ache she felt at her separation from Vivacia peaked into a sudden sharp pang of isolation. She clenched her hands in her lap for a moment, resolutely pushing aside her anxiety. There was nothing she could do, until Kyle brought Vivacia home. If he brought Vivacia home. Keffria claimed he would never abandon her and the children; Althea did not see it that way. The man had a priceless ship in his control, a vessel he did not really have any right to own. If he took it south, he could operate as if he owned the ship free and clear. He could be a wealthy man with no responsibilities save himself.

"Althea?"

She gave a guilty start. "I'm sorry."

Grag smiled understandingly. "In your position, I'm sure I would be as preoccupied. I continue to ask every ship that comes into the harbor for word of her. I'm afraid that is as much as I can do right now. Next month, when we sail again to Jamaillia, I will seek word from every ship I encounter."

"Thank you," she told him warmly. Then, as his look became too tender, she distracted him. "I have missed Ophelia. If I had not promised Mother that I would be more conservative in my behavior, I would have come calling on her. The only time I ventured down there, the Satrap's tariff guards challenged me. For the sake of propriety, I did not make an issue of it." She sighed, then changed her tone. "So Amber was able to repair Ophelia's hands."

Grag leaned back in his chair. He squinted his eyes in the afternoon sunlight. "More than repair. She had to reshape them as a whole to keep the more slender fingers proportional. When Ophelia expressed concern for the scraps of wizardwood that had to be removed, Amber made a practice of saving every scrap in a special box. They never left the foredeck. The loss of them seemed very threatening to Ophelia; I was surprised that someone not of Bingtown stock could be so perceptive to the ship's distress. Now she has even gone one step further. After consulting with Ophelia, she has gained my father's permission to refashion the larger scraps into a bracelet for the ship. She will cut the pieces into fine rods and bars and then peg them together. 'No other liveship in the harbor possesses such jewelry, made not only by a prominent artist but carved of her own wizardwood.' Ophelia is ecstatic."

Althea smiled but she was still slightly incredulous as she asked, "Your father permits Amber to work wizardwood? I thought that was forbidden."

"This is different," Grag pointed out hastily. "It is actually a part of the repair. Amber is only restoring to Ophelia as much of her wizardwood as she can. My family discussed this in great depth before my father permitted it. Amber's integrity weighed heavily in our decision. She did not attempt to take any of the scraps. We watched her, you know, for as wizardwood is so rare, even the tiniest bit has value. She has been honorable. Moreover, she has been extraordinarily flexible in completing all the work on board the ship. Even the bracelet will be carved there rather than in Amber's shop. She has had to haul quite a number of tools back and forth, and all in her guise of a slave-whore." Grag took another bite of his pastry and chewed thoughtfully.

Amber had told Althea nothing of all this. She was not surprised. There were depths of reserve to the bead-maker that she never expected to plumb. "She's quite a person," Althea observed, as much to herself as to Grag.

"My mother said the same thing," he agreed. "That, I think, has been the strangest development. My mother and Ophelia have always been very close, you know. They were friends even before she married my father. When she learned Ophelia had been injured when we were attacked, she was distraught. She had many reservations about letting a stranger work on Ophelia's hands, and she was rather piqued with my father for agreeing to it without consulting her first."

Althea grinned knowingly in answer to Grag's straight-faced minimization of Naria Tenira's legendary temper. It woke an answering grin on his handsome face. For an instant, she glimpsed a carefree sailor rather than the conservative Bingtown Trader that was his other face. Here in Bingtown, Grag was far more aware of both his family's reputation and Bingtown propriety. His sailor clothes had given way to a dark coat and trousers and a white shirt. It reminded her of her father's conservative dress when he was in Bingtown. It made him seem older, more serious and stable. Her heart gave a small leap of interest that a wicked grin could still light his face. The trader was an interesting and respectable man; the sailor was an attractive one.

"Mother insisted that she would be present when Ophelia's hands were worked on. Amber did not object, but I believe she was a bit offended. No one relishes distrust. As it turned out, she and Mother talked for hours while Amber worked, about everything under the sun. Ophelia joined in, of course. You well know that you cannot speak anywhere on the foredeck without Ophelia sharing her opinion. The result has been surprising. Mother has become virulently anti-slavery. The other day she accosted a man on the street. There was a little girl with a tattooed face carrying his parcels. Mother knocked the packages from the child's hands and told the man he should be ashamed at having such a young child away from her mother. Then she brought the girl home." Grag looked a trifle discomfitted. "I don't know what we will do with her. She is too scared to say more than a few words at a time, but my mother says the child has no relatives in Bingtown. She was torn from her family and sold, like a calf." As Grag spoke, his voice thickened with suppressed emotion. This was a new side of him.

"Did the newcomer just accept your mother taking the child?"

Grag grinned again, but there was a fierce edge to it. A glint came into his eyes. "Not gracefully. However, Lennel, our cook, was with Mother. He is not a man to accept anyone trifling with the mistress. The slave-owner stood in the street and shouted threats after them, but did little more than that. Those that took notice either sneered or laughed. What will he do? Go to the town council and complain that someone kidnapped the child he had illegally enslaved?"

"No. More likely he will go to the town council and lend his support to those who would make slavery a law as well as a fact here."

"My mother has already declared that when the Bingtown Council hears our grievances against the Satrap's servants, she will bring up the matter of slavery as well. She intends to demand that our laws against it be enforced."

"How?" Althea asked bitterly.

Grag just looked at her. In a quiet voice he said, "I do not know. But it should at least be attempted. We have looked aside from it. Amber says that if the slaves truly believed we would support their liberty, they would not be so fearful to admit they were truly slaves. They have been told by their masters that if they are defiant and claim freedom, they will be tortured to death and that no one will interfere."

Althea felt a terrible coldness well up in her. She thought of the child Naria had claimed. Did she still fear torture and death? What would that do to anyone, to grow up under such a shadow?

"Amber feels that with genuine support, they would rise up and walk away from their slavery. They far outnumber their masters. She also feels that if Bingtown does not act soon to restore their rightful freedom, there will be a bloody rebellion that will ruin the whole city."

"So. We help them regain their rightful freedom soon, or we will all go down in flames when they take it for themselves?"

"Something like that." Grag lifted his mug of beer and drank thoughtfully.

After a long moment, Althea heaved a sigh. She took another sip of her tea and stared off into the distance.

"Althea. Don't look so woebegone. We're doing all that can be done. We go before the Council tomorrow night. Maybe we can bring them to their senses about both the Satrap's tariffs and slavery in Bingtown."

"Perhaps you're right," Althea agreed glumly. She did not tell him that she had not been considering slavery or tariffs. She had been looking at the handsome and good-hearted young man across the table from her and waiting. She waited in vain. She felt only affectionate friendship. She had sighed, wondering why a decent and respectable man like Grag Tenira could not stir her heart and senses as Brashen Trell had.

HE NEARLY WENT AROUND TO THE BACK DOOR. THEN SOME REMNANT OF old pride made him stride up to the front and ring the bell. He refused to look down at himself as he waited. He was not ragged, nor dirty. The yellow silk shirt was of the finest quality, as was the scarf at his throat. The dark blue trousers and short jacket he wore had seen some mending, but the work of his own needle never shamed a good sailor. If the fabric and cut were more suited to the pirates of the isles than to a Bingtown Trader's son, well . . . Brashen Trell was likely more one than the other these days. There was a small cindin burn at the corner of his mouth where he had fallen asleep while indulging, but his current mustache hid most of that. A small smile came and went on his face. If Althea got close enough to see it, he doubted she'd be thinking about it. His quick ears detected the light scuff of a serving girl's step in the passageway. He took off his hat.

A well-rigged young woman opened the door to him. She looked him up and down, plainly disapproving of his rakish clothes. She returned his cheery grin with an affronted stare. "Did you wish something?" she asked him haughtily.

He winked at her. "I could wish for a more courteous greeting, but I doubt that would get me one. I'm here to see Althea Vestrit. If she is not available, I'd like to meet with Ronica Vestrit. I've news that won't wait."

"Indeed? Well, I'm afraid it will have to, as neither of them is at home at present. Good day."

The inflection of her voice plainly said it was not at all a good day that she wished him. He stepped forward quickly to catch the edge of the door before it could close.

"But Althea is back from sea?" he pressed, needing to hear those words spoken.

"She has been home from sea for weeks. Let go!" she spat at him.

His heart lurched with relief. She was home, safe. The girl was still tugging at the door he gripped. He decided the time for tact was past. "I won't leave. I can't. I bring important news. I won't be put off by a serving girl's tantrum. Let me in, right now, or both your mistresses will be greatly displeased with you."

The little maid fell back a step, gasping in shock. Brashen took the opportunity to step into the entryway. He glanced about himself, frowning at what he saw. This entryway had always been the captain's pride. It was still clean and bright, but the woodwork and brass no longer gleamed. He missed the warm scents of beeswax and oil. He even saw wisps of a high cobweb in a corner. He had no time to see more. The housemaid stamped her small foot at him indignantly. "I am not a servant, you misbegotten bit of wharf-trash. I am Malta Haven, daughter of this household. I'll thank you to take your stench out of my home."

"Not until I've seen Althea. I'll wait as long as I need to. Put me anywhere, I'll sit still and mind my manners." He peered at the girl more closely. "It *is* Malta! Beg pardon, I didn't recognize you. The last time I saw you, you were in a little girl's frocks." He attempted to make amends for his earlier slight. He smiled down on her. "My, don't you look grand today? Are you and your friends playing a tea party, then?"

His attempt at disarming friendliness was a disaster. The girl's eyes went wide, and her upper lip sneered back from her teeth in disdain. "Who are you, sailor, to dare speak to me so familiarly, in my father's house?"

"Brashen Trell," he said. "Former first mate for Captain Vestrit. Beg pardon for not saying so sooner. I bring news of the liveship *Vivacia*. I need to see your aunt or grandmother immediately. Or your mother. Is she at home?"

"She is not. She and Grandmother have gone into town, to discuss spring planting arrangements. They will not be back until later. Althea is off doing whatever it is that currently amuses her. Sa knows when she will wander in. However, you can tell your news to me. Why has the ship been so long delayed? Will they be much longer?"

Brashen cursed his own dull wits. The prospect of seeing Althea had displaced some of the gravity of his news in his mind. He looked at the girl before him. He was bringing tidings that her family ship had been seized by pirates. He would not be able to tell her if her father were still alive. That was not news he was going to deliver to a child at home by herself. He ardently wished that she had allowed one of the servants to open the door to him. He wished even more that he had had the sense to hold his tongue until an adult was present. He chewed his lip, then winced as it tugged at the cindin sores. "I think you had best send a boy down to the town, to ask your grandmother to come home right away. This is news she should receive first."

"Why? Is something wrong?"

For the first time, the girl spoke in her own voice, not a parody of an adult's. Oddly, it made her seem more mature. The sudden fear in her voice and eyes went to Brashen's heart. He stood tongue-tied. He didn't want to lie to her. He didn't want to burden her with the truth without her mother or aunt to help her absorb the blow. He turned his hat in his hands. "I think we had best wait for an adult to be here," he suggested firmly. "Do you think you could send a lad to find your mother or grand-mother or aunt?"

Her mouth twisted, and he almost saw her fears turn to anger. Her eyes glinted with anger as she crisply replied, "I shall send Rache. Wait here."

With that command, she marched away and left him standing in the doorway. He wondered why she had not simply summoned a servant to carry the message. She had answered the door herself also. He ventured a few steps further into the once-familiar room and peered down the hall. His quick eyes picked up minor signs of neglect there also. He cast his mind back to his walk here; the carriageway had been littered with bro-ken branches and unraked leaves. The steps had been unswept. Had the Vestrit family come on hard times or was this just Kyle being tight-fisted? He waited restlessly. The evil tidings he was bearing might be much graver than he had first imagined. The capture of their family vessel might spell their ruin. *Althea!* he thought fiercely as if he could summon her by will alone.

The *Springeve* was anchored in Bingtown Harbor. They had arrived in port today. As soon as the ship was secured, Finney had sent Brashen ashore. Finney supposed he was arranging for a buyer for the best of their loot. Brashen had come straight to the Vestrit's home instead. The por-trait of the *Vivacia* was aboard the *Springeve*, mute evidence that what he said was true. He doubted they would demand to see it, though Althea would definitely want to reclaim it. Brashen was not sure what Althea's feelings for him were right now, but she would know he was not a liar.

He tried to push thoughts of Althea away, but once turned to that topic, his mind refused to give it up. What did she think of him? Why did it matter so much to him? Because it did. Because he wanted her to think well of him. They had not parted well, and he had regretted that ever since. He didn't believe she would hold his rough jest against him when they met again. She wasn't like that; she wasn't some prissy female to take grave offense at an awkward joke. He closed his eyes a moment and

almost prayed he was right. He thought more than well of her. He thrust
his hands in his pockets and paced a turn around the hallway.

ALTHEA STOOD IN AMBER'S SHOP, IDLY RUNNING HER HANDS THROUGH A
basket of beads. She fished one out at random, and looked at it. An apple.
The next was a pear, and the next was a cat, its tail curled around its
body. At the door, Amber bid her customer farewell, promising that she
would have his selections strung into a necklace by this time tomorrow.
As the door shut behind him, Amber rattled a handful of beads into a
small basket, and then began to restore the rejected wares to their shelves.
As Althea came to help her, Amber picked up their earlier conversation.

"So. Naria Tenira will confront the Bingtown Council about slavery?
Is that what you came to tell me?"

"I thought you'd want to know how persuasive she'd found you."

Amber smiled, pleased. "I already knew, of course. Naria told me. I
scandalized her by saying I wished I could be there."

"The meetings are for Trader folk only," Althea protested.

"She said the same," Amber replied affably. "Is that what brought you
here so swiftly?"

Althea shrugged. "I hadn't seen you in awhile. And I couldn't face
going home to the accounts or to Malta. Someday, Amber, I'm going to
shake that girl until her teeth rattle. She is so infuriating."

"Actually, she sounds as if she's a lot like you." At Althea's outraged
glare, Amber amended, "As you would have been if your father had not
taken you to sea."

Althea observed reluctantly, "Sometimes I wonder if what he did was
kind."

It was Amber's turn to be surprised. "Would you have it otherwise?"
she asked quietly.

"I don't know." Althea ran her hands through her hair distractedly.
Amber watched in amusement.

"You're not playing the role of a boy anymore. You'd best smooth out
that mess you just made."

Althea groaned, and patted at her hair. "No. Now I'm playing the
role of a Bingtown woman. It's equally false to me. There. Does it look all
right now?"

Amber reached across the counter to push a lock of Althea's hair
back into place. "There. That's better. False, how?"

Althea bit her lip for a moment. Then she shook her head. "False in
every way. I feel trapped in these clothes; I must walk a certain way, sit a
certain way. I can scarcely lift my hand over my head without the sleeves
binding me. The pins in my hair give me a headache. I must speak to
people according to proper protocol. Even to stand here, speaking inti-

mately with you in your shop, is potentially scandalous. But worst of all, I must pretend to want things I don't really want." She paused briefly. "Sometimes I almost convince myself I do want them," she added confusedly. "If I could want them, life would be easier."

The bead-maker made no immediate reply. Amber picked up the small baskets of beads. Althea followed her as she walked to an alcove at the back of the store. Amber let down a rattling curtain of hand-carved beads to shield them from casual eyes. She sat down on a tall stool by a worktable. Althea took a chair. The arms of it bore the marks of Amber's idle whittling.

"What don't you want?" Amber asked kindly as she began to set the beads out on the table before her.

"I don't want all the things a real woman would want. You made me realize that. I don't dream of babies and a pretty house. I don't want a settled home, and a growing family. I'm not even sure I want a husband. Today Malta accused me of being odd. It stung worse than anything else she flung at me. Because it's true. I suppose I am. I don't want any of the things a woman is supposed to want." She rubbed her temples. "I should want Grag. I mean . . . I do want Grag. I like him. I enjoy his company." She stared at the front door as she added more honestly, "When he touches my hand, it warms me. But when I consider marrying him and all that would go with it . . ." She shook her head. "It's not what I want. It would cost too much. Even though it would, perhaps, be wise."

Amber said nothing. She was setting out bits of metal and wooden spacers. She measured off several lengths of gleaming silken thread, and then began to knot them together into a woven rope. "You don't love him," Amber suggested.

"I could. I don't allow myself to love him. It's like wanting something you can't possibly afford to buy. There is no reason not to love him, save that there is so much . . . attached to him. His family. His inheritance. His ship, his position in the community." Althea sighed again, and looked miserable. "The man himself is wonderful. But I can't bring myself to give up everything I'd have to surrender to love him."

"Ah," Amber said. She fitted a bead to the woven strand and knotted it in place.

Althea traced an old carving on the chair's arm. "He has expectations. They don't include me captaining my own liveship. He'd want me to settle down and manage things for him. I'd make a home for him to come back to, and raise our children and keep our household in order." Her brows knit over her dark eyes. "I'd do everything that needed to be done so that he could sail off without any worries save the ship." Bitterness came into her voice. "I'd do all the things that made it possible for him to live the life he wanted." She spoke the next words sadly. "If I decide to love Grag, to marry him, it would cost me everything else I've ever wanted to do with my life. I'd have to lay it all down for the sake of loving him."

"And that's not what you want to do with your life?" Amber asked.

A sour smile twisted Althea's mouth. "No. I don't want to be the wind in his sails. That's what I want someone else to do for me." She sat up straight suddenly. "That is . . . that didn't come out right. I'm not explaining this very well."

Amber looked up from her work to grin at her. "On the contrary, I think you are uncomfortable only because you have stated it so plainly. You want a mate who will follow your dream. You don't want to give up your own ambitions to make someone else's life possible."

"I suppose that's true," Althea admitted reluctantly. An instant later she demanded, "Why is that so wrong?"

"It isn't," Amber assured her. A moment later she added wickedly, "As long as you're male."

Althea leaned back in her chair and crossed her arms stubbornly. "I can't help it. That's what I want." When Amber said nothing, Althea asked, almost angrily, "Don't try to tell me that that is what love is, giving it all up for someone else!"

"But for some people, it is," Amber pointed out inexorably. She bound another bead into the necklace, then held it up to look at it critically. "Others are like two horses in harness, pulling together toward a goal."

"I suppose that wouldn't be so bad," Althea conceded. Her knit brows said she did not entirely believe it. "Why can't people love one another and still remain free?" she demanded suddenly.

Amber paused to rub her eyes, then tug thoughtfully at her earring. "One can love that way," she conceded regretfully. "But the price on that kind of love may be the highest of all." She strung her words together as carefully as she strung her beads. "To love another person like that, you have to admit that his life is as important as yours. Harder still, you have to admit to yourself that perhaps he has needs you cannot fill, and that you have tasks that will take you far away from him. It costs loneliness and longing and doubt and—"

"Why must love cost anything? Why does need have to be mixed up with love? Why can't people be like butterflies, coming together in bright sunshine and parting while the day is still bright?"

"Because they are people, not butterflies. To pretend that people can come together, love and then part with no pain or consequences is more false a role than pretending to be a proper Trader's daughter." She set her beads down and met Althea's gaze. She spoke bluntly. "Don't, please, convince yourself that you can bed Grag Tenira and walk away from it without diminishing both of you. A moment ago you spoke of love without need. To sate your need without love is theft. If you must have that, hire it done. But don't steal that from Grag under the pretense that it is free. I know Grag Tenira now. He cannot give you that, not that way."

Althea crossed her arms on her chest. "I wasn't thinking of doing that."

"Yes, you were," Amber asserted, her eyes back on her beads. "We all think about doing that. That doesn't make it right." She turned her work and began a new pattern of knots. In the silence she added, "When you bed someone, there is always a commitment. Sometimes that commitment is only that you will both pretend it doesn't matter." Her strangely colored eyes held Althea's for a moment. "Sometimes that commitment is made only to yourself. The other party never knows it or agrees to it."

Brashen. Althea shifted uncomfortably in her chair. Why did he always come to mind at such inopportune moments? Whenever she thought she had weeded him from her memory, the leaves of that interlude unfurled again. It made her angry all over again, but she was no longer sure it was Brashen she was angry with. She pushed such thoughts away. It was over and done with, a part of her life she was finished with. She could put it behind her. She could cover it up with other things.

"Love isn't just about feeling sure of the other person, knowing what he would give up for you. It's knowing with certainty what you are willing to surrender for his sake. Make no mistake; each partner gives up something. Individual dreams are surrendered for a shared one. In some marriages, one partner gives up almost everything she once thought she wanted. But it's not always the woman who does so. Such sacrifice is not shameful. It's love. If you think the man is worth it, it works."

She sat still for a time, pondering. Then Althea leaned forward suddenly, to ask Amber, "Do you think that if I married Grag, I'd change my mind?"

"Well. Someone would certainly have to," Amber replied philosophically.

BRASHEN VENTURED A PEEK DOWN THE HALLWAY AGAIN. WHERE WAS THE girl? Was she going to leave him standing here until the runner returned with her mother? Waiting was always hard for him. He grinned to himself, the prospect of seeing Althea lightening his heart despite the gravity of the tidings he bore. He wished he had just the tiniest end of a cindin stick to sustain him, but he had resolutely left them behind on the *Springeve*. He knew Althea disapproved of his small vice. He didn't want her to think he was the sort of man who had to carry it with him always. She already considered it enough of a fault. Well, he already knew all Althea's faults. Proximity had forced him to tolerate them for years. They didn't matter. He had come to care for her, and it was more than a single night of bedding together. That night had only made him admit what he already felt. For years, he'd seen her nearly every day. They'd shared a drink or a meal in many ports, gamed together, mended sail together. She didn't treat him like the disgraced son of a Bingtown Trader. She treated him like a valuable ship's officer, respected him for his knowledge and his ability to command men. She was a woman, but he could talk to her, beyond complimenting her gown or comparing her eyes to stars. How rare was that?

He wandered back to a window, looked out down the drive. A light footfall behind him turned him around. It was Malta again. A bit spoiled, if Althea's tales of her were true. Her eyes met his, and she smiled gravely. Her demeanor had changed yet again. "I've sent off a runner, as you suggested. If you'd like to follow me, I can offer you a cup of coffee and some morning cake." Her genteelly modulated voice was that of a well-bred young lady welcoming him to her home.

It recalled him to his own manners. "Thank you. That would be most welcome."

She gestured to the hallway, and surprised him by taking his arm. She scarcely came to the top of his shoulder. He noticed her scent now, some floral oil, violets perhaps. It wafted up from her hair. She glanced up at him once through her eyelashes as he accompanied her down the hall. The look made him reevaluate his first impression of her. Sa's breath, how fast children grew up. Hadn't she been a playmate of little Delo? The last time he had seen his little sister, she had been in disgrace for muddying her pinafore. He hadn't even set eyes on her in years. A peculiar sense of loss assailed him. He had lost more than just home and fortune when his father had disowned him.

She led him into the morning room. Coffee service and a plate of morning bread had already been set out on a small table flanked by two comfortable chairs. The opened window presented a garden vista. "I hope you'll be comfortable waiting here. I made the coffee myself. I hope it isn't too strong."

"I'm sure it will be fine," he said lamely. He felt doubly shamed. That had been what had delayed her, and yes, the Vestrit family had fallen on hard times when a daughter of the house made coffee and sliced bread for visitors. "You know my sister, don't you?" he burst out suddenly. "Delo?"

"Of course I do. Dear, sweet Delo. She is my closest friend." Again, she gave him that smile. She gestured him to a seat, and took the opposite one at the small table she had arranged. She poured the coffee, and served him the sweet seed-studded bread.

"I haven't seen Delo in years," he found himself admitting.

"You haven't? What a shame. She has quite grown up, you know." Her smile was slightly different as she added, "I know your brother also."

Brashen knit his brows at her knowing tone. "Cerwin. He is well, I trust."

"I suppose. He was the last time I saw him." She gave a small sigh and looked away from him. "I do not see him often."

Was she infatuated with young Cerwin? Brashen quickly reckoned his siblings' ages from his own. Well. He supposed Cerwin was of an age to be courting young ladies. Yet, if Delo and Malta were the same age, Malta seemed rather young to be courted. He began to feel a bit uncomfortable. Was this pretty little charmer girl or woman? She stirred her coffee, and somehow contrived to make him notice the elegance of her hands as she did so. Then she leaned across the little table and offered to spice his coffee for him. Surely, she had not intended to display quite that much bosom as she did so. He looked away but her scent still reached him.

She sat back in her chair. She lifted her coffee, sipped it, and then pushed a stray strand of hair back from her unlined brow. "You know my Aunt Althea, I believe?"

"Of course. We served together . . . on the *Vivacia*, for many years."

"Of course."

"She returned safely to Bingtown?"

"Oh, yes. Weeks and weeks ago. She came back aboard the *Ophelia*. That's the Tenira family liveship, you know." Her eyes met his squarely as she added, "Grag Tenira is very enamored of her. It has made Bingtown buzz with gossip. Not a few are startled at the idea of my headstrong aunt suddenly losing her heart to such a steady young man. My grandmother, of course, is quite thrilled. We all are. We had almost given up hope of her ever making a good match and settling down. I am sure you know what I mean." She gave a small confidential laugh, as if these were words she would not share with just anyone. She watched him so closely, as if she could see how the barbs of her words set in his heart and clawed there.

"A good match," he repeated numbly. He found himself nodding like a bob-head toy. "Tenira. Grag Tenira. Oh, he would. Be a good match, I mean. He's a good sailor, too." This last he added more to himself. It was the only thing he could think of that might have attracted Althea to Grag Tenira. Well, he was handsome, too. Brashen had heard him called handsome. He also wasn't disinherited and didn't have a fondness for cindin. The thought of the drug made him abruptly long for some, to distract him from this nasty new sensation. There might be part of a stick in his jacket pocket, but he could scarcely indulge in a waterfront vice here in front of this gently reared child.

". . . more bread, Brashen?"

He caught only her last few words. He glanced down at his untouched plate. "No. No, thank you very much. It's very good, though." He hastily took a bite of the bread. In his dry mouth, the seedy texture was like sawdust. He washed it down with a gulp of the coffee, and then realized he was eating like a deckhand at a galley table.

Malta reached across the table to lightly touch the back of his hand

with her slender little fingers. "You seem quite travel-worn. I was so upset
when I first let you in . . . I never thanked you for coming so far to bring
us tidings of my father's ship. You have come from afar, haven't you?"

"Quite a ways," he admitted. He drew away from her and rubbed his
hands together in his lap, as if that would still the tingling of her touch.
She smiled knowingly at that, and then turned her face aside. A blush
rose on her cheeks. She was aware of her flirting then, it wasn't the casual
touch of a child. He felt besieged and confused. There were too many
things to consider here. His mouth ran at the thought of even a small
piece of cindin to clear his mind. He forced himself to take another bite
of bread instead.

"You know, I look at you, and I wonder how your brother might look
if he grew a mustache. Yours is quite flattering to your jaw and lips."

Brashen lifted a hand to his own face to smooth his mustache self-
consciously. Her words were not appropriate, nor the way her eyes followed his fingers almost avidly. Brashen stood. "Perhaps I should come
back later this afternoon. Please let them know to expect me. I probably
should have sent word before I came calling today."

"Not at all." The girl remained seated. She did not stand to escort
him to the door or even acknowledge his desire to leave. "I've already
sent the runner. I am sure they will return soon. They will want to hear
news of my father and his ship as swiftly as possible."

"I am sure they will," Brashen agreed stiffly. He could not understand
this young woman. She looked at him guilelessly. Perhaps her words had
been a child's artless error. Perhaps he had been too long at sea. He sat
down, his back rigidly straight, and held his hat in his lap. "I will wait for
them, then. I am sure I have interrupted your day. Please, do not feel you
must remain with me. I shall be fine waiting here by myself."

She gave a bubble of laughter at his awkward words. "Oh, dear. I have
made you uncomfortable. I am terribly sorry. I suppose I have been too
familiar with you. It is only because you were dear Grandfather's first mate
so long that I feel you are almost a relative. Also, knowing Cerwin and
Delo as well as I do, I naturally wished to extend a warm welcome to their
brother." Her voice dropped dramatically. "I think it is so tragic that you
are no longer welcome in your family home. I have never understood
exactly what happened between you and your father. . . ." She let her
words trail off, inviting his confidence.

Spilling his guts about his family quarrel was the last thing he wished
to do now. He could not recall that he had ever been in such an awkward
situation. One moment Malta seemed an innocent child doing her best to
welcome a guest in the absence of her elders. The next she seemed like a
temptress toying with him. His news was pressing, and he wished to see
Althea, but the longer he remained here, the uneasier he felt. It was
belatedly occurring to him that perhaps this whole situation would be

seen as improper. He was, to all appearances, completely alone with a young woman of good family. He knew some fathers and brothers who had fought duels over lesser offenses. He stood again. "I fear I must go. I have other errands. I will return, late this afternoon. Please give your family my regards."

Malta made no effort at rising. He didn't wait for her to do so. "Very pleasant to have seen you again." He bowed to her, and turned to leave.

"Your brother Cerwin doesn't think I'm a child." There was a challenge in those words.

Unwillingly he turned back to face her. She had not arisen, but she had thrown back her head against the chair, baring the white column of her throat. A bit of her hair had come loose and she reached up to twine it through her fingers as she spoke. She smiled lazily. "He is sweet, like a little house cat. You, I suspect, are more like a tiger." She put a fingertip in her mouth and nibbled at it thoughtfully. "Pets can be such boring creatures," she observed.

Brashen suddenly discovered that the heart of a correctly mannered Bingtown Trader's son beat in his chest under his pirate's blouse. He was shocked to his core. There could be no mistake in her inflection. Captain Vestrit's granddaughter, in his family home, was honing her seductive wiles on him. It was outrageous.

"You should be ashamed of yourself," he said with honest indignation.

He did not turn back at her shocked gasp, but proceeded down the hall to the main door. He pulled it open to let himself out and found himself looking down into the startled faces of Ronica Vestrit and Keffria Haven. "Oh, thank Sa you've come," he exclaimed, even as Keffria demanded, "Who are you and what are you doing in our house?" She glanced about wildly as if to summon menservants to seize him.

"Brashen Trell," he told her hastily, bowing low. "I bring tidings of the *Vivacia*. Urgent and troublesome tidings."

The shock of his words instantly seized their attention.

"What is wrong? Has anything happened to Kyle? Have you word of my son, of Wintrow?" Keffria demanded immediately.

"No." Ronica Vestrit commanded. "Not here, come inside and sit down. Come, Keffria. To the study."

Brashen stepped aside to allow them to precede him. He spoke as he followed them. "Your granddaughter Malta let me in. I presumed the runner she had sent to fetch you would have prepared you for my tidings." He wanted to ask if Althea were coming, but held his tongue against that.

"No runner found us," Ronica Vestrit informed him tersely. "But I had feared that sooner or later, someone would knock at our door and the tidings would not be good ones." She ushered them into the study and shut the door firmly. "Have a chair, Trell. What do you know? You didn't sail with the *Vivacia*; I know that Kyle replaced you with a man of his own choosing. So how do you come to bear this message to us?"

How much of the truth did he owe her? If she had been Althea and they had been sitting quietly over a couple of beers, he would have told her all, and allowed her to judge him as she saw fit. Trafficking with pirates was a hanging offense; there was no denying that was what he had been doing. He wouldn't lie; he simply wouldn't tell.

"*Vivacia* has been taken by pirates." He dropped the words like an unchained anchor. Before they could recover enough to pelt him with questions, he added, "I know very little more than that. She was seen in a pirate outpost harbor, anchored up. I do not know what has become of her captain or crew. I'm sorry to tell you that, and sorrier to tell you that the pirate who has seized her is one Captain Kennit. I don't know why he went after *Vivacia*. His reputation is that of an ambitious crusader. He dreams of uniting the Pirate Isles into a kingdom for himself. To that end, he has been pursuing slaveships. The rumors say that he kills all the crew, and sets the slaves free, to gain their goodwill and that of other pirates who hate slavery as he does." He ran out of breath and words. As he spoke, Keffria had appeared to become boneless, settling deeper and deeper into her chair as if his words were taking all life from her body. She had lifted both hands to cover her mouth, holding in a wail of horror.

In contrast, Ronica Vestrit stood as if turned to wood. Her face was frozen in a rictus of despair. Her old hands clutched the back of a chair like a bird's talons gripping a perch.

After a long moment, Ronica drew in a breath. She spoke in a whisper that seemed to tax her. "Do you bring us a ransom offer?"

It shamed him. The old woman was quick-witted. She had seen the cut of his clothes, and guessed where he had been making his living. She thought he was Kennit's go-between. The shame burned him, but he could not fault her for it. "No," he said simply. "I know little more than I've told you, and half of that is rumor and gossip." He sighed. "I do not think there will be a ransom offer. This Captain Kennit appears very pleased with his prize. The ship, at least, I suspect he will keep. I know nothing of the men who were aboard her. I'm sorry."

The silence that welled up now seemed chilling. His tidings had changed the course of their lives. With a score of words, he had slain their hopes. The ship was not merely delayed. Her captain would not come home with coin to restore their fortunes. Instead, whatever they had left to muster must be sacrificed for a ransom, if they were fortunate enough to receive a ransom offer. The news he had brought ruined the Vestrit family. They would hate the bearer of such tidings. He waited for the storm to break.

Neither of them wept. Neither of them screamed, nor accused him of lying. Keffria buried her face in her hands. "Wintrow," she said very softly. "My little boy." Ronica aged before his eyes, her shoulders sagging, the lines in her face graving more deeply. She groped her way into her chair and sat in it, staring. A horrible weight of responsibility settled on Brashen. What had he expected? He groped after vanished imaginings in which Althea had been fiery-eyed with anger, and turned to him as her friend to aid her in rescuing her ship. This was the reality. He had dealt the final crushing blow to a family who had once befriended him.

There was a sudden squawk, a thudding on the door, and then it was flung open. Althea entered, pushing a disheveled and struggling Malta before her. "Keffria! This brat was eavesdropping again. I'm tired of her spying, sneaking ways. It isn't worthy of anyone in this family—Brashen? What are you doing here? What's happened, what is going on?" Althea let go of Malta so suddenly that the girl sat down flat with a thud on the floor. She stared at him wild-eyed, her mouth open as if he had knocked the wind out of her lungs.

He stood and took a step toward her. His story spilled out. "The *Vivacia* has been captured by pirates. I saw her anchored up in a pirate stronghold, with the Raven flag flying from her masthead. That's Kennit. I'm sure you know his reputation. It is said he kills the full crew of every slaver he captures. I don't know the crew's fate."

A piercing wail from Malta blasted away all other responses. She drew a second breath, and came to her feet. She charged Brashen, swinging her fists wildly. "No. It's a lie, it's a lie! Father said he would come home, he was going to make everything right! He is going to come home and make us rich again and throw out Althea and make everyone treat me well! You're only saying that, you pig. It isn't true, it isn't true. My father can't be dead, he can't!"

He caught one of her wrists, and then the other after she had hit him twice. He expected she would surrender. Instead, she kicked him sharply twice in the shins. "Malta! Stop that!" Ronica commanded sharply while Keffria cried out, "Stop it, stop it. It won't solve anything."

Althea was more direct. She strode up, seized Malta by the hair on the back of her head and pulled her sharply back. The girl cried out in pain. Brashen promptly released her wrists. Then Althea shocked him by pinning Malta in a rough embrace. "Stop it, stop it now," she whispered hoarsely to the struggling girl. "It won't do any good. Save your strength and your wits. We can't waste them fighting each other. We have a common enemy now. We have to put everything we have toward rescuing them. Malta. Malta. I know this is terrible, but we have to cope, not thrash about in hysteria."

Malta quieted abruptly. Then she thrust Althea savagely away and staggered clear of her aunt before turning to accuse her. "You're happy this happened. You are! You don't care anything about my father, you never did. All you want is that ship. You hope he is dead, I know you do! You hate me. Don't pretend to be my friend." She clenched her teeth and glared at Althea. A moment of stark silence filled the room.

Althea's voice was stone. "No. I'm not your friend." She pushed her mussed hair back from her face. "Most of the time, I don't like you at all. But I am your aunt. Fate has made us family, and now it has made us allies as well. Malta. Put aside your airs and flouncing and sulking. Set your mind to this problem. It is what we all must do. We need to get our family ship back and rescue any of her crew who may still be alive. That is the only problem we can put our energies to right now."

Malta looked her up and down suspiciously. "You're trying to trick me. You still want the ship for yourself."

"I still want to command the family ship," Althea agreed easily. "That's true. But that quarrel will have to wait until *Vivacia* is safely back in Bingtown. Right now, that is what all of us want. It is rare when the women of this family agree on anything. So, while we do, you need to stop behaving like a hysterical girl with the brains of a chicken."

Althea's gaze swept to include her mother and sister. "None of us can afford to give way to our emotions right now. We have only one course that I can see. We need to raise money for a ransom. A substantial one. That is, frankly, our best chance of getting both ship and crew back uninjured." She shook her head. "It sticks in my craw to have to buy back what is ours, but that is our most practical way to regain it. If we are fortunate, he will take our money and return what is ours. Brashen is right, however. I have heard of this Captain Kennit. If he pursued the *Vivacia*, it is because he means to keep her. If that is so, we can only pray to Sa that he has been wise enough to keep her family members and familiar crew alive to keep her sane. So, you see, Malta, I have reasons of my own for hoping your father and brother are alive and well." Althea delivered this wry aside with a pained clench of a smile.

In a lower voice she went on, "The Bingtown Trader Council meets tomorrow night. They are supposed to give the Tenira family a hearing on the Satrap's tariff, the presence of the so-called Chalcedean 'patrol ships' and slaves in Bingtown. I've promised Grag I'll be there to support his father's views. Mother, Keffria, you should come as well. Rally any others that you can. It is time the Bingtown Traders were awakened to all that is going on. The worsening piracy and their increasing boldness is yet another part of the Satrap's mess. When the time is right, we need to bring up the *Vivacia*'s situation and ask for support from at least the other liveship families, if we cannot sway all the Traders to help us. This is something that affects us all. At the risk of setting off Malta again, I will add that it directly relates to the slavery issue. If Kyle hadn't been using *Vivacia* as a slaver, this would not have befallen her. It is well known that Kennit targets slaveships. It is also known," she added in a slightly louder voice as Malta took a breath to interrupt, "that the pirate activities are why we have these Chalcedean privateers tied up in our harbor. If Bingtown itself takes a stand against the pirates, perhaps we can show the Satrap we don't need his patrol boats and we don't intend to pay for them." She turned and looked out the window at the waning afternoon. "And if we succeed in all that, perhaps we can waken all Bingtown to the fact that we don't need Jamaillia or the Satrap at all. That we can take care of ourselves now." Those words were very softly spoken but they sounded clear in the quiet room.

Althea gave a sudden deep sigh and her shoulders drooped. "I'm hungry. Isn't that stupid? Brashen brings me the worst possible news that I can imagine, and somehow I still get hungry at dinner time."

"No matter what befalls you, your body tries to go on living." Ronica spoke the heavy words with the experience of a survivor. She moved stiffly as she crossed the room to her granddaughter. She held out her hand to her. "Malta. Althea is right. We must stand as a family now, putting aside all quarrels with each other." She lifted her eyes and smiled grimly around at them all. "Sa's breath. Look what it takes to make us remember we are family. I feel ashamed." She returned her gaze to her granddaughter. Her empty hand waited, hovering. Slowly Malta extended her own. Ronica took it. She looked deep into the girl's angry gaze. Suddenly she gave her a brittle hug. Malta cautiously returned it.

"Malta and Papa aren't bad anymore?" a young voice wondered aloud. All heads turned to the boy in the doorway.

"Oh, Selden!" Keffria cried in weary dismay. She pulled herself up from her chair and went to her young son. She tried to hug him but he pulled stiffly free. "Mama, I'm not a baby!" he cried in annoyance. His eyes went past his mother to Brashen. He considered him gravely. He cocked his head. "You look like a pirate," he decided.

"I do, don't I?" Brashen said. He squatted down to be on a level with the small boy. He smiled and held out a hand. "But I'm not. I'm just an honest Bingtown sailor, a bit down on my luck." For a moment, he believed it was true. He could almost forget the stub end of a cindin stick his wayward fingers had found in the corner of his jacket pocket.

CHAPTER SIXTEEN

Taking Charge

ALTHEA WATCHED HIM LEAVE. SHE HAD NOT JOINED HER MOTHER TO WALK him to the door. Instead, she had fled to a maid's chamber in the upper story of the house. She had left the dusty room dark, and did not even lean too close to the window lest Brashen look back and chance to see her. The moonlight washed the gaudy color from his clothes. He walked slowly, not looking back, his gait as rolling as if he strode a deck instead of a carriage drive.

Althea had been lucky she had been struggling with Malta when she first entered the study that evening. No one had remarked on her red cheeks or lost breath. She did not think that even Brashen had realized her moment of panic at seeing him. The stricken expressions that Keffria and Mother had worn had near stilled her heart. For one ghastly instant, she had imagined that he had come to her mother to confess all and offer to redeem Althea's shame by marrying her. Even while she reeled from the severity of Brashen's real tidings, she had felt a secret relief that she did not have to admit publicly what she had done.

What *she* had done. She accepted that now. Amber's words had made her confront herself on that issue weeks ago. She was almost ashamed now that she had tried to hide behind excuses. What they had done, they had done together. If she wanted to respect herself as a woman and an adult, she could not claim otherwise. She had only spoken otherwise, she decided truthfully, because she had not wanted to be blamed for such an irresponsible act. If he had really tricked or coerced her into bed with him, then she could justify the pain she had felt since then. She could have been the wronged woman, the seduced innocent, abandoned by a heartless sailor. But such roles insulted both of them.

She had not been able to meet his eyes tonight, nor yet look away from him. She had missed him. The years of shipboard camaraderie, she told herself, outweighed the harsh way they had parted. Time and again, she had stolen glances at him, storing his image in her mind as if she were satisfying some sort of hunger. The devastating news he had brought still tore at her heart, but her traitor eyes had studied only the bright darkness of his eyes, and how his muscled shoulders moved under his silk shirt. She had noticed a cindin sore at the edge of his mouth; he was still using the drug. His freebooter's garb had appalled her. It hurt and disappointed her that he had turned pirate. Yet, such clothes suited him far better than the sober dress of a Bingtown Trader's son ever had. She disapproved of everything about him, yet the sight of him had set her heart racing.

"Brashen," she said hopelessly to the darkness. She shook her head after his departing form. She had regrets, she told herself. That was all. She regretted that bedding with him had destroyed their easy companionship. She regretted that she had let herself do such an inappropriate thing with such an inappropriate person. She regretted that he had given up and not become the man her father had believed he would. She regretted his poor judgment and weak character. That was all she felt. Regrets.

She wondered what had brought him back to Bingtown. He would not have come all this way just to tell them *Vivacia* had been captured. At the thought of her ship, the pain in her heart wrenched one notch tighter. Losing her to Kyle had been hard enough; now she was in the hands of a pirate capable of murder. It would mark the ship. There was no escaping that. If she ever did recover *Vivacia,* she would be very different from the lively and spirited ship that had left Bingtown over a year ago.

"As different as I am from whom I was then," she said aloud to the night. "As different as he is." She watched Brashen until the darkness swallowed him.

MIDNIGHT HAD COME AND GONE BEFORE MALTA MANAGED TO SLIP AWAY from the house. The family had all eaten in the kitchen like servants, making a late meal off what was there. They had included Brashen in their company. When Rache had come in later from her day off in town, the family and Brashen had moved to her grandfather's study and continued their discussion. Even Selden had been included, much to Malta's disgust. All he did was ask stupid questions, which would not have been so bad, except that everyone kept trying to answer them in ways that he would understand, while insisting that he should not be scared. Finally he fell asleep on the hearth. Brashen had offered to carry him up to his bed and her mother had actually allowed that instead of rousing the little bug.

Malta drew her cloak more tightly about her. It was a fine summer night, but the dark cloak helped both camouflage her and kept the dew at bay. Her slippers and the hem of her gown were already soaked. It was much darker outside at night than she had expected. The white pebbled walkway that led to the oak tree and the gazebo reflected the moonlight to guide her feet. In some places, grass sprawled over the path. Wet brown leaves, unraked since autumn, clung to the bottoms of her slippers. She tried not to think of slugs and worms mashed under her feet.

She heard a rustle in the bushes to her right and stopped with a gasp. Something hastened away through the underbrush, but she remained frozen, listening. Once in a great while, mountain cats were seen near Bingtown. It was said they would carry off small livestock, even children. She longed to go back to the house, but she reminded herself she must be brave. This was no prank or test of her will. What she did now, she did for her father's sake.

She was sure he would understand.

She had found it very ironic that Aunt Althea had implored her to unite with her family to get the ship and her father back. Even her grandmother had made a fine show with that squishy hug. The truth was, neither of them thought Malta could do anything to help, save stay out of trouble. Malta knew the opposite was true. While Mother wept in her bedchamber and boiled wine as an offering to Sa, and Aunt Althea and her grandmother lay awake thinking of what might be sold off to raise coin, only Malta would act. Malta alone realized that she was the one who could rally others to their aid. Her resolve hardened as she thought about it. She would do whatever she had to do to bring her father safely home. Then she would see to it that he knew who had truly made a sacrifice for him. Who said that women could not be brave and daring for the sake of those they loved? Fortified with this thought, she picked her way along the path.

A weird glow through the trellised roses sent a shiver up her spine. A soft yellow light flickered and swayed. For a second all the spook tales she had ever heard about the Rain Wilds assailed her. Had Reyn set something to watch over her, and would it think she was betraying him? She almost turned back until a slight breeze brought her the scent of burning candle wax and the jasmine perfume that Delo lately favored. She crept toward the oak. From its deeper shadow, she discerned the source of the glow. Yellow light shone gently through the slats of the old gazebo, outlining the leaves of the ivy that draped the structure. It seemed a magical place, romantic and mysterious.

Cerwin awaited her there. He had lit a candle to guide her to him. Her heart surged and raced. It was perfect, a minstrel's romantic tale. She was the heroine, the young woman wronged by fate and her family, beautiful, young and heartbroken over her father's captivity. Despite all that her unloving family had done to her, she would be the one to make the ultimate sacrifice that saved them all. Cerwin was the young man who had come to deliver her, for his manly young heart thundered with love for her. He could not do otherwise. She stood still in the fickle moonlight, savoring the drama of it all.

She walked softly until she could peek inside the leafy door. Two figures waited inside. Delo was huddled up in a corner in her cloak, but Cerwin paced back and forth. It was his motion that made the candle's light erratic. His hands were empty. She frowned to herself. That didn't seem right. Reyn would have brought her flowers at least. Well, perhaps whatever Cerwin had for her was small. Maybe it was in his pocket. She refused to let it spoil the moment.

Malta paused only to push back her hood, shake out her hair and spread it carefully over her shoulders. She scraped her teeth over her lips to redden them, then entered the spill of light from the gazebo. She walked forward with a dignified pace, her face grave. Cerwin noticed her immediately. She stopped where she could be half in shadow. She turned her face to the candlelight's caress and opened her eyes wide.

"Malta!" he whispered in a voice choked with suppressed emotion. He strode toward her. He would sweep her up in his arms. She braced herself for that, but instead he halted and then dropped to one knee before her. His head was bowed and she could see only his dark curly hair. In a tight voice he said, "Thank you for coming. When midnight passed and you were not here, I feared—" He gasped in a breath that was almost a sob. "I feared I had no hope at all."

"Oh, Cerwin," she murmured sorrowfully. From the corner of one eye, she noted that Delo had crept to the door of the gazebo and was peeking out at them. For a moment, it annoyed her. It spoiled the mood to have Cerwin's little sister watching them. She pushed the thought away. Ignore her. It didn't matter. Delo couldn't tell anything without getting in big trouble herself. Malta took a step closer to Cerwin. She set her pale hands to his dark head and ran her fingers through his curls. He caught his breath at her touch. She turned his face up to hers. "How could you think I would not come?" she asked him gently. She gave a soft sigh. "No matter what sorrows batter me, no matter what danger to myself . . . you should have known I would come."

"I dared to hope," he admitted. When he looked up at her, she was shocked. He strongly resembled Brashen, yet he suffered in the comparison. She had thought Cerwin manly and mature. Now, after she had watched Brashen for an evening, Cerwin appeared a callow youth. The comparison annoyed her. It made her conquest less of a triumph. He caught her two hands, then dared to kiss each of her palms before releasing them.

"You must not," she murmured to him. "You know I am promised to another."

"I will never allow him to have you," he vowed.

She shook her head. "It is too late. The tidings your brother brought us tonight have made me see that." She looked aside from him to stare wide-eyed into the night forest. "I have no choice but to fulfill my fate. My father's life depends on it."

He surged to his feet. "What are you saying?" His voice was a low cry. "What news came . . . my brother brought it? Your father's life . . . I don't understand."

For an instant her voice tightened with real tears. "Pirates have captured our family ship. Brashen was kind enough to bring us word of it. We fear my father and brother may already be dead, but if they are not, if any chance remains . . . oh, Cerwin, somehow we must find the money to ransom them. And yet, how can we? Humbling as it is, I know you are aware of our financial difficulties. Once word gets out that our ship has been taken, our creditors will close in like sharks." She lifted her hands to her face. "I do not know how we will feed ourselves, let alone find money to ransom my father. I fear I will be wed off to the Rain Wilder immediately. As much as that distresses me, I know it is what I must do. Reyn is a generous man. He will help us to get my father back. If marrying him is what it will take . . . I do not mind . . . so much." Her voice cracked on these final words. She swayed, genuinely overcome by her cruel fate.

He caught her in his arms. "You poor, brave child. Can you imagine that I would allow you to go to a loveless marriage, even for the sake of your father?"

She whispered against his chest. "The choice is not ours, Cerwin. I will offer myself to Reyn. He has both the wealth and power to help me. That will be what I think of when . . . that time comes when . . . I must accommodate him." She hid her face against his shirt as if ashamed to speak of such things.

Cerwin clutched her upper arms more tightly. "Never," he promised her. "That time will never come." He took a breath. "I do not claim to be as wealthy as a Rain Wilder. But all I have, and all I ever will have, I put at your service." He held her a little away so he could look down into her face. "Did you think I would do less than that?"

She shrugged her shoulders helplessly. "I did not think you could," she admitted. "Your father is still the Trader of your family. Poor Brashen is proof that he runs his household with a firm hand. I know what your heart bids you to do, but, in reality—" she shook her head sadly— "there may be little you can actually command."

"Poor Brashen!" He snorted disdainfully, distracted from her real problem. "My brother brought about his own misfortunes. Do not pity him. Your other words are true, and I do not deny them. I cannot put the entire Trell fortune at your disposal, but—"

"As if I would ask that! Oh, Cerwin, what must you think of me? That I come to you at night, at risk to my reputation, to ask for money?" She turned aside from him in a swirl of cloak that briefly revealed the white cotton nightgown she wore beneath it. She heard Delo's in-drawn gasp. She scuttled out of the gazebo to stand beside Malta.

"You are practically naked!" she scolded her. "Malta, how could you!"

There. If Cerwin had been too dense to notice it before, he knew it now. Malta drew herself up with dignity. "I had no choice. I had but one chance to slip out of the house to meet you, and I took it. I don't regret it. Cerwin has been gentleman enough to ignore it and not shame me. It is not as if I chose to come to him this way. Cannot you understand that my father's life is at stake, Delo? This is not an ordinary time, and the ordinary rules do not apply." She set her hands pleadingly over her heart.

She watched Cerwin's reaction from the corner of her eye. He was staring at her with horrified admiration. His eyes traveled her body as if he could see through her cloak. "Delo," he said brusquely, "it is of no importance. You are such a child, to make much of it. Please. Allow me to speak to Malta privately."

"Cerwin!" Delo protested in outrage.

He had made her angry, calling her a child. Malta did not want that. An angry Delo might gossip too much. Malta stretched out a languid hand to her. "I know you are only trying to protect me. I love you for it. Nevertheless, I am sure that your brother would never do me harm." She met Delo's eyes. "You see, I know your heart, and that tells me much of his. You are honorable people. I do not fear to be alone with him."

Eyes shining, Delo stepped back and away from them. "Oh, Malta. You see so much." Obviously moved, she retreated once more to the gazebo. Malta looked back at Cerwin. She gathered her cloak in tightly to cover herself, well aware that doing so accented the smallness of her waist and the fullness of her hips. Then she looked up at him with a shy smile.

"Cerwin." She said his name, then gave a sigh. "It shames me that I must speak so plainly, but my need forces me to it. I do not ask all that you have and all you will ever possess. Whatever you can offer me, discreetly and comfortably, I shall gratefully accept. But more important to me would be for your family to join forces with mine. Tomorrow night there is to be a Traders' Council meeting. I shall be there. Please come. If you can move your father to attend and speak out for us, it would help us greatly. The loss of our ship and my father is not solely my family's loss. It affects all Bingtown Traders. If these cut-throat pirates do not fear to capture a liveship, what will they not take? If they do not fear to hold prisoner a Bingtown Trader and his son, who is safe?" Malta's voice had grown righteously impassioned. Her hands darted out to seize Cerwin's hands. "If your family could unite with mine in this—" she dropped her voice "—perhaps my grandmother would reconsider Reyn's courtship. Perhaps she might see there are . . . better matches."

She loosened her grip on his hands, her heart racing. Strange warmth flushed her body. Now he would take her in his arms and kiss her, and it would be like the end of a minstrel's song. She waited for the touch of his lips that would bear her up like a leaf on the wind. She half closed her eyes.

Instead, he fell to his knees before her. "I will come to the Traders' Council tomorrow night. I will speak to my father and convince him the Trells should lend their support to your family." He looked up at her adoringly. "You will see. I will prove to you and your family that I am worthy of you."

It took her a moment to find a suitable response. She had been so certain he would kiss her. What had she done wrong? "I have never doubted your worthiness," she faltered at last. She could almost taste her disappointment.

He came back to his feet slowly. He looked down at her, eyes shining. "I will be worthy of your confidence," he promised her.

She waited, thinking he might suddenly embrace her and kiss her ardently. Her skin tingled all over, awaiting his touch. She dared to look straight into his face, her eyes burning with passion. She wet her lips and parted them invitingly as she tilted her chin up toward him.

"Until tomorrow, Malta Haven," he said fervently. "You will see how well I keep my word."

Then, as if he were bidding her farewell at an afternoon tea, he bowed gravely. He turned to his sister. "Come, Delo. I had best be getting you home." He swept his own dark cloak about him and then turned and strode off into the night.

"Farewell, Malta," Delo sighed. Then she waggled her fingers at her friend. "I'll ask my mother if I may come to the Traders' Council also. Maybe we can sit together. I'll see you then." She turned abruptly and hurried away. "Cerwin! Wait for me!"

For some little time, Malta stood in disbelief. What had she done wrong? No gift token of his affection, no passionate kiss . . . he had not even pleaded to be allowed to escort her part of the way back to her house. She frowned after them. Then in an instant, she realized her error. The fault was not hers, but Cerwin's. She shook her head to herself. He was simply not man enough to live up to her expectations.

She turned and began to pick her way back to the house through the darkness. She knit her brows in thought, then self-consciously smoothed her forehead out. She certainly didn't want to end up with a lined forehead like her mother. Brashen had made her frown. He had been so rude to her at first, but then, when she was offering him coffee and flirting a bit, he had definitely reacted to her. She would wager that if he had been the one meeting her in the gazebo tonight, she would have been thoroughly kissed. A sudden shiver ran up her back at that thought. It was not that she liked him. He looked far too coarse in his pirate's silks and long mustache. He had still stunk of the ship when he came to the door, and his hands were scarred and rough with calluses. No. She felt no attraction to the man. But his sidelong glances at her Aunt Althea had stirred her interest. The sailor had watched her move like a hungry cat stalking a bird. Althea never met his eyes. Even when she spoke to him, she contrived to be looking out the window, or stirring a cup of tea or picking at her fingernails. Her avoidance of his glance had distressed him. Time after time, he had addressed his remarks directly to her. At one point she had even gone over to Selden and sat on the floor beside him, taking his hand as if her nephew could shield her from Brashen's avid eyes.

Malta didn't think her mother or grandmother had noticed, but she had. She firmly intended to find out what was between them. She would discover just what Althea knew that could make a man look at her like that. What would she have to say to make Cerwin look at her so warmly? She shook her head. No. Not Cerwin. Comparing him to his older brother had opened her eyes. He was a boy still, with no heat to his glance or power of his own. He was a poor fish, a catch she should throw back. Even Reyn had had more warmth to his touch. Reyn always brought her gifts. She reached the kitchen door and eased it open. She might, after all, use the dream-box tonight.

BRASHEN STOOD UP FROM THE TABLE. THE BEER HE HAD ORDERED WAS still untouched. As he turned and left the tavern, he saw the furtive movement of someone else claiming it. He smiled bitterly to himself. Nice place he'd chosen to drink; it was suited perfectly to the man who couldn't hold onto anything.

Outside the tavern, another Bingtown night was unraveling. He was in the roughest part of Bingtown, patronizing one of the waterfront dives that shared a street with warehouses, whorehouses and flophouses. He knew he should go back to the *Springeve*. Finney would be expecting him. But he had nothing to tell the man, and it suddenly occurred to him that he probably wouldn't go back at all. Ever. It wasn't likely Finney would come into Bingtown looking for him. Time to cut himself loose from that operation. Of course, that meant that the cindin in his pocket was the last he had. He stopped where he stood and groped for it. When he found it, it was shorter than he remembered. Had he already used some of it? Perhaps. Without regret, he tucked the last bit into his lip. He resumed walking down the darkened street. Just over a year ago, he and Althea had walked down a Bingtown street together at night. Forget it. It wasn't likely that would ever happen again. She went strolling with Grag Tenira now.

So. If he wasn't going back to the *Springeve*, where was he going? His feet had already known the answer to that. They were taking him out of town, away from the lights and up the long empty beach to where the abandoned *Paragon* rested on the sands. A smile sneered over Brashen's face. Some things never changed. He was back in Bingtown, close to penniless, and an abandoned ship was the closest thing he had to a friend. He and the ship had a lot in common. Both were outcasts.

All was peaceful under the summer starlit skies. The waves muttered and shushed one another along the shore. There was just enough of a breeze to keep him from sweating as he strode along on the loose sand. It would have been a lovely evening if he had felt good about anything.

As things stood, the wind blew emptiness through him and the starlight was cold. The cindin had energized him, but purposelessly. All it had done was given him plenty of wakefulness in which to be confused. Malta, for instance. What game, by Sa's beard, had she been playing with him? He did not know whether to feel stalked, mocked or flattered by her attention. He still did not know how to think of her, child or woman. Once her mother had returned, she had become a demure young lady, save for the occasional sharp remark delivered so innocently that it seemed accidental. Despite Malta's apparent decorum once her older relatives arrived, he had caught her eyes on him more than once that evening. He had seen her speculative gaze go from him to Althea, and her look had not been kind.

He tried to pretend that she was the reason Althea had not met his eyes. She had not wanted her young niece to guess what had passed between them. For three strides, he believed it. Then he admitted glumly to himself that she had not given him the least sign of warmth or interest. She had been courteous to him, just as Keffria had been courteous to him. No more than that, and no less. As befitted a daughter of Ephron Vestrit, she had been gracious and welcoming to a guest, even when he brought bad tidings to the family. The only time she had failed in courtesy had been when Ronica had offered him a bedchamber. Keffria had urged him to accept it, citing the lateness of the hour and how weary he looked. Althea, however, had kept silent. That had made his decision. He left.

Althea had been lovely. Oh, not as her sister was attractive, nor as Malta was beguiling. Keffria and Malta were careful and constructed in their beauty. The touch of paint, the brush of powder, the careful arranging of hair and selection of clothing all combined to set off their best features. Althea had come in from the streets, her sandals dusty, her hair tendriled with perspiration at her brow and the back of her neck. The warmth of summer was on her cheeks, and the liveliness of Bingtown's market shone in her eyes. Her skirt and blouse were simple garments, chosen for freedom of movement rather than fineness of weave. Even her struggle with Malta when she first entered the room had impressed him with her vitality. She was no longer the boyish hand she'd been on the *Reaper,* nor even the captain's daughter from *Vivacia.* Her stay in

Bingtown had been kind to her hair and skin. Her attire was softer and a bit less pragmatic. She looked like a Trader's daughter.

Hence, unattainable.

A hundred might-have-beens passed through his mind. If he were still heir to the Trell fortune and Trader status. If he had listened to Captain Vestrit and saved some money. If Althea had inherited the ship and kept him on as first mate. So many ifs, but he had no more hope of winning her than of being re-inherited by his father. So, throw it away, with his other discarded futures. Walk on into the empty night.

He spat out bitterness with the fibrous remnants of the cindin stick. The dark hulk of the *Paragon* loomed ahead against the bright canopy of the starry night sky. He caught a faint whiff of wood-smoke from somewhere. As he approached, he began to whistle loudly. He knew Paragon did not like to be surprised. As he drew closer, he called out jovially, "Paragon! Hasn't anyone made you into kindling yet?"

"Who goes there?" A cold voice from the shadows halted him in his tracks.

"Paragon?" Brashen queried in confusion.

"No. I am Paragon. If I'm not mistaken, you're Brashen," the ship jestingly replied. He added in an aside, "He's no danger to me, Amber. Set aside your staff."

Brashen peered through the gloom. A slender silhouette stood between him and the ship, tension in her stance. She moved, and he heard the clatter of hardwood on stone as she leaned her stick on a rock. Amber? The bead-maker? She sat down on something, a bench or stacked stone. He ventured closer. "Hello?"

"Hello." Her voice was cautiously friendly.

"Brashen, I'd like you to meet my friend Amber. Amber, this is Brashen Trell. You know something of him. You cleaned up after him when you moved in." There was breathless excitement in Paragon's boyish voice. He was obviously enjoying this encounter. There was an element of adolescent brag in his voice as he teased Brashen.

"Moved in?" Brashen heard himself query.

"Oh, yes. Amber lives inside me now." A hesitation. "Oh. You were probably coming to me for a place to sleep, weren't you? Well, there is plenty of room, you know. It's only the captain's quarters that she has taken over, and stored a few things in my hold. Amber? You don't mind, do you? Brashen always comes to sleep here when he has no other place to stay, and no more money."

The pause was just a trifle longer than was polite. Brashen heard a touch of uneasiness in Amber's voice as she replied, "You belong to yourself, Paragon. It's not up to me who you welcome aboard."

"I do, do I? Well, if I belong to myself, why are you so intent on buying me?" Now he teased her, hooting like a boy at his own joke.

Brashen found nothing humorous about it. What business had she with the liveship? "No one can buy a liveship, Paragon," he corrected him gently. "A liveship is a part of a Trader's family. You could not sail without a family member aboard you." In a quieter voice, he added, "It isn't even good for you to be out here by yourself so much."

"I'm not by myself, not anymore," the figurehead protested. "Amber comes out almost every night to sleep aboard me. And every ten-day, she takes a holiday and spends the whole afternoon with me. If she buys me, she won't sail me. She's going to just have me leveled up, and she's going to create some cliff-gardens over there, and . . ."

"Paragon!" Brashen rebuked him almost sternly. "You belong to the Ludlucks. They can't sell you and Amber can't buy you. Nor are you some great flowerpot to be decorated with vines. Only a cruel person would tell you such things." He glared at the slender figure sitting silently in the shadows.

Amber flowed to her feet. She advanced on him, shoulders squared, as if she were a man about to challenge him to a fight. Her voice was tight but even as she said, "If what you claim is true, then the cruelty originates with the Ludlucks. They have left him here to brood and rot, all these years. Now, when times are changing and it seems that all of Bingtown can be bought, they entertain offers from New Traders. They would not make Paragon into a 'great flowerpot.' No. They'd chop him up into bits and sell him off as trinkets and curiosities."

Brashen was struck dumb with horror. Instinctively he reached out a hand to the ship's silvery hull in a calming gesture. "That can't happen," he assured him in a husky voice. "All of the Traders would rise up in arms before they'd let such a thing happen."

Amber shook her head. "You've been gone a long time from Bingtown, Brashen Trell." She turned and kicked at the sand. Sparks flew up from the fading coals of a campfire. She stooped and, a moment later, tiny flames blossomed. Brashen watched in silence as she awakened the fire with twigs and then larger sticks of wood. "Sit down," she invited him in a weary voice. In a conciliatory tone, she added, "This has begun badly. Actually, I have looked forward to your returning to Bingtown. I had hoped that you and Althea might work together to aid me in this. She has grudgingly agreed that my acquiring Paragon might be the best thing for him. If you join your voice to hers, perhaps we could all go to the Ludlucks and make them see reason." She lifted her gaze to his disapproving stare. "Would you care for a cup of tea?"

He sat, lowering himself stiffly to perch on a driftwood log. He tried to keep his voice conversational as he said, "It is hard for me to believe Althea would ever support the sale of a liveship."

"I but pointed out the facts to her and she concurred." In the firelight, she rolled her eyes toward Paragon. The small jerk of her head was a plain indication she didn't want to discuss details in front of the ship. Curiosity burned in Brashen, but he recognized the wisdom. Paragon was in a cheery mood tonight. There was no sense in awakening the quarrelsome side of him. For now, the best course was to humor them both and collect what information he could. "So. I know Paragon is happy to see you and will want to know all of your adventures. How long have you been back in Bingtown?" Amber went on in a natural voice.

"We just anchored up today," he replied. A silence fell after his words. The oddness of the situation swept over him. Amber was conducting this as if she were a Bingtown matron hosting a tea.

"And will you be staying long?" she prodded him.

"I don't know. I came back to tell Althea I had seen *Vivacia*. Pirates have captured her. I don't know if Kyle and Wintrow are alive. I don't know if any of the crew is alive." The words spilled from him before he could consider the wisdom of sharing this information.

There was true concern in Amber's voice as she asked, "Althea knows this? How did she react?"

"She is devastated, of course. Tomorrow she goes to the Bingtown Council to seek their aid in recovering the ship. The damnable part of it is that this Kennit most likely doesn't want a ransom. He wants to keep the ship. If Wintrow and Kyle are still alive, he'll probably have to keep them as well to keep the ship sane—"

"Pirates." Paragon's voice was almost dreamy save for the terror in it. "I know about pirates. They kill and kill and kill on your decks. The blood soaks in, deeper and deeper, until your wood is so full of lives you cannot even find your own. Then they chop off your face and open your seacocks and you go under. The worst part is, they leave you to live." His voice broke into a boyish treble before it tremored into silence.

Brashen's eyes met Amber's. Hers glittered with unspoken horror. She and Brashen rose as one, both reaching out toward the ship. His voice stopped them. "Don't touch me!" His voice was deep and hoarse, a man's frantic command. "Be gone from me, you traitorous vermin! Feckless, dung-crawling rats! You have no souls! No creature with a soul could endure doing what you did to me!" He turned his face from side to side blindly. His huge hands, knotted into fists, swung back and forth before him defensively. "Take your memories away from me. I do not want your lives. You are drowning me! You are trying to make me forget who I am . . . who I was. I will not!" This last he roared out in defiance. Then his voice dropped low into a wild laugh, followed by a string of mocking obscenities.

"He's not talking to us," Amber assured Brashen in a low tone, but he was not so sure. He made no move to touch the ship. Neither did she. Instead, she took his arm, turned him away from the ship and walked him down the beach into the darkness. The sounds of Paragon's rabid curses and imprecations followed them. When the light of the fire no longer touched their faces, she halted and turned to him. She still spoke in a hushed voice. "His hearing is exceptionally keen." She glanced back at him. "He's best left alone at times like this. If you try to talk him back to rationality, he only gets worse." She shrugged helplessly. "He has to come back on his own."

"I know."

"I know that you know. I think you understand that he can't take much more of this. Every moment of every day, he dreads them coming for him. He cannot even sleep to escape it. Almost every day now, he retreats into his madness. I try to let nothing trouble him, but he is not stupid. He knows that his survival is threatened and that there is very little he can do to defend himself." Even in the dark, he could feel the strength of her gaze. "You have to help us."

"There is nothing I can do. I don't know what the ship or Althea Vestrit told you about me to make you think I have some kind of influence, but it's not true. The truth is the opposite. Anything I support, proper Bingtowners will righteously oppose. I'm as much of an outcast as that ship. Your cause is more likely to succeed without me." He shook his head at her. "Not that I think it can succeed at all."

"So. I should just give up now?" she asked mildly. "Just let him spiral down into madness until the New Traders come to haul him away and chop him up? What will we say to one another afterwards, Brashen? That there was nothing we could do, that we never believed it would really happen. Will that make us innocent?"

"Innocent?" He was incensed at her suggestion he was somehow responsible for this mess. "I've done nothing wrong, I intend nothing wrong. I *am* innocent!"

"Half the evil in this world occurs while decent people stand by and do nothing wrong. It's not enough to refrain from evil, Trell. People have to attempt to do right, even if they believe they cannot succeed."

"Even when it's stupid to try?" he asked with savage sarcasm.

"Especially then," she replied sweetly. "That's how it's done, Trell. You break your heart against this stony world. You fling yourself at it, on the side of good, and you do not ask the cost. That's how you do it."

"Do what?" he demanded, truly angry now. "Get myself killed? For the sake of being a hero?"

"Perhaps," she conceded. "Perhaps that. But it is definitely how you redeem yourself. How you become a hero." She cocked her head and eyed him appraisingly. "Don't tell me you've never wanted to be the hero."

"I've never wanted to be the hero," he defied her. Paragon was still cursing someone defiantly. He sounded drunken and rambling. Brashen turned his head, to stare at the ship. The yellow glow of firelight danced on his chopped face. What did this woman expect of him? There was

nothing he could do to help the ship, nothing he could do to help anyone. "All I ever wanted to do was live my own life. And I'm having damn
little success at that."

She laughed low. "Only because you keep standing back from it. And
turning aside from it. And avoiding it." She shook her head. "Trell, Trell.
Open your eyes. This horrible mess is your life. There is no sense in
waiting for it to get better. Stop putting it off and live it." She laughed
again. Her eyes and voice seemed to go afar. "Everyone thinks that courage is about facing death without flinching. But almost anyone can do
that. Almost anyone can hold their breath and not scream for as long as it
takes to die. True courage is facing life without flinching. I don't mean the
times when the right path is hard, but glorious at the end. I'm talking
about enduring the boredom, and the messiness, and the inconvenience
of doing what is right." She cocked her head and considered him. "I think
you can do that, Trell."

"Stop calling me that," he hissed. His surname was like salt in a
wound.

She suddenly gripped his wrist. "No. You stop. Stop thinking you're
the son your father disowned. You're not who he expected you to be; that
doesn't mean you aren't somebody. Nor are you perfect. Stop using every
mistake you make as an excuse to fail completely."

He jerked his wrist free of her grip. "Who are you, to speak to me of
these things? What are you, to even know these things?" With chagrin,
he finally realized the only possible source of her knowledge. Althea had
been talking about him. How much had she told Amber? He looked in
her face and knew. Althea had told her everything. Everything. He
turned and walked swiftly away from her. He wished the darkness could
completely swallow him.

"Brashen? Brashen!" She hissed out the call.

He kept walking.

"Where will you go, Trell?" It was a hoarse cry in the darkness.
"Where will you go to get away from yourself?"

He didn't know. He couldn't answer.

THE SLIPPERS WERE RUINED WITH DAMP. MALTA FLUNG THEM INTO A COR-
ner of her closet and took down a warm robe. Her night stroll had chilled
her despite the mildness of the season. She took the dream-box down
from its shelf. The gray powder she had hidden inside a larger bag of
headache herbs. She fished it out and brushed the crumbles of herbs from
the outer bag. A shiver of excitement ran over her as she tugged open the
laced mouth. She up-ended it into the dream-box and shook it out carefully. A fine powder of dream dust hung glittering in the air. She sneezed

violently, and hastily shut the lid of the box. The back of her throat felt odd, numb and yet warm. "Shake the box well, wait, and then open the box by the bedside," she instructed herself. As she crossed the room to her bed, she shook the box. She drew back the coverings of her bed, climbed in and then put the open box by her bed. With a puff, she blew out her candle and lay back on her pillows. She shut her eyes and waited.

Waited.

Anticipation was betraying her. She could not fall asleep. Resolutely, she kept her eyes closed. She tried to think sleepy thoughts. When that failed, she focused her thoughts on Reyn. She found him much more attractive after Cerwin's disappointing performance. When Cerwin had taken her in his arms, he had seemed thin compared to Reyn's broad chest during his one stolen embrace. She considered it. Certainly, Reyn would not have missed a chance to steal a kiss. Her heart beat faster at the thought.

Reyn raised a storm of conflicting emotions in her. His gifts and attention made her feel important. His wealth was attractive, especially after a whole year of penury. Sometimes she did not mind his veiled face and gloved hands. They made him mysterious. She could look at him and imagine a handsome young man hidden beneath them. When he led her with such grace through intricate dance steps, she felt both his strength and his agility in his light touch upon her hand and back. Only occasionally did she wonder if his veil hid a warty visage with mis-shapen features.

When they were apart, her doubts assailed her. Even worse was the sympathy of her friends. One and all, they were certain he must be a monster. Half the time, Malta suspected they were just jealous of the gifts and attentions he showered on her. Maybe they just wanted him to be ugly, out of envy for her good fortune. Oh, she did not know what she felt or how she believed. Nor was she falling asleep. She had wasted the dream-box powder. Nothing had come out right. She tossed in her bed, both mind and body restless with longings she scarcely understood. She wished her father had come home to make everything right.

"I WANT TO COME OUT. WHY WON'T YOU HELP ME?"

"I can't. Please. Understand that I can't, and stop pleading with me."

The imprisoned dragon was contemptuous. *"You won't. You could, but you won't. All it would take is sunlight. Open the shutters and let in the sunlight. I would do the rest."*

"I have told you. The chamber you are in is buried. Once, I am sure, there were great windows and shutters to open and close them. But the whole structure is buried now. Earth covers you, and trees grow in it. You are beneath a whole forested hillside."

"If you were truly my friend as you claim to be, you'd dig me out and free me. Please. I need to be free. Not just for my own sake, but for the sake of all my kind."

Reyn shifted in his bed, rucking up the covers. He felt he was not truly asleep, nor was he dreaming; yet he was not awake either. The dragon vision had become an almost nightly torment now. When he slept, the dragon looked into him, at him, and through him with great copper eyes the size of cartwheels. Her eyes spun, the colors whirling all about the great elliptical pupils. He could not look away from them, nor could he break free of the dream and wake up. She was imprisoned in her wizardwood cocoon, and he was imprisoned in her.

"You don't understand," he moaned in his sleep. "The shutters are buried, the dome is buried. Sun will never shine into that chamber again."

"Then open the great doors and drag me out. Put rollers beneath if you have to, and use teams of horses. Drag me out, I don't care how. Just deliver me to the sunlight."

He could not make her understand anything. "I can't. You are too big for one man to move alone, and no one would aid me. Even if I had many workers and teams of horses, it would do no good. That door will never open again. No one even knows how it originally opened. Besides, it is buried. Before we could open it, it would take scores of men working for months to move the dirt. Even then, I don't think the door could be opened. The structure is cracked and weakened. If the door was moved, I think the whole dome would give way. You would be buried more deeply than you are now."

"I do not care! Take the chance, open the door. I could help you discover how to do it." Her voice became seductive. *"I could give you all the secrets of the city. All you would have to promise is that you would open the door."*

Somewhere, his head moved against his sweat-dampened pillow in denial. "No. You would drown me in memories. It would do neither of us any good. That way lies madness for my kind. Do not even tempt me."

"Attack the door, then. Axes and hammers must make it give way. Let it fall on me if it must. Even if it collapsed and killed me, that would be more freedom than this. Reyn, Reyn, why don't you free me? If you were truly my friend, you would free me."

He writhed before her heart-stricken words. "I am your friend. I am. I long to free you, but I cannot do it alone. I must win others to my cause, first. Then we will find a way. Be patient, I pray you. Be patient."

"Starvation does not know patience. Madness does not know patience. They are inexorable. Reyn, Reyn. Why can't I make you understand what you are doing with your cruelty? You are killing us all, for all time. Let me out! Let me out!"

"I can't!" he roared. He opened his eyes to his darkened bedchamber.

He sat up in bed, breathing like a wrestler. The sweaty bedding twisted about him, binding him like a shroud. He writhed out of it and walked naked to the center of the room. The window was open and the night air cooled his overheated body. He ran his hands through his thick curly hair, standing it up to let it dry. He scratched at the newest growth on his scalp, then resolutely dropped his hands. He walked to the window and looked up.

The Rain Wild settlement of Trehaug was suspended in the trees along the banks of the Rain Wild River. From one side of his home, he could look down on the rushing river. From the other, he could look up through the trees to the Old City. A few lights still burned up there. The work on the excavation and exploration never really ceased. When one was working in the deepest chambers, it made little difference if it was day or night outside. It was eternal darkness within the hill. Just as it was forever black inside the wizardwood coffin in the Crowned Rooster chamber.

He once more considered telling his mother of these nightmares but he knew how she would react. She would order the last wizardwood log to be split. The immense soft body inside would be tumbled out onto the cold stone floor, and the precious wizardwood "log" would be reduced to planks and timbers for a ship. It was the only substance the Rain Wilders had ever discovered that seemed impervious to the acid water of the river. Even the trees and bushes that lined the river survived only so long as their bark was intact. The moment anything scored them, the river began to devour them. As for the long-legged silver birds that fed in the shallows, Reyn had seen even those with knotted sores on their legs. Only wizardwood seemed to impart protection against the milky water of the Rain Wild River. And the Khuprus family possessed the last and greatest log.

If he had his way, he would find a way to expose it to sunlight and see what emerged from it. The log would likely be destroyed in the process. One rotting old tapestry seemed to show such a hatching. A flabby white creature reared its head from a soggy wreckage of wizardwood. It gripped fragments in its jaws as if devouring the remnants of its prison. Its eyes were savage, and the almost-human creatures witnessing it seemed to be stricken with awe or fear. Sometimes, when he looked at it, he knew his idea was madness. Why take a chance on freeing such a frightful being?

But it was the last one of its kind. The last real dragon.

He went back to his bed. He lay down and tried to find some thought that would let him rest but not sleep. If he slept, the dragon dream would seize him and pull him down once more. Wearily, he considered Malta. Sometimes when he thought of her, delight and anticipation filled him. She was so lovely, so spirited and so fresh. In her willfulness, he saw strength unrealized. He knew what her family thought of her. It was not without reason. She was stubborn and selfish and not a little spoiled. She was the kind of woman who would fiercely defend herself. Whatever she desired, she would pursue single-mindedly. If he could win her loyalty to himself, then she would be perfect. Like his mother, she would protect and guide her children, holding fast to wealth and power for them, long after Reyn himself was in his grave. Others would say his wife was ruthless and amoral in defense of her family. But they would say it with envy.

If he could win her over to him. There was the rub. When he had left Bingtown, he had been certain of his victory. But she had not used the dream-box to contact him. He had had one correctly worded note since he'd last seen her. That was all. He rolled over disconsolately and closed his eyes. He drifted down to sleep and a dream.

"Reyn. Reyn, you have to help me."

"I can't," he groaned.

The darkness parted and Malta came toward him. She was ethereally beautiful. Her white nightdress blew in an otherworldly wind. Her dark hair flowed with the night, and her eyes were full of its mystery. She walked alone in the perfect blackness. He knew what that meant. She had come seeking him. She had set no stage, composed no fantasy. She had lain down to dream, thinking only of him.

"Reyn?" She called again. "Where are you? I need you."

He composed himself, then entered the dream. "I'm here," he said softly, not wishing to startle her. She turned to him and her eyes swept up and down his dream self.

"You were not veiled, last time," she protested.

He smiled to himself. He had chosen a realistic representation of himself, soberly clothed, veiled and gloved. He suspected that the nightgown she wore was what she truly had on tonight. He reminded himself of how young she was. He would not take advantage of her. Perhaps she did not completely understand the power of the dream-box. "Last time, you brought many ideas to our dream. As did I. We let them mingle and lived what followed. Tonight, we bring only ourselves. And whatever else we wish."

He lifted an arm, and swept it across the darkness. A landscape unfurled in its wake. It was one of his favorite ancient tapestries. Starkly black leafless trees offered globes of gleaming yellow fruit. A silver path wound between the trees, then ran off to a fortress in the distance. The floor of the forest was thickly mossed. A fox with a rabbit in his jaws peered at them from a bramble. A couple, too tall to be completely human, he with copper hair, she with gold, embraced in the foreground. His body pressed hers against the black bole of a tree. Reyn had visualized them as frozen in time, but the woman suddenly took a sighing breath and turned her head to accept the man's kiss more deeply. He smiled to himself. She learned to play so quickly, this Malta.

Or did she even know she had done it? She broke her eyes away from the ardent couple. She stepped closer to him and lowered her voice as if fearful of disturbing the phantoms. "Reyn, I need your help."

He had thought that distressed plea had been a shadow of his earlier dragon dream. "What is wrong?"

She glanced over her shoulder at the ardent couple. The man's hand moved slowly to the throat of the woman's robe. Malta snatched her eyes away. He could feel her focus herself on him. "Everything that could be wrong is wrong. Pirates have captured our family ship. The pirate who has the ship has a reputation of killing all crew members on the prizes he takes. If my father still lives, we hope to ransom him. But we have little enough money as it is. If our creditors discover we have lost our liveship, they will not lend us more. More likely they will demand swifter repayment of what we already owe." Her eyes wandered unwillingly back to the man and woman. Their love play was becoming more intimate. It seemed to distract and agitate her.

Congratulating himself on his self-control, Reyn took her unresisting hand. He willed another path through the forest. They walked slowly along it as he led her away from the amorous duo. "What do you want me to do?"

"Kiss me." The voice was commanding.

The words were not Malta's. They had come upon another couple, beneath another tree. The young man gripped the woman by her shoulders masterfully. He looked down into her proud, upturned face. She gave him a look of icy disdain, but he lowered his mouth to hers. Against his will, Reyn's blood stirred. The woman struggled briefly, then clasped the back of the man's head to hold his mouth against hers. Reyn looked away, disturbed by the force of it. He tugged Malta's hand and they walked on.

"What can you do?" Malta asked.

He considered. He did not think that this was the sort of thing usually discussed in shared dreams. "Your mother should write to my mother. They are the ones who should discuss this, not us."

He wondered what his mother's reaction would be. In coming to him for help, Malta seemed to have forgotten that the Khuprus family now held the note on the liveship. Not only were they one of the creditors that Malta now feared, but the pirated ship had secured that debt. It was a tangled situation. The magic of the liveships was to be carefully guarded, guaranteed by the purchaser never to fall into the hands of outsiders. When he had persuaded his mother to buy the Vestrit note on the ship, her long-range view was that the ship would be given as a bridal gift to the Vestrit family. He had expected his own children would eventually inherit it. The complete loss of the ship would be a substantial financial blow to anyone. He was sure his mother would be spurred to action, but he was not sure what action. He had never been interested in the financial business of the family. His mother, eldest brother and stepfather handled all that. He was the explorer and scholar. He mined out the discoveries that they turned into coin. What they did with that coin had not concerned him. Now he wondered if he had any say in it.

Malta was outraged instantly. "Reyn, we are talking about my father. I cannot wait for my mother to talk to your mother. If he is to be rescued, we must act now."

He felt emasculated. "Malta. I have no power to help you directly. I am a younger son, with three older siblings."

She stamped her foot angrily. "I don't believe you. If you care for me at all, you will help me."

She sounded just like the dragon, he thought in sudden dismay.

It was a dangerous thought to have in a dream-box setting. The earth suddenly trembled under their feet. A second, harder shudder followed the first. Malta clutched at a tree to keep from falling. "What was that?" she demanded.

"An earthquake," he replied calmly. They were common enough in Trehaug. The suspended city swayed with the living trees that supported it and took little harm. The quakes, however, often did great damage to the excavation work. He wondered if this were a real earthquake pushing its way into the dream, or an imagined one.

"I know what a quake is." Malta sounded annoyed with him. "The whole Cursed Shore is prey to them. I meant that sound."

"Sound?" he asked uneasily.

"Like scrabbling and scratching. Don't you hear it?"

He heard it all the time. Waking and sleeping, the sound of the dragon's claws working feebly against its tomb haunted him. "You can hear it, too?" He was astounded. He had learned to ignore what he had always been told was his imagination.

Before he could reply, everything began to change. The colors of the forest suddenly grew bright and new. There was a strong fragrance of ripening fruit on the warm breeze. The texture of the mosses underfoot became coarser, while the path suddenly sparkled in sunlight. The blue of the sky deepened. This was no longer Reyn's memory of a tapestry. Someone else was adding to the dream-box vision, and he did not think it was Malta.

When thunderclouds began to boil up along the horizon, he was certain of it. He glanced up fearfully as the rising winds sent ripe fruit plummeting from the trees. One spattered into seeds and pulp right by Malta's feet. The rich smell of its spilled nectar was decadent.

"Malta. We should part now. Tell your mother that . . ."

Lightning cracked the sky overhead. Thunder followed instantaneously. Reyn felt his hair stand on end and a peculiar smell rode the wind. Malta cowered low and pointed wordlessly up at the sky. The erratic winds lashed her hair wildly and pressed her nightdress up against her body.

A dragon hovered above the trees. The powerful beat of her wings spurred the winds. Even the cloud-dimmed light of the sun could not diminish her glory. She was iridescent. Colors chased one another over her silver body and wings. Her eyes were copper. "I have the power," she declared. Her voice split the sky. The branch of a nearby tree cracked and fell heavily to the earth. "Free me and I will aid you. I promise you this." Her wings lifted her to the sky where she turned a slow, dazzling loop. Her long serpentine tail lashed the sky behind her.

Rain began suddenly to fall, a torrent that drenched the humans. Malta fled shivering to the shelter of Reyn's arms and cloak. He put his arm around her. Even in the shadow of the hovering dragon, he was aware of the warmth of her skin through the damp cloth of her nightdress. From beneath his cloak, Malta squinted up at the beast. "Who are you?" she cried loudly. "What do you want?"

The dragon threw back her head and roared her laughter. She swept past them and rose again into the sky. "Who am I? Do I look so foolish as to gift you with my name? No. You will not come to control me that way. As to what I want . . . a trade. My freedom, in exchange for this ship you mention, and if your father is still aboard it, his life. What say you? An easy trade, is it not? A life for a life?"

Malta looked to Reyn. "Is she real? Can she help us?"

Reyn stared up at the dragon above them. She beat her wings heavily as she rose into the storm-torn sky. Up and up she rose, growing smaller with distance. She shone like a star against the dark gray clouds. "She's real. But she can't help us."

"Why not? She is immense! She can fly! Couldn't she just go to where the ship is and . . ."

"And what? Destroy the ship to kill the pirates? Possibly, if you truly thought that was wise. Possibly, if she were truly free and flying. But she isn't. She is only showing herself to us, in this dream, as she imagines herself to be."

"How is she really?"

Reyn abruptly realized how close he had come to a very dangerous topic. "She's trapped, far beneath the earth, where no one can free her." He took her arm and hurried her down the path, to where he had willed a sturdy little cottage into existence. He opened the door and Malta darted inside gratefully. He followed her, shutting the door behind them. A small fire illuminated the simple little room. Malta gathered up her hair in a bundle and squeezed the water from it. She turned back to him, raindrops still glistening on her face. The firelight danced in her eyes.

"How is she trapped?" Malta demanded. "What would we have to do to free her?"

He decided to tell her enough to be honest. "A long time ago, something happened. We're not sure what. Somehow, an entire city was buried under a heavy layer of earth. It was so long ago that trees have grown in the earth above it. The dragon is in a chamber deep within the buried city. There is no way to free her." He put all the finality he could muster into his words. Malta looked stubbornly unconvinced. He shook his head at her. "This is not the dream I imagined we would share."

"Couldn't she be dug out? How can she be alive, buried so deeply?" Malta cocked her head at him and narrowed her eyes. "How do you even know she is there? Reyn. There is something you are not telling me," she accused him.

He straightened his back and stood his ground. "Malta, there are many things I cannot tell you. I would not ask you to betray the secrets of the Bingtown Traders. You must trust me that I have told you all I honorably can." He crossed his arms on his chest.

She stared at him for a time. Then she lowered her eyes. After a moment, in a lowered voice she said, "Please do not think ill of me. I did not realize what I was asking of you." Her voice grew throaty as she added, "I look forward to a time when there will be no secrets between us."

A blast of wind buffeted the cottage walls. Reyn suspected it was the dragon flying over them. "Free me!" Her long wild call slid down the sky to them. "Free me!"

At the sound of the dragon's voice, Malta's eyes grew wide. A second wave of wind hit the cottage, rattling the shutters, and she was suddenly in his arms. He held her close and felt her trembling. The top of her head came only to his chin. Her hair was damp under his touch when he stroked it. When she turned her face up to his, he fell into the bottomless gaze of her eyes. "It's only a dream," he assured her. "Nothing here can hurt you. Nothing here is quite real."

"It seems very real," she whispered. Her breath was warm on his face.

"Does it?" he asked in wonder.

"It does," she assured him.

Cautiously he lowered his mouth to hers. She did not avoid his kiss. The thin layer of veil between their lips was an almost pleasant coarseness. Her arms came around him and held him with awkward inexperience.

The sweetness of the kiss clung to him as the power of the dream-box faded and he drifted into ordinary sleep. "Come to me." Her words reached him faintly. "Come to me at the full moon."

"I can't!" he cried out, desperate that his words reach her. "Malta, I can't!"

He awakened saying the words into his pillow. Had she heard him?

He closed his eyes and tried to will himself back into sleep and the shared dream. "Malta? I cannot come to you. I can't."

"Is that what you say to all females?" Somewhere a voice laughed in wicked amusement. Claws twitched feebly against iron-hard wizardwood. *"Don't fret, Reyn. You cannot go to her. But I shall."*

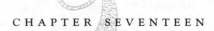

CHAPTER SEVENTEEN

Marooned

THE MOON STOOD CLEAR IN THE SKY AND THE TIDE WAS HIGH WHEN KENnit decided it was time to keep his promise. It had taken some careful maneuvering, but everything was in place and ready. No sense in wasting time. He swung his leg over the side of the bunk and sat up, scowling when a sleepy Etta lifted her head from the pillows. He wanted no interference from anyone tonight. "Go back to sleep," he commanded her. "If I need you, I'll tell you."

Instead of looking chastened, she gave him a fond and drowsy smile, then closed her eyes again. Her placid acceptance of his independence was almost unnerving.

At least she was coming to accept that he didn't need her damn help with everything. She had been tiresomely helpful in the weeks of his convalescence. Several times, he'd had to roar at her before she would retreat and let him take care of himself.

He reached for the waiting peg and slipped his stump into the cup on the end. The harness of leather that secured it to his body still seemed awkward, but he was becoming accustomed to it. Pulling his trousers on past it was another difficulty. He frowned at it. The woman would have to come up with a better arrangement. He would tell her so in the morning. His belt held only a long sheathed dagger now. A sword was a useless vanity to a man who had to balance on one leg. He dragged on his boot, then took up the crutch that leaned against the bunk. He thudded his way across the room. Teetering precariously, he buttoned on a shirt and then donned a vest. A fine broadcloth coat went over it all. He added a clean kerchief and his usual items to his pocket. He tugged his collar straight and made sure his cuffs were even. Tucking the crutch firmly under his arm, he left his cabin, shutting the door quietly behind him.

All was at peace on the anchored vessel. The ship had been tidier and better run since he had reduced the crew in Divvytown. Most of the rescued slaves had been glad to leave the crowded ship. Some had wished to remain. He had sieved those rigorously. Some had simply not been able sailors. Others were too surly. Not all those with multiple tattoos across their faces were free spirits who would not bow to slavery. Some, quite simply, were men and women too stupid to learn their tasks well and do them willingly. He did not want them any more than their former owners had. A dozen former slaves, victims of Sa'Adar's influence, had insisted on remaining aboard. Kennit had graciously allowed it. It had been his only concession to their claim to own the ship. Doubtless, they still hoped for more. Doubtless they would be disappointed. Three others he had kept aboard for his own reasons. They would serve their purposes tonight.

He found Ankle leaning on the forward railing. Not far from her, Wintrow was sprawled in the deep sleep of exhaustion. Kennit permitted himself a small smile. Brig had taken his request that the boy be kept very busy for a few days literally. The girl turned to the tapping of his peg on the deck. Ankle's wide dark eyes watched him approach with trepidation. She was not as fearful as she had been at first. A few days after he had taken the ship, Etta had put a stop to the freed men and crew using her for sex. The girl herself had not seemed to object, so Kennit had seen no problem with it, but Etta had insisted she was too addled by ill use to know how to resist their advances. Later Wintrow had told him what he knew of the girl. Ankle had gone mad in the hold and crippled herself struggling against her fetters. Wintrow believed she had been normal when she had first been put belowdecks. No one on board seemed to know anything else about her, not even her name or age. A shame, Kennit supposed, that her mind was gone. She would always limp. She was worse than useless aboard the ship, for she ate food and took up space that could have been given to an able man. He would have put her off in Divvytown if both Etta and Wintrow had not interceded for her. When Vivacia, too, had spoken out in her behalf, Kennit had allowed himself to be swayed. Nevertheless, it was time to be done with her. It was the kindest thing to do. A pirate ship was not a nursery for blighted souls.

He made a small gesture to her to come to him. She advanced a single hesitant step.

"What will you do with her?" Vivacia spoke softly from the shadows.

"I mean no harm to her. You know me well enough now to understand that." He glanced toward Wintrow. "But let's not wake the lad." He made his suggestion in a kindly tone.

The figurehead was silent for a time. "I sense you believe you are doing what is right for her. But I cannot see what that is." After a time, she added, "You block me. There are portions of your heart that you have never allowed me to see. You keep secrets from me."

"Yes. Just as you keep secrets from me. You have to trust me in this. Do you?" He made a small test of the question.

She was silent. He walked forward, past Ankle, who cowered slightly as he passed her. He took her place on the forward rail and leaned down to the ship. "Good evening, sweet sea-lady," he greeted the ship, as if they were the first words he had spoken to her. His utterance was little more than a whisper on the evening wind.

"It is more like a good night, gentle sir," she replied in kind.

He extended his hand to her and she twisted to reach up her large fingers to touch his. "I trust you are well. Tell me." He gestured at the surrounding panorama of scattered islands. "What do you think of my islands, now that you have seen a bit of them?"

She made a warm sound in her throat. "There is a unique beauty to them. The warmth of the water, the drifting mists that veil and reveal them . . . even the birds that flock here are different. More colorful, and more tuneful in their songs than most seabirds. I have not seen such plumage since Captain Vestrit took me on a voyage far to the south-lands. . . ." Her voice trailed away.

"You still miss him, don't you? I'm sure he was a fine captain, and showed you many wondrous places. But if you trust me, my lady, you and I shall see places even more exotic, and have adventures even more excit-ing." There was an almost jealous note in his voice as he asked, "Do you recall him that well? I had thought you were not quickened then."

"I recall him like one recalls a good dream in the morning. Nothing is sharp, but a scent, a horizon, the taste of a current, will seem familiar and a memory comes with it. If Wintrow is with me, it is sharper. I can convey to him far more detail than I can speak."

"I see." He changed the subject. "Nevertheless, you have never been in these parts before, have you?"

"No. Captain Vestrit avoided the Pirate Isles. We passed them by, keeping as easterly a course as we could. He always said it is easier to avoid trouble than to deal with it."

"Ah." Kennit looked past her, to the *Marietta* also rocking at anchor. Sometimes he missed Sorcor. It would have been handy to have him here for this night's work. Still, one best keeps a secret alone. He recalled abruptly what he had come on deck to do. "On that, I would have to agree with him. So, my lady, if you will excuse me, I need to avoid some trouble tonight. Think of me, until I return."

"I shall." There was puzzlement in her voice. He tapped away from her, his crutch and peg making an odd rhythm as he swung across the deck. He gestured to Ankle to follow him. She came slowly, limping, but she came. When he reached the captain's gig, he told her, "Stay here. I'll take you for a ride." He made motions as he spoke, to be certain his command was clearly conveyed. She looked anxious, but obediently sat down on the deck.

He left her sitting there in darkness. He passed the sailor on anchor watch and acknowledged him with a nod. The sailor bobbed his head but made no comment. Captain Kennit had always done as he pleased on the ship. He even sensed that the crew was more confident now that he had resumed his erratic tours of the ship. It reassured them that all was well with their captain.

He could move almost swiftly now, with a stride and a swing on his crutch, when he chose. It was not without discomfort. Wintrow seemed to think he would build callus as time passed. He hoped so. Sometimes the leather cup that held his stump chafed abominably, and his armpit would ache at the end of the day from the bruising of the crutch's impact.

Moving quietly was more of an effort than moving swiftly, but he managed. He had taken the time to ascertain where Sa'Adar slept every night and he made his way there with confidence. Even in the fitful light of the widely spaced lanterns, he knew his way. When he came to the reclining man, he stood still, looking down on him. Sa'Adar was not asleep, so Kennit made no pretense of waking him. In a very soft voice, he said, "If you would see justice done to Kyle Haven, rise and follow me now. Silently."

In apparent confidence, he turned his back on the man and walked away from him. He did not deign to look back. His keen ears picked up the soft footfalls of the priest following him. He had judged him well. The air of mystery and secrecy drew him to come alone, without waking his comrades. Kennit strode on past other sprawled and sleeping men until he came to two others he had chosen earlier. Dedge slept with his arm thrown protectively over Saylah. She was curled around her own belly. He nudged Dedge twice with the tip of his crutch. He indicated the man's companion as well, and then moved on. Obedient as a good dog, the man nudged the woman awake and silently followed him.

They moved through the mostly sleeping ship. Those who did stir or open an eye were wise enough to keep their thoughts to themselves. Up on the deck once more, Kennit led them into the aftercastle. He stopped at the chamber where Kyle Haven was confined. A curt nod of his head to the map-faces made his will known. Dedge unceremoniously opened the door and entered the chamber. Kyle Haven started up from his untidy bunk. His hair straggled wildly down his shoulders. There was a stink of unwashed flesh and urine in the room, reminiscent of the slave hold. Kennit wrinkled his nose against it. His voice was mild as he stood in the door and suggested, "You should come with us, Captain Haven."

Haven's wild glance circled those who faced him. Sa'Adar was smiling. "You're going to kill me, aren't you?" he asked hoarsely.

"No." Kennit didn't particularly care if the man believed him or not. He turned to his map-faces. "See that he comes with us, silently." He lifted one eyebrow at Haven as he added, "I don't particularly care what they have to do to ensure the silence. Your cooperation is not essential, but it would be easier for both of us." He turned away without seeing who would comply or how. Sa'Adar annoyed him by hurrying to catch up with him.

"Aren't you going to wake the others? So they can witness this?"

Kennit halted in mid-stride. He didn't bother to face the other man. "I believe I said I wanted silence," he observed.

"But—"

The move came so naturally. He did not even think about doing it. He caught his weight on his good leg, braced a shoulder against the wall and lashed out solidly with the crutch. Sa'Adar caught the blow against his thighs and staggered back. He clutched at the wall, mouth open with pain. Kennit turned away from him. If the companionway had been wider, the pirate reflected, the arc of the blow would have been more effective. He considered this as he continued his swinging stride to the deck. It might be something he should practice.

He halted by the captain's gig and waited for the others to catch up. It pleased him that Haven had kept silent without being gagged or clubbed. Obviously, the man believed in his power. Perhaps he also realized that anyone roused by his cries would be unlikely to help him. Whatever his reasoning, his compliance made everything much easier. Ankle got to her feet as the others came up. Kennit looked at his map-faces. "Fetch the chest. You know which one. Then prepare to launch the boat." The man immediately obeyed him. The others waited silently. No one was stupid enough to ask any questions.

He rode in the bow of the boat. Ankle sat in the stern near the chest, and the two map-faces took one set of oars, the priest and Captain Haven the other. Kennit pointed the way. From time to time, he quietly commanded changes in their course. He guided them between two small islands and into the lee of a third. Only when they were out of sight of both his ships did he finally point toward a fourth island that was their true destination.

Even then, he did not permit the map-faces to land on the beach of Keyhole Island. He had them row on until they came to the mouth of a small bay. Kennit was well aware that it was more than a bay. What appeared to be an island was in fact little more than a wall of forest-topped cliffs, shaped like a near closed horseshoe. The bay filled its interior. One large island and a smaller one dotted the interior bay. The sky was beginning to gray as he directed the rowers wordlessly toward the shore of the larger interior island.

From the water, it looked like any other small island. It had an unremarkable shoreline, and was forested with scrubby trees and coarse brush. Kennit knew that on the other side of the island, there was a good deep-water anchorage, but for his purposes tonight, the rocky beach was sufficient. At his gesture, the map-faces took the boat into shore. He sat in it like a king on a litter as all the others clambered over the side and seized the gunwales to run it up on the shore. They were scarce clear of the waves before Haven predictably let go of the boat and made a run for it. "Get him," Kennit commanded tersely.

A well-aimed rock from one of the map-faces felled him. Wintrow's father scrabbled on the rocky beach, but before he could come to his feet, Sa'Adar was upon him, seizing him by the throat and slamming his head to the ground. Kennit was annoyed. "Bind the captain's hands behind him and bring him. See that the priest doesn't harm him," he ordered his map-faces. To Ankle he said, "Assist me. But only if I say I need it." The girl squinted at him but seemed to understand. She shadowed him.

While the map-faces were prying the two cursing combatants apart and restraining them, Kennit clambered from the gig. The rock and sand of the beach were trickier for both his peg and his crutch than the smooth decks of the *Vivacia* had been. Stones shifted under his weight and sand gave way unexpectedly. Traversing it was going to be more difficult than he had supposed. He gritted his teeth and tried to make his turtle's pace look measured and deliberate rather than labored. "Well? Follow me!" he snapped at them when they stood watching his progress. "Bring the chest."

He found the old path without too much trouble. It was overgrown. Probably the pigs and goats were the only creatures keeping it open now, he reflected to himself. Few others beside himself had ever come to this beach, and it had been years since he had passed this way. A slippery pile of fresh pig droppings confirmed his theory. He navigated carefully around them. Ankle was right behind him. Next came the priest and Saylah carrying the chest between them. Dedge followed, manhandling Haven to make him keep pace. Haven was not being quiet, but Kennit no longer really cared. They could do what they wished to the captain, as long as he arrived intact. He was sure they understood that.

For a short time the trail led gently uphill. Then it dipped and began to wind down into the gently rolling interior of the island. Kennit paused for a moment on the lip of that small valley. Forest gave way to tussocky pastureland. A grazing goat lifted his head and regarded them warily. Little had changed. To the west, he saw a tiny thread of smoke rising toward the sky. Well. Maybe nothing at all had changed. The path gave a twist then headed through the forest toward the smoke. Kennit followed it.

The damn crutch was eating a hole in his armpit. It needed more padding. More cushioning was needed in the stump cup, too. He set his teeth and refused to show his discomfort. Sweat was trickling down his back before he reached the clearing. He halted once more on the edge of it. Dedge swore in wonder. The woman muttered a prayer. Kennit paid no heed to them.

Before him stretched the tidy garden, laid out in neat well-tended rows. Chickens cackled and scratched in a pen just beyond a small henhouse. From somewhere, a cow lowed questioningly. Beyond the garden were six cottages, once as alike as peas in a pod. Now five of the thatched roofs sagged pitifully. Smoke rose from the chimney of one that retained a roof. Other than that pale moving pillar, all was still. Beyond the cottages, the upper story and shingled roof of a larger house were visible. Once this had been a small and prosperous freehold. Now this handful of houses was all that remained. Years of careful planning had gone into it. The entire settlement had been laid out with loving precision. It had been an ordered and tidy world, designed especially for him. That had been before Igrot the Terrible discovered its existence. Kennit's eyes traveled slowly over all of it. Something stirred inside him, but he stifled it before the emotion could make itself known.

He took a slow, deep breath. "Mother!" He called out. "Mother, I'm home!"

For two breaths, nothing happened. Then a door was slowly opened. A gray-haired woman peered out. She squinted in the early morning light as she peered about the yard. She finally spotted them on the far side of the garden. She lifted a hand and clutched at her throat, staring wide-eyed. She made a small sign against wild spirits. Kennit gave a sigh of exasperation. He began to pick his way through the garden, his crutch and peg awkward in the rows of softened earth. "It's me, Mother. Kennit. Your son."

As it always had, her caution exasperated him. He was halfway across the garden before she was all the way out the door. She was barefoot, he noted with distaste, and dressed in cotton tunic and trousers like a peasant. Her pinned up hair was the color of wood-ash. Never a slender woman, she had thickened with the years. Her eyes widened as she finally recognized him. She hurried toward him at an inglorious trot. He had to suffer the indignity of her squashy embrace. She was weeping before she even reached him. Over and over, she pointed at his missing leg, gabbling in sorrow and query.

"Yes, yes, Mother, it's all right. Now have done." She clutched at him, weeping. He seized her hands firmly and set them back from himself. "Have done!"

Years ago, her tongue had been cut out. Although he had had nothing to do with that and had sincerely deplored it at the time, over the years he had come to see it was not an entirely unfortunate incident. She still talked endlessly, or tried to, but since the event he could steer the conversation as he wished it to go. He told her when she agreed with him, and when a topic was settled. As now.

"I can't stay long, I'm afraid, but I've brought you a few things." He turned her determinedly and led his awe-stricken cavalcade toward the intact cottage. "The chest has a few gifts for you. Some flower seeds I thought you would like, some cooking spices, some cloth, a tapestry. A bit of this, a bit of that."

They reached the door of the cottage and went inside. It was spotlessly tidy. Bare. On the table were smoothed shingles of white pine. Brushes and dyes were laid out beside them. So, she still painted. Yesterday's work still rested on the table, a wildflower done in intricate and realistic detail. A kettle of water bubbled on the hearth. Through the door into the second room, he glimpsed the neatly made bed. Everywhere he looked, he saw signs of a simple and placid life. She had always liked things that way. His father had loved opulence and variety. They had complemented one another well. Now she was like half a person. The thought suddenly agitated him beyond his self-control. He paced a turn around the room, then seized Ankle by the shoulders and thrust the girl forward.

"I've thought of you often, Mother. See, this is Ankle. She's your servant now. She's not very bright, but she seems clean and willing. If she turns out not to be, I'll kill her when I come back." His mother's eyes flew wide in horror and the crippled girl crouched down, babbling for mercy. "So, for her sake, do try to get along well together," he added almost gently. Already he wished he were back on the deck of his ship. Things were so much simpler there. He gestured at his prisoner.

"And this is Captain Haven. Say hello and then good-bye for now. He will be staying, but you needn't bother much about him. I'll be putting him down in the old wine cellar under the big house. Ankle, you will remember to give him some food and water now and then, won't you? At least as often as you were fed and watered aboard the ship, right? That seems fair to everyone, now doesn't it?" He waited for answers but they were all gaping at him as if he were mad. All save his mother, who clutched the front of her blouse and wrung the fabric between her hands. She looked distressed. He thought he knew the problem. "Now, remember, I have given my word that he is to be kept safe. So I insist you do just that. I'll chain him up well, but you must see to the food and water part. Do you understand?"

His mother gabbled frantically at him. He nodded in approval. "I knew you wouldn't mind. Now. What have I forgotten?"

He glanced at the others. "Oh, yes. Look, Mother. I've brought you a priest, too! I know how you like priests." His eyes drilled Sa'Adar. "My mother is very devout. Pray for her. Or bless something."

Sa'Adar's eyes went wide. "You're mad."

"Scarcely. Why do people always accuse me of that when I'm arranging things to my liking instead of theirs?" He dismissed the priest. "Now, these two, Mother, are going to be your neighbors. They have a baby on the way, they've told me. I'm sure you'll like having a little one around, won't you? They're both handy at heavy work. Perhaps the next time I come to visit, I'll find things in better repair. Perhaps you'll be living in the big house again?"

The old woman shook her head so violently that her gray hair flew free of its pinning. Her eyes went wide with some remembered pain. She opened her mouth in a quavering cry. It revealed the stump of her tongue. Kennit looked aside in distaste. "This cottage does seem quite cozy," he amended. "Perhaps you are better off here. But that doesn't mean we should stand by and let the big house fall down." He glanced at the map-face couple. "You two may choose one of the cottages for yourself. As may the priest. Keep him well away from the captain. I promised Wintrow that his father would be kept somewhere, intact, where the boy no longer needed to worry about him or deal with him."

For the first time, Kyle Haven spoke. His jaw dropped and his mouth gaped for a moment. He strangled, and then the furious words roared out of him. "This is Wintrow's doing? My son did this to me?" His blue eyes flew wide in hurt and justified hatred. "I knew it. I knew it all along! The treacherous little viper! The cur!"

Kennit's mother cowered from his vehemence. Kennit casually back-handed Haven across his mouth. Even supporting himself on his crutch, Kennit managed sufficient force that the captain staggered backward. "You're upsetting my mother," he pointed out coolly. He gave a short sigh of exasperation. "I suppose it's time I put you away. Come along, then. You two bring him." This he addressed to his map-faces. Turning to the girl, he commanded her, "Make some food. Mother, you show her where the supplies are. Priest, stay here. Pray or something. Do whatever my mother wishes you to do."

The map-faces hustled Captain Haven out the door. As Kennit followed, Sa'Adar announced, "You can't command what I do. You can't make me your slave."

Kennit glanced back at him. He gave him a small smile. "Perhaps not. However, I *can* make you dead. It's an interesting choice, don't you think?" He turned and left without a backward glance.

The map-faces awaited him outside. Haven sagged between the well-muscled pair. Disbelief warred with despair in his face. "You can't do this. You can't abandon me here."

Kennit merely shook his head to himself. He was so weary of people telling him that he could not do what he obviously could. He did not bother to look at his followers as he led the way to the big house. The pebbled path was overgrown, the flowerbeds long gone to weed and ruins. He pointed it out to the map-faces. "I'd like this tidied. If you don't know anything about gardening, ask my mother for direction. She knows a great deal about it." As they came around the front of the house, he did not look at the remains of the other structures. There was no sense in dwelling on the past. Grass and creeping vines had long ago overpowered and cloaked the burnt remains. Let it lie so.

Even the big house had taken some damage in that long ago raid. There were scorch marks on the planked walls where the flames from the neighboring structures had threatened to set it ablaze as well. Such a night of flames and screams that had been, as the supposed allies revealed their true intent. Such an orgy of cruelty as Igrot indulged to his sensual limits. The smells of smoke and blood were forever intermingled in his memories of that night.

He climbed the steps. The front door was not locked. It had never been locked. His father had not believed in locks. He opened the door and strode in. For an instant, his memory leaped and showed him the interior as it once had been. Education and travel had sharpened his tastes since then, but when he was a child, he had found the hodge-podge of tapestries and rugs and statuary luxurious and rich. Now he would have scoffed at such a mish-mash of trash and treasures, but then his father had reveled in it and the boy Kennit with him. "You'll live like a king, laddie," his father would say. "No. Better yet, you'll be a king. King Kennit of Key Island! Now doesn't that have a fine ring? King Kennit, King Kennit, King Kennit!" Singing that refrain, his father would scoop him up and swing him wildly about, capering drunkenly around the room. King Kennit.

He blinked his eyes. He saw the stripped walls and the bare floor of what was actually little more than a plantation house, not the aristocratic mansion his father had pretended it to be. Kennit had considered refurbishing the house many times. In the rooms upstairs were stored more than enough art and furniture to eclipse the house's former tawdry glory. It was his carefully gleaned collection, the finest of his troves, brought here a bit at a time in great secrecy. But that was not what he wanted. No. He would restore it with what Igrot had stolen from them. The same paintings, the same tapestries and rugs, chairs and chandeliers. Someday, when the time was right, he would go after all of it, bring it back here, and put it all back just as it had been. He would make it right. He had promised that to himself more times than he cared to remember, and now the fulfillment of that promise was within his grasp. All that Igrot had ever stolen from anyone was now his by right. A small hard smile formed on his mouth. King Kennit indeed.

His mother wanted no part of it. When he was younger, during the savage years, he would climb onto her lap, hug her neck tightly, and try to whisper his plans for vengeance into her ear. She would desperately and fearfully shush him. She had not even dared dream of revenge. Now she no longer wanted luxuries and wealth on display. No. She trusted to her simple life to protect her. Kennit knew the truth of that. No one can have so little that someone else can find nothing to envy. Poverty and simplicity were not shields from the greed of others. If you had nothing left to steal, they'd take your body and enslave it.

For all his musings, he did not pause or tarry. He led his cavalcade briskly through the hall and back to the kitchen. He opened the heavy door and left it ajar as he led them down the steps to the cellar beneath. It had been painstakingly dug down into the rocky bones of the island. There were no windows but he didn't bother kindling a torch. He didn't plan to be down there that long. It was evenly cool, winter and summer. It had been a good wine cellar. No sign of that use of it remained now. The rusty chains on the floor and some odd stains recalled its later use as a makeshift dungeon and torture chamber for those who had displeased Igrot. Now it could serve that purpose again.

"Chain him up," he directed his map-faces. "Make sure you fasten him tight and true. There are some rings driven into that back wall. Fasten him to one of those. I don't want him trying to bother little Ankle when she comes with his food and water. If she comes with his food and water."

"You're trying to frighten me." From somewhere, Captain Haven had found a last measure of aplomb. "I'm not easily scared. The only problem is that I have no idea what you want from me. Why don't you simply tell me?" He even managed to keep his voice steady as the male map-face led him down the steep steps. The woman had gone ahead to rummage for chains while her docile and implacable mate dealt with the man. "Regardless of what my son has told you, I am not an unreasonable man. Everything is negotiable. Even if you keep the ship and the boy, you could get a handsome ransom for me. Have you thought of that? I am worth far more to you alive than dead. Come. I'm not a stingy man. This profits no one."

Kennit smiled sardonically. "My dear captain, not all of life is about profit. Sometimes it is about convenience. This is convenient for me."

Kyle maintained his composure. He struggled savagely but silently when the rusty manacles were snapped about his ankles. It did him no good. His time shut up in his cabin had wasted him. Either of the map-faces alone could have bested him. Together they handled him as if he were a recalcitrant five-year-old. The lock was stiff but the old keys hanging on the ring by the kitchen door still turned it. Kennit thought he knew the precise moment the man broke. It was at the quiet snap of the lock being fastened. That was when he began cursing. He swore oaths of vengeance and called down the wrath of a dozen gods on them as they climbed the stairs and left him there. As they closed the door, shutting him into the dark and dank, he began to scream. The door to the wine cellar was heavy and well fitted. When it shut, it cut off his screams, just as Kennit had recalled. He hung the keys back on their peg.

"Be sure you show Ankle the way here. I want him kept alive. Do you understand?"

The woman nodded. Seeing her do so, Dedge nodded also. Kennit smiled, well pleased. These two would do fine here. Life on Key Island would offer them more than their wildest dreams. They would have their own cottage, plenty of food, peace and a place to raise their child. So simply had he bought their lives from them, he reflected. Strange how men would resist slavery savagely, only to sell themselves for a simple chance at life.

As he walked back to the big house, they followed at his heels. He spoke over his shoulder to them. "My mother can show you all you need to know about the island. Pigs are plentiful. There are goats as well. Almost anything you need, the island can provide. If it is outside the big house, you can help yourself to what you need. All I ask in return is that you do the heavier chores for my mother. That, and be sure the priest never attempts to leave. If he does, simply put him in the cellar with the captain. Encourage him to amuse my mother." He stopped and looked back at them when they reached the cottage door. "Is there anything I've forgotten?" he asked them. "Anything you don't understand?"

"It's all quite clear," the woman replied quickly. "We'll keep our end of the bargain, Captain Kennit. Make no mistake." She rested one hand atop her belly, as if pledging to the child within rather than to him. That as much as anything they had done convinced him he had chosen well. He nodded, well satisfied with himself. He was rid of Sa'Adar without the bad luck associated with killing a priest. Kyle Haven would be where neither he nor Wintrow had to fret about him, yet he was still available to be ransomed off later if Kennit chose to do so. The disposal of the others had been convenient. They had rowed the boat ashore and seen that neither the priest nor the captain gave trouble. Yes. He had planned well.

He went into the cottage and glanced around. The priest stood in a corner, his arms folded on his chest. He did not look as if he were praying. His mother crouched over the open chest, aahing and clucking over the contents. She had already donned the turquoise earrings. As he entered the room, Ankle gimped the short distance from the hearth to the table with a platter of fresh flat bread. There was a bowl of berry preserves on the table, and a slab of yellow spring butter. Beside the butter, herb tea was steaming from the cracked lid of a pot. The table was set with odds and ends of crockery. Not a cup matched its fellow. Kennit knew a moment's annoyance. Although those gathered here would never leave this island, he did not like anyone to see his mother living in such circumstances. When he was king, it would not do for such tales to be noised about. "Next time I come to visit, I shall bring you a proper tea set, Mother," he announced. "I know you are fond of these old pieces, but really . . ."

He let the words trail off as he helped himself to a piece of warm bread. His mother gabbled away at him as she poured him a cup of tea and offered him the only chair at the table. He seated himself gratefully. The crutch head was beginning to chafe him severely. He slathered his bread with butter and heaped it with preserves. His first bite nearly swept him away on a wave of sensory memories. These humble foods, still so delicious to his palate, were like ghosts. They belonged to the world of a very small boy, coddled and indulged and safe beyond all imagining. All that had been betrayed nearly thirty-five years ago. Odd, that such a sweet taste could summon up such bitterness. He ate the rest of his bread and three more pieces, caught between enjoyment and painful memory.

The others joined him in the meal, obeying his mother's gestures to stand about the table. Only the priest demurred. His supercilious stare included Kennit. It did not bother the pirate. Hunger would cure him of his snobbery soon enough. For now, it was an oddly pleasant gathering. His mother gabbled on in her singsong way. The map-faces responded to her gestures and mouthing with nods and smiles, but few words. Her dumbness seemed contagious. Ankle appeared almost competent in this humble setting. She took up the brush and swept the ashes back into the hearth without being told. Her eyes had already lost some of their bruised look. Kennit knew a moment's reconsideration of her. He had wanted a docile servant for his mother; he hoped this girl did not recover too much of her spirits.

He finished his tea and rose. "Well. I must be going. Now, Mother, don't start to carry on. You know I can't stay."

Despite his words, she caught at his sleeve. The pleading look in her eyes spoke eloquently but he chose to misunderstand. "I won't forget the tea cups, I promise you. I'll bring them the next time I come. Yes, all done with pretty little designs, I'll remember. I know what you like." As he set her hands firmly away from his sleeve, he spoke over her shoulder to the others. "See that you mind well, Ankle. I shall expect to see a fine, fat baby when next I call, Dedge. No doubt there will be another on the way by then, eh?" He felt quite patriarchal as he said this. It occurred to him that eventually he could select others to come and live here. It could become his secret kingdom within a kingdom.

As he stepped away from his mother, she surrendered, as she always did. She sank down onto the chair, bowed her head into her hands and wept. She always wept. It made no sense to him. How many times had she found that tears solved nothing? Yet still, she wept. He patted her gingerly on the shoulder and headed for the door.

"I am not staying here," the priest declared.

Kennit paused to stare at him. "Oh?" he queried pleasantly.

"No. I'm going back to the ship with you."

Kennit considered this. "A pity. I am so sure my mother would have enjoyed having you here. You're certain you won't reconsider?"

The pirate's smooth courtesy seemed to rattle Sa'Adar. He looked all around himself. Kennit's mother still wept. Ankle had approached her and was cautiously patting the old woman's shoulder. Dedge and Saylah looked only at Kennit. Their alert and expectant waiting reminded Kennit of well-trained hunting dogs. He made a small hand motion; the two map-faces relaxed slightly but remained attentive. The priest looked back at Kennit.

"No. I will not stay. There is nothing here for me."

Kennit gave a small sigh. "I was so sure you'd stay. Certain of it. Well. If you will not stay, at least do something for my mother before you depart. Bless the house or cow."

Sa'Adar gave him a disdainful look. It was as if the pirate had given him a command more suited to a horse or dog. He looked over his shoulder at the weeping woman. "I suppose I could do that."

"I know you could. Take your time. As you have noticed, I do not move swiftly these days. I'll await you at the beach." Kennit shrugged. "You can row the boat for me."

Kennit could see the priest weighing this. He knew the pirate could not outrun him. There was small chance he could launch the gig alone. Sa'Adar gave a grudging nod. "I'll be right along. I'll put a blessing on her house and garden."

"How kind of you," Kennit enthused. "I shall wait for you on the beach, then. Farewell, Mother. I shan't forget your tea cups."

"Captain?" Saylah dared to ask softly. "Will you want any help to launch the boat?" She gave the priest a narrowed, sideways glance as she spoke. Her offer was plain.

He managed a smile. "No, thank you all the same. I am sure the priest and I can manage it. You stay here and get settled in. Farewell." He tucked his crutch more securely under his arm and began his swinging trek back to the boat.

The ground of the garden was soft. After that, his path led uphill. Kennit was more tired than he had realized. Nevertheless, he persevered until he was out of sight of the cottage before he paused to rest. He mopped sweat from his face and considered. He decided he did not need to fear treachery from the priest. Not just yet, anyway. Sa'Adar needed him to return to the ship. He would not be welcomed aboard without the captain.

He took up a more leisurely pace. Once he stopped, and listened to the rustling of a pig in the brush. It did not come his way and he soon went on. He almost expected the priest to overtake him before he reached the beach, but he did not. Perhaps he was bestowing a very lengthy blessing upon the house. That would please his mother.

The sand of the beach was loose and dry. His peg dragged through it. He was so weary. He could scarcely lift his leg high enough for the peg to clear the sand. He reached the gig and sat down. The tide was coming in. Soon the boat would be almost afloat, but it promised to be a long row back to the ship. Had he overestimated his strength? The warmth of the day and the aching fatigue of his body worked against him. He wanted to drowse. He wanted to sit still and drift in the warm afternoon. Instead, he massaged his aching armpit where the crutch had chafed him. He spurred himself, wondering if the priest delayed to visit Captain Haven. No. Dedge would not allow that. Not unless they had been in league all along. If that were so, they would come soon to kill him. They would have killed his mother already, of course. They would have found his treasure, carefully stowed in the big house. They would come to kill him, because he had been stupid. What would they do then? They could not return to the ship. Alternatively, could they? Was there enough treasure there to buy Sorcor and Etta, Wintrow and Brig? Perhaps. His heart grew cold with anger at his own stupidity. Then he smiled a wolf's smile. Perhaps there was enough treasure to buy human hearts. But not Vivacia's. The ship had already come to love him. He knew that. One could not buy nor steal the heart of a liveship. The heart of a liveship was true.

Igrot had proved that, many years ago.

Kennit smiled as he prepared himself and waited.

When the priest finally came, he tramped like an angry man. So, Kennit thought to himself, you did try to sway Dedge to your cause. You failed. Turning his head to regard Sa'Adar, Kennit became certain of his conjecture. He had the rumpled look of a man who has narrowly averted a bad beating by fleeing. His face was redder than the walk back to the boat would explain. As he approached, Kennit climbed into the gig and seated himself on the rowing seat. He did not bother with a greeting. "Push it out into the water."

Sa'Adar glared at him. "It would be easier if the gig were empty."

"Probably," Kennit agreed affably. He didn't move.

The man was not soft, but he was not a hardened sailor either. He set his hands to the gig and pushed. Nothing happened. "Wait for a wave," Kennit suggested.

Sa'Adar gritted his teeth but obeyed the suggestion. The bottom of the gig grated on the sand and then abruptly bobbed free. "Keep pushing or she'll beach again," Kennit warned him as he took up the oars. Soon Sa'Adar was wading alongside, trying to pull himself over and into the boat. Kennit pulled steadily at the oars. It had been some time since he had rowed a boat, but his body remembered it well enough. He braced his peg against the bottom of the boat to keep from slipping. Even so, it was difficult to pull evenly on the oars. A wave of desolation engulfed him as he decided that nothing would ever be completely as it had been. He had lost a part of his body and for the rest of his life, all his actions would have to compensate for what was missing.

"Wait!" Sa'Adar complained as he scrabbled to get aboard. Kennit ignored him and continued to row. Sa'Adar was still only halfway in when the next wave lifted the gig. The priest clambered aboard like a landsman, gasping and shivering as the brisk sea wind hit his soaked clothing. Once he was well aboard, Kennit shipped the oars. It pleased him that even with a peg and crutch, he moved more gracefully than Sa'Adar as he shifted his seat. The priest, arms clutched about himself, sneered at him. "You expect me to row?"

"It will warm you," Kennit pointed out.

He sat in the bow, holding his crutch, and watched Sa'Adar struggle. Rowing a gig, even on a calm day, soon becomes serious work. There was a rising wind and a bit of a chop for him to contend with also. He worked the oars unevenly. Sometimes they skipped and splashed across the top of the water. Even when they bit well into the water, their progress was slow. Kennit was unconcerned. He could see Sa'Adar's impatience to be back aboard the ship in the furious energy he poured into his task. He decided to engage him in conversation as well.

"So. Are you satisfied with the justice meted out to Captain Haven?"

Sa'Adar had little breath to spare, but could not resist making speeches. "I wanted to see him before I left. To spit on him one more time and wish him joy of his chains and darkness." He caught his breath. "Dedge would not let me. He and Saylah both turned on me." Another breath. "But for me, they'd be slaves in Chalced right now. They would not be together still, and Saylah's child could celebrate his birth with a tattoo on his face." He was panting now.

"Keep her nose into the waves. You see that point there, on that island? Where the two trees stand separate from the forest? Fix your eyes on that and row toward it."

Sa'Adar gave an exasperated scowl. "One man cannot row this! You should take the bench beside me and help. It took four rowers to get us ashore."

"The boat was more heavily laden then. Besides. I am greatly wearied from our hike. Remember that I am a man still recovering from a grievous injury. But in time, perhaps, I shall take a turn at the oars and let you rest." Kennit turned his face to the breeze and closed his eyes to slits. The bright sun danced on the moving water. Suddenly even his weariness felt good. This was something he had needed to do. He had taken independent, physical action on his own. He had proved to himself that he could still sway others to his will with little more than words. His body had been diminished, but it was sufficient to his ambition. He would triumph. King

Kennit. King Kennit of the Pirate Isles. Would he someday have a palace on Key Island? Perhaps after his mother had died, he could establish himself there. As his father had once foreseen, the opening to the bay in Keyhole Island could be easily fortified. It would make a wonderful stronghold. He was still building his towers when Sa'Adar spoke again.

"Should we be able to see the ships by now?"

Kennit nodded. "If you were pulling at the oars like a man, instead of slapping and skipping them on the water, we'd have cleared the point of that island by now. Then, we'd be able to see the ships, though we would still have a long row ahead of us. Keep rowing."

"The journey did not seem to take this long last night."

"Things never seem to take as long or be as hard when someone else is doing the work. It is much like captaining a ship. It seems easy, when someone else is doing it."

"Do you mock me?" It is hard to be disdainful when one was out of breath, but Sa'Adar managed it.

Kennit shook his head sadly. "You do me wrong. Is it mockery to tell a man a thing he should have learned long ago?"

"That ship . . . by rights . . . is mine. We had . . . already taken it . . . when you came." Sa'Adar's breath was coming harder.

"There. You see. If I had not come alongside and put a prize crew aboard, the *Vivacia* would be at the bottom now. Not even a liveship can sail herself completely."

"We would have . . . managed." Sa'Adar abruptly flung the oars down. One started to slip through the oarlock into the water. He snatched at it, and pulled it half into the boat. "Damn you, take a turn at this!" he gasped. "I am as good as you are. I will be treated like your slave no longer."

"Slave? I have asked no more of you than I would of any ordinary seaman."

"I am not yours to command. I never will be! Nor will I give up my claim to the ship. Wherever we go, I shall be sure that all hear of your injustice and greed. How so many can adulate you, I do not know! There is your poor mother, abandoned to a harsh life alone for Sa knows how long! You return to visit her for less than half a day, leaving only a trunkful of trinkets and a half-wit servant to wait on her. How can you treat your own mother so? Is not a man's mother to be ever revered as the symbol of the female aspect of Sa? Nevertheless, you treat her as you treat everyone else. As a servant! She tried to speak to me, poor thing. I could not make out what distressed her so, but it was not a lack of tea cups!"

Kennit could not help himself. He laughed aloud. It incensed the other man so that his face grew even redder. "You bastard!" he spat. "You heartless bastard!"

Kennit glanced about. It wasn't far to the point of the island now. He could manage it. Once there, if he grew too weary, his coat tied to an oar and waved would bring someone from either the *Marietta* or the *Vivacia*. They would be watching for him by now.

"Such language, from a priest! You forget yourself. Here. I'll row for a bit, while you recover."

That quelled him. Sa'Adar rose from the rowing bench. In a stiff half-crouch, he waited for Kennit to change places with him as he rubbed at his aching back. Kennit tried to rise from his own bench, but sat down again heavily. The small vessel rocked. Sa'Adar cried out and made a wild grab for the gunwales. Kennit grimaced in embarrassment. "Stiff," he grunted. "Today has taken more out of me than I thought." He sighed heavily. He narrowed his eyes at the disdainful look on the priest's face. "Still. I said I would row and I shall." He picked up his crutch, took a firm grip on it, and then extended the tip towards Sa'Adar. "When I give the word, you heave me to my feet. Once I'm up, I'll wager I can move about."

Sa'Adar gripped the crutch end. "Now," Kennit told him, and tried to rise. He sat down heavily once more. He set his jaw in grim determination. "Again," he commanded the priest. "And this time, put your back into it."

The weary man took a double-handed grip on the crutch. Kennit made better his own clutch upon it. "Now!" he commanded him. As the priest heaved, the pirate suddenly thrust forward, shoving with all his strength upon the crutch. It hit the priest in the chest and he went flailing wildly backwards. Kennit had hoped for a clean splash overboard. Instead, the man fell athwart the gunwales, almost out of the boat but not quite. Quick as a tiger springing, Kennit flung himself forward. He kept his weight low, as the landsman had not. He gripped one of Sa'Adar's feet and lifted it high. The man went over, but as he went he launched a kick at Kennit that slammed his bare foot hard into Kennit's face. Kennit's head rocked back on his shoulders; he felt the warm gush as blood flowed from his nose. He wiped it hastily on his sleeve, then scrabbled to the rower's bench and took up the oars. He seated the oars well in the oar-locks and began to pull mightily.

An instant later, the priest's head bobbed up in the boat's wake. "Damn you!" he shouted. "Sa damn you!"

Kennit expected the man's head to go under again. Instead, he struck out after the boat with long powerful strokes. So, he was a swimmer. Kennit had not reckoned on that. It was a pity the sea was warmer here in these island waters. He couldn't count on cold to kill him quickly. He might have to do it himself.

Kennit did not strain. Instead, he set a steady pace and pulled on the oars. He had not lied to Sa'Adar. He had been stiff, but this was loosening him up. The priest swam with the swift, frantic strokes of a desperate man.

He was gaining on the small boat; his body offered far less resistance to the waves than the lightened boat did. When he was within a stroke or two, Kennit carefully shipped the oars and drew the dagger from his belt. He moved to the stern and waited. He did not try for a killing stroke. He would have had to extend himself too far to do that easily and might end up being dragged into the sea by the priest. Instead, each time the drowning man reached for the boat, he slashed at his hands. He cut his reaching palms, he slashed the back of his knuckles when his grip closed on the stern. Kennit was silent as death itself while the priest cursed him, screamed, and then begged for his life. When he seized hold of the side and clung there stubbornly, the pirate risked a blinding slash across the man's face. Still he clutched the side, begging and praying to be allowed to live. It infuriated Kennit. "I tried to let you live!" he roared at him. "All you had to do was what I wanted you to do. You refused me! So!"

He risked a stab and the dagger went deep into the side of the man's throat. In an instant, his hands were warm and slick with blood thicker and more salt than the sea itself. The priest fell away suddenly. Kennit released the haft of the dagger and let him go. For a wave, then two, he bobbed facedown on the water. Then the sea swallowed him up.

Kennit sat for a time, watching the empty water behind the boat. Then he wiped his hands down the front of his coat. Slowly he moved back to the rower's bench. He took up the oars in hands that had begun to blister. It didn't matter. They would hurt, but it did not matter. It was done, and he would live. He knew it as surely as he knew his luck still rode with him.

He lifted his eyes and scanned the horizon. Not so far to go and he'd be where the ships' lookouts could spot him. He smiled to himself. "I'll wager Vivacia sees me before any of them. I'll wager she knows right now that I'm coming back to her. Watch for me, my lady! Cast about those lovely eyes!"

"Perhaps I should open those eyes for her," suggested a small voice close by. Kennit nearly lost his grip on the oars. He looked at the long silent charm strapped to his wrist. His own features in miniature, encarmined now in blood, blinked up at him. The small mouth opened, and a tiny tongue emerged to lick his lips as if they were parched. "What would she think of her captain bold, if she knew you as well as I do?"

Kennit grinned. "Methinks she would think you a liar. She has been with me, and knows my deepest heart. She and the boy both have. And they love me still."

"They may think they have," the charm conceded bitterly. "But only one creature has ever seen to the bottom of your dark, dirty heart and still chosen loyalty to you."

"You refer to yourself, I assume," Kennit hazarded. "You have little choice in the matter, charm. You are bound to me."

"As tightly as you are bound to me," the charm replied.

Kennit shrugged. "So we are bound to one another. So be it. I suggest you make the best of it, and do the duty you were created to do. Perhaps that way, we shall both live longer."

"I was never created for any duty to you," the charm informed him. "Nor does my life depend upon yours. But for the sake of another, I will do what I can to preserve you. At least for a time."

The pirate made no further reply. The blisters on his right palm broke stingingly. An expression, part grimace, part grin, lit Kennit's dark face. A little pain was nothing. His luck was holding. With luck, a man could do much.

CHAPTER EIGHTEEN

Wishes Fulfilled

"WHAT HAVE YOU DONE WITH MY FATHER?"

Kennit looked up from the tray of food Wintrow had just placed before him. The pirate was freshly attired, washed and combed. That final effort had exhausted him. All he wanted right now was his food. Etta's flapping and whining about how worried she had been the whole time he was gone had been taxing enough. After she'd laid out fresh clothing for him, he'd banished her from his room. Nothing was more irritating to his nerves than someone fretting. He would not tolerate that atmosphere for his dinner. He ignored the lad. He picked up a spoon in his sore hand and stirred the soup before him. Pieces of carrot and fish bobbed to the top.

"I beg you. I have to know. What have you done with my father?"

Kennit looked at the boy, a sharp reply on the tip of his tongue, and relented. Wintrow's face was as pale as such a tanned and swarthy lad could be. He stood very straight and still, as if composed. The quickness of his breath and his teeth clenched on his lower lip betrayed him. His dark eyes were haunted. He supposed the youngster felt bad, but one had to take responsibility for one's choices. "I only did what you asked me to do. Your father is now somewhere else. You don't have to worry about him, you don't have to see him or contend with him." Before Wintrow could ask, Kennit added, "He is safe. When I keep a promise, I don't keep it halfway."

Wintrow rocked slightly forward. He looked as if he'd been punched in the belly. "I didn't mean it," he said in a hoarse whisper. "Not like this, not just vanished away while I slept. Please, sir. Bring him back. I'll take care of him and make no complaints."

"I'm afraid I can't do that," Kennit pointed out affably. He gave Wintrow a small smile to reassure him, but rebuked him gently with, "Next time, be sure you want what you ask for. I went to a great deal of trouble to arrange this for you." He took a spoonful of the soup. He wanted to eat in peace. It was time to put an end to Wintrow's impertinence. "I had expected you to be grateful, not remorseful. You asked for this. I've granted it. That's all there is to say about it. Pour me some wine."

Wintrow moved woodenly to obey him. Then he stepped back from the table and stood as if frozen, his eyes fixed on the wall. Fine. Kennit put his attention on his food. The exercise had given him a marvelous appetite. His muscles ached and he planned to rest after his meal, but other than that, he felt keen-edged and competent. This had been good for him. He'd have to get out and move about more, once Etta had padded his crutch and stump-cup for him. He tried to decide if he could adapt his peg to allow him to climb the rigging again. Even in miserable times, he'd loved going aloft. The wind up there always seemed cleaner, and the possibilities of life as broad as the horizon.

"There was blood all over your coat. And the side of the gig." Wintrow's stubborn words broke into his reverie and his dining.

Kennit sighed and set his spoon down. Wintrow was still staring at the wall, but his rigidity suggested that he was trying to control shaking. "The blood was not your father's. If you must know, it was Sa'Adar's." Sarcasm crept into his voice. "Please don't tell me that you have revised your feelings about him as well."

"You killed him because I hated him?" There was panicky disbelief in Wintrow's voice.

"No. I killed him because he would not do as I wanted him to do. He really left me no choice. His death is no loss to you. The man had only contempt for you and your father." Kennit lifted his wine and drained off the glass. He held it out to Wintrow. The youth moved as jerkily as a puppet as he refilled the glass.

"And Ankle?" he dared to ask in a sickened voice.

Kennit slammed his glass to the table. Wine leaped out and soiled the white cloth. "Ankle is fine. They are all fine. Sa'Adar is the only one I killed, and I only killed him because I had to. I saved you the trouble of having to do it later for yourself. Do I look so foolish as to waste my time on unnecessary actions? I will not sit here and be badgered by a ship's boy! Clean up this mess, pour me fresh wine and then leave." The look Kennit gave him had cowed many a larger man.

To the pirate's surprise, it suddenly kindled an answering spark in the boy's eyes. Wintrow straightened himself. Kennit sensed he had pushed the boy across some sort of boundary. Interesting. Wintrow advanced to the table and removed the food and the soiled cloth with a silent, savage efficiency. He restored it, carefully poured more wine, then spoke. He dared to let his anger sound in his voice. "Do not ever lay your deeds at my door. I do not kill people who inconvenience me. Sa gives life, and every life he forms has a meaning and a purpose. No man has the ability to understand fully Sa's purpose. Rather I must learn to tolerate those others until they have lived to fulfill Sa's purpose. I am a part of his intention for this world, but my part is no more important than anyone else's."

Kennit had leaned back in his chair and crossed his arms on his chest while Wintrow tidied the table and preached. Now he sighed out through his nose. "That is because you are not destined to be a king." A thought occurred to Kennit and he could not control his smirk. "Meditate on this, priest. Perhaps I am one of those you must learn to tolerate until I can fulfill Sa's purpose." When the glower on Wintrow's face only darkened at this jest, Kennit laughed aloud. He shook his head. "You take yourself so seriously. Run along now. Go talk to the ship. I think you'll find her course aligns closer with mine than yours just now. I mean it. Run along. Send Etta to me on your way."

Kennit whisked his hand at the door. He turned his attention back to his interrupted meal. The boy took his time about leaving and shut the door a bit loudly. Kennit shook his head. He was getting too fond of Wintrow and allowing him too many liberties. If Opal had taken that tone with him, he'd have worn stripes before sunset. He shrugged at his own leniency. That had always been one of his faults. He was too kind-hearted for his own good. He shook his head to himself and let his thoughts wander back to Key Island.

"WHY DIDN'T YOU WAKE ME?" WINTROW DEMANDED. HIS UNRESOLVED ANger at Kennit still roiled within him.

"I told you." Vivacia reacted stubbornly to his tone. "You were weary and deeply asleep. I did not see any harm in what he was doing. You could not have stopped him anyway. So I saw no sense in waking you."

"He must have come right up here to get Ankle. She was here when I fell asleep." A sudden suspicion jabbed him. "Did he tell you not to wake me?"

"And if he did?" Vivacia asked, affronted. "What difference would it make? It was still my decision."

Wintrow looked down at his feet. The depth of his hurt surprised him. "Once you would have been more loyal to me. You would have wakened me, whether you thought it was wise or not. You must have known I would have wanted that."

Vivacia turned her head and looked out across the water. "I fail to see your point."

"You even sound like him," Wintrow said miserably.

His unhappiness spurred her more than his anger had. "What do you want me to say? That I am sorry Kyle Haven is gone? I am not. I have not known a moment of peace since he took command. I am glad that he is gone, Wintrow. Glad. And you should be glad, also."

He was. That was the rub. Once she would have known that, but now she was so taken with the pirate, she considered only Kennit's view. "Do you need me anymore?" he asked her abruptly.

"What?" It was her turn to be shocked. "Why ask such a thing? Of course, I need . . ."

"Because I thought that if you were happy with Kennit, perhaps he'd let me go. Both of you could just put me ashore on the mainland. I could make my own way back to the monastery and my life. I could put all this behind me, as something I couldn't change anyway." He paused. "You'd be rid of me also, just as you are rid of my father."

"You sound like a jealous child," she retorted.

"You haven't answered my question."

In that moment, she did. She opened herself to him, and he felt her pain at his hard words.

"Oh," Wintrow said softly. That was all. His gaze followed hers. The *Marietta* rocked at anchor so close by that Wintrow could see the face of the man on watch. Sorcor had not been pleased when an anxious Brig had sent to ask if he had word of the captain. The new, closer position of the other ship reflected his renewed watchfulness.

She cut to the heart of the squabble. "Why are you jealous that I care for Kennit? You would do away with the bond you and I share, if you could. He is the opposite. He strives so earnestly to build a tie between us. He speaks to me as no one else ever has. He comes up here, while you are off and about your tasks, and he tells me stories. Not just tales from his life, but folk-tales, and stories he has heard from other people. And he listens to me when I speak. He asks me what I think, and what I would like to do. He tells me his plans for his kingdom and the people he will rule. When I make a suggestion, he is pleased. Have you any idea how nice that is, to have someone tell you things and listen in return to what you say?"

"I do." It put him in mind of his monastery, but he did not say the words aloud. He did not need to.

"I do not know why you will not give him a chance," she suddenly burst out. "I cannot claim to know him as I know you. However, this we both have seen; he harbors more affection and goodwill toward you than your father ever did. He thinks of others. Ask him, sometime, to show you the plans he has drawn for Divvytown. He has given it great thought, how he would build a tower to warn them of danger, and where he would put the wells to have cleaner water. Askew, too. He has drawn a chart of Askew, with a breakwater to improve the harbor, and docks drawn in. If only they would listen to him and live their lives as he directed, things would be so much better for them. He wants to make things tidy and better. Moreover, he wants to be your friend, Wintrow. Perhaps what he did to Kyle was high-handed, but you did request it. He could have gained the goodwill of the slaves by turning Kyle over to them. His torture and death would have been a spectacle for Divvytown that would have brought Kennit great renown. Surely, you must know that. Alternatively, he could have ransomed him back to your mother, beggaring the Vestrit family in the process of enriching his own coffers. He did neither of those things. Instead, he simply set that nasty, small-hearted man aside, in a place where he cannot hurt you or others."

She drew a breath, then seemed out of words. Wintrow felt overwhelmed by what she had said. He had not known Kennit dreamed such dreams. Her reasoning seemed valid, but her defense of the pirate still stung him. "That is why he is a pirate, I suppose. To do good?"

The ship was insulted. "I do not pretend he is selfless. Nor that his methods are above reproach. Yes, he savors power and longs for more of it. When he gains it, he does good with it. He frees slaves. Would you prefer he stood and spouted platitudes about the brotherhood of man? What is all your longing to return to your monastery, but a desire to retreat from what is wrong in the world?"

Wintrow gaped in wordless astonishment. A moment later, she bravely confessed, "He has asked me to pirate with him. Did you know that?"

Wintrow tried to remain calm. "No. But I expected it." Bitterness broke through in his voice.

"Well? What would be so wrong with it?" she demanded defensively. "You see the good he does. I know his ways are harsh. He has admitted that to me himself. He has asked me if I would be able to cope with what I must witness. I have told him honestly of that horrid night when the slaves rose. Do you know what he said?"

"No. What did he say?" Wintrow struggled to master his emotions. She was so gullible, so naïve. Didn't she see how the pirate was playing her?

"That it was like cutting off his leg. He had suffered a long misery, thinking it might get better if he did nothing. You made him see he had to endure a far greater pain before his anguish could be over. He believed in you, and you were right. He asked me to recall all I had shared of the slaves' torment, and then to consider that in other ships, that torment continued. It is not piracy, but surgery he performs."

Wintrow's lips had been folded tightly. Now he opened them to say, "So Kennit plans to only attack slaver ships after this?"

"And those who profit from slavery. We cannot seize every slaveship between Jamaillia and Chalced. However, if Kennit's just wrath is felt by all who traffic with slavery, and not just those who run slaveships, soon all will be forced to think about what they do. Those merchants who are honest and good will turn against the slavers when they see what they have brought down on them."

"You don't think the Satrap will renew his patrols of this area? His patrol ships will hunt down and destroy the pirate colonies in an effort to be rid of Kennit."

"Perhaps he will try but I do not believe he will succeed. Kennit champions a holy cause, Wintrow. You of all people should see that. We cannot be turned aside by the prospect of pain or risk. If we do not persevere in this endeavor, who will?"

"Then you have told him you will pirate for him?" Wintrow was incredulous.

"Not yet," Vivacia replied calmly. "But tomorrow I intend to."

ALTHEA'S TRADER ROBE SMELLED OF CAMPHOR AND CEDAR. HER MOTHER had stored it to keep the moths from the wool. Althea shared the moth's opinions of the smells. The cedar would have been tolerable, in a milder dose. The camphor made her feel giddy. She had been surprised to find the robe still fit her. It had been several years since she had worn it.

She crossed the room and sat down in front of her glass. A feminine young woman looked back at her. Sometimes her days as ship's boy aboard the *Reaper* seemed like a dream. Since she had returned home, she had put on weight. Grag had expressed his approval of how her figure had rounded out. As she brushed out her glossy black hair and then pinned it up sedately, she had to admit she was not displeased with the change. The plainly cut Trader's robe was not especially flattering to her. Just as well, she told herself as she turned slowly before the glass. She did not want to be seen as an ornamental female tonight, but as a sober and industrious Trader's daughter. She wanted her words to be taken seriously. Nonetheless, she paused to add a bit of scent to her throat, and a touch of color to her lips. Garnet earrings, a recent gift from Grag, swung from her ears. They went well with the magenta robe.

It had been a busy day. She had gone personally to petition the Bingtown Council. They had said only that they would consider it. They did not have to hear her. Keffria was the Trader of the family, not Althea, and she had stiffly told her sister that she, too, would speak tonight if the opportunity presented itself. Althea had composed a note to let Grag know of the taking of the *Vivacia*, and sent Rache off to deliver it. After that, she had gone herself to Davad Restart's, both to give Davad the news about the piracy and to ask the Trader if he would give them a ride to the Council. Davad had been properly horrified, but also reluctant to believe anything "that Trell rascal" said. He assured her that if the story proved true, he would stand by them in their trouble. Althea noticed that that offer had not extended to his wallet. She knew Davad better than to expect financial assistance from him. His affection and his money were kept well separated. Then she had returned home, helped Rache bake the week's bread, staked the beans in the kitchen garden and tied up the plants, and thinned the green fruit on the plum and apple trees. It had taken a good scrubbing to make herself presentable again.

Yet, all her frantic activity had not been enough to keep Brashen Trell from intruding on her thoughts. Hadn't her life been complicated enough without him coming back to Bingtown? Not that he had anything to do with her life, really. Right now, every moment of her time should have been occupied with thoughts of Vivacia or the Traders' Council meeting. Or Grag. Instead, Brashen stood there, at the edge of every thought, opening a whole realm of other possibilities. To contemplate any of them made her uneasy. She pushed him away, but images of him kept returning: Brashen sitting at the kitchen table, drinking coffee and nodding to her mother's words; Brashen's head bent over little Selden as he lifted the boy to carry him off to bed; Brashen standing, legs braced as if on a deck, staring out the window of her father's study into the night. Or, she reminded herself tartly, Brashen, repeatedly feeling in the corner of his jacket pocket for the cindin that undoubtedly was there. The man was the victim of his own bad decisions. Let him go.

Althea hurried out to the entry. She didn't want to be late for the meeting tonight. There were too many portentous things on the agenda. To her surprise, Malta was already waiting there. She ran a critical eye over her niece, but found nothing to correct. She had expected Malta to overindulge in paint, scent and jewelry, but she looked almost as sedate as Althea did. The flowers in her hair were her only ornamentation. Yet even simply attired in her Trader robe, the young girl was breathtaking. Althea looked at her and could not fault the young men who admired her. She was growing up. Over the past day and a half, she had shown far more maturity than Althea had thought she possessed. It was a shame that it had taken a family crisis to bring it out in her. She tried to push her nervousness aside and reassure her niece.

"You look very nice, Malta."

"Thank you," the girl replied distractedly. She turned to Althea with a frown. "I wish we weren't riding to the meeting with Davad Restart. I don't think it looks good."

"I agree with you." Althea was surprised that Malta had even considered it. Althea herself was fond of Davad, as one is fond of an eccentric and occasionally boorish uncle. For that reason, she struggled to ignore the wrong-headedness of his current politics. She agreed with her mother. Davad Restart had been a friend of the family too long to let a political disagreement come between them. Althea just hoped her association with him would not weaken her presentation to the Council. She must seem whole-hearted and righteous in her support of the Tenira family. It would be humiliating beyond repair if she was regarded as a silly woman who would take sides based on the opinion of the man closest to her. She wanted to be heard as Althea Vestrit, not as a girl infatuated with Grag Tenira.

"Does a carriage and a team truly cost that much? There is the whole summer season of balls, teas and parties ahead of us. We cannot always be depending on Davad. Think how that looks to the other Trader families," Malta went on plaintively.

Althea knit her brows. "There is the old carriage. If you are willing to help me, we could clean and oil it. It's very dusty, but sound. Then we could look into hiring a team and a driver." She crossed the room to peer out the window. Then she turned and grinned wickedly at Malta over her shoulder. "Or I could manage the reins myself. When I was your age, Hakes, our coachman, used to let me drive occasionally. Father didn't mind, but Mother never approved."

Her niece gave her a cool look. "That, I think, would be more humiliating than riding in Restart's rattletrap."

Althea shrugged and looked out the window again. Every time she thought she had established some sort of link with Malta, the girl would rebuff her.

Her mother and Keffria entered the room just as Davad's carriage pulled into the drive. "Let's not wait," Althea suggested, and opened the entry door before Davad could leave the carriage. "Once Davad is inside, he'll want wine and biscuits before we leave again. I really don't think we have time," she added at her sister's disapproving stare.

"I don't want to be late," her mother conceded. They all trooped out to the carriage. Before the surprised coachman was completely off the box, Althea had tugged the carriage door open. She shooed her relatives in ahead of her. Davad obediently squeezed over to make room. Althea sat down next to him. His musk-based perfume was nearly as dizzying as the camphor on her robes. Well, it would not be a long journey. Keffria, Mother and Malta settled facing them. Davad signaled the driver and the carriage jolted forward. The rhythmic squeaking of the carriage spoke of neglect, as did the grit in the seams of the upholstered seats. Althea frowned to herself but made no comment on it. Davad had never been adept at getting the best from his servants.

"Just look what I've brought for you," Davad announced. He produced a small beribboned box. Opening it himself, he presented them with an assortment of sticky jelly candies, the sort Althea had doted on when she was six. "I know they're your favorites," he confided to them as he helped himself to one and then passed the box around to the others. Althea gingerly took one of the sticky treats and popped it in her mouth. Keffria made brief eye contact with her sister as she was handed the box. The look they exchanged was one of fond tolerance for Davad. Keffria took a red one.

Davad himself beamed satisfaction at them. "Well! Don't you all look beautiful! I shall be the envy of every man at the Traders' meeting, arriving with a carriage full of such loveliness. I shall have to lay about me with a stick just to drive the young men back from the door!"

Althea and Keffria smiled dutifully to the extravagant compliment, as they had smiled to his compliments since they were children. Malta looked affronted, while Mother commented, "Davad, you are always full of such flattery. Do you think we believe you after all these years?" She frowned and added, "Althea, would you straighten Davad's scarf for him? The knot has worked around to under his ear."

Althea saw her mother's true concern. There was a blotch of gravy or some such predominantly displayed on the fine yellow silk. The scarf was not appropriate with his Trader robe, but she knew better than to try to persuade Davad to take it off. Instead she untied and re-knotted it for him in such a way that the stain scarcely showed.

"Thank you, my dear," he said fondly as he patted her hand gratefully. Althea smiled back and glanced at Malta to find her staring in distaste. She quirked one eyebrow at her young niece, asking her understanding. She could understand Malta's avid dislike of Davad. When Althea stopped and considered Davad's recent actions, she knew the same disgust. He had stooped to the low practices of the New Traders, and then surpassed them by aiding them against his own class. Ignoring the censure of the other Traders, he always spoke out for them at the Trader meetings now. He had acted as go-between for many of the more desperate Bingtown Trader families and the New Traders avid to buy their ancestral lands. Rumor said that he bargained keenly to get the best terms, not for the Trader involved, but for the newcomers. It was hard for her to believe half of what she had heard gossiped about Davad. She was forced to accept that he not only used slaves on his property now, he trafficked in them. That was bad enough, but by far the worst rumor she had heard was that he was somehow involved in the efforts of New Traders to buy the *Paragon*.

Now she studied the avuncular man beside her and wondered. At what point would her loyalty be strained to breaking? Would they reach that point tonight?

To distract herself, she made conversation. "Well, Davad, you always know the most amusing gossip in Bingtown. What is the best tale you've heard today?" She expected nothing more than mildly scandalous. Davad was very strait-laced in his ways.

He smiled at her compliment and patted his stomach complacently. "The juiciest rumor I have heard today is not about Bingtown, my dear, although if it turns out to be true, it will definitely have a most profound effect upon all of us." He looked around at each of them, securing his audience. "This I have from a New Trader. One of his messenger birds brought it from Jamaillia City." He paused, tapping his forefinger against his smiling lips as if he considered the wisdom of sharing his news. He wanted to be coaxed.

Althea indulged him. "Do go on. We are always interested in the goings-on in Jamaillia."

"Well." He leaned back in the seat. "You all know, I am sure, of that unfortunate fuss last winter. The Khuprus family . . . indulge me, Malta, I know their boy is enamored of you, but this is politics I'm talking, not romance. . . . The Khuprus family came to Bingtown on behalf of the Rain Wild Traders, to stir up trouble between us and the Satrap. I tried to talk sense to them, but you recall what a mob scene that meeting was, Ronica. Well. Anyway. The result was that a delegation of Bingtown Traders set off for Jamaillia City, with our original charter, with the intent of demanding the Satrap live up to the ancient document. How could they believe such antiquated agreements could be forced to apply to our modern age? Nevertheless, off they went. And they were received courteously, and told firmly that the Satrap would consider their position. And we heard no more." He glanced about to see if they were paying attention. It was all old news, but Althea listened dutifully. Malta stared out the dusty window.

Davad leaned forward over his belly and lowered his voice, as if he feared the driver might be listening. "You have all heard the rumors that the Satrap promised to dispatch an envoy to Bingtown. We have all been expecting his arrival any day now. Well, the rumor I have heard is that there is no envoy. No! Instead, the Satrap himself, high-hearted adventurous young man that he is, has decided to come himself. It is said he will travel in disguise, with only a few choice Companions of his Heart, but well escorted by his Chalcedean honor guards. He hopes, it is said, to show Bingtown that he still considers our settlement to be as tightly tied to Jamaillia and the Satrapy as any of the cities in Jamaillia itself. When folk realize what he has endured to make this trip, and the concern he has that Bingtown remain loyal to him, well, I don't see how they can refuse to be more reasonable. How many years has it been since a reigning Satrap last visited Bingtown? Not in our lifetimes, eh, Ronica? Some of the New Trader families who have heard the rumor are already planning balls and parties such as Bingtown has never seen before. Oh, what a time to be a lovely and single young woman, eh, Malta? Don't be too hasty in accepting that Rain Wilder's suit, now. Perhaps, with my connections, I can arrange an invitation to a ball where you may catch the eye of the Satrap himself!"

His words produced the shock he'd been hoping for. Even Malta stared at him wide-eyed. "The Satrap? Here?" queried her mother in disbelief.

"He'd have to be out of his mind." Althea didn't realize she'd spoken the words aloud until Davad turned to stare at her. "I mean, such a long and hazardous journey to undertake so impulsively!"

"Even so, he is on his way. So flies the rumor bird. Now, not a word of this to anyone, you understand?" He did not truly expect that last warning to be heeded. He always appended it to every bit of gossip he shared.

Althea was still mulling over his tale when the driver pulled the horses in. The carriage came to a halt, and then gave a final bounce back. "Allow me," Davad said, and leaned over Althea to reach the door handle. As the driver tugged from the outside, Davad put his wide shoulder against the inside of the door and shoved. The door flew open and Althea caught at the portly man's robe to keep him from spilling out. The driver reluctantly offered Davad his hand. The Trader exited the carriage, then proudly handed down each of the Vestrit women in turn.

Grag Tenira was loitering at the top of the steps outside the Traders' Concourse. He had girt his dark blue Trader robe up in the old seafarer style. It showed a substantial amount of well-muscled legs and sandaled feet. Somehow, he managed to look both the daring sailor and the serious Trader. He was, she admitted to herself, a very handsome man. His wandering eyes told her that he was watching for her arrival. She had sent him a message at dawn about the seizure of the *Vivacia*. His immediate reply had been as warm and supportive as she could wish. He would stand beside her, and even do his best to see that she received time to speak at this meeting. He had written that his family and Ophelia shared her concern for Vivacia.

She smiled as she caught his eye, and he gave her a white-toothed grin in response. His smile froze when he glimpsed her escort. Althea quietly excused herself and hastened up the Concourse steps to meet Grag. He bowed formally over her extended hand. As he straightened, he murmured, "I should have thought to send a carriage for you. Next time, I shall."

"Oh, Grag. It's only Davad. He has been a family friend for a long time. He would be very hurt if I refused to ride with him."

"With friends like that, it is no wonder that the Vestrit fortune is foundering," Grag observed tartly.

For an instant her heart turned to ice. How could he imply such a thing? But his next words reminded her of how grievous his own situation was, and her feelings towards him softened.

"Ophelia has been asking after you. She herself commanded wine boiled as an offering to Sa on Vivacia's behalf. She wanted you to know that." He paused, then smiled fondly. "She is completely bored with being tied up at the tariff dock. Now that the work on her hands is finished, she longs to sail again. Nevertheless, every time I promise her that we shall get back out to sea as soon as we can, she begs that I find a way for you to come along. I told her I could think of only one." He grinned engagingly at her.

"And that was?" Althea asked curiously. Did he mean to offer her employment on the *Ophelia?* Her heart quickened at the idea. She loved the matriarchal old ship.

He reddened and looked aside, but the smile still played about his mouth. "A hasty wedding and a bridal voyage. I suggested it in jest, of course. Such a scandal as that would raise! I expected Ophelia to scold me roundly. Instead, she thought it a wonderful idea." He gave her a sidelong glance. "Incidentally, so did my father. She brought it up to him, not I."

He paused and looked at her expectantly, as if he had asked her a question. But he had not, not directly. Even if she had been passionately in love with him, she could scarcely have accepted such an offer while her own family liveship was in danger. Didn't he realize that? She could not keep the confusion from her face. Her distress only deepened when she glimpsed Brashen Trell standing at the bottom of the steps to the Concourse. Their eyes met, and for an instant, she could not look away.

Grag interpreted her confusion as having a different source. "I don't truly expect you to consider it," he said hastily. He tried not to look hurt. "Not here, not now. We both have too many other concerns just now. Tonight may resolve some of them. I hope it does."

"As do I," she responded, but it was difficult to put much warmth into her voice. Too much was going on behind his shoulder. Brashen looked at her as if she had stabbed him to the heart. He had not changed his clothes since she had last seen him: the loose yellow shirt and dark trousers he wore made him look like a foreigner amongst all the robed Traders.

Grag followed her gaze. "What's he doing here?" he demanded, as if she would know. He took her arm as he spoke.

"He brought us word of the *Vivacia*." Althea looked up at Grag as she replied quietly. She didn't want Brashen to think they were staring at him and discussing him.

He met her eyes, his brow furrowed. "Did you ask him here, then?"

"No." She gave a small shake of her head. "I don't know why he's here."

"Is that Amber with him? Why is she here? Why are they together?"

Althea had to look. "I don't know," she murmured.

Amber was dressed in a simple gold-brown robe, almost the same shade as her many-plaited hair that hung over her shoulders. She had come from somewhere to stand close beside Brashen. She said something low to him. Her expression was not pleasant, but she wasn't looking at Brashen or Althea. She was glaring, her eyes yellow as a cat's, at Davad

Restart. Some vexatious fate had ordained that every facet of Althea's life would collide with every other tonight. Davad Restart had fixed his eyes on Grag Tenira. He was hastening toward them.

Davad was already huffing up the Concourse steps but her mother succeeded in reaching Althea first. Keffria and Malta were but a step behind her. Ronica and Grag greeted one another. Then her mother looked directly in Grag's eyes. "My daughter Althea may sit with you, Grag, if you wish. I know you have important matters to discuss."

Grag bowed formally. "Ronica Vestrit, you honor the Teniras with your trust. I vow we shall be worthy of it."

"I, too, thank you for allowing this," Althea replied formally to her mother. She had to admire the woman's foresight. Now she could take Grag's arm and steer him into the hall before Davad puffed up to them. At least *that* confrontation would be avoided. This Althea did, urging Grag along in a fashion just short of hasty. She tried not to wonder how her hurried departure would look to Brashen.

Inside the great hall, she followed Grag. She was aware of other people noting their passage. For her to be seated with his family during such a meeting was a public acknowledgment of serious courtship. For just an instant, she wanted to pull away from him and rejoin her family. But to leave him now would look as if they had had an abrupt disagreement. Instead she put a gracious smile on her face and allowed Grag to seat her between his mother and his sister. His mother was gray-haired and formidable in a solid Trader way. His younger sister gave Althea the grin of a fellow conspirator. They exchanged quiet greetings as the hall began to fill with people and conversation. Grag's mother and sister conversed softly, offering their condolences on the capture of the *Vivacia*, but Althea found herself unable to do more than nod to the conversation. A sudden nervousness gripped her. She prayed the Council would allow her to speak. Repeatedly, she rehearsed her thoughts. Somehow, she had to make the other Traders see that rescuing the *Vivacia* was a concern for all Bingtown, not just the Vestrit family.

The shuffling and hubbub that preceded the Traders' Meeting seemed to go on forever. Half a dozen people made a point of coming by the Tenira bench to exchange greetings. Althea set a smile to her face and held it there. They seemed to expect that she and Grag would be giddy over their courtship rather than concerned about the matters at hand. Her irritation receded when Grag's mother gave a wink. In a very low voice, she murmured, "It is good that you are here. They will take all of us more seriously if it is plain we stand together." His sister gave Althea's hand a brief squeeze. Althea felt warmed by their regard, but also a bit uneasy. She was not sure if she wished to be claimed this swiftly.

Conversation died as the Traders' Council members ascended the dais. They all wore the white robes that indicated they had surrendered their family alliances for now, to be loyal only to the greater good of Bingtown. Several black-robed order keepers took their places along the walls. Traders' Meetings sometimes became too lively. Their function was to keep the audience civil.

Althea scanned the members of the Council as they greeted one another and took their places at a long table on the dais. She felt suddenly shamed that she could put names to so few of them. Her father would have known which were his allies and which his opponents. She had no such expertise. The chimes that indicated the beginning of the meeting rang. Voices quieted. Althea breathed a brief prayer to Sa to guide her words.

She could have made it a much longer prayer. In a wordy opening speech, the Council head declared that there were several topics to cover, so he thought it best to dispense with the simpler disputes first. Althea lifted a querying eyebrow at Grag; she thought this meeting had been specially requested to hear the Tenira family concerns. He knit his brows and gave a small shrug.

They were subjected to a heated discourse between two Trader families over water rights to a creek that bounded their properties. One man had cattle to water; the other Trader wished to divert water to his fields. It was a lengthy argument settled by the Council's obvious decision that they must share the water. An arbitrator group of three was appointed to aid them in deciding how. As soon as the argumentative pair had bowed to one another and resumed their seats, Althea sat up expectantly.

She was doomed to disappointment. The next dispute was not so easily settled. One Trader's prize bull had impregnated the herd of a neighboring Trader. Both claimed to be the injured party. One wanted substantial stud fees; the other countered that he had wished to use a different bull, hence this year's crop of calves was not what he had desired. One claimed the other's servant had sabotaged his fence; the second claimed the bull's owner had been negligent in confining his animal. The Council had great difficulty with this one. They retired to a back room where they could debate more freely. During this recess, the audience shifted restlessly or chatted with neighbors. When the Council returned, they announced that the calves should be sold as soon as they were weaned, and the profits divided between the two Traders. The bull's owner would be responsible for fortifying the fence. This did not suit either Trader, but the Council's decision was binding. Both Trader families rose and stalked out angrily. To Althea's dismay, several other families also rose and followed them. She had hoped they would be able to address the Traders themselves as well as the Council.

The head of the Bingtown Traders' Council consulted a tablet before him. "The Tenira family has requested time to address the Council for the purpose of disputing the Satrap's tariffs levied against the liveship *Ophelia* and her detention at the tariff docks due to their failure to pay."

No sooner had the head of the Council announced this than a Trader stood to address the Council. They recognized Trader Daw, who spoke his obviously rehearsed words quickly. "This is not a proper matter for the Traders' Council. Trader Tenira's grievance is with the Satrap's tariff office, not with another Trader. He should take it up with them, and let the Council devote its precious time to matters that concern us all."

With a sinking heart, Althea noted that Davad Restart was seated right next to Daw, nodding soberly to his words.

Tomie Tenira stood. The old sea-captain's taut shoulders strained the sleeves of his Trader's robe. His fists were knotted at his sides. He strove to keep the anger from his voice. "When was the Traders' Council reduced to a nanny quelling squabbles between siblings? What is the Traders' Council, if not Bingtown's voice? The grievance I present is not between the tariff officer and me. It is about an unjust tax levied against all ship owners. Our original charter called for fifty percent of our profits to go to the Satrap's coffers. Outrageous as that is, our forebears agreed to it, and I willingly abide by it. However, nowhere in that charter are these tariffs mentioned. Moreover, no document anywhere says that we must tolerate murdering, thieving Chalcedean mercenaries in our harbors." Tomie Tenira's voice had begun to shake with fury. He strangled into silence, trying to regain control of himself.

Davad Restart came to his feet. Althea felt ill.

"Council members, all Jamaillian merchants pay tariff to the Satrap. Why should we be any different? Is he not our good and just ruler? Do not we owe him support to maintain the reign that benefits all of us? These tariffs go to maintain the docks and facilities in Jamaillia City, as well as to pay for those who patrol the Inside Passage against piracy. The very qualities Trader Tenira disparages in the Chalcedeans are those that make them excellent defenders against piracy. If he does not care for their services, then perhaps he should . . ."

"The Chalcedean 'patrol ships' are no more than pirates themselves! They stop legitimate ships, with no other intent than extortion. All here know how my liveship *Ophelia* was injured defending herself from such an unwarranted intrusion. Bingtown ships have never willingly submitted to being boarded by foreigners. Are you suggesting we accept it now? The tariffs began simply, as reasonable fees. Now they are so complicated to figure that we must accept the word of a hired scribe as to what we owe. The tariffs have one purpose only: to make it unprofitable for us to trade anywhere except Jamaillia City. They steal our profits to bind us more tightly to their purse strings. Anyone who has tied up in Jamaillia recently can testify that the charges we are paying are not going for dock maintenance there. I doubt if anything has been spent on those docks in the last three years."

A general rumble of agreement, with some laughter, followed his last statement. "My ship's boy damn near fell through the last one we tied up to," someone in the back called out.

Daw stood again quickly, inserting his words into the pause. "Council members, I suggest you adjourn to see if you should even be hearing this matter before you accept any more testimony about it." He glanced about. "Evening draws close to night. Perhaps we should save this matter for a later meeting."

"We are well within our purpose in hearing this, I believe," the head of the Council replied, only to have two lesser members immediately shake their heads in denial. This necessitated another withdrawal to the private room.

This time the room was less patient and social while they were gone. Folk got up and milled about. Trader Larfa of the liveship *Winsome* came to stand before Tomie Tenira. He did not lower his voice as he announced, "Count on me, Tomie. No matter how it goes here. If you want, give the word now. Me and my sons will be with you, and we'll go right now and untie your ship from that damned tariff dock." Two tall young men behind him nodded soberly to their father's offer.

"You wouldn't be alone," offered another man, one Althea didn't recognize. Like Trader Larfa, he was flanked by his sons.

"Let us hope it doesn't come to that," Tomie said quietly. "I would like this to be something Bingtown acts on, not the Tenira family alone."

At that moment, a shouting match broke out elsewhere in the room. Althea half stood and craned her neck. She could see little, due to others standing up between her and the dispute, but it seemed to center where Traders Daw and Restart had been seated. "You liar!" someone accused. "You did and you know you did. Without you, the damn New Traders would never have become so deeply entrenched here." Another voice muttered a bland denial. The Council's order keepers were already moving to quell the disturbance. Althea felt her nails bite into her palms. The room was on the edge of breaking into violence, Trader against Trader.

"This serves no one!" she heard herself announce bitterly. By chance, her voice had sounded in a lull in the noise. Heads turned toward her. Even Grag and Tomie Tenira were looking at her in astonishment. She took a breath. If she waited, the Council might well adjourn for the night. Precious time would be lost. This might be her only chance to speak. "Look at us! We squabble like children, Trader against Trader. Ask yourself who wins that battle? We need to find agreement here. We need to speak of the larger matter that confronts us. What is Bingtown becoming? Are we going to bow our heads to the Satrap's rules, accept his tariffs and restrictions, no matter how heavy they become? Will we tolerate his hirelings tying up in our harbor? Will we pay to feed and outfit them, so they can stop our ships and fleece them before they reach port? Why?"

Every eye in the room had turned to her. Some people were resuming their seats, willing to hear what she had to say. She glanced down at a seated Grag. He gave her a nod of encouragement. She felt his mother reach up and take her hand. She gave it a squeeze before releasing it. Althea felt heady with power. "My father told me, two years ago, that it would come to this. I am not the Trader he was, but I do not hesitate to repeat his wisdom. A time will come when Bingtown must stand on its own, and determine its own future. That is what he told me. I think that time is now."

She looked around the room. Keffria, hand over her mouth, stared at her in horror. Davad's face was as red as a turkey's wattle. Some women looked scandalized that one of their sex should speak out so in public. But other Traders nodded, or looked seized by her words. She drew another shuddering breath. "There is too much we can no longer tolerate. These so-called New Traders usurp our lands. They know nothing of our ancient sacrifices, nothing of our blood bonds with the Rain Wild Traders. They mock our laws with their tattooed slaves. The Satrap is no longer content with half our profits. He will take all we have bought with blood and sell it for coin to his new friends, be they New Traders or Chalcedean privateers!"

"You're talking rebellion!" someone in the back of the room accused.

Something inside her turned over. Step forward and admit it, she counseled herself. "Yes. I am," she said calmly.

She was unprepared for the hubbub that broke out at her words. From the corner of her eye, she became aware of the order keepers closing in on her. She also became aware that they were having a difficult time reaching her through the assembly. Folk were not stepping aside. Legs were thrust out, or benches shoved in their paths. Nevertheless, the order keepers would reach her soon and eject her. She had but a few more moments.

"My father's ship!" Her voice rang out over the noise. The room quieted somewhat. "The *Vivacia*, a liveship of Rain Wild make, has been taken by pirates. I know that some of you have heard the rumors. I stand to tell you it is the truth. The unthinkable has happened. Pirates have taken a Bingtown liveship. Do you think the Satrap's Chalcedean mercenaries will help me recover her? If by chance she does fall into their hands, do you think they will respect a Bingtown claim to her? She will be taken to Jamaillia City, as if she were plunder, and kept there. Think but a moment of the Rain Wild River, and you know what that would mean! I need your help. Bingtown, please, I beg you, stand firm with me. I need money and a ship to go after my birthright."

She had not meant to say those words. Her mother gave her a

stricken glance of disbelief. Her thought was plain. Althea was making a public claim on the ship as her own. She had meant to speak for her family, but her heart had chosen the words.

"The Vestrit family brought that on themselves!" someone shouted. "They let their family ship sail with a foreigner as captain. Shame on them! She talks a good wind, she does, but whom did she ride in with? Davad Restart and, gentlemen, we all know where he stands. Her wild talk is a New Trader trap. If we rise in defiance of the Satrap, we cannot expect him to be fair with us. We need to reason with the Satrap, not set ourselves up against him." Some were nodding and muttering agreement.

"Why don't the damn Chalcedean patrol boats go out to rescue the *Vivacia?* Isn't that what all the new tariffs are about, paying them to run off the pirates? Why don't they get out there and show us what our money bought?"

"She talks against Chalcedeans, but her own sister married one!" someone else sneered.

"Kyle Haven can't help his blood. He's a good captain!" someone defended him.

"Ephron Vestrit left his ship in that foreigner's hands," another added. "He lost it. That's a Vestrit problem, not a Bingtown crisis. If they want the ship back, let them pay ransom on it."

Althea stood on tiptoe, craning to identify the speaker. "Trader Froe," Grag told her in a low hiss. "Never stood up for anything in his life. Pinches his coins so tight, they come away with his fingerprints on them."

As if he had heard the words, Froe asserted, "I'm not giving her one copper shard of mine. They shamed their ship, and Sa took it from them. I heard she was being used as a slaver . . . any liveship worth her salt would rather turn pirate than that!"

"You can't mean that!" Althea was outraged. "You can't dismiss her like that. There is a boy on that ship, my nephew. However you regard his father, you cannot deny he is Trader stock. The ship herself is Bingtown—"

Beside her, Grag stepped to block one order keeper, but another stepped past him to seize Althea's arm. "Out!" he told her firmly. "The Council is recessed. No one is to speak right now. You do not even have the Council's permission to speak. She is not the Trader for the Vestrit family!" he added more loudly as others raised their voices in protest of Althea's treatment. "In the interest of order, she must go!"

It was the spark in the kindling. A bench overturned with a crash. "No!" Althea cried out in horror, and for a wonder, they heeded her. "No," she said more softly. She put a light hand on Grag's arm. He slackened his grip on the order keeper he had been restraining. "I didn't come here to cause trouble. I came here to ask for help. I've asked. I also came to stand up in favor of the Tenira family. It is wrong for Ophelia to be detained at the tariff dock. They have no legal claim on any of her cargo." In a lower voice she added, "If any of you want to help the Vestrit Traders, you know where our home is. You will be welcomed and you will hear our full tale. But I won't be named as the one at fault for a riot in the Traders' Concourse. I'm leaving now. Peacefully." To Grag, she murmured, "Don't follow me. Stay here, in case the Council reconvenes. I'll wait outside."

Head up and unescorted, she moved through the crowd. She knew she could do no more good here tonight. Others seemed to share her opinion. Those Trader families who had brought small children with them were herding them out, apparently for their safety. All over the room, the order had broken down. Traders stood in small knots, some talking quietly, others arguing with wild hand gestures and raised voices. Althea picked her way past all of them. A glance showed her that her own family had remained. Good. Perhaps they might yet have a chance to speak out officially for rescuing Vivacia.

Outside it was a deceptively peaceful summer night. Crickets were chirping. The brightest stars were pricking their way into the twilight sky. Behind her, the Traders' Concourse hummed like a hive of disturbed bees. Some families were departing on foot, others entering carriages. Despite herself, she glanced about for Brashen, but saw no sign of him or Amber. Reluctantly, Althea turned her steps toward Davad's carriage. She would sit there and wait for the general adjournment of the meeting.

It was nearly at the end of the long line of carriages. She reached it, then halted in horror. The driver had vanished. The team, old and placid as they were, snorted restively and pawed. Blood ran down the door of the carriage, thick and black in the twilight. A slaughtered pig, its throat cut wide, lolled halfway out the carriage window. "SPY" was written in blood over the Restart coat of arms. Althea felt dizzy with disgust.

Behind her, the meeting seemed to have come to a close. Traders were streaming from the Concourse. Some conversed in loud, angry voices. Others hissed in whispers, glancing about suspiciously for eavesdroppers. Her mother was the first to reach her side. "The Council adjourned. They'll have a private meeting to see if they can hear—" Her words halted as she saw the pig. "Sa's breath," she gasped. "Poor Davad. How could anyone do this to him?" She glanced about as if the culprits might still be lurking.

From somewhere, Grag appeared. After one horrified look, he took Althea's arm. "Come away," he said quietly. "I'll see that you and your family get safely home. You don't want to be involved in this."

"No," she agreed grimly. "I don't. Neither does Trader Restart, I'll wager. I won't abandon him here, Grag. I can't."

"Althea, think! This isn't someone's impulsive nastiness. Someone planned this. This pig was brought here, for this purpose, before anyone spoke to the Council. It's a serious threat." He tugged at her arm.

She spun to confront him. "That's why I can't let Davad face it alone. Grag, he is an old man, with no real family left. If his friends abandon him, he's alone."

"Maybe he deserves to be alone!" Grag kept his voice low. He kept glancing at the knot of gawkers forming around the carriage. He obviously wanted to get away from it. "How can you accept how he thinks, Althea? How can you let him drag your family into this?"

"I don't accept how he thinks. I accept who he is. He is a wrong-headed old fool, but he has been like an uncle to me for as long as I can remember. Whatever he has done, he doesn't deserve this."

She looked past Grag to see Davad approaching the carriage. Trader Daw was at his side, their arms linked. They seemed to be congratulating themselves. Daw saw the pig first. His jaw dropped. An instant later, he unhooked his arm from Davad's and scuttled off without a word. Privately Althea hoped a slaughtered pig waited in his carriage as well.

"What's this? I don't understand this. Why? Who has done this? Where is my driver? Did the coward run off, then? Look at the leather, it's ruined, it's completely ruined." Davad flapped his arms about like a flustered chicken. He stepped close to his carriage, peered at the pig, then stepped back. He sent a bewildered look round at the crowd that had gathered. In the back, someone guffawed loudly. Others simply stared. No one expressed horror or disgust. They were watching him, to see what he would do.

Althea's eyes traveled from face to face. They seemed strangers to her, more foreign than Jamaillian New Traders. She did not know Bingtown anymore.

"Please, Grag," Althea whispered. "I'll stay with him and get him home. Would you take my mother, sister and niece? I don't think Malta should have to deal with this."

"I don't think any of you should have to deal with this," Grag said acidly, but he was too well-bred to refuse. Althea had no idea what he said to her mother and Keffria that made them leave so quietly. Young Malta merely looked elated at the prospect of leaving in a finer carriage than the one she had arrived in.

As they walked away, Althea took Davad's arm. "Calm down," she told him quietly. "Don't let them see you are rattled." Heedless of the blood, she jerked the door of the carriage open. The stubborn carcass rode in the window still. It was a runty pig; no one had sacrificed good stock to do this. In death, its bowels had relaxed. The stench of pig manure spilled out with it. Althea reminded herself that blood was no stranger to her. She'd seen far too much slaughter in the Barrens to be put off by a bit of pig blood now. Boldly she seized the dead animal's hind legs. A sharp tug freed it from the window. She let it drop to the street. She glanced at Davad, who stared at her wide-eyed. Blood and offal had soiled the front of her robe. She ignored it.

"Can you climb up onto the box?" she asked him.

He shook his head dumbly.

"Then you'll have to ride inside. The other seat is almost clean. Take my handkerchief. The scent on it will help."

Davad said not a word. He took the kerchief, and climbed ponderously into the carriage, making small distressed sounds the whole time. He was scarcely inside before Althea slammed the door behind him. She did not look about at the gawkers. Instead she walked around the team, had a quiet word with the horses, and then clambered up on the box. She took up the reins. She had not done this in years, and never with a team she didn't know. She kicked off the brake and shook the reins hopefully. The horses started forward at an uncertain walk.

"From sailor to driver. That's the girl for Grag! Think of the money they'll save on hired help!" cried someone in the crowd. Someone else hooted loudly in appreciation. Althea kept her eyes forward and her chin up. She slapped the reins on the team, and they lurched into a trot. She trusted they'd know the way home, even in the gathering dark.

She wasn't sure if she did, anymore.

CHAPTER NINETEEN

Aftermath

"YOU'RE HOME, DAVAD. COME OUT."

The door was stuck, and Davad wasn't trying to open it. In the gloom, Althea could just see the pale shape of his face. He huddled in a corner of the seat, his eyes tightly shut. She braced a foot against the carriage and jerked on the door again. It popped open and she nearly fell backwards. It wouldn't have hurt her robe. It stank of pig blood, dung and her own sweat. The drive home had been nerve-wracking. All the way home, she had expected to either run the carriage off the side of the road or be accosted by Davad's enemies. Now they had reached his own front door, but no steward or stable boy came to greet them. Random lights shone in the windows of his house, but for all the greeting the master received, it might as well have been abandoned. A single lantern burned feebly by the doorpost.

"What's your stable boy's name?" Althea demanded in irritation.

Davad gawked at her. "I . . . I don't know. I don't talk to him."

"Fine." She threw back her head and bellowed in her best first mate's style. "Boy! Get out here and tend to these horses. House steward! Your master is home!"

Someone lifted a corner of a curtain and peered out at them. She heard footsteps inside the house, and then caught a glimpse of movement in the shadowy courtyard. She turned toward it. "Get out here and take these horses."

The slender figure hesitated. "Now!" she barked at him.

The boy that emerged from the shadows was no more than eleven years old. He came as far as the horses' heads, then halted uncertainly.

Althea snorted in exasperation. "Oh, Davad, if you can't learn to manage your servants, you should hire a house steward who can." Her tact was all worn away.

"I suppose you're right," Davad agreed humbly. He clambered down from the carriage. Althea stared at him. In the ride from the Concourse to his home, Davad had become an old man. His face sagged, bereft of the cockiness that had always characterized him. He had not been able to avoid the manure and blood. It smeared his clothes. He held his hands out from himself in distaste and distress. She looked up to meet his eyes. He looked apologetic and hurt. He shook his head slowly. "I don't understand it. Who would do something like this to me? Why?"

She was too tired to answer so large a question. "Go inside, Davad. Have a bath and go to bed. Morning is soon enough to think about all this." Absurdly, she suddenly felt he needed to be treated like a child. He seemed so vulnerable.

"Thank you," he said quietly. "There's a lot of your father in you, Althea. We didn't always agree, but I always admired him. He never wasted time in parceling out blame; like you, he simply stepped up to solve the problem." He paused. "I should have a man escort you home. I'll order up a horse and man for you." He did not sound certain he could do it.

A woman came to the door and opened it. A slice of light fell out. She peered out, but said nothing. Althea's temper snapped. "Send out a footman to help your master into the house. Have a hot bath drawn for him and lay out a clean robe. See that hot tea and a simple meal is prepared for him. Nothing spicy or greasy. Now."

The woman darted back into the house, leaving the door ajar. Althea heard her passing on the commands shrilly.

"And now you sound like your mother as well. You've done so much for me. Not just tonight, but for years, you and your family. How can I ever pay you back?"

It was the wrong moment to ask her such a question. The stable boy had come. The lamp revealed a spidery tattoo by the side of his nose. The ragged tunic he wore was scarcely longer than a shirt. He cowered from Althea's black-eyed stare.

"Tell him he's not a slave anymore." Her voice was flat.

"Tell . . . I beg your pardon?" Davad gave his head a small shake, as if he could not have heard her correctly.

Althea cleared her throat. It was suddenly difficult to have any sympathy for the little man. "Tell this boy he's not a slave anymore. Give him his freedom. That's how you could pay me back."

"But I . . . you can't be serious. Do you know how much a healthy boy like that is worth? Blue eyes and light hair are favored in Chalced for house servants. If I keep him a year and teach him some valet skills, do you know how much coin he'd be worth?"

She looked at him. "Far more than you paid for him, Davad. Far more than you could sell him for." Cruelly, she added, "How much was your son worth to you? I've heard he was fair-haired."

He blanched and stumbled backwards. He grasped at the carriage, then jerked his hand away from the blood-sticky door. "Why do you say such a thing to me?" he wailed suddenly. "Why is everyone turning against me?"

"Davad . . ." She shook her head slowly. "You have turned against us, Davad Restart. Open your eyes. Think what you are doing. Right and wrong is not profit and loss. Some things are too evil to make money from them. Right now, you may be gaining handsomely from the conflict between the Old and New Traders. But this conflict will not go on forever, and when it does end, there you will be. One side will see you as a runagate, the other as a traitor. Who will be your friends then?"

Davad was frozen, staring at her. She wondered why she had wasted her words. He would not heed her. He was an old man, set in his ways.

A footman came out of the door. He was chewing something and his chin shone with grease. He came to take his master's arm, then cringed away with a gasp. "You're filthy!" he exclaimed in disgust.

"*You* are lazy!" Althea retorted. "Help your master in and see to his needs, instead of stuffing your belly in his absence. Promptly, now."

The footman reacted to her tone of command. Gingerly, he extended his arm to his master. Slowly Davad took it. He took a few steps, then halted. Without turning, Davad spoke. "Take a horse from my stable to get home. Shall I send a man with you?"

"No. Thank you. I don't need one." She wanted nothing from him anymore.

He nodded to himself. He added something quietly.

"I beg your pardon?"

He cleared his throat. "Take the boy, then. Stable boy. Go with the lady." He took a breath and spoke heavily. "You are free." Davad walked into the house without a backward glance.

SHE HAD A MINIATURE OF HIM. SHE HAD BEGGED HIM TO SIT FOR IT, shortly after they were married. He had told her it was a foolish notion, but she was his bride, and so he gave in. He had not been gracious about sitting for it. Pappas was too honest an artist to paint Kyle Haven with patient eyes, or to leave out the small fold of annoyance between his brows. So now as Keffria looked at Kyle's portrait, he regarded her as it seemed he always had, with annoyance and impatience.

She tried to cut past the layers of hurt in her heart to discover a core of love for him. He was her husband, the father of her children. He was the only man she had ever known. Yet, she could not honestly say that she loved him. Odd. She missed him and longed for him to return. It was not just that his return would mean the return of the family's ship and her son. She wanted Kyle himself. Sometimes, she thought, having someone stronger to depend on was more important than having someone you loved. At the same time, she needed to settle things with him. Over the months that he had been gone on this trip, she had discovered there were words she had to say to him. She had decided she would force him to respect her, even as she had learned to demand respect from her mother and sister. She did not want him to vanish from her life before she had wrung that respect from him. If she did not gain it, she would always wonder if she had ever been truly worthy of it.

She closed the miniature's case and set it back on the shelf. She badly wanted to go to sleep, but wouldn't until Althea was safely home. She found her feelings for her sister closely mimed those she had for her husband. Every time she felt that she and Althea had regained some remnant of sisterly closeness, Althea would reveal that she still played only for herself. Tonight, at the meeting, she had made it clear that the ship was what she cared about, not Kyle nor Wintrow. She wanted the ship back in Bingtown so she could challenge Keffria for ownership of it. That was all.

She left her bedroom and drifted through the house like a wraith. She peeked in on Selden. He was deeply asleep, careless of all the problems that beset his family. When she came to Malta's closed door, she tapped on it lightly. There was no reply. Malta, too, slept with the deep ease that children had for rest. She had behaved so well at the meeting. On the ride home, she had made no mention of the near riot, but had put Grag Tenira at ease with her casual conversation. The girl was growing up.

Keffria went down the stairs. She knew she would find her mother in her father's study. Ronica Vestrit, too, would not sleep until Althea returned. If they were going to stay up, they might as well do it together. As she passed through the hall, she heard a light footfall on the front porch. That would be Althea. Keffria frowned in annoyance when she knocked at the door. Why couldn't she go around to the unlocked kitchen door? "I'll get it," she called to her mother and went to unlatch the big front door.

Brashen Trell and that bead merchant stood on the porch. He was wearing the same clothes as when she had last seen him. His eyes were bloodshot. The bead merchant looked composed. Her expression was friendly but offered no apology for the late hour. Keffria stared at them both. This went beyond the boundaries of all courtesy. It was rude enough of Brashen to come calling so late, unannounced, but he had also brought an outsider with him. "Yes?" she asked uncomfortably.

Her restraint didn't seem to bother him. "I need to talk to all of you," he announced without preamble.

"About what?"

He spoke quickly. "About getting your ship and your husband back. Amber and I think we've come up with a plan." As he nodded toward his companion, Keffria noted a sheen of sweat on his face. The night was mild and pleasant. The feverishness of his face and manner was alarming.

"Keffria? Did Althea come in?" her mother called from down the hall.

"No, Mother. It's Brashen Trell and ah, Amber, the bead-maker."

This brought her mother swiftly to the door of the study. Like Keffria, she was in her night-robe and wrapper. She had taken her hair down. With the long graying strands of it around her face, she looked haggard and old. Even Brashen had the good grace to look a bit embarrassed. "I know it is late," he apologized hastily. "But . . . Amber and I have conceived of a plan that might benefit all of us. Greatly." His dark eyes met Keffria's squarely. It seemed to take an effort on his part. "I believe it might offer us our only chance of bringing your husband, son and ship safely home."

"I do not recall that you ever had any great warmth or respect for my husband," Keffria said stiffly. If Brashen Trell had been alone, she might have felt more kindly toward him, but his strange companion put Keffria's hackles up. She had heard too many peculiar things about her. She did not know what these two were after, but she doubted it would be to anyone's benefit but their own.

"Warmth, no. Respect, yes. In his own way, Kyle Haven was a competent captain. He just wasn't Ephron Vestrit." He considered her stiff stance and cold eyes. "Tonight, at the meeting, Althea asked for help. That's what I've come to offer her. Is she home?" His bluntness was appalling. "Perhaps at a more suitable time . . ." Keffria began, but her mother cut her off.

"Let them in. Bring them to the study. Keffria, we don't have the luxury of being picky about our allies. Tonight, I am willing to listen to anybody's plan to make our family whole again. No matter how late they come calling."

"As you will, Mother," Keffria said stiffly. She moved aside and let them enter. The foreign woman dared to give her a sympathetic glance. The woman even smelled odd as she passed Keffria, to say nothing of her strange coloring. Keffria had no quarrel with most foreigners. Many of them were both charming and fascinating. But this bead-maker made her uneasy. Perhaps it was the way the woman assumed equality, no matter what company she was in. As Keffria followed them reluctantly down the hall to the study, she tried not to think of the nasty rumor about this woman and Althea.

Her mother did not seem to share her misgivings. Despite the fact that she and Keffria were both in their house-robes, she welcomed them in. She even rang Rache to ask her to bring in some tea for their visitors. "Althea has not returned home yet," Ronica told them before Brashen could ask. "I'm waiting up for her."

He looked concerned. "That was a harsh prank played upon Trader Restart. I wondered at the time if worse awaited him at home." He stood abruptly. "You probably have not heard. Bingtown has been very dis-

turbed tonight. I think I had best go seek for Althea. Have you a horse I
might borrow?"

"Just my old—" Ronica began, but at that moment, there was a noise
at the door. Brashen stepped into the hall to view the entry with an
alacrity that betrayed his concern.

"It's Althea, and a boy," he declared, and strode off to meet her as if
this were his home and she the guest. Keffria exchanged a look with her
mother. Although Ronica looked only puzzled, Keffria was feeling increasingly affronted by his odd behavior. Something was not right about that
man.

SHE TRIED TO TAKE THE BOY'S HAND TO LEAD HIM TO THE DOOR, BUT HE
drew back from her touch. Poor lad. How badly had he been treated, to
fear the simple touch of a hand? She opened the door and gestured him
inside. "It's all right. No one's going to hurt you. Come inside." She spoke
slowly and reassuringly. She wasn't sure he even understood her. He
hadn't spoken a word since they'd left Davad's house. It had been a long
weary walk in the dark, with only dark thoughts to occupy her. She'd
failed badly tonight. She'd talked out of turn at the Council's meeting,
and possibly hastened its early adjournment. The Council hadn't even
formally agreed to hear their concerns. She'd been forced to face what
Davad Restart had become; she feared there were many other Traders who
had slid down just as far. And her quick tongue had burdened her with a
boy she had no means to care for. She'd brought that down on herself.
She wanted nothing so much as a bath and her bed, but she supposed
she'd have to see to the boy's needs first. At least, little else could go
wrong tonight. Then she thought of facing Keffria and her mother after
all she'd said to the Council. Her mood plummeted.

The boy had come up the steps but made no move to go inside.
Althea opened the door wide, and stepped inside. "Come on in," she
coaxed.

"Thank Sa you're all right!"

She jumped and spun about at the deep masculine voice behind her.
Brashen was bearing down on her. Relief shone on his face, to be instantly replaced by a frown. A moment later he was chewing her out as if
she were an incompetent deckhand.

"You're damn lucky you weren't waylaid. When I heard you'd driven
Restart's carriage off, I couldn't believe it. Why would you throw in with
an ass like that, with feelings running so high against . . . oh. What *is*
that?" He halted a step away from her, his expression changing. He lifted
a hand to his nose.

"S'not me!" The boy beside her piped up indignantly. A Six Duchies'

twang twisted his tongue. "S'her. She's got shit aloover 'er." At Althea's
outraged glare, he shrugged apologetically. "Y'do. Y'need a bat' " he added
in a small voice.

It was the final blow. It was too much to endure. She transferred the
frown to Brashen. "Why are you here?" she asked. The words came out
more bluntly than she'd intended.

Brashen's eyes traveled up and down her filthy robe before coming
back to her face. "I was worried about you. As usual, you seemed to have
survived your impulses. But, set that aside, I have something very important to discuss with you. Regarding going after Vivacia. Amber and I
think we have a plan. You might think it's stupid, you probably won't like
it, but I think it will work." He spoke hastily, his words coming too fast as
if challenging her to disapprove. "If you'll only listen and think about it,
you'll come to find it's really the only way to save her." He met her eyes
again. "But that can wait. The boy is right. You should wash first. The
smell is pretty bad." A small smile came and went on his face.

It was too close an echo of his words when they'd parted in Candletown. Was he mocking her, to remind her of that, here and now? How
dare he speak so familiarly to her, inside her own home? She scowled at
him. He opened his mouth as if to speak, but the boy's voice cut him off.
"Nothen' stenks wors'n peg shet," the boy agreed cheerily. "Doon't let her
get et on'yer," he cautioned Brashen.

"Small chance of that," she told them both coldly. She met Brashen's
eyes. "You can let yourself out," she told him. As she stalked by him, he
gaped after her. The boy she could forgive; he was only a lad, in a foreign
place and a strange situation. Trell had no such excuse for his manners.
She'd had too long a day to listen to anything from him. She was exhausted, filthy and, Sa help her, hungry. Light and voices came from her
father's study. She'd have to face her mother and Keffria as well.

By the time she reached the door of her father's study, she had put a
façade of calmness on her face. She stepped into the pleasant room, well
aware that the smell of pig offal preceded her. She'd get it over quickly.
"I'm home, I'm safe. I brought a little boy with me. Davad was using him
as a stable boy. . . . Mother, I know we cannot take on any more burdens
just now, but he was tattooed as a slave and I simply couldn't leave him
there." The look on Keffria's face was one of social horror. Althea's explanation halted as she met Amber's eyes. She was here, too?

The slave-boy stood in the doorway, pale eyes wide. His gaze darted
from person to person. He did not speak. When Althea attempted to take
his arm to pull him into the room, he snatched his hand away from her.
She gave a false laugh. "I think it's the blood and dung. He didn't want to
ride with me on the horse; that's what kept me so long. When I couldn't
get him to mount with me, we left the horse and came home on foot."

Althea glanced about for rescue. Keffria was staring past her. Althea glanced over her shoulder. Brashen Trell stood slightly behind her, arms crossed, looking very stubborn. He met her gaze steadily. His expression didn't change.

"Come in, boy. No one will hurt you. What's your name?" Ronica sounded weary but kind. The lad stayed where he was.

Althea abruptly decided to escape, at least for now. "I'm going up to bathe and change. I won't be long."

"It won't take long for me to tell you our idea," Brashen countered pushily.

Their gazes locked. She refused to look aside from him. He himself smelled of smoke and cindin. Who did he think he was? She wasn't going to let him bully her here in her father's house. "I'm afraid I'm much too tired to listen to any more from you, Brashen Trell." Her voice walked a thin line between correct and cold as she added, "I believe it's far too late for conversation." The line of his mouth flattened. For a moment, he almost looked hurt at her rebuff.

Rache coming into the room interrupted their standoff. She carried a tray with a large pot of tea and cups on it. There was a small plate of spice cakes, just enough to be polite. The boy didn't move from where he stood, but he flared his nose and snuffed after them like a dog.

"Althea." Her mother's tone more reminded than rebuked. "I, at least, am interested in what Brashen has to propose. I think we need to consider every possible solution to our situation. If you are that tired, we will, of course, excuse you. But I'd rather that you returned." Her mother's gaze traveled to the serving woman. She smiled at her apologetically. "Rache, if you don't mind, I think we'll need more cups. And something more substantial than spice cakes for the boy, please." Ronica's voice was as measured and controlled as if this were an everyday occurrence.

Her mother's courtesy jabbed at Althea's conscience. This was still her father's house. She softened her tone. "If you wish, Mother. If you'll excuse me, I'll only be a few moments."

KEFFRIA POURED FOR THEIR ODD GUESTS. SHE TRIED TO MAKE POLITE CON-versation, but her mother stared at the cold grate while Brashen paced the room. Amber chose to sit cross-legged on the floor not far from where the boy hovered. She ignored Keffria's attempts at small talk. Instead, she lured the slave-boy with bits of cake, as if he were a shy puppy, until he finally snatched a whole cake from her hand. Amber did not seem to think her own behavior odd or outrageous at all. She smiled proudly when the boy stuffed the whole cake into his mouth. "You see," she said to him quietly. "Folk are kind here. You're safe now."

Althea was true to her word. Rache had scarcely come back with more tea, cups and a plate of warmed food for the boy before she returned. She must have washed with cold water to be so quick, Keffria thought to herself. She was attired in a simple house-robe. Her wet hair had been braided and pinned up severely. The cold water had rouged her cheeks. She somehow managed to look both tired and freshened. Without any apologies, she helped herself to tea and cakes. She glanced at Amber, then went to join her on the floor. The boy sat on the other side of her, completely engrossed in his food. She addressed her first words to Amber. "Brashen says you have a plan to save the *Vivacia*. He also told me I wouldn't like it, but that I'd come to see it was the only way. What is it?"

Amber gave Brashen a sidelong glance. "Thank you for preparing her so well," she said with dry sarcasm. She lifted her shoulders in a shrug followed by a sigh. "It is late. I think I should state it briefly, and then leave you all to think about it." The woman flowed smoothly to her feet, as if a string attached to her head had lifted her from the floor. She advanced to the center of the room and looked around at all of them to be sure of their attention. She smiled at the boy, who was wolfing down the food on the platter. He was aware of nothing save the next bite. Amber sketched a small bow and began. She put Keffria in mind of an actor on the stage.

"I propose this. To recapture a liveship, let us use a liveship." Her gaze touched each of them in turn. "The *Paragon*, to be precise. We buy, lease or steal him, put a crew aboard with Brashen in command and go after the *Vivacia*." In the shocked silence that followed, she added, "If you suspect my motive in this, be assured that at least half of it is to save the *Paragon* from being turned into lumber. I think your good friend Davad Restart could be instrumental in getting the Ludlucks to part with the ship for a reasonable price. He has seemed to have their ear for the outrageous offers the New Traders have been making. Perhaps he might be willing to seize this opportunity to save face with the Old Traders. Perhaps that is even truer after tonight's events. I'm willing to put up everything I own as part payment for the ship. So. What say you?"

"No." Althea spoke flatly.

"Why not?" Malta demanded. She stepped into the room from the hallway. She wore a wrapper of thick blue wool over her white night-gown. Her cheeks were pink from sleep yet. She glanced about the room. "I had a nightmare. When I woke up, I heard your voices. I came down to see what was going on," she offered by way of explanation. "I heard you say we might be able to send a ship after Papa. Mama, Grandmother, why should Althea be able to forbid us to do this? It seems a sensible plan to me. Why not go rescue Papa ourselves?"

Althea began to tick the reasons off on her fingers. "Paragon is mad.

He has killed whole crews before; he might again. *Paragon* is a liveship, who should not be sailed by anyone except his family. He hasn't been sailed in years. He hasn't even been floated. I don't think we have the coin to both buy the *Paragon* and refit him as he would need. Moreover, if we do this, why should Brashen be captain? Why not me?"

Brashen gave a snort of laughter. His voice broke strangely. "And there you have her real objection!" he observed. He drew out a kerchief and wiped perspiration from his brow.

No one else laughed. There was a feverish note to his behavior that even Althea seemed to notice. She frowned at Amber, but the woman did not deign to notice it. Keffria decided that perhaps it was her turn to be blunt. "Forgive me if I sound skeptical. I do not see why either of you should wish to become involved in this. Why should a foreigner wish to risk her whole fortune on a mad liveship? What does it profit Brashen Trell to risk his life for a man who found his seamanship unsatisfactory? We could gamble what is left of the Vestrit finances, only to lose it all, if you never returned."

Brashen's eyes flashed. "I may be disinherited, but that does not mean I am totally without honor." He paused and shook his head. "Plain words, tonight, will serve us all best. Keffria Vestrit, you fear I'd take the *Paragon* and turn pirate. I could. I don't deny that. But I wouldn't. Whatever differences Althea and I may have, I think she'll still vouch for my integrity. I know your father would have."

"Speaking for myself," Amber added smoothly, "I've already told you that I wish to prevent the *Paragon* from being dismantled. We are friends. I am also a friend of your sister Althea. In addition, this is something that I feel I am called to do. I can explain it no better than that. I'm afraid you'll have to take my offer at face value. I can offer you no other assurances."

A silence fell in the room. Brashen slowly folded his arms on his chest. His brow was deeply lined. He fixed his gaze on Althea and stared at her, in a challenge that made no pretense of courtesy. Althea refused to meet it. She looked instead at her mother. Malta fidgeted, looking from one adult to another.

"I'll come back tomorrow evening," Brashen said suddenly. He waited until Althea glanced at him. "Think it over, Althea. I saw the mood of the Traders as they left tonight. I doubt that you'll get any other offers of aid, let alone a better one." He paused. In a softer voice he spoke only to her, "If you want to speak to me before then, leave a message at Amber's shop. She knows where to find me."

"Are you living aboard *Paragon?*" Althea's voice sounded hoarse.

"At nights. Sometimes." Brashen's voice was non-committal.

"And how much cindin have you used today?" she suddenly demanded. There was a cruel edge to the question.

"None at all." Brashen permitted himself a bitter smile. "That's the problem." He glanced at Amber. "I think I had best be going now."

"I think I need to stay a bit longer." Amber sounded almost apologetic.

"As you see fit. Well. Good evening to you all, then." Brashen sketched a bow.

"Wait!" Malta's plea sounded sharp. "Please, I mean. Please wait." Keffria thought she had never heard such anxiety in her daughter's voice. "May I ask some questions? About Paragon?"

Brashen focused his entire attention on her. "If you're asking my permission, certainly."

Malta shot a pleading look around the room. "If he is going to leave us to think on this, then . . . it is like you are always telling me, Grandmother. We cannot argue with numbers. Nor can we make decisions without them. So, to consider this at all, we first need to know the numbers."

Ronica Vestrit looked snared between shock and approval. "That's true."

Malta took a breath. "So. My Aunt Althea seems to think that the *Paragon* will need many repairs before he can sail. But I have always heard the wizardwood doesn't rot. Do you think he needs to be refitted?"

Brashen nodded. "Not as much as if he were a ship of ordinary wood, but yes, there is much to be done. The *Paragon* is an old ship. Far more wizardwood was used in his construction than in later liveships. Those parts of him that are wizardwood are sound. Much of the rest of him is in surprisingly good condition. I think wizardwood repels many of the boring worms and pests much as cedar repels moths. But there is still a great deal of work and supplies he would need. New masts, new canvas, new lines. Anchors, chain and a ship's boat, plus a kit for the kitchen, carpenter tools, a medicine chest . . . all of the things a ship must carry aboard it to become its own little world. Many of his seams should be re-caulked. A lot of his brightwork needs replacing. Amber has restored much of his interior wood and fixtures, but there is still a great deal to be done.

"There would be the further expense of buying the foodstuffs necessary to stock the ship for the voyage. We'd need a secret store of money or goods, in the hopes we can make a ransom offer for the ship and men. Weapons, also, would have to be bought, in case Captain Kennit refuses to dicker, and if we can afford any deck machines, they'd have to be installed. And there would have to be some coin up-front to hire hands for the voyage."

Althea found her voice. "Do you believe you'll find any decent sailors willing to sign aboard the *Paragon?* I think you are forgetting his reputation as a killer. Unless you are willing to pay above top wages, why should a good hand ship out on such a vessel?"

Keffria could hear that Althea was trying to keep her voice civil. She suspected that her sister's interest was roused despite her disparagement of the idea.

"It would be a problem," Brashen conceded easily. He pulled out the kerchief again and wiped his face. His hands trembled very slightly as he carefully refolded it. "There might be a few who would sign on simply for the daring of it. There are always some sailors with more guts than brains. I'd start with the *Vivacia's* old hands first, asking those of your father's crew that Kyle discharged. Some of them might go for the sake of the ship herself, or your father's memory. For the rest—" He shrugged. "We would end up with the dregs and the troublemakers. A great deal would depend on whom we could get as first mate. A good mate can make a working crew out of near anything, if he's given a free hand."

"What's to keep them from turning on you when—"

"Numbers!" Malta broke in irritably. "There is no sense in worrying about 'what ifs' until we know if it is financially possible." She went to her grandfather's old desk. "If I give you paper and ink, can you write up for us what you think it would cost?"

"I'm not an expert," Brashen began. "Some things would have to be done by professionals and—"

"Assuming you'd find any shipwrights willing to work on the *Paragon*," Althea chimed in sarcastically. "His reputation is bad. And assuming the Ludlucks give permission and—"

Malta's hands clenched into fists on the paper she had taken from the drawer. Keffria thought she would ball it up and throw it to the ground. Instead, the girl closed her eyes for a moment and drew a deep breath. "Assuming all that, then. How much money? And can we possibly get it? Until we answer those questions, there is no point in asking others!"

"We may just as easily be defeated by these other factors as by a lack of money!" Althea snorted in exasperation.

"All I am saying," Malta said in a tightly controlled voice, "is that we should consider those factors in the order in which they may defeat us. If we have no money to hire hands, then we don't have to worry about who will or will not sail for us."

Althea stared at the girl. Keffria felt her muscles tighten. Althea could be sharp-tongued. If she mocked Malta now, when the girl was trying so hard to be pragmatic, Keffria would not even try to control her temper.

"You're right," Althea said suddenly. She looked suddenly at their mother. "Do we have any reserves left at all? Anything not entailed, anything we can sell off?"

"There are a few things," Ronica said quietly. She absently twisted the ring on her finger. "What we must recall is that whether or not we have possession of the liveship, a payment comes due soon. The Khuprus family will expect . . ."

"Don't consider that," Malta said quietly. "I will accept Reyn's suit. I will set a date for our wedding, on condition that my father is home to attend it. I think that will win us a reprieve from that debt, and perhaps some financial help to launch the *Paragon*."

A profound silence filled the room. To Keffria, it seemed that the room filled with stillness as a bucket brims with clear water. It was not just the quiet. It was a moment of cognizance. She looked at her daughter and suddenly saw her as someone else. The spoiled and stubborn girl who would stop at nothing to get her own way was suddenly a young woman who would sacrifice anything, even herself, to rescue her father. This unswerving act of will was rattling. Keffria bit her tongue to keep from telling her that Kyle wasn't worth it. He would never understand that what his daughter had been ready to sacrifice was not a moment's brave word but her whole life. No one, she thought, can be worth another's entire life spent in subservience. She glanced at the slave-boy, so silently watching them all, but found herself considering her marriage. A bitter smile bent her mouth. One woman had already made that sacrifice for Kyle Haven.

"Malta. Please do not make such a decision under these circumstances." The power in her own voice surprised her. "I do not dispute that it is your decision to make. Proof enough of your womanhood is that you are willing to make it. I simply ask that you delay such a course until all others have been explored."

"What other courses?" Malta asked hopelessly. "Through all our troubles, no one has come to our aid. Who do we think will help us now?"

"The Tenira family might," Althea offered quietly. "Some few of the other liveship owners may come forward and . . ."

"They're going to be too busy with their own problems for some time," Brashen broke in. "I'm sorry. It's hard for me to think straight tonight. I keep forgetting you probably don't know what else went on. There was a riot at the tariff docks tonight. Tenira and some of the others went down in force. They moved *Ophelia* out to the center of the harbor and a whole fleet of small boats went out to unload her. The cargo has been scattered all over Bingtown. Tenira gave it away rather than pay any tariffs on it. But that didn't stop the Chalcedeans from trying to interfere."

"Sweet Sa, have mercy. Was anyone hurt?" Ronica demanded.

Brashen's smile was not a friendly one. "The Bingtown harbor master is quite upset about two sunken galleys. Unfortunately, they went down right near the tariff docks. No large ships are going to be able to get in there to tie up for a time. Sa only knows when they'll find a way to raise them. . . ."

"They burned going down," Amber added. She sounded both sad-dened and satisfied. She added casually, "Part of the tariff dock caught as well. When we left, some of the Satrap's warehouses were still burning."

Brashen's tone challenged Althea, "You might concede there was good reason to be concerned for your safety, on such a night."

"You were down there?" Althea looked from one to the other. "All those fires . . . too many to be one accidental fire spreading. This was planned in advance, wasn't it? Why didn't I know?"

"Ophelia and I have become very good friends," Amber replied eva-sively.

"Why wasn't I told?"

"Maybe it wasn't a fit place for a Trader's daughter to be." Brashen shrugged. More sourly, he added, "Perhaps Grag cares enough for you that he wouldn't want to risk you being arrested also."

"Grag was arrested?"

"For a short time. They found the Chalcedean guards who were sup-posed to be holding him, but Grag himself has disappeared." He permitted himself a small smile. "I understand that he's fine, however. I'm sure you'll hear from him in a day or so. Surely he wouldn't leave his lady love in suspense."

"How do *you* know so much? How did you happen to be down there?" Althea's anger was building. She had flushed a deep scarlet. Keffria could not understand why she was so upset about this. Did she wish she had been at a riot, instead of driving Davad home?

"When I saw a band of disgruntled Traders form up and leave the meeting early together, I followed them. When I saw their real intent, I joined them. As did a good many others along the way." He paused. "Later, I heard some talk about what had been done to Davad Restart's carriage. And what some wished to do to him. If I'd been there, I would never have allowed you to drive that carriage off alone. What Tenira was thinking, I don't—"

"I've told you before, I don't need you to look after me!" Althea was suddenly savagely angry. "I don't need anyone's help."

Brashen folded his arms on his chest. "Oh, that's obvious, now. I'm only puzzled as to why you stood up at the Traders' meeting and asked for the help you now refuse."

"I don't need help from *you!*" Althea clarified fiercely.

"I do." Keffria found her sister's shock almost satisfying. She met Althea's glare with a calm look. "You seem to have forgotten that I, not you, am the Trader for this family. I am not so proud as to turn away the only help we may be offered." Keffria switched her glance to Brashen. "What do we need to begin this? Where do we start?"

Brashen tilted his head toward Malta. "The little one is right. We need money to start." He nodded next to Ronica. "And the captain's lady

will have to push Davad Restart to make him present this offer favorably
to the Ludlucks. Any other liveship owners who would add their approval
would help. Maybe Althea could get her sweetheart to put in his word on
this. I know a few of the liveships, and I'll speak to them directly. You
might be surprised how much pressure a liveship can put on his family."
He took a breath and briefly rubbed his temples. He put his kerchief away
slowly. "Althea is right. Getting crew will be a problem. I'll start on that
immediately, put word out in the taverns that I'm hiring a lively crew of
daring men. Those that come will half expect to turn pirate. They may
turn away at the name of Paragon, but . . ."

"Ay'll go. Ay'll sail wiff you."

The boy blushed a bit when they all stared at him, but he didn't lower
his eyes from Brashen's face. The plate of food looked as clean as if it had
been washed. With the meal, the boy seemed to have taken on substance
and spirit as well.

"That's a brave offer, lad, but you're a bit small yet." Brashen could
not quite keep the amusement from his voice.

The boy looked indignant. "I feshed wiff my Da, 'fore the slave raiders
kem. Know ma way roun' a deck." He shrugged his thin shoulders.
"D'ruther do that'n shovel hosshit. Hosses stink."

"You're free now. You can go anywhere you want. Wouldn't you
rather go home to your family?" Keffria asked him gently.

His narrow face stilled. For an instant, it seemed as if her words had
muted him again. Then he shrugged. His voice was harder and less boyish
as he said, "Nothern but ashes'n bones there. D'ruther go back ta sea.
S'my life, right? Freed, am't I?" He looked about defiantly as if he expected them to revoke that.

"You're free," Althea assured him.

"Then 'm gone wiff him." He tossed his head at Brashen, who shook
his head slowly.

"There's another idea," Malta broke in suddenly. "Buy a crew. I've
seen some tattoo-faced sailors about Bingtown. Why couldn't we just buy
some sailors?"

"Because slavery is wrong," Amber pointed out dryly. "On the other
hand, I know some slaves who might be willing to risk punishment by
running away and joining the crew. They were stolen from homes and
families in the pirate isles. They might be willing to take part in a chancy
venture, if they were promised the opportunity to go home. Some might
even know something of the waters."

"Could we trust slave sailors?" Keffria asked hesitantly.

"On the ship, they wouldn't be slaves," Brashen pointed out. "If it's a
choice between an able-bodied runaway and a broken-down drunk, I'll
hire the runaway. A little gratitude from a man given a second chance at
life can go a long way." He looked suddenly thoughtful as he said this.

"Who put you in charge of hiring?" Althea protested. "If we're going to do this, I'll want the final say on my crew."

"Althea, you can't be thinking of sailing with them," Keffria protested.

"How could you think I would not? If we are going after the *Vivacia*, I must be on board." Althea stared at her sister as if she were crazy.

"It's completely inappropriate!" Keffria was aghast. "The *Paragon* will be an unreliable ship, with a motley crew, going into dangerous waters, possibly into battle. You can't possibly go. What would people think of the Vestrits if we allowed you to sail on such a ship?"

Althea's eyes grew flinty. "I worry more about what people would think if we were content to let others take all the risks of regaining our family ship. How can we say it is a vital errand and ask our friends for aid, but then say that it isn't worth one of the family taking a risk?"

"I think she should, actually." This astonishing statement from Brashen left several of them gaping. He addressed his remarks to Keffria, acknowledging that the decision actually rested with her. "If you don't make it plain that this is a Vestrit venture, you won't get any of the other Traders to support it. They'll see it as entrusting a liveship to a ne'er-do-well, disinherited Trader's son and a foreigner. And if, I hope when, we regain the *Vivacia*, the ship will need Althea. Badly." He met eyes cautiously as he added, "But I do not think she should sail as captain, mate or even crew. This is going to be a tough crew, one that will be kept in line by fists and brawn, initially, anyway. The type of men we'll end up with aren't going to respect anyone who can't pound them to the deck if he has to. You don't qualify. And if you're working alongside them, they aren't going to give you respect. They'll test your abilities at every turn. Sooner or later, you would get hurt."

Althea's eyes narrowed. "I don't need you to look after me, Brashen Trell. Remember? I've proved my abilities, and they're not based just on body strength. My father always said it was a poor captain who had to keep his crew in line by blows."

"Maybe because he felt that was the first mate's job," Brashen retorted. He modified his tone as he added, "Your father was a fine captain with a wonderful ship, Althea. He could have paid low wages and still had good men willing to work for him. We won't have his options, I'm afraid." Brashen yawned abruptly, then looked embarrassed. "I'm tired," he said abruptly. "I need to get some sleep before we do anything further. I think we at least know what our difficulties will be."

"There is one other problem we haven't addressed at all tonight," Amber interjected. They all looked at her. "We can't assume the *Paragon* will enter into this willingly. He has many fears of his own. In some ways, he's a frightened boy. The dangerous side of the coin is that he is an angry man, just as often. If we are going to do this, I think it is essential that he do it willingly. For if we try to force him to do it, there is no possibility of success."

"Do you think it will be hard to persuade him?" Ronica asked.

Amber shrugged. "I don't know. Paragon is completely unpredictable. Even if he is agreeable at first, he may change his mind a day or a week later. It is something we must take into account on this venture."

"We'll cross that bridge when we come to it. First, we must get Davad Restart to get the Ludlucks to agree to our plan."

"I think I can prevail there," Ronica said in a voice that had a cool steel edge to it. Keffria felt a moment of sympathy for Davad. "I think I shall have the answer to that before noon tomorrow. I see no point in delaying this."

Brashen sighed heavily. "We are in agreement, then. I will return tomorrow afternoon. Good night, Ronica and Keffria. Goodnight, Althea." There was a very subtle change to his tone as he bid her sister goodnight.

"Goodnight, Brashen," Althea returned his farewell in a similar tone.

Amber, too, bid them farewell. As Althea prepared to walk them to the door, the slave-boy also stood. Keffria knew a moment of exasperation with her sister's impulsive behavior. "Don't forget, you have to find a place for the boy to sleep," she told Althea.

The boy shook his head. "Not here. 'm gone wiff him." He tossed his head at Brashen.

"No." Brashen made the single word final.

"Freed, am't I?" the boy protested stubbornly. He cocked his head and stared at Brashen. "Ken't stop me."

"Don't bet on that," Brashen told him ominously. In a kinder voice he added, "Boy, I can't take care of you. I've got no home to go to; I'm on my own."

"Me, too," the boy insisted calmly.

"I think you should let him go with you, Brashen," Amber suggested. She had a strangely speculative look on her face. With a wry twist to her mouth, she added, "It might not be the best of luck to turn away your first willing crewman."

"S'right," the boy asserted cockily. "El ken't respect a man who don't dare. Dare tek me. Y'on't regret it."

Brashen squinted his eyes shut tightly and shook his head. But as he left the room the boy followed him, and he made no motion to discourage him. Amber followed with a small smile on her face.

"Do you think they can bring Papa home?" Malta asked in a small voice after they had left the room.

While Keffria was trying to decide how to answer that, her mother spoke. "Our finances are foundering, my dear. There is no point to refusing this risk. If it succeeds, it may save the family fortunes. If they fail, we will sink a bit faster. That is all."

Keffria thought it a cruel thing to say to a child, but to her surprise, Malta nodded slowly. "I was thinking the same thing myself," she observed.

It was the first time in the last year that she had spoken in a completely civil tone to her grandmother.

CHAPTER TWENTY

Piracy

WITH THE PREY IN SIGHT, ALL HER DOUBTS EVAPORATED LIKE THE MORNING mists on a sunny day. Wintrow's shared soul searching, all his anxieties and structured morality, fell away from her like paint peeling off quickened wizardwood. She heard the lookout's shout as the sail came into view and something ancient stirred in her: time to hunt. When the pirates on her deck took up the lookout's fierce cry, she herself gave voice, like the shrill ki-ii of a stooping hawk. First the sail and then the ship came into sight, fleeing madly from the *Marietta*. Sorcor's smaller vessel hounded the prey as *Vivacia*, concealed behind a headland, swooped out to join the chase.

Her crew drove her on as she had never been driven, piling on canvas until her masts and spars strained to hold the wind's breath. The canvas billowing wide, the whistle of the wind past her cheeks stirred in her memories that were not born in human lives. She lifted her hands and, fingers crooked like talons, reached after the fleeing ship. A wild thundering filled her heartless, bloodless body, quickening her to frenzy. She leaned forward, sleeking her planked body to a fleetness that made her crew whoop with excitement. White spume flew as she cut the waves.

"You see?" Kennit cried out in triumph as he clung to her forward rail. "It is in your blood, my lady! I knew it! This is what you were made for, not some sedate toting of cargo like a village woman with a bucket of water. After them! Ah, they see you; they see you, look how they scramble! But it will avail them nothing."

Wintrow dug his fingers into the railing beside Kennit. Tears streamed from the corners of his eyes in the harsh kiss of the salt wind. He made not a sound. His jaws were clenched tight, near as tight he held the disapproval inside him. But the wild pounding of his heart betrayed him. His blood sang with this wild pursuit. His whole soul quivered in anticipation of the capture. He might deny this enthusiasm to himself, but he could not hide it from her.

Kennit and Sorcor had not chosen this prey randomly. The rumor of the *Crosspatch* had reached Sorcor's ears weeks ago. More recently, with his captain's continuing recovery, he had shared the news with Kennit. Captain Avery of the *Crosspatch* had bragged, not only in Jamaillia City but in several smaller ports as well, that no pirate, no matter how daring or righteous would dissuade him from the slave trade. It had been a foolish boast, Kennit had told Vivacia. Avery's reputation was already well-known. He carried only the finest cargo, educated slaves suitable for tutors, house servants and estate managers. He transported the best of Jamaillia's civilized wares as well: fine brandies and incenses, perfumes and intricate silver work. His customers in Chalced expected the extravagantly fine from him, and paid accordingly for his goods.

While his ship represented a rich target, it was not one that Kennit would have ordinarily chosen. Why challenge a ship that was fleet and well armed, crewed by well-disciplined men, when there was easier prey to seize? But Avery had spoken once too often and once too recklessly. Such impudence could not be tolerated. Kennit, too, had a reputation to uphold. Avery had been foolish to challenge it.

Kennit had gone to the *Marietta* more than once to plan this capture with Sorcor. Vivacia knew they had discussed the best places for such an ambush, but knew little more of his plans than that. Her curious questions had received only evasive answers.

As the two ships scissored toward their quarry, Vivacia considered Wintrow's words of last night. He had bluntly condemned Kennit. "He hunts this ship for glory, not righteousness," he had said accusingly. "Other slavers carry far more slaves aboard them, in great misery and deprivation. Avery, I have heard, does not chain his charges, but lets them move freely belowdecks. He is generous with both food and water, so his merchandise arrives in good condition and brings fine prices. Kennit chooses to pursue Avery's ship, not out of hatred of slavery, but for wealth and fame."

She had pondered his words for some time. "That is not how he feels about it when he thinks of it," she answered. She had not elaborated on that topic further, for she herself was not completely certain of what Kennit felt. She knew there were depths to him that he concealed from all. She tried a new tack. "I do not think the slaves below his decks will be less grateful for their freedom than those held in squalor and deprivation. Do you think slavery is acceptable, if the slave is treated like a prized horse or dog?"

"Of course not!" he had retorted and from there, she had steered the conversation into channels she could negotiate more nimbly.

It was only today that she had finally put a name to the emotional undercurrent in Kennit when he spoke of the *Crosspatch*. It was the lust of the hunt. The small ship that fled so fleetly before them was a thing of beauty, as irresistible to Kennit as a fluttering butterfly is to a cat. Pragmatic as he was, he would not have chosen this challenging prey. Neither could he resist the contest once he had been taunted to it.

AS THE DISTANCE BETWEEN THE VIVACIA AND THE LITTLE TWO-MASTED *Crosspatch* closed, Wintrow felt a queasy anticipation build inside him. Repeatedly, he had warned Kennit that no blood must be shed on the *Vivacia*'s decks. He had tried to explain to the pirate that the ship must forever carry the memories of the slain, but he could not convey to him how wearisome a load they were. If Kennit did not heed him, if the pirate permitted the fighting to reach her decks, or worse, chose to execute prisoners on her decks, Wintrow did not think the ship could handle it. When Wintrow had gone to plead that *Vivacia* not be put to piracy, Kennit had listened with a bored air, and then dryly asked him why he thought he had captured the liveship? Wintrow had chosen to shrug and keep silent. Further pleading might only drive Kennit to prove his mastery of both ship and boy.

The crew of the *Crosspatch* was aloft, working the sails desperately. If the *Marietta* alone had pursued her, the *Crosspatch* might have escaped. The liveship was not only fleeter than the two-master, but in a position to crowd her over in the channel. For an instant, Wintrow thought the *Crosspatch* was going to slip past them and gain open water. Then Wintrow heard an angry command shouted, and saw the slaver spill wind from her sails in a frantic effort to avoid going aground. Minutes later, the *Marietta* and *Vivacia* boxed her. Grapples soared from the *Marietta*, to fall and bite into the decks of the *Crosspatch*.

Her crew gave up their efforts to flee and fell to the tasks of defense. They were well prepared. Firepots were launched, to shatter and splatter flames on the *Marietta*'s hull and deck. Men donned light leather armor and took up blades with casual competence. Other men with bows slung over their shoulders were moving swiftly up the *Crosspatch*'s rigging. On the *Marietta*, some pirates tended to the defense of their own vessel, smothering the flames with wet canvas, while others worked the catapults. A steady rain of rocks fell upon the *Crosspatch*. Meanwhile the grapples pulled the unfortunate ship ever closer to the *Marietta*, where a blood-thirsty boarding party crowded the rails in anticipation. The fighters aboard the *Marietta* outnumbered the crew of the *Crosspatch* substantially.

Aboard the *Vivacia*, men lined the railing enviously. They catcalled and whooped advice to their pirate brethren. Archers ascended the *Vivacia*'s rigging, and a random rain of arrows began to fall on the crew and deck of the *Crosspatch*. That was the extent of their participation in the battle, but it was a deadly one. The fighters trying to defend the *Crosspatch* had to remember there was a second enemy at their backs. Hissing arrows skewered those who forgot. Kennit held the *Vivacia* back at the edge of the action, her bow pointed toward the conflict. He stood on the foredeck, his hands clutching the railing. He spoke in a low voice as if he were instructing her. Every now and then, a gust of wind would bring his muttered words to Wintrow's ears, but they were obviously intended for Vivacia. "There, you see him, first across the railings and onto the enemy's deck, him in the red kerchief, that's Sudge, a fine rascal, always has to be first. Behind him, now, that's Rog. The lad idolizes Sudge, which may get him killed someday—"

The figurehead nodded to his words, while her eyes drank in the scene. Her fists were clenched at her chest, her lips parted with excitement. When Wintrow reached to her, he felt her confused enthusiasm. The emotions of the men aboard, a mixture of lust, envy and excitement, beat against her like a rising tide. A separate strand of emotion was Kennit's pride in his men. Like a horde of ants, the brightly clad pirates surged onto the *Crosspatch*'s deck and spread the battle. The wind and the open water between the ships muffled the curses and screams. If Vivacia was aware that the arrows that flew from her own rigging were piercing human flesh, she gave no sign of it. Distanced here, the slaughter was a spectacle of motion and color. There was pageantry to it, drama and suspense. A man fell from the rigging of the *Crosspatch*. He struck a spar, tangled briefly about it, and then crashed down to the deck. Wintrow winced at the impact but Vivacia didn't even blink. Her attention was fixed on the foredeck, where the captain of the vessel battled Sorcor. Captain Avery's fine blade glistened like a silver needle as he darted it at the more ponderous pirate. Sorcor turned the blade with a short sword in his left hand, and made his own attack with the long sword in his right. Death was dancing between them. Vivacia's eyes were bright.

Wintrow gave Kennit a sidelong glance. Here, at a distance, she could see the excitement and action of the battle, but she was insulated from the horror. Blood did not spatter her decks, and the wind carried away the smoke and the screams of the dying and wounded. Like a stain spreading, the pirates flowed slowly but surely over the deck of the captured vessel. Vivacia saw it all, but she was detached from it. Did Kennit seek to accustom her to violence by a gradual introduction?

Wintrow cleared his throat. "Men are dying over there," he pointed out. "Lives are ending in pain and terror."

Vivacia quickly glanced at him, then back to the battle. Kennit was the one who replied. "They brought it on themselves," he pointed out. "They chose this, knowing well there was a chance they would die. I do not speak only of my own brave men, who leap willingly to battle. Those on board the *Crosspatch* expected to be attacked. They invited this. They proclaimed their readiness with their boasts. Recall that they were well supplied with leather jerkins, swords and bows. Would they have such things aboard if they did not expect battle, if they did not know they *deserved* to be challenged?" Kennit gave a deep laugh. "No," he answered himself. "That is not slaughter you see over there. It is a contest of wills. One could even say it is but a physical manifestation of the eternal conflict between righteousness and injustice."

"People are dying," Wintrow repeated stubbornly. He tried to put conviction in his words, but found his certainty fading before the pirate's persuasive words.

"People are always dying," the pirate agreed smoothly. "As you and I stand here on this deck, we are fading already, withering with the briefness of summer flowers. Vivacia will outlive us all, Wintrow. Death is not bad. She absorbed several deaths, did she not, to allow her to quicken? Think of it this way, Wintrow. Is it our lives she witnesses each passing day, or our deaths? You can as easily say one as the other. Yes, there is pain and violence. They are a part of all creatures, and of themselves are not evil. The violence of a flood tears a tree from the riverbank, but the nurturing soil and water the flood brings more than compensate. We are warriors for right, my lady and I. If we must sweep away evil, let us do it swiftly, even if it involves pain."

His voice was low and rich as distant thunder, and as stirring. Somewhere in that seamless logic, Wintrow knew there were loose threads. If he could but find one, he could unravel the man's whole argument. He retreated to a line he had read in a book. "One of the differences between good and evil is that good can endure the existence of evil and still prevail. Evil, however, is always ultimately vanquished by good."

Kennit smiled genially and shook his head. "Wintrow, Wintrow. Think what you have said. What kind of murky good can tolerate evil and permit it to go on? Good that fears for its own comfort and safety does that, and transforms itself from true good to blinkered complacency. Shall we turn away from the misery in that ship's hold, saying, 'Well, we are all free men here. That is the best we can do, and they will have to look out for themselves?' Surely that is not what you were taught in your monastery."

"That is not what I meant!" Wintrow retorted indignantly. "Good endures evil as a stone can endure rain. It does not tolerate it, that is . . ."

"I believe it is over," Kennit interjected smoothly. Bodies were splashing over the side of the *Crosspatch*. No serpents rose to receive them. Swift and clean, the ship had never attracted a following of the beasts. The *Crosspatch*'s pennant was torn down. A red and black Raven flag swiftly replaced it. The hatches were opened. Slaves began to emerge onto the deck. Kennit glanced over his shoulder. "Etta. Have the ship's boat readied. I want to go and inspect our catch." He turned to Wintrow.

"Care to go along, lad? It might be instructive for you to witness the gratitude of those we have saved. It may change your mind about what we do."

Wintrow shook his head slowly.

Kennit laughed. Then his voice changed. "Come with me anyway. Briskly now, no dawdling. I'll educate you in spite of yourself."

Wintrow half suspected that the pirate's true motivation was to keep him from speaking privately with Vivacia about all they had just witnessed. Kennit wanted his words to be the ones she considered as she pondered the taking of the *Crosspatch*. Wintrow clenched his jaws but turned to obey the pirate's bidding. He could endure. He was shocked when Kennit threw an arm across his shoulders. He leaned on him as if for support. The captain's voice was affable as he said, "Learn to lose graciously, Wintrow. For you aren't really losing. You're gaining what I have to teach you." Kennit's grin twisted as he assured him, "I have much to teach you."

Later, as they were seated in the ship's boat, being propelled across the water to the *Crosspatch*, Kennit leaned down to speak in Wintrow's ear. "Even a stone is worn down by the rain eventually, my boy. No shame to the stone in that." He patted him affably on the shoulder and then sat up straight on his seat. He beamed satisfaction as he looked across the sparkling water toward his prize.

THE GUSTY WIND BROUGHT ALTHEA THE RANDOM NOTES OF A PIPE AS SHE hurried through the woods behind her home and then clambered down the cliffs. She had promised to meet Brashen and Amber at the beached ship by noon. Together they would give him the news. Anxiety was a nasty ball in the pit of her stomach as she wondered how Paragon would react. The pipe notes that came to her ears were not quite music; it sounded like experimentation to her. Some child, probably, at play on the beach.

The deepness of the notes should have prepared her for the sight of the blind figurehead blowing into an oversized shepherd's pipes. The self-absorbed look on his face transformed him. The lines were smoothed from his brow, and the set of his shoulders was no longer so defensive. He looked a completely different creature from the spooky and suspicious ship she had befriended so long ago. She knew a brief moment of jealousy that Amber had been able to work such a change in him.

The oversized pipes were obviously more of Amber's work. Althea shook her head at what she suddenly perceived as a lack in herself. In all the years she had known Paragon, she had never thought to give him the sort of gifts Amber did. The bead-maker gave him toys and trinkets, things to busy his hands and his mind. Althea had been his friend for years, but had never perceived him as anything other than a failed live-ship. She was fond of him, and saw him as a person, not a thing. Never-theless, her image of him had never changed. He was a ship that had disappointed his trust, an unsafe vessel that would never sail again. Am-ber had unlocked the part of him that was a lively, if stunted, child and responded to that. It had made all the difference in Paragon's spirit.

Althea knew a moment's hesitancy as she drew closer. The ship was blissfully unaware of her as he played. The figurehead had originally been carved as a bearded, craggy-faced warrior. Years ago, a hatchet or axe had chopped away his eyes. Now, despite the wild beard and shaggy locks, what remained of his face looked oddly boyish. She had come to join Brashen and Amber in convincing him to once more confront the task at which he had spectacularly failed. She was coming to take away this sunny day and the boyish creature playing his pipes. She would ask him to do that which he most feared. What would it do to him? For the first time since Brashen had suggested the plan, she truly wondered how it would affect Paragon. Then she thought of Vivacia and hardened her heart. He was a liveship. He had been created to sail and, if she could restore that to him, it would be greater than any trinket Amber had ever given him.

She refused to think about what it would do to them all if he failed again.

She smelled a cook-fire. Now that the summer weather had warmed, Amber did most of her cooking outside on the beach. Within the Para-gon, she had wrought a gradual change, some of which Althea approved and some of which horrified her. The captain's quarters now gleamed with polished and oiled woodwork. The brassware had been buffed to a sheen. The vandalized cupboards and wrenched hinges had all been lovingly restored. The room was redolent of linseed oil, turpentine and beeswax. In the evenings when Amber lit a lantern inside the chamber, all was honey and gold.

Dismaying was the trap door she had cut in the floor that led down into the hold. Both Brashen and Althea had been initially outraged on seeing it. She had tried to explain to them that she had wanted swifter access to the holds for her supplies, but neither of them accepted that. No ship, they explained, had a trap door in the captain's chamber. Even securely bolted and covered with a fine carpet, it offended Althea.

Amber had restored other parts of the ship as well. The galley stove had been cleaned and polished. Although Amber did most of her cooking on the beach, she kept her pans and supplies there. How she coped with the cant of the deck, Althea was not sure. Amber would only say that restoring these places seemed to make Paragon feel better, and so she had done it. The entire ship had been swept free of sand. Those bits of wind-flung moss and seaweed that had managed to cling to the ship had been cleared away. She had burned cleansing herbs in smoke-pots throughout the ship to drive out both the damp and the insects. Doors, windows and hatchcovers were all tight now. All these things she had done before the re-launching of *Paragon* had been discussed. For an instant Althea pondered that, then set her speculations aside.

"Paragon!" she called to him.

He took the pipes away from his lips and grinned in her direction. "Althea! You've come to visit."

"Yes, I have. Are Brashen and Amber here as well?"

"Where else?" he asked jovially. "They're inside. For some reason, Brashen wanted to look at the linkage to my rudder. Amber is with him. They'll be out in a bit."

"Your pipes are lovely. Are they new?"

He looked abashed. "Not quite. I've had them for a day or so, but I still can't play anything. Amber says it doesn't matter if I don't follow a tune. Amber says that as long as the sounds please me, the music is mine. But I want to be able to play them."

"I think Amber is right. The playing of tunes will come in time, as you get used to them."

The shrieking of disturbed gulls turned Althea's head. Far down the beach, two women were making their way toward the ship. A portly man trundled along behind them. Althea frowned. They were early. She hadn't even broached the subject to Paragon yet, and soon he would discover it had been decided without him. She had to get Brashen and Amber out here quickly, before they arrived.

"What disturbed the gulls?" Paragon demanded.

"Just some walkers on the beach. I'd like to, uh, have a cup of tea. Do you mind if I go aboard and ask Amber for the use of her kettle?"

"Go ahead, I'm sure she won't mind. Welcome aboard."

She felt like a traitor as he unconcernedly lifted the pipes to his lips again. In a very short time, his entire life would be changed. She scrambled up the rope ladder that was Brashen's most recent contribution to Amber's abode and made her way across the sloping deck to the aft hatch. She was clambering down a ladder when she heard their voices at the bottom.

"It seems to be in good condition," Brashen was saying. "But it's hard to tell with the rudder wedged in the sand. Once the ship is freed, then we'll have to check how it moves. Grease wouldn't hurt anything, however. We could put Clef on it."

Despite her worry, Althea had to smile. The slave-boy was an extreme annoyance to Brashen, according to Brashen. Yet, somehow he seemed to have already slipped into the role of ship's boy. Brashen gave him all the small, uncomplicated tasks that no one else had time to do. The boy had spoken true when he said he knew his way around a deck. He seemed completely comfortable living aboard the derelict ship. Paragon appeared to have accepted him much more swiftly than the boy had adapted to the living figurehead. Clef was still very shy of speaking directly to Paragon. A blessing, Althea decided, considering the secret they had been concealing from the ship for the last week.

Davad Restart had not been easy to persuade. To Ronica, he had initially denied all knowledge of any bargains concerning Paragon. Ronica had been unrelenting in insisting that he did know about the offers and counter-offers. Moreover, she insisted that only he could negotiate this delicate contract. When he had finally admitted that he did know of the bargaining for Paragon, Althea had left the room. Disgust filled her. He was a Bingtown Trader, born of the same traditions she was. How could he have considered doing that to a liveship? How could he sink to tempting the Ludluck family with money to agree to so heinous a thing? What he had done was traitorous, cruel and wrong. For money and for the sake of gaining influence with the New Traders, he had betrayed his heritage. Beneath the disgust churned her hurt. Davad Restart, source of sweets and pick-a-back rides when she was tiny, Davad, who had watched her grow up and sent her flowers on her sixteenth birthday. Davad the betrayer.

Ronica and Keffria had handled what she now thought of as a ransoming. Althea had not been able to bring herself to take any part in it. She avoided Davad, for she did not think she could speak to him civilly, yet she dared not offend him.

She dropped the rest of the way down the ladder. As her boots thumped the deck, she announced, "The others are coming. Mother is just down the beach. I'm afraid Trader Restart has chosen to tag along as well. I hope he has the good sense to keep his mouth shut, but I doubt it. Have you spoken to Paragon yet?" Her eyes were on Amber. It was easier so. There was no enmity between Brashen and her, but no comfort either.

"Not yet!" Amber looked stricken. "I wanted you to be here. I did not expect the others so soon."

"They're early. We could send Clef down the beach to them, to ask them to wait until we signal them."

Amber pondered a moment. "No. I think the sooner it is done, the better. He will rant and pout, I fear, but I suspect that secretly he may rejoice, also." She gave a small sigh. "Let's go."

Althea followed Amber up the ladder, with Brashen close behind her. Out on the beach again, they found Clef sitting on a rock before Paragon. Clef's face was bright red; he was trying to catch his breath. Paragon blew on his pipe, making an abrupt farting sound, and they both went off into gales of laughter. The ship lifted his free hand to smother his giggles, but the boy laughed loud and heartily. Althea halted and stared. Behind her, Brashen joined in their laughter. The *Paragon* turned blindly toward them and grinned. "So, here you are."

"Here we are," Amber agreed. "All of us." She approached the figurehead, then reached up a gloved hand to touch his forearm. "Paragon. We are all here because we want to speak to you about something. Something very important."

The laughter faded from his face, replaced by uncertainty. "Something bad?"

"Something good," Amber said soothingly. "At least, we all think so." She looked around at the others and then glanced down the beach. Althea followed her gaze. Her mother and Amis Ludluck would be with them very soon. "It's about a chance we have to do something good, with your help. We can't do it without you."

"I'm not a child," the ship said. "Speak plainly." His anxiety was building. "How could we be together? What good thing?"

Amber rubbed at her face nervously. She glanced again at Althea and Brashen, then focused herself on the ship. "I know you're not a child. I'm not doing this well, because I am so afraid you won't want to join us. Paragon, here it is. You know of the Vestrit family's liveship, Vivacia. Pirates have captured her. You know all about it. You've heard us talking about it, wondering what to do. Well. Althea wants to go and rescue them. Brashen and I want to go, too." She took a breath. "We want you to be the ship that takes us there. How would you feel about that?"

"Pirates," he said breathlessly. He scratched at his beard with his free hand. "I don't know. I do not know. I like you all. I like being with you. No ship should be left with pirates. They're terrible creatures."

Althea began to breathe again. It was going to be all right.

"Have the Ludlucks said they'll take me there?"

Brashen coughed nervously. Amber glanced around, inviting one of them to speak, but neither offered. "The Ludlucks will allow you to take us there."

"But who . . . you can't mean there won't be a member of my family aboard?" He was incredulous. "No liveship sails without a member of his family aboard."

Brashen cleared his throat. "I'll be there, Paragon. After all the years we've known one another, you're as close to family as I have. Would I do?"

"No. No, Brashen." The ship's voice rose nervously. "I like you, I do, but you're not a Ludluck and I am. You're my friend, but not my family. I can't sail without a family member aboard." He shook his head, emphasizing it. "They wouldn't let that happen to me. That would be like them saying that they'd given up on me forever, that I'll never, ever be any good. No." He gripped the shepherd's pipes with both hands, but still they shook. "No."

Althea's mother and Amis Ludluck had halted. Amis was staring at the *Paragon*. She crossed her arms in front of her and set her mouth in a flat line. Althea read both denial and rejection there. She was glad the ship was blind. Davad was puffing, striving to close the distance and catch up with them.

"Paragon," she said calmingly. "Please. Listen to me. It has been years since there was a Ludluck aboard you. You have been alone, save for us. Nevertheless, you have survived. I think you are different from most liveships. I think you have a sense of yourself apart from your family. I think you have learned to be . . . independent."

"I survived only because I could not die!" he roared suddenly. He lifted the pipes high in one hand, as if he would dash them at her. Then, in a great show of self-control, he reached over his shoulder to set the precious instrument on his canted foredeck. He was breathing hard through his nose as he turned back to her. "I live in pain, Althea. I live at the edge of madness! Do you think I do not know that? I have learned . . . what have I learned? Nothing. Only that I must go on, and so I go on. An emptiness devours me from within and is never satiated. It eats my days, one at a time, consuming second after dripping second, and every day I grow less, but I never manage to wink out." He gave a sudden, wild laugh. "You say I have a self apart from my family? Oh, I do. Yes, I do, a self with talons and teeth, so full of misery and fury that I would rend the world to shreds if I could only make it all stop!" His voice had risen to a roar. He suddenly flung his arms wide and threw his head back. He shrieked out a cry, inhumanly loud, unbearably sad. Althea clapped her hands over her ears.

From the corner of her eye, she saw Amis Ludluck turn and run away. Her mother spun after her. Althea watched as Ronica caught up with her and grabbed her arm. She halted her and turned her around. Althea knew she was remonstrating with her, but had no idea what she was saying. Davad was beside them now, tut-tutting and wiping his sweating face with a silk kerchief. Althea knew what had happened. Amis Ludluck had changed her mind. Althea was sure of it. She had lost her only chance to rescue Vivacia. It would not have been so devastating if she could believe Paragon had won, but she could not believe that, either. The Ludlucks would not sell Paragon, but they would not sail him. He would stay here on the shores of Bingtown, getting older and crazier with each passing year. Althea wondered if she would do the same.

Amber was standing dangerously close to Paragon. One hand rested on his hull. She was talking softly to him. He wasn't paying any attention. He had dropped his shaggy head into his hands and was weeping, shoulder-shaking sobs like a heart-broken child. Clef had drawn closer, staring up wide-eyed at the overcome ship. He clenched his teeth on his lower lip. His fists were knotted at his sides.

"Paragon!" Amis Ludluck shouted his name.

He jerked his scarred visage up from his hands and stared sightlessly about. "Who's that?" he demanded frantically. He rubbed at his cheeks, as if to wipe away tears he had not eyes to cry. He was plainly distressed at having a stranger witness his grief.

"It's Amis Ludluck." The woman sounded defensive. Her graying hair had blown out of her summer bonnet, and her shawl flapped in the wind. She said no more than that, waiting for his reaction.

The ship looked stunned. He opened and closed his mouth twice before he found words. "Why have you come here?" His voice and tone were surprisingly reserved, that of a man rather than a boy. Misery shone from him. He dragged in a breath, composed himself even more. "Why, after all these years, have you come to speak to me?"

She looked more shaken than if he had shouted at her, Althea thought. She fumbled for words. "They've told you, haven't they?" she finally asked him lamely.

"Told me what?" he asked her mercilessly.

She straightened herself. "I've sold you."

"You can't sell me. I'm part of your family. Could you sell your daughter, your son?"

Amis Ludluck shook her head. "No," she whispered. "No, I could not. Because I love them and they love me." She lifted her gaze to stare up at the disfigured ship. "That is not true of you." Her voice went suddenly shrill. "For as long as I can remember, you have been the bane of my family. I was not even born when last you sailed away, but I grew up with the pain of my mother and grandmother at their losses. You disappeared and the men of our family went with you, never to return. Why? What was it you wished to punish us for, save that we were your family? It would have been bad enough if you had never returned. At least we would have been able to wonder. We could have imagined that you had all gone down together, or that they still lived somewhere, alive but unable to get back to us. Instead, you had to come back, to prove to us that you had killed once more. Yet again, you had slain the men of the family who had made you and left the women to mourn.

"Here you have been, for thirty years! A constant reproach to my family, a symbol of our shame and our guilt. Every ship that passes in or out of the harbor sees you here. There is no one in Bingtown who does not have an opinion as to why you failed. Most lay the blame at our door. We have been called greedy, reckless, selfish and cold-hearted. Some say we deserved what befell us. As long as you are here, we can never forget, nor forgive ourselves. It would be better by far if you were gone. They are willing to take you and we are more than willing to be rid of you." She doused them all with her poisonous words. The pain Althea felt for Paragon left her speechless. The woman's eyes bulged with madness. Perhaps, after all, Paragon was made of the same stuff as the Ludlucks.

"We were a powerful family, before you! You were to have been our

glory, the *Paragon* of our success. Instead, it beggared our fortune to pay
for you, and all you ever brought us was misery and despair. Well? Will
not you at least deny it? Speak, oh wondrous ship! After all these years,
tell me why? Why did you turn on them, why did you kill our dreams, our
hopes, our men?" She finally stopped and stood panting with the force of
her emotions. Beside her, Ronica Vestrit looked sickened. But the look on
Davad Restart's face was the most arresting. He looked disquieted, and yet
a sort of righteousness shone in his eyes.

"The Rain Wild River," Davad said quietly. "Nothing good ever came
out of the Rain Wilds. Poisonous magic, insidious sickness. That is all that
ever . . ."

"Stop it," Amber hissed. "Shut up and go away. Go away now. He
knows. Here. Here it is, take it, it is yours, it's all yours. All I have, in
exchange for him. As I promised." From around her neck she took a key
on a leather thong. She flung it at Davad's feet. It hit a beach rock and
rang a clear note before it bounded onto the sand. He leaned down
laboriously to pick it up. Althea recognized the massive key to the shop
on Rain Wild Street. He dropped it into his pocket. Amis Ludluck stood
looking up at the ship. A few tears had tracked down her withered cheeks,
but she didn't weep now. She just stared at Paragon, her mouth set in
silence.

Above her, Paragon crossed his arms on his chest. His head was lifted.
If he had had eyes, they would have been staring out to sea. The bunched
muscles of his jaws clamped his mouth tightly shut. He was as still as if
carved of ordinary wood.

Davad took Amis Ludluck's arm and tugged. "Come along, Amis. I'll
take you home now. Then I'll go and secure your shop for you. I think
you've made the best of a bad bargain. I think we all have. Good day,
Ronica, Althea. Remember, this transaction did not begin with me."

"We'll remember," Althea said flatly. She didn't watch them go. She
stared up at the unmoving and silent ship. Guilt gnawed at her. Why had
she thought that if Amis Ludluck came down here, she would persuade
Paragon to go willingly? Ludluck spite was legendary in Bingtown. Why
had she thought the woman would not turn it on her own abandoned
ship? Suddenly, it all seemed insane. To set sail on a mad ship, in the dim
hope of seeking out and recovering her family's liveship was an errand for
a fool. Who else could believe in the success of such an undertaking?

"Paragon?" Amber said quietly. "Paragon, she's gone now. Everything
is going to be all right, you'll see. It's for the best. You'll be with people
who care about you now. Out on the sea again, where a ship belongs.
When you next return to Bingtown, you'll be a hero. All will see your
value then, even the Ludlucks. Paragon?"

Clef crept out from behind Brashen. He slipped up to the ship and shyly set a hand to his planking. He looked up at the still figurehead above him. "Sometimes," he said earnestly, "Y'ave t'be yer own fam'ly. When yer all at's left ov et."

Paragon did not speak.

THE *CROSSPATCH* WAS AS PRIME A CATCH AS ANYTHING HE'D EVER TAKEN. A rare elation filled Kennit as he was hoisted onto her deck. Etta was waiting for him, to hand him his crutch. There was a double spice to this victory. Not only was it his first substantial catch since he had been healed, but Wintrow was here to witness it. He could almost feel the wonder in the boy at his heels. Well, let him gawk about at the spit-and-polish little vessel, and rethink his measure of Captain Kennit. Did young Wintrow think he was some one-legged rascal, fit only to catch stinking slaveships? Let him look about at this, and know Kennit for one of the best freebooters that had ever sailed the Inside Passage.

His satisfaction expressed itself as magnanimity toward the crew and Sorcor in particular. When the red-handed rogue hastened up to report to him, Kennit shocked him with a hearty clap on the shoulder and a "Well done! As nice a bit of piracy as I've ever seen! Any hostages?"

Sorcor grinned, elated at such praise. "Just ship's officers, Captain. It was like you said it would be; the others were as much fighters as sailors. None of them wanted to lay down weapons and take up with us. Gave them a chance twice, I did. Told them, yield, we'll let you sign articles with us. But they wouldn't. Damn shame, too. There was some fine fighters aboard, but the only ones left are the ones who came here with me." Sorcor grinned at his own joke.

"The ship's officers, Sorcor?"

"Confined below. Their mate took a couple bad knocks to the head before he'd go down, but he'll be fine. There's a pretty tally of other loot, too. The slaves are okay. Some are a bit rattled at the sudden change, but they'll come round."

"Losses?" Kennit stumped along briskly.

Sorcor's grin faded. "Heavier than we expected, sir. These were fighters, and they went down blades in hands. We lost Clifto, Marl and Burry. Kemper's short an eye. A few of the others took minor damage. Opal got his face laid open to his teeth. He's wild with the pain; I sent him back to the *Marietta* already. He was screaming something awful."

"Opal." Kennit considered a moment. "Have him sent over to *Vivacia*. Wintrow will do what he can with him in a bit. Lad has a knack for healing. I notice you've made no mention of yourself, Sorcor."

The big pirate grinned and made a deprecatory gesture at his bloodied left sleeve. "Two swords to his one and he still managed to cut me. I'm ashamed of myself."

"Nevertheless, we'll have it seen to. Where's Etta? Etta! See to Sorcor's arm, there's a good lass. Wintrow, you'll come with me. Let's take a quick look at what we've won today."

It was not a quick look. Kennit deliberately led the boy through every hold. He showed him tapestries and rugs rolled and wrapped in canvas for the journey. He showed him casks of coffee beans and chests of tea, thick ropes of dream herbs coiled in stoppered clay pots and glistening spools of thread in gilt, red and purple. All of this, Kennit explained to him, was the fruit of slavery. Pretty as they might be, they had been bought with blood. Did Wintrow think it right that men such as Avery and his backers be allowed to keep their ill-gotten gains? "As long as slavery is profitable, men will traffic in it. Greed was what brought your own father into this game. It was his downfall. I intend to see that it is the downfall of all who trade in human flesh."

Wintrow nodded slowly. Kennit was not sure if he was completely convinced of the captain's sincerity. Perhaps that didn't matter. As long as he could cite righteous reasons for piracy and battle, the boy would have to agree with him. That would make it easier to sway the ship to his will. He threw an arm around Wintrow's shoulders and suggested, "Let's go back to Vivacia. I wanted you to see this, and hear from Sorcor himself that we offered those wretches a chance to live. What more could we have done, eh?"

It was the perfect endnote. He should have known it was too good to last. As he and Wintrow emerged onto the deck, three female slaves hurried toward him. Before they could reach him, Etta stepped in front of them, stopping them with her hand on the hilt of her blade. They cowered together as she stared at them. Etta spoke to Kennit. "Bit of a problem here. These three are insisting they don't want to be freed. They want to be ransomed with the captain and mate."

"And why is that?" Kennit asked in cool but civil tones. He ran his eyes over them. They were all comely women, young and smooth-skinned. Their slave tattoos were tiny pale things, barely visible in the sunlight.

"The stupid bitches think they'd rather go on being slaves than have to find their own lives in Divvytown. Used to being rich men's pets, they are."

"I'm a poet, not a whore," one woman broke in angrily. "Captain Avery came to Jamaillia City to buy me especially for Sep Kordor. He is a wealthy noble and well known as a fair-handed master. If I go to him, he will provide for me and let me pursue my art. If I go with you, who knows what I must do to support myself? Even if I continue to compose, who will be my audience, save thieves and cut-throats in a backwater scum-town?"

"Maybe you'd rather sing for the serpents?" Etta suggested sweetly. She drew her blade and touched the tip lightly to the woman's belly above her navel. The poet refused to flinch. She gave her head a shake and stared at Kennit instead.

"And you two . . . are you poets also?" Kennit asked lazily. They shook their heads.

"I weave tapestries," one replied huskily.

"I am a body servant, skilled in massage and the lesser healings," the other said when Kennit fixed his eyes on her.

"And . . . let me guess . . . all of you are for the Sep whoever . . . the very rich man with many servants?" Kennit's jovial tone woke an answering sparkle in Etta's eyes. She casually put more pressure on her blade, to nudge the first one back into line with the others. The other two slaves nodded.

"There, you see." Kennit turned away from them, dismissing them with a wave of his hand. "That is what slavery does, Wintrow. A rich man buys their talents for his own glory. He buys them for money, and they do not even know they are whores. Not one has enough pride to speak her own name. They have become a part of their master already."

"What shall I do with them?" Etta called after him as he limped away.

He gave a small sigh. "They wish to be slaves. Put them with the others to be ransomed. Sep Kordor bought them once: he may as well buy them again." Inspiration struck Kennit. "Whatever they bring in ransom, we will divide amongst those who have chosen freedom. It will give them a better start." Etta nodded in slow consternation before she herded her charges away. Kennit turned to Wintrow at his side. "You see, I do not force people to my way of thinking. I won't force you, nor Vivacia. I think you are already coming to see that I am not the wicked pirate you supposed me to be."

As they strolled toward the rope chair that would return Kennit to the *Vivacia*'s boat, he asked Wintrow, "Have you ever imagined what it would be like to be captain of your own ship? A sweet little vessel like this, perhaps?"

Wintrow looked around before he answered. "She's a lovely ship. But, no, my heart does not lie in that direction. Given my freedom, I'd still return to my monastery."

"Your freedom? Wintrow! The tattoo on your face means nothing to me. Do you still consider yourself a slave?" Kennit feigned astonishment.

"No. A tattoo does not make me a slave," Wintrow agreed. He closed his eyes tightly for a moment. "It is my blood that binds me to Vivacia almost as firmly as chains. The bond between us grows stronger with every passing day. I think that perhaps, I could still leave her and find completeness in a life dedicated to Sa. But that would be a selfish act, one that would leave her forever hollowed by my absence. I do not think I could find serenity, knowing that I had left her."

Kennit cocked his head. "And you do not think she could ever accept me in your stead? For I only want what will make the both of you happy. Your monastery for you, if it can be managed without destroying the ship's spirit."

Wintrow shook his head slowly. "It would have to be someone of my blood. Someone who shares a family tie with the ship. Only that could keep her from going mad at the abandonment."

"I see," Kennit said pensively. "Well. That does leave us in a fix, doesn't it?" He patted the boy's shoulder comfortingly. "Perhaps I shall be able to think of something that would make us all happy."

THE WATER MOVING AGAINST THE HULL MADE A PLEASANT SOUND. *VIVACIA* was underway once more, flanking the *Crosspatch* with *Marietta*. Kennit wanted all three ships well away from the ambush site. Kennit had told Etta that ransom was more swiftly paid when preceded by uncertainty. The *Crosspatch* would simply disappear for a time. He would take the ship to Divvytown first, to show off his prize and his captives. In a month or two, he would arrange for word to be sent to Chalced that the ship and the survivors could be ransomed. The cargo he would dispose of himself. Etta had already helped herself to some of it. She smoothed the fabric that lay across her lap, marveling yet again at its texture before putting more thread on her needle.

The night was dark around the ships now. Kennit himself was on the wheel. Etta tried not to be annoyed at that. After all the time he had spent talking with the ship earlier today, it seemed as if he could rest now. It had been a long day for all of them. She herself had sewn up Sorcor's arm. The big man had sat still, teeth clenched in a grin of pain as she closed the long slash up his arm. She didn't enjoy such work, but at least he hadn't been screaming like poor Opal.

They had brought Opal over to the *Vivacia* to heal him. He'd struggled as they pinned him down on the foredeck as if they were going to flog him. A sword cut had laid open his cheek and nose to the bone. The gash had to be stitched closed if he was ever going to eat normally again. Evening was falling; they hung a lantern and the light fell upon him in a circle. There had been a surgeon on the *Crosspatch* among the slaves. At Wintrow's earnest request, Kennit had sent for him as well. Opal would not allow anyone to touch the wound. When Wintrow tried to hold the flesh together for the surgeon to stitch, the boy had shrieked and thrown his head about so wildly they had given it up. The surgeon had decided they must bleed him to ease the force of the pain, and this he had done until Opal had subsided. Etta had watched for a time whilst Kennit had spent the time explaining the process to the ship. The pain the boy endured was necessary: he could not be healed without it. Kennit compared it to the necessary killing he did in his effort to rid these waters of slavers. Wintrow had scowled at the words, but his task of catching Opal's blood had kept him busy. He had been very conscientious about it, insisting that canvas be put down thickly to keep even a drop from staining the liveship's decks. Eventually Opal's hoarse cries of pain subsided to muted little sighs and they took up their needles to make the boy's face whole again. He would never be as pretty as he had been, but he would be able to eat. It had been Opal's first time to be part of a boarding party. Bad luck had caught him, that was all.

Etta finished the last looping stitches of the hem. She bit off the thread, stood up and unfastened her skirt. It fell to the floor around her feet in a scarlet puddle. She stepped into her new creation, drew it up and fastened it at her waist. She did not know the proper name for this fabric. It had a crisp texture, crinkling deliciously under her hands as she smoothed it. It was a cedar green, but when she moved, it caught the lamplight in watermarks on the fabric, making the color ripple gently. The feel of the cloth pleased her the most. She ran her hands over it again, sleeking it against her hips. It made a slight crackling sound. Kennit would like it. He could appreciate sensation, at those times when he let himself focus on it.

Not that those times had been as frequent lately as she could hope for. She looked into the glass in his cabin and shook her head at herself. Ungrateful woman. It had not been that long since he was flat on his back, burning with fever. She should be grateful that he had recovered his manly appetites at all. She had heard that some never did after they had been maimed. She picked up a brush and drew it through her thick hair, sleeking it down. She was letting it grow longer. Soon it would be to her shoulders. She thought of his hands in her hair and his weight upon her, and felt her blood stir. When she had been a whore, she had never imagined she would come to this. Longing for a man's touch, rather than wishing they would just get on with it and finish. Then again, she had never imagined that she would feel jealous of a ship.

Now that was foolishness. She lifted her chin to put scent on her throat. She sniffed it critically. This was a new fragrance, also taken from the Crosspatch just today. Spicy and sweet. She decided it would do. She resolved to have more faith in Kennit. Didn't he have enough on his mind, without her giving in to feelings of jealousy? Foolish jealousy at that. It was a ship, not a woman.

She drifted about the cabin, tidying after Kennit. He was always drawing or writing something. Sometimes she watched him, when he allowed it. The skill fascinated her. His pen moved so swiftly, scratching down the precise marks. She paused to look at some of the scrolls before she rolled them and moved them to his chart table. How did he remember what all the little marks meant? It was a man's skill, she supposed. From the deck outside, she heard Brig's voice raised in command. Shortly thereafter, she heard the anchor going down. So they would stop for the night. Good.

She left the cabin and went looking for Kennit. She made her way to the foredeck. Wintrow sat cross-legged on the deck by Opal, keeping vigil with him. She looked down on the injured ship's boy. The stitches had drawn the edges of the cut together. That was all that could be said for their work. She crouched down to touch his brow. As she did so, her skirts crinkled pleasantly around her. "He feels chilled to me," she observed.

Wintrow glanced up at her. He was paler than Opal. "I know." He snugged a blanket more closely about his patient. More to himself than to her, he added, "He seems so weak. I am sure the surgeon did what was best. I wish the night was warmer."

"Why not take him below, away from the night chill?"

"I think he takes more good from being here than he would from being below."

She cocked her head at him. "You believe your ship has healing powers?"

"Not on the body. But she lends strength to his spirit, and helps it heal the body."

She straightened up slowly, but remained looking down on him. "I thought that was what your Sa did," she observed.

"It is," he agreed.

She could have mocked him then, asking him if he still needed a god if he had this ship. Instead, she suggested, "Go get some sleep. You look exhausted."

"I am. But I'm going to sit with him tonight. It doesn't seem right to leave him alone."

"Where did the surgeon go?"

"Over to the *Marietta*. There are other injured men there. He's done what he could do here. Now it is up to Opal."

"And your ship," she could not resist adding. She glanced about the foredeck. "Have you seen Kennit?"

Wintrow glanced toward the figurehead. It took her a moment to pick out his silhouette, for he shared a shadow with Vivacia. "Oh," she said quietly. She did not usually seek him out when he was talking to the ship. But having asked after him aloud, she could not very well just walk away. Trying to appear casual, she joined him at the bow rail. For a time, she did not speak. He had selected a small cove in one of the lesser islands for their anchorage. The *Crosspatch* rocked nearby, and the *Marietta* just beyond her. They showed few lights, but those few zigzagged away in reflections on the water. The wind had died off to an insistent breeze that made a faint music in the rigging. So close to land, the smell of the trees and plants was as strong as the salt water. After a moment, she observed, "The attack went well today."

"Are you telling me that because you think I don't know it?" He put a small bite of sarcasm on his words.

"Will you do it again? Use that channel that way?"

"I might." His brief answer chilled her effort at conversation.

The ship was blessedly silent, but Etta still felt her presence as an intrusion. She wished they were on board the *Marietta*. There she could have contrived to move closer to him and make him aware of her. Here, the ship was like a duenna. Even in the privacy of the cabin, Etta felt her presence. She smoothed a hand down her skirt, taking pleasure in the crinkle and rustle of the fabric.

"Before we were interrupted," Vivacia said abruptly, "we were discussing plans for tomorrow."

"We were," Kennit conceded. "At first light, we sail for Divvytown. I need a good place to stash the *Crosspatch* until she is ransomed. And I wish to put the slaves aboard her onto land as soon as possible. So we shall start back for Divvytown."

They were ignoring her. Etta's jealousy simmered, but she refused to stalk off.

"And if we encounter other ships?" the ship continued.

"Then it will be your turn," Kennit said quietly.

"I'm not sure if I'm ready. I still don't know . . . all the blood. The suffering. Humans feel such pain."

Kennit sighed. "I suppose I should not have brought Opal aboard. I was worried about the boy and wanted him near me. I didn't think you would mind."

"I don't, really," Vivacia added hastily.

Kennit went on speaking as if he hadn't heard her. "I don't enjoy watching his pain, either. But what sort of a man would I be to turn away from it? Shall I turn aside from one who has taken hurt for my sake? For four years, my ship has been the only home that he has known. He wanted to be part of the boarding party today—Oh, how I wish Sorcor had stopped him! I know he did it to impress me." Kennit's voice choked with emotion. "Poor lad. Young as he is, he was still willing to risk everything for what he has come to believe in." His words came tighter as he said, "I fear I have been the death of him. If I had not undertaken this crusade . . ."

Etta could not help herself. She had never heard Kennit speak such words. She had never imagined he carried such a depth of pain inside him. She stepped close to him and took his hand. "Oh, Kennit," Etta said softly. "Oh, my dear, you cannot take it all upon yourself. You cannot."

For an instant, he stiffened as if affronted. The figurehead glared at her. Then Kennit turned and to her shock, he dropped his head down to rest it on her shoulder. "But if I do not?" he asked wearily. "Oh, Etta, if I do not take this on, who will?"

Her heart broke with tenderness for the strong man who suddenly leaned on her. She lifted her hand to the back of his head. His hair was silky under her touch as she stroked it. "It will come out right. You'll see. Many love you and will follow you. You must not take it all upon your own shoulders."

"Whatever would I do without them? I could not go on." His shoulders shook briefly, as if he suppressed a sob. He coughed instead.

"Captain Kennit," Vivacia said in dismay, "I did not mean that I don't share your ideals. I only said I was not sure if I was ready to completely—"

"It's all right. No, really, it's all right." His reply cut off the ship's even as his tone dismissed her words as mere courtesy. "We have only known one another a short time. It is far too soon for me to ask you to throw your fate in with mine. Good night, Vivacia." He drew in a long breath, let it out as a sigh. "Etta, my sweet. I fear my leg pains me tonight. Could you help me to our bed?"

"Of course." It touched her. "Bed would be wisest. There was some scented oil on the *Crosspatch*. I took some; I know how your crutch makes your back and shoulder ache. Let me warm the oil and rub them for you."

He leaned on her as she assisted him away from the railing. "Your faith in me gives me such strength, Etta," he confided to her. He stopped suddenly and she halted beside him, confused. With an odd deliberation, he took her chin in his hand and turned her face up to his. He leaned down and kissed her slowly. Sensation washed through her, not just the warm press of his lips on hers and his strong arms around her, but the openness of this demonstration of affection. He ran his hands over her, the fabric of her skirt crackling to his touch as he snugged her close to him. He had placed her on a pinnacle for all to see his feelings as he kissed her. She felt glorified by it. He broke the kiss at last, but kept his arms around her. She trembled like a virgin.

"Wintrow," Kennit said quietly. Etta turned her head to find the young man looking up at them wide-eyed. "If anything happens with Opal, in the night. You will come to me right away?"

"Yes, sir," Wintrow whispered. His eyes traveled over both of them. Awe like hunger was in his eyes.

"Come, Etta. To our bed. I need the comfort of your closeness. I need to feel your belief in me."

To hear him speak such words aloud dizzied her. "I am beside you always," she assured him. She took his crutch from him to help him descend to the main deck.

"Kennit," Vivacia called after him. "I believe in you. In time, I will be ready."

"Of course you will," he said politely. "Good night, ship."

It took a year to cross the deck and another before she could close the door of their cabin behind them. "Let me warm the oil," she offered. But as she held it over the lamp, he limped over to her. He took the half-warmed oil from her hands and set it aside. For an instant, he frowned at her, his brows knit as if she presented a problem. She looked at him questioningly. He braced his crutch under his arm and lifted his hands to her throat. He caught his lower lip between his teeth as his large hands struggled with the fine ribbon that closed her shirt. She put her hands up to untie it for him, but with amazing gentleness, he set them aside. "Allow me," he said softly.

She shivered as he painstakingly negotiated the ties and buttons of her clothes. He drew off each separate piece and dropped it to one side. Never before had he done such a thing. When she stood naked before him, he took up the dish of oil. He dipped his fingers in it. "Like this?" he asked her uncertainly. His trailing fingers left shining tracks on her breasts and belly. She gasped at the lightness of his touch as he anointed her. He bent his head to kiss the side of her throat. He herded her gently toward the bed. She went willingly, though puzzled at this strange behavior.

He lay himself down beside her and touched her. He watched her face the whole time, taking note of her every reaction. He leaned close to her and whispered into her ear. "Tell me what to do, to please you." The admission shocked her. He had never done this before; she was the first woman he had ever tried to please. It made her catch her breath. Suddenly his boyish incompetence was sweepingly erotic. He offered no resistance as she took his hands and guided them on herself. Never had he offered her this dominance; it was heady.

He was not an apt pupil. His touch was hesitant, and as sweet as honeysuckle nectar. She could not look long at his intent face; she feared she would weep if she did, and he would not understand that. Instead, she surrendered herself to him. She watched him learn, guided by the sudden intake of her breath and the other small sounds that she could not control. A pleased smile began to hover around his mouth and his eyes grew brighter. She could almost see him learn that being able to bring her this much pleasure was a form of mastery. As the realization grew in him, his touch grew surer, but never rough. When he finally joined his body to hers, her release was immediate. Then came the tears she could not restrain. He kissed them away and began again.

She lost track of time. When her entire body was so satiated and so sensitized that his touch was almost painful, she spoke quietly. "Please, Kennit. Enough."

A slow smile came to his face. He eased away from her, letting cooler air touch them both. Suddenly he leaned over and flicked the tiny skull charm at her navel. She winced at the impact. The little ring of wizardwood that pierced her navel protected her from both diseases and pregnancy.

"Does this come off?" he asked her brusquely.

"It could," she conceded. "But I am careful. It has never . . ."

"And then you could get pregnant."

Her breath caught in her throat. "I could," she admitted guardedly.

"Good." He lay down beside her with a contented sigh. "I might want you to have a child. If I wanted you to have a baby, you'd do that for me, wouldn't you?"

Her throat clenched so she could scarcely speak. She whispered, "Oh, yes. Yes."

NIGHT WAS DEEP WHEN KENNIT AWAKENED TO A SCRATCHING AT THE DOOR. "What is it?" he called hoarsely. Beside him, the woman slept on deeply.

"It's Wintrow. Captain Kennit . . . sir. Opal's dead. He just . . . died."

That wasn't good. The whole idea had been that Opal would endure pain, and then survive it. He was supposed to be an object lesson for Vivacia. Kennit shook his head in the darkness. Now what? Could it be saved?

"Captain Kennit?" Wintrow sounded desperate.

Kennit pitched his voice low. "Don't question it, Wintrow. Accept it. That's all we can do. We are, after all, only men." He sighed loudly, and then put concern in his voice. "Go get some rest, lad. Tomorrow morning is soon enough to face this sorrow." He paused. "I know you tried, Wintrow. Don't feel you have failed me."

"Sir." After a moment, he heard the soft pad of the boy's feet as he moved away. Kennit lay back down. So. What would he say to the ship tomorrow? Something about a sacrifice, something that made Opal seem noble and inspiring instead of just dead. The words would come to him, if he just relaxed and trusted to his luck. He put his arms up above his head and leaned back on his pillows. His back ached abominably. He had had no idea that women had such stamina.

"Vivacia is roiling with jealousy. But that was what you intended, wasn't it?"

He turned slightly toward the charm on his wrist. "If you know so much, why do you ask so many questions?"

"To hear you admit what a cad you are. Do you feel anything at all for Etta? Are not you ashamed at all at what you do to her?"

Kennit was offended. "Ashamed? She has not suffered at my hands.

On the contrary, I gave her a night tonight that she will never forget." He stretched, trying to ease his aching muscles. "And at no small cost to myself," he added petulantly.

"Such a performance," the little wizardwood face muttered sarcastically. "Did you fear the ship would not know it if she did not cry out with pleasure? I assure you, Vivacia is keenly aware of you at all times. It was your efforts on Etta's behalf that scalded her, not any pleasure Etta took."

Kennit rolled over and spoke more softly. "So. How aware of the ship are you?"

"She guards against me," the charm admitted reluctantly. "But there is still much I can tell. She is far too large, and all around me. She cannot completely conceal her awareness from me."

"And Wintrow? Can you sense him through her? What does he feel tonight?"

"What? Do you need to know more than how he sounded when he came to bring you the news? He was devastated by Opal's death."

"Not about Opal's death," Kennit said impatiently. "I saw him watching us, when I kissed Etta in front of Vivacia. It surprised me. Does he have feelings for the whore?"

"Don't call her that!" the charm warned him in a low growl. "If you speak of her like that again, I shall tell you nothing."

"Does he find Etta attractive?" Kennit persisted doggedly.

The charm relented. "He is naïve. He admires her. I doubt he would presume to find her attractive." The small voice paused. "Your little display tonight set him thinking for a time. He will contrast that with Opal's death."

"An unfortunate coincidence," Kennit muttered. He fell silent, considering how he could make Wintrow more aware of Etta. He should have her wear more jewelry, he decided. Boys were always attracted to sparkly things. He would display her as an attractive possession.

"Why did you ask her about a baby tonight?" the charm demanded abruptly.

"A passing thought. A child might be useful. Much depends on how Wintrow develops."

The charm was baffled. "I don't understand what you are suggesting. I suspect if I did, I would find it repugnant."

"I don't see why," Kennit replied easily. He composed himself for sleep.

"How could a child be useful to you?" the charm demanded a few moments later.

"I won't be quiet until you answer me," it added when some silence had passed.

Kennit drew a weary breath and sighed it out. "A child would content the ship. If Wintrow becomes too intractable, if he interferes with me persuading the ship to obey me willingly, well, he could be replaced."

"With your own child, by Etta?" the charm asked incredulously.

Kennit chuckled sleepily. "No, of course not. Now you are being ridiculous." He stretched and turned his back to Etta. He curled up and closed his eyes. "Wintrow would have to father the child. So it would be of the ship's family." He gave a deep sigh of satisfaction, then frowned to himself. "I imagine a baby aboard would be a nuisance. It would be simpler if Wintrow learned to accept his fate. The boy has great potential. He thinks. I simply have to school him to think my way. Perhaps I shall take him to the Others' oracle. Perhaps they could persuade him it is his destiny."

"Let me speak to him instead," the charm offered. "Perhaps I could persuade him to kill you."

Kennit chuckled appreciatively and released himself into sleep.

CHAPTER TWENTY-ONE

Salvage

THE BREEZE OFF THE WATER WAS THE ONLY THING THAT MADE WORKING tolerable. The summer sun beat down from the cloudless sky. When Brashen looked out across the waves, the reflected light was dazzling. The brightness pounded spikes of pain into his brow. The only thing that made him scowl more deeply was the workmen moving lackadaisically, performing their tasks without energy or enthusiasm.

He stood braced on the slanting deck of the *Paragon*. He shut his eyes for a moment then re-opened them and tried to consider the task from a fresh perspective. The ship had been hauled out on the beach over a score of years ago. Abandoned and neglected, the elements had had their way with him. Were it not for his wizardwood construction, he would be no more than a skeleton. Storms and tides had conspired to push the *Paragon* to the limits of the high-tide line. The passage of years had heaped sand against his hull. He now lay with his keel toward the water, heeled over on the sandy beach. Only the very highest tides now touched him.

The solution was deceptively easy. The sand must be shoveled away. Timbers shoved under the hull would act as skids. Put a heavy counterweight on the top of his shattered main mast to lay him even further over on his side. At the highest tide at the end of the month, anchor a barge offshore. Run a line from the *Paragon* to the barge's stern windlass. With men on shore with levers to urge him down the skids and men on the barge working the windlass, the ship would slide on his side toward the water. The counterweight on his hull would keep him heeled over and allow him to float in shallower water. Once they got him into deeper water, they'd right him.

Then they would see what happened next.

Brashen sighed. A man could describe the whole operation in a breath or two. Then he could work for a solid week and be no closer to the solution.

All around the ship, men toiled with shovels and barrows. Heavy timbers had been floated in on yesterday's high tide. Securely roped together, they awaited use on the beach. Near them was another raft of roller logs. If all went well, eventually *Paragon* would ride them down the beach to be re-launched. If all went well. Some days that seemed like a vain hope.

The new crew of workmen moved sluggishly in the hot sun. Hammers rang in the summer air. There was rock under the sand. In some places it could be chipped away to allow the skids under the ship. In others, the workers were trying to set levers under the hull. Then there would be a massive effort of lifting, so that other levers could be grounded even more deeply. Each shifting placed new wracks on the old vessel.

After all the years of lying on his side, there was bound to be some shifting of timbers and planks. From what Brashen could see, the hull was not too badly racked, but the ship would have to be lifted before he could be sure. Once he was upright and floating free . . . and he prayed *Paragon* would float freely . . . the real work would begin. The entire hull would have to be trued up before it could be re-caulked. Then a new mast would have to be stepped. . . . Brashen abruptly stopped the chain of thought. He could not think that far ahead, or he would become completely discouraged. One day and one task at a time were all his aching head could handle.

He absentmindedly ran his tongue about inside his lower lip, feeling for a piece of cindin that wasn't there. Even the deep sores from the addictive drug were starting to heal now. His body seemed able to forget the drug faster than his spirit. He longed for cindin with an intensity as relentless as thirst. He'd traded away his earring for a stick two days ago, and regretted it. Not only had it set him back in forgetting the drug, but the cindin had been poor quality, no more than a tease of relief. Still, if he'd had even a shard of silver to his name, he would not have been able to resist the urge. The only coins he possessed were those in the bag Ronica Vestrit had entrusted to him. Last night he'd awakened drenched in a cold sweat, his head pounding. He'd sat up until dawn, trying to rub the cramps from his hands and feet while he stared at the dwindling purse. He'd wondered how wrong it would be to take a few coins to set himself right. The cindin would help him to stay alert longer and have more energy for this task. Towards dawn, he had opened the bag and counted the coins out into his hand. Then he had put them back and gone into the galley, to brew and drink yet another pot of chamomile tea.

Amber, sitting there and whittling, had wisely said nothing. He was still amazed at how easily she had adapted to his presence. She accepted his coming and going without comment. She still occupied the captain's cabin. Time enough to make that space his own when the *Paragon* floated free once more. For now, he had slung his hammock in the tween decks. Living in the canted ship became more challenging daily as the angle of the deck grew ever sharper.

"Paragon, no!"

Amber's voice, raised in disbelief, coincided with the immense crack of a timber. Voices cried out in alarm. Brashen scrambled forward, arriving on the foredeck just in time to hear a timber strike ringingly against a rocky outcrop of the beach. All around Paragon, the workers were retreating from the ship. They called warnings to one another, pointing not just at the thrown timber but at the trench it had made in the beach when it landed. Without a word, his face expressionless, Paragon refolded his thick arms on his muscled chest. He stared blindly out across the water.

"Damn you!" Brashen cried out with great feeling. He glared around at the workers. "Who let him get hold of that timber?"

A white-faced oldster replied. "We was setting it in place. He reached down and snatched it away from us. . . . How in Sa did he know it was there?" The old man's voice was full of superstitious dread.

Brashen clenched his hands into fists. If it had been the ship's first display of sulkiness, he might have been surprised. But every day since they began, he had created one delay after another. His displays of temper and strength made it difficult for Brashen to keep workers. Through them all, Paragon had spoken not one civil word to Brashen.

Brashen leaned over the railing. From the corner of his eye, he spotted Althea, just arriving at the ship for the day's work. She looked puzzled at the frozen scene. "Get back to work!" he bellowed at the men who were gawking and nudging one another. He pointed at the thrown timber. "Pick that up and put it back in place."

"Not me!" one worker declared. He wiped sweat from his face, then tossed his mallet to the sand. "He could have killed me, just then. He can't see where he's throwing stuff, even if he did care. And I don't think he does. He's killed before, everyone knows that. My life is worth more than you're paying me for a day's work. I'm gone. I want my pay."

"Me, too."

"Same for me."

Brashen clambered over the railing, then dropped lightly to the beach. He didn't let his face show how the pain shot to the top of his skull. He advanced on the men in a show of aggression, praying he wouldn't have to back it up. He thrust his face into that of the first man who had spoken. "You want to get paid, you stick around and finish out your day's work. You walk now, you don't get a copper." He scowled round at the lot of them and hoped his bluff would work. If these ones walked, he didn't know where he would find others. They were the dregs of the taverns, men who would only work long enough to earn coins for the night's drinking. He had had to offer them better wages than they could get anywhere else to lure them out to the bad-luck ship. As the men about him muttered discontentedly, he barked, "Take it or leave it. I didn't hire you for half a day's work, and I'm not paying for half a day's work. Get under that timber, now."

"I'll work," one of the men offered. "But not up here, not where he can reach me or crush me with a thrown timber. I won't do that."

Brashen spat in disgust. "Work on the aft keel then, lionheart. Amber and I will take the bow, if none of you here has the courage to do so."

A slow and evil smile spread across Paragon's face. "Some prefer a quick death, some a slow one. Some don't care if their sons are born legless and blind like this cursed ship. Pick up your mallets and work on. What care you about what happens tomorrow?" In a lower voice he added, "Why should you expect to live that long?"

Brashen had spun to confront the ship. "Are you talking to me?" he demanded. "All your days of silence, and then you say that to me?"

For an instant, the *Paragon*'s face changed. Brashen could not say what emotion was displayed there, but it froze his soul and squeezed his heart. An instant later, it was replaced with a supercilious stare. The figurehead took a breath and settled into stillness.

Brashen's temper snapped. The brightness of the day blazed inside his skull, igniting the pain to unbearable heat. He snatched up one of the buckets of drinking water that the workers had left near the bow. With every ounce of strength he had, he dashed it in Paragon's face.

The entire ship shuddered and Paragon gave an angry roar. Water dripped from his beard and ran down his chest. Below him on the sand, Brashen dropped the now-empty bucket. He roared at the ship, "Don't pretend you can't hear me. I'm your captain, damn it, and I won't tolerate insubordination from you nor anyone else. Get this through your wooden head, Paragon. You're going to sail. One way or another, I'm dragging you out into the water again and putting canvas on your bones. Now you have a choice, but you'd better choose fast, because I am all out of patience. You can go out of here listing and wallowing, sulking like a brat, and the whole damn fleet will watch you go that way. Or you can lift your head up and sail out of here like you don't give a damn about anything that anyone has ever said about you. You have a chance to prove them all wrong. You can make them eat every foul thing they've ever said about you. You can sail out of here like a Bingtown liveship and we'll go give some pirates a bloody bad time. Or you can prove they were right all along and that I was the fool. I'm telling you this because that is the only thing you have a choice in. You don't get to decide whether you're going or not, because I'm the captain and I already decided that. You're a ship, not a flowerpot. You were meant to sail and it is what we are going to do. Are we clear on that?"

The ship clenched his jaws and crossed his arms on his chest. Brashen spun about and snatched up a second bucket. With a grunt of effort, he dashed it up into the figurehead's face. Paragon recoiled, sputtering with shock.

"Is that clear?" Brashen bellowed. "Answer me, damn you!"

Around him, the workmen were transfixed with awe. They waited for him to die.

Althea had gripped Amber's arm. The bead-maker's eyes blazed with outrage. Only that hold kept her from charging out between Brashen and the ship. With a sign, Althea warned her to keep silent. Amber clenched her fists, but kept her tongue still.

"It's clear," Paragon finally replied. The words were clipped and unrepentant. But he had answered. Brashen clung to that tiny triumph.

"Good," Brashen replied in a surprisingly calm voice. "I leave you to think about your choice. I think you can make me proud. I have to get back to my work. I intend that when you sail, you'll look as sharp as the first time you were put into water." He paused. "Maybe we can make them eat every slur they ever uttered about me, too."

He turned back to Amber and Althea with a grin. Neither woman returned it. After a moment, it faded from his face. He took a breath and shook his head in resignation. In a low voice, he spoke only to them. "I'm doing my best with him, the only way I know how. I'm sailing. I'll do or say whatever I must to get this ship in the water." He glared at their disapproving silence. "Maybe you two need to decide how badly you want this to happen. But while you're thinking, we're the bow work crew. Maybe tonight I can hire some new workers who aren't afraid of him, but I can't waste daylight on it now." He pointed at the flung timber. "We're putting that back in place." In the quietest voice he could summon, he added, "If he thinks you're afraid of him . . . if he thinks he can get away with behaving like this . . . we are all lost. Paragon included."

It was the start of a long, sweaty day. The skid timbers were massive. In a fit of perversity, Brashen spared neither of the women nor himself. He worked in the sun until he felt his brain boiling inside his skull. They dug away dry sand and hauled it away. The rocks they encountered were always wedged together in layers, or just slightly larger than one person could move. He drove his body relentlessly, punishing it for its unceasing itch for cindin. If either Althea or Amber had asked for quarter, he could have given it. But Althea was as stubborn as he was, and Amber amazingly tenacious. They matched the pace he set. More, as they worked under the nose of the figurehead, they included Paragon in the conversation, ignoring his stubborn silence.

The efforts of two mere women and their lack of fear seemed to shame the hired workmen. First one, and then another came to join them at the bow. When Amber's friend Jek walked out from town to see what they were doing, she gave them a couple of hours of her strong back as well.

Clef came and went, underfoot as often as he was helpful. Brashen snarled at the boy as frequently as he praised him, but his stint as a slave had given him a thick skin. He worked doggedly, handicapped more by his size than any lack of skill. He had all the makings of a good hand. Against his conscience, Brashen would probably take him along when they sailed. It was wrong, but he needed him.

The other workmen on the ship watched them surreptitiously. Perhaps it shamed them to see the women working where they had refused to go. They stepped up the pace of their own labors. Brashen had never expected that such a sorry lot of dock scrapings would have any pride left. He seized the opportunity to push them harder.

THE AFTERNOON WAS SWELTERING INSIDE THE MORNING ROOM. OPENING the windows hadn't helped; there wasn't a breath of air stirring. Malta plucked at the collar of her dress, pulling the damp fabric away from her skin.

"I remember when we used to drink iced tea here. And your cook would make those tiny lemon pastries." Delo sounded more fretful about Malta's reduced circumstances than Malta herself. In fact, it rather irritated Malta to have her friend so pointedly noticing all the deficiencies in her home.

"Times have changed," Malta pointed out wearily. She walked over to the open window and leaned out to look at the neglected rose garden. The bushes were blooming voluptuously and sprawling, rejoicing in their lack of discipline. "Ice is expensive," she pointed out.

"My papa bought two blocks yesterday," Delo said negligently. She fanned herself. "Cook is making ices for dessert tonight."

"Oh. How nice." Malta's voice was void of expression. How much of this did Delo expect her to take? First, she had shown up in a new dress with a fan and a hat to match. The fan was made of spice paper, and gave off a pleasant scent when she used it. It was the newest vogue in Bingtown. Then Delo hadn't even asked how the ship was coming along, or if they'd received a ransom note yet. "Let's go out in the shade," Malta suggested.

"No, not yet." Delo glanced around the room as if servants might be spying. Malta almost sighed. They didn't have servants to eavesdrop. With a great show of secrecy, Delo pulled a small purse from inside the waistband of her skirt. In a lowered voice, she confided, "Cerwin sent you this, to help you in these troubled times."

For an instant, Malta could almost share Delo's enjoyment of this dramatic moment. Then it fluttered away from her. When she had first learned of her father's abduction, it had seemed exciting and fraught with tragedy. She had thrown herself into exploiting the situation to the limit of its theatrical possibilities. Now the days had passed, one after another, full of anxiety and stress. No good news had come. Bingtown had not rallied to their side. People had expressed sympathy, but only as a courtesy. A few had sent flowers with notes of commiseration, as if her father were already dead. Despite her plea to Reyn that he come to her, he had not. No one had rallied to her.

Day after day had ground by in deadly, boring desperation. It had slowly come to Malta that this was real, and that it might be the death knell for her family's fortune. She could not sleep for thinking of it. When she did fall asleep, her dreams were disturbing ones. Something stalked her, determined to bend her to its will. The dreams she could remember were like evil sendings from someone determined to break her hopes. Yesterday morning she had awakened with a cry, from a nightmare in which her father's wasted body washed up on the beach. He could be dead, she suddenly realized. He could already be dead and all these efforts for nothing. She had lost spirit that day, and had not been able to recover hope or purpose since then.

She took the little purse from Delo's hand and sat down. Her friend's discontented expression showed that she had expected a more passionate response. She feigned examining it. It was a little cloth purse, extensively embroidered and closed with gilt strings. Cerwin had probably bought it especially for this gift. She tried to take some pleasure in that. But thoughts of Cerwin were not as exciting as they had once been. He hadn't kissed her.

She still hadn't recovered from that disappointment. But what had followed was even worse. She had believed that men had power. The very first time she ever asked one to use that power for her, he failed her. Cerwin Trell had promised her he would help, but what had he done? At the Trader meeting, he had stared at her most improperly. Half the people there must have noticed it. Did he get up and speak when Althea was asking the Traders to help? Had he nudged his father to speak? No. All he had done was make calf eyes at her. No one had helped her. No one would help her.

"*Free me and I will aid you. I promise you this.*" The words of the dragon from the dream she had shared with Reyn suddenly echoed in her head. She felt a twinge of pain, as if a string pulled tight between her temples had suddenly become tauter. She wished she could just go and lie down for a time. Delo cleared her throat, abruptly reminding Malta that she was just sitting there, holding Cerwin's gift-purse.

Malta tugged open the neck of the bag and spilled the contents out into her lap. There were some coins in it, and a few rings. "Cerwin is going to be in big trouble if Papa finds out he gave those rings to you," Delo told Malta accusingly. "That little silver one is one Mama gave him for doing well at his lessons." She crossed her arms and looked at Malta disapprovingly.

"He won't find out," Malta told her bleakly. Delo was such a child. The rings were scarcely worth the trouble of selling them. No doubt, Delo thought this little bag a magnificent gift, but Malta knew better. She had spent the entire morning on the household books, and knew that what was in this purse was barely enough to hire two good workmen for a week. She wondered if Cerwin had as little knowledge of finances as Delo did. Malta hated helping to keep the accounts, but she understood money far better now. She recalled the rush of chagrin she had felt when she discovered just how foolishly she had spent the coins her father had given her. They should have been enough for a dozen dresses. Those small gold pieces had been worth far more than was in this bag. She wished she had them back now. They would have gone much further toward getting that ship off the sand than what Cerwin had given her. The boy simply did not grasp the size of her problem. It was as disappointing as the lack of a kiss.

"Why didn't he say anything at the meeting?" she wondered aloud. "He knows what is at risk. He knows what it means to me. But he did nothing."

Delo was huffy. "He did. He did everything he could. He talked to Papa at home. Papa said it was a very complicated situation and that we could not get involved."

"What is complicated?" Malta demanded. "My father has been kidnapped and we must go and rescue him. We need help!"

Delo folded her arms on her chest and cocked her head. "That is a Vestrit matter. The Trell family cannot solve it for you. We have trading interests of our own to maintain. If we invest money in a search for your father, what will the return be for us?"

"Delo!" Malta was shocked. The pain she felt was genuine. "We are talking about my father's life . . . the only one who truly cares what becomes of me! This isn't about money and profit!"

"Everything eventually comes down to a profit," Delo declared harshly. Then her expression suddenly softened. "That is what my father said to Cerwin. They argued, Malta. It frightened me. The last time I remember two men shouting at each other was when Brashen lived at home. He used to argue with my father all the time. . . . At least, he would stand there like a stick while my father roared at him. A lot of it I don't remember. I was little. They always sent me out of the room. Then, one day, my father told me that Cerwin was my only brother now. That Brashen would never be coming home again." Delo's voice faltered. "The arguing stopped." She swallowed. "It's not like your family, Malta. You all argue and shout and say terrible things, but then you hold together. No one is thrown out forever, not even your Aunt Althea. My family isn't like that. There isn't room in my family for that." She shook her head. "If

Cerwin had kept arguing, I'm afraid I'd have no brothers at all now." She looked at Malta in a direct appeal. "Please. Don't ask my brother to help you with this. Please."

The plea rattled Malta. "I'm . . . sorry," she said awkwardly. She had never thought that her experiments with Cerwin would affect anyone besides him. Lately, everything seemed so much bigger and far-flung than it once had. When she had first heard that her father was taken, it had not seemed real. She had used it as an opportunity to indulge her sense of the tragic. She had play-acted the role of a stricken daughter, but she had really believed that any day at all, her father would come home. Pirates could not really have taken her papa. Not brave, handsome Kyle Haven. Nevertheless, slowly it had become real. At first, she had feared that he would never come home to make her life better. Only now was she realizing he might never come home at all.

She scooped the coins and rings back into the purse. She offered it to Delo. "You should take this back to Cerwin. I don't want him to get in trouble." It also wasn't enough to do her any good, but she wouldn't mention that.

Delo looked horrified. "I can't. He'd know that I'd said something to you. He'd be furious with me. Please, Malta, you have to keep it, so I can tell him I gave it to you. Also, he asked me to ask you to write him a note back or send him a token."

Malta just looked at her. Sometimes, lately, she felt like she had run out of ideas and plans. She knew she should stand and pace a turn about the room. She knew she should say something like, "There are so few things left I can call mine . . . most of them I have sold to raise money to rescue my father." At one time, that would have seemed so fine and romantic. She had felt like a heroine in a story when she had emptied her jewelry box onto the table that first day. She had put her bracelets and rings and necklaces out and then sorted them into piles as Grandmother and Aunt Althea and her own mother were doing. It had seemed like a ritual for women. The little muttered comments were like prayers. *This is gold, this is silver, this is old-fashioned, but the stones are good.* And all the little stories they had told one another, stories they already knew. "I remember when Daddy gave me this, the very first ring I ever had, look, it won't even go on my little finger now." Or, Grandmother saying, "These still smell so lovely," and Althea adding, "I remember the day Papa chose those for you. I remember asking him why he was buying perfume gems, when he didn't like Rain Wild goods, and he said you wanted them so badly he didn't care." They shared stories as they sorted out gold and jewels that were suddenly memories of better times. But no one had flinched, no one had held anything back, not even their tears. Malta had even wanted to put out the things Reyn had given her, but they had all told her that she must keep them, for if she eventually refused his suit, then they all must be returned. That morning was both dismal and shining in her memory. Odd. That day she had felt more like a woman grown than any time before then.

But in the days since then, there had been only the reality of the empty jewelry box gaping at her from her dresser. She had things she could have worn, a child's ornaments, enameled pins and shell beads, as well as the things from Reyn, but somehow she could not wear them while the other women of her family went ringless and unornamented. She rose and went to the small writing desk. She found a pen, ink and a sheet of thin paper. She wrote quickly. "Dear friend, thank you so much for your expression of caring in our time of need. With great sincerity." The words reminded her of the correct thank-you notes she had helped pen to those who had sent flowers to them. She signed it with her initials, then folded it and sealed it with a drop of wax. As she gave it to Delo, she wondered at herself. Even a week ago, she would have carefully composed any missive she sent Cerwin. She would have filled it with innuendoes and words that seemed to say a great deal more than they did. She managed a sad smile. "The words are bland. I feel much more than I dare commit to paper."

There. That would leave him some hopes. It was all she had the energy for on this hot day.

Delo took it and slipped it into her cuff. She looked around the room. "Well," she said disappointedly. "I suppose I should go home."

"I'm not much company today," Malta admitted. "I'll walk you out."

At the door, a pony trap and a man to drive it awaited Delo. That, too, was new. The Trell family was obviously preparing to present Delo as a young woman at the midsummer ball. Malta would be presented at the same ball. She and her mother were using the fabric from several older dresses in the house to create a new gown for her. Her slippers would be new, as would her headpiece and her fan. At least, so she hoped. Nothing was certain anymore. She imagined she would ride there in Trader Restart's old carriage. It was yet another humiliation that she could not face just now.

Delo hugged her and kissed her on the cheek at the door. She did it as if it were a trick she had recently learned. It probably was, Malta reflected bitterly. Many of the young girls of the better families received instruction in the finer points of etiquette before they were presented. Another small thing that Malta would never have. She shut the door while Delo was still waving farewells with her new fan. It was a petty revenge, but she felt better for it.

She took the small bag of coins and the rings to her room. She spilled them out on her bed. They had not grown. She looked at it and wondered how she could make this small addition to their ship fund without explaining where it came from. She frowned. Could she do nothing right?

She scooped the coins and baubles into the bag and tucked it into her blanket chest. She flung herself down on her bed to think.

The day was too hot and there was too much work to do. There was weeding in the kitchen garden, and herbs to gather, tie and hang. Her dress for the Summer Ball was still only half finished. She had not the heart to work on it, not after seeing Delo's new finery. Malta was sure that everyone would know it was made over from old dresses. She recalled how she had dreamed of her first Summer Ball. She had visualized herself in an extravagant gown, entering on her father's arm. She smiled bitterly and closed her eyes. It was almost as if she were under a curse. Anything sweet, wonderful, and romantic that she ever imagined, she would never have.

She counted her disappointments drowsily. No lovely dress and carriage for the ball. No dashing sea-captain father to escort her. Cerwin had failed her; he didn't even know when to kiss a girl. Reyn had not come to her. She hated her life. All the problems were too big. She was trapped in a life she was helpless to change. The day was too hot. She was suffocating in its embrace. It was so stuffy.

She tried to roll over but there was not enough room. Perplexed, she tried to sit up. Her head thudded against a barrier. Her uplifted hands met only damp, shredded wood. The dampness, she suddenly realized, was from her own breath. She opened her eyes to blackness. She was trapped in here, trapped, and no one cared. She lifted frantic hands to press against whatever enclosed her. "Help me! Let me out of here! Someone help me!" She shoved against her boundaries, pushing with her hands, her elbows, her knees and feet. Nothing gave way. It only made the enclosure seem smaller. The only air she had to breathe was already warm and moist from her breath. She tried to scream, but there was not even enough air for that.

"It's a dream," she told herself. She forced herself to be very still. "This is a dream. I am safe in my own bed. All I have to do is wake up now. Wake up." She stretched and contorted her eye muscles, trying to open her eyes. She could not. There was not even enough room for her to bring her hands up to her face. She began to pant convulsively in fear. A whine escaped her.

"Do you see, now, why he must free me? Help me. Make him free me and I promise I will help you. I will bring back your father and the ship. All you have to do is make him free me."

She knew that voice. She had heard it echoing through her dreams since she had shared the dream with Reyn. "Let me out," she begged the dragon. "Let me wake up."

"Will you make him help me?"

"He says he cannot." Malta could scarcely find breath for the words. "I think he would if he could."

"Make him find a way."

"I can't." A second layer of darkness was closing in on her as she panted. She was going to faint. She'd suffocate in this dream. Could someone faint in a dream? Could she die in a dream? "Let me out!" she cried faintly. "Please. I have no control over Reyn! I can't make him do anything."

The dragon chuckled, a deep rich laugh. *"Don't be foolish. He is only a male. You and I, we are queens. We are destined to master our males. It is the proper balance of the world. Think about it. You know how to get what you want. Take it. Free me."*

Malta felt herself abruptly flung up into darkness. The boundaries around her were gone. She clawed for purchase but her outstretched hands found nothing. She tumbled through blackness while the wind screamed past her. She fell heavily onto a yielding surface.

She opened her eyes to her bedroom, to a hot summer day and bright light streaming in the open window. *"Remember."* Someone spoke the word right by her ear. She heard it. But no one was there.

EVENING FOUND THEY HAD DONE MORE THAN IN ANY TWO OTHER DAYS. Even so, Brashen wondered how many of the workmen would return tomorrow. He could not blame them. He no longer understood why he himself stayed on. It wasn't his ship at risk, nor his nephew. When he asked himself why he continued he came back to the negative that he had nothing better to do. The *Springeve* had vanished from the harbor the second night after he had jumped ship. No doubt Finney had smelled a rat, and decided to cut his losses and run. There was no going back to that life.

Seldom did he concede to himself that this was the only way he could be near Althea. Pride wouldn't let him. She showed him less attention than she paid Clef. At least she smiled at the boy. He stole a glance at her. Her hair was sweated to her skull. She wore loose white trousers and a roomy tunic of the same fabric. Sand clung to her garments and her damp skin. He watched her walk over to the water buckets. She drank deeply, then splashed water up on her face and neck. The ache of wanting her near choked him. He reminded himself that she was all but promised to Grag Tenira. Tenira wasn't a bad hand. He'd be a wealthy man some-day. Brashen tried to feel satisfaction for her. She could have done worse. She could have been content with a disinherited Trader's son. He shook his head and tossed his mallet to the sand. "That's a day!" he called abruptly. The light was fading anyway.

Althea and Amber retired to the galley while Brashen paid off the crew. Brashen lingered with his book and pen after the last workman had left, toting up his figures and shaking his head over them. Ronica Vestrit

had given him a free hand with the funds to restore the *Paragon*. Althea
had been surprised to find that his shipwright's knowledge extended far
beyond what she would have expected of a mate. He had taken satisfaction in her surprise, but it did not make his task any easier. He agonized
over the trade-off between the best quality of material and the best trades-
men to do the job. Often enough, he couldn't get the workmen he preferred anyway. The *Paragon*'s reputation was well established, and his
recent behavior confirmed it. Most of the shipwrights claimed they were
not superstitious but that their other customers would turn away a man
who had worked on such a ship. What excuse they gave didn't matter to
Brashen. The delay did. Time was their greatest enemy. With every passing day, the task of tracking *Vivacia* from where Brashen had last seen her
became more difficult. Moreover, the work must be timed to the tide. An
exceptionally high tide was expected at the end of the month; Brashen
hoped it would be the one to float the *Paragon*. The most frustrating part
was that much of the work they could reasonably do themselves could
only be done after the more massive tasks were completed. Each job
depended on the one before it.

By the time he went to join the women, they were no longer in the
galley. He followed the soft sounds of their voices and found them sitting
on the slanting stern of the ship. Side by side, legs dangling, they could
have been two ship's boys idling furtively. Amber had taken to binding
her honey-colored hair back in a tail. It was not a flattering change; the
bones of her cheeks and the line of her nose were too sharp to be feminine. In contrast, even with a smudge of tarry dirt down her cheek,
Althea's profile made his heart turn over. She was not softly feminine.
Instead, she was female in a cat-like way that was as much threat as it was
enticement. And she was unaware of it. He looked at her, and wished
fervently he had never touched her. It was not just that he had somehow
spoiled it so that she would not even meet his glance anymore. The worst
was that he could not look at her without recalling the taste of her skin
and the honesty of her body. He closed his eyes for a moment. Then he
opened them and made his way aft.

Amber and Althea both held teacups that steamed. A fat ceramic pot
sat between them with an extra cup beside it. Brashen poured a cup for
himself. He considered sitting down between them, then decided to
stand. Amber was staring out to sea. Althea was running her fingertip
around the rim of her cup and watching the waves. Their conversation
had died at his approach. Amber sensed the awkwardness. She glanced up
at him. "Early start again tomorrow?"

"No," Brashen said succinctly. He took a sip of his tea and added, "I
don't think so. I suspect I'll spend the morning hunting up new workers."

"Not again," Althea groaned. "What did I miss?"

Brashen took a breath as if to speak, then clamped his jaws and shook his head.

Althea rubbed her temples. "At least, he was talking to you again?" She offered the words to Amber hopefully.

"Not to us," Amber said dejectedly. "He had lots of things to say to the work crew, though. Mostly nasty whispered stuff, before he got onto how their children would be born without legs and blind, because they'd worked near a cursed ship." In bitter admiration, she added, "He was very descriptive."

"Well. That's creative. At least he didn't throw any more timbers after the first one."

"Maybe he's saving some for tomorrow," Brashen pointed out.

They shared a discouraged silence. Then Amber asked sadly, "Well. Have we given up, then?"

"Not quite yet. Let me finish this cup of tea while I ponder how hopeless it all is," Brashen replied. He frowned as he turned to Althea. "Where were you this morning, anyway?"

She didn't look at him as she answered. Her voice was cool. "Not that you have a right to ask, but I went to see Grag."

"I thought Tenira was still in hiding. Price on his head, and all that." Brashen's voice was very detached. He sipped his tea and looked at the water.

"He is. He found a way to send me word. I went to see him."

Brashen shrugged one shoulder. "Well, at least that solves one problem. When we run out of money, you can always turn him in to the Satrap's ministers. We can use the reward to hire still another work crew." He showed his teeth in a grin.

Althea ignored the remark to tell Amber, "Grag said he wished he could offer help to me, but his own situation makes everything difficult. His family got a fraction of what the *Ophelia*'s cargo was worth. And they have resolved not to trade in Bingtown or Jamaillia until the Satrap rescinds the unfair tariffs."

"Didn't the *Ophelia* sail a few days ago?" Brashen asked determinedly.

Althea nodded. "She did. Tomie thought it best to take her out of Bingtown Harbor before any more galleys arrived. The Satrap's tariff ministries have been making threats to seize the ship. They are now claiming that the Satrap can regulate where liveships trade, and that Rain Wild goods can be sold only in Bingtown or Jamaillia City. I doubt that they could enforce that, but Tomie saw no sense in waiting for trouble. The Tenira family will continue to battle them, but he won't put Ophelia in the middle of it."

"If it was me," Brashen said speculatively, "I'd take her up the Rain Wild River. Nothing except another liveship could follow her up there."

He cocked a head. "That's the plan, isn't it? Grag will be smuggled up-river on another liveship to rejoin them there. Am I right?"

Althea gave him a sidelong glance and a shrug.

Brashen looked offended. "You don't trust me?"

"I promised not to tell anyone." She looked at the water.

"You think I'd pass the word about?" He was outraged. What kind of a man did she think he was? Did she really think he would let his rivalry with Grag go that far?

"Brashen." She sounded at the end of her patience. "It is not that I don't trust you. I gave him my word to keep silent. I intend to keep it."

"I see." At least, she was finally speaking directly to him. A question burned in him. He cursed himself, but asked it anyway. "Did he ask you to go with him?"

Althea hesitated. "He knows I have to stay here. He even under-stands that I have to sail when the *Paragon* goes." Althea scratched her chin, then scraped at the dirt on her cheek. Irritably, she added, "I wish I could make Keffria understand that. She's still squawking to Mother that it isn't proper. She doesn't approve of me being down here to help. She hates the way I dress when I come down here to work. I don't know what she would approve. Perhaps I should sit at home and wring my hands in distress."

Brashen knew she was trying to change the subject. He couldn't leave it alone. "Sure, Grag knows that you have to go after *Vivacia*. But he still asked you to come with him, didn't he? He still wanted you to go. You probably should. Cut your losses. Wager on the winner. None of the Traders really expects we'll succeed. That's why none of them have of-fered help. They think it would be a waste of time and money. I'll bet Grag had all kinds of sound reasons why you should abandon us, including that we'll never get this derelict off the sand." Brashen thudded his heels on the ship's hull. He felt a sudden, irrational rush of anger.

"Don't call him a derelict!" Amber snapped.

"And stop whining," Althea added nastily.

Brashen stared at her, outraged. Then he raised his voice in a shout. "Derelict! Piece of beach junk! You hear me, Paragon? I'm talking about you."

His words echoed from the sea cliffs behind them. Paragon made no reply. Amber glared at him, breathing out sharply through her nose. "That isn't going to help anything," she scolded.

"Instead of starting quarrels with everyone, why don't you go panhan-dle some cindin?" Althea asked him sarcastically. "We all know that is your real problem."

"Yeah?" Brashen set his cup down. "And I know what your real prob-lem is."

Althea's voice went soft and deadly. "You do, do you? Well, why don't you tell us all plainly?"

He leaned close to her. "Your real problem is that last winter you finally figured out who you are, and you've spent every day since then trying to deny it. It scared you so you ran home to try and forget it."

His words were so different from what she had expected that Althea was struck dumb. He almost grinned at her astonishment. She gawked up at him where he stood over her on the slanting deck. "And to make it perfectly clear," he added in a softer voice, "I'm not talking about anything that happened between you and me. I'm talking about what happened between you and yourself."

"Brashen Trell, I have no idea what you're talking about!" Althea declared quickly.

"You don't?" He did grin then. "Well, Amber does, sure as Sa has balls and tits. I've known that she's known all about *that* since I got back to Bingtown. It was on her face the first time she looked at me. Funny that you'll talk to her about it, but not me. But I told you. That isn't the issue. You went out and you found out that you weren't a Trader's daughter. Oh, you're Ephron Vestrit's daughter, all right, and no mistake about that. But you aren't bound to this damn town and its traditions any more than he was. He didn't like the cost of trading up the Rain Wild River, so, by Sa, the man stopped trading there. He went out and found his own contacts and his own trade goods. You're like him, right down to the bone. If they wanted to weed that out of you, they're too late. You can't change that about yourself. You should stop pretending.

"You can't really settle down and be Grag Tenira's female half. It'll break both your hearts if you try. You're never going to stay home and make babies for him while he goes out to sea. You talk big about family and duty and tradition, but the reason you're going after the *Vivacia* is that you want your own damn ship. And you intend to get out there and take it. If you can just find the guts to leave Bingtown again, that is."

The words had spilled out of him. He found himself out of breath, and almost panting. Althea stared up at him. He wanted so badly to reach down and pull her up into his arms. He'd kiss her. She'd probably break his jaw.

She finally found her tongue. "You could not be more wrong," she declared, but there was no strength in her words. Beside her, Amber hid her smile in her teacup. When Althea glared at her accusingly, she shrugged. Sudden embarrassment claimed Brashen. Disdaining the rope ladder, he clambered over the railing and dropped lightly to the sand. Without another word or look back, he stalked off to the bow of the ship.

Clef had a small cook-fire going. Cooking the evening meal was his task. The work on the ship kept him busy in many ways. He had gone to fetch more drinking water for the men after Brashen had flung their ration at Paragon. He sharpened tools, he ran errands, and when evening came, he fetched supplies from the Vestrit home and fixed food for them. Ronica Vestrit had told them they were welcome to eat at her table, but Amber had courteously refused, saying she did not feel comfortable leaving Paragon alone. It had been a handy excuse for Brashen. There was no way to conceal his anxiety; sitting at a polite table would have strained him past the breaking point.

Sa, he wished he had just one tiny nubbin of a cindin stick left. Just enough to make his skin stop tingling with longing. "So. What's for supper?" he asked the boy.

Clef gave him a fish-eyed stare but didn't reply.

"Don't you start with me, boy!" Brashen warned him, his temper flaring again.

"Fesh soup, sir." Clef scowled as he clacked the wooden spoon about in the pot. He looked at the soup as he defiantly muttered, "He'n't junk."

So that was what had tweaked the boy. Brashen softened his voice. "No. Paragon isn't junk. So he shouldn't behave like beach junk." He turned to look up through the gathering darkness at the figurehead that loomed silently above them. He addressed Paragon more than the boy. "He's a damn fine sailing ship. Before this is all over, he'll recall that. So will everyone else in Bingtown."

Clef scratched his nose and then stirred the pot. " 'zee bad luck?"

"Is he bad luck," Brashen corrected him wearily. "No. He just had bad luck, from the very beginning. When you have bad luck, and then heap your own mistakes on top of it, sometimes you can feel like you'll never get out from under it." He laughed without humor. "I speak from experience."

"Y'got bad luck?"

Brashen frowned. "Speak plain, boy. If you're going to sail with me, you have to be able to make yourself understood."

Clef snorted, "I say, ya got bad luck?"

Brashen shrugged. "Better than some, but worse than most."

"Turn yer shert about. My da tole me, t'change yer luck, change yer shert."

Brashen smiled in spite of himself. "It's the only shirt I've got, lad. Wonder what that says about my luck?"

ALTHEA STOOD SUDDENLY. SHE DASHED THE TEA OUT OF HER CUP ONTO THE beach. "I'm going home," she announced.

"Farewell," Amber replied neutrally.

Althea slapped the stern rail. "I always knew he'd throw that at me some day. I always knew it. It was what I feared all along."

Amber was puzzled. "Throw what at you?"

Even alone on the isolated ship, she lowered her voice. "That I bedded with him. He knows he can ruin me with that. All he has to do is brag to the right person. Or the wrong person."

A glint came into Amber's eyes. "I have heard people say some stupid things when they were frightened or hurt. But that is among the stupidest. Althea, I don't believe that man has ever considered that as a weapon. I don't think he has a braggart's nature. Nor do I believe he would ever deliberately hurt you."

An uncomfortable silence held for a time. Then, she admitted, "I know you're right. Sometimes I think I just want a reason to be angry with him." She crossed her arms on her chest. "But why does he have to say such stupid things? Why does he have to ask me questions like that?"

Amber let the questions hang for a moment. Then she asked one of her own. "Why does it upset you so much when he does?"

Althea shook her head. "Every time I start to feel good about what we're doing, he . . . and we had a good day today, Amber. Damn him! We worked hard, and we worked well together. It was like old times. I know how he works and how he thinks; it's like dancing with a good partner. Then, just when I start thinking that it's going to be comfortable between us again, he has to . . ." Althea's voice trailed off into silence.

"Has to what?" Amber pressed.

"He has to ask me a question. Or he says something."

"Something more than, 'Get under that beam!' or 'Pass me the mallet'?" Amber inquired sweetly.

Althea smiled miserably. "Exactly. Something that reminds me of how we used to talk when we were friends. I miss it. I wish we could go back to it."

"Why can't you?"

"It wouldn't be right." She scowled to herself. "There's Grag, now, and . . ."

"And what?"

"And it could lead to more, I suppose. Even if it didn't, Grag wouldn't approve."

"Grag wouldn't approve of you having friends?"

Althea scowled. "You know what I mean. Grag wouldn't like me being friends with Brashen. I don't mean polite friends. I mean, as we used to be. Comfortable. Feet up and beer on the table."

Amber laughed softly. "Althea, in a short time, we're all going to sail off in his ship. Do you expect to use tea-party manners with someone you work with each day?"

"Once we sail, he won't be Brashen. He'll be the captain. He's already rubbed my nose in that. No one gets chummy with the captain."

Amber cocked her head and looked up at Althea in the darkness.

"Then why are you worrying about it? It sounds to me like time will cure all."

Althea spoke in a very low voice. "Maybe I don't want it cured. Not that way." She looked at her hands. "Maybe I need Brash's friendship more than Grag's approval."

Amber shrugged one shoulder. "Then maybe you should start talking to him again. And say something more than 'Here's the mallet.' "

CHAPTER TWENTY-TWO

A Change of Heart

VIVACIA WAS SEETHING. WINTROW FELT AS IF HE WERE IN THE PRESENCE OF a bubbling pot that was perpetually on the verge of boiling over and scalding everyone. The worst part was that he could do nothing to calm her. She not only would not allow herself to be calmed; she actively repelled any attempts to soothe her.

It had gone on for nearly a month, now. Wintrow sensed in her the vengeful purpose of a child who has been told she is too small to do something. Vivacia was determined to prove herself, and not just to Kennit. Her defiant enthusiasm included Wintrow. In the days since Opal had died on her deck, her resolve had grown and strengthened. She would turn pirate. Every time Wintrow tried to dissuade her, she became more stubborn. More troubling was that she grew more remote from him every day. She was reaching out toward Kennit so strongly that she had left Wintrow behind and alone.

Kennit sensed her turmoil. He was well aware of the feelings he had stirred in her. The pirate did not ignore her. He spoke gently to her and treated her with all courtesy. But he no longer courted her. Instead, he had turned the sun of his face onto Etta, and in his light, the woman bloomed extravagantly. Like a spark set to tinder, he had kindled her. She walked the decks like a tigress on the prowl, and all heads turned to watch her pass. There were a few other women aboard; Kennit had permitted some of the freed women to remain aboard, but in contrast to Etta, they seemed only moderately female. The puzzling thing to Wintrow was that he could not name any specific change she had made in herself. She dressed as she always had. Despite Kennit's presentations of jewelry, she seldom wore more of it than a tiny ruby earring. Instead, it was as if the ash had been brushed from a coal to reveal the fire burning within. She had not stopped working the deck; she still flowed up the rigging with pantherish speed; she still talked and laughed with the men as her sail needle flashed in the sun. Her tongue was as sharp as ever, her humor as biting. Yet, when she looked at Kennit, even across the deck, the life in her seemed to multiply. Captain Kennit, for his part, seemed to revel in her glory. He could not pass her without touching her. Even bluff Sorcor near blushed at the sight of them together on the deck. Wintrow could only watch them in amazement and envy. To his chagrin, every time Kennit caught him looking at them, he would raise his eyebrow at him. Or wink.

The entire crew responded to this new stimulus. Wintrow would have expected jealousy, or discontent as the captain flaunted his lady. Instead, they took pride in him, as if his virility and his possession of this desirable woman did credit to them all. The morale on the ship had leaped to a higher level than Wintrow had ever known. The new crew members were blending seamlessly with the old. Any discontent the freed slaves had felt had evaporated. Why clamor to possess a ship when one could be a part of Kennit's own crew on his ship?

Vivacia had witnessed three more piracies since Opal had died. In each case, they had been small cargo vessels, not slavers. Wintrow knew the pattern. The channel Kennit and Sorcor had selected was admirably suited to these ambushes. Sorcor lurked to the south of them. He selected the ships and started the chase. Vivacia waited at the head end of the channel. Her task was to run the pursued vessel onto the rocks. Once the prey was aground, the pirates from the *Marietta* moved in to pick their prey clean of whatever they fancied. The small cargo ships were not well manned or defended. To give Kennit credit, he did not slaughter their crews. There was little bloodshed, for once the ships were grounded, resistance flagged. Kennit did not even hold them for ransom. He simply took the cream of their cargo, and let them go with a stern warning to spread the word that Kennit of the Pirate Isles would not tolerate slavers passing through his waters. He did not name himself as king. Not yet. All three ships had managed to limp away from their encounters with him. The word would spread swiftly.

Vivacia both sulked and chafed at being held back from the action. Like a child dismissed from adult conversation, she was no longer invited to discuss piracy or politics with Kennit. He spent most of his evenings aboard the *Marietta* with Sorcor and Etta. It was there that they planned their attacks and celebrated their victories. When the pirate and his lady returned late at night, Etta was always decked with Kennit's latest gifts to her. Merry with wine, they would immediately retreat to their chamber. While Wintrow suspected this was a deliberate ploy to make Vivacia both curious and jealous, he did not speak of it to her. She would not have tolerated hearing it from him.

Between piracies, the life of the pirates was almost indolent. Kennit still kept his crew occupied, but he fed them well from the plundered vessels, and gave them time for both gaming and music. He included Wintrow in these pursuits, often summoning him to his cabin. Not for

Kennit simple games of dice or cards. He challenged Wintrow to games of strategy, not chance. Wintrow had the uneasy feeling that the pirate was evaluating him. Often, before the long afternoons were over, the game would lie forgotten between them while Kennit quizzed him on the philosophy of Sa. The second ship they had raided had been carrying a good store of books. Kennit was a voracious reader and shared his trove with Wintrow. Wintrow could not deny these interludes were pleasant ones. Sometimes Etta would sit in on both the game and the discussion. Wintrow had come to respect her lively intelligence, which was at least the match of Kennit's, though less schooled. She kept up well with both of them as long as they were speaking in generalities; it was only when they discussed the views of particular philosophers that she would grow first taciturn, and then withdrawn. One afternoon when Wintrow deliberately made an effort to include her, he stumbled onto her deficiency. He attempted to pass the book they were discussing to her. She would not accept it from his hands.

"I can't read it, so don't bother," she had declared angrily. She had been perched on a bench behind Kennit, gently massaging his shoulders as they talked. Now she abruptly stood and walked to the door of the chamber. Her hand was on the latch when Kennit's voice stopped her.

"Etta. Come back here."

She turned to face him. For the first time since he had met her, Wintrow saw a flash of defiance in her eyes as she looked at Kennit. "Why?" she challenged him. "So I can see all the more clearly how ignorant I am?"

A spasm of anger passed over Kennit's face. Wintrow watched him smooth his features, then hold his hand out to the woman. "Because I wish you to," he said, almost gently. She came back to him, but gazed at the book he picked up as if it were a hated rival. He held it out to her. "You should read this."

"I can't."

"I wish you to."

She clenched her teeth. "I don't know how!" she raged. "I never had teachers or lessons. Not unless you count the men who taught me my trade before I was even a woman! I'm not like you, Kennit, I . . . ."

"Quiet!" he barked at her. Again, he held the book out to her. "Take this." It was an order.

She snatched it from his hand and stood holding it as if it were a sack of offal.

Kennit shifted his attention to Wintrow. A very slight smile played about his face. "Wintrow will teach you to read it. Barring that, he will read it to you." He glanced back at Etta. "He will have no other tasks aboard ship until he has completed this one. I don't care how long it takes."

"The crew will laugh at me," Etta protested.

Kennit narrowed his eyes. "Not for long. It's difficult to laugh with one's tongue cut out." He took a breath, then smiled. "And if you wish to keep these lessons private, so be it. You may use these chambers. I will see that you have sufficient time alone and undisturbed to complete this task." He gestured at the other plundered books scattered about the chamber. "There is much here for you to learn, Etta. Poetry and history as well as philosophy." Kennit leaned forward. He captured Etta's hand and drew her closer. With his free hand, he stroked her hair back from her face. "Don't be stubborn. I wish you to enjoy this." He shot Wintrow a peculiar, flickering glance. It was almost as if he wished to be sure he was watching them. "I hope it will bring great pleasure and learning to both of you." He brushed his lips across her face. Etta closed her eyes to his touch. But Kennit's eyes were wide open, and watching Wintrow.

Wintrow was acutely uncomfortable. In some unnatural way, he felt included in the embrace. "You must excuse me," he muttered, rising hastily from the gameboard. Kennit's voice stopped him at the door.

"You won't mind teaching Etta. Will you, Wintrow?" There was little query in his voice. He held the woman close to him and looked at Wintrow over her bent head.

Wintrow cleared his throat. "Not at all."

"Good. See that you begin soon. Today, in fact."

As Wintrow fumbled for an answer, he heard the now familiar cry. "Sail!" He felt a shock of relief. The thunder of running feet resounded throughout the ship. "On deck!" Kennit barked, and Wintrow sprang gratefully to obey. He flung himself out the door and ran while the pirate was still reaching for his crutch.

"There! There it is!" Vivacia was crying as Wintrow gained the foredeck. She scarcely needed to point. Even at this distance, the wind carried the taint of the slaver. The ship that hove into sight was the filthiest, most dilapidated vessel that Wintrow had ever seen. Her hull gleamed with slime where waste had slopped over her side. She rode low in the water, obviously overloaded. Her unevenly patched jib puckered with the wind. A sporadic gushing of water from her indicated that her bilge pumps were being manned, probably by slaves. Some small part of Wintrow reflected that it was probably a constant effort to keep the wallowing ship afloat. In her wake were visible the additional V's of serpents trailing her. The loathsome creatures seemed to sense the panic on board, for they lifted their great maned heads and looked back at the *Marietta*. There were at least a dozen of the beasts, their scaled bodies gleaming in the sun. Wintrow felt ill.

Vivacia leaned forward, her face avid. Her eagerness was so great, she almost seemed to pull the ship after her. "Look at them, look at them flee!" Her crooked fingers and outstretched arms reached after the ship.

As her crew sprang to set her sails for the pursuit, the wind put its power to their backs.

"It's a slaver. Kennit will kill them all," Wintrow warned her in a low voice. "If you help him capture that ship, all the crew will die."

She spared him one glance back. "And if I do not, how many slaves will die each day of their voyage?" She fixed her gaze on her prey once more and her voice hardened. "Not all humans are worthy of life, Wintrow. At least our way preserves the most lives. If she sails on as she is, it will be a miracle if any on board survive the journey."

Wintrow scarcely heard her. He was watching, incredulously, as the slaver began to pull away from the *Marietta*. The distance between the two vessels widened. The slaver was not blind to opportunity, nor to the new threat the *Vivacia* represented. The over-laden ship made for the center of the channel. The *Marietta* was too far behind her. Without the pirate ship to crowd her, the pincer technique had but one jaw. Incredibly, the slaver would escape.

Kennit set his crutch down on the foredeck, and then hauled himself up the rest of the way. Once on the deck, he struggled to his feet and tucked his crutch under his arm. Etta was nowhere in sight. Laboriously he made his way over to the railing to join them. Once there, he shook his head in disappointment. "Those poor souls. The slaver is getting away. I'm afraid they're doomed to their fate."

There would be no killing today. Wintrow felt a moment of relief. Then Vivacia screamed. The cry was one of thwarted lust. In that instant, the ship picked up speed. Every plank and sail suddenly aligned to their best use. The whoops and calls of the crew grew fierce as the gap between *Vivacia* and the slaver began to close. Her intentness caught Wintrow's awareness like a butterfly snared in a spider's web. "My lady!" Kennit exclaimed in vast approval. It was benediction and Vivacia glowed with satisfaction. Wintrow felt it heat him. Kennit was barking commands. Behind him, he heard the rattle of blades and the jests of men making ready to go and kill other men. Challenges and bets were exchanged as the boarding party readied itself. Grapples and lines were brought out on deck, while laden archers moved hastily to their places in *Vivacia's* rigging.

Vivacia ignored them all. This was her pursuit, her kill. The men on board her she heeded not at all. Dimly Wintrow was aware of his own body. His hands were set like claws to the bow rail and the wind of their passage lashed his hair. Vivacia suffocated his small self in her greater energy. As in a dream, he saw the slaver grow larger before him. The stench of her grew stronger, and the scurrying men on her decks wore fear-stricken faces. He heard the voices of the pirates raised in excitement as the grapples were thrown and the first volleys of arrows loosed. The screams of those the arrows found and the muffled roar of the terrified slaves belowdecks were like the cries of distant shorebirds. He was far more keenly aware of the *Marietta* suddenly gaining on them. She threatened to steal the kill from Vivacia. The ship would not tolerate it.

Vivacia literally leaned over and grasped at the other ship as the grappling lines were pulled tight. Her clawing fingers reached nothing but the avidity on her face terrified the crew of the slaver. "At them! At them!" she cried out mindlessly, heedless of the orders Kennit was trying to give. Her fierce blood lust was contagious. The moment the span between the ships was leapable, the boarding party began their exodus.

"She has done it! Our beauty has done it! Ah, Vivacia, never did I suspect you had such speed and skill!" Kennit was worshipful in his praise.

A wave of purest adoration for Kennit flowed through Wintrow. The ship's emotion completely overwhelmed his own fear of what would follow now that the slaver had been captured. The figurehead twisted about to lock eyes with Kennit. The admiration that passed between them was the mutual recognition of predators.

"We will hunt well together, we two," Vivacia observed.

"That we shall," Kennit promised her.

Wintrow felt adrift. He was linked to them but they ignored him. He was irrelevant to what they had just discovered in one another. He could sense them connecting on a deeper, more basic level than any he had ever attained. What, he wondered dimly, did they acknowledge in one another? Whatever it was, he felt no answering echo in himself. Across a body-length of water, there was another deck, where men were fighting for their lives. Blood was flowing there, but what flowed here, between the liveship and the pirate, was something even thicker.

"Wintrow. Wintrow!" In a sort of daze, the boy heard his name and turned to it. Kennit's grin was white and wide as he indicated the captured ship. "With me, lad!"

He found himself following Kennit across the railing and onto a foreign deck where men struggled, cursed and screamed. Etta suddenly flanked them, a drawn blade in her hand. She strode with a pantherish awareness of all around her. Her black hair shone sleek in the sunlight. Kennit himself carried a long knife, but Wintrow was weaponless and wide-eyed in this strange world. His mind cleared somewhat as he left *Vivacia's* wizardwood behind, but the chaos he plunged into was nearly as numbing. Kennit strode across the deck fearlessly. Etta had placed herself on his right side, adjacent to his crutch. They threaded their way across the filthy and stinking deck. They passed by men intent on killing one another and circled around a man curled in a pool of blood on the deck. An arrow had skewered him, but the fall from the rigging had done more damage. His face was hideous as he grinned with his pain, his eyes crinkled as if in merriment while blood trickled from his ear and into his scruffy beard.

Sorcor came bounding across the deck toward them. Evidently, the *Marietta* had caught up swiftly, once she put her mind to it. She had grappled the slaver from the other side. The embattled crew never had a chance. The drawn blade in Sorcor's hand dripped while his tattooed face shone with savage satisfaction. "Just about done here, sir!" he greeted Kennit affably. "Just a few live ones left up on the poop. Not a real fighter amongst them." A wild yell punctuated his comment, followed by a flurry of splashing. "And one less now," Sorcor remarked cheerily. "I've got some men opening hatch covers. It's a stinking hole belowdecks. I think they have got as many bodies chained up down there as they do live men. We're going to have to take the survivors off fast. This ship is making water like a sailor pissing beer."

"Do we have room for them all, Sorcor?"

The stocky pirate waggled his eyebrows in a shrug. "Most likely. It'll crowd both our ships, but when we rejoin the *Crosspatch*, we can transfer a lot of them to her. I'd say that about fills us up, though."

"Excellent." Kennit nodded almost absently. "We'll be making for Divvytown, after we pick up the *Crosspatch*. Time to let out the word as to how well we've done."

"I'd say so," Sorcor grinned.

A blood-smudged pirate hastened up to the group. "Begging your pardons, sirs, but the cook wants to yield. He's holed up in the galley."

"Kill him," Kennit told the man in annoyance.

"Begging your pardon, sir, but he says he knows something that would make it worth our while to let him live. Says he knows where there's treasure."

Kennit shook his head in wordless disgust.

"If he knew where there was treasure, why wasn't he going after it instead of hauling slaves in this tub?" Etta demanded sarcastically.

"Don't know, ma'am," the sailor apologized. "He's an old 'un. Missing an eye and a hand. Claims he used to sail with Igrot the Bold. That's what got us thinking. Everyone knows that Igrot knocked off the Satrap's treasure barge and that lot was never seen again. Maybe he does know. . . ."

"I'll take care of it, Captain," Sorcor promised in irritation. "Where's he at?" he demanded of the hand.

"Hold on a moment, Sorcor. Perhaps I'll have a word with this cook." Kennit sounded both intrigued and suspicious.

The young pirate looked uncomfortable now. "He's holed up in the galley, sir. We got the door half kicked down, but he's got a lot of knives and choppers in there. Pretty good at throwing them, too, for an old man with one eye."

Wintrow saw a change come over Kennit's face. "I'll talk to him. Alone. You see to getting the slaves up and out of the holds. She's starting to list."

Sorcor was used to taking orders. He didn't hesitate, just bobbed his head and turned. He was already barking orders as he strode away. Wintrow became aware of slaves. They were standing on the deck in listless groups, blinking at the sunlight. Coated with filth, shivering in the shock of the fresh air, they looked bewildered at the sudden change. The smell and the dazed faces suddenly took him back to the night the slaves emerged from *Vivacia*'s hold. A wave of pity swept over him. Some of them were so feeble they had to be helped to stand. Slave after slave emerged from the holds. He looked at them, and knew the ineffable rightness of what Kennit had done. To eliminate this misery was right. But his method of achieving it . . .

"Wintrow!"

There was a spark of annoyance in Etta's voice. Wintrow was standing, staring while Kennit was moving swiftly and with purpose across the deck. The list to the ship was becoming more perceptible every moment. There was no time to waste. He hurried after them.

As he crossed the deck, he heard the roaring of serpents, followed by a sudden splashing. They were throwing bodies to the creatures. An appreciative murmur and laughter rose from the watching pirates as the serpents squabbled over the feed.

"Leave off that!" he heard Sorcor bellow. "They'll have all the dead soon enough. Get the slaves out of the hold and onto the other ships. Swiftly, now! I want to cut this wreck loose as soon as we can."

The galley was in a low deckhouse. Blades drawn, a cluster of pirates huddled around the door, unaware of Kennit's approach. As Wintrow watched, one kicked the barricaded door. It brought a volley of curses from the man cornered within and then a blade appeared in the small opening. "I'll cut the first man what tries to come through. Get your captain. I'll yield to him, and him alone." The mocking pirates only crowded closer. They reminded Wintrow of a pack of dogs with a cat up a tree.

"He's here," Kennit announced loudly. The laughing, grinning men suddenly sobered. They fell back from the door, making way for him. "Be about your work!" Kennit ordered them brusquely. "I'll deal with this."

They dispersed quickly, but not willingly, with many a backward glance. The rumor of treasure was enough to hold any man's interest, but Igrot's treasure was legendary. Plainly, they would have liked to stay and hear what bait the man would trade for his life. Kennit ignored them. He lifted his crutch and gave the door a thump. "Come out," he commanded the cook.

"You the captain?"

"I am. Show yourself."

The man peeped one eye around the door, then darted back out of sight. "I got something to trade. You let me live, I'll tell you where Igrot the Bold stashed his loot. The whole lot. Not just all he got from the treasure barge, but all he took afore that."

"No one knows where Igrot hid his treasure," Kennit declared with confidence. "He and his whole crew went down together. No one survived. If anyone had, they would have plundered his trove a long time ago." With amazing stealth, Kennit eased forward to stand immediately beside the doorjamb.

"Well, I did. Been waiting for years to get to where I could go back and get it. But I never was in the right position. Anytime I'd a told, all I woulda got is a knife in the back. And not just any man could go after it. It would take a special ship. A ship like you got, just the same as Igrot once had . . . and I'm sure you're taking my drift now. There's places as a liveship can go that no other can follow. But now, well, I told you enough. You keep me alive, I'll lead you there. But you gotta let me live."

Kennit didn't reply. A stillness came over him. He was poised motionless beside the door. Wintrow glanced at Etta. She was as silent and motionless as Kennit. Waiting.

"Hey! Hey, you, Captain, what say you? Is it a deal? It's more treasure than you can ever imagine. Heaps of it, and half of it magical Bingtown Trader stuff. You could just walk right in and take it. You'll be the richest man alive. All you got to do is say I can live." The cook sounded jubilant. "That's a fair trade, isn't it?"

The ship's list had begun to increase markedly. Wintrow could hear Sorcor and his men hurrying the slaves along. One man's voice raised suddenly. "He's dead, woman. Nothing we can do. Leave him." A woman's sudden wail of anguish floated on the sea wind, but around the door, all was silent. Kennit made no reply to the cook.

"Hey? Hey, Cap, you out there still?"

Kennit's eyes narrowed as if in thought. Something almost like a smile played about his mouth. Wintrow felt a sudden shiver of nervousness. It was time to finish this and get off this ship. It was taking on water, and as the vessel grew heavier, the sea gained more power over it. He took a breath to speak but Etta elbowed him sharply. What happened next occurred simultaneously. Wintrow was left staring, trying to comprehend. Did Kennit's knife hand move first or did he glimpse the motion of the man peering around the door? The two objects came together as swiftly and synchronously as clapping hands. Kennit's blade sank deep into the man's good eye and then was pulled out. The man's body tumbled back out of sight. "There are no survivors from Igrot's crew," Kennit asserted. He took an uneven breath. When he looked around, he blinked as if awakening from a dream.

"Stop dallying here. This ship is going down," he exclaimed in annoyance. Bloody knife still gripped in his hand, he stalked back to the *Vivacia*. Etta walked almost beside him. The woman appeared unfazed by what had just happened. Wintrow trailed them numbly. How did death happen so swiftly? How could the whole equation of a man's life be so swiftly reduced to zero? What he had done was an immense shock to the youth. A brief extension of the pirate's hand, and death bloomed. Yet, the holder of the knife felt nothing. Wintrow felt scored by his association with the man. He suddenly longed for Vivacia. She would help him think about this. She would say there was no justification for the guilt that he felt.

Kennit's boot had no sooner touched the deck of the *Vivacia* than the ship called out to him. "Kennit! Captain Kennit!" Her voice boomed in assertive command. There was a note in it that Wintrow had never heard. Kennit grinned in hard satisfaction. "Get the slaves settled and cut that hulk loose!" he ordered brusquely. He glanced at Wintrow and Etta. "See that they are made as clean as possible. Keep them aft." He turned and hastened away from them and toward the figurehead.

"He wants to be alone with her." Etta stated it as blunt fact. Jealousy flamed in her eyes.

Wintrow looked down at the deck to keep her from seeing the same thing in his face.

"FOR A MAN IN HIDING, YOU LIVE IN STYLE," ALTHEA OBSERVED, SMILING.

Grag grinned, well pleased with himself. He leaned back in the small chair he was perched in, rocking it back on two legs. He reached overhead to bat casually at a cut-tin lantern that hung from the tree branch above him. "What is life, without style?" he asked rhetorically. They both laughed aloud easily.

The swinging lantern scattered light around them dizzily. Patterned candlelight danced in the darkness of his eyes. He wore a dark shirt, open at the throat, and loose white trousers. When he moved his head, the light gleamed warmly on his gold earring. The summer sun had bronzed him; his coloring made him seem a part of the forest evening. When his teeth flashed white in a smile, he seemed the easy-going sailor lad from Rinstin. He looked about the clearing in front of the cottage and sighed peacefully.

"I hadn't been up here in years. When I was a little boy, before I began sailing with Da, Mother used to bring us all up here for the hottest part of the summer."

Althea glanced about the little garden. The house was little more than a cottage, with the forest encroaching almost to the door. "Is it cooler up here in the summer?"

"A bit. Not much. But you know how Bingtown can stink in the summer. We were up here the year the Blood Plague first struck. None of us got it. Mother always believed it was because we avoided the evil humors of the city that summer. After that, she insisted on bringing us here every year."

They both fell silent for a time, listening. She imagined this cabin and garden as a lively place, inhabited by a woman and her children. Not for the first time, Althea wondered how her life would have been different if her brothers had survived the Blood Plague. Would her father have taken her on the ship? Would she be married by now, with children of her own?

"What are you thinking?" Grag asked her gently. He let his chair drop forward, then leaned his elbows on the table. He rested his chin in his hands and regarded her fondly. A bottle of wine, two glasses and the remains of a cold supper cluttered the table. Althea had brought the food up with her. The note that had come to the house had actually been from Grag's mother to hers. It had begged her mother's pardon, then asked if it would be possible for Althea to run a discreet errand for the Tenira family. Keffria had raised her eyebrows, but perhaps her mother had decided that Althea had no reputation left to protect. She had returned a note granting her leave.

A horse had been waiting for her in a Bingtown stable. Althea had set out with no clear knowledge of her destination. As she passed a small tavern on the outskirts of Bingtown, a loiterer had hailed her and pressed a note into her hand. The note directed her to an inn, where she half expected to find Grag. Instead, when she arrived there, she was offered a fresh horse and a man's hooded cloak. The mount that awaited her had laden saddle packs. Still another note accompanied him.

There had been an air of both mystery and adventure to tracking Grag down, but never did Althea forget that it was serious as well. In the days since Ophelia had defied the Satrap's tariff minister, Bingtown had grown more divided. The liveship's swift departure from the harbor had been a wise decision, for three new Chalcedean patrol vessels had arrived shortly thereafter. This "timely" arrival had sparked suspicions that the tariff ministry had closer ties to Chalced than perhaps even Jamaillia knew. Someone had broken into the minister's quarters, and messily killed a cote of homing pigeons there. The tariff warehouses that had survived the Council night fires had been torched twice since then. This had led to the Chalcedean mercenaries guarding the minister's quarters by night as well as ostensibly patrolling the harbor and adjacent waters. Some of those Old Traders who had initially been more conservative were now more sympathetic to those who quietly spoke of independence from Jamaillia.

Grag Tenira had become a focus for the tariff minister's grievances with the town. There was a large price on his head. Brashen's suggestion that Althea could sell Grag for enough money to re-launch *Paragon* had been a jest, but not an exaggeration. If Grag did not put himself out of harm's reach soon, even those loyal to him might be tempted by the soaring bounty.

So now, as she sat in the summer evening's mellow breeze and looked across at him, she felt a sense of foreboding. Grag had to act and soon. She had spoken to him of it before, and now she ventured, "I still do not understand why you linger near Bingtown. Surely, you could slip out of town on one of the liveships. I am only amazed that the Satrap's agents have not deduced that you would be here. It is well known that your family has a cabin in the Sanger Forest."

"So well known that they have been here twice and searched it. They may come again. But if they do, they will find it as empty and abandoned as the last times."

"How?" Althea was intrigued.

Grag laughed, but not lightly. "My great uncle was not the most moral of men. The family rumor is that he kept many a tryst up here. That is why there is not only a wine cellar concealed behind a false wall in the root cellar, but a tiny chamber behind that. And there is a very expensive sympathy bell, with its partner installed in the foot bridge you crossed."

"I heard nothing when I crossed the bridge," Althea protested.

"Of course not. It's a tiny one, but very sensitive. When your passage rang it there, its partner answered up here. Thank Sa for the magic of the Rain Wilds."

He lifted his glass in a toast to their Rain Wild brethren, and Althea drank with him. She set her glass down and dragged him back to her topic. "Then you intend to remain here?"

He shook his head. "No. It would only be a matter of time before they caught me. Supplies must be brought up. The folk in this area know that I am here. Many of them are Three Ships families. Good people, but not rich. Eventually, one would give in to temptation. No, I am leaving and very soon. That is why I begged my mother to arrange this visit. I feared your family would forbid it; I knew it was not proper for me to seek to see you alone in these circumstances. Desperate times beget desperate measures." He looked apologetic.

Althea gave a soft snort of amusement. "I don't think Mother gave it that much thought. I'm afraid my childhood reputation as a rebellious hoyden has followed me into adulthood. What would be scandalous for my sister to do is ordinary behavior for me."

He reached across the table to put his hand over hers. He pressed it warmly, then possessed it. "Is it wrong for me to say that I am glad it is so? Otherwise, I would never have come to know you well enough to love you."

The bald admission left her speechless. She tried to move her mouth to say she loved him too, but the lie would not come. Odd. She had not known it would be a lie until she tried to speak the words. She took a breath to say something true: that she had come to care for him as well, or that she was honored by his words, but with a shake of his head, he cut her off.

"Don't speak. You don't have to say it, Althea. I know you don't love me, not yet. In many ways, your heart is even more cautious than mine is. I knew that from the beginning. Even if I had not, Ophelia was at great pains to tell me so when she was instructing me in how to woo you." He laughed self deprecatingly. "Not that I sought her advice. In many ways, she is a second mother to me. She does not wait for me to ask for her advice."

She smiled gratefully. "I find no fault with you, Grag. There is nothing you have done to turn back my feelings. My life has given me no time, of late, to dwell on hopes or dreams for myself. My family's problems weigh heavily on me. Lacking grown men in our line, the duty falls squarely on me. No one else can go after the *Vivacia*."

"So you have told me," Grag conceded, in a voice that did not concede complete agreement. "I have given up the hope that you might go with me now. I suppose that even in times such as these, that would be seen as too hasty a wedding to be seemly." He turned her hand over in his and brushed his thumb over her palm. It sent a shiver of pleasure up her arm. He looked down at her hand as he asked, "But what of later? Better times will come . . ." He considered his own words and then gave a bitter laugh. "Or worse ones, perhaps. I would like to tell myself that in time, you will stand beside me and join my family. Althea. Will you marry me?"

She closed her eyes and knew a moment of pain. This was a good man, an honest and upright man, handsome, desirable, even wealthy. "I don't know," she told him quietly. "I try to look ahead, and imagine a time when my life will be my own, to arrange as I will, but I cannot see that far. If all goes well, and we win the *Vivacia* back, then I will still challenge Kyle for possession of her. If I win her, then I will sail her." She met his eyes honestly. "We have spoken of this before. I know you cannot leave Ophelia. If once more I possess Vivacia, I will not leave her. Where does that leave us?"

His mouth twisted wryly. "You make it hard for me to wish you success, for if you win all you desire, I lose you." At the dawn of her frown, he laughed aloud. "But you know I do. Nevertheless, if you do not succeed . . . well, I will be waiting for you. With Ophelia."

She lowered her eyes and nodded to his offer, but in her heart she felt a small chill. What would it be to fail? A lifetime ahead with no ship of her own. The *Vivacia* gone forever from her life. Grag's wife, aboard his ship as a passenger, minding her little ones lest they fall overboard. Seeing her sons grow up and sail away with their father while she stayed home and ran a household and married off her daughters. The future suddenly seemed a tightening net, webbing her in. She tried to breathe, tried to convince herself that her life would not be like that. Grag knew her. He knew her heart was at sea, not at home. But, just as he accepted her duty to her family now, once they were married he would expect her to do her duty to him. Why else did sailors take wives, save to have someone at home to mind the house and raise the children?

"I can't be your wife." Incredulously, she heard her say the words aloud. She forced herself to meet his eyes. "That is what truly keeps me from loving you, Grag. Knowing that that would be the price I must pay. I could love you, easily, but I could not live in your shadow."

"In my shadow?" he asked in confusion. "Althea, I don't understand. You would be my wife, honored by my family, the mother of the Tenira heir." There was genuine hurt in his voice. He groped for words. "More than that, I could not offer. It is all and everything I have to offer any woman I marry. That and myself." His voice sank to a whisper. "I had hoped it would be enough to win you." Slowly he opened his hand. It was as if he released a bird.

Reluctantly she drew her hand back. "Grag. No man could offer me more than that, or better."

"Not even Brashen Trell?" he asked roughly. His voice thickened on the words.

A terrible coldness welled up inside her. He knew. He knew she had bedded with Trell. She was glad she was sitting down. She tried to control her face even as she fought the roaring in her ears. Sa, she was going to faint! This was ridiculous. She could not grasp the extent of her reaction to his words.

He stood suddenly, and walked a short distance away from the table. He stared off into the night forest. "So. You love him, then?" His words were almost accusatory.

Guilt and shame had dried her mouth. "I don't know," she managed hoarsely. She tried to clear her throat. "It was just something that happened between us. We'd both been drinking, and the beer was drugged and . . ."

"I know all that." He dismissed it brusquely. He still did not look at her. "Ophelia told me all that, when she warned me. I didn't want to believe her."

Althea lowered her face into her hands. *Warned him.* The sudden gaping loss gutted her. She suddenly doubted that Ophelia had even liked her. "How long have you known?" she managed to ask.

He sighed heavily. "The night she urged me to kiss you, and I did . . . she told me later. I suppose she felt, oh, I don't know, guilty. Afraid that I might get hurt, if I fell too deeply in love with you, and then found out you weren't . . . what I expected."

"Why didn't you tell me before this?"

She lifted her head to see his lop-sided shrug. "I thought it wouldn't matter. It bothered me, of course. I wanted to kill the bastard. Of all the low things to do . . . but then Ophelia told me that you might have feelings for him. Might even be a bit in love with him?" It was a half-hearted question.

"I don't think I am," she said in a low voice. The ambivalence in her own voice surprised her.

"That's twice," Grag observed bitterly. "You know you don't love me. But you aren't sure about him."

"I've known him a long time," she said lamely. She wanted to say she didn't love him. But how could you know someone that long, be friends with someone that long, and not feel some kind of love for him? It was not that different from her relationship with Davad Restart. She could despise the Trader's actions, and still recall a kindly, avuncular bumbler. "For years, Trell was a friend and a shipmate. And what happened between us doesn't change those years. I . . . ."

"I don't understand at all," Grag said softly. She still heard the undercurrent of anger in his voice. "He dishonored you, Althea. He compromised you. When I found out, I was furious. I wanted to call him out. I was sure you must hate him. I knew he deserved to die. I thought he would never dare return to Bingtown after what he had done. When he did, I wanted to kill him. Only two things held me back. I could not do so without revealing the reason for challenging him. I didn't want to shame you. Then, I heard he had called at your home. I thought, perhaps, he was going to offer to do the honorable thing. If he had and you had refused him . . . Did he offer? Is that what this is about, do you feel some sort of obligation to him?"

There was desperation in his voice. He was struggling so hard to understand.

She stood up from the table and went to stand beside him. She, too, looked into the darkened forest. Shadows of twigs and limbs and trunks tangled and obstructed each other. "He didn't rape me," she said. "That is what I must admit to you. What happened between us was not wise. But it wasn't violent and I was as much to blame as Brashen."

"He's a man." Grag spoke the words uncompromisingly. He crossed his arms on his chest. "The blame is his. He should have been protecting you, not taking advantage of your weakness. A man should control his lust. He should have been stronger."

She felt struck dumb. Was this really how he viewed her? As a weak and helpless creature, to be guided and protected by whatever man happened to be closest to her? Did he honestly believe she could not have stopped Brashen if she had wanted to? She felt first a rift, and then a building anger. She wanted to rip him with words, to force him to see that she controlled her own life. Then, as swiftly as it had come, the anger fled. It was hopeless. She saw her liaison with Brashen as a personal event that had involved only the two of them. Grag viewed it as something that had been done to her, something that must change her forever. It affronted his whole concept of society. Her own shame and guilt had not come from a sense of wrongdoing, but from a fear of what the discovery could do to her family. The two views seemed radically different to her. She knew, with a sudden deep certainty, that they could never build anything together. Even if she could have given up her dreams of a ship of her own, even if she had suddenly decided she wanted a home and children to cherish, his image of her as a weak and defenseless woman would always humble her.

"I should leave now," she announced abruptly.

"It's dark," he protested. "You can't go now!"

"The inn isn't far, once I'm past the bridge. I'll go slowly. And the horse seems very steady."

Finally, he turned back to look at her. His eyes were wide, his face vulnerable as he pleaded, "Stay. Please. Stay and talk. We can resolve this."

"No, Grag. I don't think we can." An hour ago, she would have touched his hand, would have wanted to kiss him good-bye at least. Now she knew she could never get past the barriers between them. "You're a good man. You'll find a woman who is right for you. I wish you all the best. And when next you see Ophelia, give her my best wishes also."

He followed her back into the circle of dancing light from the cut-tin lanterns. She picked up her wine glass and drank the last swallow from it. When she looked around, she realized there was nothing further to do here. She was ready to leave.

"Althea."

She turned to the bereft tone of his voice. Grag suddenly looked very boyish and young. He met her eyes bravely and did not try to hide his pain. "The offer stands. I'll wait until you come back. Be my wife. I don't care what you've done. I love you."

She searched for true words she could say to him. "You have a kind heart, Grag Tenira," she said at last. "Farewell."

CHAPTER TWENTY-THREE

Consequences

SERILLA HAD NOT LEFT THE CAPTAIN'S CABIN SINCE SHE HAD BEEN dragged there. She ran her hands through her bedraggled hair and tried to decide how long that had been. She forced herself to review the events in her mind, but her memories would not stay in proper order. They jumped and jiggled about, the moments of terror and pain leaping up to demand her attention even as she refused to think about them.

She had fought the sailor sent to bring her. Serilla had wanted to go with dignity, but found she could not. She had held back until he dragged her. When she struck him, he had simply picked her up and slung her over one wide shoulder. He stank. Her efforts to strike and kick him had amused not only him, but also the other members of the crew who had observed her humiliation. Her screams for help had been ignored. Those of the Satrap's party who had witnessed her abduction did nothing. Those who had chanced to see her kept their faces carefully expressionless, turning away from her plight or closing the doors they had peeped out. But Serilla could not forget the expressions on Cosgo and Kekki as they watched her hauled away. Cosgo smiled in smug triumph, whilst Kekki roused from her drugged stupor to watch in fascinated titillation. Her hand had lingered on Cosgo's thigh.

Her captor had borne her into an unfamiliar part of the ship. He shoved her into the captain's darkened cabin, then latched the door behind her. Serilla did not know how long she had waited there. It seemed hours, but how could one measure time in such circumstances? She had cycled from rage to despair to terror. Fear had been with her constantly. By the time the man actually arrived, Serilla was already exhausted from shouting, weeping and pounding on the door. At his first touch, she physically collapsed, near fainting. Nothing in her scholarly upbringing or days at court had ever prepared her for anything like this. He easily overcame her efforts to push him away. She was like a spitting kitten in his hand. He raped her, not savagely, but matter-of-factly. The discovery of her virginity made him exclaim in surprise, and curse in his own language. Then he went on with his own pleasure.

How many days ago had that been? She did not know. She had not left the cabin since then. Time was broken up into when the man was there and when he was not. Sometimes he used her. Other times he ignored her. He was impersonal in his cruelty. He did not notice her in any other way; he made no attempt to win her affection. He showed her the same courtesy he gave to the chamber pot or spittoon. He never spoke to her. She was there to use, when he felt the need. If she made it difficult, with resistance or pleading, he would hit her. He delivered the open-handed blows casually, with a lack of effort that convinced her his intent strength would be far greater. One slap loosened two of her teeth and left her ear ringing for hours. The lack of malice with which he struck her was more frightening than the blows. Hurting her was of no concern to him.

At some early point in her captivity, she had contemplated revenge. She had rummaged about in the room, looking for anything that might serve as a weapon. The man was not a trusting soul. His chests and cupboards were locked, and did not give way to her prying. But she did find on his desk documents that indicated her suspicions were well founded. She recognized a chart of Bingtown harbor, and a map of the area around the mouth of the Rain Wild River. Like all such maps she had ever seen, there were great blank spaces. There were letters there as well, but she did not read the Chalcedean language. The documents contained mention of money and the names of two high Jamaillian nobles. It might have been information about bribes; but it might also have been a bill of lading. She put everything back exactly as she had found it. Either she had not done a good job, or the beating he gave her that night was for a different offense. It quenched her last thoughts of resistance or revenge. She no longer even thought of survival. Her mind retreated, leaving her body to function on its own.

After a time, she had learned to eat the leavings from his meals. He did not eat often in his cabin, but provided her no other food or drink. She had no clothing left intact, so she spent most of her time huddled in the corner of his bed. She no longer thought. When she tried to fumble her way out of her confusion, she found only ugly alternatives. All thought was fear. Today, he might kill her. He might give her to his crew. He might keep her forever, all the rest of her life, in this cabin. Worst of all, he might return her to the Satrap, a broken toy that no longer amused him. Eventually, he would get her pregnant. Then what? This present that she endured had irreparably destroyed all her futures that might be. She would not think.

Sometimes she stared out the window. There was little to see. Water. Islands. Birds flying. The smaller ships that accompanied them. Sometimes the smaller ships disappeared, to rejoin them a day later. Sometimes they showed sign of battle, scorched wood or tattered sails or chained men on the deck. They raided the small outlaw settlements of the Inside Passage as they discovered them, taking loot and captives as slaves. They seemed to be doing well at it.

Someday, they would get to Bingtown. When that thought came to Serilla, it was like a tiny crack through which light shone. If she could somehow escape in Bingtown, if she could get ashore, she could conceal who she had been and what had happened to her. That was very important to her. Her mind recoiled from continuing this life. She could no longer be Serilla. Serilla was a soft and pampered academic, a gently reared scholar, and a court woman of words and thoughts. She despised Serilla. Serilla was too weak to fight off this man. Serilla had been too foolishly proud to accept the Satrap's offer to bed him instead of the Chalcedean. Serilla was too cowardly to plot how to kill the captain, or even how to kill herself. Even knowing that Bingtown was her last hope in the world, she could not focus her mind enough to form an escape plan. Some vital part of herself had been, if not destroyed, suspended. She detached herself from Serilla, and shared the world's contempt for her.

The end of her ordeal came as abruptly as it had begun. A sailor unlocked the cabin one day and gestured for her to follow.

She clutched the blanket to herself as she cowered on the captain's bed. Steeling herself for a blow, she dared to ask, "Where are you taking me?"

"Satrap." The one word was his reply. Either he spoke no more of her language than that, or he considered it ample. He jerked his head toward the door again.

She knew she had to obey. When she stood and wrapped the blanket about herself, the sailor did not try to take it from her. The gratitude she felt for this brought tears to her eyes. When he was sure she was following, he led the way. She followed him cautiously, as if she were venturing into a new world. Blanket clutched tightly around her, she emerged from the cabin. She kept her eyes cast down and hurried along. She tried to go to her old cabin, but a shout from her guide made her cringe. She fell in behind him once more, and he took her to the Satrap's quarters.

She expected he would knock at the door. She had hoped to have at least that much time to prepare herself. He didn't. He flung the door of the cabin open and gestured impatiently for her to enter.

She stepped forward into a noisome flow of overly warm air. In this warm weather, the smells of the ship itself had ripened with that of sickness and sweat. Serilla recoiled but the sailor was merciless. He seized her shoulder and pushed her into the room. "Satrap," he said, and then shut the door firmly.

She ventured into the stifling room. It was still and dim. It had been tidied, in a careless sort of way. Discarded garments hung on backs of chairs rather than littering the floor. The censers for the Satrap's smoke herbs had been emptied but not cleaned. The smell of stale smoke choked the room. Plates and glasses had been cleared from his table, but the sticky circles from the bottoms of the bottles remained. From behind the heavy curtains on the great window came the sound of a single determined fly battering its head against the glass.

The room was accusingly familiar. She blinked slowly. It was like awakening from a bad dream. How could this room with its domestic clutter still exist so unchanged after all she had been through? She stared around, her daze slowly lifting. While she had been held captive and raped repeatedly, a single deck away, life had gone on for the Satrap and his party. Her absence had changed nothing for them. They had continued to drink and dine, to listen to music and play games of chance. The litter and mess of their safely ordinary lives suddenly enraged her. A terrible strength flooded her. She could have smashed the chairs against the table, could have shattered the heavy stained glass of the windows and flung his paintings and vases and statues into the sea.

She did not. She stood still, savoring her fury and containing it until it became her. It was not strength, but it would do.

She had believed the room was deserted. Then she heard a groan from the disheveled bed. Clutching her blanket about her, she stalked closer.

The Satrap sprawled there in a wallow of bedding. His face was pale, his hair sweated to his brow. The smell of sickness was thick about him. A blanket thrown to the floor beside the bed stank of vomit and bile. As she stared down at him, his eyes opened. He blinked stickily, then appeared to focus on her. "Serilla," he whispered. "You've come back. Thank Sa! I fear I am dying."

"I hope you are." She spoke each word clearly as she stared at him. He cowered from her gaze. His eyes were sunken and bloodshot. The hands that clutched the edge of his blanket trembled. To have lived in fear for all those days, and then discover that the man who had given her over to such treatment was now sickened and wasted was too great an irony. In his illness, his wasted face finally resembled his father's. That brief resemblance both stabbed and strengthened her. She would not be what Cosgo had tried to make her. She was stronger than that.

She abruptly discarded her blanket. She walked naked to his wardrobe and flung the doors of it wide. She felt his eyes on her; she took a vengeance in that she no longer cared. She began to pull out and then discard his garments, searching for something clean she could put on. Most of his clothing stank of his drug-smokes or perfumes, but she finally found a loose pair of white pantaloons, and then a red silk shirt. The trousers were too ample for her. She belted them up with a finely woven black scarf. An embroidered vest covered her breasts more appropriately. She took up one of his hairbrushes, cleaned it of his strands, and then began to bring her own dirty locks into order. She ripped the brush through her brown hair as if she could erase the Chalcedean's touch from it. Cosgo watched her in dull consternation.

"I called for you," he offered her weakly. "After Kekki sickened. By then, there was no one else left to tend me. We were all having such fun, before the sickness came. Everyone got so sick, so quickly. Lord Durden died right after our card game one night. Then the others began to get sick." He lowered his voice. "I suspect it is poison. None of the crew has been ill. Only me and those loyal to me. In addition, the captain does not even seem to care. They sent servants to tend me, but many of them are sick and the rest are fools. I have tried all my medicines, but nothing eases me. Please, Serilla. Don't leave me to die. I don't want to be tipped overboard like Lord Durden."

She braided her hair back from her face. She studied herself in the mirror, turning her face from side to side. Her skin had gone sallow. On one side of her face, the bruises were fading. There was caked blood inside one of her nostrils. She picked up one of his shirts from the floor and wiped her nose on it. Then she met her reflection's gaze. She did not recognize herself. It was as if a frightened, angry animal lurked behind her eyes. She had become dangerous, she thought to herself. That was the difference. She gave him a glance. "Why should I care? You gave me to him, like a leftover bone thrown to a dog. Now you expect me to care for you?" She turned to face him and stared into his eyes. "I hope you die." She spoke the words slowly and individually, willing him to understand how completely she meant them.

"You can't hope that!" he whined. "I am the Satrap. If I die, with no heir, all Jamaillia will fall into disorder. The Pearl Throne has never been unoccupied, not for seventeen generations."

"It is now," she pointed out sweetly. "And however the nobles are managing now is how they will manage when you are dead. Perhaps they won't even notice."

She crossed the room to his jewelry boxes. The best quality would be in the ones most stoutly locked. Casually she lifted an ornately carved box over her head. She dashed it to the floor. The thick carpeting on the deck defeated her. She would not humiliate herself by trying again. She would content herself with simple silver and gold instead. She opened compartments of a different chest randomly, chose earrings for herself and a throatpiece. He had let her out as if she were a whore he owned. He could pay well for what he had done to her, in a multitude of ways. What she took now might be her only source of wealth when she left him in Bingtown. She decked her fingers with rings. She looped a heavy chain of gold about her ankle. Never had she worn such jewelry. It was almost like armor, she thought. Now she wore her worth on the outside of her body instead of within. It built her anger.

"What do you want from me?" he demanded imperiously. He tried to sit up, then sank back with a moan. The command was gone from his voice as he whimpered, "Why are you being so hateful to me?"

He seemed so genuinely incredulous that she was jolted into an answer. "You gave me over to a man who raped me repeatedly. He beat me. You did it deliberately. You knew what I was suffering. You did nothing. Until you needed me, you cared nothing for what became of me. You were amused by it!"

"I do not see that you took great hurt from it," he declared defensively. "You are walking and talking and being as cruel to me as you always were. You women make so much of this! After all, it is what men naturally do to women. It is what you were made for, but refused to grant me!" He plucked petulantly at his blankets and muttered, "Rape is nothing but an idea women created, to pretend that a man can steal what you have an infinite supply of. You took no permanent harm from it. It was a rough jest, I admit, and ill considered . . . but I do not deserve to die for it." He turned his head and faced the bulkhead. "No doubt when I am dead, you will experience more of it," he pointed out with childish satisfaction.

Only the truth of his last statement kept her from killing him at that moment. The depth of her contempt for him was suddenly boundless. He had no concept of what he had done to her; worse, he seemed incapable of understanding it. That this was the son of the wise and gentle Satrap who had made her a Companion was inconceivable. She pondered what she must do to ensure her survival. He inadvertently gave her the answer.

"I suppose I must give you presents and honors and bribes before you will take care of me." He sniffled a little.

"Exactly." Her voice was cold. She would be the most expensive whore he had ever created. She went to a desk that was securely fastened to the bulkhead. She unburdened it of discarded clothing and a forgotten plate of moldy dainties. She found parchment, a pen and ink. She set them out, then dragged a chair across to seat herself. The change in her posture reminded her of how her whole body ached. She paused, frowning to herself. Going to the door, she jerked it open. The sailor on duty there looked at her questioningly. She made her voice imperious.

"The Satrap requires a bath. Have his tub brought, with clean towels, and buckets of hot water. Very quickly." She shut the door before he could react.

She returned to the desk and took up her pen.

"Oh, I do not wish a hot bath. I am too weary as it is. Cannot you wash me where I lie?"

Perhaps she'd allow him to use the water when she was finished with
it. "Be quiet. I'm trying to think," she told him. She took up the pen and
closed her eyes for a moment, composing her thoughts.

"What are you doing?" Satrap Cosgo asked.

"Drawing up a document for you to sign. Be quiet!" She considered
terms. She was inventing a whole new position for herself, as the Satrap's
permanent envoy to Bingtown. She would need a salary, and allowance
for suitable quarters and servants. She inked in a generous but not outrageous amount. How much power should she allot to herself, she wondered, as her pen inscribed the flowing characters on the parchment?

"I'm thirsty," he whispered hoarsely.

"When I am finished, and you have signed this, then I will get you
some water," she told him reasonably. In fact, he did not seem very ill to
her. She suspected it was a combination of some true illness, sea-sickness,
and wine and pleasure herbs. Put that with a lack of servants and Companions fawning over him, and he believed he was dying. Fine. It well
suited her purposes that he believe he was dying. Her pen paused for an
instant in its flight and she tilted her head as she considered. There were
emetics and purges in the medical stores he had brought with them.
Perhaps, in the course of "caring" for him, she could see that he did not
recover too swiftly. She needed him alive, but only as far as Bingtown.

She set her pen aside. "Perhaps I should take time to prepare a rem-
edy for you," she conceded graciously.

HIGH
SUMMER

CHAPTER TWENTY-FOUR

The Ringsgold

THE TANGLE HAD GROWN. MAULKIN SEEMED TO TAKE BOTH PLEASURE AND pride in this. Shreever had more mixed feelings. While the larger contingency of serpents that traveled with them now assured greater protection against predators, it meant that food supplies had to be shared. She would have felt better if more of the serpents were sentient, but many of those who followed the tangle were feral creatures who gathered with them only out of instinct.

As they traveled and hunted together, Maulkin closely observed the feral serpents. Any that showed signs of promise were seized when the tangle paused for rest. Kelaro and Sessurea usually overpowered the chosen target, bearing him down and letting him struggle against their combined weight and strength until he was gasping. Then Maulkin would join them, to shake loose his toxins and weave his body through the winding loops of the memory dance while they demanded that the newcomer recall his own name. Sometimes it worked, sometimes it did not. Not all of those who could recall their own names were able to retain their identities for long. Some remained simple, or drifted back into their animalistic ways by the next tide. But some few did recover and hold on to higher thought. There were even a few who followed the tangle aimlessly for a few days, and then suddenly recalled both names and civilized manners. The core group of serpents had grown to twenty-three, while easily twice that number ghosted behind them. It was a large tangle. Even the most generous provider could not keep them all satisfied.

Every rest period, they pondered the future. Maulkin's answers seldom satisfied them. He spoke as plainly as he could, and yet the words were confusing. Shreever could sense his own bewilderment behind his prophecies; her hearts went out to him. Sometimes she feared that the others might turn on him out of frustration. She almost longed for the days when it was only herself and Sessurea and Maulkin, seeking for those answers. When she whispered as much to Maulkin one evening, he rebuked her. "Our folk have dwindled. Confusion besets us from all sides. If any of us are to survive, we must gather as many as we can. It is the simplest law of the Plenty. A multitude must be born for a few to survive."

"Born," she said, the question unspoken.

"The recombination of old lives into new lives. It is what we all hear summoning us. Our time to be serpents is over. We must find She Who Remembers. That one will guide us, to where we can seek rebirth as new creatures."

His words made her shudder her whole length, but with dread or anticipation, she could not say. Others had drawn close to hear his words. Their questions swarmed thick as capelin on a moonlit tide.

"What sort of new creatures?"

"How can we be reborn?"

"Why is our time over?"

"Who will remember for us?"

Maulkin's great copper eyes spun slowly. Color rippled his length. He struggled. She could sense it, and wondered if the others did as well. He strained to reach beyond himself, grasping at knowledge and bringing back only disconnected fragments. It drained him more than a full day of traveling. She also sensed that he was as discontented with his fragmentary answers as the others were.

"We will be as we once were. The memories you cannot understand, the dreams that frighten, come from that time. When they come to you, do not chase them away. Ponder them. Pursue them into the open and share them." He paused, and when he spoke again, it was more slowly and with less certainty. "We are long past due to change, so long past due that I fear something has gone terribly wrong. Someone will remember for us. Others will come to protect us and guide us. We will know them. They will know us."

"The silver provider," Sessurea asked quietly. "We followed, but she knew us not."

Sylic twined uneasily through the heart of the resting tangle. "Silver. Silver-gray," he hissed. "Do you remember, Kelaro? Xecres found the great silver-gray creature and called us to follow it."

"I do not recall that," Kelaro trumpeted softly. He opened and closed his huge silver eyes. They spun with shifting color. "Except, perhaps, as a dream. A bad dream."

"It attacked us when we gathered close around it. It threw long teeth at us." Sylic turned a slow knot through his length, pausing when he came to a scar gouged deep. The scales that had grown over it were thick and uneven. "It bit me here," the scarlet whispered hoarsely. "It bit me but it did not devour me." He turned to look deep into Kelaro's eyes, as if seeking confirmation. "You tore its tooth from my flesh for me. It had pierced me and it stayed in me, festering."

Kelaro lidded his gaze. "I do not recall," he replied regretfully.

A rippling ran the length of Maulkin's body. His false-eyes shone brighter than they had in a very long time. "The silver being attacked you?" he asked incredulously. "He attacked you!" Anger was a rip tide in his voice. "How could it be that one who gives off the smell of memories turns on those who come to him for help?" He lashed his great head back and forth, his mane coming erect with toxins. "I do not understand!" he suddenly bellowed out. "There are no memories of this, not even the taste of a memory! How can it be that these things happen? Where is She Who Remembers?"

"Perhaps they forgot," Tellur said with black humor. The slender green minstrel had not gained much strength since he had recalled his own name. The effort of maintaining his identity seemed to consume all his energy. How he had been before he had forgotten himself, no one could say. Now he was a dour-humored, sharp-tongued whip. Despite recalling who he had been, he could seldom bring himself to sing.

Maulkin whipped about suddenly to face him. His mane was full standing, his colors rippling. "They forgot?" he roared in outraged astonishment. "Have you seen this in a memory or dream? Do you recall a song that speaks of a time when all forget?"

Tellur sleeked his mane to his throat, making himself smaller and less significant. "It was a jest, great one. An evil jest from a sour minstrel. I beg pardon for it."

"A jest with perhaps a grain of truth in it. Many of us have forgotten. Could the ones who remember, the memory keepers of us all, have likewise failed in their tasks?"

A despondent silence greeted his question. If it was so, it meant they were abandoned. They had no future save to wander, until one by one their minds failed and grew dark. The serpents gripped one another tighter, holding fast to what little future might remain to them. Maulkin abruptly tugged free of them all. He turned an immense circle and then began a series of slow looping turns. "Think with me!" he invited them all. "Let us consider if this could be true. It could account for much. Sessurea, Shreever and I saw a silver being, one that smelled like She Who Remembers. She ignored us. Kelaro and Sylic saw a silver-gray creature. When Xecres, the leader of their tangle, sought memories of him, he attacked them." He whipped his body about suddenly to confront the others. "Is that so different from how you all behaved, as you lost your memories? Did not you ignore one another, not replying to my questions? Did not you even attack your fellows as you vied for food?" He arched backwards, revealing his white underbelly as he flashed past them. "It is so clear!" he trumpeted. "The minstrel has seen through to the heart of it. They have forgotten! We must force them to remember us!"

The tangle was silent, awe-stricken. Even the mindless serpents who gathered in random tangles of their own at rest times had disengaged to watch Maulkin's jubilant dance. The wonder that shone in so many eyes shamed Shreever, but her doubt was too strong. She voiced it. "How? How can we make them recall us?"

Maulkin suddenly darted at her. He looped her, wrapped her, and drew her forth from the tangle to join in his sensual weaving. She tasted his toxins as she moved beside him. They were besotted with joy, intoxicatingly free. "Just as we have re-awakened the others. We shall seek one, confront one, and demand that that one name its name."

As she had danced with him, entwined and intoxicated, it had been so easy to believe it was possible. They would seek out one of the silver creatures who smelled like memories, force it to remember its purpose and to share its memories with them. And then . . . then they would all be saved. Somehow.

Now, as she looked up at the shape passing between them and the light, she wondered. They had been days seeking a silver. Once they had caught the scent of one, Maulkin had allowed them only brief pauses for rest. Their purposeful pursuit had near exhausted some of them. Slender Tellur had lost color and bulk. Many of the feral serpents had dropped behind as Maulkin sustained the pace. Perhaps they would catch up with them later; perhaps they would never see them again. For now, Shreever had thoughts only for the bulky creature that moved purposefully above them.

The tangle ghosted along in his shadow. Now that they had actually caught up with him, even Maulkin seemed daunted by their task. In bulk, the silver creature far surpassed any of the serpents. In length, he was the equal of even Kelaro.

"What will we do now?" Tellur asked bluntly. "We cannot wrap such a creature and drag it down. It would be like wrestling a whale!"

"Actually, that would not be an impossible task," Kelaro observed with the confidence of his size. He brought his mane up aggressively. "It would be a battle, but there are many of us. We would prevail."

"We shall not begin with force," Maulkin informed him. Shreever watched him gather his strength. Sometimes it seemed to her that the spark of his vitality burned as brightly as ever, but that his physical being dwindled as it burned. She wished she could convince him to conserve himself, but that unending argument was best not begun. The prophet-seer stretched himself to his full length. A swift ripple undulated his whole body, waking his false-eyes to bright gold. Slowly his ruff blossomed about his throat, until every spine of his mane stood stiff and welling venom. His great copper eyes spun with purpose. "Await my call," he directed them.

They obeyed as he left them and swam up toward the great silver shape.

This one was not a provider. He had not the taint of old blood and waste to him that was the hallmark of the hulks who bestowed flesh upon them. This creature moved more swiftly, though he had neither fins nor flippers that Shreever could discern. He had a single flipper-like append-age at the back of his rounded belly, but he did not appear to use it to move. Rather he slid through the Plenty effortlessly, with his upper body basking in the Lack. Maulkin matched his pace. He did not seem to have gills, eyes or a mane, but Maulkin hailed him anyway. "Maulkin's tangle gives you greeting. We have traveled far, in search of One Who Remem-bers. Are not you such a one?"

He gave no sign of hearing Maulkin. His speed did not slow nor vary. His scent did not change. It was as if he were completely unaware of the serpent. For a time, Maulkin kept pace with him, waiting patiently. He hailed him again, but again there was no response. He suddenly lashed himself to greater speed, to place himself ahead of the silver one. Then, with a shuddering shake of his mane, he released a stunning cloud of toxin.

The creature passed through it without even slowing. He seemed unfazed by the toxins. It was only after he had passed that Shreever sensed something from him; a thin shivering from the silvery body, a faint scent of uneasiness. It was so slight a reaction, scarcely a response at all, but still she took courage from it. He might pretend to ignore them, but he was aware of them all the same.

Maulkin felt the same, for he suddenly whipped his body in front of the creature, where he must pause or collide with him. "I am Maulkin of Maulkin's tangle! I do demand your name!"

He struck Maulkin. He ran him down as if he were kelp. But Maulkin was not kelp, to be brushed aside. "I demand your name!" he bellowed. He flung his full length against the silver creature. His tangle followed him. They could not wrap the silver one, though they tried. They could nudge and bump him. Cobalt Kelaro even rammed him, striking a blow that near stunned the serpent, while Sessurea battered the creature's sin-gle flipper. Every member of the tangle released their most potent toxins, so that they passed through cloud after cloud of their own poisons. Their attack slowed and baffled the great creature. He hesitated in his course. Shreever heard shrill keening. Did he sing into the Lack, even under the full light of the sun? Disoriented and gasping in the wild array of toxins, she rose to lift her head out into the Lack.

It was there she found his face and flippers, unlike any she had ever beheld. He had no mane, but spread great white wings above him, like a gull coming to rest on the face of the Plenty. Parasites infested his body. They hopped and clung to his upper body and wings, making shrill cries. At the sight of her, their agitation increased. Emboldened, she lifted as much of her length up as she could. She flung herself into the gray one's face. "Who are you?" she trumpeted. She shook her own small mane, lashing him with her stinging cells, spattering him with her toxins. "Say your name! Shreever of Maulkin's tangle demands that you remember for her!"

He cried out as her toxins struck him. He lifted his flippers to his face and pawed at himself. The parasites scampered madly over his back, trumpeting in their tiny voices. The silver one suddenly leaned far over. Shreever thought he would dive to escape her; then she saw that it was not by his own will that this was done. Maulkin had united his tangle's efforts. Their combined force pushed upon him, making him wallow far to one side. His white wing clipped the water. A parasite fell, buzzing shrilly, into the Plenty. One of the feral serpents surged forward to snatch it up.

They had only to be shown once. The entire school of them then converged on the silver one. With a violence that surely Maulkin had never intended, they battered and rocked the creature. He cried out wildly and swung his flippers about in frantic efforts to strike his attackers. This only enraged the feral serpents more. They added their undisciplined toxins to those already clouding the Plenty. Fish stun and shark repellent battered her senses. The feral serpents were doing most of the work now, while Maulkin and his tangle circled the embattled creature, repeating over and over their demands for his name. More and more of the parasites plummeted into the water. The creature's great white wings flapped wildly as they dipped into the Plenty, first on one side and then the other. Finally, when the creature was laid over almost completely on his side, Kelaro flung his great length out of the Plenty. He crashed down on the creature's unprotected flank. Swiftly other serpents joined him, both sentient and feral. Some leaped up to seize his stiff limbs and fluttering wings. The silver creature tried to roll back, but there were too many of them. He could not overcome them. Their weight overwhelmed him and drew him under, away from the Lack and deeper into the Plenty. As they pulled him down, the parasites tried to leap free of him, but snapping jaws awaited every one of them.

"Your name!" Maulkin insisted as they bore him down. "Tell us your name!"

The creature bellowed and gesticulated wildly, but gave them no words. Maulkin darted at him, wrapping his length around the creature's forepart. He shook his mane right in the creature's face, discharging toxins in a thick cloud. "Speak!" he commanded him. "Remember for us. Give us your name! What was your name?"

He struggled, his tiny head and forelimbs convulsing in Maulkin's grip while the disproportionate bulk of his body remained stiff and unyielding. Some of his smaller brittle limbs broke away while his wings grew wet and heavy. Still, he struggled to rise to the top of the Plenty. They could not drag him completely down, though the tangle managed to hold him below the Lack.

"Speak to us!" Maulkin commanded him. "Just one word. Just your name and we will let you go. Reach for it, reach back for it. You have it. We know you do. We can smell the thickness of your memories."

He battered wildly at the prophet. His mouth gaped and stretched with his sounds, but no sense came out of him. Then he suddenly went still. His eyes, small and brown, went wide. His mouth gaped once, twice. Then he suddenly relaxed in Maulkin's grasp. Shreever lidded her eyes. The silver-gray creature was dead. They had killed him, to no good end.

Then he suddenly spoke. Shreever's attention snapped back to him. His voice was thin, almost bodiless. His puny forelimbs tried to encircle Maulkin's thick body in an embrace. "I was Draquius. I am no more. I am a dead thing, speaking with the mouth of memories." His trumpet was shrill and weak, barely audible.

The tangle grew still, gathering closer in awe. Draquius spoke on. "It was the time of the change. We had swum far up the river, to where the memory silt was fine and thick. We had spun our cocoons, encasing ourselves in thread woven of memory. Our parents laved us with the silt of memories, gave us our names and their memories to share. They watched us, our old friends. They celebrated our time of change, under the blue skies. They cheered as we wallowed from the river to the sunny banks, to let the light and the heat dry our cases while we transformed ourselves. Layer upon layer of memories and silt they wrapped us in. It was a season of joy. Our parents filled the skies with their colors and songs. We would rest through the time of cold, to awaken and emerge when the days turned hot and long." He closed his small eyes, as if pained. He clung to Maulkin as if he were part of his own tangle.

"Then the whole world went wrong. The earth shook and split. The very mountains were shattered and oozed hot red blood. The sun dimmed; even within our cases, we felt it fade. Hot winds blew over us, and we heard the cries of our friends as it snatched the breath from their lungs. Yet even as they fell, gasping, they did not forsake us. They dragged us into shelter, many lives ago. They could not save many of us, but they tried. I give them that, they tried. It was only for a time, they promised. Only until the dust stopped raining down, only until the skies shone blue again. Only until the earth stopped quaking. But it did not stop. The earth trembled daily and the mountains burst into fire. The forest burned and the ash fell down over all, stifling everything. The river flowed thicker than blood with it. The air was choked with it, and where it settled, it covered all life in a layer of ash. We called out to them from inside our cocoons, but after a time, they did not answer. Without the sun, we could not hatch. We lay in the deep darkness, wrapped in our memories, and waited."

The tangle and its followers were silent. They remained as they were, draped on his stiff limbs and wings, wrapped over his bulky body. Maulkin breathed out a thin cloud of toxin in his face. "Speak on," he commanded him gently. "We do not understand, but we listen."

"You do not understand?" He laughed thinly. "I do not understand. After a very long time, another people came. They were like and not like those who had sought to save us. We called out to them joyously, sure they had come at last to deliver us from the darkness. But they would not hear us. They brushed our airy voices away, dismissing us as less than dreams. Then they killed us."

Shreever felt hope grow tiny within her.

"I heard the screams of Tereea. I could not grasp what was happening. She was with us; then she was gone. A time passed. Then they attacked me. Tools bit into my cocoon, splitting it open while it was still thick and heavy, strong with my memories. Then . . ." He became perplexed. "They threw my soul out onto the cold stone. It died there. But the memories remained, trapped in the layers of the cocoon. They sawed me into planks and from them created a new body. They made me anew in their own image, gouging away until they had shaped me a face and head and body such as they wear. And they drenched me in their own memories, until one day I awoke as someone else. *Ringsgold* they named me, and so I became. A liveship. A slave."

A silence flowed through them all when he was still. He had used words that Shreever did not know, spoken of things she could not grasp. A terrible dread flowed chill over her. She knew that his tale was a monumental one, a tale of an ending of all her kind, but she did not know why. She was almost glad she could not comprehend the tragedy. Maulkin, still wrapped around him, had lidded his eyes. His colors had gone pale and sick.

"I will mourn you, Draquius. Your name conjures echoes of memories in my soul. Once, I think, we knew one another. But now we must part as unremembered strangers. We will let you go."

"No! Please!" Draquius' eyes went wide and he strove to cling to Maulkin. "Do not let go of me. You speak my name and it rings in my heart like the bugling of the Dragon of Dawn. For so long, I have forgotten myself. They kept me always with them, never letting me have solitude, never allowing my old memories to surface. Layer on layer of their little lives they spread atop mine, until I believed I was one of them. If you let me go, they will reclaim me. It will all begin again, and perhaps, never end."

"There is nothing we can do for you," Maulkin apologized sorrowfully. "There is nothing we can do for ourselves. I fear you have told us the ending of our own tale."

"Undo me," Draquius pleaded in his thin little voice. "I am no more than the memory of Draquius. If he had survived, he would have been one of your guides, to bring you safely home. But he did not. I am all that is left, this poor shell of a life. I am memories. No more than that, Maulkin of Maulkin's tangle. I am a tale with no one left to tell me. So take my memories for your own. Had Draquius survived his transformation, he would have devoured his shell and taken all his memories back into himself. He did not. So take them for yourselves. Preserve the memories of one who died before he could trumpet his own name across the sky. Remember Draquius."

Maulkin lidded his great copper eyes. "It will be a poor memorial, Draquius. We do not know how much longer we can sustain our own lives."

"So take mine, and draw strength and purpose from it." He loosened his grip on Maulkin and folded his sticklike forelimbs across his narrow chest. "Free me."

In the end, they obeyed him. They crushed and tore, splintering him into pieces. Some of his body, they discovered to their shock, was no more than dead strips of plants. But all that was silver and smelled of memories, they took and devoured. Maulkin ate that part of him that was shaped as a head and forebody. Shreever did not think he suffered, for he did not cry out. Maulkin insisted that all partake of Draquius' memories. Even those who were feral were subtly urged to the sharing.

The silver threads of his memories had dried long and straight and hard. When Shreever took her portion in her jaws, she was surprised to feel it soften and melt. As she took it in, memories dawned bright in her mind. It was as if she swam from clouded water to clear. Faded images of another time came to mind and glowed bright with color and detail. She lidded her eyes in ecstasy and dreamed of wind under her wings.

CHAPTER TWENTY-FIVE

The Launch of the Paragon

THE HIGH TIDE WOULD COME JUST AFTER DAWN SO THE FINAL WORK WAS completed in a frenzy by lanternlight. Brashen stalked and cursed through the work site the whole night. The *Paragon* had been laid over and nudged as far toward the water as Brashen could manage without putting too much stress on the wood. With jacks and struts inside the hull, the ship had been brought groaning closer to true. Some preliminary caulking had been done, but not too much. Brashen wanted the planking free to shift as the water lifted the hull. A ship must be flexible to withstand the pounding of waves and water. *Paragon* must be allowed enough freedom to allow the water and hull to come to terms with each other. The full length of his keel was exposed now. Brashen had rung it with a hammer; it seemed sound. It ought to be, it was silver-gray wizardwood, hard as stone. Nevertheless, Brashen would not trust anything to be the way it *should* be. His experience with ships told him those were precisely the things that went wrong.

He had a thousand worries about the re-floating of the ship. He took it for granted that *Paragon* would leak like a sieve until his planking swelled again. Old joists and timbers, left in one position for so many years, might spring or split as they took up the tensions of a floating vessel once more. Anything could happen. He wished fervently that they had had a larger budget, one that would have allowed the hiring of master shipwrights and workers to oversee this phase of the salvage. As it was, he was using the knowledge he'd personally gained over the years, much hearsay and the labor of men who were usually sleeping off drunks at this hour. It was not reassuring.

But repeatedly, his anxiety crested at Paragon's attitude. It had shown little improvement during the course of the work. The ship now spoke to them, but his temperament fluctuated wildly. Unfortunately, the spectrum of his emotions seemed to encompass only the darker ones. He was angry or bleak, whining miserably or ranting insanely. In between, he sank into a self-pitying melancholy that made Brashen wish the ship truly was a boy, simply so he could shake him out of it.

Brashen suspected that discipline and self-control was something the ship had never truly learned. That, he explained to Althea and Amber, was the root of all Paragon's problems. No discipline. It would have to come from them until Paragon learned to manage himself. But how did one discipline a vessel? The three of them had considered that question over mugs of beer several nights before the peak tide.

The evening was muggy. They sat on driftwood logs on the beach. Clef had lugged the beer out from town for them. It was cheap beer and, even at that, too dear for their budget. But the day had been exceptionally long and hot, and Paragon especially difficult. They had convened in the shade of his stern. He had reverted today to his most infantile behavior, which included name-calling and sand-throwing. With the ship laid over on the beach, he could reach a near-unlimited supply. Brashen felt prickly from the sand stuck in his sweaty hair and down the back of his neck. Shouting and cursing him had no effect on him. In the end, Brashen had simply hunkered down and done the necessary work while making no response to the showers of sand from Paragon.

Althea had shrugged one shoulder. Brashen could see black, gritty sand trapped along her hairline. "What can you do? He's a bit large to spank. You can't send him to bed, let alone without any supper. I don't think there is any way to discipline him. We may have to resort to bribes."

Amber set down her mug of beer. "You're speaking of punishments. The issue is discipline."

Althea looked thoughtful for a moment. "I suppose they are two different things, though I don't know how you separate them."

"I'm ready to try anything to make him behave. Can you imagine the difficulty of sailing him as he is? If we don't make him more tractable soon, all of this work will have been for nothing." Brashen voiced his deepest fear. "He could turn on us. In a storm, or a confrontation with pirates . . . he could kill us all." In a lower voice, he forced himself to add, "He's done it before. We know he is capable."

It was the one topic they had never openly discussed. Odd, Brashen thought. Paragon's madness was something they dealt with every day. They had spoken often of many aspects of it, but never bluntly considered it in its entirety. Even now, a silence followed his words.

"What does he want?" Amber asked them all. "Discipline must come from within himself. He must desire to be co-operative, and that desire is only going to be based on what he wants. Ideally, we can hope that that is something we can either provide, or deny him, based on his behavior."

She sounded troubled as she added, "He's going to have to learn there are consequences for bad behavior."

Brashen had smiled wryly. "That will be almost harder on you than it is on him. I know you can't stand to see him unhappy. No matter how rotten he is, you always go to him when evening comes, to talk to him or tell him stories or play music for him."

Amber looked down guiltily, toying with the fingers of her heavy work gloves. "I can feel his pain," she confessed. "So much has been done to him. So often, he has been left with no choices. And he is so confused. He fears to hope for the best, for whenever he has dared to hope in the past, all joy has been snatched from him. So he has made up his mind to believe, from the outset, that every man's hand is against him. He acts to hurt before he can be hurt. That's a thick wall to break through."

"So. What can we do?"

Amber closed her eyes tight, as if in pain. Then she opened them. "What is hardest, and hope it is also what is right." She had risen then and walked the length of the hauled down ship to the bow. Her clear voice carried to them when she spoke to the figurehead. "Paragon. You have behaved badly today. Because of that, I won't be coming to tell you stories tonight. I'm sorry it has to be this way. If you behave tomorrow, I will spend time with you tomorrow night."

Paragon's silence was very brief. "I don't care. You tell stupid, boring stories anyway. What makes you think I want to hear them? Stay away from me forever. Leave me alone. I don't care. I never cared."

"I'm very sorry to hear that."

"I don't care, you stupid bitch! Didn't you hear me? I don't care! I hate you all!"

Amber's step was slow and heavy as she came back to them. She resumed her seat on the log without a word.

"Well. That went well," Althea observed dryly. "I can see that his behavior will improve in no time."

The words came back to haunt Brashen as he paced yet another circuit of the work site. Everything was ready and in position. Nothing more could be done until the tide came in. A heavy counterweight attached to what was left of *Paragon*'s mast would ensure that the ship did not right himself too swiftly. Brashen looked out to the work barge anchored offshore. He had put a good man out there, one of the few of his new crew that he actually trusted. Haff would be watching for Brashen's flag signals and supervising the crew on the capstan that would drag the *Paragon* back toward the water. Inside the *Paragon* would be other men, ready to man the bilge pumps continuously. His biggest fears were for the side of *Paragon* that had been in contact with the abrasion and insects of the beach for all those years. He had done what he could from the inside of the hull. He had a weighted sheet of canvas to drop down along that side of the hull, as soon as the ship was in the water and righted. If, as he expected, water rushed through the gaps between those planks, the flow would press the canvas up against the hull, where the fabric would at least slow it. He might have to re-beach the *Paragon*, with that side up, for extended chinking and caulking on that planking. He hoped not, but was resigned to do whatever he must to make the ship seaworthy.

He heard a light step on the sand behind him. He turned to find Althea squinting out to the barge. She nodded when she saw the man on watch there. He jumped when she patted his shoulder. "Don't be so worried, Brash. It will all come together."

"Or it won't," he muttered sourly in reply. Her touch and reassurance, the affectionate shortening of his name, startled him. Of late, it seemed to him that they were resuming the casual familiarity of shipmates. She at least met his eyes when she spoke to him. It had made the work situation more comfortable. Like himself, she probably realized that this voyage would demand their co-operation. It was no more than that. He resolutely quenched the brief spark of hope that had kindled. He kept the conversation centered on the ship.

"Where do you want to be for this?" he asked her. It had been agreed that Amber would stay near Paragon and talk him through it. She had the most patience with him.

"Where do you want me?" Althea asked humbly.

He hesitated, biting his tongue. "I'd like you belowdecks. You know what trouble looks like and sounds like before it becomes a disaster. I know you'd rather watch from up here, but I'd like to have someone I trust down below. The men I put on the pumps have muscle and endurance, but not much sea time. Or wits. I've got a few hands down there with mallets and oakum. You move them around as you see fit as he starts to take on water. They seem to know their business, but watch them and keep them working. I'd like you moving around down there, looking and listening and letting me know how we're doing."

"I'm there," she assured him quietly. She turned to go.

"Althea," he heard himself say aloud.

She turned back immediately. "Was there something else?"

He ransacked his mind for something intelligent to say. All he wanted to ask her was if she had changed her mind about him. "Good luck," he said lamely.

"To us all," she replied gravely, and left.

An incoming wave ran up across the sand. The white foam at the edge of it lapped against the hull. Brashen took a deep breath. This was it. The next few hours would tell all. "Everyone, get to your places!" he barked. He twisted his head and looked up at the top of the cliffs above the beach. Clef nodded that he was paying attention. He held two flags at the ready. "Signal them to start taking up the slack. But not too much."

Out on the barge, the men at the turnstile leaned into their work. Someone took up a slow-paced chantey. The rough music of the men's deep voices reached to him over the water. Despite all his reservations, a grim smile broke out on his face and he took a deep breath. "Back to sea with us, Paragon. Here we go."

EACH INCOMING WAVE WASHED CLOSER TO HIM. HE COULD HEAR IT. HE could even smell the water coming closer. They had shoved him down and weighted him and now they would let the waves swallow him up. Oh, he knew what they said, that they were going to re-float him. But he didn't believe them. He knew this was his punishment, coming at last. They would weight him down and pull him out under the water and then they would leave him there for the serpents to find. It was, after all, what he deserved. The Ludluck family had waited a long time, but they would finally take their vengeance today. They would send his bones to the bottom, just as he had done to their kin.

"You're going to die, too," he said with satisfaction. Amber perched like a sea-bird on his cockeyed railing. She had told him, over and over, that she was going to stay with him through the whole thing. That she wouldn't leave him, that everything was going to be fine. She'd find out. When the water finally rushed over them and pulled her down, too, she would found out how wrong she had been.

"Did you say something, Paragon?" she asked him courteously.

"No." He crossed his arms on his chest again and held them tightly against his body. He could feel water the full length of his hull now. The waves pushed at the sand under him like little tunneling insects. The ocean worked its greedy fingers up under him. Each wave that brushed him was a tiny bit deeper. He felt the rope from his mast to the barge grow tighter. Brashen shouted something, and the pressure steadied but did not increase. The men's work song stilled. Inside him, Althea called out in a carrying voice, "So far, so good!"

The water crept under him. He shivered suddenly. The next wave might lift him. No. It came and went and he still rested on the sand. The next one, then. No. Well, then, the next . . . Wave after wave came and went. He was in an agony of anticipation and fear. Despite all his expectations, when he first felt that tiny bit of lift, the grating of hull against sand as he floated for a fraction of a second, he whooped in surprise.

He felt Amber tighten her grip convulsively. "Paragon! Are you all right?" she called out in alarm.

Suddenly, he had no time for her fears. "Hang on!" he warned her jubilantly. "Here we go!" But wave after wave kissed against him and

Brashen did nothing. Paragon could feel the sand shifting under him as the sea ate at it. He felt, too, a great stone revealed by the retreating sand.

"Brashen!" he called out in annoyance. "Get onto it, man! I'm ready! Tighten that line! Have them put their backs into it!"

He heard the heavy sound of splashing. Brashen ran up to him, through licking waves that must be thigh-high on the man by now. "Not yet, Paragon. It's not quite deep enough yet."

"Cark you if it isn't! Do you think I'm so stupid I don't know when I'm floating? I can feel myself starting to lift on every wave, and there's a damn big rock under me. If you don't start moving me down the sand I'm going to be pounding up and down against it soon."

"Easy, then. Don't get excited, I'll take your word for it! Clef! Signal them to get started. Slow and easy now!"

"Screw that! Tell them to put their backs into it now!" Paragon countermanded Brashen's order. "You hear me, Clef?" he bellowed when no one made any response. They had damn well better be listening to him, he thought savagely. He was tired of them treating him like a child.

The line on his mast stub tightened with an abruptness that made him grunt.

"Heave!" Brashen shouted, and the men with the levers strained against them. They rocked him up, but not quite enough. Once he started moving, he was supposed to tip forward onto a roller wedged under his hull. They would have been smarter to haul it out of there. Now it was only going to act as a wedge.

"HEAVE!" Brashen shouted as the next wave peaked. Suddenly he bumped up and onto the roller. "TIGHTEN THAT LINE!" Paragon felt Brashen scramble aboard him. Suddenly he was moving, sliding down the beach, deeper and deeper into the incoming water. It was cold, ghastly cold after his years of lying out in the sun, and he gasped with the shock of it.

"Steady. Steady. It's going to be all right. Take it easy. They'll right you as soon as the water is deep enough. Hang on. It's going to be all right."

From inside him, he heard Althea call, "We're making water, but I think we're under control. You, get onto that pump! Don't wait for it to fill up, do it now!"

He felt the thudding of mallets inside him as someone packed oakum into a seam that had opened. Althea's raised voice indicated they weren't doing it fast enough to suit her. He was sliding, sliding on his side down the beach, into ever-deeper water. Now as each wave hit him, he rocked. Both design and his own instinct tried to bring him upright, but the damn counterweight on his mast was holding him over.

"Cut the weight loose! Let me come upright!" he bellowed angrily.

"Not yet, lad. Not quite yet. Just a bit more. I've set a buoy, and as soon as we're past it, I'll know your keel will clear. Steady now, steady."

"Let me up!" Paragon shouted, and this time he could not keep a note of fear out of his voice.

"Soon. Trust me, lad. Just a bit further."

In his years ashore, he had almost become accustomed to his blindness. But it was one thing to lie immobile and see nothing. It was quite another to suddenly be in motion, on the breast of the unpredictable sea once more, and to have no idea where he was or what was near him. A driftwood log could pound against him, an unseen rock could hole him, and he would have no warning until it happened. Why wouldn't they let him come upright?

"All right, let it go!" Brashen suddenly yelled. The line that had been attached to the counterweight was loosened. Slowly he began to come upright, and then sudden as a cork, the next wave righted him. Amber gave an abrupt yell of surprise, but held on. Cold water suddenly washed against and below him on both sides. For the first time in over thirty years, he stood straight and tall. He flung his arms out and gave a roar of triumph. He heard Amber echo it in a wild laugh even as within him Althea shouted in alarm.

"Get on those pumps! Now! Brashen, let go the canvas as soon as you can!"

He heard the thunder of feet and wild shouting, but he didn't care. He wasn't going to sink. He could feel it. He stretched his arms, his back and his shoulders. As the water bore him up, he extended his awareness throughout his body. He could almost feel how his planks and beams should go. He took a deep breath and tried to bring himself into alignment. He listed suddenly to starboard. There was a cry of surprise from Amber and an angry roar from Brashen. He lifted his hands to his temples and squeezed. It was the same old thing: something was wrong inside him. His parts didn't go together right. He shifted again, ignoring the groans and squeaks of his wood as the planks worked against each other. Slowly he began to stabilize. Dimly he was aware of the frantic work going on within him. Men manned his pumps, trying to keep up with the water streaming in through his sprung seams. He felt the sudden press of canvas against his planking. Althea was shouting at the men inside him to hurry, hurry, get that oakum tamped into place. He could feel his wood starting to swell.

Abruptly he bumped against something, and Brashen was shouting, throw a line, throw a line and make it fast, you idiot!

He groped toward the obstacle.

Amber's comforting voice reached his ears. "It's the barge, Paragon. We're alongside the work barge and they're making you fast to it. You'll be safe here."

Paragon wasn't so sure. He was still taking on water and settling lower. "How deep is it here?" he asked nervously.

Brashen's jubilant voice sounded as if he were standing alongside Amber. "Deep enough to float you. Not so deep that if you go down we'll lose you. Not that we'd let you go down. We may have to beach you again to work on your port side. For now, don't worry. It's all under control." The speed with which he hastened away seemed to belie his words.

For a time, Paragon listened. There were voices and hurrying foot-steps inside him, running feet across his deck. On the barge beside him, the work crew was congratulating one another on their work and specu-lating on how many repairs he was going to need. However, those were not the things he heard. Instead, he listened to the slap of the waves against his hull and the sound of his wood creaking and settling, even the sounds his hull made rubbing against the bumpers on the barge. Every-thing was suddenly eerily familiar and yet strange. The smells seemed sharper out here, the cries of the sea-birds louder. He rose and fell with the waves. The gentle rocking was soothing, but it was also the stuff of his nightmares. "Well," he said aloud, but quietly. "I'm afloat again. I guess that makes me a ship and not a hulk."

"I guess," Amber agreed easily. She had been so still and silent, he had almost forgotten her. Unlike all other people he had ever known, she sometimes became transparent to his senses. He knew, without even reaching, where Brashen and Althea were. A moment's reflection, and he could locate every nameless worker on his deck or in his holds. But Amber was different. She seemed, he thought to himself, more contained and isolated than any other human he had ever known. Sometimes he suspected it was deliberate; that she only shared herself when she chose to, and then only in a limited way. Not unlike myself, he reflected, and then frowned at the thought.

"Is something wrong?" she asked quickly.

"Not yet," he replied in a sour voice.

She laughed lightly, as if he jested. "So. Are you glad to be a ship again?"

"Glad or sorry, it makes little difference. You will do with me as you want to, and my feelings about it will not matter to anyone." He paused. "I admit, I did not believe you. I did not think I would float again. Not that I particularly wanted to float again."

"Paragon, your feelings matter. Somehow, I do not believe that you truly wanted to remain on that beach forever. You once told me, quite angrily, that you are a ship and a ship is meant to sail. I suspect that even if you do not enjoy this at first, it will be good for you. All living things need to grow. You were not growing, abandoned there on the beach. You were close to giving up and believing yourself a failure." Her voice was affectionate. Suddenly he could not stand that. Did they think they could force him to do something, and then pretend it was for his own good?

He laughed harshly. "On the contrary. I knew I had succeeded. I'd killed them all, every one of them who tried to oppose me. You are the ones who refuse to believe me a success. If you did, you'd have the good sense to fear me."

An instant of horrified silence followed his words. He felt her let go of his railing and stand up straight. "Paragon. When you speak like that, I refuse to stand and listen to you." Her voice held no hint of what she was thinking.

"Oh. I see. Then you are afraid?" he asked her wickedly.

But she had turned and resolutely walked away. She made no reply at all.

He didn't care. So he had hurt her feelings. So what? No one cared anything about his feelings. No one ever asked him what he wanted to do.

"Why're you like that?"

He had known Clef was there. The boy had come out to the barge with the beach crew. He didn't startle. For a time, he didn't even reply.

"Why're you like that?" the boy persisted.

"Like what?" Paragon finally asked in annoyance.

"Ya'know. Allus mad. Or crazy fightin'. Say'n stuff ta be mean."

"How else do you expect me to be?" Paragon retorted. "Joyous that they've dragged me out here? All excited to go off on a hare-brained rescue mission with them?"

He felt the boy's shrug. "Ya could be."

"I could be?" Paragon snorted. "I'd like to know how."

"S'easy. Ya decide t'be."

"You decide to be happy? I should just forget everything that has been done to me, and be happy? Tra-la-la-la? Like that?"

"Ya could." He heard the boy's nails against his scalp. "Lookit me. I coulda hated everyone o' 'em. I decided t'be happy. Decided ta take what I could get. Make a life outer it." A pause. "S'not like I'm gonna get another life. Gotta make this'n work."

"It's not that simple," Paragon snapped.

"Could be," Clef insisted. "In't no harder than decidin't'be mad allus."

The boy sauntered away slowly. His bare feet scuffed lightly on the deck. "But it's a lot funner," he called back over his shoulder.

WATER STREAMED DOWN THE INSIDE PLANKING. THE CANVAS WAS SUCKED into place and the flow was slowing. The caulkers were working swiftly and efficiently, with more skill than Althea had expected from them. The men on the pumps concerned her. They were tiring. She had gone to find

Brashen, to ask him if he had replacements for them. She ran into him as he came down a ladder. Behind him were several burly men from the barge. Before she could even speak, he tossed his head at them. "The shore crew is on the barge now. They're to spell your men on the pumps. How are we holding?"

"We're keeping up with it, and even gaining a little. The wood is swelling fast, but wizardwood does that. If he were any other liveship, I'd say he could apply himself a bit and close up half the leaks. But with Paragon, I fear even to ask him." She took a breath, waited until the pump crew was out of earshot, then added very softly, "For fear he would do exactly the opposite. How is he?"

Brashen scratched at his beard thoughtfully. "I don't know. When we were getting him off the beach, he was yelling out suggestions and com-mands as if he were eager to be afloat again. But like you, I'm afraid to assume that is so. Sometimes all it takes to plunge him into a foul temper is to assume that he is in a good mood."

"I know what you mean." She met his eyes, commiserating. "Brashen, what have we let ourselves in for this time? While he was on the beach, and he was our only hope, it seemed a viable plan. But now that we are out here . . . do you realize how completely we are in his power? He holds our lives in his hands."

For a moment, the sailor looked very tired. His shoulders sank in discouragement. Then he drew in a deep breath. "Don't stop believing in him now, Althea, or we are all lost. Don't show him any sign of fear or doubt. Paragon is more child than man. When I give Clef an order, I don't watch him to see if he'll obey. I'd never let him believe he had more power over me than I had over him. Boys can't deal with that. They'll keep groping for the limits until they find them. They only feel safe when they know where the boundaries are."

She tried to smile at him. "You speak from experience?"

The smile he returned her was a sickly one. "By the time I found the boundaries, I had fallen off the edge of the world. I won't let that happen to Paragon." He stood still for a moment, and she thought he might say more to her. Then he shrugged his shoulders, turned and hastened after the pumpers.

It reminded her she had work of her own. She moved swiftly through the ship, checking on the workers caulking the hull. Mostly, they were reinforcing and tightening work that had been done while the Paragon was on shore. In a few places, they were even removing oakum to allow the planks to swell shut. Like most Rain Wild ships, Paragon had been well and tightly constructed, his planking designed to withstand the seething water of the Rain Wild River, as well as the vagaries of ocean waves. The workmanship had withstood even the neglect of thirty years. The gray wizardwood planks actually seemed to recall how they had been fitted together. Perhaps, she dared to hope, Paragon was co-operating after all. A liveship could do much to maintain himself, if he chose to do so.

It seemed strange to move through the ship. It was the first time in all the years she had known him that his decks were level under her feet. Satisfied that her work crew was well occupied, she made a quick tour of the ship. The galley was a mess. The stove had broken loose of its stove-pipe and slid across the small room, trailing soot. Like as not, it would have to be repaired if not replaced. The master stateroom had suffered likewise. Amber's chests of belongings had spilled. A vial of scent had fallen and smashed, leaving the room reeking of lilac. As Althea stood looking about, the future became real to her. Amber would have to move her things out of here, and assume the humbler quarters befitting the ship's carpenter.

Then Brashen would move in.

She had reluctantly accepted that he must captain this ship. She did not agree with any of his arguments. Her reasons were more personal. When they recovered Vivacia, she would need to be able to step off Paragon's deck and assume command there. If she were captain of the Paragon, that would prove very unsettling to a ship that was already flighty. Whoever sailed out as Paragon's captain must stay with him for the return journey. It would have to be Brashen.

She still felt a twinge of regret as she closed the door on the chamber. Paragon had been built in the old style. The captain's quarters were by far the finest ones on the ship. Amber had done a great deal to restore the lavishly carved cabinet work and window frames. A bit of carpet covered the ill-conceived hatch she had cut between the cabin and the hold. The stained-glass windows had suffered cracks and portions of the glass were missing, but that was a minor detail. Their money would go first to pay for functional repairs.

She moved on to consider the first mate's cabin. This would be hers. Much smaller than the captain's quarters, it was still palatial in compari-son to crew quarters. She had a fixed bunk, a fold-down desk and two cupboards for her possessions. A third chamber, not much bigger than a good-sized closet, was intended for the second mate. Crew quarters were hooks in the forecastle where hammocks could be strung, and little more than that. The older liveships had not taken the crew's comfort into consideration. Cargo space had been their main goal.

When she went on deck, she found Brashen pacing about. He was restless, and yet triumphant. He turned to her immediately. "We're hold-ing steady. There's still water coming in, but no more than a two-man pump crew can keep up with. I think by tomorrow morning, he'll have tightened up. We've a bit of a list, but proper ballast should handle that." There was a light in his face she had not seen since he had sailed on Vivacia under her father. His step was brisk. "Nothing has cracked, noth-

ing sprung. Our luck on this is almost too good to believe. I knew liveships were tough, but this beats all. Any other ship that had been beached
for thirty years would be rot and kindling."

His exuberance was contagious. She followed as he strode about the
ship, pausing to shake a railing to see how much give it had in it, or open
and shut a hatch to see if it was still square. There was still a great deal of
work to do on the *Paragon*, but most of it would be refitting rather than
rebuilding. "We'll stay with the barge for a while, to let his wood swell.
Then we'll move him to the west wall to finish."

"With the other liveships?" Althea asked uneasily.

Brashen rounded on her in a manner almost challenging. "Where
else? He is a liveship."

She spoke as bluntly. "I fear what they may say to him. That a
thoughtless remark may set him off into one of his frenzies."

"Althea, the sooner we start dealing with that, the better." He
stepped closer to her and for a moment, she thought he would take her
arm. Instead, he gestured her to accompany him as he strode forward
toward the figurehead. "I think we should plunge him into a normal life.
Treat him as we would any liveship, and see how he reacts. The more we
tiptoe around him, the more tyrannical he will become."

"Do you really think it will be that simple? Start treating him normally, and he'll start behaving normally?"

Brashen flung a grin at her. "No. Of course not. But it's where we'll
begin and hope for the best."

She found herself grinning back at him. Something in her responded
to him on a level her intellect could not reach. She could not reason with
the attraction she felt. She only knew it was a pleasure to see him moving
and speaking as he once had. The bitter and cynical rogue that Kyle
Haven and Torg had created was gone. This was the man who had been
her father's first mate.

She followed him as he sauntered up to the bow railing and leaned
over. "Paragon! We've done it, old friend. You're afloat and we're going to
make them all sit up and take notice."

The figurehead ignored him. Brashen gave a small shrug and raised an
eyebrow at Althea. Not even this could daunt him, it seemed. Leaning
back on the railing, he stared off to the forest of masts that was Bingtown
Harbor. A faraway look came over his face. "Do you hate me for this?" he
asked suddenly.

For an instant, she thought he addressed the ship. But then he
glanced at her quizzically.

"For what?"

He turned to face her and spoke with a bluff honesty she remembered
well. "For standing here, as I never believed I would. For standing on my
own deck as Captain Brashen Trell of the liveship *Paragon*. Where I know

you'd love to be." Despite his efforts at gravity, a smile broke over his face. Something in it brought tears to her eyes. She turned hastily to look out over the water lest he see them. How hungry had he been for this moment, and for how long?

"I don't hate you for it," she said quietly. It was true, she realized. It surprised her that there was not even one splinter of jealousy in her soul. Instead she felt a rising joy at seeing him triumph. She gripped *Paragon's* railing. "You belong here. So does he. After all these years, he's in good hands. How could I be jealous?" She stole another glance at him. The wind stirred his dark hair. His own chiseled features could have been a figurehead. "I think my father would have slapped you on the back and congratulated you. And warned you, as I do now, that when I have my own *Vivacia* under me again, you won't hold a candle to us." She smiled at him, holding nothing back.

PARAGON HAD HEARD THEM COMING AND KNEW THEY WERE TALKING about him. Gossip, gossip, gossip. All of them were always like that. They'd always rather talk about him than to him. They thought he was stupid. They probably thought it was no good talking to him about anything. So he didn't feel a bit sneaky about listening in. Now that there was salt water around him again, he could sense them more clearly. It was not only their words that carried more clearly to his ears, but their feelings.

He lost his irritation in a brief sense of awe. Yes. He could feel them much more clearly now. Almost as clearly as he could have felt one of his own family. He reached toward them very cautiously. He didn't want them to be aware of him. Not just yet.

Their emotions were strong. Brashen was heady with triumph, and Althea shared it. Something more was there, too. Something else passed between them. He didn't have a word for it. In some ways, it felt like the salt water soaking into his wizardwood planks. Things were resuming their rightful places. Lines that had been skewed were coming back into true. He sensed the same adjustment between Brashen and Althea. The tension between them was one they accepted. It acted as a counter-force to easiness between them. He tried to find a simile for it. Like wind in his sails. Without the force against the canvas, he could not move. It was not a tension to be avoided, but one to be courted.

As they did?

It wasn't until Brashen leaned over the railing and spoke to him that he realized how close they had come. He had been so aware of them he hadn't noticed the physical distance closing. Well, he wasn't about to answer them.

Then Althea leaned on the railing also. The feelings flowed through him. From Brashen to Althea, from Althea to Brashen, it included him. The pride in Brashen's voice was not feigned. "Captain Brashen Trell, of the liveship *Paragon*." The words thrummed through the ship. Brashen spoke with more than pride. With fondness. Possession. Brashen had longed to claim him. Not just for this rescue, not because he was cheap and available. He wanted to be captain of the liveship *Paragon*. In wonder, he sensed Althea echoing his feelings. They both truly felt that he was where he belonged.

Something long closed in Paragon opened. A tiny spark of self-worth suddenly burned in his darkness. "Don't bet on it, Vestrit," he said quietly. He grinned as he felt them both start and then lean over the railing to try to see his face. His arms were still crossed on his chest, but he sank his bearded chin onto his chest in self-satisfaction. "You may think you and *Vivacia* can show us up. But Trell and I, we still have a lot to reveal. You haven't seen the half of us yet."

CHAPTER TWENTY-SIX

Compromises

"I THINK IT'S PERFECT." KEFFRIA COULD NOT KEEP THE SATISFACTION OUT of her voice.

"It's lovely," Rache echoed the sentiment. "But turn about just one more time for us. A little faster, so the skirts lift just slightly with the motion. I want to be sure the hem is perfectly even before we do the final stitching."

Malta lifted her arms carefully to avoid the pins and turned on her stockinged feet. All about them on the floor was the litter of the gown's making. Older dresses had been robbed of lace. The bright panels of fabric set into the lavish sleeves of the dress had once been the skirts of another dress.

"Ah! Like a lily floating on water, when a summer breeze ripples it. You could not be more beautiful." Rache was triumphant.

"Unless she smiled," Selden pointed out quietly. He sat on the floor in the corner of the room, his counters spread on the floor before him. Malta had been watching him. He was building castles with them, not working his problems. She was too dispirited to point out his idleness to their mother.

"Your little brother is right, Malta. The gown cannot brighten your face as a smile can. What is wrong? Are you still wishing we had had a fashionable seamstress do this?"

Of course she was! How could her mother even ask such a question? For years, she and Delo had talked of their first Summer Ball as young ladies. They'd drawn pictures of their elaborate gowns, discussed trims and seamstresses and slippers. Never again would the eyes of Bingtown fall so attentively upon them. All would see her dressed in a home-stitched dress with made-over slippers. Every waking moment of summer, she had spent longing for a miracle. It was useless even to speak of how she felt. She didn't want her mother to weep again, or her grandmother to tell her she should take pride in the sacrifices she'd made. This was the best they could do for her. What good would it do to speak of her disappointment?

"It is hard to smile these days, Mother." She took a breath. "I had always thought I would walk into the Summer Ball on my father's arm."

"As did I," Keffria Vestrit replied quietly. "It breaks my heart that you cannot have that, Malta. I still remember my first Summer Ball in a woman's gown. When they announced me, I was so nervous I thought I couldn't stand. Then Papa picked up my hand and set it on his arm. And we walked in together . . . he was so proud of me." Her voice choked suddenly. She blinked rapidly. "Wherever your father is, my dear, I am sure he is thinking of you as you are of him."

"Sometimes it feels wrong to be thinking of the summer parties after the great ball, worrying about dresses and fans and headpieces while he is a prisoner in the Pirate Isles." Malta paused. "Perhaps we should put this off one more year. Perhaps by then, he would be home."

"It's a little late now to be considering that," Grandmother put in from her chair. She was sitting in the light from the window, trying to fashion a fan from the leftover fabric. "I used to know how to do this," she muttered crossly to herself. "My fingers just aren't as nimble at this as they used to be."

"I'm afraid your grandmother is right, dear." Her mother fussed with the lace at her cuffs. "Everyone is expecting us to present you. And it would make our situation with the Khuprus family even more difficult."

"I don't think I like him anymore anyway. If Reyn were truly interested in me, he would have come to see me again." She twisted her head to look at her mother just as Rache tried to set her headdress in place. "Have you heard no more from his mother?" Rache seized her chin, straightened her head, and pinned the headdress in place.

Keffria frowned at it. "It's too big. It overpowers her face. We need to make it more delicate. Take it off, we'll try again." As Rache unpinned it, Keffria asked, "What more could she write to us? She sympathizes with our plight. They pray your father will return safely to us. Reyn looks forward eagerly to the Summer Ball." Keffria sighed and added, "And she suggested, very delicately, that two weeks after the ball, we might discuss the payment on our debt."

"Translation: she wants to see how Malta and Reyn get along at the ball," Grandmother put in sourly. She squinted at the pretty work in her hands. "They have to consider appearances just as much as we do, Malta. For Reyn to call on you too often before you are even presented would be seen as unseemly haste. Besides, it is a substantial journey from the Rain Wilds to Bingtown, not to be undertaken lightly."

Malta gave a small sigh. So she had told herself, often enough. But it seemed to her more likely that Reyn had simply decided she wasn't worth the nuisance of courting her. Perhaps the dragon had had something to do with it. She had dreamed of the dragon often since then, and the dreams varied from disturbing to frightening. Sometimes the dragon spoke of

Reyn. She said that Malta was foolish to wait for him. He would not come to help her. Her only possible hope was to somehow come to the dragon and free her. Over and over, Malta had tried to tell her that was impossible. *"When you say that,"* the dragon had mocked her, *"You are saying, really, that it is impossible for you to rescue your father. Is that what you truly believe?"* That question always left her speechless.

It did not mean she had given up. She had learned a great deal about men lately. It seemed to her that when she needed their strength or power most, they abandoned her. Both Cerwin and Reyn had vanished when she asked them for something more substantial than trinkets or sweets. Reluctantly she acknowledged a second thought. Just when she needed her own father's strength and power, he had sailed out of her life. And disappeared. It wasn't his fault. She knew that. It didn't change what she had learned. You couldn't depend on men, even powerful men, even when they truly loved you. To save her father, she was going to have to gather power to herself, and then use it.

Afterwards, she would keep it.

A thought occurred to her. "Mother. Father will not be here to escort me into the Summer Ball. Who will?"

"Well." She looked uncomfortable. "Davad Restart has offered, of course. He would be honored; I suppose he feels we owe him something for negotiating for the *Paragon* . . ." Her voice died away apologetically.

Rache gave a small snort of contempt. She ripped the seams out of the headdress as if it were Davad's face she tore apart.

"We owe him nothing," Ronica Vestrit said firmly. She lifted her eyes from her stitching to regard her granddaughter. "You have no obligation to him, Malta. None."

"Then . . . if my Papa cannot be there . . . I should like to walk in by myself."

Keffria looked troubled. "My dear, I am not sure if that would be proper."

"Proper or not, it is fitting. Let her do it."

Malta looked in astonishment at her grandmother. Ronica returned the look almost defiantly. "Bingtown has left us to stand or fall on our own. Let them see that we stand, even to our youngest daughter." Her eyes locked with Malta's and something almost like understanding passed between them. "Let the Rain Wilds know it as well," Ronica added quietly.

ALTHEA STRODE DOWN THE DOCKS ON THE WEST WALL OF THE HARBOR. AT every third or fourth step, her skirts hobbled her. She would slow for a pace or two, then forget herself and step out again. Out on the beach, she had become accustomed to the luxury of trousers. Now that Paragon was tied up in town at the liveship dock, she had to make more of an effort to conform, but this was a compromise that suited no one. Her coarse cotton work-skirt scandalized Keffria and was still too confining to suit Althea. She longed to be out to sea, where she vowed she would dress as she pleased.

"Althea!" boomed Kendry. She halted in her tracks to turn to the liveship with a grin.

"Good morning!" She waved up at him. He was riding high today, but by sundown, he'd be heavy with cargo to take upriver. Barrows of melons were being trundled aboard him as they spoke. There was little arable soil up the Rain Wild River. Most of the foodstuffs had to be brought in. Kendry made it his regular run. He trafficked in little besides food supplies and Rain Wild goods.

"Good morning, yourself, young lady!" The figurehead put his fists on the sides of his ship as if they were his hips. He looked down in mock disapproval. "You looked so like a scrub girl, I almost didn't know you."

She grinned up at his good-natured teasing. "Well, you know yourself, it takes more than one scrub girl to keep a liveship clean. I'll be all over grease and tar before the day is out. Then we'll see if you recognize me more easily."

The *Kendry* had been carved as a handsome young man. His affable grin and wide blue eyes made him a favorite on the liveship dock. Althea was long accustomed to his casual ways with her. "It'll take a rough scrubbing to get that off before the Summer Ball," he suggested wryly.

That was a more sobering topic. After much argument with her mother and sister, she had won her way. "I won't be going to the Summer Ball, Kendry. We hope to set sail before then. Besides, even if I went, who would dance with a scrub girl?" She tried to lighten her words with a smile.

He glanced about and then dropped her a slow wink. "I know a sailor who might not be dismayed at such an idea." He lowered his voice. "I'd be happy to take a message to Trehaug with me, if you'd care to send one."

So. Grag Tenira was still holed up in the Rain Wild city. She started to shake her head, then reconsidered. "I might send a note, if you didn't mind taking it."

"Always happy to do a favor for a friend." He jerked his head down the dock. In a more confidential tone he asked, "And how is our other friend doing?"

Althea suppressed annoyance. "As well as can be expected. He has his difficulties. He was very isolated and neglected for a long time, you know. And we've put him through a lot in a very short time. New rigging, new crew, not to mention that he has no true family member aboard."

Kendry shrugged his bare, broad shoulders. "Well, if he hadn't killed

so many of them, there might be a few more Ludlucks to go around." He
laughed at Althea's scowl. "Just telling you how I see it, girl. Don't
scrunch your face up at me. There isn't a ship in this harbor that doesn't
feel he brought much of his troubles down on himself. That does not
mean we do not wish him well. I would like nothing better than to see
him straighten up and redeem himself. But," he admonished her with a
lifted forefinger, "I don't think he's worth a lady taking big chances. If
things don't feel right by your sailing date, you let him go without you."
He leaned back against his ship like a boy leaning on a sunny wall.
"Maybe you'd like to take a trip up the river with me instead? Bet I could
get my captain to let you ride free."

"I'll bet you could, and I thank you for the offer. But when *Paragon*
sails, I'm aboard him. After all, it's my family liveship that we're going
after. Besides, I believe he'll do just fine." She glanced up at the sun. "I've
got to hurry, Kendry. Take care of yourself."

"Well, little one, you take care of yourself. Mind what you said. Don't
take too long about that note. I plan to be away from this dock before
noon tomorrow."

She turned and waved gaily as she walked away from him. She told
herself they meant well, all the people who wished her success and then
warned her about Paragon. Even Trell. Sometimes she had to work to
remember that.

The work had gone better than anyone had expected it to. Their
small budget had been supplemented by Amber's mysterious influence. No
less an artisan than Nole Flate had come down to volunteer his services in
setting up the canvas for the new rigging. Althea couldn't imagine what
Amber knew about Nole that had prompted the stingy old man to be so
suddenly generous with his time. Some nasty little secret, she didn't
doubt. Yesterday, a score casks of ship's biscuit had been donated by a
well-wisher who insisted on remaining anonymous. Althea suspected Amber's hand there, as well.

But the most useful had been Amber's slave recruits who quietly
arrived in the dark of night, after Brashen had sent home the regular
workers, to slip aboard *Paragon* and toil until dawn almost grayed the
skies. Then they would disperse as swiftly as they had arrived. They spoke
little and worked hard. Every face was tattooed. She hated to think what
risks they took to slip away from their masters each night. Althea suspected that when they sailed, most of the night crew would be belowdecks. They'd fill out the hired crew as fighters and seamen. How this had
been arranged, she didn't want to know. Brashen had tried to take her
into his confidence about it one afternoon. She had lifted her hands to
her ears. "A secret is kept best by one," she reminded him.

He had looked pleased.

That thought brought a smile to her own face. She shook her head at herself. Why should she care if he were pleased with her or not? He'd made very little effort to please her with his latest decision. It should have been a monumental argument, but damn Brashen had insisted on remembering his privileges as captain.

At least he had summoned her into the captain's quarters before breaking the news to her. No one would see her angry face, but the missing window meant that any passer-by might hear raised voices. Brashen had sat nonchalantly at the newly refinished chart table. He was studying a handful of canvas scraps he'd taken from a bag.

"I did as was my right. I hired my own first mate." He had cocked his head at her maddeningly. "Wouldn't you have done the same in my position?"

"Yes," she had hissed. "But I'd have hired you, damn you. I thought that was the agreement."

"No," he replied thoughtfully. He set a scrap of canvas down on the table, pushed at it thoughtfully, then seemed to decide the sketch on it was upside down. "There was no agreement about that. Save that you would sail with me . . . with the *Paragon* when he sailed. We made no other agreement. As you might recall, I suggested some time ago that you not work alongside the men, in light of the type of men I'd have to hire."

She had made a small sound of disgust. Some of them barely merited the title of men. She took a breath to speak, but he held up a hand.

"Any other ship, any other crew, you would have been first for me. You know that. But this crew will need a whip hand. Sweet reason will not sway many of these men. The real threat of a physical thrashing may."

"I could hold my own," she lied gamely.

He shook his head. "You're not big enough. They wouldn't respect you until after they'd challenged you and had it proven to them. Even if you won, it would be more violence on the *Paragon* than I am willing to risk. If you lost—" He didn't go into the consequences of that. "So I've hired a man who is big enough and strong enough that most of the men won't want to challenge him. Those that do will certainly lose. I've hired Lavoy. He is a brute, and that's one of the kinder things we can say about him. He's also a damn fine sailor. If it weren't for his temperament, he'd have risen to command years ago. I told him that I was giving him a chance on the *Paragon*. If he proves out here, all of Bingtown will know that he could be mate anywhere. He's hungry for this chance, Althea. The opportunity is what hired him; the coin I could offer was no better than he might get as a bully mate on a larger vessel. He wants to prove himself, but I suspect he doesn't have it in him. That's where you come in. I'm captain. He's the first. You will be second. We'll pin his authority between ours. Not undercut it, but moderate. Do you take my drift?"

"I suppose," she replied grudgingly. She saw the logic of it, but it still rubbed her raw. "Second, then," she conceded.

"There's something else. Something you'll like just as little," he warned her.

"And that is?"

"Amber has bought her right to be aboard. She's put more coin and time into this than any other sailor aboard, and I include us both in that. I don't know what sort of a sailor she'll make; she's told me she has little taste for traveling by ship. She's proven herself a fine carpenter, in matters both great and small. So that will be her capacity aboard the vessel. She'll bunk in with you."

Althea gave a groan of protest.

"And Jek," he added remorselessly. "She wanted to come along, she has good sea time from the Six Duchies, and she was willing to hire on cheap, 'for the dare of it' as she told me. You've seen her up the rigging when we strung it. She's nimble and fearless. I'd be a fool to refuse such a hand. I'd also be a fool to house her in with the dock scrapings we've taken on as crew. There's at least one who's been branded as a rapist, and another that even I won't turn my back on." He shrugged. "She'll bunk in with you and Amber. I'll put you on different watches, so you shouldn't be too crowded to sleep."

"We're going to be stacked like cordwood in there," Althea complained.

"Amber is as displeased about it as you are. She claims that some solitary time each day is essential to her. I've told her I'll give her some access to my room when I'm not in it. Same goes for you."

"That'll cause talk amongst the crew."

Brashen had grinned sourly. "Let's just hope that's the most unsettling thing they have to gossip about."

That was a sentiment Althea fervently shared. Even now, as she made her way down the sun-swept dock toward the ship, she prayed for an ordinary day. Let Paragon not be weeping endlessly into his hands, or reciting the same bawdy poem over and over. Some days, when she arrived and he gave her a pleasant good morning, it was like a direct blessing from Sa. Yesterday when she got to the dock, he had been holding a dead flounder some passing wag had given him. For some reason, the dead fish upset him, and yet he would not give it to her or put it down himself. Amber had finally coaxed it away from him. Sometimes she was the only one who could handle him.

Their total complement of crew members had been hired several days ago, and several times since then. Brashen would find sailors, convince them to sign aboard, and get them moved on, only to have them walk the next day. It wasn't just the bizarre things Paragon said or did. Like the smell of fear-sweat, his madness flavored the air of the ship. Those sensitive enough to feel it without knowing the source suffered nightmares, or sudden panics while working in the holds. Neither Brashen nor Althea tried to force any man to remain aboard. Althea knew it was better to lose them now than to have jittery or frightened men aboard once they set sail. It was still becoming a local joke. The mongrelized crew was unusual enough by Bingtown standards, without men jumping ship in the harbor and spreading rumors of the odd goings-on aboard the ship.

Today Paragon seemed calm enough. At least, she did not hear him ranting. As she reached his slip, the traffic along the dock seemed normal. "Hey, Paragon," she greeted him as she passed the figurehead on the way to the gangplank.

"Hey, yourself," he replied affably. Amber was sitting on the bow rail swinging her legs. Her freed hair floated on the wind. She had adopted a strange style of dress of late, loose pantaloons and a blouse with a vest. As a foreigner in Bingtown, she could get away with such things. Althea envied her.

"Any word of the *Ringsgold?*" Paragon asked as she passed him.

"Not that I've heard," she replied. "Why?"

"There's been talk that he's late returning to Bingtown. The ships that should have seen him, haven't."

Althea's heart sank in her. "Well, a lot of things can delay a ship, even a liveship," she pointed out jovially.

"Of course," Paragon replied. "Pirates. Serpents. Deadly storms."

"Unfavorable winds," Althea countered. "Delays loading cargo."

He gave a snort of contempt. Amber shrugged her shoulders at Althea. Well, at least he was rational today. Althea continued to the gangplank and came aboard. Lavoy was standing in the center of the deck. His fists were on his hips and he was glaring about with a hard eye. This was the most difficult, grating part.

"Reporting, sir," she said stiffly.

He gave her a fish-eyed look. His gaze traveled up and down her and his mouth twisted in contempt. "So I see," he said after a moment. "Supplies are coming aboard today. Pick a crew of six men and get below. Stow the goods as they come on. You know how to do that." There was just the slightest bit of a question in his voice.

"I do," she said flatly. She wasn't going to recite her credentials for him. She wore her ship's tag from *Ophelia* at her belt. It would have been good enough for anyone else on the Bingtown dock. She glanced about the deck and chose her hands for the day by jabbing a finger at them. "Haff and you. Jek. Cypros. You and Kert. Come on." She was still learning names. It wasn't made any easier by the way hands came and went. She didn't look forward to the task as she led them down to the hold.

Lavoy was running the shore crew, bringing the supplies on board and passing them down to her gang. It would be her job to load the cargo evenly and well. She suspected he would work his crew as fast and hard as he could to see if hers could keep up. There was always that sort of chivvying between mates on a vessel. Sometimes it was good-natured. This was not.

The *Paragon* had proven to be a lively ship on the water. Brashen had been most particular about his ballast, but he still rolled more than Althea liked. How he was loaded was going to be critical, especially if they were under full sail and a wind came up. Althea was divided. She didn't want to be the one responsible for his stability; at the same time, she didn't trust anyone else to do it, save perhaps Brashen. Her father had always been most particular about cargo. Perhaps she'd inherited that tendency.

Belowdecks, the air was hot and thick with ship smells. Even with the hatches open, the air was still and stagnant. She was grateful it was the smell of new tar and oakum and varnish. Before this voyage was over, the smells of aged bilge water, human sweat and rancid cooking would be added to the bouquet. For now, *Paragon* actually smelled like a new ship.

But he wasn't. Throughout him were the small signs of his usage. Initials carved in a bulkhead, old hooks where a hammock or ditty bag had been hung. Some signs were grim. Bloody handprints that suggested someone had crawled while bleeding heavily. A spatter that was obviously from a heavy blow. Wizardwood remembered. She suspected that at one time there had been a massacre on board the ship. That did not fit with Paragon's claims to have killed his crews, but any hint of a question about such things sent him into frenzy. She supposed they would never know the full truth of what he had endured.

She had been right about Lavoy. A steady stream of supplies soon threatened to overwhelm her work crew. Any fool could bring a box or cask aboard a ship quickly, she told herself. It took someone with some sea sense to know how to stow it all correctly. She worked alongside her crew. As second mate, that was expected of her. She sensed that this was part of the compromise that Brashen had offered. She still believed she could earn the crew's respect as an equal. She would get no better chance than now to prove it. She pushed Jek as hard as she did herself, taking the woman's measure to see if she was all she claimed to be. Jek appeared more at ease working alongside the men than the men did with her, but that was to be expected. Hers was the Six Duchies way. Jek measured up, and her good-natured humor eased the task. She would be a good shipmate. Althea's only concern was that she might become too friendly with the men. She had made no effort to conceal her lively appetites. Althea wondered if it would lead to later problems aboard the ship. Reluctantly, she concluded it was something she would have to bring up to Brashen. He was captain, after all. Let him handle it.

Light from the open hatches fell in squares down into the massive timbered holds. Once the crates, barrels and casks were loaded down, it was the work of muscles and bones alone to move them. Here Althea's shorter height gave her an odd advantage as she scrabbled over and around their cargo. Crates and bins were lowered down; her crew seized them by hand or snagged them with freight hooks. Container after container was shouldered into place, then blocked and wedged to prevent shifting. As barrel after barrel came down to be stowed, she reminded herself that all too soon they would likely wish they had had more to load aboard. The crew *Paragon* carried was larger than normal. They'd need enough men to fight and sail the ship at the same time. With no definite port in their plans, and no chance to re-provision, they'd load the ship as full as they could afford now. Far better to have too much than too little.

She watched her crew as she worked alongside them, quickly learning who worked well and who did as little as possible. Cypros and Kert did a fair share, but required direction. Jek was a jewel, putting her back into what she did and looking ahead to foresee possible difficulties. Semoy, an older man with a drink-reddened nose, was already pleading that a sore shoulder was troubling him. If he couldn't keep up, it was better he was off the vessel before they sailed. Of the two others, Haff was a loudmouth youngster who made no secret of his disdain for Althea's commands while Lop, a skinny man of middle years, was willing but stupid. She preferred his stupidity to Haff's near-insubordination. Soon, she knew, she would have to hash things out with Haff. She didn't look forward to it. He was larger than she was, and well-muscled. She told herself that if she handled herself correctly, it would never become a physical confrontation. She prayed to Sa she was correct.

Lavoy came down twice that morning, to inspect her work. Each time he complained about small issues. Each time she gritted her teeth and shifted the load to suit him. He was first mate, she reminded herself. If she ignored him, it would undermine his authority with the crew. The fourth time he came down the ladder, she thought she was going to grind her molars flat. Instead he looked around, and gave a grudging nod to her work. "Carry on." That was all the encouragement he offered, but she actually felt complimented by it. So he felt the need to try her mettle. He wouldn't find her slack nor insubordinate. She had agreed to this with Brashen; she'd keep her word to him.

It still made for a long day. By the time her watch was over and she emerged onto the deck, the sunny afternoon felt open and fresh. She plucked her sweat-soaked shirt free of her body and lifted her braided hair from the back of her neck. She went forward to look for Amber.

She found the ship's carpenter engaged in conversation with Brashen. She held the ends of two coils of line in her gloved hands. Althea watched silently as she awkwardly put a double sheet bend into the lines. Brashen took it from her, shook his head, undid it and tossed it back. "Do it again. Keep doing it until you can tie it with your eyes shut. If we're ever so hard-pressed that I haul you out on deck, it's likely to be in bad weather."

"That's reassuring," Amber muttered quietly, but did as he bade her. Althea marveled at how swiftly the woman adapted herself. With all of them, Brashen was quietly asserting his new status as captain of the vessel. Althea was accustomed to such a shifting of roles. She'd seen it before, on the *Vivacia*, when a deckhand rose to mate status and suddenly had to change his relationship with his fellows. She knew that sometimes it could be bloody, though she had never seen it go that far on *Vivacia*. She was willing to cede to Brashen both the distance and the respect he needed to function as captain. That distance might make it easier for both of them.

So she schooled her tongue to respect as she said, "Sir, I've a concern about the crew."

He gave her his full attention. "And that is?"

She took a breath, then plunged in. "Jek is a bit too friendly with the other hands. It may lead to problems later. While we are in port, it is one situation. Out on the open water, it may become something else."

He nodded. "I know. I've given it some thought. Most of these men have never sailed with women aboard, save for perhaps a captain's wife. I intend to gather the whole crew and speak plainly. The message will be, it won't be tolerated on board the vessel."

Amber had followed the exchange with raised eyebrows.

For the first time, Paragon spoke. "What won't be tolerated?" he asked curiously.

Althea managed not to smile. Brashen took the question seriously. "I won't tolerate any relationship between hands that affects the operation of this vessel."

Jek had approached as they were speaking. She raised one eyebrow, but kept her silence until Brashen acknowledged her. "Jek. Is there a problem?"

She had heard what they were discussing. She didn't pretend otherwise. "No, sir. Nor do I expect there to be one. I've sailed before, with mixed crews. If you don't mind my saying so, I know how to handle myself in close quarters."

Probably only Althea could tell that Brashen fought to keep from smiling. "I don't doubt that you do, Jek. My concern is mostly for the men who don't know how to govern themselves."

Jek didn't smile. "I'm sure they'll learn, sir."

Surprising them all, Paragon added, "Let's hope the lesson is not too painful for anyone."

"HE HAS SPENT THE PAST THREE DAYS ON IT. ALL I'M SAYING IS THAT IF IT'S something of value, he should know it by now. And if it isn't, there are other places I'd like to put him to work. Places that, in my opinion, show a lot more promise than that little cell." Bendir put down his pipe. "That's all I'm saying," he repeated defiantly. He cast an exasperated look at his younger brother. Reyn sat across the polished wood table. He looked harried and pale. His shirt was rumpled as if he had slept in it.

"You said much the same thing when I insisted I needed more time to puzzle out the flame jewels," Reyn retorted. "If you had listened to me then, far fewer of them would have been damaged in recovery. Some things don't happen overnight, Bendir."

"Such as your growing up, for instance," Bendir grumped to himself. He examined the bowl of his pipe. It had gone out. He set it aside. His embroidered shirt and neatly combed hair contrasted sharply with his younger brother's appearance.

"Bendir!" Jani Khuprus instantly rebuked her eldest son. "That is not fair. Reyn has told us that he is having a hard time keeping his mind on this task. We should be understanding, not condemn him for that. As I recall, you were none too focused when you were courting Rorela." She smiled fondly at her youngest son.

"He'd be a lot less distracted if he chose a sensible woman like Rorela, instead of a spoiled Bingtown girl who doesn't even know her own mind," Bendir retorted. "Look at him. He has the color of a mushroom. It's a wonder he doesn't go about walking into walls. Ever since he began court-ing this Malta, she has done nothing but torment him. If she can't make up her mind, then . . ."

Reyn leaped to his feet. "Shut up!" he told his brother savagely. "You don't know anything at all about what she's going through, so just shut up." He snatched up the ancient parchments from the table with a fine disregard for their fragility and stalked off toward the door. Jani gave her elder son an exasperated look. She hastened after Reyn to set a restraining hand on his arm.

"Please, son. Come back, sit down, and talk with us. I know the strain you are under. And I appreciate how you must share Malta's grief over her missing father."

"Not to mention *our* missing liveship," Bendir added under his breath. He had intended that Reyn hear his remark, and his brother took the bait. He spun to face this new provocation.

"That's all you care about, isn't it?" he accused him. "A good deal. A sharp bargain. You care nothing for what I feel about Malta. You could not even grant me time away from the city and transport to Bingtown last month when she first received her bad news. It's always the same with you, Bendir. Money, money, money. I find these parchments, and I want the time to make sense of them. It is not easy. There are very few written documents from the Elderlings. That makes translating what we do find difficult. I want to discover all of what they can tell us. I hope they may be a clue as to why there are so few written records. They obviously were a literate folk; there should be a wealth of books and scrolls. But where? You care nothing for solving the greater mystery that may be the key to the whole city. To you, these documents only represent one thing. Can we make a profit from what they say? If not, toss them aside and go dig up something else." As if to mock Bendir's attitude, he flung the parchments casually onto the table between them. Jani winced as they landed. It would not take much abuse to crumble them into fragments.

"Please," she said sharply. "Both of you. Sit down. There are things to discuss."

Grudgingly, they came to the table. Jani seated herself at the head of it, intentionally taking the position of authority. Bendir had become a bit too officious with his younger brother lately. It was time to take her eldest son down a notch or two. At the same time, she did not want to encourage Reyn in his sullen melancholy. Of late, it seemed that was his only mood. She, for one, was heartily sick of it. She gave them no warning before she attacked.

She leveled a forefinger at Bendir. "You have no excuse for being jealous of your brother's courtship. When you were first infatuated with Rorela, the entire family was tolerant of your antics. You spent every spare moment you had on her doorstep. I seem to recall that you demanded we redecorate an entire wing of Rooster Hall for her, painting all of it in shades of green because you said it was her favorite color. Nor would you allow me to consult with her as to whether that was truly her wish. Do you recall how she reacted to your 'surprise' for her?"

Bendir glared. Reyn grinned, an expression she had not seen on his face for some time. She wished she could have let it linger, but one had to strike while the iron was hot.

"And you have to stop acting like a lovesick boy, Reyn. You're a man. I would have expected this of you had you fallen in love at fourteen, but you are over twenty. You need to practice more restraint in how you display the heart on your sleeve. Your request to dash off to Bingtown, unannounced, at a moment's notice to us, was simply unreasonable. Your sulking since then ill becomes you. You will go downriver shortly, and you will escort your lady to her first Summer Ball. What more can you ask of us?"

Glints of anger came into his eyes. Good. If she could make them both irritated with her, chances are they would commiserate with each other. So it had always worked when they were boys.

"What more could I ask of you? I could ask a little understanding of what she is enduring! I wanted to go to her, to lend her and her family what support I could during this crisis. Instead, what have I been allowed? Nothing. You have sent off polite notes of sympathy, and say that letters directly from me to Malta would be precipitate. Mother, I intend to marry her. How can it be precipitate to ask my family to aid hers?"

"The family's resources are not yours to dispense, Reyn. You have to understand that. In your ardor, you would commit us all, far too deeply. I know it is her father and her family liveship at stake. My heart bleeds for them. It also represents a sizable investment on our part, one that may already be irretrievably lost. Reyn, we cannot throw good money after bad. No. Do not stalk off. Hear me out. What you perceive as cruel is only common sense. Should I allow you and Malta to beggar yourselves in what may be a lost cause? We've all heard tales of this Kennit. My opinion of Kyle Haven, apart from his being Malta's father, is not a high one. This I say only for your ears. He has brought this on himself. I do not say he deserved this, only that he left himself and his family and ship open to this.

"Nor can I approve of the course the Vestrits have chosen to follow in this 'rescue' attempt. Not even their own friends and neighbors are supporting them in this. It is all very ill-advised: Althea is strong-willed to the point of mulishness, they have this disowned Trader's son at the helm and some foreigner providing money. The ship they are using should never have left the beach again. Paragon is a rebuke to all of us. Our ignorance is our only claim to innocence. He should never have been built from mixed plank, but even so, the Ludlucks have a heavier share of the blame. They loaded him too heavy with cargo on deck and then piled on the sail to make up for it. He was top heavy when he went over.

"Our greed built that ship too swiftly, and their greed drove him mad. We were both to blame for what he became. Beaching him was the wisest thing that was ever done with him; refitting him has to be the most foolish."

"What other choice did the Vestrit family have?" Reyn asked quietly. "Their fortunes are teetering. They have been most honest with us about that. So they mount what effort they can with the resources they can beg or borrow."

"They could have waited," Jani declared. "It has not been all that long. Kennit is known for making his victims wait for the ransom offer. It will come."

"No, it won't. By all accounts, the man wanted a liveship, and he took one. Now there is a rumor the *Ringsgold* has vanished as well. Do you realize how vulnerable that leaves us, Mother? Pirates could come right up the Rain Wild River. We have never planned for such an emergency. We have nothing in place to stop them. I think the Vestrits have taken the only sensible action. That liveship must be recovered, at any cost. They are risking their kin and their family fortune to do so. Ultimately, they do so to protect us. And what do we do? We let them."

"What do you want us to do?" Bendir asked wearily.

Reyn leaped on this opportunity. "Forgive the liveship debt. Help fund this expedition, at the least. Take action against the Satrap, who has allowed piracy and slavery to flourish and thus precipitated this whole situation."

Bendir was instantly outraged. "Not only do you propose to risk our fortunes along with theirs, but to plunge us into a political whirlpool. This has been discussed in the Rain Wild Traders' circle. Until Bingtown commits to stand beside us, it is too soon to defy the Satrap. I am as sick as you are of his boot upon our neck, but—"

"But you'll endure it until someone else is ready to take the first risk!" Reyn finished angrily for his brother. "Just as Bingtown is ready to let the Vestrits take the first risk in challenging the pirates, and Tenira stood alone in challenging the tariff."

Jani had not foreseen the conversation venturing into this area, but she leaped at her chance. "In this, I must agree with Reyn. The situation has not improved since I last addressed the Bingtown Traders' Council, but I think the climate of opinion in Bingtown has. From the reports I received of the tariff riot, I think that if the Khuprus family took a stand, others would follow. And I think that stand must be for complete independence."

A profound silence followed her words. After a time, Reyn said in a small voice, "So much for me being the one willing to risk the complete family fortune."

"We risk it more when we do nothing," Jani declared. "It is time we aligned ourselves with like-minded persons, whether they are from The Wilds or Bingtown."

"Like Grag Tenira?" Reyn asked.

"I do not think it is coincidence he fled here. The Grove family has been hosting him; they have strong trade ties with the Tenira family."

"And strong sympathy for any who wish to stand against the Satrap," Reyn added thoughtfully.

Bendir looked surprised. "When did my little brother become so interested in politics? It seemed to me that we had to drag you to that meeting in Bingtown."

"It was well that you did. It opened my eyes to many things," Reyn replied easily. To his mother, he suggested, "We should have Grag Tenira over to dinner. With the Groves, of course."

"I think that would be a wise course." She watched her older son, and when he nodded approval, she breathed a secret sigh of relief. She would not live forever. The sooner her sons learned to work together, the better. She ventured to divert the topic. "So, Reyn. Have you made any sense of those old papers?" She nodded to the ancient parchments he had abandoned on the table.

"Some." He frowned as he drew them toward him. "There are a lot of unfamiliar words in them. What I have deciphered is both exciting and frustrating. There seems to be references to another city, substantially upriver of us." He scratched at a scaly patch on his cheek. "If I am interpreting it correctly, it would be way to the back of beyond. Almost to what some call the Mountain Kingdom. If such a city existed and we could locate it . . . well. It might represent the greatest find since Trehaug was founded here."

"A smoke dream," Bendir said dismissively. "There have been explorations up the river before. Nothing was found. If there is another city, it is likely buried deeper than Trehaug was."

"Who knows?" Reyn challenged him. "I tell you, from what I can translate, it is quite a ways upriver from us. It might have escaped destruction altogether." He looked speculative. "For all we know, the Elder race could have survived there. Imagine what they could teach us. . . ." He let his voice trail off, unaware of the worried glance that passed between his mother and brother. "I think it is worth more study. And I think I will take my questions to the dragon and see what she says."

"No." Bendir forbade it bluntly. "Reyn, I thought we were clear on that. You are to stay out of the Crowned Rooster Chamber. That log has entirely too much power over you."

"It's not a log. She's a dragon. She should be freed."

Jani and Bendir did not try to hide the look they exchanged. Bendir spoke almost angrily. "I should have cut up that damn thing a long time ago, when I first suspected you were susceptible to it. But the time wasn't right. It's the last log of wizardwood, and the biggest. The ship we build from it will be the last liveship . . . unless you are right about this other city of yours. Perhaps we might find more wizardwood there."

"You won't find it without me," Reyn pointed out quietly. "And I won't help you if you kill the dragon."

Bendir crossed his arms on his chest. Jani knew the gesture well. He was trying to contain his anger with his youngest brother. Reyn the dreamer, Reyn the scholar, so often frustrated pragmatic Bendir. She had always hoped that with time her boys would learn to complement one another. Now she feared they would always be at odds.

"There is no dragon," Bendir spoke slowly, with great finality. "Whatever was in there died long ago. It was probably mad before it died. All that is left of it is its memories. It is no more alive than liveships are truly alive. The planks absorb memories, and retain them. That is all. If it weren't true, we wouldn't be able to cut up a log and allow Bingtowners to store fresh memories in them. Anyone who talks to a liveship is really talking to himself, mingled with the family memories stored in the wood. That is all. When you talk to that log, you hear your own thoughts, as interpreted by the mad memories of some poor creature that died long before we even discovered this city." He was almost pleading as he added, "Reyn. Don't let stillborn madness speak with your voice. Put it away from you."

Uncertainty wavered across Reyn's face. Then it hardened into stubbornness. "It's easy enough to prove to me. Help me bring the log out into light and air. If nothing happens, I'll acknowledge how foolish I was."

"That would truly be a madman's bargain!" Bendir exclaimed in disgust. "That log is immense. We'd have to take the whole top of the hill off. Or excavate the slide area over the original entrance, and risk collapsing the chamber in the process. The wall above the door is cracked. Even if we knew how to open it, we risk compromising the whole wall. Reyn, you can't be serious."

"She's alive." Defiantly he added, "And she says she would be willing to aid Malta and her family. Think on that. Think of the potential of such an ally."

"Think of the potential of such an enemy!" Jani retorted angrily. "Reyn, we have been through this and through this. Even if there is some creature alive inside that log, we can't get it out, and we'd be stupid to release it if we could. Now that is over. It's finished. Do you understand me? We will not speak of this again. I forbid it."

He opened his mouth. His jaw and lower lip quivered, just as they had when he was a small child and was about to bellow forth his discontent. Then he shut his mouth with a snap. Without a word he rose from the table and turned away from it.

"We are not finished here!" Jani Khuprus warned him.

"I am."

"No. You are not. Come back to this table and tell us what you have learned from the parchments so far. I demand it."

He turned back to them. His eyes had gone cold and dark. "You demand it? This is what I demand, then. Make it worth my while. If you will not give me the dragon, then give me some of your precious money, Mother. Because one way or another, I will help my beloved. I will not go to the Bingtown Ball, take her hand, dance with her and then leave her as beggared of hope and coin as when I arrived there. I won't."

It was Bendir's turn to be outraged. "When did you stop being a member of this family? Must we bribe you to do your family duty? Should we pay you for giving back a measure of what you have taken? I will be damned first!"

"Then be damned!" Reyn replied coldly.

"Reyn." Jani tried to keep her voice reasonable. "Speak plainly. Exactly what do you ask of us? What would we have to offer you to have you surrender this dragon dream of yours?"

"Mother, I refuse—"

"Hush, Bendir. Hear what he asks before you say no." She prayed she had not given too broad a hint of her plan. Reyn had to believe he walked into this of his own will. "What are you asking for, son?"

Reyn licked his dry lips. He looked furtive and cornered, now that he finally had to speak the words aloud. He cleared his throat. "First. Forgive the Vestrits' debt for the liveship. It's but a formality anyway. It was openly acknowledged that that would be my bridal gift to Malta. Give it now, while it is needed most. Don't let her believe that we would continue to wring coins from her family when they are sorely beset. Don't make her fear," and his voice went hoarse, "don't make her fear that for the sake of coin, she must come to wed me, whether she would or not. I don't want her that way. I don't want her to fear that we will invoke the blood agreement."

"She would come to love you in time, Reyn. Don't doubt that. Many a bride who has come to the Rain Wilds reluctantly has soon learned to love—"

"I don't want her that way," Reyn repeated stubbornly.

"Then we won't invoke that part of the contract," his mother assured him.

"Fine, it's done. We'll just throw the contract away. Now. What did you learn from the parchments?" Bendir spoke brusquely, his voice thick with fury.

"There's more," Reyn said implacably.

"Oh, what else can there be? Do you wish to be Satrap of the Rain Wilds?" Bendir demanded sarcastically.

"No. Only ruler of my own life. I want to be able to go and see her whenever I wish, until we are wed and she comes here. I want an allowance issued to me, money I can spend without accountability to anyone. In short, I want you to treat me as if I were a man. You had a purse of your own when you were younger than I am now."

"Only because I also had a wife! When you are wed, you will have your income. Right now, you don't need it. I have never been stingy with you. Mother has always indulged you far above the rest of us. The more we give, the more you ask!"

"You may have that, also," Jani broke in relentlessly.

Bendir's face went from incredulous to furious. He threw up his hands. "Why am I here at all?" he asked rhetorically. "It seems I have no say in anything!"

"You are here to witness your brother giving his word to me. Reyn.

This is what we have asked of you: that you will give up the dragon dream, and not visit the log anymore. You will no longer claim a say in what becomes of the log. You will do your duty to your family, employing your skills as we ask. You will not enter the city, save with the approval of your brother and me, and then only for work we sanction. In return, we will void the contract for the liveship *Vivacia*, issue you a man's independent allowance and allow you to visit your beloved as you wish. Do you agree to this?"

She had phrased it formally. She watched her son consider it as she had taught him, going over each phrase, committing to memory the terms of the agreement. He looked from her to his brother. His breath began to come faster. He rubbed his temples, as if he waged some internal battle with himself. The terms of the contract were steep, for both sides. She was offering much to gain much. He was taking too long to reply. He would refuse. Then, "Yes. I agree." He spoke hastily, as if his words hurt him.

She let out her pent breath soundlessly. She had done it. The trap closed behind him, unsuspected. She took a deep breath to quell her queasiness at doing this to her own son. It was necessary, she told herself. Necessary, and therefore honorable. Reyn would abide by his word. He always had and always would. What was a Trader, if he was not as good as his word?

"As Trader for this family, I accept your agreement. Bendir, do you witness it?"

"I do," he agreed sourly. He would not meet her eyes. She wondered if he suspected what she had done and was disgusted by it, or if he were dismayed at the terms.

"Then let us say enough of this for tonight. Reyn, please devote another day to the parchments, and then give us the best written translation that you can. Please document any new symbols in them, and note what you think they mean. But not tonight. Tonight, we all need to sleep."

"Oh, not I," Reyn retorted with bitter amusement. "No sleep for me, I fear. Or rather, I fear that I will sleep. I'll begin tonight, Mother. Perhaps I'll have something for you by morning."

"Do not overtax yourself," she suggested, but he was already gathering up his parchments and leaving. She waited until he was out the door and then hastily stepped in front of Bendir as he approached the door. "Wait," she commanded him.

"For what?" he demanded in a surly tone.

"For Reyn to be well out of earshot," she told him bluntly. That got his attention. He looked down at her in shock.

She let a few slow minutes pass. Then she took a deep breath. "The dragon-log, Bendir. We need to be rid of it, and soon. Cut it up. Perhaps you are right; perhaps it is time the Khuprus family had a ship of our own. Or have it sawn into planks and store them. Get rid of the thing inside it. Otherwise, I fear we will lose your brother. The log, not Malta, is the root of our problems with your brother. It preys upon his mind." She took a deep breath. "I fear he will drown in the memories. He already walks a narrow path beside a precipice. I think we should keep him from the city as much as possible."

A look of concern came into his face. It eased her heart. It was unfeigned. He truly cared for his younger brother. The depth of his feelings showed in his next question. "Now? You mean, cut up the log before he goes off to the Summer Ball in Bingtown? I don't think that is wise, Mother. No matter that he has agreed to give up any say about it. That should be a happy time in his life, not one tormented by second thoughts."

"You are right. No. Wait until he is safely away. I expect he will spend a week or more in Bingtown. Do it then. Let him come home to it as something that is done and irrevocable. That will be best."

"He will blame me, you know." A shadow passed over Bendir's face. "This will not make anything easier between us."

"No. He will blame me," his mother assured him. "I will see that it is so."

NIGHT HAD FALLEN OVER THE HARBOR. PARAGON COULD SENSE IT. THE wind had shifted. Now it carried the smells of the town to his nostrils. He reached up to touch his nose. Cautiously his fingers ventured higher, exploring the splintered wreckage of his eyes.

"Are you in pain?" Amber asked him quietly.

He immediately dropped his hands from his face. "We do not know pain as humans do," he assured her. A moment later, he asked her, "Tell me about the town. What do you see?"

"Oh. Well." He felt her shift on the foredeck. She had been lying on her back, either dozing or looking up at the stars. Now she rolled onto her belly. Her body was warm against his planking. "All around us is a forest of masts. Black sticks against the stars. A few of the ships have small lights showing, but not much. But in town, the lights are many. They reflect in the water and—"

"I wish I could see them," he said plaintively. More loudly, he complained, "I wish I could see anything. Anything! It's all darkness, Amber. To be blind on the beach was bad, Amber, but after a time, I became accustomed to it. But here, in the water once more . . . I don't know who is passing me on the docks, or what vessels may come alongside me. Fire could break out on the docks, and I would not know it until it was too late. All that is bad enough, but soon we will sail. How can you expect me to venture into that vastness blindly? I want to do well. I do. But I fear I cannot."

He sensed her helplessness when she spoke. "You will have to trust us. We will be eyes for you, Paragon. If we must go into danger, I swear I will be here, right beside you, telling you all we face."

"Thin comfort," Paragon replied after a time. "That is thin comfort, I fear."

"I know. It is all I can offer."

He listened. The waves patted gently against his hull. Ropes creaked. Footsteps sounded as someone passed them on the dock. The evening sounds of Bingtown came to his ears. He wondered how much it had changed since he had last seen it. He stared ahead into a future of eternal darkness. "Amber," he asked quietly. "Was it difficult to fix Ophelia's hands? Were they badly damaged?"

"The scorching did not go deep, except in a few places. The problem was more one of keeping the proportions of finger to hand. Rather than simply carve away what was damaged, I had to rework both her hands. A good portion of the wood that I removed was not burnt at all. I think the hardest part of the task was for her to keep still, and for me to concentrate on my skill when I worried about causing her pain."

"Then it was painful?"

"Who knows? She said it was not. As you say, she also told me: liveships do not experience pain as humans do. Nevertheless, I think it was uncomfortable for her. She told me she felt a sense of loss at the wood I pared away; that was one reason I restored it to her as jewelry. She also told me that her hands felt 'wrong' when I was finished." Amber paused. "That was devastating to me. I had done the best work I could. But when I last visited her, before she sailed, she told me she had become accustomed to her new hands and that now they felt fine. She greatly desired that I would re-carve her hair for her, but Captain Tenira refused. He said they could not stay in port that long. To tell you the truth, I was grateful. Wizardwood is . . . uneasy wood. Even with my gloves on, I always felt it was trying to draw me into it."

He scarcely heard her final words. "You could cut my beard off," he suddenly exclaimed.

"What?" She came to her feet in alarm in a single fluid motion, like a bird lifting in flight. "Paragon, what are you saying?"

"You could cut my beard off, and shape it, and peg it back onto me as a new face. I'd be able to see again."

"That's a crazy idea," Amber said flatly.

"A crazy idea from a mad ship. It would work, Amber. Look how much wood is here." He reached up to seize two great handfuls of his full beard. "There is plenty enough to make me new eyes. You could do it."

"I would not dare," she said flatly.

"Why not?"

"What would Althea and Brashen say? To repair Ophelia's hands was one thing. To completely refashion a new face for you would be something else entirely."

He folded his arms on his chest. "Why should it matter what Althea or Brashen say? Do I belong to them? Am I a slave?"

"No, it's just that—"

He ignored her attempt to speak. "When you 'bought' me, did not you insist that it was but a formality for others? You said I belonged to myself. That I always had and always would. It would seem to me, then, that this should be my decision."

"Perhaps it should. That does not mean that I have to agree to it."

"Why would you refuse? Do you want me to be blind?" He felt anger shivering inside him, trying to find a way out. He swallowed it back like bile. Anger did not work on Amber. She would just walk away.

"Of course not. Nor do I want you to be disappointed. Paragon, I do not understand wizardwood. My hands tell me it is one thing, my heart tells me it is another. Working on Ophelia was . . . difficult for me. She said she had a sense of wrongness about her hands. What I sensed was something subtler. Something closer to sacrilege." Her voice went soft on the last word. He could almost feel her confusion.

"You did it for Ophelia, but you would not do it for me?"

"Paragon, there is a very great difference there. On Ophelia, I removed damaged wood. You are talking about me pegging pieces on to create new eyes for you. As I said, I don't understand the nature of wizardwood. Would those pegged-on parts become alive as you are? Or would they remain scraps of pegged-on wood?"

"Then do for me as you did for her!" Paragon burst out after an exasperated silence. "Cut away my old ruined face. Make me a new one."

Amber breathed out some words in a different language. Paragon had no idea whether she prayed or cursed. He only sensed her horror at his suggestion. "Do you know what you are advocating? I would have to rework your face entirely . . . perhaps your whole body, to make you proportional. I've never taken on a project of such magnitude. I'm a woodcarver, Paragon, not a sculptor." She huffed out a sigh of disgust. "I might ruin you. Destroy your beauty forever. How would I live with that?"

Paragon lifted his hands to his face and clawed his fingers down his ruined eyes. He laughed aloud, a bold, bitter laugh. "Amber, I would rather be ugly than blind. Right now, I am both. How could you make it worse?"

"The answer to that question is exactly what I don't want to discover," she replied nimbly. Unwillingly she added, "But I know I will think about it. Give me time to think about it, Paragon. Give yourself time to consider it well."

"Time is all I possess," he pointed out. "Time and to spare."

Kingdom's Foundation

VIVACIA RODE HEAVY IN THE WATER. HER HOLDS WERE FILLED WITH KENnit's collections. It was, the ship thought drowsily, like the feeling a man got after a large, satisfying meal. She felt satiated and pleased with herself, even though her cargo had little to do with her own efforts. Kennit's wits had earned this trove. No. His wisdom, she corrected herself. Any minor pirate might make his living by his wits. Kennit was beyond that. He was a man of both destiny and vision. She was proud to be his ship.

This last stint of sailing had not been so different from her days as a trader with Ephron Vestrit. Their first stop had been Divvytown, where the slaves had disembarked. Then there had been a meeting, mysteriously arranged, at which Kennit met a northbound ship and arranged for a ransom note to be taken to the owners of the *Crosspatch* and to Captain Avery's family. After that, Kennit had begun a systematic tour of his "share-ships" and their homeports. The *Marietta* kept them company. At every port of call, Kennit and Sorcor had gone ashore. Sometimes Etta and Wintrow had gone with them. Vivacia liked it when Wintrow accompanied Kennit. When he came back to her and told her of his experiences, it was almost as if she had been there herself. It was very different from the days when she had dreaded being parted from Wintrow for even a few hours. She supposed her sense of self had become more solid, now that she had been quickened longer. Or perhaps her need to know every detail of Kennit's life had become more pressing than her need for Wintrow's company. She had besought Kennit to conduct his business on board her, so that she might be more aware of it, but he had refused her.

"You are mine," he had told her jealously. "All your mystery and beauty I reserve to myself, my sea-lady. It pleases me that they look at you with awe and wonder. Let us keep that mystique intact. I would rather they envied and admired you from afar than that they came aboard and vainly tried to win you from me by charm or bloodshed. You are my castle and my stronghold, Vivacia. I will allow no strangers aboard you."

She could recall not just his words, but his every inflection. They had soaked into her like honey into bread. She smiled to herself, recognizing her symptoms. He had courted her and won her. She no longer even attempted to sift his words for inaccuracies or tried to probe his heart for truth. It no longer mattered. He did not seek out and number her faults; why should she inventory his?

She was anchored now in a pathetic excuse for a harbor. Why anyone would have chosen to settle there, she could not imagine. At the far end of it, the skeletal remnants of a ship were subsiding into the mud. She tried to think of the name of the place. Askew. That was it. Well, it suited the look of the town. The sagging dock, the windswept huts, all looked slightly out of joint. There were recent signs of prosperity. The board-walks that fronted the street were of new yellow lumber. Good intentions and paint covered some of the rickety houses. Someone had planted several rows of trees as a windbreak. Young fruit trees stood in a row beyond them. A herdboy kept a flock of goats well away from the trees' tender bark. Tied to the dock, amidst a clutter of smaller vessels was a larger ship. The *Fortune*, her nameplate proudly proclaimed. The Raven flag flew boldly at her mast. Even at a distance, her brasswork gleamed in the sun. The whole town, she decided, had the look of a place on the verge of becoming Someplace.

Her attention perked as a party of men left the largest building in the village and moved toward the dock. Kennit would be amongst them. She spotted him soon, in the lead, his well-wishers flanking him or trailing behind him as their local status dictated. Sorcor walked beside him. Etta, tall and thin, shadowed him with Wintrow at her side. For a time the gathering clustered on the dock. Then, with many flourishes and bows, they bid her captain farewell. As he and his party clambered down the ladder and into her gig that was moored there, the townsfolk on the dock called farewells. So it had been in every town they had visited on this circuit. Everyone loved her captain.

She watched the ship's boat approach her across the glittering water of the placid harbor. Kennit had dressed well for this visit. The black plumes on his hat nodded in the breeze. He saw her watching his approach and lifted a hand in greeting to her. The sun flashed off the silver buttons on the cuff of his jacket. He looked every bit the prosperous pirate. More, he sat in the bow of the boat as regally as any king.

"They treat him as such already," Wintrow had confided to her the last time he had told her of such a visit. "They present his share of their takings without a murmur of discontent. But it is not just that they acknowledge his right to claim a portion of their piratical profits. They bring him their internal grievances. He has passed judgment on everything from chicken thieves to unfaithful spouses. He has drawn plans for the defense of the towns, and dictates what they must build and what must be torn down."

"He is a judicious man. I am not surprised they have waited for his decisions."

Wintrow snorted. "Judicious? Only in how it furthers his own popularity. I have stood behind him and listened to their grievances as they presented them. He listens, frowns and asks questions. But in each case, he decides with the popular sentiment, even when it is clearly not just. He does not judge, Vivacia. He merely validates their opinions and makes them feel justified in them. When he has dispensed that justice, he strolls through the town, looking at this and that. 'You need a well, for better water,' he will tell them. Or 'tear down that building before it burns down and takes the rest of the town with it. Repair your dock. That widow needs a new roof on her cottage. See that she gets it.' In addition, he scatters coin to pay for what he suggests, as if it were largesse rather than returning what they gave him. He enraptures them. They adore him."

"Why shouldn't they? It sounds as if he does great good for them."

"He does," Wintrow had admitted uncomfortably. "He does. He gives them money to be kind to the poor and the old amongst them. He makes them lift up their heads and see what could be. In the last town, he commanded that they create a place for their children to gather and learn. There was one man in the town who could read and cipher well. Kennit left enough money to pay him handsomely to teach the children."

"I still do not grasp why you find that so reprehensible."

"It is not what he does. What he does is fine, even noble. It is his motive for doing it that I suspect. Vivacia, he wants to be king. So he makes them feel good. With the money they parcel out to him, he buys what they should have bought for themselves. Not because it is the right thing to do, but because it makes them think well of him and feel good about themselves. They will connect that feeling of pride with his coming."

She had shaken her head. "I still see no harm in it. In fact, I see much good. Wintrow, why are you so suspicious of him? Did you ever consider that perhaps he wants to be king of the Pirate Isles just so he can do such things?"

"Does he?" Wintrow had demanded.

To him, she owed the truth. Still. "I don't know," she replied honestly. "But I hope that he does. The results are the same, in any case."

"For now, they are," he admitted. "But I do not know what the results will be over the long run," he'd added darkly.

She mulled his words as she watched the boat approaching. The youth was too suspicious. Some small-spirited part of him could not accept Kennit as a force for good. That was all. The boat came alongside and the rope ladder was flung down to them. She always hated this part. Kennit stubbornly insisted of late that he would get himself up the ladder and back aboard his ship. It seemed to take him forever to manage the

climb. At every step she feared he would slip and fall down, to smash his
bones against the boat below him. Or worse, he might fall into the water,
to either vanish beneath the waves, or be snapped up by serpents. There
was a veritable plague of serpents this year. Never could she recall a time
when they had been so thick nor so bold. It was unnerving.

In a short time, his peg-legged step sounded on her decks. She
breathed a sigh of relief and awaited him impatiently. He always came to
see her first, whenever he rejoined the ship. Sometimes Wintrow dogged
his steps. Etta had used to, but of late, she had avoided the foredeck.
Vivacia thought that was a wise decision on her part.

This time, as she twisted her body about to greet him, she saw he was
alone. Her smile deepened and became warmer. These were the best
times, when they were alone and could speak unfettered by Wintrow's
questions and skeptical looks. He returned her smile with a smug grin.
"Well, my lady. Are you ready to take on more cargo? I've arranged for
them to ferry it out this afternoon."

"What sort?" she asked, knowing well that he delighted in enumerat-
ing his treasures.

"Well," he paused, savoring his pleasure. "Some very fine brandy in
small casks. Bales of tea. Silver bars. Some woolen rugs, in truly amazing
colors and designs. Quite a selection of books, all very well bound. Poetry,
histories, an illustrated natural history and several travel journals, quite
fine. Those I think I shall keep for myself, though I shall let Wintrow and
Etta read them, of course. Foodstuffs, sacks of wheat, casks of oil and rum.
And quite a quantity of coin, in various minting. Rufo has done quite well
with the *Fortune*. I am quite pleased with how Askew has prospered."

Vivacia's attention had been captured by the mention of the books. "I
suppose this means that Wintrow will continue to spend every spare moment he has closeted with Etta," she observed sourly.

Kennit smiled. He leaned over the railing and touched her hair, letting a heavy lock slide through his fingers as he spoke. "That's right. He
will continue to distract Etta, and she will busy him. Thus you and I shall
continue to have private time in which to talk of our own ambitions and
interests."

A shiver ran over her shoulders at his touch. She knew a moment of
delightful confusion. "Then you have deliberately paired them, to give us
more time together?"

"Why else?" He picked up another lock of her hair and weighed the
thickly carved coil. She glanced over her shoulder at him. His pale blue
eyes were closed to slits. He was, she thought, an extraordinarily handsome man, in a cruel way. "You don't mind, do you? Etta is quite ignorant,
poor thing. Whoring is such a narrow occupation. Wintrow is more patient a teacher than I could be. He will give her the tools she needs to

better herself, so that when she leaves the ship, she need not go back to whoring."

"Etta will leave?" Vivacia asked breathlessly.

"Of course. I only brought her aboard the *Marietta* for her own protection. We really have very little in common. She was kind, and useful while I was recovering from my injury. Nevertheless, it is hard to overlook that she was the source of the injury." He favored her with a narrow smile. "Wintrow shall educate her, and when she goes ashore, she will be able to do more than lie on her back." A thoughtful frown creased his brow. "I think it is my duty to leave people better than I found them, don't you?"

"When will Etta be leaving?" Vivacia tried to keep eagerness from her voice.

"Well. Our next port is Divvytown. That was her home." He smiled to himself. "But one never knows how things will develop. I shall not force her to leave, of course."

"Of course," Vivacia murmured in reply. He was twining the heavy lock of her black hair in his hand, and the tickling tip of it brushed her bare shoulder.

A package was tucked under his arm, something wrapped in coarse burlap. "Your hair is so lovely," he said quietly. "I thought of you the moment I saw this." He opened one end of it, then drew out a handful of something red. He shook it loose, and length upon length of wide red fabric unfurled, incredibly light and fine. He offered it to her. "I thought you might put it in your hair."

She was flustered. "I have never had such a gift," she marveled. "Are you sure you wish to give it to me? The sea and the wind may spoil it. . . ." Yet as she spoke she twined it through her hands. She lifted it, to place a band of it across her brow. He caught the ends and tied it for her.

"Then I should simply have to bring you more." He cocked his head, and smiled in admiration. "Such a beauty you are!" he said quietly. "My pirate queen."

WINTROW UNBUCKLED THE CARVED WOODEN COVER OF THE BOOK CARE-fully. He opened it gingerly, then sighed in awe. "Oh, this is incredible. Look at the detail here." He carried the open volume over to the window where the light fell on the artfully decorated page. "This is exquisite."

Etta came slowly to stand at his shoulder and look down on the displayed page. "What is it?" she asked.

"It's an herbal . . . a book about herbs, with drawings and descriptions and explanations of how they are to be used. I've never seen one so elaborate." Carefully he turned the page, to expose yet more beauty. "Even in our monastery library, we had nothing so fine as this. This is an incredibly valuable book." He touched his finger lightly to the page and outlined the drawing of a leaf. "See? This is peppermint. Look at the crinkles and tiny hairs on each leaf. Such an eye this artist had."

They were in the small stateroom he had once shared with his father. All signs of that time had been scrubbed away long ago. Now there was only his neatly made bunk, the small fold-down desk and a case full of manuscripts and scrolls and books. Wintrow had begun Etta's lessons in the captain's quarters, but Kennit had soon decided that they made too much clutter with their books, papers and pens. He had banished their studies to Wintrow's room. Wintrow did not mind. Never before had he had complete and unhampered access to so much written work. Certainly, he had never before even glimpsed a book to rival the quality of the one he now held.

"What does it say?" Etta asked reluctantly.

"You can read it," he encouraged her. "Try."

"The letters are all crawly," she complained, but she accepted the book he tenderly transferred into her hands. She knit her brows over it.

"Don't let that discourage you. His hand was very decorative, and some of the characters are formed elaborately. Look only at the basic forms of the letters, and ignore the flourishes. Try it."

Her finger moved slowly across the page, piecing the words together. Her mouth moved as she puzzled them out. Wintrow clamped his jaws together to keep from helping her. After a time, she drew a deep breath and began. "Of all the goodly herbs known, this is the queen. A tea brewed from fresh leaves is best for a closed head . . ."

She stopped abruptly, and closed the book carefully. When Wintrow glanced up at her face in confusion, he saw her eyes were closed as well. As he watched, tears leaked out from under her lashes.

"You can read," he confirmed for her. He stood very still, afraid to say more. It had been a very arduous journey to this place. Etta had been a difficult student. She was bright enough. But his efforts to teach her had uncovered a deep anger within her. For a time, he had been sure the anger was directed at him. She was surly, disdaining his help and then accusing him of withholding it to make her look stupid. She had a temper that did not stop at flinging a precious book across the room, or shredding expensive paper to bits. More than once, she had shoved him away as he bent over her work to correct her. Once he had raised his voice to her when he had had to explain for the fifth time that she was reversing a letter. She had struck him. Not a slap, but a closed-fist blow to his face that had sent him reeling. Then she had stalked out of the room. She had never apologized for that.

Only after days of working with her did he realize that her anger was not for him. It was for her own abysmal ignorance. She felt shamed that she did not know. It humiliated her when she had to ask him for help. If he insisted she try it on her own, she interpreted that as taunting her for her stupidity. Given her propensity for taking it out on him, she was not only a difficult student but also an intimidating one. Praising her too much was as dangerous as letting her struggle. He had tried once to escape. He had approached Kennit to beg off from this task. He had expected Kennit to order him back to it. Instead, the pirate had only cocked his head and asked him gently if he truly believed it was Sa's will that he not help Etta. While Wintrow had stood silent, struck dumb by the question, Kennit's face had suddenly changed.

"It's because she was a whore, isn't it?" he had demanded starkly. "You don't think she's good enough to benefit from such learning. You're repulsed by her, aren't you?" He asked the question with a face so kindly and understanding and yet so grieved that Wintrow felt as if the deck were rocking under him. Did he look down on Etta? Did he secretly harbor a belief in his own superiority, a belief he would have found reprehensible in anyone else?

"No—no!" he had faltered and then exclaimed, "I do not look down on Etta. She is an amazing woman. I just fear . . ."

"I think I know what you fear," Kennit had smiled indulgently. "You are uncomfortable because you find her attractive. You must not be distressed by that, Wintrow. Any healthy young man would find a sensuous woman like Etta hard to resist. She does not intend to be so tempting. Poor thing. She has been schooled to it since she was a child. Seducing a man is as natural to her as swimming is to a fish. I caution you: be very careful how you reject her. You could hurt her far more than you intended."

"It's not that! I would never . . ." he stuttered and then lost his ability to choose words. It would not have been so humiliating if he had been completely innocent. She did fascinate him. He had never spent time with a mature woman, much less alone with one. She invaded all his senses. The perfumes she wore lingered in his room after she had departed. He was aware of not only her husky voice but also the susurrus of the rich fabrics she wore. She would turn her head, and the light would dance suddenly on the sheen of her hair. He was aware of her, and sometimes she troubled his sleep. He was prepared to accept that as normal. He was less prepared for Kennit's indulgent smile.

"It's all right, lad. I could scarcely blame you if you did. I would, however, think less of you if you let that come between you and doing what we both know is right. She cannot better herself without letters,

Wintrow. You and I both know that. So do your best with her and do not be discouraged. I shall not allow either of you to give up when we are so close to success."

The days of teaching her that followed had provided a unique torture. The captain's words had made him more aware of the woman, not less. The "accidental" brush of her hand against his as they shared a book sometimes seemed contrived. Why did she wear such perfumes, if not to beguile him? Did she intend her direct stares as seduction? At some time, his awareness of her had become unmistakable attraction. From dreading his time alone with her, he had gone to living for it. He was sure it was not reciprocated. Well, almost sure. It did not matter if it was; she was irrevocably Kennit's. All the tragically romantic ballads he had ever heard, all the tales of ill-fated lovers that had once seemed so vapidly emotional now rang true in his heart.

Now, watching her face as she savored her victory, he suddenly knew that Kennit had been right. Any torment of temptation he had endured had been worth this. She could read. He had never known it was in his power to give such joy to anyone. He felt exulted by it in a way that surpassed all carnality. He had given her a gift that somehow completed himself.

She stood, clasping the exquisite book to her bosom as if it were her child. Her face, eyes closed, was turned toward the small porthole in his cabin. The light touched it, making her bronzed skin golden and glinting off the tears on her cheeks and the sheen of her hair. She reminded him of a sunflower turned toward the light. He had seen her merry before, laughing with Kennit or jesting with the other pirates. Now he saw her transfigured with joy. The two could not be compared.

Her bosom rose and then fell in a long sigh. She opened her eyes and smiled at him. "Wintrow," she said quietly. She shook her head slowly, her smile widening. "Kennit is so wise, is he not? I saw no value in you, at first. Then, I was jealous at how much he cared for you. I hated you, you know. And now, what I feel for you . . ." She hesitated. "I thought only Kennit could stir my heart as you have," she admitted quietly.

The simple words astounded him. Sternly, he told himself that she had not said she loved him, only that he stirred her heart. His own teachers had stirred his emotions. That was all she meant by her words. Even if she meant more, he'd be a fool to let himself react to them. A fool.

"Please," she said quietly. She held out a hand to him. "Help me choose a book. Perhaps the new one you said was poetry. Then let me practice with you. I want to read to Kennit tonight." She shook her head in fondness. "I almost cannot grasp that I can do this thing. He is so . . . I know, you are the one who taught me. However, he made it all possible. Can you imagine how that makes me feel? What does Kennit see in me,

Wintrow? How can I be worthy of such a man? I was a skinny little whore in Bettel's house when he first saw me. I never saw myself as more than that. How did he?" She cocked her head and her dark eyes peered into his soul, seeking her answer. He could not deny her.

"You shine," he said quietly. "Even when I first saw you. Even when I knew you hated me. There is something about you, Etta. Something in you that cannot be quenched, by hardship or ill treatment. Your soul gleams like silver beneath a patina of hard use. He is right to love you. Any man would love you."

Her eyes widened at his words. She turned aside from him, and unbelievably, a blush touched her wind-burnt cheeks. "I am Kennit's," she reminded him. She spoke the words proudly.

"I know," Wintrow said. Very softly, only to himself, he added, "I envy the man."

KENNIT'S DAY HAD BEEN A LONG ONE, FULL OF SATISFACTIONS. ASKEW WAS the last port before they returned to Divvytown. He and Sorcor had visited the homeports of every pirate ship he had created and manned with rescued slaves. Some had done better than others, but in every town he had been met with acclamation. Even bluff Sorcor had come to believe in his plan. It showed in the rough sailor's swagger. His beefy face gleamed with pride as he stood at Kennit's shoulder and listened to the tally of their takings.

Both the *Marietta* and *Vivacia* rode heavy with spoils. The loading of this last treasure had been a pleasant challenge. Young Rufo had operated the *Fortune* aggressively, taking nearly every ship they pursued, if he could trust the tales he'd been told. There had been coin aplenty, as well as freed slaves to swell their population. With the aid of the village's head woman, the young pirate had kept a tally. They had showed their record sticks to Kennit as proudly as any steward. He had listened to the accounting of every coin they had spent for lumber or fruit trees or goats. They had even hired themselves several artisans to come and live in Askew. Rufo had saved for Kennit's share the prizes that were most exotic and rare. These treasures they ceded to Kennit with the knowledge that he would take pleasure in them. He had sensed that, and made great display of his delight. It had only fueled their desire to please him more. He had promised them another ship, the next one he took. Well, and why not? They deserved it. Perhaps he would bring the *Crosspatch* here if her owners were slow to ransom her.

But even pleasure can be taxing. The type of cargo they had taken on could not be treated like crates of salt fish. He had been most particular about how it was stowed, insisting on overseeing it himself. The very best of their prizes, the smallest and most valuable items, he had ordered taken to his cabin. Now as he opened the door, he almost dreaded the delightful task of arranging these new treasures so he would not be crowded. Perhaps he would sleep first and then do it in the morning, after both ships were underway to Divvytown.

He opened the door of his cabin to a wash of golden lamplight and drifting incense. Not again. Did the woman's appetites know no bounds? He expected to find her artfully arranged upon his bed. Instead, she sat in one of two chairs she had drawn close together. A pool of lamplight illuminated her and the open book in her lap. She had on a nightdress, but it was demure rather than seductive. She almost looked like some-body's daughter.

With a glance of annoyance, he realized she had already moved his treasures. His initial response was one of swift outrage. How dared she touch his things! It was followed by a smaller wave of both resignation and relief. Well, at least they were all put away. Nothing stood between him and his bed. He limped over to the bed and sat down on the edge of it. The leather cup around his stump was chafing abominably. It needed to be relined again.

"I want to show you something I can do," she said quietly.

He gave a small sigh of exasperation. Did the woman think of nothing but her own pleasures? "Etta, I have had a very long day. Help me with my boot."

Obediently she set her book aside and came to him. She tugged his boot off, then rubbed his foot gently. He closed his eyes. "Fetch me a nightshirt."

She complied quickly. As swiftly as he removed his garments, she shook them out, folded them and returned them to his clothing chest. As he eased the cup and peg off the stump of his leg, he pointed out the abrasion to her. "Cannot you pad this thing so that it stays comfortable?"

She turned the cup, examining the lining. "Were you a less active man, it might be easier. I will try silk this time. Despite its softness, it is a sturdy material."

"Good. I'll need it by morning." He hopped onto his leg, pulled the bedding open and sat down on the linens. They were cool and clean as he lay back in them. The pillow smelled of lavender. He closed his eyes.

Her soft clear voice broke into his emptying mind:

"Our souls have loved a thousand times.
Down pathways we no longer recall, we have ventured in other lives.
I know you too well, love you too deeply, for this to be the growth of
*   mere years.*
As a river carves a course within a valley, so has your soul marked
*   mine with its passage.*
In other bodies, we have known completeness, such as never—"

He interrupted her recitation wearily. "I have never cared for the Syrenian school of poetry. They speak too plainly. Poetry should not be doggerel. If you are going to memorize something, find something by Eupille or Vergihe." He shouldered deeper into the blankets. He gave a low growl of content and surrendered himself to sleep.

"I didn't memorize it. I was reading it. I can read, Kennit. I can read."

She expected him to be surprised. He was too tired. "That's good. I'm glad Wintrow was able to teach you. Now we'll see if he can teach you what is worth reading."

She set the book aside, and blew out the lamp. It plunged the room into darkness. He heard the soft scuff of her feet as she came to the bed and crawled in beside him. He had to find somewhere else for her to sleep. Perhaps she could hang a hammock in the corner of the room.

"Wintrow says I no longer need his help. Now that I have my letters, he says I should simply explore every manuscript or scroll that comes my way. Only practice will make me read swifter, or write a better hand. That I can do on my own."

Kennit dragged his eyes open. This would not do. Grudgingly he rolled over to face her. "But you would not want that. Surely you have enjoyed the hours you have spent in his company. I know he enjoys teaching you. He has been very honest with me about what a pleasure he takes in your company." He managed a warm chuckle. "The lad is quite enamored of you, you know."

She surprised him. She made no attempt to dissemble. "I know. He's a sweet boy, and gently mannered. I understand now why you are so fond of him. He has given me a gift that I shall keep the rest of my life."

"Well. I hope you thanked him appropriately." All he wanted to do was sleep. At the same time, he could not resist this conversation. It sounded as if perhaps his scheme might bear fruit. She had called him a sweet boy. He had seen how Wintrow's eyes followed her when she was on deck. Had they acted on the impulse yet? Did she, perhaps, already carry an heir for his liveship? He slid his hand down her arm as if he were caressing her, then set his hand flat on her belly. The tiny skull still jutted from her navel. Time, he cautioned his disappointment. These things took time. If he penned them together long enough, they would breed. So it had always worked with his family's pigeons, goats and pigs when he was a boy.

"In truth, I don't know how to thank him," Etta demurred.

The answer to that was obvious to Kennit, but he refrained from stating it baldly. "I think the lad is lonely. Show him that you have become fond of him and enjoy his company. That will please him. Think of what knowledge you have that he might benefit from, and teach him. That would seem an appropriate exchange to me."

There. Was that too broad of a suggestion for her to take?

"I know so little," she faltered after a moment. "What would Wintrow learn from someone like me?"

Kennit sighed and tried again. Delicately, he reminded himself. Delicately. "Oh, I am sure you know far more of the world than he does. The boy has spent most of his life in a monastery. He may know much of letters and the arts, but he is woefully ignorant of more worldly skills. Your situation, of course, was just the opposite. So, share with him what life taught you. Teach the boy to be a man. He could have no better instructor." He stroked the length of her body.

She was silent. He could almost hear her thinking. "I would like to give him . . . Kennit, would you mind greatly if I gave him something of yours? Something from our cargo?"

This was not quite what he had in mind, but it was along the right path. Who knew where her gift giving might end, once she had started? "Do not hesitate," he encouraged her. "I am, as you know, very fond of the boy. I do not mind sharing with him what is mine."

WINTROW CAME AWAKE TO HIS DOOR OPENING. SOMEONE CAME SILENTLY into his cabin and shut the door stealthily. For a moment, fear paralyzed him. He had slept better since Sa'Adar was no more, but he had always feared that some of the ex-slaves would blame him for their leader's death. He caught his breath and held it. He tried to edge silently over in his bed. Maybe the first attack would miss him and he'd have a chance to escape. Whoever it was crossed to the small desk in his room and set something down there.

"I know you're awake," Etta said quietly. "I heard you stop breathing. Get up and strike a light."

"It's not morning," he protested in confusion. "What are you doing here?"

"I noticed that," she replied wryly. "I've come to teach you something. Some things are better learned privately. Night seemed the best time for the lessons I have come to teach."

He groped for a candle, and then stepped out into the companionway to light it at the small lamp that burned there. He brought it back to the cabin, shut the door and fixed the candle into a candlestick. When he turned to face her, he was hard put not to gasp. She wore leggings and a snug-fitting jerkin. Never before had he seen a female form so blatantly displayed. She ignored his stare. Instead, she walked around him slowly. Her eyes ran up and down his body appraisingly. The frankness of her gaze warmed his cheeks. She gave a small snort of displeasure.

"Well. It's plain you've worked hard, but not heavy. Still. You're lithe and quick. I've marked that about you. And that may be more telling in this game than muscle or bulk."

He blinked at her. "I still don't know what this is about."

"Kennit suggested it. I told him I felt a debt to you for teaching me to read. He said I should return it in kind, by teaching you something I know well. Something of my more worldly skills, as he put it. I've come to do that. Take your shirt off."

Slowly he obeyed her. He refused to think about what he was doing, or what her intentions were.

She smiled grimly. "You're sweet and smooth as a little girl. Not a hair to your chest yet. A little more muscle would please me, but that will come in time." She went back to his table, and worked the latch on the flat box there. As she opened the box, she repeated, "Some things are best learned in private. The skills of a man are among them. Were we more open with this, the crewmen would mock you. This way, you can pretend it was something you've always known how to do." When she turned back to face him, she held a dagger in either hand.

"These are for you, now. Kennit said I could give them to you. You should begin to wear one at your belt whenever we go into a port. After a time, start wearing it all the time, and sleep with it under your pillow. But, first, you have to learn how to use it."

She threw one at him suddenly. It was a toss, really, the weapon coming at him hilt first. He caught it awkwardly, but not squarely. The blade bit into his thumb. She laughed at his exclamation. "First blood to me!" A menacing light came into her eyes. "Grip that like you mean it and get ready. I'm going to teach you how to fight."

"I don't want to know how to fight," he protested in dismay. He retreated. "I don't want to hurt you."

She grinned merrily. "I'm very sure you won't. Don't worry about it in any case." She had gone into a knife-fighter's crouch, her blade at the ready. She swayed gracefully, and transferred the knife from hand to hand almost more swiftly than he could follow. Suddenly, she came at him, menacing as a tigress, her blade leading the way. "Just concentrate on keeping me from hurting you. That is always the first lesson."

CHAPTER TWENTY-EIGHT

Departure of the Paragon

"I WISH WE HAD TIME FOR MORE SEA TRIALS."

Amber gave Althea a weary look. "No time. No money. And after each one, at least two or three hands jump ship. A few more sea trials, Althea, and we'll have no crew left at all." She paused and cocked her head at Althea. "Is this the fifth time we've had this conversation, or the sixth?"

"The twenty-seventh, by my count," Brashen interjected, coming up between them. They shifted aside to make a space for him at the after rail. He joined them in staring out to the open water past the mouth of Bingtown Harbor. He gave a small chuckle. "Get used to it, Amber. Sailors have the same conversations over and over. Chief topics: the bad food, the stupid captain and the unfair mate."

"You forgot the rotten weather and the unruly ship," Althea filled in.

Amber shrugged. "I have a lot to become accustomed to. It has been years since I took an extended sea voyage. As a youth, I was a bad sailor. I hope that my living aboard here in the harbor will have schooled my stomach to a moving deck."

Althea and Brashen both grinned. "Trust me. It hasn't," Brashen warned her. "I'll try not to expect too much of you the first few days out. But if I need you, I'll need you, and then you'll have to crawl about and do your best between trips to the rail."

"You're so cheery," Amber thanked him.

A silence fell over them. Despite their easy words, they all had reservations about what they faced today. The ship was loaded, most of the crew aboard. Secreted belowdecks, unbeknownst to their hired crew, were seven slaves who had resolved to take this opportunity to escape to a new life. Althea tried not to think of them. The risk they took was not just to themselves. If anyone else discovered them before they sailed, who knew what might come of it? Nor did she know how their hired crew would react to these extra hands. She hoped they would be relieved there would be more backs to bear the work. Most likely, there would be some scuffling for position and bunking space, but that happened aboard any ship. She took a breath and told herself it would be all right. She still pitied the crowded men hidden below. The suspense for them must be agonizing.

At first light, they would sail. Althea almost wished they could just slip away now. But to sail off silently into the dimness would be an ill leave-taking. Better to wait and endure the farewells and good wishes of those who came to see them off. Better, also, to have clear light and the morning breezes to speed them.

"How is he?" Brashen asked quietly. He stared off into the distance.

"He's anxious. And excited. Eager, and scared to death. His blindness—"

"I know." Brashen was brusque. "But he's endured it for years. He got himself back to Bingtown, blind and capsized. This is no time for a risky experiment in carving wizardwood. He'll have to trust us, Amber. He has done so much to turn himself around that I don't want to risk changing any of his conditions. If you tried and failed, well," Brashen shook her head. "I think it's better for us to sail as he is. He's familiar with this hindrance. I think he can cope better with blindness he's accepted than with a great disappointment."

"But he has never accepted it," Amber began earnestly.

"Forty-two," Althea cut in. She gave a sigh but managed a smile. "We've had this conversation at least forty-two times."

Amber nodded in acceptance. She changed the subject. "Lavoy."

Brashen groaned, then laughed. "I gave him the last night in town. He'll be on deck on time. I'll vouch for that. He'll have a head, no doubt of that, and he'll take it out on the hands. That's traditional, and they'll expect it. I expect he'll drive them hard and they'll resent him. That's traditional, too. He's the best we could have hired for the job."

Althea bit her tongue firmly. She had lost count of how many times she and Brashen had wrangled about that. Besides, if they got into it again, he would probably make her admit that Lavoy was not as bad as she had expected him to be. The man had a streak of fairness in him. It was unreliable, but when it did surface, he held himself to it. He would be a tyrant. She knew that. So did Brashen. As long as he did not go too far with it, a tyrant was exactly what this crew needed.

The sea trials had exposed every weakness in their crew. Althea now knew which hands wouldn't scramble, and which ones seemed incapable of it. Some were lazy, some stupid and some slyly determined to do as little as possible. Her father, she was convinced, would have sacked the lot of them. When she had complained to Brashen, he had told her she could replace any and all of them with better men at her discretion. All she had to do was find such men and hire them at the wages he could offer.

That had ended that conversation.

"I wish we were already out there," Brashen said quietly.

"So do I," Althea agreed. And yet she dreaded it also. The sea trials had exposed more than the weaknesses of the crew. She knew now that Paragon was far more fragile than she had ever expected. True, he was a stoutly built ship. Once Brashen had arranged the ballast to his liking, he had sailed well, but he did not sail like a liveship. Althea was ready to accept that, as long as he did not actively oppose the men working his decks. What was most difficult for her was his obvious torment. Every time Brashen called a course change, the figurehead flinched. His hands would break free briefly from his crossed arms, to tremble before him. Almost instantly, he would recross his arms and hold them firm against his chest. His jaws were clenched tightly shut, but his fear simmered throughout the ship. All around her, Althea could see the crew reacting to it. They glanced at one another, up at the rigging, out over the water, all seeking the source of their uneasiness. They were too new to the ship to realize they were infected with his fear. That made them more prone to panic, not less. To tell them the cause would only have made it worse. They would learn, she had promised herself. In time, they would learn.

TRADER RESTART HAD HAD HIS CARRIAGE REPAIRED. THE UPHOLSTERY HAD been thoroughly cleaned as well. Now the doors opened and shut as they should, the springs had not groaned alarmingly as Malta climbed in, and when the horses did start, the jolt did not clack her teeth together. It all looked quite clean. As it worked its way through the busy Bingtown streets, a breeze came in the window. Still, she could not convince herself that she didn't smell dead pig. She dabbed at her face with her scented handkerchief.

"Are you all right, dear?" her mother asked her for the tenth time.

"I'm fine. I didn't sleep well last night." She turned and looked out the window and waited for her mother's next line in the dialogue.

"Well, it's natural for you to be excited. Our ship is sailing today and the ball is only eight days away now."

"Quite natural!" Davad Restart agreed heartily. He smiled round at them all eagerly. "You shall see, my dear. This shall mark the turn of all our fortunes."

"I'm sure it will," Ronica agreed, but to Malta, it sounded more as if her grandmother prayed it would be so.

"And here we are!" Davad brayed out enthusiastically, as if no one else had noticed. The carriage halted smoothly. "No, sit still, sit still," he told them as Keffria reached for the door. "The driver will open that."

The slave did indeed come to the door of the carriage, open it for them, and then assist them all out. As first Ronica and then Keffria thanked him for this courtesy, the man looked uneasy. He glanced at Davad as if expecting to be rebuked, but the Trader was too busy straightening his jacket. Malta frowned briefly to herself. Either Davad had become more prosperous lately, or he had simply decided to be freer with his money. The repaired carriage, the trained driver, Davad's new clothes . . . he was preparing for something. She made a mental note to be more watchful of the Old Trader. Foolish as Davad was socially, he had a shrewd streak for sensing profit. Perhaps there was a way to turn whatever he was doing to her family's advantage as well.

He offered his arm to her grandmother. Ronica allowed it. They were all dressed in their best summer clothes. Grandmother had insisted on it. "We cannot afford to look poor on this day," she had said, somewhat fiercely. So fabric had been salvaged from old gowns, washed, turned and pressed to make new dresses for all of them. Rache was developing into quite a seamstress. Malta had to admit she had an eye for copying the newer styles on the streets of Bingtown. Today they were almost fashionable, save for last year's parasols. Even Selden was properly dressed, in blue trousers and a white shirt. He was digging at his collar again. Malta frowned at him severely and shook her head. "A proper little Trader boy doesn't fuss with his collar," she told him.

He dropped his hand but scowled at her. "Being a proper little Trader is choking me," he returned snippily.

"Get used to it," she advised him, and took his hand.

The day was warm, the breeze fresh and the Bingtown docks as lively as always. Her mother followed her grandmother, and Malta came on her heels with Selden. She could not deign to notice them, but it was still gratifying to see the sailors' heads turn as she passed. A few made admiring, if unseemly, comments to their fellows. She kept her head up and did not change her pace. Sharp and sudden, she wished she were a Three Ships girl. She could have winked and flirted back and no one would think she had made a bad match if she attracted a hearty young sailor. She was having to live as cheaply as a fisher girl; why could not she have the carefree ways of one?

Her grandmother slowed the pace as they reached the West Wall. As they proceeded down the docks, she greeted each liveship by name. Without failure, every ship returned her greeting, and added good wishes for the *Paragon's* voyage. Some spoke the words formally, but Malta thought she detected genuine warmth from others. Ronica Vestrit thanked every ship before going on.

When they finally reached the *Paragon*, the rush of emotion she felt surprised Malta. There he was, the blind ship, the mad ship that her family had scraped and strained to refloat. He rode easily beside the dock. His brass gleamed, his wood shone. He looked like a new ship. He held his head high, his arms crossed on his muscled chest. Below his splintered eyes, his jaw was set firmly and his chin jutted. He looked nothing like the rotting old wreck she had last seen on the beach below the cliffs. Selden's small hand tightened on hers.

Her grandmother halted and looked at the figurehead. She raised her voice. "Good day to you, Paragon! A fine day to begin a voyage."

"Good day to you, Mistress Vestrit." A sudden smile cracked his beard. "I'm blind, not deaf. You needn't shout."

"Paragon!" Brashen rebuked him. He had appeared suddenly on the foredeck. Althea hastened up the docks to them.

"It's quite all right, Captain Trell. The ship is correct." Ronica Vestrit refused to take offense. "But I shall say again it is a lovely day to begin a voyage."

There followed an exchange of pleasantries between Brashen, the ship and her grandmother. Malta did not pay too much attention. She was glad the ship wasn't whining or raving. She had feared he would be in one of his mad moods today, throwing things about and shouting. She had seen him like that once, when she had ventured down to the beach to see how things were progressing. He had frightened her so that she had immediately turned around and gone back home.

Most of her attention shifted between her Aunt Althea and Brashen Trell. She still suspected there was something between them, but today she could detect no sign of it. Brashen was very much Captain Trell today. His clothes were clean and neat, his white shirt and dark blue trousers fastidiously pressed. The dark blue jacket gave him dignity. They were her grandfather's clothes, made over to his size. She wondered if he knew that, if he felt odd wearing his old captain's cast-offs. Althea was dressed unusually sedately. She wore a white blouse, and a split skirt with a matching vest. She even had her shoes on. Malta was willing to bet that these clothes were for show only. Even though she'd be acting as second mate, she suspected her aunt would revert to boy's clothes as soon as she could. There was something decidedly odd about Aunt Althea.

Her friend Amber appeared to have resolved that if people were going to stare, she'd give them a good reason. When she appeared, she wore the togs of an ordinary sailor, but every button to her trousers and shirt was a hand-carved bead. The garb was not flattering to her; it showed that she had a very spare figure, flat-chested and narrow-hipped. She wore a snugly laced vest with fanciful butterflies embroidered on it. The only part of her that seemed at all attractive to Malta was her coloring. Like some pale honey-wood was her skin and hair, and her eyes almost the same shade. She had pulled her long hair back, braided it, and then pinned it to her head. Foreign was the only word that fit her. Even her earrings did not match.

"Welcome aboard," Brashen was saying. The others had started up the gangplank. He had come down to greet them all, and was now actually offering Malta his arm as he invited her to board the ship. Not so long ago, she would have felt giddy and flattered. He was handsome enough, and challenging in a rakish way. But her fears and her dreams seemed to have scorched that part of her to death.

Once on board the ship, Althea guided them about, pointing out what had been done. Most of it was meaningless to Malta, but she kept a politely interested look on her face. Sailors busy with the last-minute tasks of readying the ship for departure stepped hastily out of their paths, but stared after her. Their eyes were too bold and their manners too crude for Malta to find it flattering. She wondered how Aunt Althea would fare amongst them in the long weeks to come. Perhaps she enjoyed it, she thought in dismay. She felt distant from all of it as she followed her mother and grandmother on a slow tour of the upper deck.

Brashen was at the top of the gangplank, where other well-wishers had begun to gather. It was gratifying to see the Bingtown Traders at least show them this much support. Most of those who came were from liveship families. Perhaps only a seafaring family could appreciate their predicament. Some were dressed as if they had planned to bid them farewell. Others were the captains or crew members of other liveships currently in port. It was, Malta decided, a substantial turnout for such a venture. A few even paused to speak to Davad. The Trader had sagaciously stationed himself by Brashen, where anyone coming aboard must greet him as well. Malta gathered that he had been able to restore slightly his reputation with the other Traders by acting as a go-between in this arrangement. Even so, the greetings they gave him were formal and brief. Davad beamed as if he didn't know any better. At the slightest excuse, he began a well-rehearsed and long-winded account of all he had done to make today possible. Malta was careful to stay out of earshot and not make eye contact with him. The man was a toad.

"Coming, Malta?" her aunt asked her with a smile. She gestured that they were about to leave the foredeck and be shown the rest of the vessel. Malta had no desire to see the holds or the smelly quarters.

"I think I shall stay here," she ventured. "It's too lovely of a day to go below."

"Well, I'm going," Selden declared boldly and tugged free of her hand.

Althea looked troubled for an instant. Her glance strayed to the crewmen nearby. Plainly, she did not think she should leave her niece in such company. Then her look suddenly cleared and she nodded. "Of course you may."

Malta glanced over her shoulder. Amber was standing behind her, leaning on the rail by the figurehead. Some sort of sign had passed between Althea and Amber. Althea now felt Malta would be safe. Interesting.

And interesting, too, to be left in the company of such a mysterious and scandalous figure as the foreign bead-maker.

"Behave yourself, Malta," Keffria cautioned her daughter worriedly, but she allowed Althea to lead her away with Grandmother. As soon as they had left the deck, Malta focused her attention on Amber. She put a social smile on her face and extended a hand toward the woman.

"Best wishes for your voyage, Mistress Amber."

The woman looked coolly amused. "Thank you, Mistress Haven." She merely inclined her head, but it was as courtly as a bow. She touched Malta's hand briefly with the tips of her gloved fingers. It sent a little shiver up Malta's arm. The woman was so strange. Amber shifted her eyes to stare out over the sea. Malta wondered if it were an attempt to end the conversation. She refused to let it die.

"It seems you have good weather for an auspicious start."

"Yes. It does indeed." Amber's voice was polite.

"And the ship seems to be in excellent condition."

"I would venture to agree with that, also."

"The crew seems fit and ready."

"Captain Trell has trained them as thoroughly as time has permitted."

"Indeed, it seems that all aspects are favorable for this voyage." Malta suddenly tired of the game. "Do you think there is any chance you'll succeed?" she asked bluntly. She needed to know. Was this all a fanciful exercise, a show of caring by her family, or was there truly a chance they might rescue her father?

"There is always a chance of anything happening," Amber replied. Her voice was suddenly serious. She turned back to face her. The intensity of her sympathy burned Malta. "And when anyone takes action to attempt to make something happen, that something becomes more likely. Many folk have taken actions to try to rescue your family's ship and your father and brother, Malta." When Amber spoke her name, Malta had no choice but to meet her eyes. They were strange eyes, and it was not just the color. Somehow, that did not matter. She could feel the other woman's words reach for her. "We have no other focus than rescuing them. I cannot promise you that we will succeed, but we shall sincerely try."

"I don't know if your words make me feel better or worse."

"What I want to tell you is that you have done all that you can. Be content with it. You have a wild young heart; right now, it is like a caged bird that batters itself against the bars. To struggle harder will only hurt you more. Wait. Be patient. Your time will come to fly. And when it does, you must be strong, not bloodied and weary." Amber's eyes went suddenly wider. "Beware of one who would claim your wings for her own. Beware of one who would make you doubt your own strength. Your discontent is founded in your destiny, Malta. A small life will never satisfy you."

Malta crossed her arms on her chest, and actually took a step back. She shook her head. "You sound like a fortune-teller," she said. The laugh that came from her lips cracked in the summer air. "How you have made my heart beat!" She tried to laugh again, to dismiss the moment as a foreigner's social gaffe.

"Sometimes I do," Amber admitted. It was her turn to look away from Malta. The woman looked uncomfortable. "Sometimes I am. But a fortune-teller is not a fortune-maker. We all make our own fortunes."

"And how is that?" Malta felt as if she had somehow taken the upper hand in the conversation. When Amber turned back to meet her eyes, that feeling vanished.

"You earn your future, Malta Vestrit." The bead-maker cocked her head at her. "What does tomorrow owe you?"

"Tomorrow owes me?" Malta repeated in confusion.

"Tomorrow owes you the sum of your yesterdays. No more than that." Amber looked out to sea again. "And no less. Sometimes folk wish tomorrow did not pay them off so completely."

Malta suddenly felt she must change the subject. She advanced to the railing and leaned on it to peer down at Paragon. "Our ship looks very handsome today!" she complimented him recklessly. "You absolutely gleam, Paragon. How excited you must be!"

As sudden as a snake striking, the ship twisted his head to look up at her. That was the chilling part. The wrecked space between his brow and nose froze her with its shattered glance. The coloring of the rest of his face was so natural, but the chopped place was silvered and splintered wood. Her tongue clove to the roof of her mouth. She gripped the railing to keep from falling. Paragon's mouth parted in a wide, white smile. It was the rictus of madness.

"Too late for her," he whispered. Malta did not know if he spoke to her or about her. "Too late for her. Wide wings hang above her. She crouches like a mouse in the owl's falling shadow. Her little heart beats to bursting. See how she trembles. But it is too late. Too late. She sees her. Knows me as well!" He threw back his head. The laughter roared from him. "I was a king!" He was incredulous in his triumph. "I was lord of the three dominions. But you have made me this. A shell, a toy, a slave!"

Perhaps lightning struck her from the still blue sky. She fell into a roaring black gulf. She tumbled, soundless, through endless black space. Then from nowhere, a flash of gold appeared. It was too large a shape for her to see it all. In an instant, it loomed too close to her to be seen. Great talons seized her, wrapping around her chest and waist. They squeezed the air from her. She clawed at them, but they were armored in scales like metal. She could not pry them loose to let herself breathe. Nor did she want to fall to her death if they let go of her. *Choose a death*, a dragon whispered. *That's all you have left, pretty little one. The choice of your death.*

No! She is mine, mine! Let her go!
Prey belongs to he who seizes it first!
You are dead. I have still a chance at life. I will not see it snatched from me!

Iridescent silver clashed suddenly with gold. Mountains collided and fought for possession of her. The talons clenched, cutting her in two. *I shall kill her before I let you take her!*

Malta had no breath to cry out. There was almost nothing left of her at all. These two were so immense; there was no room for her to exist in their world. She was going to blink out like a dying spark.

Someone spoke for her. *"Malta is real. Malta exists. Malta is here."* As if she were being wound up like a ball of yarn, the layers of herself were gradually restored to her. Someone held her against the maelstrom of forces that tried to shred her apart. It was like being cupped in warm hands. She curled tighter into herself, holding on. Finally, she spoke for herself.

"I am Malta."

"OF COURSE YOU ARE," KEFFRIA SPOKE THE WORDS COMFORTINGLY, TRYING to stay calm despite her panic. Her daughter was pale as death. The slits of her eyes showed only white. When they had heard the commotion on deck and hastened back up, she had never suspected it would be Malta. She had collapsed, and lay half in the bead-woman's arms, her head supported by one of the woman's hands. The entire ship had been rocking. The figurehead was doing it, his head bent into his hands as he wept. "I'm sorry, I'm sorry," he sniveled over and over. "Be quiet," Keffria heard Amber tell him irritably. "You did nothing. Just be quiet." Then, as they had burst through the circle of staring sailors, Keffria saw Amber look up and speak directly to Althea.

"Help me get her off the ship. Right now."

Something in the foreigner's voice brooked no argument. Althea stooped and actually lifted her niece bodily, but then Brashen was there, taking her into his own arms. Keffria had a glimpse of Amber's disfigured hands before the woman gloved them hastily. She glanced up to meet Keffria's stare. The look in the bead woman's eyes chilled her to the bone.

"What happened to my daughter?" Keffria had demanded.

"I don't know. You should go to her."

The first was obviously a lie, the second a plain truth. Keffria hastened after her daughter as Amber turned back to the figurehead and spoke to him in a low, intense voice. The ship quieted abruptly and the rocking eased. Then Selden began to cry. The boy wept at everything. It was not right for a boy to be so highly strung, and how could she be thinking of something like that at this moment? "Shush, Selden. Come with me," she snapped at him. Her son followed her, wailing. When she reached the dock, she found that Brashen had spread out his coat and lay Malta down upon it. Ronica took over Selden, patting and shushing him. Keffria sank down beside her daughter. This was terrible, an awful omen for the launch of the ship, and so improper for Malta to be stretched out unconscious like this in front of every passerby. Then she moaned and began to mutter, "I am Malta, I am Malta."

"Yes. You are Malta," she assured her daughter. "You're here and you're safe, Malta."

As if those words were a magic charm, the girl suddenly opened her eyes. She looked around dazedly, then gasped. "Oh, help me up!" she begged her mother.

"Rest a moment longer," Brashen counseled her, but Malta had already seized her mother's arm and was pulling herself upright. She rubbed at the back of her neck, winced, and then rubbed her eyes.

"What happened?" she demanded.

"You fainted," Amber told her. She had appeared suddenly at the edge of the group. Now she pushed closer to Malta and their eyes met. "That is all. I suspect the light on the water dazzled you. That can happen, you know, if you stare at the sea too long."

"I fainted," Malta agreed. She lifted a hand to pat nervously at her throat and gave a giddy little laugh. "How silly of me!"

Her words and gestures were so contrived that Keffria could not believe that anyone could accept them. But Davad bustled up, to add, "The excitement of the day, no doubt. And we all know how Malta has pined for her father. No doubt this launch of his rescue has overwrought the poor child."

Malta glared at him. "No doubt," she said in a venomous little voice. Even thick-skinned Davad seemed to feel the barb. He recoiled a bit, and looked at her oddly.

"I fainted," Malta repeated. "Dear me. I hope I have not delayed the sailing."

"Not by much. But you are right, we must be on our way." Brashen turned away from her, but before he could shout an order, Trader Ashe stepped up to him.

"Let your men save their backs. I'll have the boats from *Sea Rover* give you a tow out."

"Leave room for one from *Winsome*," Trader Larfa brayed. In a moment, half a dozen other liveship owners had offered assistance. Keffria stood, wondering if this was a belated show of good will, or simply a sign of how eager they were to have *Paragon* out of the harbor. There had been rumors that some of the other liveships found him unsettling, but no one had been crass enough to challenge his right to dock there.

"Gentlemen, I give you my thanks," Brashen had replied in such a wry voice that Keffria was certain he wondered the same things.

They did not re-board the vessel, but said their good-byes right there. Mother was more emotional than Keffria had expected her to be. Over and over, she cautioned Althea to be careful and come home safely. Althea scowled when Brashen promised to do all he could to watch over her. As she embraced her sister in their own good-bye, Keffria could only wish that things had been different between them. Her heart was so full of conflicting emotions that she could barely wish her farewell.

It was even more disturbing to turn from that and see Amber holding one of Malta's hands in her two gloved ones. "Take good care of yourself," the foreigner was saying to her. Her gaze was far too intense.

"I will," Malta had promised her. They spoke almost as if Malta were the one sailing off into the unknown. Keffria watched Amber turn away from her daughter and re-board the ship. A moment later, the bead woman reappeared on the foredeck by the figurehead. She leaned down and said something to him. The carved figure dropped his hands away from his face. He brought his head up, took in a breath that swelled his chest, and then crossed his arms on his chest tightly. His jaw set into lines of stark determination.

The lines were cast off, the final farewells and good wishes exchanged. The crews of the small rowing vessels bent to their oars and began to draw *Paragon* away from the dock and out into the waters of the harbor. Althea and Brashen joined Amber on the foredeck. Each in turn bent to speak to Paragon, but if he acknowledged them in any way, Keffria could not see it. She glanced away from the spectacle and found Malta staring raptly at the ship. She could not decide if her daughter's expression was one of terror or love. Nor, she frowned to herself, could she tell if she stared at the figure-head or Amber.

Malta gasped and Keffria immediately looked out to the ship again. The small boats were catching back the lines thrown to them. Brashen was waving his thanks as the sails began to blossom on the ship's rigging. Despite the men scampering about frantically, it was a truly graceful sight. As Keffria watched, the figurehead suddenly threw wide his arms as if to embrace the horizon. He shouted and a trick of the wind carried the words to them. "I fly again!" It was a triumphant challenge to the world. *Paragon*'s sails swelled with wind and he began to move under his own power. From his deck, a faint cheer rang out. Tears pricked Keffria's eyes.

"May Sa speed you," Malta whispered.

Keffria heard her daughter's voice break on the words. "May Sa speed you, and bring you safely home again," she herself said aloud. The breeze seemed to blow her prayer away.

CHAPTER TWENTY-NINE

Bingtown Convergence

THE FLEET THAT ACCOMPANIED THEM HAD GROWN. SERILLA THOUGHT IT would be very interesting to discover how it had been arranged for the other ships to join them en route. How long had all this been in the planning? Did anyone in Jamaillia know this show of force accompanied the Satrap as he descended upon Bingtown? She was now almost sure that the Satrap would be sacrificed to justify a Chalcedean attack on Bingtown. She clutched that morsel of knowledge to herself as if it were a gold nugget. To warn the Old Traders might be her surest way of buying their trust of her. If she had any loyalties left, they now belonged to the wondrous place she had studied for years. She lifted her eyes and stared through the night. On the horizon was a very faint glow: the lights of the Night Market rose into the starlit sky. By morning, they would arrive in Bingtown.

A sailor came to stand at her shoulder. "Satrap call for you. Want to come out, too." He clipped the words curiously with his foreign tongue.

"He can't. His health is much too delicate. But I shall go to him now."

She would have ignored his summons, except that the Chalcedean captain might hear of it. Despite her newfound strength, she still did not dare to cross him. She had encountered him twice since he had returned her to the Satrap. It shamed her that she had been unable to look at him. The first time she had turned a corner in the corridor and run into him, she had nearly wet herself with terror. He had laughed aloud as she had scuttled away from him. It was incomprehensible that she could so fear another human being. Sometimes, when she was alone, she tried to work up a fury toward him or hatred. It was useless. The captain had steeped her in terror. She could feel nothing else about him. The thought of him hastened her footsteps as she returned to the Satrap's chamber.

She ignored the Chalcedean on duty at the door. She entered a chamber that was clean and uncluttered. The fresh ocean air swept through the room from the open window. She nodded to herself with satisfaction. The servants had left her evening repast on the table, and lit the candelabra for her. There was a platter of sliced meat, and a pudding of steamed fruit and several flats of unleavened bread to accompany it. A bottle of red wine and a single goblet awaited her. Simple foods, she thought with satisfaction, prepared to her command. She was taking no chances with herself. Whatever had sickened the rest of the Satrap's company had not touched the Chalcedean captain or crew. She doubted poison, only because she could not see how anyone would profit from it. She suspected one of the more elaborate delicacies the Satrap had brought with him. Perhaps the pickled eggs and walnuts, or the fat pork pastries had gone bad.

On a smaller tray was the Satrap's meal. There was a bowl of bread soaked in hot water, and a smaller dish of steamed onions and turnips mashed together. As a treat, she would allow him some watered wine. Perhaps she would even shred some meat for him. She had stopped seasoning his food with emetics two days ago. It would not do to have him too weak when he arrived in Bingtown. She smiled, pleased with herself, and sat down to her meal. He should rally briefly before he died. As she transferred a slice of meat to her plate, she heard the Satrap stir in his bedding.

"Serilla?" he whispered. "Serilla, are you here?"

She had closed the drapes around his bed. She considered not answering him. He was so weak now that to sit up and part his own curtains would require a substantial effort. She decided to be kind.

"I'm here, Magnadon. I'm preparing some food for you."

"Oh. That's good." He fell silent.

She ate at her leisure. She had trained him to be patient. The servants were barred from his chamber, save once a day when they came in to tidy under her particular supervision. She allowed him no other visitors. His health was far too delicate, she told him. It had not taken much effort to inflate his fears of death to a stultifying level. A substantial number of his party had died from this illness. Even Serilla had been appalled at the toll it had taken. She believed she was quite safe from whatever it had been. But she had filled the Satrap's head with the idea that the disease still ran rampant on the ship.

It had not been hard. The more she restricted his food and dosed him with poppy syrup, the more tractable he became. When his eyes were wide and wandering whatever she told him became his truth. When she had first taken over caring for him, the others had been too ill to visit him, let alone intervene. Since they had recovered, she had successfully turned them back at the door. It was the Satrap's order that he not be disturbed. Serilla had had the spacious chamber to herself, save for the bed the Satrap occupied. She had been quite comfortable.

When she had finished eating, and had enjoyed a glass of wine, she carried the Satrap's tray to his bedside. She swept back the bed curtains and regarded him critically. Perhaps, she thought, she had gone too far. His skin was pallid, his face almost skeletal from lack of flesh. The bony hands that rested atop the coverlet twitched from time to time. That was nothing new; his indulgence in pleasure drugs had done that to him years ago. It was only their feebleness that made them look like dying spiders, she decided.

She sat down gently on the edge of the bed and set the tray on a low table. She smiled as she gently pushed back his hair. "You're looking so much better," she told him. She patted his hand reassuringly. "Shall we get some food into you?"

"Please," he said. He smiled up at her fondly. He was convinced she was the only one who had stood by him, the only one he could rely on. She winced from his foul breath when he opened his mouth for the spoon. He had complained yesterday that some of his teeth felt loose. Well, he would probably recover swiftly enough. Or not. He just had to live long enough to get her ashore in Bingtown and ingratiated with the Traders. She did not want him to be so strong that he could contradict her account. Anything unfortunate that he said she intended to attribute to his wandering mind.

A bit of food dribbled from his mouth. She slipped an arm around his shoulders and helped him to sit up. "Isn't that good?" she cooed to him as she spooned up some of the soggy bread. "And tomorrow we'll be in Bingtown. Won't that be nice?"

RONICA VESTRIT COULD NOT RECALL THE LAST TIME THE GREAT BELL HAD rung to summon an emergency gathering of the Traders. Dawn was barely gray in the sky above the Traders' Concourse. Ronica and her family had hastened down the hill from their home on foot, only to be picked up by Trader Shuyev's coach on its way to the meeting. Folk milled about in front of the hall, calling to one another. Who had rung the bell? Why were they summoned? Some of the Traders who were arriving were in their morning robes, summer cloaks flung hastily about their shoulders. Others were red-eyed from lack of sleep and still wearing evening dress. All had come hastening as soon as the bell had clanged out its dire warning. Many carried weapons or had swords strapped to their sides. Children clung to their parents; young boys tried desperately to look brave, but many faces showed the tracks of panicky tears. The diverse crowd of worried folk looked incongruous amongst the planters full of blooming flowers and the garlanded arches and beribboned stairs of the Concourse. The festive decorations on the hall in preparation for the Summer Ball almost seemed mocking.

"It's the Blood Plague," someone declared on the edge of the crowd. "The Blood Plague has come to Bingtown again. That's all it could be."

Ronica heard the rumor picked up and boosted along through the gathering. The muttering began to rise to a panicky roar. Then from the steps, Trader Larfa bellowed for attention. He was the owner of the liveship *Winsome*, a man usually steady to the point of dullness. This morning his cheeks were glowing red with excitement. His hair stood up in wild tufts on his head. "I rang the bell!" he proclaimed. "Listen to me, all of you! There isn't time to enter the hall and convene properly. I've already passed the word to every liveship in the harbor, and they've gone out to face them. Invaders! Chalcedean war galleys. My boy saw them at first light and came to wake me up. I sent him to the West Wall to rouse the other liveships. I don't know how many galleys are out there, but it's more than ten. They mean business."

"Are you sure?"

"How many?"

"How many liveships went out? Can they hold them back?"

The questions peppered him. He shook his fists at the crowd in frustration. "I don't know. I've told you all I know. There's a fleet of Chalcedean warships coming into Bingtown Harbor. If you've got a ship, man it and get it out there. We need to slow them down. Everyone else, bring weapons and buckets and come down to the harbor. Chalcedeans use fire. If they manage to get off their ships, they'll try to burn the town."

"What about our children?" a woman cried from the back of the crowd.

"If they're old enough to tote a bucket, bring them with you. Leave the smallest ones here with the old and crippled. They'll have to look after each other. Come on."

Little Selden stood beside her in the crowd. Ronica looked down at him. Tears were rolling down his cheeks. His eyes were huge. "Go into the Concourse, Selden," Keffria told him in a falsely cheerful voice. "We'll be back for you soon."

"Shan't!" he declared in a brittle little voice. "I'm big enough to carry a bucket." He choked back a frightened sob and crossed his arms defiantly on his chest.

"Malta will be with you," Keffria offered desperately. "She can help take care of the babies and old people."

"I'd rather carry a bucket," Malta declared sourly as she took Selden's hand in hers. For a moment she looked and sounded almost like Althea. "We're not going to hide here and wonder what is going on. Come on, Selden. Let's go."

At the top of the Concourse steps, Trader Larfa was still shouting directions. "You. Porfro. Get word to the Three Ships families. Someone take word to the New Traders' Council."

"As if they would care! Let them watch out for themselves!" someone shouted back angrily.

"It's their fault we have Chalcedeans in the harbor in the first place," someone added.

"There's no time for that now. We need to defend the city!" Larfa argued. "Bingtown is what counts, not when we got here!"

"Bingtown!" someone shouted. Others took up the cry. "Bingtown! To Bingtown!"

Wagons and carriages were already rattling out of the courtyard, headed down into the city proper. Ronica overheard someone arranging riders to take word to the outlying farms and settlements. There was no time to go home and change into different clothes, no time to wonder about missed breakfasts or shoes that were more sensible. She saw a woman and her grown daughter matter-of-factly tearing their voluminous skirts from their gowns. They discarded the hobbling fabric and in their long cotton pantaloons followed the men of their family.

Ronica seized Keffria's hand, counting on the children to follow. "Room for us?" she shouted to a passing cart. The driver halted it without a word. They piled into it, heedless of the crowding. Three young men leaped in after them. One wore a pitted sword at his hip. They were all grinning like maniacs. Their eyes were bright, their movements swift and powerful like young bulls ready to challenge one another. They smiled wide at Malta, who glanced at them and looked aside. The cart started with a jolt and Ronica seized hold of the edge. They began the trip down to Bingtown.

At one place in the road, the trees parted and Ronica had a brief glimpse of the harbor. The liveships were drawn up in the mouth of it. Men clustered on their decks, milling and pointing. Out beyond them, she saw the tall mast of a ship. The many-oared galleys of the Chalcedeans surrounded it like foul, scuttling bugs.

"They were flying the Jamaillian standard!" one young man in their cart cried out as they lost sight of the harbor.

"Don't mean a thing," another one sneered. "The cowardly buggers just want to get in close before they attack. There's no other reason for that many ships to be heading into our harbor."

Ronica agreed. She saw a sickly smile blossom on Malta's face. She leaned close to the white-faced girl. "Are you all right?" she asked her quietly. She feared her granddaughter was about to faint.

Malta laughed, a thin, near-hysterical sound. "It's so stupid. All this week, I've been sewing on my dress, thinking about Reyn, and the flowers and lights and dancing. Last night I could not sleep because my slippers displeased me so. And now I've a feeling that none of it may ever come to be." She lifted her head and her wide eyes swept over the stream of wagons, carts, and the folk beside them on foot and on horseback. She spoke with a quiet fatalism. "Everything in my life that I was sure I would do someday has always been snatched away when it was almost within my reach. Perhaps it will happen again." A far look came into her eyes. "Perhaps by tomorrow we shall all be dead and our town a smoking ruin. Perhaps my presentation will never even be."

"Don't say such things!" Keffria exclaimed in horror.

Ronica said nothing at all for a time. Then she set her hand over Malta's where she gripped the side of the cart. "This is today. And this is your life." They were comfortless words, and she was not sure where they came from. "It is my life, also," she added, and looked ahead of them, far down the winding road to Bingtown.

REYN STOOD ON THE AFTERDECK OF THE KENDRY, WATCHING THE WIDENING wake of the great liveship in the broad river. The coming of morning turned the milky water of the river to silver and made the ever-dripping canopy of the forested banks a shimmering curtain of falling jewels. The swiftness of the current and the ship's great sails carried them downriver at an incredible rate. He drew in a great breath to try to lift the heaviness from his heart. It would not go away. He bowed his head into his hands. Sliding his hands up under his veil, he scrubbed at his sandy eyes. Deep sleep seemed like a nursery tale from his childhood. He wondered if he would ever sleep well again.

"You look like I feel," a voice said quietly. Reyn startled and turned. In the dimness of the early morning light, he had not noticed the other man. Grag Tenira rolled a tiny parchment up and slipped it up the sleeve of his shirt. "But you shouldn't," he continued, his brow creasing in a frown. "Are not you to be Malta Vestrit's escort at the Summer Ball? What is there to sigh about in that?"

"Very little," Reyn assured him. He plastered a smile onto his face. "I share her concerns for her father and their missing ship. That is all, but it is a heavy concern. I had hoped that her presentation ball would be a wholly festive occasion. I fear this will overshadow it."

"If it's any comfort, the Kendry brought me word that the rescue expedition has already left Bingtown."

"Ah. I had heard your name linked with Althea Vestrit's. This word comes directly from her then?" Reyn nodded his veiled head toward the missive that still peeped from Grag's sleeve.

Grag gave a short sigh. "A farewell missive from her, before she set forth. She has great hopes for her expedition, but none at all for us. It's a very friendly letter."

"Ah. Sometimes friendly is harder than cold."

"Exactly." Grag rubbed his forehead. "The Vestrits are a stiff-necked bunch. The women are too damn independent for their own good. So everyone has always said of Ronica Vestrit. I've discovered the hard way that the same is true of Althea." He gave Reyn a bitter grin. "Let's hope your luck with the younger generation is better."

"She gives little sign of that," Reyn admitted ruefully. "But I think that if I can win her, the battle will have been worth it."

Grag shook his head and looked away from the other man. "I felt the same way about Althea. I still feel that way. Somehow, I doubt that I'll get a chance to find out."

"But you're returning to Bingtown?"

"I won't be stopping there, I'm afraid. Once we get to town, it's belowdecks for me, until we're out at sea."

"And then?" Reyn asked.

Grag gave a friendly smile but shook his head dumbly.

"Quite right. The fewer who know, the better," Reyn agreed. He returned his gaze to the river.

"I wanted to tell you personally how grateful the Teniras are for the support you've shown us. It is one thing to say you will back us. It's another to put your family fortune on the line as well."

Reyn shrugged. "It is a time when the Rain Wilds and Bingtown must stand united, or give up who and what we are."

Grag stared at the ship's white-edged wake. "Do you think enough of us will stand united for us to succeed? For generations, we have functioned as part of Jamaillia. All of our lives are patterned as closely as possible on Jamaillia City. It is not just our language and our ancestry. It is all our customs: our food, our style of dress, even our dreams for our futures. When we stand apart from that and say, We are Bingtown, what will we really be saying? Who will we be?"

Reyn concealed his impatience. What did it matter? He tried to formulate a more political answer. "I think we will simply be recognizing the reality of the last three or four generations. We are the folk of the Cursed Shores. We are the descendants of those brave enough to come here. They made sacrifices and we inherited their burdens. I don't resent that. But I won't share my birthright with those who will not make the same commitment. I won't cede my place to people who don't recognize what it cost us."

He glanced at Grag, expecting him to agree easily. Instead, the man only looked troubled. In a low voice, as if ashamed of the thought, Grag asked him, "Have you never thought of just kicking it all over and running away?"

For a moment, Reyn just stared at him through his veil. Then he observed wryly, "Obviously, you have forgotten whom you are speaking to."

Grag gave a lopsided shrug. "I've heard you could pass. If you wanted to. As for me . . . sometimes, when I am away from my ship for a while, I find myself wondering. What holds me here? Why do I stay in Bingtown, why must I be all a Trader's son must be? Some folk have kicked over the traces. Brashen Trell for instance."

"I don't believe I know him."

"No. You wouldn't. And you never will. His family disowned him for his wild ways. When I heard about that, I halfway expected him to die from it. But he didn't. He comes and goes as he pleases, lives where he wants, sails where the wind blows him. He's free."

"Is he happy?"

"He's with Althea." Grag shook his head. "Somehow, the family picked him to captain the *Paragon* for them. And they entrusted him with Althea."

"From what I've heard of Althea, she needs no man's protection."

"She would agree with that." Grag sighed. "I don't. I think Trell has deceived her in the past, and may again. . . . It eats at me. But do I rush off to find her and bring her back? Did I leap in and say, 'I'll go, I'll captain your mad ship for you, so long as I can be with you?' No. I didn't and Trell did. And that's another difference between us."

Reyn scratched at the back of his neck. Was something growing there? "I think you make a fault of what is actually a virtue, Grag. You know your duty and you are doing it. It isn't your fault if Althea can't appreciate that."

"That's just the trouble." He tugged the small missive from his sleeve, then pushed it back again. "She does. She praised me for it and wished me well. She said she admires me. That's a poor substitute for love."

Reyn could think of nothing to say to that.

Grag sighed. "Well. No point in dwelling on any of that now. If it comes to war with the Satrap, it will come soon enough. Either Althea will come back to me, or she won't. It seems there is little I can do about my life; I'm like a leaf caught in a current." He shook his head, and grinned in embarrassment at his own melancholy words. "I'm going forward to talk to Kendry for awhile. You coming?"

"No." Reyn realized how abrupt he sounded and sought to soften it. "I've got some thinking of my own to do."

Reyn watched through a gray haze of veil as Grag walked forward to the figurehead. He stuffed his hands in his pockets. Even with gloves on, he would not take a chance on leaning on the railing. The whole ship shouted to him as it was, and it was not "Kendry" that spoke to him.

He had traveled aboard liveships before and never had this problem. The dragon had done something to him. He wasn't sure what, or how, but it frightened him. He had broken his bargain with his mother and elder brother to pay her a final visit. It was wrong, but so was abandoning her without trying to make her see that he had done his best. He had begged her to let him go; she had seen how hard he had tried. Instead, she had vowed that she would devour his soul. "As long as I am a prisoner here, Reyn Khuprus, so shall you be also," she had cursed him. She had twined herself through his mind like a black vein in marble, mingling with him until he was no longer certain where she left off and he began. It frightened him worse than anything else she had ever done. "You are mine!" she had declared.

As if to underscore her words, the entire floor of the chamber had trembled. It was only a tremor, a common occurrence on the Cursed Shores. It was not even a large one as quakes went, but never before had he been in the Crowned Rooster Chamber when one struck. His torch showed him the frescoed walls undulating as if they were draperies. He ran, fleeing for his life, with her laughter echoing inside his mind. He could not escape it. As he fled, he had heard the unmistakable sound of corridors giving way. The deadening rush of damp earth followed the clattering of falling tile. Even when he reached the outside and bent over, hands on his knees, trying to reclaim his breath, he could not stop shaking. There would be work tomorrow, and for days to come. Tunnels and corridors would have to be shored up. If it was bad, sections of the buried city might have to be abandoned. All would have to be inspected laboriously before there could be any new explorations. It was precisely the sort of work that he hated.

"Toil away," the dragon's voice had bubbled merrily in his mind. "You might be able to shore up the walls of this dead city, Reyn Khuprus. But the walls of your mind will stand no more against me or my kind."

It had seemed an idle threat. What worse could she do to him than she had already done? But since then, his dreams had been plagued with dragons. They roared and battled one another, they stretched out on rooftops to sun themselves, they mated atop the lofty towers of an exotic city. He was witness to it all.

It was not a nightmare. No. It was a dream of extraordinary brilliance and complexity. They trafficked with beings that were almost human, yet were subtly different. They were tall, with eyes of lavender or copper, and the shades of their flesh were subtly different from any folk he had ever encountered in his real life.

His real life. That was the problem. The dreams were far more compelling than his waking hours. He saw cities of the Elderkind and came tauntingly close to understanding their history. He suddenly grasped the wideness of their streets and corridors, the broad yet shallow steps, the height of the doors and the generous windows. The vastness of their constructions had been to accommodate the dragons that shared the city. He longed to venture inside the buildings, to linger close to the people as they strolled in the markets or ventured out on the river in their gaily painted boats. He could not.

In the dream, he was with the dragons and of the dragons. They regarded their two-legged neighbors with tolerant affection. They did not consider them peers. Their lives were too short, their concerns too shallow. Reyn, while he dreamed, shared that attitude. It was the dragon culture he steeped in, and their thoughts began to color his, not just sleeping but in waking times as well. The emotions they felt were a hundred times as strong as anything Reyn had ever experienced was. Human passion, intense as it might be, was but a snap of the fingers compared to the enduring devotion of a dragon to his mate. They treasured one another, not just through years but through lives.

He saw the world with new eyes. Cultivated fields became a patchwork quilt flung across the land. Rivers, hills and deserts were no longer barriers. A dragon, on a whim, went where a man might not venture in his entire lifetime. The world, he saw, was at once much greater and far smaller than he had known.

The curse of such dreams manifested itself slowly. He awoke unrested, as if he had never slept at all. The potency of his other life drew him. He spent his human days in a fog of discontent and restlessness. He regarded his own existence with disdain. A double curse of weariness dogged him. He longed to sleep, but sleep gave him no rest. Yet he desired sleep, not to rest, but to leave his dreary human life behind and immerse himself once more in a draconian world. His life as a man had become a string of weary days. The only thoughts that could still stir his heart at all were thoughts of Malta. Even in those fancies, he could not shake the dragon's curse, for in his mind's eye Malta's hair shone like the scales of a black dragon.

Behind all his thoughts and dreams, in words almost too soft to hear and yet never silent, came the mourning of the trapped dragon in the Crowned Rooster Chamber. "*No more, no more, no more. They are all gone and dead, all the great bright ones. And it is your fault, Reyn Khuprus. You ended them, by cowardice and laziness. You had it in your power to create their world anew, and you walked away from it.*"

That had been the sharpest of his torments. That he had it within his power, she believed, to free her and bring true dragons back into the world.

Then he had stepped aboard the *Kendry,* and his torment took an even more cruel turn. The *Kendry* was a liveship; the bones of the ship's body were wizardwood. Generations ago, Reyn's ancestors had pounded wedges into a great wizardwood log within the Crowned Rooster Chamber. They had split the immense trunk open, and plank after plank of lumber had been sawn and peeled from it. One immense chunk had been taken whole, to form the figurehead.

The soft, half-formed creature within had been unceremoniously spilled out onto the cold stone floor of the chamber. Reyn twisted inside every time he thought of that. He had to wonder: had it squirmed? Had it mouthed airless cries of pain and despair? Or, as his brother and mother insisted, had it been a long dead thing, an inert mass of tissue and nothing more than that?

If there was nothing for the Khuprus family to be ashamed of, why had it always been kept secret? Not even the other Rain Wild Traders knew the full secret of the wizardwood logs. Although the buried city was their mutual property, the Trader families had long ago established their territories within it. The Crowned Rooster Chamber and the odd sections of wood within it had long ago been ceded to the Khuprus family. It was ironic that, at the time, the immense logs had been considered of little value. An accident had revealed their unique properties, or so Reyn had always been told. Exactly how that had happened, he had never been able to discover. If any of his living family knew the tale, they had held it back from him.

The *Kendry* held nothing back. The figurehead was that of a smiling and affable young man. No one was more knowledgeable about the ways of the Rain Wild River. In previous times, Reyn had enjoyed many pleasurable conversations with him. Since the dragon's curse had fallen on him, the figurehead could no longer abide him. The smile faded from Kendry's lips, the words died unspoken in his mouth when Reyn approached him. The young man's face became, not hostile, but apprehensive at the sight of the Rain Wilder. He would regard Reyn watchfully, forgetting all conversation. The crew of the *Kendry* had noticed his odd behavior. Although none had been so bold as to remark on it, Reyn felt the pressure of their attention. He avoided the foredeck entirely.

Yet if Kendry felt anxious at the sight of Reyn, Reyn's emotions ran sharper and deeper. For Reyn knew that deep within his fibers, down past the affable face of the handsome young man, there lurked the spirit of a furious dragon. Whenever Reyn slept, even if he so much as dozed off in a chair, the buried spirit awaited him. Savagely the creature mourned the death of all he had once been. He railed at the fortune that had torn away his wings and replaced them with flapping canvas. Instead of talons for seizing prey, he had soft little paws with appendages like wilted tubers. He who had once been a high lord of three kingdoms was now confined to the surface of water, pushed about by the wind, ridden with humanity like vermin on a dying rabbit. It was intolerable.

He knew it, even if the smiling figurehead did not. Now Reyn knew it, too. He knew the spirit that lurked in the bones of the *Kendry* thirsted for revenge. He feared that his presence on board the liveship was strengthening those buried memories. If those recollections could ever break through to the surface, what would Kendry do? On whom would his vengeance fall harshest? Reyn was terrified the dragon would discover who he was: the descendant of those who had tumbled him unborn from his cradle.

SERILLA STOOD ON THE DECK OF THE SHIP. BESIDE HER, TWO STOUT Chalcedean sailors held the Satrap. He was prone on a makeshift litter devised from oars and canvas. The wind had brought a faint reddening to his cheeks. She smiled down on him fondly. "Let me speak for you, Magnadon. You need to conserve your strength. Besides, these are only sailors. Save your words for when you address the Traders' Council."

In his ignorance, he nodded gratefully to her words. "Just tell them," he instructed her. "Tell them I want to get off this ship and onto shore as swiftly as possible. I need a warm room with a good bed and fresh food and—"

"Shush, now. You'll tire yourself. Let me serve you in this." She leaned down to tuck the blankets about him more snugly. "I won't be gone long, I promise you."

That, at least, was true. She meant to make all haste. She hoped to persuade the Bingtown ship to take only herself and the Satrap to their town. There was no sense in having any of the others from the Satrap's party along. Their stories might only prove confusing to the Traders. She intended that her tale would be the one told first and most convincingly. She straightened up and pulled her cloak more tightly about her. She had chosen her clothes with care, and even insisted on time in which to dress her hair. She wished to appear imperious, and yet somber. In addition to the subtle jewelry she wore, the toes of her slippers were heavy with several pairs of the Satrap's best earrings. Whatever became of her, she did not intend to begin anew in poverty.

She ignored the Chalcedean captain who stood scowling nearby. She advanced to the railing. She looked across the space of open water that separated the ships and did her best to make eye contact with the group of men on the other ship. The carved figurehead of the ship glared at her fiercely. When it lifted its arms and crossed them defiantly on its chest, she gasped softly. A liveship. A real liveship. In all her years in Jamaillia, she had never seen one. Beside her, the Chalcedean crewmen muttered and several made the hand signs they believed would ward off magic. Their superstitious dread made her stronger. She harbored no such fears. Drawing herself up to her full height, she took a deep breath and pitched her voice to carry.

"I am Serilla, Heart Companion to the Magnadon Satrap Cosgo. My area of expertise is Bingtown and its history. He chose me to accompany him here. Now, weakened by illness and in sore distress, he chooses me to come to you and present you with his greetings. Will you send a boat for me?"

"Of course we shall!" a portly man in a wide yellow vest declared, but a bearded man shook his head.

"Quiet, Restart! You're only here on my suffrance. You! Companion. You say you will come to us. You alone?"

"I, alone. To make known to you the Satrap's will." She lifted her arms wide, holding her cloak open. "I am a woman, and unarmed. Will you let me cross to you and hear my words? There has been a great misunderstanding here."

She watched them confer. She felt confident that they would take her. The worst that could befall her was that she would become their hostage. Even that would get her off this hellish ship. She stood tall and still, the wind blowing her hair into gradual disarray. She waited.

The bearded man came back to the railing. He was obviously the captain of the liveship. He pointed at the Chalcedean captain. "Send her across in your boat! Two sailors at the oars, no more."

The captain actually glanced at her before he looked at the Satrap. It sent a small shiver of triumph through her. Did her rapist finally realize that she had taken a share of power for herself? She cautioned herself to discretion and cast her eyes down. For the first time, her hatred of him was the equal of her fear. Someday, she thought, I might be strong enough to kill you.

Once it was settled, things happened quickly. She was bundled into the boat as if she were cargo rather than a person. The boat itself seemed alarmingly small and lively. The waves lifted and dropped it, and an inordinate amount of water splashed over the sides on their way to the Bingtown ship. When she reached the other ship, a young sailor descended to meet her. The most frightening part of the episode was having to stand up in the boat. As a wave lifted the tiny vessel within reach, the sailor leaned out and scooped her into an arm like a cat snatching a mouse from under a cupboard. He said not a word, nor did he allow her time to feel more secure before he dashed up the ladder with her.

Once they reached the deck, he set her on her feet. For a moment, her ears roared and her heart thundered so that she scarcely heard the introductions the bearded man barked at her. When a silence fell and she realized they were all staring at her, she took a breath. It was suddenly daunting to stand here, in the middle of a group of strange men on the deck of a liveship. Suddenly Jamaillia was so far away, it almost didn't exist. She willed it back to reality with her words.

"I am Serilla, Heart Companion to the Magnadon Satrap Cosgo. He has come a long way to hear your grievances and resolve them." She looked at the faces of the men. They were all listening intently. "On the journey here, he was taken gravely ill, along with many of his party. When he realized how sick he was becoming, he took steps to assure that his mission would be completed successfully, no matter what became of him." She reached deep inside her cloak, to the pocket she had stitched there just last night. She drew out the rolled parchment and proffered it to the bearded man. "In this document, he appoints me as his Envoy in Residence to the Bingtown Traders. I am authorized to speak for him."

Several of the men looked incredulous. She decided to risk it all rather than not have them take her seriously. She opened her eyes wide and looked at the bearded man beseechingly. She lowered her voice, as if she feared the Chalcedeans might hear. "Please. I believe the Satrap's life is in danger, as does he. Think on it. Would he ever have ceded so much power to me if he thought he was going to reach shore alive? If it is at all possible, we must get him off the Chalcedean ship and to the safety of Bingtown." She glanced fearfully back at the Chalcedean ship.

"Say no more," the captain cautioned. "These words should be for the Bingtown Traders' Council. We will send a boat for him immediately. Do you think they will allow him to leave?"

She shrugged helplessly. "I but ask you to try."

The captain scowled. "I warn you, lady. There are many in Bingtown who will consider this but a ploy to get into our good graces. Feelings for the Satrapy have run foul of late, for you have not . . ."

"Please, Trader Caern! You are distressing our guest. My lady Companion, please, allow me. I shall be proud to extend to the Satrap the hospitality of Restart Hall. Although we Traders may seem a bit divided at the moment, I am sure that you shall find that the hospitality of Bingtown lives up to its legendary standards. For now, let us get you off this windy deck and into the captain's sitting room. Come along. Fear nothing. Trader Caern will send off a boat for the Satrap. You shall have a hot cup of tea and tell us all about your adventures."

There was something almost comforting in the broad man's assumption that she was a helpless, trusting female. She set her hand atop his forearm and allowed him to escort her away.

CHAPTER THIRTY

Shakedown

"IF SHE LEAVES HER GEAR BAG STICKING OUT FROM UNDER HER BUNK ONE more time, I'm going to kill her."

Althea half-rolled over in her bunk, then worked the rest of the way over on her elbows. The bunk was so damn narrow she could not even roll all the way over in it. She peered down at Amber. The carpenter stood, hands on her hips, and teeth clenched, glaring at Jek's gear bag. She was panting as if she had just run the rigging.

"Calm down," Althea cautioned her. "Take a breath. Tell yourself it doesn't really matter that much, it's just the cramped quarters." She grinned. "Then kick it as hard as you can. You'll feel much better."

For an instant, Amber stared at her. Her eyes were flat and hard as her namesake. Then she turned wordlessly and kicked Jek's duffel under her bunk. With a sigh, she hunched down onto her own bunk. It was immediately under Althea's. Althea heard her trying to arrange herself in it. "I hate this," she muttered savagely after a few moments. "I've seen coffins that were bigger than this bed. I can't even sit up all the way."

"If we get into any weather, you'll be glad it's so tight. You can brace yourself and still manage to sleep," Althea advised her.

"Now there's something to look forward to," Amber muttered.

Althea hung her head over the edge of her bunk and peered down at her curiously. "You're serious, aren't you? You really hate this that much?"

Amber didn't look at her. She stared at the bulkhead that was in front of her nose. "All my life, I've always had somewhere I could go to be alone. To go without solitude is like going without salt."

"Brashen offered you the use of his room, when he is not in it."

"It used to be my room," Amber said without rancor. "Now it is his, with his things in it. That is all the difference in the world. I cannot settle myself in there. I feel like an intruder. Nor can I latch the door against the world."

Althea pulled her head back up. She racked her brains. "It would not be much, but you could curtain your bunk with canvas. It would be a tiny space, but Jek and I would respect it. Or you could learn to climb the rigging. Up at the top of the mast is an entirely different world."

"Exposed to everyone's view," Amber suggested sarcastically. But there was a note of interest in her voice.

"Up there, the sky and the ocean are so large that the little world below you does not matter. In reality, once you are up the mast, you are almost invisible to anyone on deck. Take a look up there the next time you're on deck."

"Perhaps I shall." Her voice was low again, almost subdued.

Althea judged it was best to leave her alone. She had seen this before, in new sailors. Either Amber would adapt to shipboard life, or she'd crack. Somehow, Althea could not imagine her going to pieces. She had an advantage over most new hands in that she had not come to the sea to make an exciting new life for herself. The adventurers fared the worst: they woke up on the fifth day to realize that the monotonous food, enforced companionship and general squalor of the crew quarters were the norm of the glorious new life they had embarked upon. Those were the ones who not only broke, but often took others with them.

Althea closed her eyes and tried to sleep. Soon enough she'd have to be out on deck again and she had problems of her own to wrestle. The weather had been fair and the *Paragon* was sailing as well as any ordinary ship would have. The ship had not been jolly, but he had not descended into one of his morose moods, either. For those blessings, she thanked Sa. The other side of the coin was that she was having problems with the crew. In fact, she was having the very kind of problems that Brashen had predicted she would, damn him. Somehow, that made it impossible to go to him for advice. She had been so cocky, back on the beach. She had been sure she could handle herself and the men under her command. Now her crew seemed bent on proving the opposite.

Not all of them, to be fair, she reminded herself. Most, she thought, would have fallen into line well enough, if not for Haff. He bucked her at every opportunity. Worse, he was charismatic. The others easily fell in with his attitude. He was handsome, clean and engaging. He always had a cheery word or a jest for his shipmates. He sprang to it readily when another man was in trouble. He was the ideal shipmate, well liked by the rest of the crew. His own natural leadership, she decided wearily, was exactly why he was always at odds with her. Her sex was the rest of the issue. He seemed to have no problems taking orders from Brashen or Lavoy. That was another reason why she could not take her grievances to them. This was something she'd have to unknot for herself.

If the man had been openly insubordinate, she could have dealt with it openly. But he defied her subtly and made her appear incompetent to her crew. She imagined herself making that complaint to Brashen and winced. Haff was clever. If she was paired with him, hauling on a line, he held back his strength, forcing her to work to the limits of hers. The one time she had told him to put his back into it, he had looked shocked at her rebuke. The other men had glanced at them in surprise. Paired with anyone else, Haff always did more than his share. It made her look weak.

She was not as strong as the men she worked alongside. She could not change that. Nevertheless, damn him, she did her share, and it humiliated her when he made the others think she could not keep up. When she set him to a task on his own, he did it swiftly and well. He had an air of rakish showmanship that turned the simplest job aloft into a feat. Disdain for her command and a certain relish of risk: uncomfortably, she recalled a young sailor named Devon who had shared those traits and how she had admired him. No wonder her father had gotten rid of him.

Haff's other trick was to defer to her as a woman rather than as the mate in command. He would make a sly show of stepping aside to allow her to precede him, or offering her a rope or tool as if it were a cup of tea. This last brought snickers from the other men, and today Lop had been fool enough to imitate it. He had been clumsily obvious as he bobbed his head obsequiously to her. Their positions had been right and she had delivered a substantial kick to his butt that had sent him down the companionway ahead of her. There had been a general laugh of support for her, ruined when some faceless wag called, "No luck, Lop. She likes Haff better'n you." From the corner of her eye, she had seen Haff grin broadly at the remark and waggle his tongue. She had pretended not to have seen, simply because there was no good way to deal with it. She thought she had pulled it off until she saw the look on Clef's face. Disappointment was writ large on his face. He had turned aside from her, shamed by her shame.

That as much as anything had convinced her she had to act the next time Haff stepped out of line. The problem was, she still had no idea what to do. Second mate was a hard position to hold down. She was both of the crew and above them. Neither officer nor honest seaman, she had to walk this line alone.

"What would you like to do about Haff?" Amber asked her quietly from the bottom bunk.

"It spooks me when you do that," Althea complained.

"I've explained it before. It's an obvious trick, used at every fair you've ever been to. You've been shifting about up there as if your bunk is full of ants. I simply picked the most likely cause of your anxiety."

"Right," Althea replied skeptically. "To answer your question, I'd like to kick him in the balls."

"Exactly the wrong tack," Amber told her in a superior way. "Every man that witnessed it would wince and imagine himself in Haff's place. It would be seen as a whore's trick, a woman hitting a man where he is most vulnerable. You can't be seen that way. You have to be perceived as a mate giving an uppity hand a take-down."

"Suggestions?" Althea asked warily. It was unnerving to have Amber cut so swiftly to the heart of a problem.

"Prove you're better than he is, that you deserve to be second mate. That's his real problem, you know. He thinks that if you stepped aside and became a passenger, he'd step up into your spot."

"And he would," Althea conceded. "He's a competent sailor and a natural leader. He'd be a good second, or even a first."

"Well, there's your other option. Step aside and let him be second."

"No. That's my spot," Althea growled.

"Then defend it," Amber suggested. "But because you're already on top, you have to fight fair. You have to show him up. Wait for your moment, watch for it, then seize it. It has to be real. The rest of the crew has to have no doubt. Prove you're a better sailor than he is, that you deserve what you've got." Althea heard Amber shift in her own bunk.

Althea lay still, pondering a disturbing idea. Was she better than Haff? Did she deserve to be mate over him? Why shouldn't he take the position from her? Althea closed her eyes. That was something she'd have to sleep on.

With a muttered oath, Amber kicked at her footboard, then turned her pillow over. She settled down, only to shift again an instant later.

"I haven't your gift. Why don't you tell me what's bothering you?" Althea called down.

"You wouldn't understand," Amber complained. "No one can."

"Try me," Althea challenged her.

Amber took a long breath and sighed it out. "I'm wondering why you aren't a nine-fingered slave-boy. I'm wondering how Paragon can be both a frightened boy and a cruel-hearted man. I'm wondering if I should be aboard this ship at all, or if I was supposed to stay in Bingtown and watch over Malta."

"Malta?" Althea asked incredulously. "What does Malta have to do with any of this?"

"That," Amber pointed out wearily, "is exactly what I would love to know."

"SOMETHING IS WRONG, SIR! WITH DIVVYTOWN, I MEAN."

Gankis stood framed in Kennit's stateroom door. The old pirate looked more distressed than Kennit had ever seen him. He had taken off his hat and stood wringing it. Kennit felt his stomach turn with a sudden premonition. He didn't let it show on his face.

He raised one eyebrow queryingly. "Gankis, there are many things wrong with Divvytown. Which particular one has brought you to my door?"

"Brig sent me, sir, to tell you the smell is bad. The smell of Div-vytown, that is. Well, it's always bad, coming into Divvytown, but now it's real bad. Like wet ashes—"

There. Like an icy finger in the small of his back. The moment the old hand mentioned it, Kennit was aware of it. It was faint inside the closed cabin, but there. It was the old smell of disaster, one he had not scented in a long time. Odd, how a smell brought memories back sharper than any other prod to the senses. Screaming in the night, and flowing blood, both slick and sticky. Flames, lifting to the sky. Nothing quite like the smell of burned houses, mixed with death.

"Thank you, Gankis. Tell Brig I'll be up shortly."

The door shut behind the sailor. He had been very troubled. Div-vytown was as close to a homeport as this crew had. They all knew what the smell meant, but Gankis hadn't been able to bring himself to say it. Divvytown had been raided, probably by slavers. It was not an unusual event in a pirate town. Years ago, under the old Satrap, there had been fleets of raiding ships that had cruised these waters just for that purpose. They had found and wiped out a great many of the old pirate strongholds. Divvytown had weathered those years, undiscovered. In the lax years of the old Satrap's dying reign and Cosgo's incompetent one, the pirate towns had been undisturbed. They had learned both carelessness and prosperity. He had tried to warn them, but no one in Divvytown would listen to him.

"The circle is closing."

He glanced down at the charm on his wrist. The be-damned thing was more nuisance than luck-piece anymore. It spoke only when it suited it, and then it mouthed nothing but threats, warnings and bleak prophe-cies. He wished he had never had it created but he could scarcely get rid of it. There was far too much of himself in it to trust it if it fell into other hands. Likewise, to destroy a living sculpture of one's own face must invite a like destruction to oneself. So he continued to tolerate the little wizardwood charm. Someday, perhaps, it might be useful. Perhaps.

"I said, the circle closes. Do you not take my meaning? Or are you growing deaf?"

"I was ignoring you," Kennit said pleasantly. He glanced out the window of his stateroom. The Divvytown harbor was coming into sight. Several masts stuck up from the water. Beyond them, the town had burned. The jungly forest beyond the town showed signs of scorching. Divvytown's docks had survived as freestanding platforms that pointed at the shore with charred-off beams. Kennit felt a pang of regret. He had come back here, bringing his richest trove ever, in the expectation that Sincure Faldin could dispose of it at a tidy profit. No doubt, he had had his throat slit and his daughters and wife were dragged off for slaves. It was all damnably inconvenient.

"The circle," the charm went on inexorably, "seems to be composed of several elements. A pirate captain. A liveship for the taking. A burned town. A captive boy, family to the ship. Those were the elements of the first cycle. And now, what do we have here? A pirate captain. A liveship for the taking. A captive boy, family to the ship. And a burned town."

"Your analogy breaks down, charm. The elements are out of order." Kennit moved to his mirror, then leaned on his crutch as he made a final adjustment to the curled ends of his mustache.

"I still find the coincidence compelling. What other elements could we add? Ah, how about a father held in chains?"

Kennit twisted his wrist so that the charm faced him. "Or a woman with her tongue cut out? I could arrange one of those, as well."

The tiny face narrowed its eyes at him. "It goes around, you fool. It goes around. Do you think that, once you have set the grindstone in motion, you can escape your ultimate fate? It was destined for you, years ago, when you chose to follow in Igrot's footsteps. You will die Igrot's death."

He slammed the charm facedown on his table. "I will not hear that name from you again! Do you understand me?"

He looked at the charm again. It smiled up at him serenely. On the back of his hand, blood spread under the surface of his skin. He tugged on his shirt cuff to conceal both the charm and the bruise with a fall of lace. He left his cabin.

The stench was much stronger on deck. The swampy harbor of Div-vytown had always had a stink of its own. Now the smells of burned homes and death joined it. An uncommon silence had fallen over his crew. The *Vivacia* moved like a ghost ship, pushed slowly by a faint wind over the sluggish water. No one cried out, nor whispered or even moaned. The terrible silence of acceptance weighed the ship down. Even the figurehead was silent. Behind them, in their wake, the *Marietta* came in a similar pall.

Kennit's eyes went to Wintrow, standing on the foredeck of the *Vivacia*. He could almost feel the numbness they shared. Etta was beside him, gripping the rail and leaning forward as if she were the ship's figure-head. Her face was frozen in a strange grimace of disbelief.

The destruction was uneven. Three walls of a warehouse stood, like hands cupped around the destruction within. A single wall of Bettel's elegant bagnio still stood. Here and there, isolated hovels had failed to catch well enough to burn. The soggy ground the town was founded on had saved these few places.

"There's no point in tying up here," Kennit observed to Brig. The young first mate of the *Vivacia* had drifted up wordlessly to his side. "Bring her about and let's find another port."

"Wait, sir! Look! There's someone. Look there!" Gankis raised his voice boldly. The scrawny old man had climbed the rigging, the better to look down on the town's destruction.

"I see nothing," Kennit declared, but an instant later, he did. They came drifting in from the jungle, in ones and twos. The door of one hovel was flung open. A man stood in the open door, holding a sword defiantly. His head was bound in a dirty brown bandage.

They tied up to the skeletal pilings that were the remnants of the main dock. Kennit rode in the bow of the ship's boat as it carried him ashore. Sorcor in the *Marietta*'s boat kept pace with him. Both Etta and the boy had insisted on accompanying him. Grudgingly, he had said that the whole crew might have a brief shore time, provided a skeleton crew always manned the ship. Every man aboard seemed intent on getting ashore, to prove the destruction to himself. Kennit would have been content simply to leave. The burned town unsettled him. He told himself there was no telling what the desperate survivors might do.

The Divvytown survivors had gathered into a crowd before either gig touched the shore. They stood like ragged, silent ghosts, waiting for the pirates to land. Their silence seemed ominous to Kennit, as did the way he felt every pair of eyes follow him. The boat nudged suddenly into the mucky shoreline. He sat still, his hands gripping his crutch as the crew jumped out and dragged the boat further up. He did not like this one bit. The shining muck of the beach was black, with a thin oily overlay of greenish algae. His crutch and his peg were bound to sink into the muck as soon as he got out of the boat. He was going to look very awkward. Worse, he would be vulnerable if the crowd decided to rush him. He remained seated, staring over the crowd and waiting for some definite sign of their temperament.

Then, from the *Marietta*'s boat, he heard Sorcor exclaim, "Alyssum! You're alive!" The burly pirate was instantly over the side. He sloshed through the water and muck up to the waiting crowd. It parted before his charge. He seized a shrinking girl in his arms and swept her to his barrel chest. It took Kennit a moment to recognize her. The bedraggled creature had been much more fetching when Sincure Faldin had presented her and her sister Lily as prospective brides for Kennit and Sorcor. He recalled that Sorcor had seemed infatuated with the girls, but he had never suspected that he had continued the courtship. Sorcor stood gripping Alyssum Faldin now like a bear with a calf in its hug. She had wrapped her pale arms around the pirate's thick neck and was holding on to him. Amazing. Tears were rolling down her cheeks, but Kennit was willing to suppose they indicated joy. Otherwise, she would most likely be screaming as well. So the girl was glad to see him. Kennit decided it was safe to get out of the boat.

"Give me your arm," he told Wintrow. The boy looked pale. It would be good to give him something to do.

"The whole town is gone," he said stupidly as he climbed over the side and held out his arm to the pirate.

"Some might think that an improvement," the pirate captain observed. He stood in the boat, regarding the filthy water with distaste. Then he stepped over the side, peg first. As he had feared, it plunged into the soft muck. Only the boy's shoulder saved him from going knee deep, and he still nearly lost his balance. Then Etta was there, gripping his other arm and steadying him as he clambered out. They slogged up the mucky shore until they reached firmer ground. He spotted a rock protruding from the muck and chose that as a stopping place. He planted his peg firmly atop it and looked around.

The devastation had been thorough. The new growth of jungle in the scorched areas told him that the raid had likely been weeks ago, but there was no sign that anyone had tried to rebuild. They were right. It was pointless. Once the slavers had discovered a settlement, they would return again and again until they had harvested every person there. Divvytown, one of the oldest of the pirate settlements, was dead. He shook his head to himself. "I don't know how many times I told them they needed to put up two watchtowers and some ballista. Even one tower with a watchman would have given them enough warning that they could have fled. But no one would listen to me. All they could worry about was who would pay for it."

It was satisfying to have been so right, and no one could argue that he had not warned them. Usually his suggestions had been met with mockery, or the accusation that he just wanted to gather power to himself. Yet several of the survivors turned to him with accusing eyes. One man flushed scarlet with sudden anger as he pointed at Kennit and declared, "You! You are responsible! You brought the Chalcedeans down on us!"

"I?" Kennit was incensed. "I just told you, it was I who warned you that this was coming. If you had listened to me, there would be many more survivors here now. Who knows? You might have even been able to defeat the raiders and seize their ships!" Kennit gave a snort of contempt. "I am the least to blame for what happened here. If you wish to blame anyone, blame your own pig-headed stubbornness!"

It was the wrong tone to take. Almost instantly, Kennit knew that. Too late.

The crowd rolled toward him like ice avalanching off an iceberg. He had that same sense of an inevitable wave of destruction. Etta, damn her, loosened her grip on his arm. Would she run? No. Her hand had fallen to her knife. Much good that would do against so many, but he appreciated the sentiment. He loosened his shoulders with a quick roll and took his hand from Wintrow's shoulder. He waved the boy aside. Kennit had his own knife: they wouldn't take him down cheaply. He summoned the small smile to his face and waited for them, his peg braced on his rock.

He was shocked beyond words when the boy also drew a knife, a very valuable knife indeed, and stepped in front of him. Beside him, Etta gasped and then gave a snort of amusement. A glance at her showed a wild proud smile dawning on her face. It was perhaps the most frightening sight Kennit had ever seen. Well he knew that she enjoyed cutting up men. At least she was on his side this time. He heard splashing and the sloppy sounds of boots running through the mire as his crew formed up behind him. Only four men had come ashore with him. Some part of his mind registered that Vivacia was shouting something; she saw what was going on, but there was nothing his ship could do for him now. By the time she put out another boat and sent more men ashore, it would be over. He stood his ground and waited.

The crowd rolled up to him, and then flowed ominously around him. Behind Kennit, the men at his back turned to face outward. Tension hummed in the air. Faced with a determined group of armed men, no one in the mob wanted to be the first to engage. The red-faced man he now confronted he recalled as a tavern owner: Boj, that was his name. He carried a cudgel that he tapped meaningfully against his leg, but he stayed out of the boy's knife reach. The others stood, waiting for him to attack. Kennit suspected Boj suddenly did not relish being leader of this mob. A glance to the side showed him Sorcor flanking the mob with his own sailors from the *Marietta*. The girl had vanished. Kennit had no time to wonder where. A look passed between the two men; Sorcor needed no sign from him. He would do nothing until it became inevitable. Then he would cut his way to Kennit as swiftly as he could.

Boj glanced warily over his shoulder at his followers, then smiled with cold satisfaction at the ones that had surrounded the pirate. Sure of his backing, he confronted Kennit. He had to look over Wintrow's head to lock eyes with him. "It is your fault, you scummy bastard. You're the one that stirred things up, pirating slaveships. Had to show off, you couldn't be content with just making a living. You and your talk of being a king. A ship here, a ship there, that boy with a crown in Jamaillia didn't care. Not until you come along. The Satrap was leaving us alone, until you stirred the pot. You got into his pocket personal. Now look what you've done to us. We've got nothing left. We're going to have to find a new place, and rebuild from the ground up. Chances are we'll never find as good a hiding place as Divvytown was! We were safe here, and you destroyed that. The raiders that came here were looking specifically for you." Suddenly he slapped the cudgel meaningfully against his hand. "You owe us, is how I see it. Whatever you got on that ship, we are taking, so we can find

ourselves a new hiding spot. Choose now how we get it. If you don't want
to share easy, well . . ." He swung the cudgel with a whistling motion.
Kennit refused to flinch.

More folk had emerged from the trees. Plainly, there were more survivors than he had first thought, but this whole confrontation was a foolish
one. Even if they killed him here on the beach and wiped out his men,
they could scarcely expect both ships to yield to them. They'd simply sail
away. It was stupid; mobs were usually stupid. And deadly. He let his
smile widen as he composed his words.

"Hiding. Is that all you can think of?"

The sound of Wintrow's voice shocked Kennit. It rang out, clear as a
bard's, laden with contempt, and pitched, Kennit realized, to reach not
just the men in front of him but those coming in from the jungle as well.
Wintrow still held his knife low and ready; where had he learned that?
But the boy obviously had other intentions than fighting the crowd.

"Shut up, kid. No one has time for more talk!" Boj weighed his cudgel
threateningly. He eyed Kennit over Wintrow's head. "Well, King Kennit?
Easy or—"

"Of course you have no time for talk!" Wintrow's voice rang clear
over Boj's. "Talk would require brains, not brawn. No one here ever has
time for talk, not even when it would have saved you. Kennit tried to
show you. You can't hide from what is happening outside your little town.
Sooner or later, the rest of the world catches up with you. Kennit tried to
warn you. He told you to fortify the town, but you wouldn't listen. He
brought slaves here and set them free amongst you, but you would not
look at them and see yourselves! No, you'd rather hide here in the muck
like some garbage-eating crab, and trust that the world will never take
notice of you! It doesn't work that way. If you'd listen to him now, you'd
find out how to be men again. I've seen the sketches in his room. This
harbor could be fortified. Divvytown could declare itself. You could dredge
this stinking slough you call a harbor and claim a place on the traders'
charts. All you'd have to do is stand up and say, we are a people, not a
band of outlaws and Jamaillia's outcasts. Choose a leader and stand up for
yourselves. But no. All you want to do is splatter some more brains, work
some more death and then go hide under another rock until the Satrap's
raiders dig you out again!"

The boy had run out of breath. Kennit hoped the others could not see
his trembling. He pitched his voice low, as if for Wintrow alone, but he
knew his words would carry. "Give it up, son. They wouldn't listen to me,
they won't listen to you. This is all they know. Fighting and hiding. I've
done what I could to try to teach them to be free men." He shrugged one
shoulder. "They'll do what they'll do." He lifted his eyes and looked over
the crowd. Some of the tattooed faces he saw were vaguely familiar.
Slaves he had brought here as free men, he realized, as one after another

they dropped their eyes from his gaze. One slave, braver than the rest, suddenly stepped apart from the mob.

"I'm with Kennit," he said simply, and crossed the small space to stand with Sorcor's sailors. Half a dozen others followed him wordlessly. The mob began to shift restlessly as its numbers dwindled. Some of those who had come down from the jungle's edge stood apart from them, plainly reluctant to take sides. Nothing seemed as clear as it had a few moments before.

A woman's voice was raised suddenly. "Carum! Jerod! Shame upon you! You know what he says is true! You know it!" It was Alyssum. She was standing in the *Marietta*'s boat. Sorcor must have put her there. She pointed accusingly at the young men as she named them. "Vahor. Kolp. You teased Lily and me, saying Father had offered her hand to a madman and mine to his first mate. And what did my mother tell you? That they were men who saw how the future could be! Men who were trying to help us be more than a village on the edge of nothing. And now she is dead! Dead! Kennit didn't kill her. Our stupidity did! We would not listen to him. We needed a king to protect us, but we mocked his offer!"

Kennit's shirt stuck to his back with perspiration. By now, both the *Marietta* and the *Vivacia* would have put out more boats. If he could just keep them from attacking him for a few moments longer, he would soon have enough men at his back to sway the odds more in his favor. He would still probably die. The boy in front of him and the woman at his side would at most slow down one or two of them. Then he would die, once they pressed him and he had to step away from the rock that braced his peg. He would die.

Some of the folk in the back of the crowd were standing more loosely. They had stepped slightly apart from their fellows, and struck poses more listening than threatening. Boj was not one of them. He and the five or so men standing closest to him stood with their shoulders raised and elbows out, gripping their weapons hard. The resistance from the other survivors only seemed to inflame Boj's anger. The young man at his side was most likely his son. Boj's breath came faster and harder, while his mouth worked as if he could not find words sharp enough. "You're wrong!" he roared suddenly. "It's his fault! His fault! He brought them down on us!" His voice rose into a shriek, and then he leaped forward, cudgel swinging. The crowd behind him was suddenly in motion, surging forward like a wave.

Boj's cudgel swept the place where Wintrow's skull had been. The boy had ducked, but not deeply enough. Kennit saw the glancing blow snap his head to one side. He expected the boy to go down. He planted his crutch and lifted his knife to defend himself. A young tough had engaged Etta's blade. She'd be no help to him.

As Kennit raised his blade, Wintrow suddenly sprang up again between him and Boj. Like a sapling blown to one side but not snapped, the boy swept back to his stance. The shock showed plain on Boj's face, but the fool had already drawn his cudgel back for a blow intended to kill Kennit. His chest was wide open; no doubt the tavern keeper was accustomed to a bar between himself and his victim. Wintrow's knife slammed into the man, punching through his shirt and vest and into his hard belly. Wintrow screamed as he did it, a cry of both horror and hate. Boj roared, injured, but far from dead.

The fighting closed in from all sides. Kennit could hear Sorcor roaring curses to encourage his men as they sliced through the crowd toward him. He heard the shrieks of women, and knew that some folk fled the fight. Everything was happening at once, yet Kennit felt he stood in an island of stillness. Etta was down in the mud with her man, shrieking, stabbing and wrestling. Kennit was dimly aware of the other fighting going on about him. He heard yells from the water, probably the men in the boats shouting their frustration at not landing yet. Behind him, two men grappled in the mud. One kicked out and clipped the end of his crutch, sending him staggering a half step into the mud. Boj's cudgel came crashing down on Wintrow's shoulder as the boy pulled out his knife and punched it into the man again. Kennit heard a solid smack as the cudgel connected and Wintrow's yell of pain and then he staggered into them. He caught himself on Boj and used his own knife. His crutch was gone; his peg sank into the mud, throwing him to one side. Boj's dying flail with the cudgel just missed him. Kennit fell across Wintrow, and then Boj came down upon them both like a tree falling. The weight of the tavern keeper slapped Kennit down into the shining mud.

The sheer indignity of it energized Kennit more than any anger. With a roar, he threw the heavier man off him. A slice of his knife across Boj's throat made sure of him. He scrabbled up onto his good knee, and saw Etta back-down in the mud. She gripped two-handed the wrist of a powerful man who was trying to plunge a knife into her with one hand while throttling her with the other. Kennit shoved his knife into him just to the right of the man's lower spine. The man shrieked and spasmed in the shock of his pain. Etta used the moment to turn the knife from herself into the man's gut. With the same thrust, she rolled out from under him and came to her feet, crying, "Kennit, Kennit!" She was filthy. She scrabbled through the mud toward him, then stood over him protectively with her knife. It was too humiliating. Kennit struggled to stand.

As swiftly as the melee had begun, it was abruptly over. His pirates were left standing. Anyone in the mob who had truly wanted to fight was down. The rest had withdrawn a safe distance. Somehow, Sorcor had contrived to cut through the thick of it, as usual. As Kennit lost his balance and sat back in the mud, Sorcor casually dispatched a wounded Divvytown man and stepped across the remaining space between them, extending a broad hand dripping both mud and blood. Before Kennit could object, Sorcor had seized him by his jacket front and set him back on his feet. Etta found his crutch and offered it to him. It, too, was thick with muck. He accepted the filthy thing and tried to look nonchalant as he tucked it under his arm.

At his feet, Wintrow had managed to get as far as his knees. In his right arm, he cradled his left, but he still gripped his knife as well. This Etta noticed and she gave a proud laugh. Heedless of his moan, she seized him by the back of his shirt and hauled him upright. To Kennit's surprise, she gave the boy a rough hug. "You didn't do too badly, for your first time. Next time, duck deeper."

"I think my arm is broken," he gasped in reply.

"Let me see." She seized his left arm and worked her hands up it. Wintrow gave an involuntary cry and tried to pull away from her, but she held him fast. "It's not broken. If it were broken, you would have passed out when I did that. I think it might be cracked a bit, though. You'll get over it."

"Help me get to firmer ground," Kennit demanded, but it was Sorcor who took his arm and helped him along. Etta and Wintrow followed together. For an instant, that rankled. Then he reminded himself that it was his intention to throw Etta and Wintrow together. They passed the handful of men who had died, and one who sat with his head bowed over his slit belly. The other Divvytown folk had fallen back to a safe distance. One of his crewmen had been gashed on the leg, but for the most part, they were unharmed. The outcome did not surprise Kennit. They had had the advantage of full bellies and decent weapons, experienced fighters against town brawlers. Only the odds had been against him, and a few deaths had quickly changed that.

Once he was where he could stand on his own, Kennit wiped his hands firmly down the front of his hopelessly spoiled trousers. He glanced past the crewmen who encircled him protectively to the ruins of the town. Nowhere to take a bath, nowhere to have a quiet drink, nowhere to sell his booty. Nothing left of Divvytown. No point in staying. "Let's get out of here," he said to Sorcor. "There's a man in Bull Creek with a link to Candletown. Last time we were there, he was bragging he could get us better prices for our swag. Maybe we'll try a bit with him."

"Sir," agreed Sorcor. Then he hung his head as if studying the sand between his big boots. "Sir, I'm taking Alyssum."

"If you must," Kennit replied in some annoyance. When the big man lifted his head, there were glints of anger deep in his eyes. "And of course you must," Kennit amended hastily, shaking his own head sadly. "For what is left for the poor girl here? You're the only protector she has now, Sorcor. I see it as your duty. You must."

Sorcor was nodding gravely. "Just as I saw it myself, sir."

Kennit looked with distaste at the trampled muck he must pass through on his way back to the boat. He must manage it so that it looked no more difficult for him than for anyone else. He took a firmer grip on his mud-slicked crutch. "Let's go, then. There's nothing left for us here."

He cast a wary eye at the folk that still huddled in clusters, staring at them. None looked prone to attack, but one never knew. As he glanced at them, one stepped out boldly to stand before the rest. "You're leaving us here, like this?" He was incredulous.

"How else would I leave you?" Kennit demanded.

Again, Wintrow surprised him. "You've made it very apparent he's not welcome here. Why should he waste his time on you?" The boy sounded sincerely disdainful.

"It wasn't us that jumped him!" the man cried out, affronted. "It was them other troublemakers, and they're all dead now. Why should we be punished for what they done?"

"It also wasn't you that jumped in to save him," Wintrow snapped back. "That shows you have learned nothing. Nothing! You still believe that the evil that befalls another is nothing to you. Let another man be taken slave, let another town be raided, let someone else be slaughtered on the beach right in front of you. It won't matter to you until it's your own throat being slit, and we haven't time to wait for that. Other towns are glad to listen to what he says, glad to profit from his leadership. Divvytown is dead. It was never on a chart, and it never will be. Because the people in it were already dead."

The boy's voice had a power to it. The very people he was reviling drew closer, moving as if drawn in like fish on lines. Some scowled, some looked shamed. Some still wore the dazed look of people whose bodies have survived some widespread disaster while their minds fled. They came toward the boy. Even stranger, the men of the crew parted, to let Wintrow stand before his audience unblocked. When the boy fell silent, the quiet that followed his words echoed his accusation.

"Other towns?" someone finally asked from the crowd.

"Other towns," Wintrow confirmed. "Towns like Askew. They took the ship that Kennit gave them and put it to use. With the wealth that came in, they bettered the lot of all. They no longer hide, but venture out and declare to the world that they are there and they are free. They trade openly, and they challenge slaveships that seek to pass. Unlike you, they took Kennit's words to heart. They fortify their harbor and live free."

"That won't work for us," a woman objected. "We can't stay here! The raiders know where our town is. They'll be back. You must take us with you. You must! Our only hope is to flee. What else are we to do?"

"What else?" Wintrow mused. He stood up on his tiptoes. He looked about the squalid harbor as if mentally comparing it to something. "There!" He pointed to a low bluff. "That is the spot where you could start. You rebuild, but you begin with a tower there. It need not be very tall to command a view of the lagoon. With a man keeping watch there . . . nay, even a child on watch there could have warned you all in time to flee or fight. You would have survived the last raid."

"You're suggesting we rebuild Divvytown?" a man asked skeptically. His hand described an arc to indicate the remnants of the buildings. "With what?"

"Oh, I see. You have better prospects elsewhere?" Wintrow asked him dryly.

When the man made no reply, he went on. "Rebuild it with what you do have. Some of the lumber is salvageable. Cut trees now and put them to dry for more lumber later. Raise the ships in the harbor. If they will not sail again, put their planks to use elsewhere." Wintrow shook his head as if he could not fathom their stupidity. "Must it all be laid out for you? Make your stand here. Was this not your home? Why are you allowing them to drive you from it? Rebuild, but this time, do it right, with fore-thought for defense, for trade, for clean water. The docks should never have been built here! They should run out from there. You gave the best ground to the warehouses. Put your homes and businesses there, and build the warehouses on pilings over there, where a ship can come right up to the door. It was all in Kennit's plans; he saw it clearly. I cannot believe that you did not ever see it for yourselves."

Few things appeal so much to the heart of a man as a fresh start. Kennit watched them look about with new eyes and then exchange glances. Almost as quickly, he saw a sly look steal over several faces. There was opportunity here, a chance to better what they had lost. Those who had been newcomers or poor were suddenly on an equal footing with everyone else. He would wager that whoever had owned the ships had been dragged off in chains. Someone would be smart enough to claim what was left.

Wintrow raised his voice like a prophet proclaiming. "Kennit is a good man, who has always cared for you, even when you spurned his offers of help. You have never been far from his heart. I doubted his motives at first. I feared him. But I can tell you this now. I have seen into his heart, and I believe now what he believes. Sa has put a destiny upon him. Kennit will be King of the Pirate Isles. Will you be one of his cities, or will you vanish?"

Kennit's ears rang. He could not believe for an instant what he was hearing. Then his heart seized it. The boy was his prophet. Sa had sent him Wintrow, a priest of his own, to open the eyes of others to his destiny. That was what he had felt, when he had first set eyes on the lad. The connection of king to soothsayer had linked them. It was not, as the charm had accused, some brutish urge to repeat the past. Wintrow was his prophet. His luck embodied.

Even stranger events followed as the miracle unfolded. A man stepped forward, declaring, "I'm going to stay here. I'm going to rebuild. When I got away from my master in Jamaillia City and fled here, I thought I was a free man. But now I see I wasn't. The boy's right. I won't be free until I stop running and hiding."

One of the freed slaves came to stand beside him. "I'm here. I have nowhere else, nothing to my name. I start again here." One of his fellows came mutely to join him. Slowly the whole crowd edged closer.

Kennit set a muddy hand on Wintrow's shoulder. The boy turned his head to look up at him and the admiration in his eyes near blinded the pirate. For an instant, he truly felt something, a pang of some emotion so sharp he could not tell if it was pain or love. His throat closed. When he did speak, his words came out softly and folk drew nearer still to hear him. He felt like a holy man. No. Like a wise and beloved king. He smiled down on his people. "You have to do it together. It cannot be every man for himself. Begin with the tower, yes, but at its foot, raise a shelter that all can share until your homes are restored. Dig for your water instead of taking it from the slough." He looked around at the faces of the folk listening to him. They came to him like lost, bedraggled children; they were finally ready to hear him. He could correct their lives for them. They would let him show them how they should live. His heart swelled with triumph. He turned to Etta at his side.

"Etta. Go back to *Vivacia*, to my stateroom. Bring the plans from my desk; they are labeled clearly. Do you know the ones I mean?"

"I can find them. I can read," she pointed out gently. She touched his arm briefly, her smile warm, then turned to commandeer two men to row for her.

He called after her, "Tell the crew to make all secure. We will be here for a time, helping Divvytown rebuild. The *Marietta* has sacks of wheat aboard. Have them start ferrying the wheat ashore. These people are hungry."

A murmur ran through the crowd. A young woman stepped forward. "Sir. You do not need to stand out here. My house is still standing, and I have a table. I can draw water for washing as well." She made a self-effacing gesture. "It is poor lodging, but I would be honored."

He smiled at her, and then looked around at all his loyal subjects. "That would be most welcome."

CHAPTER THIRTY-ONE

The Calm

"MALTA, YOU HAVE USED TOO MUCH POWDER. YOU LOOK PALE AS A GHOST," Keffria rebuked her.

"I haven't used any," the girl replied listlessly. She sat in her shift before the mirror, staring into the glass. Her shoulders were slumped, her hair but half brushed. She looked more like a weary serving girl at the end of her day's work than a Trader's daughter just an evening away from her presentation at the Summer Ball.

Keffria's heart went out to her. She had come into her room, expecting to find her daughter primping and sparkling with excitement. Instead, the girl looked dazed. The summer had been too hard on her. She wished that somehow she could have spared Malta the drudgery and scrimping. Above all else, Keffria wished that this ball could have been as they had both imagined it. Malta was not the only one who had looked forward to this for years. Keffria, too, had dreamed of the proud moment when her only daughter would walk into the Traders' Concourse on her father's arm, to pause in the entry and be announced to the gathered Old Traders. She had dreamed of an extravagant gown for her daughter, a presentation of fine jewelry to commemorate the occasion. Instead, she would soon lace Malta into a dress concocted from older gowns. Her only jewelry would be gifts from Reyn, rather than a woman's wealth bestowed by her father. It was neither fitting nor proper, but what else were they to do? It rankled.

She saw her own frown in the mirror over Malta's shoulder. Self-consciously, she smoothed it from her face. "I know you didn't sleep well last night, but I thought you were going to rest this afternoon. Didn't you lie down?"

"I did. I couldn't sleep." Malta leaned closer to the mirror, pinching at her cheeks to try to bring up some color in them. After an instant, she seemed caught in her own reflection. "Mother?" she asked quietly. "Do you ever look at yourself and wonder if there is someone else inside?"

"What?" Keffria took up the hairbrush. Under the guise of smoothing

Malta's hair, she felt her skin. She was not feverish. If anything, her skin seemed too cool. She lifted the heavy flow of Malta's hair. As she began pinning it up, she reminded her, "You need to wash the back of your neck. Or is that a bruise?" She bent closer to look at the pale blue spot. She brushed at it, and Malta flinched away. "Does that hurt?"

"Not exactly. It buzzes, when you touch it. What is it?" Malta twisted her head to try to see it in the mirror, but could not.

"It's just a grayish-blue spot, about the size of a fingertip. It looks like a bruise. Did you bump yourself, when you fainted on the ship?"

Malta frowned distractedly. "Perhaps. Does it show much? Should I powder it?"

Keffria had already dipped her fingers in the talc. With a quick dab, the smudge disappeared. "There. No one else will even notice it," she said comfortingly. But Malta had already gone back to staring at her face in the mirror.

"Sometimes I don't know who I am anymore." Malta spoke quietly, but her voice was apprehensive rather than dreamy. "I'm not the silly little girl I was last summer, all in a hurry to grow up." Malta bit her lower lip and shook her head at herself. "I've tried to be responsible and learn all the things you've tried to teach me. A part of me knows that they are important. But, in all honesty, I hate the fussing with numbers and the constant juggling of this debt against that one. That isn't who I am, either. Sometimes I think of Reyn or another young man, and my heart flutters and I think I could be so happy if I could just have him. But a few minutes later, that all seems like pretend, like a little girl being mother to her dolls. Or worse, it seems that I just want the man because he is who I wish I were . . . if that makes sense. When I try to think who I really am, all I feel is tired and somewhat sad in a way that doesn't have tears. And when I try to sleep and I dream, the dreams seem foreign and distorted. Then when I wake up, the dreams seem to follow me, and I find myself thinking someone else's thoughts. Almost. Does anything like that happen to you?"

Keffria was at a loss. Malta had never spoken like this before. She put a falsely bright smile on her face. "My dear, you are just nervous, and it is making you have all these odd thoughts. Once we arrive at the ball, your spirits will rise. This will be quite a ball, such as Bingtown has never seen." She shook her head. "Our problems all seem quite small to me when I consider all that is happening in Bingtown. Here we are, block-aded in our own harbor by Chalcedean galleys that claim to be the Sa-trap's patrol. The Satrap himself and most of his entourage are staying with Davad Restart. The Satrap will be coming to the ball tonight, with several of his Companions. That alone will make Bingtown history. Even those who most ardently oppose Jamaillia will be endeavoring to get a moment with him. Some say we are at the brink of war, but I prefer to believe that the Satrap intends to correct the wrongs done us. Why else would he have come so far?"

"And brought so many fine Chalcedean galleys and mercenaries?" Malta added with a skewed smile.

"I have heard it was to protect himself from pirates on his trip up," Keffria told her. The girl sounded altogether too disillusioned for her years. Had they done this to her? Had their discipline, lessons and chores destroyed the selfish flighty girl and replaced her with this weary, cynical young woman? It squeezed her heart to think so.

"Did they let the other ship come in? The one with the nobles aboard? I heard that the New Traders were quite upset about them being turned back. Many claimed to have relatives aboard."

"Not the ship, no, but they allowed the nobles themselves to come ashore in small boats. Many of them were ill, or suffered injuries in their many battles with the pirates on their way here. It was only common mercy to let them come ashore. Besides, as you say, they have kin here, among the New Traders. They are not Chalcedean mercenaries. What harm can they do us?"

Malta shook her head. "No more than their relatives have already done, I suppose. After the great panic when all those ships came into the harbor, I expected we would exercise more caution. We spent near the whole day in Bingtown, filling buckets and barrels with water. Not to mention hours standing about with no idea what was happening out on the ships during the confrontation."

Keffria shook her head in exasperation at the memory. "That is because nothing was happening out there. Our ships held a line across the harbor mouth, and the Chalcedean galleys formed up across the sea entrance. I am glad all parties were reasonable and there was no bloodshed."

"Mother, there has been no trade since then. Trade is the lifeblood of Bingtown. There is no bloodshed when someone is strangled, but it is murder all the same."

"The Chalcedeans let the *Kendry* into the harbor," Keffria pointed out. "With your young man aboard."

"And they closed up the blockade behind him. Were I the captain of the *Kendry*, I would not have brought him in. I suspect they only let him through to have one more liveship corraled in the harbor. You know they fear our liveships since Ophelia stood up to their galleys." A mirthless light dawned in Malta's eyes.

Keffria tried again. "Davad Restart has promised us that he will see you are personally presented to the Satrap and his Companions. That is a great honor, you know. There are many distinguished matrons in Bingtown who will envy you that. Yet, I suppose you will hardly have eyes for the Satrap, once Reyn arrives. The Khuprus family is always known to distinguish itself in matters of dress. Your young man will probably be resplendent. You will be the envy of every girl at the ball. Most young ladies spend their presentation ball dancing with fathers, uncles and cousins, or standing modestly beside mothers and aunts. I know I certainly did."

"I would throw both Reyn and the Satrap aside, could I have but one dance with my father," Malta observed to herself. "I wish there was something I could do to bring him home. Something besides this eternal waiting." She sat for a time in utter stillness staring into the mirror. Suddenly, she drew herself up straight and looked hard at her reflection. "I look awful. I have not slept well in weeks; my dreams when I do sleep allow me no rest. I shall not go to my presentation looking like this; it is too important an opportunity. May I borrow rouge from you, Mother? And something to make my eyes look brighter?"

"Of course." Keffria's relief was so intense her head swam. She knew this Malta. "I'll bring it to you right now, while you finish dressing your hair. Both of us need to get ready. Davad could not send his coach for us, of course; it will be much too busy, ferrying his grand visitors to the ball. But between your grandmother and me, we have scraped up enough for a hired coach. It will be coming soon, and we had best be ready."

"I intend to be ready," Malta replied determinedly, but it did not sound as if she were speaking of rouge and dresses.

SERILLA'S PLANS WERE IN TOTAL DISARRAY. NOT ONLY HAD THE YOUNGER sons from the second ship managed to talk their way ashore, they had brought with them the remainder of the Satrap's entourage from the main ship. The only positive aspect of that, as far as Serilla was concerned, was that her clothing and possessions had been brought ashore as well. In the days since then, not only had her control over the Satrap withered away but he had recovered his strength with amazing rapidity. A healer had declared the Satrap was mending well and given Serilla the credit. Cosgo still believed that she had saved his life, but with Kekki and his pleasure drugs restored to him, his dependency was fading. Their host seemed bent on nourishing him with every rich food imaginable and cosseting him with constant entertainment.

Cosgo's restored vitality had set her plans awry. She had had to scramble to modify her position. The scroll that Cosgo had signed had been secreted in the knotted sleeve of one of her gowns. She herself had not brought up its existence since she had first shown it on the ship. When one Trader had asked her about it, she had smiled and assured him that since Cosgo had regained his health, it would not be needed. Cosgo himself did not seem to recall it existed. A special convening of the Bingtown Traders' Council had been scheduled. She hoped that before then she would find some opportunity to shift power in her favor once more. For now, she must abide.

She looked out the window of the chamber Trader Restart had given her. She was definitely in the provinces, she reflected to herself. The gardens below had a willful, jungle look to them. The chamber itself, though large, was both outdated and musty with disuse. The bedding smelled of cedar and storage herbs, and the hangings were of a style that her grandmother would recognize. The bed was uncomfortably tall; she suspected it had been designed to protect the sleeper from rats and mice. The chamberpot was right under the bed instead of in a separate alcove. The housemaids only brought her warm wash water twice a day, and there were no fresh flowers in her room. The household had provided the Companions with only one personal maid, and Kekki had kept the poor girl at a dash since then. Serilla had had to tend to her own needs. That suited her, at present. She had no desire to allow any stranger access to the items concealed in her room.

But, it was not the niceties that had fascinated her when she had chosen Bingtown as her area of expertise. This pioneer town had managed to survive. All other attempts to colonize the Cursed Shores had failed. In all she had ever read or heard of Bingtown, nothing had ever explained that to her satisfaction. Why had it survived and prospered? What had set it apart from all those other tragic efforts? Had it been the people, the location or purest luck? There was a mystery to be probed here.

Bingtown was the main settlement on the Cursed Shores. It was surrounded by a network of outlying villages and farms, yet for the number of years it had existed, it had not grown as large as one would have expected. The population did not thrive. Even the influx of the Three Ships Immigrants had been only a temporary swell in population. Families were small, with rarely more than four surviving children. The wave of New Traders threatened to displace the old Bingtown Traders with their sheer number, not to mention the slaves they had brought in with them. The growth was not welcome. Bingtown resisted the idea of expanding into the surrounding countryside. The reason offered was that much of the ground was too boggy, and that tilling up what looked like a wild pasture usually transformed it into a marsh by the next spring. Good reasons. But Serilla had always suspected there was something more going on.

Take, for example, the so-called Rain Wild Traders. Exactly who were they?

They were not mentioned, at least by that name, in any charter issued by a Satrap. Were they a group of Bingtown Traders that had splintered off? A native people who had intermarried with the Bingtown folk? Why were they never openly discussed? No one ever spoke of a city on the Rain Wild River. Yet there must be one. All the most fascinating goods from

Bingtown were always touted as being from the Rain Wilds. Little more than that was said about them. Serilla was convinced that the two secrets were linked. In all her years of delving, she had never found the bottom of that mystery.

Now she was here, in Bingtown itself. Or, at least, on the outskirts of it. Through the trees, she could catch just a glimpse of the lights of the town. How she longed to go and explore it. Since she had arrived, their host had insisted that they remain in his home and rest. It was a tactic she suspected of being more to Trader Restart's advantage than theirs. While the Satrap and his Companions lodged with him, there would be a constant stream of visitors through his doors. She suspected, from the disused state of her chamber, that Trader Restart had not enjoyed such a jolt of popularity in many years. Yet, she was more than willing to smile and greet the Traders, both Old and New, that came to call. Every association that she could form, every woman she could dazzle with casual tales of palace life in Jamaillia, was one more foothold in her new home. For so she still intended to make it. Perhaps her opportunity to seize power had slipped away, but she still had a hope of making Bingtown her home.

As she leaned on the railing of the small balcony, the whole house trembled gently. Again. She stood straight and backed away from the edge and into her room. The earth had shivered almost daily since her arrival here, but the local folk seemed to pay it no mind. The first time it had happened, she had started up from her seat, exclaiming in surprise. Trader Restart had merely shrugged his round shoulders. "Just a little shiver, Companion Serilla. Nothing to be concerned about." The Satrap had already been too doused with Restart's wine to notice it. As it always did, the tremor passed. Nothing had fallen, no walls had cracked. She heaved out a small sigh. That was a part of the Cursed Shores; the restlessness of the earth under her feet. If she intended to make a life here, she had best get used to it. She squared her shoulders firmly and turned her mind to the business at hand.

Tonight, her dream would come true. She would see Bingtown. She shut the tall window and went to the wardrobe to select clothing. She was to be a guest at some sort of summer assemblage the Traders held. She gathered that by their standards, it was quite an affair. It was for the Bingtown Traders only: outsiders were admitted only if they had married into a Bingtown Trader family. Young women would be presented as being of age, and she had heard some rumors of offerings of friendship exchanged between the Bingtown Traders and the Rain Wild Traders. Now that, she told herself, was a fascinating internal distinction, one that was not spoken of in Jamaillia. Why were offerings exchanged? Did one group subjugate the other? Questions, questions.

Serilla frowned at her jewelry. She could scarcely wear what she had filched from the Satrap's chests. Kekki or one of the others would be sure to recognize it and comment upon it. While she was sure that, given enough time alone with the Satrap, she could make him "recall" giving it to her, she did not want the situation to arise in public. With a small sigh, she restored the jewelry to its hiding place inside a slipper. She would have to go unadorned.

Yesterday, one of Davad Restart's visitors had sought to distinguish herself by bragging the gossip that Reyn Khuprus of the Rain Wild Traders was actually already courting a young girl who was to be presented to-night. The other Old Traders present had sternly hushed her. Then the woman, one Refi Faddon, had been bold enough to defy them, pointing out that surely the Satrap and his Companions would be introduced to young Khuprus at the ball. What was the point of concealing who he was?

Davad Restart himself had intervened. The host, who had been al-most stiflingly accommodating to that point, suddenly invoked his power. "But you cannot discuss young Khuprus without mentioning the Vestrit family and the young lady in question. In her father's absence, I regard her reputation to be my responsibility. I shall not tolerate any gossip about her. But I shall ensure that you shall meet her personally after her presen-tation. She is a dazzling young lady. Now. Shall we have more cakes?"

He had effectively ended the conversation. While some of the Bingtown Traders had regarded him with approval, a few of the others had rolled their eyes at his circumspect ways. Interesting. She could sense the pull and stress of power at play here. This Davad Restart seemed to be some sort of a bridge between the Old and New Traders. Circumstance seemed to have landed them in an ideal position, for both sides of the divided society seemed moderately comfortable in calling on Davad. While the New Traders brought the Satrap extravagant gifts and invita-tions to their homes, the Bingtown Traders brought only their dignity and implied power. She did not think the Satrap had made a particularly good impression on the Old Traders, nor they on him. It would be interesting to see how things proceeded. There was so much going on here; it was so much livelier than the staid and stagnant court at Jamaillia. Here, if a woman was bold, she could make a place for herself. She pulled a gown from the wardrobe and held it against her. It would do, she decided. It was simple, but well made; surely, that would be appropriate for an evening among provincial folk.

Changing into the gown necessitated baring her body. She resolutely turned her back to the mirror in the room while she dressed. Yesterday morning, as she dressed, a casual look in the mirror had revealed to her that the deep bruises on her back and the back of her thighs had faded to shades of green, brown and yellow. Yet, that brief betraying glance had suddenly swept her back into horror and helplessness. She had been caught there, staring at herself. Suddenly a deep shuddering, more kin to convulsion than trembling, had taken her. She had sat down abruptly on the edge of her bed, and taken great breaths to keep the deep sobs from tearing out of her. Tears would have been a relief. Even after she had managed to dress, she had been unable to force herself out the door and down to breakfast. They would know. They would all know. How could anyone look at her and not know how badly she had been hurt?

It had taken her until noon to compress her feelings and master them again. The panic had passed, and she had been able to join the party, pleading a morning headache as excuse for her absence. Since then, she had wondered if it were strength or a sort of madness that let her pretend she was normal. As before, she resolved to create for herself a place where no man had authority over her. She lifted her chin as she touched scent to her throat. Tonight, she told herself. The opportunity might come tonight. If it did, she would be ready.

"HOW DO YOU STAND THE VEIL?" GRAG TENIRA ASKED REYN. "I THOUGHT I was going to die of suffocation in the carriage on the way here."

Reyn shrugged. "One gets used to it. I have lighter ones than the one I loaned you, but I feared you might be recognized if you were not veiled heavily."

They sat together in a guest chamber in the Tenira home. A small table had been bustled in, laden with bread, fruit, plates, glasses and a bottle of wine. From the hallway outside came the heavy tread of the servants bringing Reyn's trunks and chests up the stairs. Grag's discarded Rain Wild garb was strewn across the bed. He tousled up his sweaty hair to cool himself, and then advanced on the table. "Wine?" he offered Reyn.

"It would be most welcome, little cousin," Reyn replied wryly.

Grag gave a half-laugh, half-groan. "I don't know how to thank you enough. I had not intended to come ashore in Bingtown at all. Yet here I am, not only on shore but back in my family's home, for however brief a time. If you had not been willing to aid me in this ruse, I fear I would still be cowering in the *Kendry*'s hold."

Reyn accepted the glass of wine, deftly slipped it under his veil and drank. He gave a sigh of satisfaction. "Well," he balanced it, "if you had not extended me the hospitality of your home, I'd be standing outside the inn with my cases. The town is crawling with New Traders and the Satrap's minions. My rooms at the inn were long ago given away." Reyn paused uncomfortably. "With the harbor blockaded, and the inns full, I do not know how long I will have to beg hospitality of you."

"We are more than happy to welcome you both." These words came from Naria Tenira as she pushed into the room carrying a tureen of steaming soup. She kicked the door closed behind her and scowled at Grag as she set the soup down on the table. "It is a relief to have Grag at home, and know he is safe. Do have something hot to eat, Reyn," she invited him before rounding on her son and demanding, "Put that veil back on, Grag. And the gloves and hood. What if I had been a serving girl? I have told you, I trust no one. For as long as you are at home, we must carry on the pretense that you are a Khuprus from the Rain Wilds, guesting with us. Otherwise, you endanger your own life. Since we spirited you out of town, the offer for your capture has only gone up. Half the vandalism to New Trader businesses and the Satrap's ministries that has gone on in your absence has been attributed to you."

She turned from her son and began dishing up soup for Reyn as she continued, "You're near a hero to some of the young men in town. I fear it is all getting out of hand, and the Satrap's minister has made you the scapegoat for it. The Traders' sons dare one another to 'Tenira' a warehouse, and all know what is meant by that." She shook her head as she set food before Reyn. "No matter how quietly your sisters and I live, folk still turn and whisper when we go into town.

"You are not safe here, son. I wish your father were here. I declare, I am at my wit's end to know how to protect you." She pointed commandingly at the discarded veil.

"I'm a bit old to be hiding behind your skirts, Mother," Grag protested as he picked up the veil with distaste. "I'll put this on after I've eaten."

"I'm a bit old to hope to have another son if they kill you," she pointed out in a soft voice. She gathered up the gloves and handed them to him. "Put them on now, and get used to them," she begged him. "This disguise is your only hope. Sa alone knows when the Kendry or any other ship will get out of Bingtown. You must continue to play the part of a Rain Wilder, and play it convincingly." She looked at Reyn beseechingly. "Will you help him?"

"Of course."

"I've given word to the servants that you are both excessively private young men. They are not to enter without knocking. To honor you, I've told them, Grag's sisters themselves will see to tidying the room daily." She turned a severe glance on her son. "Don't abuse that, Grag, however humorous you might find it."

Grag was already grinning widely.

She ignored him and turned to Reyn. "I must beg your pardon that I ask you to share your garments with my son. It seems the best way to preserve the masquerade."

Reyn laughed self-deprecatingly. "I assure you, in my nervousness about the ball, I have probably brought enough garments to well clothe half a dozen young men."

"And I, for one, am looking forward to both the elegance and the mystery of being a Rain Wild son at the Bingtown Summer Ball," Grag chimed in. He held up the veil and peered around the corner of it at his mother.

She looked dismayed. "Be serious, Grag. Stay at home, here, where you are safe. Reyn, of course, must go, as must your sisters and I. But—"

"It would look decidedly odd for me to have come all the way from the Rain Wilds and then not attend the ball," Grag pointed out.

"Especially as we have announced him as my cousin," Reyn agreed.

"Could not we say he was taken ill?" Naria Tenira pleaded.

"Then surely it would be expected that someone would stay with me here. No, Mother, I think the least attention will be paid to me if I continue to play my role as expected. Besides. Do you think I could resist the chance to see the Satrap face-to-face?"

"Grag, I beg you, none of your wildness tonight. You shall go, then, as you seem so set on it. But I beg you, do not be tempted to do anything to call attention to yourself." She fixed him with a grave stare. "Remember, the trouble you bring down may fall upon others besides yourself. Your sisters, for instance."

"I'll behave like a very gentlemanly Rain Wilder, Mother. I promise. But if we are not to be late, we must all make haste now to get ready."

"Your sisters were ready long ago," Naria admitted wearily. "They have only been waiting for me, not that it takes long for an old woman like myself to dress. I do not pay as much attention to primp and powder as they do."

Grag leaned back in his chair with a soft snort of disbelief. "That means that we have plenty of time to eat, bathe and dress, Reyn. No woman in my family can be ready to do anything in less than half a watch."

"We shall see," Reyn told him pleasantly. "You may find that attiring yourself as a Rain Wilder takes longer than you think. A Rain Wild man seldom uses a valet or body servant. It is not our way. And you must practice, at least a bit, how to sip a glass of wine through a veil. Put it on. I'll show you now, so my 'cousin' doesn't disgrace me at the ball this evening."

THE INSIDE OF THE HIRED COACH SMELLED LIKE STALE WINE. HER mother had insisted on inspecting the seats before she had allowed Malta to sit down on them. Her grandmother had insisted on inspecting the coachman before she allowed him to drive them. Malta had felt impatient with both of them. The excitement of her presentation had finally sparked her. Despite the hired coach and her made-over dress, her heart was beating faster than the rattling of the horse's hooves.

The Traders' Concourse had been transformed. Scores of tiny lanterns had been set out in the gardens and ground surrounding it. In the late summer evening, they seemed reflections of the stars in the clear sky. Arches erected over the walks were garlanded with greenery. Pots of sweet-scented night-blooming flowers, imported from the Rain Wild, added their eerily glowing blooms to the colors of the walkways. All this Malta glimpsed from the window. It was so hard to resist the urge to hang her head out the window like a child. Their hired coach joined a line of carriages and coaches. As each reached the steps before the main entrance, it paused and footmen opened the doors and handed down the ladies. Malta turned to her mother. "Do I look all right?" she asked anxiously.

Before Keffria could answer, Malta's grandmother replied quietly, "You are the loveliest thing to grace this gathering since your mother was presented."

The most shocking thing was not that she had said it with such sincerity. What amazed Malta was that, at that instant, she believed it, too. She held her head a notch higher and waited for her coach's turn.

When the footman opened the door at last, her grandmother descended first, followed by her mother. Then they stood to either side, as if they were already presenting her, whilst the footman helped her step down from the coach. She stood between them, and then little Selden, groomed and scrubbed, came out to offer his grandmother his arm. She took it with a smile.

The night was suddenly a mystical and magical place. Little glass cups in different hues held candles that edged the steps to the entrance. Other families clad in their best and bearing their symbolic offerings to the Rain Wild Traders were making their way into the hall. Keffria, as Trader for the Vestrit family, carried their offering. It was a simple tray of carved wood, one that Grandfather had brought back from the Spice Isles long ago. On it were six little pots of homemade preserves. Malta knew that the gifts were largely symbolic, gestures of remembered bonds and kinship. Even so, she could remember when the gift had been lengths of rainbow hued silk so heavy that Papa had had to help Grandfather carry them. It did not matter, she told herself stoutly.

As if her grandmother sensed her uncertainty, she whispered, "The receiver of the gifts tonight is none other than our old friend Caolwn Festrew. She has always loved our sweet cherry preserves. She will know we thought especially of her when we prepared this gift. All will be well."

All will be well. Malta lifted her eyes to the top of the steps. The smile that dawned on her face was genuine. All would be well. As Rache had shown her and she had practiced on the steps at home, she set her hands lightly on her skirts and lifted them just enough to help them skim the ground. She kept her chin up, her eyes on her destination, as if she had never even considered she might trip over her own skirts. She preceded her mother and grandmother this night as she climbed the steps and entered the bright mouth of the Traders' Concourse.

Within, the wide hall was scarcely recognizable to her. It blazed with light and color. Malta felt dazzled by it. They were amongst the early arrivals. The musicians were playing softly, but as yet there was no dancing. Instead, folk stood in small knots conversing. At the far end of the hall were the long tables, set with snowy cloths and gleaming service for the communal meal that was the final symbolism of their shared kinship. Malta noted that the raised dais that was reserved for the visiting representative of the Rain Wilds and the Bingtown Council members had been enlarged. No doubt, the Satrap and perhaps his Companions would share the high table as well. For an instant, she wondered whether it was display or honor afforded him.

She glanced back for the rest of her family. They were already caught up in the social ritual of recognizing friends and greeting them. She had a few moments to herself to look around. Technically, she smiled to herself, this was her last time as a child, free to mingle without social restraint. After her presentation, she would be bound by all of Bingtown's unspoken rules. She would take one last unchaperoned stroll around the Concourse.

Then her attention was caught by a figure at once familiar and strange. Delo Trell swept up to her in a wave of scent and rustling fabric. Sparkling blue stones shone at her throat and wrists and on the fine silver chains that secured her upswept hair. Her eyes and mouth were expertly painted. She carried herself scrupulously erect, and the polite expression on her face was as still as a doll's painted smile. Malta blinked her eyes, intimidated by this woman grown. Delo regarded her coolly. Yet for all that, Malta suddenly realized, she was still Delo Trell. Malta found herself smiling widely at her old friend. She caught both her hands in hers, squeezed them warmly and heard herself say, "Here we are! Did you ever really believe we would be here?"

Delo's painted face of pleased interest held steady. For an instant, Malta's heart lurched within her. If Delo snubbed her now—then Delo's smile cracked just a fraction wider than it had been. She pulled Malta closer and whispered, "I was so nervous all day I was afraid to eat for fear I would get the trots. Now that I am here, I am so hungry that my stomach is growling like a bear. Malta, what shall I do if I am dancing or talking with someone and it makes a noise?"

"Look at someone else accusingly," Malta suggested facetiously. Delo nearly giggled, then remembered her new dignity. She lifted her fan swiftly to cover her face.

"Walk with me," Delo begged her friend. "And tell me all you have heard of what is going on in Bingtown! Whenever I come into the room, Papa and Cerwin stop speaking about it. They say they don't want to frighten me with things I can't understand. Mama talks only of how to hold my elbows in, or what to do if I drop something at the table. It drives me mad. Are we truly on the brink of war? Kitten Shuyev said she had heard rumors that while we were all at the ball tonight, the Chalcedeans might sweep in and burn the whole city and kill us all!" She paused dramatically, and then leaned closer to whisper behind her fan, "You can imagine what she said they would do with us!"

Malta patted her friend's hand comfortingly. "I scarcely think they would attempt that, while the Satrap, with whom they are supposedly allied, is in our midst. All the Traders would have to do is take him hostage. That he came ashore with the first group, without Chalcedean guards, is why we can believe he has truly come to mediate and negotiate. Besides, we are not *all* at the ball tonight. The liveships maintain their vigil in our harbor, and I have heard that many Three Ships families patrol with their boats as well. I think it is safe for us to relax and have fun."

Delo shook her head in amazement at her friend. "How do you do it? You comprehend things so well. Sometimes you sound almost like a man when you talk."

Malta was taken aback for a moment, then decided the comment had been intended as a compliment. She nearly shrugged, then remembered to act the lady. She lifted one eyebrow instead. "Well, as you know, the women of my family have had to take care of themselves lately. My mother and grandmother believe it is more dangerous for me not to know these things." She lowered her voice. "Had you heard that the Chalcedeans did admit the *Kendry* through the blockade? He came in late, so I have had no word, yet I dare to hope that Reyn was aboard."

Instead of looking pleased for her, Delo looked troubled. "Cerwin will not rejoice at that news. He had hoped to claim a dance or two with you tonight . . . and perhaps more, if your beau was not here."

Malta could not resist. "Surely I am permitted to dance with whom I please tonight? I have not given my promise to Reyn yet." Some of her old giddiness swept through her. "I shall certainly save a dance for Cerwin. And perhaps for others as well," she added mysteriously. As she had just given herself permission, her eyes swept over the gathered folk, lingering on the young men. As if they were surveying a tray of dainties, she invited Delo, "And who do you think your first dance will be with?"

"My fourth, you mean. I have a father, a brother and an uncle who will claim dances with me, after I am presented." Her brown eyes suddenly went wide. "I had the most awful dream last night. I dreamed that at the moment I was presented and was making my curtsey, the stitches in my dress all came out and my skirt fell off! I woke up shrieking. Can you imagine a worse dream than that?"

A tiny chill went up Malta's spine. For a moment, the brightness of the ball dimmed and the music seemed to fade. She clenched her teeth and willed the darkness away. "Actually, I can. But, look, the servants are ready at the refreshment table. Let's go and get something to still the bear in your stomach."

DAVAD RESTART WIPED HIS SWEATY PALMS ON THE KNEES OF HIS TROUSERS. Who would ever have believed it? Here he was, going to the Summer Ball as he had for so many years, but not alone this time, oh no. Not this year. Across from him in the coach sat the Satrap of all Jamaillia, and beside him the lovely Companion Kekki in an astonishing gown wrought of feathers and lace. Beside him was the less flamboyant, but still important, Companion Serilla in her demure cream gown. He would escort them into the ball, he would sit at table with them and he would introduce them, to all Bingtown society tonight. Yes.

He would show them all.

How he wished his beloved wife had survived to see this triumph.

The thought of Dorill put a brief shadow across his victory. She and the boys had been claimed years ago, when the Rain Wilders brought the Blood Plague down the river. So many had died then, so very many. The plague had most cruelly spared him, left him to live alone, speaking to the memories of his family, always imagining what they would say, what they would think of all he was doing each day. He took a breath and tried to recapture his satisfaction in the moment. Dorill would be pleased and proud. He was sure of it.

And the other Bingtown Traders would concede that he was as shrewd and foresighted a trader as they had ever seen. Tonight he was going to bring it all together. The Satrap himself would dine with them, and they would remember all that Jamaillia and elegant society meant to Bingtown. In the weeks to come, he would be at the Satrap's side as he and his Companions healed the rift between the Old and New Traders. He could not begin to imagine the trade benefits that would bring to his door. Not to mention that he would finally recapture his social stature with the Bingtown Traders. They'd have to welcome him back into their midst and admit that, over the years, he had seen more keenly than they had.

Davad smiled to himself as he considered the final capstone to his evening's plans. Lovely as Kekki and Serilla were, they were drab compared to Malta Vestrit. They were fine as Companions, as advisors and intellectuals. But tonight it was Davad's intention to introduce the Satrap to his future consort. He was so certain the young man would be smitten with Malta that he could already almost imagine the festivities for their wedding. There would have to be two ceremonies, one in Bingtown and a second, grander one in Jamaillia. He would certainly attend both of them.

It would save the Vestrit fortune and redeem him in Ronica's eyes. It would link Bingtown and Jamaillia forever. Davad Restart would be remembered forever as the man who had reconciled the towns. Years from now, the Satrap's children would call him Uncle Davad.

He chuckled warmly to himself, swept away on the glorious tide of his future. He realized that Companion Serilla was looking at him uncertainly. His heart suddenly went out to the woman. No doubt, the Satrap would have no further need of her, once he was married to a woman who was Bingtown born and raised. He leaned toward her and patted her knee companionably.

"Don't fret about your gown," he whispered to her. "I am sure that all of Bingtown will honor you for your position, no matter what you are wearing."

For an instant the poor thing just stared at him wide-eyed. Then she smiled. "Why, Trader Restart. How kind of you to attempt to be comforting!"

"Not at all, not at all. I simply wish to put you at your ease," he assured her, and leaned back in the seat of his carriage.

It was going to be a momentous evening in his life. He was sure of it.

CHAPTER THIRTY-TWO

The Storm

"MALTA! DELO! YOU SHOULD NOT BE JUST WANDERING ABOUT. IT IS NEARLY time for you to be presented." Her mother sounded both exasperated and amused as she added, "Delo, I saw your mother just a few moments ago, and she was looking for you over by the fountain. Malta, you come with me!"

They had both taken refuge behind one of the columns by the entrance, and had been spying on the late arrivals to the ball. Kitten, they agreed, had the finest dress; it was a pity she had not the figure for the neckline she had chosen. Tritta Redof had a headdress that was far too big for her, but her fan was exquisite. Krion Trentor had put on weight since he had begun courting Riell Krell, and had lost his melancholy poetic face. How had they ever thought he was handsome? Roed Caern was as dark and dangerous as ever. Delo had near swooned at the sight of him, but oddly enough, Malta had caught herself thinking that his shoulders were not nearly as wide as Reyn's.

Veiled and hooded Rain Wild folk arrived to mingle with their Bingtown counterparts. Malta looked in vain for Reyn. "How will you know him when he gets here? They all look the same, muffled like that," Delo complained. In a line worthy of the girl she had been last year, Malta sighed back, "Oh, I shall know him, never fear. My heart always leaps at the sight of him." For a moment Delo had stared at her wide-eyed, and then they had both broken down in gales of smothered laughter. As they whispered and spied, all the spring's awkwardness between them was forgotten. Delo had assured Malta that the fabric of her dress was far richer than anything that could be bought nowadays, and that the cut of it suited her tiny waist quite well, while Malta had sworn that Delo did not have thick ankles, and that even if she did, no one could see them tonight anyway. It was as girlish and gay as she had felt in a long time. As Malta obediently followed her mother away, she wondered that she had ever wanted to leave such things behind and become a woman.

A screen trellised with flowers provided an alcove for the young women to be presented tonight. The fathers who would present them and then escort them into the Concourse for the first dance shifted restlessly outside, while within anxious mamas made last-minute adjustments to hair and hemlines. They had drawn lots, and it seemed the hand of fate that she would be presented last. Girl after girl was led away. Malta felt as if she could not get enough breath. As Keffria tugged a few stray hairs up and into place, she whispered to Malta, "Reyn has not arrived yet. I suppose he was delayed because the *Kendry* arrived so late. Do you want me to tell Davad to take the first dance with you?"

Malta looked at her mother in horror, but to her shock, Keffria grinned wickedly. "I thought that might remind you that there are worse things than having to stand alone during the first dance of your formal presentation."

"I shall wait it out and think of Papa," Malta assured her. Her mother's eyes shimmered suddenly with tears, and then Keffria was tugging at the neck of her gown, saying, "Now be calm, keep your head up, mind your skirts and oh, it's your turn now!" The last words came out as a half-sob. Malta was suddenly blinking away tears of her own. Half-blinded by them, she stepped from behind the screen, to take her place in the circle of torchlight at the top of the stairs.

"Malta Vestrit, the daughter of Kyle Haven and Keffria Vestrit, is presented now to the Bingtown Traders and the Rain Wild Traders. Malta Vestrit."

For a moment, she was angered because they named her by her Trader name. Did not they think her father was good enough for their company? Then she accepted it as the Bingtown way. She would do him proud. He might not be here to extend an arm to her and descend the steps with her, but she would walk as his daughter. Head up, but eyes cast down, she sank in a slow curtsey to the assembled folk. As she came back up, she lifted her eyes. For a moment, the people seemed far too numerous, the stairs too many and too steep. She thought she might faint and go tumbling down them. Then she took a deeper breath and began her slow descent to the floor.

Below her on the dance floor, the other girls and their papas awaited her in a half circle. It was her time, and her moment. She wanted it to last forever, and yet, as she reached the bottom of the stair, she felt grateful. As she joined the line of young women and their fathers, she lifted her eyes to look about the room. The folk of Bingtown and the Rain Wild displayed themselves in their finest clothes. Many were not so prosperous in years past, and it showed. Yet they all carried themselves proudly, and smiled at this latest crop of eligible young women. She did not see Reyn. Soon the music would strike up, and the young girls would be whirled away to it. She would be left standing alone while they danced. It fit so well with all the rest of her life, she thought bitterly. Then the impossible happened.

Things became worse.

On the dais across the room, wedged into a chair between a pale young man and the head of the Bingtown Council, sat Davad Restart. Rather, she devoutly wished he had been sitting. He had half stood up, to lean across the table and frantically waggle his fingers at her. In an agony of humiliation, she lifted her hand slightly and waved her fingers at him. He didn't stop. Instead, once he was sure she had seen him, he made frantic gestures for her to cross the empty dance floor and come up to the dais. Malta was dying. She longed to faint, but could not. The leader of the musicians, who was awaiting the signal from the dais to begin the music, looked puzzled. At last, she realized she had no other choice. This nightmarish moment would not be over until she had left the safety of the other young women and their papas and crossed the vast expanse of the empty floor alone and presented herself to Davad to hear his congratulations.

So be it.

She drew a deep breath, took one glance at her grandmother's shocked white face, and then began her slow crossing of the dance floor. She would not hurry. That would be even more unseemly. She kept her head up, and lifted her skirts to allow them to float across the polished floor. She tried to smile as if this were something she had expected, as if it were a perfectly normal part of her presentation. She fixed her eyes on Davad and recalled the dead pig stuck in his carriage window. She managed to keep the smile, despite the roaring in her ears. Then she was standing before the dais. At that moment, she suddenly realized that the pale young man seated next to Davad must be the Satrap of all Jamaillia.

She had just been humiliated before the Satrap of all Jamaillia and two of his Companions. The elegant women of the court were looking down at her in tolerant condescension. Now she would faint. Instead, some sort of instinct took over. She sank down before the dais in a low curtsey. Through the blood pounding in her ears, she heard Davad say enthusiastically, "This is the young woman I told you about. Malta Vestrit of the Bingtown Traders. Is not she the fairest young blossom you have ever seen?"

Malta could not rise. If she stood now, she would have to look at their faces. Here she crouched, in her pieced-together gown and her made-over slippers and—

"You did not exaggerate at all, Trader Restart. But why is this sweet flower unaccompanied?" Jamaillian accent, and a languid tone. The Satrap himself spoke of her.

The leader of the Bingtown Council took pity on her and signaled the musicians. The tentative opening notes of the music suddenly flowed through the hall. Behind her, proud fathers escorted their daughters onto the dance floor. The thought of it suddenly was anger instead of pain. She came to her feet and lifted her eyes to meet the Satrap's indulgent stare. She spoke out clearly in answer to his question.

"I am alone, Magnadon Satrap, because my father has been taken by pirates. Pirates that your Chalcedean patrol vessels did nothing to stop."

The other people on the dais gasped. The Satrap dared to smile at her, "I see this little one has the spark of spirit to match her beauty," he observed. As the hot flush colored Malta's cheeks, he added, "And at last I have met one Bingtown Trader who admits that the Chalcedean galleys are simply my patrol vessels." One of his Companions chuckled throatily at this cleverness, but the Bingtown Council did not look amused.

Her temper got the better of her. "I shall concede that, sir, if you will concede they are ineffective. They have left my family bereft of both our ship and my father."

The Satrap of all Jamaillia rose to his feet. He would order her dragged off and killed now, she decided. Behind her, in the room, the musicians played on and the couples whirled. She waited for him to summon guards. Instead, he announced, "Well, as you blame me for your father's absence, there is only one way I can rectify this."

She could not believe her ears. Could it really be this simple? Ask for it, and get it? Breathlessly, she whispered, "You will command your ships to rescue him?"

His laugh rang out through the music. "Certainly. That is their purpose, you know. But not right this moment. For now, I shall do my best to correct this tragic situation by taking his place on the dance floor with you."

He rose from his place on the dais. One of his Companions looked shocked; the other horrified. Malta turned her eyes to Davad Restart, but there was no help there. He was beaming at her fondly and proudly. When her eyes met his, he nodded swift encouragement. The faces of the Bingtown Council members were carefully blank. What was she to do?

The Satrap was leaving his seat, and now he was descending the steps to the dance floor. He was taller than she and very lean, his skin so aristocratically white as to be almost pallid. His clothing was unlike any she had ever seen on a man; it was soft and flowing, in pastel hues. His pale blue trousers were cuffed tight to his ankles above his low soft shoes. The loose folds of his saffron shirt shawled about his throat and shoulders. As he came closer to her, she could smell him, foreign smells, a strange perfume, a clinging smokiness on his breath. Then the most powerful man in the world bowed to her and held out his hand for hers.

She was frozen.

"It's all right, Malta, you may dance with him," Davad Restart an-

nounced benignly. He chuckled to the others on the dais. "Such a shy
and sheltered little thing she is. She scarcely dares touch his hand."

His words gave her the power to move. She felt cold and yet tingly as
she set her hand in his. The Satrap's hand was very soft as it closed
around hers. To her shock, he set his other hand on the back of her hips
and drew her body closer to his. "This is how we dance this measure in
Jamaillia," he told her. His breath was warm on her upturned face. There
was so little space left between them she feared he would feel her heart
beating. He led her into the dance.

For five steps, she was awkward, off balance, moving behind the measure. Then suddenly the music caught her, and it was as easy as if she were
holding Rache's hands and moving to her count around the morning
room. The other dancers, the brightly lit room, even the music faded
around them. There existed only this man and the motion as their bodies
kept time together. She had to look up to see him. He smiled down at her.

"You are so tiny, like a child. Or a lovely little doll. The fragrance of
your hair is like flowers."

She could think of no reply to such compliments, not even to thank
him. All her coquetry had been erased from her mind. She tried to speak,
but could only ask, "Will you truly send your ships to rescue my father?"

He raised one thin eyebrow. "Certainly. Why shouldn't I?"

She lowered her eyes, then closed them. The music and his body
leading hers were all she needed. "It seems too easy." She shook her head,
a tiny motion. "After all we have endured . . ."

He gave a small laugh, high as a woman's. "Tell me, little bird. Have
you lived all your life in Bingtown?"

"Of course."

"Well, then. You tell me. What can you really know of how the world
works?" Suddenly, he drew her even closer, so that her breasts almost
brushed his chest. She gasped and stepped back from him, stumbling out
of rhythm with the music. He caught the step easily and kept her moving.

"Are you shy, little bird?" he asked merrily, but his hand tightened on
hers almost cruelly.

The music had ended. He let go of her hand. When she glanced
around, she heard the murmur of many-footed rumors running. All eyes
looked toward them, although none quite stared. He bowed to her, deeply
and graciously. As she sank into a curtsey, he breathed, "Perhaps we
should speak later about rescuing your father. Perhaps you can better
convey to me just how important it might be to you."

She could not rise. Were his words a threat? Because she had stepped
away from his touch, he would not send the ships to rescue her father?
She wanted to cry out after him to wait, wait. But he had already turned
away from her. A Bingtown matron with her own daughter beside her had
claimed his attention. Behind her, the music was starting again. She

managed finally to rise from her curtsey. She felt as if all the air had been knocked out of her. She had to get off the dance floor.

She walked between the couples unseeingly. She caught a glimpse of Cerwin Trell; he seemed to be coming toward her, but she could not bear that just now. She hurried on, searching the crowd for her mother, her grandmother, even her little brother. All she wanted was some safe refuge for a few moments until she could gather herself. Had she just destroyed her father's chance of swift rescue? Had she made a fool of herself before all of Bingtown?

A touch on her arm made her gasp. She recoiled from it as she turned to see who it was. He was veiled, hooded and gloved like any other Rain Wilder, but she knew it was Reyn. No one but he could take the secretive garb of a Rain Wilder and turn it to such elegance. His veil was black lace, but gilt and silver cat's eyes outlined where his eyes would be. The hood that covered his hair and the back of his neck was secured with an elaborately folded cravat of shimmering white silk. His soft white shirt and black trousers revealed as much of his physique as his veil and hood concealed of his features. The breadth of his shoulders and the depth of his chest were accentuated by his slim waist and narrow hips. His light dancing boots were filigreed with silver and gilt to match his veil. He held a glass of wine toward her. Softly he said, "You are pale as snow. Do you need this?"

"I want my mother," she said stupidly. To make it worse, she repeated it more desperately. "I want my mother."

Reyn's whole stance stiffened. "What did he say to you? Did he hurt you?"

"No. No. I just . . . I want my mother. Now."

"Of course." As if it were the most normal of behaviors, he tapped a passing Trader on the shoulder and handed him the glass of wine. Reyn turned back to Malta. "This way." He did not offer her his arm or try to touch her in any way. Did he sense that just now she could not have tolerated it? Instead, he gestured gracefully with a gloved hand, and then walked slightly in front of her, parting the crowd for her. Folk stared after them curiously.

Keffria came swiftly through the crowd, as if she had been seeking her. "Oh, Malta," she cried out in a low voice, and Malta braced herself for the inevitable recrimination. Instead her mother went on, "I was so worried, but you handled yourself beautifully. Whatever was Davad thinking? I was trying to get to you after you danced and he dared to catch hold of my arm and advise me to tell you to come to him, that he could see you got another dance with the Satrap."

Malta was trembling all over. "Mother. He said he would send ships to rescue Papa. But then—" She faltered, and suddenly wished she had said nothing. Why tell her mother? It would have to be her own decision.

How important was it to her that her father be rescued? She knew exactly what he had insinuated to her. It was unmistakable. The choice was hers. If she was the one who would have to pay the price, did not the decision belong to her alone?

"And you believed him?" Reyn butted in incredulously. "Malta, he was toying with you. How could he toss out such an offer as if it were a bit of flattery? The man has no compunctions at all, no ethics. You are barely more than a girl, and he torments you like this. . . . I should kill him."

"I am not a girl," Malta asserted coldly. Girls did not have to face decisions such as this. "If you believe I am such a child, where are your ethics in courting me?" She hardly knew what she was saying. She needed to be alone somewhere, to think about what the Satrap had offered, and what he had implied the price was. Her tongue flew on without her mind. "Or is this how you seek to make your claim exclusive, the first time another man shows an interest in me?"

Her mother caught her breath sharply. Her eyes flitted from Reyn to Malta. "Excuse me," she murmured, and fled their lovers' quarrel. Malta scarcely noticed her going. A moment ago, she had longed for her. Now she knew her mother could not help her with this.

Reyn actually took a half-step backwards. The silence quivered like a bowstring between them. Abruptly he sketched a bow toward her. "I beg your pardon, Malta Vestrit." She actually heard him swallow. "You are a woman, not a child. But you are a woman newly admitted to society, with little experience in the ways of low men. I thought only to protect you." He turned his veiled face to watch the dancers as they moved through the formal steps of a multi-partnered dance. His voice lowered as he added, "I know that rescuing your father is foremost in your thoughts. It is a vulnerability in you just now. It was cruel of him to offer to help you."

"Odd. I thought it was cruel of you to refuse me when I begged your help. I now see you intended to be kind." She heard the icy scorn in her own voice and recognized it. *This is how my father quarrels with my mother,* she thought, *turning her own words against her.* Something in her wanted to stop this, but she did not know how. She needed to think, she needed time to think, and instead everything just kept happening. The only presentation ball she would ever have was whirling on around her, she might be able to get the Satrap to save her father, and instead of all the other girls watching enviously as her elegant beau danced with her, she was standing here having a stupid quarrel with him. It wasn't fair!

"I did not intend to be kind. I intended to be truthful," he said quietly. The music had ended. The dancers were leaving the floor or securing new partners. Reyn's words fell in the silence, not loudly, but enough that several heads turned their way. Malta sensed that he was as uncomfortably aware of the attention as she was. She tried to put a small smile on her face, as if his words were some kind of a witticism, but her cheeks felt hot and stiff. At that moment, someone cleared his throat behind her. She turned her head.

Cerwin Trell swept a low bow to her. "Would you allow me the next dance?" There was a small challenge in his voice, almost as if the words were directed to Reyn rather than to her. Reyn took it up.

"Malta Vestrit and I were sharing a conversation," he pointed out in a dangerously pleasant voice.

"I see," Cerwin retorted, his voice equally controlled. "I thought she might more enjoy sharing a dance with me."

The first strains of the music threaded through the hall. Folk were staring at them. Without asking her, Reyn took her hand in his. "We were just about to dance," he informed Cerwin. His other hand caught her waist, and as easily as if he lifted a child, he suddenly whirled her into the dance.

It was a spirited tune, and she found she could either dance or stumble awkwardly after his grip on her hand. She chose to dance. She quickly caught up a finger-pinch of her skirts to display her lively feet, and then deliberately embellished the sprightly dance. He met her challenge without missing a beat, and suddenly it took every bit of her concentration to match herself to him. For a moment, she was aware of the effort, and then they moved as one. Couples who had been stealing peeks at them suddenly moved aside to cede them more of the dance floor. She caught a fleeting glimpse of her grandmother as Reyn twirled her through a step. The old woman was smiling fiercely at her. She found, with surprise, that she herself was smiling in genuine pleasure. Her skirts floated as he turned her through the elaborate steps. His touch on her waist was sure and strong. She became aware of his scent, and was not sure if it was a perfume he wore or the musk of his skin. It did not displease her. She was almost aware of the admiring looks from the spectators at the ball, but Reyn was at the center of her thoughts. Without quite intending to, she closed her fingers firmly on his, and his grip on her hand strengthened in response. Her heart lifted unexpectedly.

"Malta." It was only her name he spoke. It was not an apology for anything, but it was an affirmation of all he felt for her. A wave of feeling washed through her in response. She suddenly perceived that the incident with the Satrap was separate entirely from what was between herself and Reyn. It had been her error to even mention it in his presence. It had nothing to do with him or with her relationship with him. She should have known it would only upset him. At this moment, for now, neither of them had to think about anything outside of what they were together. That was the language of this dance. For this space of time, they moved perfectly together and understood each other. That was what she should be savoring.

"Reyn," she conceded, and smiled up at him. The quarrel was swept away by their moving feet, trodden down and forgotten. Too soon the music was ending and he spun her gracefully through the closing measure, then caught her briefly in his arms to halt her movement. It caught her breath as well. "When we move together, like this," she whispered shyly. "I almost feel we are destined to always move as one."

He held her a moment longer in his arms than was strictly proper. It set her heart to racing. She could not see his eyes, but she knew he looked down into her face. He spoke softly. "All you have to do, my dear, is trust me to lead you in your steps," he told her indulgently.

His patronizing words popped the bubble he had created around them. She stepped free of his embrace, to drop him a very formal curtsey. "I thank you for the pleasure of the dance, sir," she told him coolly. "You will excuse me now." As she rose, she nodded a farewell to him. She turned and walked away as if she knew where she was going. From the corner of her eye, she saw him start to come after her, only to have a Rain Wild man hasten up to him and catch him by the arm. Whatever the man wanted of him seemed more important than his pursuit of her. He halted and turned to him. Fine. She kept walking. The agitation in her heart would not let her stand still. Why did he have to spoil everything like that? Why did he have to say such condescending words to her?

She could not see anyone she knew. Not her mother or grandmother, not a girl of her acquaintance, not even Davad Restart. She saw the Satrap, surrounded by a circle of Bingtown society matrons. She could scarcely intrude on that group. The musicians had struck up another tune. She moved toward a table laden with wine and glasses. It would have been more proper for a young man to bring her refreshment. It was suddenly so awkward to be alone. She imagined that every eye in the room tracked her solitary movement.

She was almost there when Cerwin stepped in front of her. She had to stop to keep from bumping into him. "Perhaps we can dance now?" he asked gently.

She hesitated. It would anger Reyn or perhaps fill him with jealousy. But she no longer wished to play such games. This was complicated enough without that. As if Cerwin sensed her reservations, he nodded somberly to the dance floor. "It did not take him so long to decide on a new partner."

In disbelief, she turned to see what he indicated. Her heart stood still in her chest. Reyn moved gracefully through the languid dance steps with one of the Satrap's Companions in his arms. It was not even the beautiful one. It was the unadorned woman in the cream gown that he held close and listened to so attentively.

"No," Cerwin whispered. "Don't stare. Put your head up and look at me. Smile. And off we go."

With a frozen little smile, she set her hand in his. He gathered her in and they moved out onto the dance floor with all the grace of two dogs circling one another. His dance stride was short after matching himself to Reyn. She felt like she lurched about in his arms. He seemed blissfully unaware of this awkwardness. Instead, he smiled down at her. "At last, I find you in my arms," he said softly. "I thought my dreams would never come true. Yet here you are, presented as a woman! And that Rain Wild fool has cast you aside for someone he can never hope to possess. Ah, my Malta. Your hair gleams so that it dazzles me. The fragrance of your hair intoxicates me. I could never dream to possess a more precious treasure than your tiny hand in mine."

The compliments rained down on her. She set her teeth in a smile and endured them. She tried not to watch Reyn dance with the other woman. His veil made it hard to tell, but it seemed that she had captured his attention completely. Not once did his head turn in her direction.

She had lost him. That simply, that quickly. One tart word too many, and the man was gone. She actually felt as if her heart had been tugged out of her chest, leaving only an empty space. Foolishness. She had not even decided whether or not she loved him. So that could not be it. No. It was that he had claimed to love her, and she had foolishly believed him. Obviously, he had lied to her. It was only injured pride that she felt, she was sure of it. It was only that she felt angry because he had made a fool of her. Why should she care at all? She was right now dancing in the arms of another man, a very handsome man who obviously doted on her. She didn't need Reyn. She had never even seen his face; how could she love him?

She felt suddenly dizzy as she glimpsed Reyn bending his head, to speak to the Companion more privately. The woman answered earnestly and at length. Malta nearly stumbled, and Cerwin tightened his grip on her. He was uttering some nonsense about how pink her lips were. What in Sa's name did he expect her to reply to such inanity? Should she compliment his teeth, or the cut of his shirt? She actually heard herself say, "You look very handsome tonight, Cerwin. Your family must be proud of you."

He smiled as if she had praised him to the stars. "Such words from your lips mean so much to me," he assured her.

The music ended. He reluctantly released her and she stepped back from him. Her traitorous eyes sought out Reyn. He bowed low over the Companion's hand, and then gestured toward the doors that led out into the lantern-lit garden and walks of the Traders' Concourse. She tried to find some hardness or resolve to cling to, but all she felt was the desolation of her soul.

"May I bring you some wine?" Cerwin asked her.

"Please. I should like to sit down for a while."

"Of course." He offered his arm to escort her.

WHEN GRAG GRIPPED REYN'S ARM, REYN HAD SPUN TO FACE HIM AND nearly struck him. "Not now! Let me go!" he protested. Malta was walking away from him. That milky-skinned Trell boy was cutting hastily through the crowd to reach her. This was no time for a friendly word on the dance floor.

But Grag gripped his arm more tightly and spoke in a low, urgent voice. "One of the Satrap's Companions just danced with me."

"That's wonderful. I hope it was the pretty one. Now let go." He craned his neck trying to follow her progress through the crowd.

"No. You should ask her for the next dance. I want you to hear for yourself what she told me. Afterwards, come and find me in the gardens, near the pin oak on the east walk. We need to decide who else to tell, and what actions to take."

Grag's voice was taut with tension. Reyn didn't want this now. He attempted levity. "I need to speak to Malta first. Then we'll discuss burning warehouses."

Grag didn't release him. "It's not a jest, Reyn. It won't wait. I fear we may be too late already. There's a conspiracy against the Satrap."

"Go join it," Reyn advised him in annoyance. How could he think about politics just now? Malta was hurt. He could almost feel her pain himself, it was so intense. He had hurt her and now she was wandering through the crowd like a lost kitten. He needed to speak to her. She was so vulnerable.

"The Chalcedeans and some of his own nobles plan to kill him. Bingtown will take the blame for it. They'll raze us to the ground, with the blessings of all Jamaillia. Please, Reyn. It has to be now. Go and ask her to dance. I have to find my mother and sisters and ask them to start arranging for some of the other Traders to meet us outside. Go ask her. She's in the plain cream-colored gown, over by the high dais. Please."

Malta had vanished. Reyn shot Grag a look that he seemed to feel even through his veil. The Trader's son let go of Reyn's arm. He shrugged his shoulders then gave an angry shake of his head. Grag hastened away.

Slowly, his heart sinking inside him, Reyn turned and made his way toward the Satrap's Companion. She was watching for him. As he approached, she made some witty remark to the woman she was conversing with, nodded and began to move away. He intercepted her and gave her a short bow. "Would you honor me with a dance, Companion?"

"Certainly. It would give me great pleasure," she replied formally. She lifted her hand and he took it in his gloved one. The first strains of the music began. It was a slow melody, traditionally a lovers' dance. It would give couples both old and young an excuse to hold one another as they moved slowly to the dreamlike music. He could be taking Malta in his arms right now, soothing her hurt and his own. Instead, he found himself matched with a Jamaillian woman nearly as tall as himself. She made an excellent dance partner for him, graceful and light-footed. Somehow that only made it worse. He waited for her to speak.

"Did your cousin pass on my warning to you?" she finally asked.

Her directness shocked him. He strove to be contained. "Not really. He merely said you had told him something interesting, something he wished me to hear for myself." He put quizzical concern in his voice, nothing more.

She gave an impatient snort. "I fear we have no time for tiptoeing about like this. It occurred to me on the way here tonight that this would be the perfect time for them to put their plot in motion. Here you are, all gathered together, Bingtown Traders and Rain Wild Traders, with the Satrap in your midst. All know how strong the feelings run against the New Traders and the Satrap's Bingtown policies. What better time to set off a riot? In the confusion, the Satrap and his Companions will be killed. Then the Chalcedeans can move with just anger to punish you all."

"A nasty little scene. But who does it profit? Why?" His voice said he found it improbable.

"It profits those who banded together to plan it. The Jamaillian nobles are tired of a self-indulgent boy who knows nothing of ruling except how to spend the treasury on himself. Chalced gains Bingtown for its own province, to plunder as it pleases. They have long claimed that this territory of the Cursed Shores was rightfully theirs."

"Jamaillia would be foolish to give Bingtown up to Chalced. What other province yields such a rich harvest to the Satrapy?"

"Perhaps they believe it is better to yield Bingtown as part of a bargain than to simply lose it to the Chalcedeans as a conquest of war. Chalced grows stronger and more warlike. Internal strife and Northland raiders paralyzed the Six Duchies for years. That kingdom used to keep Chalced occupied. In the years since the Red Ship Wars, the Six Duchies have been occupied with rebuilding. Chalced has become a powerful nation, rich with slaves and ambition. They push to the north, in border skirmishes. But they also look south. To Bingtown and its rich trade. And the Rain Wild River lands."

"Lands?" Reyn gave a snort of contempt. "There is so little . . ." He halted his words abruptly, recalling to whom he was speaking. "They are fools," he finished succinctly.

"On the ship, coming here—" For a moment, the woman seemed to have sudden difficulty speaking, as if she could not catch her breath. "I was held captive for a time in the captain's quarters." He waited, then leaned closer to capture her soft words. "There were charts in his room.

Bingtown Harbor. The mouth of the Rain Wild River. Why else would he have such things, if he did not intend to use them?"

"The Rain Wild River protects its own," Reyn declared boldly. "We have nothing to fear. The secret ways of the river are known to none but our own."

"But tonight, there are many of you here. Representatives from many Rain Wild families, I am told. If they were taken hostage in the plundering of Bingtown, can you be sure that none of them would reveal your Rain Wild secrets?"

Her logic was relentless. Suddenly, small inconsistencies made sense. Why else allow the *Kendry* through the blockade and into the harbor? "They would have allies among the New Traders here," he said half-aloud, thinking of all the new folk who had just come ashore as well. "People whose ties to the slave trade in Chalced are as strong or stronger than their links to Jamaillia. People who have lived amongst us and learned enough of our ways to know that both Bingtown Traders and Rain Wild Traders would be gathered here tonight."

"If I were you, I would not be positive that there were not such folk among the Bingtown Old Traders as well," she pointed out quietly.

A trickle of cold suspicion ran through him. Davad Restart. Of course. "If you knew of this plot, why did you come to Bingtown?" he demanded of her.

"Obviously, if I had known, I would not have come," she retorted. "I have only this evening gathered enough of the pieces to grasp the whole picture. I am telling you this not only because I do not wish to die, but because I do not wish to see Bingtown fall. All my life, Bingtown has been the center of my studies. I have always wanted to come here: it is the city of my dreams. So I connived and begged to get the Satrap to allow me to come. Now that I am here, I do not want to be a witness to its death throes, any more than I want to die here before I have fully comprehended its wonders."

"What do you suggest we do?"

"Act before they do. Take the Satrap and his Companions hostage, yes, but keep us safe. Alive, he is a bargaining chip. Dead, he is the spark that ignites the fire of war. Not all the Jamaillian nobles can be involved in this. Send a message out somehow, to alert those who are loyal to the Satrapy. Tell them what is transpiring here. They will mount an effort to aid you, if you promise to return Cosgo unharmed. There will be war with Chalced, but eventually, there is always war with Chalced. Take the time I have given you by this warning, and secure the town as best you can. Gather supplies; hide your children and families. Get word to the folk up the Rain Wild River."

He was incredulous. "But you say it is most likely that they will act tonight. There is no time for any of that!"

"You are wasting time dancing with me now," she pointed out acidly. "You should be getting the word out right now. I suspect there will be incidents in the streets tonight. Fires, brawls, whatever it will take to ignite riots in the city. It will spread out to the ships in the harbor. Someone, intentionally or by accident, will give the Chalcedeans an excuse to attack. Perhaps they will simply receive a message that the Satrap has been killed." She looked unerringly into his veiled eyes. "By morning light, Bingtown will be burning."

The music was ending. As he and his partner slowed and then stopped, it seemed prophetic. He stood a moment in the silence, her hand still in his. Then he stepped away from her with a bow. "The others are gathering outside, in the gardens. We should join them," he suggested. He gestured to the door.

As if someone had literally tugged his heartstrings, he turned and looked across the room. Malta. Walking away with her hand on Cerwin Trell's arm. He could not simply leave the gathering like this, not without a word. He turned back to Companion Serilla. "Just outside the doorway, there is a pathway that goes to the east. It isn't far and the lanterns will all be lit tonight. Will you be comfortable, walking alone? I shall join you as quickly as I can."

Her look said it was unforgivably rude. But she said, "I am sure I shall be fine. Do you think you will be long?"

"I hope not," he assured her. He did not wait to see what she would think of such a vague answer. He bowed again and left her by the door. The music was starting again, but he cut swiftly across the dance floor, narrowly avoiding the whirling couples. He found Malta sitting alone. When he stood before her, she looked up quickly. The sudden light of hope in her eyes could not quench the fear that was there. "Reyn—" she began, but he cut her off before she could apologize.

"I have to go somewhere. It's very important. I may not be back this evening. You'll have to understand."

"Not be back . . . where? Where are you going? What is so important?"

"I can't tell you. You'll have to trust me, just now." He paused. "I'd like you to go home as soon as possible. Would you do that for me?"

"Go home? Just leave my presentation ball and go home while you go and do 'something more important'? Reyn, this is impossible. The meal has not been shared, the gifts of our kinship have not been offered— Reyn, we've only shared one dance! How can you do this to me? I've looked forward to this all my life, and now you say I should hurry home, because you've found something more important to do?"

"Malta, please understand! This isn't something I chose. Fate doesn't respect our wishes. Now . . . I have to go. I'm sorry, but I have to go." He longed to tell her. It wasn't that he didn't trust her. It was her family's connection to Davad Restart that worried him. If Davad was a traitor, it was important that he believe their plot was still secret. What Malta did not know, she could not accidentally betray.

She looked up at him and her eyes flashed darkly. "I think I know exactly what it is that is more important to you than I am. I wish you joy of it." She looked aside from him. "Good evening, Reyn Khuprus."

She was dismissing him, as if he were a recalcitrant servant. He doubted she would heed his advice to go home. He stood still in an agony of indecision.

"Excuse me."

The jostle was deliberate. Reyn turned. Cerwin Trell glowered at him. He held two glasses of wine. For a moment, Reyn's control teetered in the balance. Then something like despair clutched his heart. There wasn't time. He could stay and pursue this squabble now, but it could not be resolved. If he stayed, by morning they might all be dead.

The hardest part of turning and walking away was knowing that by morning they might all be dead, no matter what he did. He did not look back at all. If Malta had looked stricken, he would have had to return to her. If she had been simpering at Trell, he would have had to kill the boy. No time. Never any time to live his own life. He left the Traders' Concourse and plunged into the torch-tattered darkness outside.

MALTA DANCED THREE MORE TIMES WITH CERWIN. HE SEEMED BLITHELY unaware of how her feet dragged through the steps. After her effortless grace in Reyn's arms, dancing with Cerwin seemed an awkward physical effort. She could not quite match his step or the beat of the music. The adoring compliments he showered upon her rattled against her nerves like hailstones. She could hardly stand to look into his earnest, boyish face. All the life and beauty had gone out of the ball. The whole gathering seemed diminished by Reyn's departure. It suddenly seemed there were fewer couples on the dance floor, less laughter and talk in the room.

Bleakness welled up from the bottom of her soul, inundating her again. She could recall that she had been briefly happy earlier today, but the memory seemed shallow and false. As the music faded, it was a relief to see her mother at the edge of the dance floor, gesturing unobtrusively for Malta to come to her.

"My mother summons me. I'm afraid I have to go."

Cerwin stepped back from her, but caught both her hands in his. "Then I shall let you go, but only because I must, and I pray you, only for a brief time." He bowed to her gravely.

"Cerwin Trell," she acknowledged him, and then turned and left him.

Keffria's face was solemn as her daughter approached her. The concern in her eyes didn't change, but she managed a smile as she asked, "Have you had a good time, Malta?"

How to answer that? "It has not been what I expected," she replied truthfully.

"I don't think anyone's presentation ball is quite what one expects." She reached for Malta's hand. "I hate to ask this of you, but I think we should leave soon."

"Leave?" Malta asked in confusion. "But why? There is still the shared meal, the presentation of the gifts—"

"Hush," Keffria bid her. "Malta, look around you. Tell me what you see."

She glanced about herself hastily, then perused the room more carefully. In a low voice she asked, "Where have all the Rain Wild Traders gone?"

"I don't know. A number of Bingtown Traders have vanished as well, without any explanation or any farewell. Grandmother and I fear there is some trouble afoot. I went outside for a breath of air, and I smelled smoke. The blockade of the harbor has increased tension in the city. We fear a riot or outbreak of some kind." Keffria looked slowly about the room. She kept the calm smile on her face as if she discussed the ball with Malta. "We feel we would all be safer at home."

"But," Malta began and then fell silent. It was hopeless. All joy and light had gone out of the evening anyway. To stay here would just extend the death throes of her dream. "I shall do as you think best," she abruptly conceded. "I suppose I should tell Delo farewell."

"I think her mother already took her home. I saw Trader Trell speaking to his son just a moment ago, and now I do not see Cerwin either. They'll understand."

"Well, I don't," Malta replied sourly.

Her mother shook her head. "I am sorry for you. It is hard to see you come of age in such troubled times. I feel you are being cheated of all the things we dreamed you would do. But there is nothing I can do to change it."

"I know that feeling," Malta said, more to herself than to her mother. "Sometimes I feel completely helpless. As if there is nothing I can do to change any of the bad things. Other times, I fear I am simply too cowardly to try."

Keffria smiled a genuine smile. "Cowardly is the last word I would use to describe you," she said fondly.

"How will we get home? The hired coach will not be back for hours."

"Grandmother is talking to Davad Restart. She will ask if his coach could take us home. It would not take long. It would be back long before the ball is scheduled to end."

Grandmother came hastening up to them. "Davad is reluctant to see us leave, but he has agreed to loan us the use of his coach." She scowled suddenly. "But there is a condition on it. He demands that Malta come and bid the Satrap farewell before she leaves. I told him I thought that improper and putting herself forward, but he insists on it. I feel we have no time to argue. The sooner we are home, the safer we shall be. Now, where has Selden got off to?"

"He was with the Daw boys a moment ago. I'll find him." Keffria abruptly sounded both weary and harassed. "Malta, do you mind? Grandmother will be with you, so you needn't be afraid."

Malta suddenly wondered how much they had deduced about her earlier encounter with the Satrap. "I'm not afraid," she retorted. "Shall we meet you outside?"

"I suppose that will work. I'll go and find Selden."

As she and her grandmother crossed the floor, Ronica Vestrit spoke. "I think we shall host a tea ten days from now. The group of women presented this year is not large. Shall we invite them all?"

Malta was startled. "A tea? At our home?"

"In the garden, I think. We should be able to trim it up decently. Now that the berries are ripening, we could make little tarts to serve. In my day, such little tea parties often had a theme." Grandmother smiled to herself. "My mother held one for me, in which everything was lavender or violet. We ate tiny candied violets, and sugar cakes tinted purple with blueberry juice and the tea was flavored with lavender. I thought it tasted dreadful, but the idea of it was so lovely I didn't mind." She chuckled aloud.

Grandmother was trying to make her feel better. "Our lavender is blooming very well this year," Malta pointed out with an effort. "If we are deliberately old-fashioned, then no one will remark if we use the old lace tablecloths and doilies. And the old china, perhaps." She tried to smile.

"Oh, Malta, this has all been so unfair to you," Grandmother began. Then, "Chin up; cheery smile. Here comes Davad."

He bore down on them like a big gander in a poultry yard. "Well, I do think it is tragic, just tragic, to hurry this sweet girl home like this. Is her headache truly that bad?"

"Devastating," Malta replied quickly. So that had been her grandmother's ruse. "I am not accustomed to such late hours, you know," she added sweetly. "I told Grandmother I only wished to bid you good night and thank you for your kind offer of your coach. Then we shall be on our way."

"Oh, my poor little sugarplum! Surely, you will at least bid the Satrap good evening. After all, I have already told him you must leave, and I've come to escort you while you say good-bye."

That sealed her doom. No gracious way out. "I suppose I could manage it," Malta said faintly. She set her hand on Davad's arm, and he hastened her across the room to the high dais, with Ronica Vestrit hurrying after them.

"Here she is, Magnadon Satrap," Davad announced grandly before Malta had even caught her breath. He did not seem to notice that he had interrupted a conversation Trader Daw was having with the Satrap.

The Satrap turned a languorous glance on Malta. "So I see," he said slowly. His eyes moved over her casually. "Such a shame you must leave so soon. We have had only the briefest of conversations, and on such an important topic."

Malta could think of nothing to say. She had sunk into a deep curtsey the moment the Satrap deigned to notice her. Now Davad rather ungracefully took her arm and hauled her to her feet again. The act made her appear clumsy; she felt the blood rush to her face. "Aren't you going to tell him good night?" Davad prompted her as if she were a backward child.

"I wish you a good evening, Magnadon Satrap. I thank you for the honor of your dance." There. That was dutiful and correct. Then, before she could forbid herself the hope, she added, "And I pray you will soon act on your offer to send rescue for my father."

"I fear I may not be able to, sweet child. Trader Daw tells me there is some unrest down in the harbor tonight. Surely my patrol vessels must stay in Bingtown until it is subdued."

Before Malta could decide if he expected an answer to that, he was turning to Davad. "Trader Restart, would you have your coach summoned? Trader Daw feels it might be safest for myself to leave the ball early. I shall be sorry not to witness all of your quaint festival, of course, but I see I am not the only one to prefer caution over entertainment." His languid arm swept the ballroom. Malta glanced around reflexively. The crowd had thinned substantially, and many of those who remained were gathered in small anxious groups and talking. Only a few young couples still moved across the dance floor in apparently blissful ignorance.

Davad looked uncomfortable. "I beg your pardon, Magnadon Satrap. I had just promised Trader Vestrit and her family the use of my coach to get her safely home. But it will return quite swiftly, I promise you."

The Satrap rose, stretching like a cat. "It will not need to, Trader Restart. Surely, you cannot have intended to send these women off by themselves? I shall accompany them to their home, to see them safely there. Perhaps young Malta and I shall have a chance this evening to continue our interrupted conversation." The smile he gave her was a lazy one.

Her grandmother swept forward in a rustle of gown. She curtseyed low, near demanding that the Satrap recognize her. After a moment, he nodded at her irritably. "Lady," he acknowledged in a flat voice.

She rose. "Magnadon Satrap, I am Malta's grandmother, Ronica Vestrit. We would, of course, be honored to have you call upon us, but I fear our household is a very humble one. We could scarcely accommodate your visit tonight; at least, not in the manner in which you are no doubt accustomed to being welcomed. We would, of course—"

"My dear lady, the whole purpose of travel is to experience that which one is not accustomed to. I am sure I shall find your household accommodating. Davad, you will see to sending my personal servants over tonight, will you not? And my trunks and baggage."

The way he spoke, it was not a request. Davad bobbed an acquiescent bow. "Certainly, my lord Magnadon. And—"

"Your coach is outside by now, surely. Let us take our leave. Trader Daw, bring Companion Kekki's wrap and my cloak."

Davad Restart made a last brave attempt. "Magnadon Satrap, I fear we shall be very crowded in the coach—"

"Not if you ride on top with the driver. Companion Serilla seems to have vanished. Be it upon her own head. If she will not attend me as she should, then she must bear the consequences. Let us leave."

So saying, he rose from his seat on the dais, descended to the floor and set off for the main door. Davad hurried after him like a leaf caught in a ship's wake. Malta exchanged a look with her grandmother and then they both followed. "What are we to do?" Malta whispered worriedly to her.

"We shall be courteous," her grandmother assured her. "And no more than that," she added in a dangerously low voice.

Outside, the night was mild and pleasant, save for a distinct odor of smoke on the breeze. The Concourse had no view of Bingtown proper. There was no way to tell what was on fire, or where, but just the smell of it put shivers up Malta's back. Cloaks and wraps were brought hastily and the coach came around. Ignoring his own Companion, the Satrap took Malta's arm and assisted her into the coach first. He followed her and sat down by her on the ample seat. He gave Davad a look. "You will have to ride up top with the driver, Trader Restart. Otherwise, we shall be unforgivably crowded. Ah, yes, Kekki, you shall sit here, on the other side of me."

That left the opposite seat for her grandmother, mother and Selden. Malta felt wedged in the corner, for the Satrap sat uncomfortably close to her, his thigh nearly brushing hers. She tried not to look alarmed, but folded her hands modestly in her lap and gazed out the window. She was suddenly exhausted. She desired nothing so much as to be alone. The coach rocked as Davad climbed up awkwardly to take a seat next to the coachman. It took a while for him to settle and then the driver spoke to the horses. The coach moved out smoothly, leaving behind the lights and the music. As the darkness closed around them and the sound of the ball dwindled, the driver kept the horses to a sedate pace. No one spoke inside the coach. It seemed to fill with the night. The overloaded coach creaked companionably as its wheels rumbled over the cobbled road. It was not peace but numbness that settled over Malta. All the merriment and life had been left far behind them now. She feared she might doze off.

Companion Kekki broke the silence. "This summer celebration was very interesting to me. I am so pleased that I could witness it."

Her vapid words hung in the air, then Ronica exclaimed, "By Sa's breath! Look at the harbor!"

There was a break in the trees lining the road. Atop the coach, both Davad and the coachman swore in disbelief. Malta stared. It seemed as if the whole harbor were on fire, for the flames were reflected in the water and doubled there. It was not just a warehouse or two; the entire waterfront seemed to be burning, as well as several of the ships. Malta stared in horror, scarcely hearing the exclamations and speculation of the others. Well she knew that only fire could kill a liveship. Had the Chalcedeans known that as well? Were the ships that battled the flames out near the mouth of the harbor liveships or the ships and galleys the Satrap and his party had come on? But they had only that brief glimpse and the distance was too great to be sure what she had seen.

"Perhaps we should go down there and see for ourselves," the Satrap suggested boldly. He raised his voice. "Coachman! Take us down to the harbor!"

"Are you mad?" Ronica exclaimed, heedless of whom she addressed. "That is no place for Selden or Malta just now. Take us home first, then do as you will!"

Before the Satrap could reply, the coach gave a lurch as the coachman whipped up his horses. As blackness closed around them once more, Ronica exclaimed, "What can Davad be thinking, to travel at such a pace in the darkness? Davad? Davad, what are we doing?"

There was no direct reply to her query, only muffled shouts exchanged atop the coach. Then Malta thought she heard another voice. She seized the windowsill and leaned out of it. Behind them, in the darkness, she thought she caught a glimpse of something. "I think some horsemen are coming up behind us quickly. Perhaps Davad is just trying to get out of their way."

"They must be drunk, to gallop their horses at night on this road," Keffria exclaimed in disgust. Selden was climbing up on the seat, trying to get to the window to look out. "Sit down, child! You're trampling my dress," she exclaimed in annoyance. Suddenly Selden was thrown to the floor as the coachman cracked his whip and the horses suddenly surged forward against their harness. The coach rocked heavily now, shifting them back and forth against one another as it swayed. If they had not been packed so tightly together, they would have been sliding about inside the coach.

"Don't lean against the doors!" her mother commanded her wildly, while Ronica cried out, "Davad! Make him slow the horses! Davad!"

As Malta clung desperately to the windowsill to keep from being thrown about, she glimpsed sudden movement outside it. A horse and rider had pulled abreast of them. "Yield!" he shouted. "Halt and yield to us, and no one will be hurt!"

"Highwaymen!" Kekki exclaimed in horror.

"In Bingtown?" Ronica retorted. "Never!"

Yet now there was another horse and rider on the other side of the coach. Malta glimpsed him, and then she heard the driver shout something. A wheel bumped wildly, and she was thrown against the side of the coach as it slewed to one side. For an instant, it seemed to recover. All would be well, she told herself, and then the opposite side of the coach simply sank with an abrupt lurch. She was flung hard against the Satrap who sprawled against Companion Kekki. Incredibly, she was falling sideways, and then the roof of the coach was somehow almost under her. A door flew open beside her. She heard a scream, a terrible scream and saw a sudden great flash of white light.

"DAVAD IS DEAD." RONICA VESTRIT SPOKE THE WORDS SO CALMLY, SHE could hardly believe it was her own voice. She had come across his body in the darkness, groping her way up the steep and uneven slope toward the road. She knew it was Davad by the heavy embroidery on his jacket. She was glad it was too dark to see his body. The heavy warm stillness and the stickiness of blood were overwhelming enough. She could find no pulse at his throat, only blood. There was no whisper of breath. She believed from the drenching of blood down the back of his jacket that his skull had been crushed, but she could not bring herself to touch him anymore. She crawled away from him.

"Keffria! Malta! Selden!" She called the names wildly but without strength. Nothing made sense. Above her, she could see the bulk of the coach between her and the uneven light of torches. There were voices up there, and people moving in the darkness. Maybe her children were up there.

The hillside was steep and brushy. She could not clearly recall how she had gotten out of the coach. She could not understand how she could be so far away from it. Had she been thrown clear?

Then to her ears came Keffria's voice. She wailed, "Mama, mama!" just as she had used to call when she was a child and tormented by nightmares.

"I'm coming!" Ronica called. Prickly bushes caught at her and she fell again. The entire left half of her body stung as if she had lost the skin off it. But that could be managed, that could be ignored, forgiven and forgotten, if she could just find the children. She fell again.

It seemed to take a long time to get up. Had she fainted? She could see nothing at all now, not the coach, nor the flickering light. Had there been people moving about or had she imagined that? She listened hard. There. A sound, a squeaking of breath, or weeping. She scrabbled toward it.

In the darkness, she found Keffria by touch. The squeaking had been her sobbing. She cried out when Ronica touched her, then clutched at her wordlessly. Little Selden was in her lap. The boy was curled in a tight little ball. The tension of his muscles told Ronica that he was alive. "Is he hurt?" were her first words to her daughter.

"I don't know. He won't speak. I can't find any blood."

"Selden, come here. Come to Grandma." He did not resist her but he did not try to come to her. She felt the boy over. No blood, nor did he cry out at her touch. He simply huddled, shivering. She gave him back to Keffria. For a miracle, neither of them seemed seriously injured. Keffria had some broken fingers, but more than that she could not tell, nor could Ronica see. The trees were too dense. No moonlight or starlight reached them to help them search.

"Malta?" Ronica asked at last. She would not mention Davad before Selden.

"I haven't found her yet. I heard the others, at first. Then I called . . . I thought I heard you, but you didn't come. Malta never answered."

"Come. Let's get back up to the road. Perhaps she is there."

In the dark, she more felt than saw Keffria nod. "Help me with Selden," she said.

Ronica hardened her voice. "Selden. Mama and I cannot carry you. You are too big a boy for that. Remember how you helped with the buckets, the day the ships first came? You were brave then. Now you must be brave again. Come. Take my hand. Stand up."

He did not react at first. Nonetheless, she took his hand and tugged at it. "Come, Selden. Get up. Take your mother's good hand. You're strong. You can help us both get up this hill."

Very slowly, the child unfolded himself. Each of them took a hand, and between the two of them, they hauled him up the hill. Keffria carried her injured hand curled to her chest. No one spoke much, except words of encouragement to the boy interspersed with calling Malta's name. No one replied. The noise they made had stilled the night birds. The only sounds were those they made themselves.

The coach lay on its side. Here, closer to the road, the trees were thinner and starlight reached through to the ground. It showed Ronica the end of her world in shades of black and white. One dead horse was still tangled in its traces. Between the coach and the road uphill of it, the saplings were bent and snapped.

They searched all around the coach. Neither of them spoke of what they were really doing. They searched the ground for Malta's body, feeling about in the dark. After a time, Keffria said, "She might have been trapped inside the coach."

The coach lay on its side on the steep slope, with its roof pointing downhill. The coachman's booted feet stuck out from under it. Ronica and Keffria both noticed them, but neither pointed them out to the other. Selden had seen enough tonight. He did not need to be shown that. He did not need to wonder, as they did, if Malta's body was under there, too. Ronica guessed that the coach had rolled at least twice before coming to rest. Even now, it did not look stable. "Be careful," she cautioned her daughter in a low voice. "It may slide further down the hill."

"I'll be careful," Keffria promised uselessly. Then she clambered slowly up the undercarriage of the coach. She gasped once as her injured hand slipped. She lay on the side of the vehicle, looking in the window. "I can't see a thing," she called down to them. "I'll have to climb down inside it."

Ronica listened to her wrestle with the door. She managed to drag it open. Then she sat on the edge of the opening for a moment, before lowering herself inside. Ronica heard her sharp exclamation of horror. "I stepped on her," Keffria wailed. "Oh, my baby, my baby."

The silence stretched all the way to the stars and back. Then Keffria began to sob. "Oh, Mother, she's breathing! She's alive, Malta's alive!"

CHAPTER THIRTY-THREE

Proofs

IT WAS ALMOST DAWN WHEN SHE SLIPPED QUIETLY INTO HIS CABIN. NO doubt, she thought he was asleep.

Kennit was not. When they had first returned to the ship, Etta had assisted him through a hot bath and into clean clothing. Then he had shooed her out of his cabin, and spread out the plans for Divvytown on the chart table. He set out his straight-edge, dividers and pens, and considered his previous effort with a scowl. He had been working from memory when he created it. Today, as he painstakingly stumped over the areas in question, he swiftly saw that some of his ideas were unworkable. He set out a new sheet of vellum and began work afresh.

He had always loved this type of work. It was like creating his own world, a tidy and orderly world where things made sense and were arranged to their best advantage. It took him back to the days of his very early boyhood, when he had played on the floor beside his father's desk. The floor had been earth in that first home he remembered. When his father was sober, he worked on his plans for Key Island. It was not only his own grand manor house that he drew. He inked in the cottages in a row where the servants would live, designating how large the garden plots for each would be, and even calculating how much space each crop would need. He had sketched out the stable and the barn, the pens for the sheep, arranging them so that the manure piles would be handy to the garden plots. He had planned a bunkhouse for the ship's crew members should they want to sleep ashore. He set each structure in place so that the roads might run straight and level. It was the plan for a perfect little world on a hidden island. Often he had taken young Kennit on his lap, to show him his dream. He had told him tales of how they would all be happy here. All had been laid out so well. For a brief time, the dream had prospered.

Until Igrot came.

He had pushed that thought away, shoved it down to the back of his mind as he worked. He was working on the layout for the shelter at the base of the watchtower when the charm suddenly spoke. "What is the purpose of this?" it demanded.

Kennit scowled at the squiggle of ink his start had caused. He blotted it carefully away. It would still leave a mark. He would have to sand it out of the vellum. He frowned as he leaned to the work again. "The purpose of this design," he said, more to himself than to the insolent charm, "is that this structure can double as a safe haven in case of attack, as well as a temporary shelter until their homes are rebuilt. If they put a well here, inside, and fortify the outside structure, then—"

"Then they could starve to death instead of being carted off for slaves," the charm observed brightly.

"Raiding ships don't have that type of patience, usually. They are after a quick, easy capture of plunder and slaves. They are not likely to besiege a fortified town."

"But what is the purpose of these plans? Why do you take such an interest in creating a better town for folk you secretly despise?"

For a moment, the question stymied him. He looked down at his plans. The folk of Divvytown were truly not worthy to live in such an orderly place. It did not matter, he discovered. "It will be better," he said stubbornly. "It will be tidier."

"Control," the charm corrected him. "You will have left your mark on how they live their lives. I have decided that that is what you are all about, Kennit. Control. What do you believe, pirate? That if you get enough control, you can go back and control the past? Make it all un-happen? Put your father's precise plan back to work, bring his little para-dise back to life? The blood will always be there, Kennit. Like a smear of ink on a perfect plan, the blood sinks in and stains. No matter what you do, when you walk into that house, you will always smell the blood and hear the screams."

He had thrown down his pen in fury. To his disgust, it had left a snake's trail of blood across his plans. No, not blood, he told himself angrily. Ink, black ink, that was all it was. Ink could be blotted and bleached away. So could blood. Eventually.

He had gone to bed.

In the darkness, he had lain awake and waited for Etta to come in. But when she did come in, she came slinking in like a cat after a night's hunt. He knew where she had been. He listened to her disrobe in the darkness. She came softly to the side of the bed she slept in and tried to slip under the covers.

"So. How was the boy?" he asked her in a hearty voice.

She gasped in surprise. He saw her silhouette as she set her hand to her heart. "You startled me, Kennit. I thought you were asleep."

"Obviously," he observed sarcastically. He was angry, he decided, not because she had slept with the boy. He had intended that all along, of course. It was that she thought she could deceive him about it. That meant she thought he was stupid. It was time to divest her of that notion.

"Are you in pain?" she asked him. Her concern sounded genuine.

"Why do you ask?" he asked in return.

"I thought that might be what kept you awake. I fear Wintrow was injured more seriously than we thought. He did not complain this afternoon, but tonight his arm was so swollen he scarcely could get his shirt off."

"So you helped him," Kennit decided pleasantly.

"Yes. I made a poultice for him. It took the swelling down. Then I asked him some questions about a book I've been trying to read. It seemed to me a foolish book, for all it spoke about was how to decide what was real in one's life and what was the product of how one considered life. Philosophy, he named it. A waste of one's time, I told him. What is the good of pondering how one knows that a table is a table? He argued that it makes us think about how we think. I still think it is foolish, but he insists I should read it. I had not realized how long we had argued until I left his room."

"Argued?"

"Not angrily. Discussed, I should have said." She lifted the coverlet and slid into the bed with him. "I've washed," she added hastily as he shrugged away from her touch.

"In Wintrow's room?" he asked nastily.

"No. In the galley, where the water can be kept hot more easily." She settled her body against his and sighed. A moment later, she asked, almost sharply, "Kennit, why did you ask me that? Do you mistrust me? I am faithful to you."

"Faithful!" The word shocked him.

She sat up abruptly in the bed, her action snatching the blankets off him. "Of course, faithful! Faithful always. What did you think?"

This could be a barrier to all his plans for her. He tugged at the blanket and she lay back down beside him. He formulated his words carefully. "I thought that you would be with me for a time. Until another attracted you." He shrugged lightly, more disturbed than he liked to admit. Why should it be so hard to admit this? She was a whore. Whores were not faithful.

"Until another attracted me? Such as Wintrow, you mean?" She laughed a rich throaty chuckle. "Wintrow?"

"He is closer to your age than I am. His body is sweet and young, scarcely scarred and possessed, I might add, of two legs. Why would not you find him more desirable?"

"You are jealous!" She said it as if he had just presented her with a diamond. "Oh, Kennit. You are being silly. Wintrow? I started to be kind to him only because you asked it of me. Now, I have come to see his value. I see what you wanted to show me about him. He has taught me much, and I am grateful for that. But why would I trade a man for an untried youth?"

"He is whole," Kennit pointed out. "Today he fought as a man. He killed."

"He fought today, yes. But that scarcely makes him a man grown. He fought for the first time, with a blade we gave him and the skills I taught him. He killed, and that act consumes and torments him tonight. He spoke long about it, the wrong of taking from a man what Sa alone could give him." She lowered her voice. "He wept about it."

Kennit groped to follow. "And that made you despise him as less than a man."

"No. It made me pity him, even as I wanted to shake him out of it. He is a youth torn between his natural gentleness of spirit and his need to follow you. He himself knows that. He spoke of it tonight. A long time ago, when we were first thrown into one another's company, I said things to him. Commonsense things, such as finding his life in what is instead of longing after what could be. He took those things to heart, so seriously, Kennit." She lowered her voice. "He now believes that Sa has steered him to you. Everything, he says, that happened to him since he left his monastery carried him toward you. He believes that Sa gave him over to slavery so that he might better understand your hatred of it. He fought the idea for so long. He says that he resisted it because he was jealous of how his ship swung so quickly to you. That jealousy blinded him and made him seek out faults in you. But over the last few weeks, he has come to see it is Sa's will for him. He believes he is destined to stand beside you, speak out for you and fight for you. Yet, he dreads the last. It tears him."

"Poor boy," Kennit said aloud. It was hard to sound sympathetic with triumph racing through his heart. He tried. It was almost as good as if she had slept with the boy.

Etta's hands came up to rest on his shoulders. She kneaded gently at his flesh. Her cool hands were pleasant. "I tried to comfort him. I tried to tell him it might be chance, not destiny, that has put him here. Do you know what he said?"

"That there is no chance, only destiny."

Her hands paused. "How did you know?"

"It is one of the cornerstones of Sa's teachings. That destiny is not reserved for a few chosen ones. Each man has a destiny. Recognizing it and fulfilling it are the purpose of a man's life."

"It seems a burdensome teaching to me."

Kennit shook his head against the pillow. "If a man can believe it, then he can know he is as important as any other man. He can also know that he is no more important than any other is. It creates a vast equality of purpose."

"But what of the man he killed today?" Etta asked.

Kennit snorted softly. "That is Wintrow's hurdle, isn't it? To accept that someone is destined to die at his hand, and that he is destined to wield the knife. In time Wintrow will see that it was not his doing that slew the man at all. Sa brought them both together, to fulfill their destinies."

Etta spoke hesitantly. "Then you, too, believe in Sa and his teaching?"

"When it fits my destiny to do so," Kennit told her loftily, and then laughed. He suddenly felt inexplicably good. "This is what we shall do for the lad. We'll get the Divvytown construction under way, and then we'll take Wintrow to the Others Island. I'll let him walk the beach, and have an Other tell his fortune from what he finds." He grinned in the darkness. "Then I'll tell him what it means."

He rolled over into her reaching arms.

AT LEAST ONE BARREL OF THEIR SALT PORK HAD GONE BAD. THE CASKS that held fatty pieces of meat floating in brine should have been tight. The smell meant that the cask had been broached, either in loading or by other cargo shifting against it. The leaking brine and rotting meat not only stank, it would contaminate any other food it contacted. The stench was coming from a forward hold, one with little headspace. Food supplies in kegs, boxes and barrels filled it snugly. The cargo would have to be shifted, the offending cask disposed of and anything it had leaked onto would have to be cleaned up or discarded. Brashen had discovered the stench on one of his prowls of the ship. He'd given the task to Lavoy, who had passed it on to her. She had put two men onto it at the beginning of her watch. Now, as dawn reached over the face of the water, she had come down to see how they had progressed.

The sight that met her eyes infuriated her. Only about half the cargo had been shifted. The stench was as strong as ever; there was no sign that the cask had been discovered, or any cleaning done. The hand hooks they should have been using to move the kegs and crates were both sunk into an overhead beam. Lop sat on a cask, hunching his tall, skinny frame over the crate before him, his pale blue eyes intent on three walnut shells. Opposite him was Artu, his dirty fingers flickering and dancing over the shells. "Which one, which one," he was humming in the old trickster's chant as he deftly shifted the shells. The slick scar of the old brand on his cheek caught the lantern's fading light. This was Brashen's rapist. Lop was merely stupid, and prone to idleness, but Althea hated Artu. She never worked near him if she could help it. The man had glittery little eyes, dark as a rat-hole, and a puckered mouth that was constantly wet. So engrossed was he in cheating Lop out of his money that Artu was completely unaware of her. He stopped the shells with a flourish, and his darting tongue wet his lips again. "And which one has the bean?" he demanded, wiggling his eyebrows at Lop.

Althea strode up and kicked the crate, making all the shells jump. "Which cask has the rotten meat?" she roared at them.

Lop turned amazed eyes up at her. Then he pointed at the over-turned shells. "There's no bean!" he exclaimed.

She seized him by the back of his shirt collar and shook him. "There never is!" she told him, and then shoved him to one side. He gaped at her.

She turned on Artu. "Why haven't you found that cask and cleaned it up?"

He came to his feet, licking his lips nervously. He was a small, bandy-legged man, more quick than strong. " 'Cause there ain't one to find. Me and Lop, we shifted all the cargo in this hold, looked at it all and found nothing. Right, Lop?"

Lop goggled at her, his large pale eyes wide. "We didn't find it, ma'am."

"You didn't move all the cargo. I can smell it! Can't you?"

"Just ship stink, that's all. All ships smell like that." Artu shrugged elaborately. "When you been on as many ships as I have," he began condescendingly, but Althea cut him off.

"This ship doesn't stink like that. And it never will as long as I'm a mate on it. Now get that cargo shifted, find that rotten meat and clean it up."

Artu scratched at a boil on the side of his neck. "Our watch is almost up, ma'am. Maybe the next watch'll find it." He nodded to himself in satisfaction and gave Lop a conspiratorial nudge. The lanky sailor echoed Artu's grin.

"Tidings for you, Artu. You and Lop are on watch down here until you find it and clean it up. Clear? Now get on your feet and start shifting this cargo."

"That ain't fair!" Artu cried out as he came to his feet. "We worked our watch! Hey, come back here! That ain't fair!"

His grubby fingers caught at her sleeve. Althea tried to jerk free, but his grip was amazingly strong. She froze. She wouldn't risk a struggle she might not win, nor a torn shirt, with this man. She met his gaze with narrowed eyes. "Let go," she said flatly.

Lop stared, wide-eyed as a boy. He'd caught his lower lip between his teeth. "Artu, she's second mate," he whispered nervously. "You're gonna get in big trouble."

"Mate," Artu snorted in disgust. Quick as a flea's hop, he shifted his grip from her sleeve to her forearm inside it. His dirty fingers bit down hard on her flesh. "She ain't no mate, she's a woman. And she wants it, Lop. She wants it bad."

"She wants it?" Lop asked dimly. He looked at Althea in consternation.

"She ain't screaming," Artu pointed out. "She's just standing here, waiting for it. I think she's tired of getting it from the captain."

"She'll tell," Lop complained in confusion. It took so little to confuse the man.

"Naw. She'll scream and wiggle a bit, but we'll leave her smiling. You'll see." Artu leered at her. He wet his pursed little mouth. "Right, matey?" he taunted her. He grinned, showing brown-edged teeth.

Althea met his gaze squarely. She could not show fear. Her mind was racing. Even if she screamed, no one would hear her down here. The ship might be aware of her, but she couldn't count on Paragon. He had been so spooky lately, imagining serpents and floating logs and yelling out sudden warnings, that most likely no one would pay attention to him. She would not scream. Artu was looking at her, his little eyes shining. He'd like her to scream, she realized. He and she both knew that when he was finished with her, he'd have to kill her. He'd try to make it look like an accident, falling cargo or whatever. Lop would say whatever Artu told him to say, but Brashen would not be fooled. Brashen would likely kill them both, but she wouldn't be around to watch him do it.

The cascade of thoughts tumbled through her mind in less than a breath. She was on her own here. She'd sworn to Brashen she could handle this crew. Could she?

"Let go, Artu. Last chance," she told him evenly. She managed to keep the tremor out of her voice.

He backhanded her with his free hand, the blow so swift she never saw it coming. Her head snapped back on her neck. She was stunned for an instant, dimly aware of Lop's distressed, "Don't hit her," and Artu's, "Naw, that's how she wants it. Rough."

His hands scrabbled over her body, pulling her shirt loose from her trousers. Her revulsion at his touch was what brought her back. She struck out at him with all her strength, body punches that he didn't seem to feel. His body was as hard as wood. He laughed at her efforts and she knew an instant of despair. She couldn't hurt him. She would have fled then, but his grip on her arms was tighter than a vise, and the disarray of cargo made a quick escape impossible. He forced her up against a crate. He released one of her arms to grip the front collar of her shirt. He tried to tear it, but the stout cotton held. With her one free hand, she punched hard in and up at the base of his ribs. She thought he flinched.

This time she saw his blow coming. She threw her head to one side and he punched the crate behind her instead of her face. She heard the wood splinter with the force of his blow and heard him shout hoarsely. She hoped he had broken his hand. She tried to gouge his eyes, but he snapped at her, biting her wrist hard and drawing blood. They over-balanced, and went down. She twisted desperately, trying not to land beneath him. They fell on their sides amongst the crates and boxes. It made for close quarters. She drew her arm back and delivered two short, hard jabs to Artu's belly.

She had a glimpse of Lop towering over them. The great dolt was hitting himself in the chest in his distress. His mouth hung open, wailing. No time to think.

She grabbed a handful of Artu's hair and slammed his head against the keg behind him. For an instant, his grip on her slackened. She did it again. He kneed her in the gut, driving all the breath out of her. He rolled on top of her and pressed her down. With a knee, he tried to force her legs apart. She cried out in fury, but could not draw her arms back to get in a decent punch. She tried to pull her legs up to kick at him but he had her pinned. He laughed down at her, his breath foul in her face.

She'd seen it done. She knew it would hurt. She threw her head back as far as she could, then tried to slam her forehead against his. She missed and cracked her forehead against his teeth. They cut her forehead as they broke off in his mouth. He screamed high in pain and was suddenly leaning back from her, his hands to his bloody mouth. She followed him up, hitting him as hard as she could, not caring where her punches landed. She heard one of her knuckles pop and felt a flash of pain in her hand, but kept hitting as she managed to come up to her feet. Once she was standing in the confined space between the crates, she kicked him instead. When he was lying on his side, balled up and moaning, she stopped.

She pushed her loose bloody hair back from her forehead and stared around her. Hours seemed to have passed, but the lantern still flickered and Lop still gaped at them. She had never realized how half-witted the man was until now. He was chewing on his knuckle and as her eyes met his, he shouted at her, "I'm in trouble, I know, I'm in trouble." His eyes were both defiant and scared.

"Find that keg of rancid meat and get it overboard." She stopped to catch another breath. "Clean up the mess. Then you're off watch."

She suddenly hunched over, hands on her knees, and took several deep breaths. Her head was spinning. She thought she would throw up, but managed not to. Artu was starting to uncurl. She kicked him again, hard. Then she reached overhead to the freight gaff. She grabbed the hook by the handle and twisted it free of the beam.

Artu rolled his head and stared up at her with one blood-caked eye. "Sar, no!" he begged. He threw his hands up over his head. "I didn't do nothing to you!" The pain of his broken teeth seemed to have completely disabled him. He waited for the blow to fall.

Lop gave a wordless shout of horror. He frantically began moving crates and kegs, looking for the spoiled meat.

For answer, she grabbed a handful of Artu's shirt, and punched the freight hook through it. Then she headed toward the ladder, determinedly hauling him after her. He came kicking and squalling and trying to get to his feet. She paused and gave the handle of the hook a twist. The canvas of his shirt twisted with it, binding his arms in tight to his body. She dragged him on, almost a dead weight behind her. She supplemented her ebbing strength with her anger. She could hear Paragon shouting but couldn't make out his words. By this time, a few heads had appeared at the hatch and were peering down curiously. They were from Lavoy's watch. That meant the first mate was most likely on deck now. She didn't look at them as she clambered up the steps dragging the struggling Artu behind her. She put all her determination into reaching the deck.

As she finally emerged above, she heard muttered comments as the hands asked one another what was going on. Those about the hatch fell back. As she hauled Artu up behind her, the exclamations became curses of awe. She caught one glimpse of Haff, staring wide-eyed at her. She headed for the port railing, dragging Artu after her. He was moaning and mewling, "I didn't do nothing to her, I didn't do nothing!" His complaints were muffled by his own hands held protectively over his broken teeth and bloody mouth. Lavoy looked at them incuriously from his post on the starboard railing.

Brashen suddenly appeared on the deck. His shirt was open and he was barefoot, his hair unbound. Clef trailed after him, his mouth still tattling. The captain took in the situation at a glance. Brashen stared in horror at her bloodied face and disheveled clothing, but only for an instant. Then he glanced about for the mate.

"Lavoy! What is going on here?" Brashen roared. "Why haven't you put a stop to this?"

"Sir?" Lavoy looked puzzled. He glanced over at Althea and Artu as if he had only just now noticed them. "Not my watch, sir. The second seems to have it well in hand." He hardened his voice to that of command as he asked her, "Am I correct? Can you handle your task, Althea?"

She halted where she stood to look at him. "I'm throwing the rotten meat overboard, like you ordered. Sir." She put another half-twist on the hook as she spoke.

For a moment, all was still. Lavoy transferred his quizzical look to Brashen. The captain shrugged. "Carry on." He began fastening his shirt as if it did not concern him. He lifted his eyes to look over the water and see what sort of weather lay before them.

Artu howled like a kicked dog and began to struggle. She dragged him closer to the rail, wondering if she would really do it. Suddenly Lop appeared on deck. He was carrying two buckets; the smell told her what they held. "I found the bad meat. I found it," he bellowed and rushed past her to the railing. "Cask was smashed. It is all over down there, but we'll get it cleaned up, right Artu? We'll get it cleaned up." He heaved one load over the side. As he lifted the second bucket, a serpent's head broke the water.

It snapped at the fall of foul meat as Lop staggered back, screaming.

"Serpent! Serpent!" Paragon added his roar to the sudden commotion.

Althea let go of the cargo hook. Artu scrambled backwards from the railing, the hook handle clacking against the deck as he went. For a long instant, she and the serpent stared at one another, eye to eye. Its scales were the green of new spring foliage, with immense eyes as yellow as dandelions. Each individual scale overlapped two others in a precise pattern that begged the eye to follow it. The largest scales on its back were bigger than her hand, while around the eyes its scales were tinier than grains of wheat. For a moment, the beauty of the immense animal transfixed her. Then it opened jaws that could have easily engulfed a whole man. She looked into a shockingly red mouth edged with rows of teeth. It shook its head back and forth with a questioning roar. She stood stockstill. It closed its mouth and stared at her.

She caught movement from the corner of her eye. A man running with a boat hook. At the same instant came Brashen's shouted warning, "Don't anger it! Leave it alone!"

She turned and flung herself at Haff. The sailor brandished the long gaff like a weapon, shouting, "I'm not afraid!" The pallor of his face told a different story. She caught at his arm and tried to stop him.

"It just wants food. Leave it alone. It might go away. Haff. Leave it alone!"

He shook her off impatiently. Her bruised hands were suddenly too sore to grip. She fell away from him as he spurned her. In horror, she watched him swing the hook.

"No!" Brashen roared, but the gaff was already in motion. It struck the animal on the snout, glancing harmlessly off the overlapping scales until the hook reached a nostril. More by chance than aim, the hook caught there and dug in.

In horror, Althea watched the creature throw its head back. The gaff went with it and Haff held on with the game stupidity of a pit dog. In an instant, the serpent seemed to double in size. Its neck swelled, and an immense ruff of poisonous quills suddenly stood out stiff around its face and throat. It roared again, and this time a fine spray flew from its mouth. Where it struck the deck, the wood smoked. Althea heard Paragon cry out in distress. The drift of poison stung Althea's skin like a sunburn. Haff shrieked as he was engulfed in a fog of the stuff. He let go of the gaff and fell bonelessly to the deck. He was either unconscious or dead. The serpent abruptly cocked its head, eyeing the prone man. Then it darted its head at Haff.

She was the only one close enough to do anything. Even if the only thing she could do was stupid, she could not watch the serpent just eat the man. She sprang and caught the wooden handle of the gaff. It felt pitted and splintered from the serpent's breath. She grasped it, and threw her weight against it to jerk the creature's head off target. From somewhere, Lop had appeared. He flung an empty wooden bucket at the serpent's head. In the same motion, he grabbed Haff's ankles and dragged him back.

That left Althea as the serpent's sole target. She tightened her grip on the gaff and shoved with all her might. She expected the wood handle to give way at any moment. Momentarily, her push and the serpent's pain turned the creature's head away from her. It breathed another rush of spittle that pocked Paragon's deck. The liveship shrieked again. Behind her, other voices were raised, Lavoy commanding men to put on sail, men yelling in anger or terror, but above all was the ship's amazed and furious cry. "I know you!" Paragon roared. "I know you!" Amber shouted a question but Althea could not make it out. She gripped the hook desperately. The haft was weakening in her hands, but it was the only weapon she had.

She did not know Brashen had joined her until he struck the serpent with an oar. It was a pitiful weapon against such a creature, but it was all that was close to hand. Abruptly, her hook came loose from the creature's nostril. Unencumbered now, it shook its maned head, spattering the deck with smoking poison. As the head came toward them, Althea leveled the gaff like a pike and charged. She was aiming for the great eye, but missed as the serpent swiveled its head toward Brashen. Instead, the tip of the boat hook struck a color-spot on the creature just behind its jaw hinge. To her shock, the tip of the hook plunged into the flesh easily, as if she had stabbed a ripe melon. With all her strength, she shoved it as deep as it would go. The hook followed the tip into the animal's flesh. With a jerk, she set it.

In agony, the serpent flung its head back. "Get away!" she cried needlessly to Brashen. He had already ducked and rolled away. She gave a final jerk on the hook. It tore flesh, and smoking hot poison ran down the serpent's own neck. It shrieked, fountaining poison and blood from its wide-open mouth. It shook its head wildly, snatching the gaff from her numbed hands. She sat down hard and stared helplessly up at the thrashing creature. Some of its poison landed harmlessly in the sea, but some spattered across Paragon's deck and side. The ship cried out wordlessly and a tremor ran through his wooden body. As the serpent fell back and sank beneath the waves, Brashen was already shouting for buckets, seawater and brushes. "Get it off the deck! Now!" He roared from where he crouched on his hands and knees. His face was scalded scarlet by the serpent's venom. He rocked back and forth as if he were trying to rise but could not. She feared he was blinded.

Then from the bow came the wild cry that chilled Althea's blood. "I knew you!" the *Paragon* bellowed. "And you knew me. By your poisons, I know myself!" His wild laughter rose on the wind. "Blood is memory!"

HOW MUCH COULD THE WORLD CHANGE IN ONE NIGHT, RONICA VESTRIT wondered?

If one stood on a chair in Althea's old bedroom and looked out the window, there was a partial view of Bingtown and the harbor over the intervening treetops. Today, peer as she might, all she could see was smoke. Bingtown was burning.

She clambered stiffly down from the chair, and picked up the armful of linens from Althea's bed. She would use it to make bundles for them to carry as they fled.

She remembered far too much of the long walk home in the darkness. Malta had lurched along between them like a crippled calf. After a time, Selden had come out of his daze and begun to cry. He wailed endlessly, demanding to be carried, as he had not been in years. Neither of them could do it. Ronica had gripped his hand in hers and towed him along, with her other arm about Malta's waist. Keffria had gripped Malta's upper arm and helped her along while she carried her own injured hand curled to her chest. The walk had been eternal. Twice riders had passed them, but despite their cries for help, the horsemen had simply thundered past.

Daybreak came late, for the smoky air extended night's hold on the land. Night had been more merciful. Daylight revealed their tattered clothes and scraped flesh. Keffria was barefoot, her shoes lost in the wreck. Malta shuffled along in the ragged remnants of slippers never intended for the street. Selden's shredded shirt clung to his raw back; he looked as if he had been dragged by a horse. Malta had struck her forehead. Blood had dried in macabre stripes down her face. Both her eyes were blacked and closed to slits. Ronica looked at the others and could imagine how she looked.

They spoke hardly at all. Once, Keffria observed, "I forgot all about them. The Satrap and his Companion, I mean." In a lower voice she asked, "Did you see them?"

Ronica shook her head slowly. "I wonder what happened to them," she had replied, although in truth she did not. She did not wonder anything about anybody except her own just now.

Malta spoke thickly through her puffed mouth. "The horsemen took them away. They looked for the other Companion, and when they found that I was not she, they just left me there. One of them said I was nearly dead anyway."

She fell silent again. The silence lasted the rest of the way home.

Like a string of battered beggars, they limped up the unkempt drive to Vestrit Manor, only to find the door latched and barred to them. Keffria had given way to tears then, pounding weakly on the door as she sobbed. When Rache came to let them in at last, she carried a stick of kindling in her hand as a makeshift club.

Somehow, half the morning had passed since then. Wounds had been bathed and dressed. Their fine and bloodied ball clothes were heaped in the hallway. Both the youngsters were in bed, sleeping heavily. With Rache's aid, both Ronica and Keffria had bathed and changed clothes, but as yet there was no rest for them. Keffria's fingers had swollen to agony. That left Ronica and Rache to gather provisions and spare clothes for all of them. Ronica was not sure what was going on in Bingtown below, but armed horsemen had taken the Satrap and his Companion from the coach last night and left the rest of them to die. The town was burning. The haze was too thick to see what was taking place in the harbor. She would not wait for the chaos to reach her door. They had her old saddle mare and Selden's fat pony. They could not take much with them, but, she reflected bitterly, there was precious little of value left. They'd go with their lives. Ingleby Farm had been part of her bridal portion. It would take them at least two days to get there. She wondered what old Tetna, the caretaker, would think of her. She had not seen her ancient nursemaid in years. She tried to pretend she looked forward to it.

When the pounding came at the door, she dropped the linens in the hallway. She wanted to run away. She could not. She stood alone between whatever was at the door and the children of her family. She saw Rache venture out from the kitchen, her kindling in hand. Ronica stepped briefly into the study. It had been Captain Vestrit's conceit to keep a marlinespike on the corner of his desk. It was still there. She had it in her hand as she stood inside the door and demanded, "Who's there?"

"Reyn Khuprus! Please. Let me in!"

Ronica nodded at Rache, but did not put down the marlinespike. The serving woman undid the latch and bolt. As the door swung open, Reyn recoiled in horror at the sight of the battered old woman.

"By my honor, I prayed it was not true!" he cried. "And Malta?"

Ronica stared at the young Rain Wild man. He was still dressed in his elegant evening wear, but the smells of dust and smoke clung to him. He had been in the thick of it. "She's alive," Ronica said flatly. "Davad Restart is dead. As is the coachman."

He did not seem to hear her words. "I swear, I did not know. She came in a hired coach, they told me you all arrived in a hired coach. I expected her to leave that way. Please, please. Is Malta all right?"

Ronica made the connection. Cold enveloped her. "Your men left her to die. In fact, they told her she was dying. That should tell you something of her condition. Good day, Reyn Khuprus." She motioned to Rache, who began to close the door.

Reyn flung himself bodily against it. Rache could not hold it against him. He stumbled into the hall, then straightened and faced them. "Please, please. There is so little time. We've driven the galleys from the harbor mouth. I came to get Malta, to get all of you. I can get you out now, and up the Rain Wild River. You'll be safe up there. But there isn't much time. The *Kendry* will sail soon, with or without us. The galleys could return and close the harbor at any time. We have to go now."

"No." Ronica said flatly. "I think we'll take care of our own, Reyn Khuprus."

He spun away from her abruptly. "Malta!" he cried. He sprinted down the hallway toward the wing of bedchambers. Ronica started after him, only to suddenly grasp at the wall, her head reeling. Her body would betray her now? Rache took her arm and helped her follow Reyn.

The young Rain Wilder had gone mad. He roared Malta's name as he raced down the hall, flinging doors open. He reached Malta's room just as Keffria came flying out of hers at the end of the hall. He looked inside, gave a cry of anguish, and disappeared into her room.

"Don't you touch her!" Keffria cried, and raced toward the door. But Reyn reappeared in the door, Malta, wrapped in a blanket, in his arms. She was as white as the bandages that bound her head. Her eyes were closed and her head lolled against him.

"I'm taking her," he said defiantly. "The rest of you should come, too. But that's up to you. I can't force you to come with me, but I won't leave Malta here."

"You have no right!" Keffria cried. "Is this the new way of your folk, to abduct their brides?"

Reyn gave a sudden wild laugh. "By Sa, she dreamed true! Yes! I take her now. I have the right. 'By blood or gold, the debt is owed.' I claim her." He babbled the crazy words. He looked down into her face. "She is mine," he asserted.

"You cannot! The payment is not due—"

"It will be soon, and you cannot possibly amass it. I'm taking her, while she is still alive. If I must do it this way, then I shall. Come with me, I beg you. Don't make it be like this for her." He turned to face Keffria. "She will need you. And Selden is not safe here, not if the Chalcedeans over-run the town. Would you see your little son with a slave tattoo on his face?"

Keffria's hands flew up to cover her mouth in horror. She looked at Ronica. "Mother?" she asked through her fingers.

Ronica decided for all of them. "Get the boy. Go quickly, take nothing, just go."

SHE STOOD ON THE PORCH AND WATCHED THEM RIDE AWAY. REYN HELD Malta bundled before him on the horse. Keffria rode their old mare and a stoic Selden sat his fat old pony. "Mother?" Keffria asked a last time. "The horse can carry two of us. It is not so far for her."

"Go. Go now," Ronica repeated, as she had already said over and over. "I'm staying. I have to stay."

"I can't leave you like this!" Keffria wailed.

"You must. It is your duty to your family. Now go. Go! Reyn, take them away from here before their only chance is gone." Only to herself did she add, "If Bingtown is going to end in blood and smoke, I will see it. And I must see to burying Davad."

Rache stood at her side on the porch. They watched until they were out of sight. Then Ronica sighed heavily. Everything was suddenly so simple. Reyn would get them out of the harbor and to safety. There was only herself to worry about now and she had stopped caring what became of her a long time ago. She felt a faded smile come to her scratched face. She turned to the former slave at her side and took her hand.

"Well. A quiet moment at last. Shall we have a cup of tea?" she asked her friend.

SOMEONE KNOCKED HARD ON THE CABIN DOOR. ALTHEA GROANED. SHE opened one eye. "What?" she demanded from her bunk.

"Captain wants to see you. Now." Clef's boyish voice, officious with the command, reached through the door.

"He would," she muttered to herself. To the door she announced, "I'm coming." She clambered stiffly down from her bunk.

It was afternoon, but felt like the middle of the night to her. She should have been sleeping. She looked around the small room blearily. Jek was on watch, and it looked as if Amber had stayed with Paragon. Althea had given up on him, at least for now. After the incident with the serpent, the ship had ranted for a time, phrases that taunted Althea because they almost made sense. "Blood is memory," he had proclaimed. "You can spill it, you can devour it, but you can never erase what it holds. Blood is memory." He had repeated it until she thought she would go crazy, not with the recitation but with her failure to grasp the meaning. It was at the edge of her understanding.

She picked up her shirt. In some places, it was stiff with her own blood, in others the serpent's venom had eaten holes. The thought of pulling the rough cotton on over her blistered and bruised body made her shudder. With a groan, she crouched down to drag her gear bag out from under Amber's bunk. There was a light cotton shirt in there, a "town" shirt. She dug it out and pulled it on over her sore flesh.

Paragon had finally subsided to confused muttering. Then he had fallen silent, in that terrible impervious silence that was his retreat from the world. It had seemed to Althea that there was almost a smile on his mouth, but Amber had been frantic with worry. When Althea had left her, the bead-maker had been sitting out on the bowsprit, playing her pipes. Nursery tunes, she called them, but they were no songs Althea had ever known. Althea had passed the work crews that were scrubbing the venom and blood from Paragon's pitted decks. She had paused to marvel at the damage done so swiftly to the iron-hard wood. It had melted gouges and dips into the deck. Then she had come back to her cabin and crawled into her bunk.

How long ago had that been? Not long enough. And now Brashen had sent Clef to roust her out. He probably wanted to tell her how she should have handled it. Well, that was the captain's prerogative. She just hoped he talked fast, or she'd fall asleep in his face. She belted up her trousers and went to face her doom.

At the door of his cabin, she smoothed her hair back from her face and tucked in her shirt. She wished vainly that she'd stopped to wash up after the fight and before she'd gone to bed. At the time, it had seemed too much trouble. Too late now. She rapped smartly at the door and waited for Brashen's "Enter."

She shut the door behind her and then stared. Forgetting herself, she cried out, "Oh, Brashen!"

His dark eyes were shocking in his scarlet face. Huge watery blisters stood up on his cheeks and brow like a Rain Wilder's warts. The tattered remains of the shirt he had been wearing hung across the back of a chair. He wore his fresh shirt loosely, as if he could scarcely bear the touch of it against his skin. He showed his teeth in a grimace meant to be a smile. "You look no better," he offered her. He made a small gesture at the washbasin in his room. "I've left you some warm water in the pitcher."

"Thank you," she said awkwardly. He turned his back to her as she took him up on his courtesy. She hissed when she first lowered her bruised hands into the basin; then as the stinging eased, she thought she had never felt anything so good.

"Haff's going to be all right. He got it worse than either of us. I had the cook wash him down with fresh water. Poor bastard could hardly stand it. He's all over blood blisters. It ate the clothes right off his body, and still did that to him. That handsome face will bear some scars, I suspect." He paused, then pointed out, "He disobeyed your order as well as mine."

Althea lifted the warm washrag to her face. Brashen had a mirror fixed to the wall, but she hadn't dared look in it yet. "I doubt that he remembers that right now."

"Perhaps not now. But as soon as he's out of bed, I'll see that he does. If he'd left the damn serpent alone, it might have gone away. His actions endangered the whole ship and crew. He seems to think he knows better than mate or captain what to do. He discounts your experience and mine. He wants a bit of stepping on."

"But he is a good hand," Althea pointed out reluctantly.

Brashen did not falter. "When I'm finished stepping on him, he'll be a better hand. One that obeys."

She supposed there was a small rebuke for herself in there, in that she hadn't taught Haff that lesson herself. She bit her tongue and looked at herself in the mirror. Her face looked scalded. She ran her fingers lightly over it; it was pebbled stiff with tiny blisters. Like the serpent's scales, she thought, and snagged for a moment in the memory of its beauty.

"I'm taking Artu off your watch, and putting him on Lavoy's," Brashen went on.

Althea stiffened where she stood. Her father's eyes, black with anger, stared back at her from the mirror. She kept her voice cold. "I don't think that's fair. Sir." She ground the last word out between her teeth.

"Neither do I," Brashen agreed easily. "But he begged Lavoy on his knees, and the man finally gave in to be rid of him. Lavoy promised him every dirty duty he could find on the ship, and Artu wept tears of gratitude. What on earth did you do to him?"

Althea bent over the washbasin and lifted a double handful of water to her face. She rubbed it gently over her face. It dripped red-tinged back into the basin. She examined the cut at her hairline; she'd done that on Artu's teeth. She spoke through clenched teeth as she washed it out more thoroughly. "The captain should never be too interested in that sort of thing."

Brashen gave a soft snort of laughter. "That's funny. Clef came running to get me, and I came, my heart in my throat. Clef said Paragon was shouting that you were being killed. Then I got there, and here you were, hauling Artu along on a freight hook. I looked at that, and I thought to myself, 'Sa's breath, what would Captain Vestrit say to me if he could see her now?'"

She could see the back of his head in the mirror. She scowled at it. Would he ever understand that she could take care of herself? She remembered that Artu had bitten her arm. She folded back her sleeve, and cursed silently at the uneven row of tooth marks. She dipped her fingers into Brashen's soap, and rubbed at them. It stung. She would rather that a rat had bitten her.

He went on in a softer voice. "All that came to mind was Ephron Vestrit's voice saying, 'If the mate is handling it, the captain shouldn't see it.' He was right. He never interfered with me when I was settling small matters aboard the *Vivacia*. Even Lavoy knew that. I shouldn't have said a word."

It was almost an apology. "Lavoy's not so bad," Althea offered in return.

"He's coming around," Brashen agreed sagely. He suddenly crossed his arms on his chest. "I'll leave, if you'd like to make fuller use of that water."

"No, thank you. Sleep is what I need most. I do appreciate the offer. I don't smell that bad, do I?" The unfortunate words were out before she recalled how he might take them.

A little silence stood like a wall. She'd overstepped the bounds.

"You never did," he admitted quietly. "I was just angry. And hurt." He was still facing away from her, but she saw his shrug in the mirror. "I had thought there was something between us. Something that—"

"We're better as we are now," Althea broke in quickly.

"Undoubtedly," he said drily.

The silence stretched out. She looked at her battered hands. Every knuckle was swollen. When she flexed the fingers on her right hand, it felt like there was sand in the joints. Still, they moved. More to break the silence than to ask, she queried, "If you can move your fingers, that means nothing is broken, right?"

"It means nothing is badly broken," Brashen corrected her. "Let me see."

Knowing it was a mistake, she still turned and held out her hands to him. He came to her and took both of her hands in his. He moved her fingers and felt the bones of her hands. He shook his head over her knuckles, and winced when he saw the teeth marks on her wrist. He released one of her hands and lifted her chin. He looked at her face critically. She found herself examining his face in return. Even his eyelids showed blisters, but his dark eyes were clear. It was a miracle he hadn't lost his sight. The open collar of his shirt exposed standing welts on his chest. "You're going to be all right," he told her. He cocked his head and nodded to himself. "You're a tough woman."

"You probably saved my life when you distracted that thing with the oar," she suddenly remembered.

"Yes. I'm a dangerous man with an oar." He still held her hand. Without warning, he drew her closer. When he leaned down to kiss her, she did not step away. She lifted her face to his. His mouth was gentle on hers. She closed her eyes to it and refused to be wise. She refused to think at all.

He broke the kiss. He drew her closer but did not embrace her. For just an instant, he rested his chin on top of her head. His voice was deep. "You're right. I know you're right. We're better as we are." He sighed heavily. "That doesn't make it any easier for me." He released her hand.

She could not think of anything to say to that. It was not easy for her, either, but to tell him that would only make it harder for both of them. He'd said she was a tough woman. She proved it by walking to the door. "Thank you," she said softly at the door. He made no reply and she went out.

She passed Clef standing in the companionway. He was kicking one bare heel against the wall and chewing his lower lip. She frowned at his idleness. "Peeking at keyholes isn't right," she told him severely as she passed.

"Neither is kiss'n' ther cap'n," he replied insolently. With a grin and a flash of dirty soles, he was gone.

CHAPTER THIRTY-FOUR

Oracle

"I DON'T LIKE THIS." VIVACIA SPOKE SOFTLY, BUT HER WORDS THRUMMED through him.

Wintrow was stretched belly down on the foredeck, letting the early sun touch him. He had discarded his blanket during the muggy night, but his shirt was wrapped around his head. The new warmth of the sun soothed the ache in his arm, but the light from it nagged his headache into wakefulness. He was resigned to it. He had to wake up soon anyway. How he longed to just lie still. All the others seemed long recovered from the injuries taken at Divvytown. He felt a weakling that a couple of blows from a club still bothered him. He pushed away the idea that his injuries hurt more because he had killed the man who had given them. That was a silly superstition.

He rolled over onto his back. Even through the shirt and his eyelids, the light danced on his eyeballs. Sometimes it seemed he could see things in the patterns. He clenched his eyelids, and green flashes snaked across his vision like darting serpents. He loosened his eyes and the color became paler and took the shape of sunbursts.

The days of high summer were dwindling now, falling away one after another as the year inexorably carried them toward autumn. So much to have happened in the passing of a handful of months. When they had left Divvytown, half a dozen motley structures, constructed of wood old and new, had already risen from the ashes. A wooden tower as tall as a ship's mast was already manned, while one of stone took slow shape around it. The folk there called Kennit king. It was a term of affection as much as title. "Ask the king," they would advise one another, and nod to the tall peg-legged man with the scroll of papers always tucked under his arm. Their last sight of Divvytown had been the Raven flag flapping boldly from the flagstaff atop the tower. "Here To Stay" was embroidered beneath the bird's outstretched wing and rapacious beak.

Vivacia was now anchored, fore and aft, in Deception Cove off Others Island. The tide was swelling in around them. Kennit had said this was the only safe anchorage of the island. When the tide was fullest, he and Wintrow would leave the ship and row in to the shore. They were here to seek the oracle. Kennit had insisted that Wintrow walk the Treasure Beach.

Farther offshore, the silhouette of the *Marietta* was just visible in a drifting fog bank. She would stand off and watch them, coming closer only if they appeared to need aid. The peculiar weather had everyone unsettled. To look out to sea was like peering across a distance into a different world. The *Marietta* ghosted in and out of the mist; here in the cove, all was breathless warm sunlight. The silence cupped Wintrow's ears and made him sleepy.

"I do not like being here," the ship insisted.

Wintrow sighed. "Neither do I. Some find them exciting, but I have always feared omens and portents. At the monastery, some of the acolytes would play with crystals and seeds, casting them out and reading what they foretold. The priests tolerated it, more or less. A few were amused by it, saying we would learn better as we grew. At least one said we'd be better off playing with knives. My instincts led me to agree with him. All of us stand on the edge of the future; why venture off the precipice? I believe there are true oracles, who can peer ahead and see where one is destined to tread. But I also think that there is a danger in—"

"Not that," the ship said sharply. "I know nothing of that. I remember this place." A note of desperation crept into her voice. "I remember this place, but I know I've never been here. Wintrow. Is it your memory? Have you been here before?"

Wintrow spread his hands flat on the deck, opening himself to her. He tried to be comforting. "I have never been here, but Kennit has. You have become close with him. Perhaps it is his memories that are mingling with yours now."

"Blood is memory. His blood has soaked into me and I know his memory of being here. It is the memory of a man. But when last I was in these waters, I slipped through them, swift and sleek. I was new and young. I began here, Wintrow. I began here, not once, but many times."

She was troubled. He reached for her, and felt the swift shadows of memories so old she could not grasp them. They flitted away from her, soft-edged and elusive as the sunlight patterns under his eyelids. The glimpses he caught disturbed him. He knew them as well as she did. Wings against the sun. Sliding deep-water images framed in green light. These were the images of his deepest sleep, fever shapes too bright and hard to meet the light of day. He tried to mask his uneasiness. "How could you begin many times?" he asked her gently.

She pushed her glossy black hair back from her face and pressed her temples as if it would ease her. "It's all a circle. A circle that turns. Nothing stops, nothing is lost, and it all goes spiraling on. Like thread on a spool, Wintrow. Around and around it goes, layering on in circles, and yet it is always the same piece of thread." She shivered suddenly in the sun, hugging herself. "This is not a good place for us."

"We won't be here long. No more than the turning of one tide. It will be—"

"Wintrow! Time to go!" Etta's voice broke into his words.

He ran his hand along the wizardwood planking of the deck. "It will be all right," he assured her. He jumped swiftly to his feet and hurried off to join the others, unwinding his shirt from his head as he went. He dragged it on and tucked it in. Despite his reservations, his heart beat faster at the prospect of landing on Others Island.

KENNIT WATCHED WINTROW'S FACE AS HE PUSHED THE OAR. THE TRACES OF his pain were there to see—a pinch of white about his mouth, a sheen of sweat on his forehead—but the boy wasn't whining. Good. Etta sat on the bench next to Wintrow and manned an oar also. They kept pace with the other two rowers. Kennit sat in the bow, his back to the beach. He spared a glance for the *Vivacia*. He trusted her safety to her as much as the man he'd left in charge. Jola was the new mate. He'd given the man a direct command to defer to the ship's wisdom if they disagreed. It was a strange order, but he'd ignored the query on the man's face. In time, as Jola proved himself, perhaps Kennit would trust him more. Kennit had been sorry to let Brig go, but he had earned a ship of his own. Kennit had given him the ship they had managed to raise from the Divvytown harbor. An ample measure of coin went with it, and the order to obtain some lumber and hire some stonemasons for the tower. After that, Brig was to stop a few slaveships, and rebuild Divvytown's population. Most of Brig's new crew was from Divvytown; Kennit had chosen men and women with family in Divvytown, to be sure the ship would not be tempted to abandon their mission. He nodded to himself, pleased with how he had managed it all. His only unanticipated factor was Sorcor's new tie to the town. Alyssum had been pregnant by the time they had left. Sorcor already wanted to return as soon as they had finished at the Others Island. Kennit had had to remind him sternly that as a family man he had to earn a respectable living. He could scarcely return to Alyssum with empty pockets, could he? Especially as Sincure Faldin had not been in town when the slavers struck. Any day now, the man and his sons would return. Sorcor should be ready to show her father that he could provide well for his daughter. That had re-ignited the man's fervor for piracy with a fierceness Kennit had not expected, either. Truly, there was more to Sorcor than he had first suspected.

The bow of the boat grated against the black sand of the beach, snapping his mind back to the present. He looked about the somber little cove as the rowers jumped over the side and dragged the boat up onto the shore. Rocky walls and evergreens fenced the small beach. Little had changed here since his last visit. The green-scummed bones of some large animal were tangled in the rocks. The roots of one tree on the cliff above had given way; the dark evergreen now dangled tip-down to the sand. Seaweed was tangled in its dying branches. A narrow path climbed the cliff via a crack in the black wall of stone.

Kennit clambered from the boat to the shore. Squidgy seaweed bladders, blue mussels and white barnacles on the glistening black rocks made the footing treacherous for his crutch. He threw an arm across Etta's shoulders in mimicry of affection. "Etta and Wintrow will be coming with me. You two wait here for us." The rowers muttered uneasy agreement as Kennit surveyed the steep path without enthusiasm. He had a long hike ahead of him, over a stony trail. For a moment, he doubted the wisdom of his decision. Then his eyes met Wintrow's gaze. The youth was nervous, but anticipation danced in his eyes. For a sharp instant, Kennit felt that sense of connection again. Wintrow was so like himself as a lad. Sometimes he had felt that same rush of excitement, usually when they had sighted a particularly rich plum of a ship. An instant later, the faint smile on his face turned to a grimace of distaste. He rejected the memory. No. He had never truly shared anything with Igrot. After all the man had subjected him to, he felt nothing for his memory except disdain. "Let's go," he said so sharply that Wintrow jumped slightly. Kennit started up the narrow defile, leaning on Etta.

By the time they reached the crest of the first hill, Kennit's shirt was sweated to his chest. He had to stop to rest. It was the day, he told himself. It was warmer than it had been last time he was here. Under the trees, the heat became more oppressive despite their shade. The pebbly path that led through the Others' domain was as precisely kept as ever. The last time he had passed this way, the charm on his wrist had told him that there was a spell on this path, to keep travelers from straying. Now, as he glanced off into the green shadows of the verdant forest, he dismissed it as so much nonsense. Who would want to stray from a straight and level path to venture through such a leafy maze? He took out his kerchief and wiped his face and neck. When he looked around, he realized the other two were waiting for him.

He scowled at them. "Well? Are you ready? Let's go on." The gravel of the path shifted unpredictably under his crutch and his peg. The constant small struggle to correct his balance multiplied the distance for him as the path meandered down this hill and up the next. At the top of the second rise, when he stopped to catch his breath, he suddenly reached a conclusion.

"They don't want me here," he said aloud. The trees seemed to echo his words back in agreement. "The Others are making it hard for me, trying to turn me back. But I won't give up. Wintrow shall have his oracle." As he lifted his kerchief again, he caught sight of the charm strapped to his wrist. Its face was frozen in a clownish smile, the mouth ajar, the tongue lolling out. It mocked him. Deliberately he set his thumbnail to its brow and scraped it down, but as always, the iron-hard wood defied him. The face of the charm did not even flicker an eyelid. He lifted his glance to the other two, to find them watching him in consternation. Casually he brushed his thumb over the charm again, as if he had been flicking dirt from it.

He made a difficult decision. "Wintrow. Go ahead of us. I think it might be better for you to walk the Treasure Beach alone, undistracted by my presence. I might inadvertently prompt you to pick up something you were not destined to discover. I would not wish to taint the prophecy. Go along, now. Etta and I will be there for the Other's pronouncement. That is all that really matters. Go now."

Wintrow looked uncertain. He exchanged a glance with Etta, who gave a tiny shrug. Kennit felt his fury rising. "Do you question my order? Go!"

His roar sent the boy haring off down the path.

"Good." Kennit put satisfaction into the word. He shook his head after him. "Wintrow must learn two things from me: to obey, and to be able to act on his own." Once more, he set his crutch under his arm. "Follow me. Not too swiftly, for I wish Wintrow to have plenty of time alone on the beach. These things are not to be rushed."

"To be sure," Etta agreed. She glanced about the forest. "This is a strange place. Seldom have I seen such beauty. Yet it forbids itself to me." As if suddenly fearful, she moved to take his free arm. He shook his head to himself. Helpless females. He wondered why the charm had been so insistent that he bring her along. Not that he had consulted the charm about this venture; the damnable thing had insisted on offering its opinion, not once but repeatedly. "Take Etta, you must take Etta with you," it had exhorted. Now look at her. He would have to take care of her, he supposed.

"Come along," he told her firmly. "If you stay to the path, nothing will hurt you."

WINTROW RAN. NOT FROM ETTA AND KENNIT; HE FELT HALF A COWARD TO have abandoned them there. He ran from the forest itself, that cupped him like a trapped mouse in its palms. He ran from the overwhelmingly strange beauty of the threatening flowers and the poignant fragrances that both tempted and repulsed him. He fled even from the whispering of the leaves set to gossiping of his death by the hot breath of the wind. He ran, his heart pounding in his chest more from fear than exertion. He ran until the path spilled him out on a wide-open tableland. Before him was suddenly the blue arch of the sky over the open sea. A crescent beach spread out, framed at its tips by toothy cliffs. He halted, gasping for breath, wondering what he was supposed to do now.

Kennit had told him little. "It's simple. You walk the beach, you pick up whatever interests you, and at the end of the beach, an Other will greet you. He will ask of you the piece of gold. You give it to him; just put it on his tongue. Then he will tell you his prophecies for you." Kennit had lowered his voice to confide skeptically, "Some say there is an Oracle on the island. A priestess say some, a captive goddess say others. The legend is that she knows all the past, everything that has ever been. Knowing all that has gone before, she can predict the shape of the future. I doubt this to be true. I saw nothing of the kind when I was there. The Other will tell us what we need to know."

When he had tried to ask for more details, Kennit had become impatient. "Wintrow, stop dithering. When the time comes, you will know what to do. If I could tell you everything you would find and do on the island, we would not need to go there. You cannot always depend on others to live and think for you."

Wintrow had bowed his head and accepted the rebuke humbly.

Increasingly, Kennit said such things to him. Sometimes Wintrow felt the man was grooming him for something, but he was not sure what. Since Divvytown, he had accepted that there was far more to Kennit than he had ever suspected. He had followed at Kennit's heels all of one long afternoon, dragging a bag of stakes and a mallet. Kennit paced the distances, and jabbed a hole with his peg where he wanted each stake driven. Some described the edges of a road, others the corners of the houses. When they finished and looked back, Kennit seemed transfixed. Wintrow had stood beside him, trying to see what he saw. Kennit broke the silence. "Any fool can burn a town," he observed. "They say that Igrot the Bold burned a score of towns." He gave a snort of contempt. "I shall raise a hundred. I shall not be remembered with ashes."

Wintrow had accepted him then as a man of vision. And more. He was a tool of Sa.

He scanned the scene from left to right. Kennit had told him to walk the beach. Where was he supposed to start? Did it matter? With a shrug, he turned his face to the wind and began walking. The tide was still going out. Once he reached the tip of the beach's crescent, he'd turn and start his search. He would walk the whole beach seeking for his destiny.

The bright sun beat down on his head. He muttered at his stupidity in not bringing a bandana. He kept his eyes down on the beach as he walked, but saw nothing out of the ordinary. Tangles of skinny black seaweed, empty crab shells, wet feathers and bits of driftwood marked the limits of the tide's reach. If objects like this were to foretell his future, he did not think the prophecies would be earth-shaking.

Towards the tip of the crescent beach, the sand gave way to outcroppings of black rock. The tableland behind him had risen to the height of a ship's mast and showed its underpinnings of slate and shale. The tide had retreated fully, baring the normally covered black shelves. Their cracked and pitted surfaces cupped tidepools full of life. Such things had always beckoned Wintrow. He glanced back at the trail from the forest. There was still no sign of Kennit and Etta. He had a bit of time. He wandered out onto the rocks, stepping carefully. The seaweed underfoot was treacherously slick, and a fall would land him on barnacles, blue mussels and cone caps.

The isolated pools harbored anemones and seastars. Tiny crabs scuttled from oasis to oasis. A gull came down to join him in his inspection. He knelt briefly by one tidepool. Anemones of red and white bloomed in its shallows. A touch of his finger stirred the surface of the still water. In a flash, the delicate petals of the creature folded away from him. He smiled, rose and went on.

The sun was warm on his back; it eased the ache in his shoulder. There were no sounds save the wind, the water and the gulls. He had almost forgotten the simple pleasure of walking an isolated beach on a pleasant day. He did not realize he had rounded the headland until he glanced back. He could not see the beach anymore. A survey of the cliffs above him showed him that it would be death to be trapped here by an incoming tide. They rose black and sheer. Except . . . He stepped back farther from the bluff and squinted up. There was a fissure there, or perhaps something more. A narrow sloped trail led across the cliff's face. It was not very high, no more than the height of two men. Before he had truly considered the wisdom of it, he had started up it.

If it was a trail and not an accident of nature, whatever had made it was more sure-footed than he was. It was not wide enough for him to walk comfortably on it; he had to face the rock and edge up it. It ascended the face of the rock sharply. It shone underfoot with sparkly slime like a slug's dried track. One moment it seemed slippery, the next tacky. It suddenly seemed higher than it had from the beach; if he fell there were only rocks and barnacles to land on. Still, he had come this far, he would satisfy his curiosity. He came to a sudden indentation in the rock, the beginning of the chimney. He stepped inside and found his way blocked by bars of metal. He stepped close to peer past them.

A very narrow fissure in the rock extended all the way to the cliff top. Sunlight reached down timidly from an opening high above. Someone had chiseled and ground out a cave within it, not much larger than a coach. Inside the wrought cave, the rock floor sloped sharply away. Water from a high tide was trapped there in a dark still pool. He could see light reflected from its surface.

So what was the purpose of the bars? To keep people out, or to keep something in? He set his hands to one of the bars and tried to rattle it. It did not budge, but he could rotate it. It grated against the stone, and suddenly the surface of the pool erupted.

Wintrow stepped back so quickly he nearly fell over the edge. The pool was deeper than it looked to contain such a creature. Then, as it continued to regard him with immense gold eyes, he became bold enough to venture back to the bars. He clutched them in his hands and stared.

The sea serpent confined in the cave was stunted, its body marked with the limits of the pool. Its head was the size of a pony. Its body was so convoluted, he could not guess the length. It was a pale yellow-green, like a glowing fungus. Unlike the scaled sea serpents he had glimpsed from the deck of the *Vivacia*, this one looked plump and soft as an earthworm. Its body bore thick layers of callus where it had rubbed against the rocky walls of its prison. He suddenly realized that it must have grown to fill the pool. It had been captured and confined when small. He suddenly knew that this was the only world this creature had ever known. He glanced about himself. Yes. A high tide would just reach the lip of this fissure, bringing with it new salt water. And food? He didn't think so. Someone must bring it food.

It roiled in the confines of the pool, no more than a shifting of its tail from one side to the other. The effort corkscrewed its body. He watched with pity as it worked each segment of its serpentine body, trying to ease the twist on it. It could not, not completely. It stared at him expectantly.

"So you're used to being fed," he observed. "But why are you kept here? Are you a pet? A curiosity?"

The creature canted its head as if intrigued by his words. Then it dipped its immense brow down into the pool to wet it once more. The movement was an effort in the confined space. When it tried to lift its snout, its whole body kinked and bound. He watched it struggle, its length bulging up out of the water and scraping against stone smoothed by many such wedgings. It gave a cry like a raven's sharp caw, then suddenly snapped its head free again. Wintrow felt sickened. A fresh scrape showed on the side of its face. A thick greenish ichor oozed from it.

He set his hands once more to the bars. He could turn each in its socket, but they were set deep in stone both above and below. He could not budge them from their beds. He knelt at the base of them, to see how they had been fitted. He found the answer under his feet. He brushed away sand and sea detritus, to find the fine seams of worked stone. Above him, the sockets for the bars had been painstakingly drilled into the stone. A slight discoloration at the edge of one suggested it might have been a slot cut in the stone, one that had been filled in to the shape of the bar afterward. He visualized it to himself. The long bars would have been brought in, inserted at a sharp angle into the deep holes above and swung into place. The stones that secured them at the base had then been set. An examination of the seams proved him correct. He tried lifting each bar in place. Each had some play, some more than others. Yes. Now that he knew how it had been done, could he undo it?

The Treasure Beach and Kennit forgotten, he knelt on the floor in the alcove. He brushed sand and detritus away with his hands, then took off his shirt and cleaned the floor down to stone. The fine knife that Etta had given him became a tool for cleaning the sand and tired mortar from the fine cracks where the stones were joined. As he worked painstakingly, the creature watched him. From its interest, it almost seemed to know that its freedom was at stake. He gauged its girth against the spacing of the bars. At least three of them would have to come out, he guessed, and possibly four.

The mortar was old and crumbly. If the mortar was his only enemy, he would have won easily. But the blocks themselves had been cut and fitted with the precision of a master. He worked until his calloused hands broke new blisters. His knees ached from kneeling on the stone. He leaned close to the seam and blew sand and mortar out of his way. He tried his fingers in the crack. They would just slip inside. If he could get a grip, would he have the strength to lift the stone? He pulled with all his strength, and thought he felt the block slide fractionally. He took up his knife and went back to work while the serpent watched him with spinning golden eyes. His injured shoulder began to ache.

ETTA WAS BATHED IN SWEAT BEFORE THEY GOT TO THE BEACH. BY TAKING his arm, she was able to help Kennit along without being too obvious about it. Sometimes she looked at what fate had done to the man and she wanted to shriek in fury. And loss. The tall, strong body that had once intimidated her was taking on a cripple's twist as muscles on one side of his body compensated for the loss of his leg. She saw how he planned what he would or would not do, all with an eye to keep from disgracing himself with any show of weakness. His tigerish spirit had not dwindled; his ambitions had not lessened. She only feared that the heat of the fires that drove him might consume his weakened body.

"Where is he?" the pirate demanded. "I don't see Wintrow."

She shaded her eyes and looked up and down the beach. "I don't see him either," she said uneasily.

The curved shoreline was black sand and rock backed by the table-land. There was nothing large enough to conceal him. Where could he be? She blinked her eyes against the glare of sun on the water. "Could he have walked the beach already? Would the Others have met him and taken him somewhere?"

"I don't know," Kennit growled. He lifted his arm and pointed to the far end of the beach, where a separate finger of land separated itself from the shore. "Down there is the alcove cliff, where all the treasures are kept on display. If he walked the beach and met an Other, it might take him there, to deposit whatever he had found. Damn! I should have been here with him. I wanted to hear what the creature would say to him."

She thought he would blame her then, accuse her of dawdling on the path or otherwise delaying him. Instead, he settled his crutch under his arm and nodded at the alcove rock. "Help me get there," he growled.

She surveyed the loose dry sand and the stretches of uneven black rockface that made up the beach and her heart sank. The tide was at full ebb now. Soon it would turn and gradually cover the beach once more. The men at the boat expected them to return by high tide. It would make more sense for her to run ahead and see if Wintrow was there first, instead of forcing Kennit to lurch the length of the beach. She nearly spoke out. Then she straightened her spine and took Kennit's arm. He knew all those things as well as she did. He had said to help him get there. She would.

THE BACKS OF HIS HANDS WERE SCRAPED AND BLEEDING AND HIS ARM WAS throbbing by the time he lifted the first block from its bed. It had been heavier than he expected, but the tight fit had been the biggest obstacle. He braced his hands against the floor as he sat by the block, and then used both his feet to shove it out of the way. The base of one bar was now exposed. He stood up, arched his aching back and then gripped the bar in both hands. He lifted it. It grated against the stone as he raised it, and the serpent in the pool suddenly lashed its tail in excitement.

"Don't get your hopes up yet," Wintrow grunted. The bar of metal was heavier than he had expected. The higher he lifted it, the longer it seemed to be. He braced his shoulder against it, took a fresh grip and lifted again. He suddenly saw the end of the bar. He pulled it at an angle, and was rewarded with a shower of old mortar from above. He lost his grip on the bar, but it did not slide back into the hole. It fell with a heavy thud to the stone. He caught his breath, took another grip on the shaft and dragged the loose end of it toward the cave's entrance. It came slowly, screaming in protest as the metal scraped and dragged against the stone. When the top finally came free, it overbalanced him. He lost his footing and fell, while the length of metal clashed to the stone with a ringing like a hammer on an anvil. It echoed in the small cave.

Wintrow stood up. "Well. That's one," he told the serpent.

Transparent lids briefly covered the great gold eyes. It lifted its head from the water and shook it. A fleshy starburst suddenly bloomed around its throat. When it twisted in the water, he now saw that a faint pattern ran the length of its body. The variation in color reminded him of the eyes on a peacock's tail. He abruptly wondered if the display meant it was angry. Perhaps it felt threatened by what he did. The poor creature had probably been confined here all its life. Maybe it thought he threatened its lair.

"Next time the water rises, you'll be able to go free. If you want to." He spoke the words aloud, knowing they were just noises to it. It probably couldn't even interpret the reassuring tone of his voice. He knelt and went to work on the next block.

This one went much faster. The mortar had long ago weakened into clumps of sand. He had the empty space vacated by the other block; it gave him room to wiggle this one. He sheathed his knife and took a grip on the block. He did not even have to lift it all the way out of the hole. Once he had pushed it to one side, he went to work on the bar. This second one was looser than the first, and he had the knack of it now. As the metal shrieked against the stone and mortar rained down once more, it suddenly came to Wintrow that perhaps someone would be angry at what he had done. Perhaps all this noise would attract their attention.

As the pole clattered to the stone, Wintrow jumped aside to avoid it. Then he went to the mouth of the fissure and peered out. There was no one in sight. But another threat was immediately visible. The tide had turned and was creeping back in over the stones. There were storm clouds on the horizon. The wind seemed to be blowing the tide in with its force. Bladderwort that had lain flat on the rock now swayed with the incoming water. The rising tide could trap him here. Even if it did not, there were other matters to consider: the Treasure Beach, the Oracle and the boat that was expecting them to return by high tide.

Kennit was probably furious with him.

He stood, cradling his sore arm, and watched the tide spilling up over the slope of the beach. It was coming fast. He had no control at all over that one factor. If he stayed, he was going to be trapped here. As it was, he was going to get wet wading around the headland.

He'd have to leave. He'd done all he could.

He heard a sound from within the fissure, a metal bar rolling on stone. Frowning, he stepped back within, and then gasped at what he saw.

It had heaved itself out of the pool and flung itself at the walls of its prison. Its head, turned sideways, was wedged in the opening he had created. Its dwarfed and twisted body was still powerful as it lashed and thrust against the confines of the pool. "No, go back!" he cried futilely. "It's too small! There's no water yet!"

It could not understand him. The animal lunged again against the bars, but only succeeded in wedging itself more tightly. It screamed its frustration, the starburst around its neck standing out as it raged. It tried to jerk its head back through the bars, but could not. It was stuck.

With a sinking heart, he realized he was stuck as well. Wintrow could not leave it like that. Its gills worked as frantically as its gasping jaws. He did not know how long it could survive with its head out of the water. There was already an air of desperation to the lashing tail. If he could just loosen one more bar, perhaps it could slip back into the pool. It wouldn't be free, but it wouldn't be dead.

If he hurried, he might live, too.

He approached it gingerly to see which bar would be best to work on. Its wedged struggles had actually loosened one of the blocks. It had also coated it with slime. That wasn't going to make lifting it any easier. He took up one of the bars he had worked loose. It was horribly long, but at least he wouldn't have to touch it. Any trapped animal might bite, and if one that size bit, not much would be left of him.

He shoved the freed bar between two of the remaining bars and used it as a lever. Unfortunately, this meant pushing the bar even tighter against the creature. It roared, but surprisingly it did not strike at him. The block of stone that secured the bar at the base grated against its fellows as it shifted. Wintrow immediately repositioned his lever in the widened crack between the blocks. The pole was too damn long. It jammed against the walls of the fissure. But finally it worked, shoving the stone over a bit. Now for the bar.

"Don't hurt me!" he cautioned the creature as he approached it, and for a wonder it seemed to understand his intention if not his words. It stilled, gills working heavily. Or perhaps it was simply collapsing as it died. He couldn't think about that, nor about the passing time. He seized the bar in his hands and lifted it up.

He screamed.

His hands burned and froze to the slime-coated metal. But the agony on his skin was as nothing compared to the agony of knowing. He knew her pain, and he grasped suddenly the torment of a sentient creature imprisoned for time past his ability to imagine. With her, he breathed the scalding air. His tender skin cracked and stung in the dryness, while he knew with terror that soon it would be too late. She must escape now, or it would soon be too late for all of them.

He convulsed away from the bar. The strength of his body's rejection of the pain flung him to the floor of the prison. He lay there panting. Nothing in his life had ever prepared him for that blast of sharing. Even the bond he had with the liveship was a clumsy and insensitive bridge compared to that joining. For a brief moment, he had been unable to distinguish between himself and the creature.

No. Not creature, not unless he too was to be considered a creature.

She was no less than he was; as he considered all he had experienced, he wondered if she was more.

An instant later, he was on his feet. He tore his shirt off, wrapped it about his hands and approached the bar again. This time he had to recognize the intelligence that was fading in the great gold eyes. He seized the bar in his muffled grip and lifted. It was difficult, for whatever coated the bar made it slippery. He heaved up on it twice before he lifted it from its deep bed in the stone. The moment it had cleared the lip of the block, the sea serpent surged against it. Her greater bulk pushed it aside as if it were a straw. Wintrow went with it, not only flung forcefully aside by her passage but also brushed with the slick coating of her scaled hide. It seared him where it touched his flesh. He cried out as he saw even his heavy canvas trousers fraying away like crumbling ashes. He knew her determined intent. It appalled him.

"No water below!" He conveyed the information with voice and thought as forcefully as he was able. "Rocks. Only rocks. You'll die."

Death is preferable.

She undulated past him, length after coiled length of her spilling out of the imprisoning pool like thread unwinding from a spool. As she passed, he was aware of the tremendous effort it took for her to move her cramped and distorted body. This was an act of desperation. She was not sure if she fled to freedom or death. But she knew she left captivity behind.

Yes. Sorry to have killed you.

"It's all right," he muttered. He was not even sure if he was dead. He was outside himself. No. Bigger than himself. It was like the trances at the monastery, when he worked his stained glass, but bigger, much bigger. The pain of his scalded flesh was no more significant than an annoying splinter in the heel. *Ah*, he sighed. *Now I see you clearly. You were there all along. The serpents and the dragons in my windows, in all my art. How did you know I'd come to you?*

How did you know to come to me? She wondered in reply.

But she did not wait for an answer. She spilled out of the fissure. He braced, unwilling to hear the impact of her heavy body on the rocks below. But her very size saved her that. Her length reached from the floor of the cave to the beach below. She lowered her fore-section until it met the beach, and then drew the rest of her body down after herself in undulations like an inchworm. Strange. He was no longer touching her but was still aware of her. The hot sun shone down on her. Sand clung to her. She rolled helplessly on the barnacle-coated rocks. The last of her strength was spent. She needed the water to take up her weight; she needed to moisten her gills. The incoming tide just kissed against her belly. It wasn't enough. She had striven so hard, just to die on the beach. So hard a battle, only to become food for crabs and seagulls.

Something was happening to Wintrow. His entire body was reacting now. His eyes were puffing shut, while his breath whistled in and out of his thickened throat. His eyes and nose streamed, his skin felt stripped. Yet he was standing, and staggering to the edge of the fissure. His useless tattered shirt still wrapped one of his hands. He could see the green-gold body of the serpent on the beach below him. He could feel her baking in the heat. He would go down to her.

The narrow path defied him. On his third edging step, he simply fell backwards off the cliff-face. He landed on the serpent's yielding body. She broke his fall, but it was all the comfort of falling into a sizzling frying pan. He shrieked in pain. Too much, she was too much to know, and whatever coated her skin was eating his away. He rolled away from her, to land on barnacle-crusted rocks. A wave rushed in, licked tentatively at his face and rushed away. The cool of the water was a blessing, the salt a stinging curse against his raw flesh.

The Plenty.

All the longing of an immortal heart was encapsulated in that single word. His shirt was still wrapped about his out-flung arm. The ragged fabric was heavy with seawater. He gathered it to his chest and crawled to her. The world was so dim, yet the afternoon sun still beat hot on him. Or was it hot on her? He managed to shake out the remnants of his wet shirt. He flung it over one of her gills. It covered such a small part of her head.

It eases me, nonetheless. We all thank you.

"We?" He mouthed the word, but did not think that was how she shared his thought.

My kind. I am the last who can save them. I am She Who Remembers. Even now, it may be too late. But if I am not too late, and I can save them, we will remember you. Always. Take comfort in that, creature of a few breaths.

"Wintrow. My name is Wintrow."

The next wave reached them, lapping a trifle higher. She thrashed feebly in its touch and managed to heave herself a bit closer to the water. It was not enough. Selfishly he wondered if he could roll far enough away from her to stop sharing her pain. His own was quite enough. Then it all seemed like far too much trouble. He lay still and waited for the next wave to lift him so he could swim away to join his kind.

AT THE FIRST SCREAM, KENNIT HALTED IN HIS TRACKS. "WHAT IS THAT?" HE demanded.

The sound had echoed oddly. "I don't know," Etta had replied uneasily. She glanced wide-eyed around them. She suddenly felt very small and exposed. The path and the sheltering forest had been left far behind them. Here was only open sand and rock, glaring sun and the endless water. On the horizon, she glimpsed black clouds. The wind blew stronger, with a promise of rain in it. She was not sure what she feared, but knew there was nowhere to hide from it. She could see nothing threatening; the scream seemed sourceless. An ominous silence followed it.

"What should we do?" Etta asked.

Kennit's pale eyes skimmed the beach in all directions, then glanced up to the tableland behind them. He, too, saw nothing. "Continue to the alcove rock," he began, and then halted.

Etta followed the direction of his eyes. The creature she beheld had not been there a moment before. She was sure of it. There was nowhere it could have concealed itself, and yet now suddenly it was there. The erect part of it was as tall as Kennit, and a heavier sluglike body trailed behind it. As she stared at it, it flung out flexible limbs from its upper body. They were impossibly graceful, bonelessly unfolding, with outstretched long-fingered hands at the end. The fingers were webbed. Its body was gray-green and gleamed damply where it was not covered by a pale yellow cloak. Its flat eyes glared at them menacingly. "Go back!" it warned them. "Go away! She is ours!" The hissing, thrumming voice was thick with menace. Even the smell of the creature was frightening, though she could not think why. She only knew she wanted to get as far away from it as possible. It was too foreign. Too Other. She seized Kennit's arm. "Let's get away from here," she pleaded, tugging at his arm.

It was like tugging at a statue. He set his muscles and resisted her. "No. Stand still, Etta. Listen to me. It's a magic, a glamour he has cast at us. He suggests your fear to you. Do not give way to it. He is not so frightening." With a small, superior smile, he tapped the charm at his wrist. "I am impervious to it. Trust me."

She tried to listen to his words but could not. The wind brought the creature's stench to her, a smell she instinctively recognized. Dead and rotting human. It revulsed her, as did the pressure of that flat-eyed stare. She wanted to cover herself, to be out of reach of those eyes. "Please," she begged Kennit, but he had locked gazes with the Other. He shook off her grip with a strength that surprised her. He had forgotten her. She could run, if she wished.

She did not know where she got the strength to stand still and watch. Kennit baited the Other with a courage she found unthinkable. Crutch tucked under his arm, he first stepped toward it. It raised itself higher, spreading its wormy limbs. She could see the webbing between its long fingers. "Go back!" it warned him.

Kennit only smiled and shrugged his shoulders. "This way," he told her and led her toward the trailhead for the forest path. Relief flooded her. They were leaving. As he trudged toward the path through the shifting sand, she slunk along at his side. Kennit kept glancing back over his shoulder at the creature. She did not blame him, but she could not bear to look at it. Etta caught the edge of his sleeve and he allowed her to cling to him as he stumped along.

He suddenly halted and turned to her, grinning. "There. Now we know. And we will beat the Other to it."

She glanced fearfully over her shoulder. The creature was undulating rapidly over the sand, yet for all its effort, it seemed to move slowly. Again, the wave of terror shook her as the smell of the creature overwhelmed her. She could not still her shaking.

"Stop being afraid," Kennit commanded her uselessly. "See how it hastens down the beach, as soon as it thinks we are fleeing. Whatever it seeks to protect is down that way. Come. Help me go as swiftly as we can."

She closed her eyes in an agony of terror. "Kennit, please. It will kill us."

"Etta!" He took her upper arm in a grip like a vise and shook her. "Do as I say. I will protect you. Now come."

He positioned his crutch once more under his arm and then took off down the beach. He moved like a long-legged creature, swinging on his crutch as he almost ran. Stone and sand shifted under him, but he compensated. From behind them came a cry of outrage from the Other. When it was echoed, Etta glanced back fearfully. There were more Others. They seemed to rear out of the very earth or ooze up from the sand. She ran like the wind after Kennit. She stumbled once, her hands skidding on rocks and sand. She scrabbled to her feet, her palms stinging and her boots full of pebbles. She ran.

She caught up with Kennit just as they heard the second scream. Kennit blanched suddenly. "That's Wintrow!" he gasped. "I know it is. Wintrow! We're coming, boy, we're coming." Incredibly, he increased his pace. She loped at his side. The Other flowed after them, humping their bodies along as if they were walruses. Some carried short trident-headed spears.

Her mouth was dry and heart hammering when they reached the end of the beach. There was nothing to be seen, save the rocky headland rising before them. Kennit glanced from left to right, searching for a trail, or some sign. He threw his head back, and drew a deep breath. "Wintrow!" he bellowed.

There was no reply. He looked back at the oncoming wave of creatures. The wind off the water had increased, and the first warm raindrops spattered against the sand. "Kennit," she panted desperately. "The tide is coming in. The boat will be expecting us. Perhaps Wintrow went back there, to the boat."

Then they heard a shriek of pain.

Etta froze but Kennit did not hesitate. The pirate waded out into the incoming water, crutch and all. She was not even sure that was the direction the sound had come from. In the rising wind, it was hard to be sure. Still, she followed him. Salt water joined the rocks and sand in her boots. She glanced fearfully back. The Others were still coming. The sight of them paralyzed her with fear. Then with a sudden howl, wind and rain struck her. The brightness of the day vanished. All was dim and gray as she stumbled through the waves after Kennit. She clutched at his sleeve, as much for her guidance as to help him stand against each wave.

"Where are we going?" she shouted through the summer squall.

"Don't know. Around the headland!" The sheeting rain had drenched his black hair to his shoulders and molded it to his skull. Rain dripped from his long mustache. He swayed as each wave washed past him.

"Why?"

He did not answer her. He just forged on and she went with him, clinging to his sleeve. The rain was beginning to lose the warmth of the summer day and the waves were cold. She tried to think only of what they were doing, and not worry about the boat on the other side of the island. They would not leave them here. They would not.

Kennit gave a sudden shout and pointed. "There! He's there!"

Around the headland was a short rocky beach backed by black slate cliffs. Wintrow's body rose and fell with the waves that washed past him. Next to him was an immense greenish-yellow thing. From the way it wallowed back and forth in the water, it was alive. Suddenly it lifted a huge head, and her eyes resolved the contorted shape. It was a stranded sea serpent. Immense gold eyes swirled at her. Another wave washed past them, almost lifting its body. It ducked its head under the seawater and then lifted it again. Then it slowly reared its head higher and shook it. Suddenly a great fleshy mane stood out around its throat. It opened a huge red mouth lined with long white teeth and roared against the wind and the rain.

"Wintrow!" Kennit bellowed again.

"He's dead," Etta shouted to him. "He's dead, my love, killed by the serpent. It's no use. Let's go while we can."

"He's not dead. He moved." There was so much frustration in his voice, he sounded almost grief-stricken.

"A trick of the waves." She pulled gently at his arms. "We have to go. The ship."

"Wintrow!"

This time the lifting of the boy's head could not be mistaken. His features were scarcely recognizable, he was so battered. His swollen mouth moved. "Kennit," he moaned.

She thought it was a cry for help. Then the boy dragged in a breath and cried out, "Behind you. The Abominations!"

A web-fingered hand wrapped bonelessly around her thigh. Etta screamed. Her heart hammered and her ears roared as she spun to face it. Flat fish eyes stared at her from their frontal setting in a blunt bald head. It gaped its mouth open at her, the lower jaw dropping, opening wide enough to engulf a man's head.

She never saw Kennit draw his blade. She only saw the knife slice through the elastic flesh. The limb stretched before it parted. The Other belched a roaring protest. It gripped at its severed stump. Kennit reached down swiftly and unwrapped the clinging hand from her thigh. He flung it back at the Other. "Do not let them scare you to death!" he bellowed at her. "Pull your knife, woman! Have you forgotten who you are?" He turned from her in disdain to meet the next one.

The question snapped something in her, or perhaps it was the feel of her knife's hilt in her hand. She pulled it free of its sheath and then lifted her head to shriek her defiance at these creatures that strove to ensorcel her. She slashed at an Other, scoring its rubbery flesh in passing. It ignored her, flowing through the water with a grace it had lacked on land. Kennit had finished the one that had grabbed at her, but no others attacked her. They were avoiding them to fan out and encircle the stranded serpent and Wintrow.

"Ours!"

"She is our goddess!"

"You cannot steal our Oracle!"

"What is found on the Treasure Beach must always remain!"

The Others belched their words out like the croaking of frogs. They surrounded the serpent. Some lifted menacingly the short jabbing spears they carried. What did they think to do? Slay the serpent? Herd it somewhere?

Whatever they intended, Wintrow was bent on opposing them. He had dragged himself to his feet, but how he could stand, Etta did not see. His body was swollen like a sea-claimed corpse. His eyes were slits beneath an overhang of puffy brow. But he opposed the waves to slog around the serpent and stand between her and her tormentors.

He raised his voice. "Abominations! Stand back. Let She Who Remembers go free, to fulfill her destiny."

His words rang oddly, as if he spoke by rote in a language he did not know. A wave nearly knocked him down. The lift of it raised the serpent's bulk. Her coiling tail found purchase. She slid a short distance toward the sea. A few more waves, and she would free herself and be gone.

The Others seemed to realize it as well. They surged forward, jabbing at her to urge her shoreward. One closed with Wintrow as well. The boy's puffy hand groped at his waist and found his knife. He drew it out and tried to assume a fighter's crouch. That simple act, taught to him by her, cut her to the heart. Her own knife was naked in her hand, and she stood there, idle, while he died? Never. She sprang forward with a sudden shriek. She sloshed wildly through the water, and when she got close, plunged her knife into the creature's sluglike hindquarters. It bounced off the squamous flesh. It had no weapon, but it did not hesitate to attack. Wintrow got in one good cut before the Other seized his knife hand by the wrist. The boy abruptly stood stock-still. Etta could guess the terror that sank to his heart at its touch.

Her second jab cut deep, and she gripped the hilt with both hands and dragged on the blade, opening the Other up. It didn't bleed. She wasn't even sure it felt anything. She stabbed it again, higher. Kennit was suddenly at her side, slashing at the hand that gripped Wintrow. The Other sidled away from them, dragging Wintrow with it.

Then the serpent's head arched down from above them. Her jaws seized the Other, engulfing his head and hunched shoulders. She lifted the creature from the water and then flung it disdainfully aside. Wintrow stumbled, thrown off balance by the struggle. Kennit immediately seized his arm. "I have him. Let's go!"

"She must escape. Don't let them trap her. She Who Remembers must go to her kind!"

"If you mean the serpent, she'll do whatever she pleases, with no need of help from us. Come on, boy. The tide is coming in."

Etta took Wintrow's other arm. The boy was near blind with the swelling, and his face was discolored in shades of red. Like a crippled caterpillar, the three lurched toward the headland through the driving rain. The waves had gained strength now, and the water never fell lower than their knees. The surge of the sea rattled the stones and sucked the sand from beneath their feet as they struggled on. She did not know how Kennit kept his footing, but he clung to both Wintrow and his crutch and struggled gamely on. The headland jutted out from the shore. They would have to go deeper yet if they expected to circle it and get back to the beach. She refused to think of the long hike across the island, to a boat that might not be there anymore.

She glanced back only once. The serpent was free now, but she had not fled. Instead, one by one, she was seizing the Others in her jaws. Some she threw as broken wholes, others fell from her jaws sheared in half. Beside Etta, over and over, Wintrow uttered a single word with obsessive hatred. "Abomination! Abomination!"

A larger wave hit them. Etta lost the sand under her feet for an instant, then found herself stumbling as the wave passed. She clung to Wintrow, trying not to fall. Just as she was recovering her feet, another wave took them all. She heard Kennit's yell, then she was holding frantically to Wintrow's arm as she went under. The water that flooded her nose and mouth was thick with sand. She came up gasping and treading water. She blinked sandy water from her eyes. She saw Kennit's crutch float past her. Instinctively she snatched at it. Kennit was on the other end. He came hand over hand toward her, and then gripped her arm hard. "Make for the shore!" he commanded them, but she was disoriented. She flung her head around wildly, but saw only the sheer black cliffs, the foaming water at the base of them and a few chunks of floating Other. The serpent was gone, the beach was gone. They would either be pounded against the rocks, or pulled out to sea and drowned. She clung desperately to Kennit. Wintrow was little more than a dead weight she towed. He struggled faintly in the water.

"Vivacia," Kennit said beside her.

A wave lifted them higher. She saw the crescent beach. How had they come to be so far from it, so fast? "That way!" she cried. She felt trapped between the two of them. She leaned toward the shore and kicked frantically, but the waves drew them inexorably away. "We'll never make it!" she cried out in frustration. A wave struck her face, and for a moment, she gasped for air. When she could see again, she faced the beach. "That way, Kennit! That way! There is the shore!"

"No," he corrected her. There was incredulous joy in his face. "That way. The ship is that way. Vivacia! Here! We are here!"

Wearily Etta turned her head. The liveship came driving toward them through the pouring rain. She could already see the hands on the deck struggling to get a boat into the water. "They'll never get to us," she despaired.

"Trust the luck, my dear. Trust the luck!" Kennit rebuked her. With his free hand, he began to paddle determinedly toward the ship.

HE WAS DIMLY AWARE OF HIS RESCUE. IT ANNOYED HIM TREMENDOUSLY. HE was so alive, so full of memory and sensory recall, he just wished to be still and absorb it. Instead, they kept clutching at him. The woman kept shaking him and shrilling at him to stay awake, stay awake. There was a man's voice. He kept yelling at the woman to keep his face up, keep his face out of the water, he's drowning, can't you see? Wintrow wished they would both shut up and leave him alone.

He remembered so much. He remembered his destiny, as well as recalling all the lives he had led before this one. Suddenly it was all so clear. He had been hatched to be the repository of all memory for all serpents. He would contain them until such time as each was ready to come to him, and with a touch renew their rightful heritage. He would be the one to guide them home, to the place far up the river where they would find both safety and the special soil from which to create their cases. There would be guides awaiting them at the river, to protect them on their journey upriver and to stand watch over them as they awaited their metamorphosis. It had been so long, but he was free now, and all would be well.

"Get Wintrow in first. He's unconscious."

That was the man's voice, exhausted but still commanding. A new voice shouted, "Sa's breath! There's a serpent! Right under them, get them aboard, quick, quick!"

"It brushed him. Get the boy in, quick!"

A confusion of movement, and then pain. His body had forgotten how to bend; it was too swollen. They bent him anyway, seizing him tightly by his limbs as they pulled him from the Plenty into the Lack. They dropped him onto something hard and uneven. He lay gasping, hoping his gills would not dry out before he could escape.

"What is that stuff on him? It stung my hands!"

"Wash him off. Get that stuff off him," someone advised some-one else.

"Let's get him to the ship first."

"I don't think he'll last that long. At least get it off his face."

Someone scrubbed at his face. It hurt. He opened his jaws and tried to roar at them. He willed toxins, but his mane would not stand. It was too painful. He slipped back from this life, into the previous one.

He spread his wings wide and soared. Scarlet wings, blue sky. Below, green fields, fat white sheep to feed on. In the distance, the shining towers of a city gleamed. He could hunt, or he could go to the city and be fed. Above the city, a funnel of dragons circled like bright fish caught in a whirlpool. He could join them. The people of the city would turn out to greet him, singing songs, so pleased he had honored them with a visit. Such simple creatures, living scarcely for more than a few breaths. Which pleasure was more tempting? He could not decide. He hovered, catching the wind under his wings and sliding up the sky.

"Wintrow. Wintrow. Wintrow."

A man's voice, beating against his dream and breaking it into pieces. He stirred reluctantly.

"Wintrow. He hears us, he moved. Wintrow!" The woman added her voice to the man's.

That most ancient of magics, the binding of a man by the use of his name, gripped him. He was Wintrow Vestrit, merely a human, and he hurt, he hurt so badly. Someone touched him, making the pain sharper. He could not escape them now.

"Can you hear me, boy? We're nearly to the ship. Soon we can ease the pain. Stay awake. Don't give up."

The ship. Vivacia. He recoiled in sudden horror. If the Others were Abomination, what was she? He drew in a breath. It was hard to take in air, and harder to push it out as words. "No," he moaned. "No."

"We'll be on Vivacia soon. She'll help you."

He could not speak. His tongue was too swollen in his mouth. He could not beg them not to return him to the ship. A part of him still loved her, despite knowing what she was. How could he bear it? Could he keep what he knew from her? For so long, she had believed she was truly alive. He must not let her know that she was dead.

THE SEA HAD NEVER OPPOSED THEM AS IT DID NOW. ETTA CROUCHED IN the stern with Wintrow's sodden body in her arms. The four sailors on the oars fought them. The whites showed all around their eyes as they struggled. There seemed to be one current for *Vivacia* to contend with, and another that gripped the small boat and tugged at it like a dog with a bone. The rain lashed down and the wind added its push to the water's pull. Kennit huddled in the bow. His crutch had been lost when they hauled him from the water. Etta could scarcely see him for the rain that sheeted down between them. Kennit's hair was sleeked to his skull and his mustache had straightened completely in the wet. In one breathless break in the rain, Etta thought she glimpsed the *Marietta* far offshore. Her sails hung limp from her spars and sunlight glinted off her decks. In the next breath, Etta blinked the rain from her lashes. She told herself that what she had seen was impossible.

Wintrow was a heavy weight atop her legs. If she bent her head over his face, she could hear breath hiss in and out of him. "Wintrow. Wintrow, keep breathing. Keep breathing." If she had come upon his body anywhere else, she would not have known him. His fat, shapeless lips moved vaguely, but if he spoke it was without sound.

She lifted her eyes. She could not bear to look at him. Kennit had come into her life and taught her how to be loved. He had given her Wintrow, and she had learned to be a friend. Now the damn serpent was going to steal that from her, just as she had discovered it. Her salt tears blended with the rain running down her face. She could not bear it. Had she learned to feel again, only to have to feel this? Could any amount of love ever be worth the pain of losing it? She could not even hold him as he died, for the slime still on him ate into her clothes and the abrasion of her touch wiped away his skin. She cradled him as loosely as she could, while the ship's boat rocked and reared wildly and never seemed to get any closer to the *Vivacia*.

She lifted her face and peered through the storm. She found Kennit staring at her. "Don't let him die!" he commanded her loudly.

She felt impotent. She could not even tell him how helpless she felt. She saw him crouch and thought he would crawl through the boat to help her somehow. Instead he suddenly stood, peg and foot braced. He turned his back on her and the rowers and faced into the storm that opposed them. He threw back his head to it. The wind flapped his white shirt-sleeves against his arms and streamed his black, black hair out behind him.

"NO!" he roared into it. "Not now! Not when I am so close! You can't have me and you can't have my ship! By Sa, by El, by Eda, by the God of Fishes, by every god nameless and not, I swear you shall not have me nor mine!" He held out his hands, his fingers like claws, as if he would grapple with the wind that defied them.

"KENNIT!"

Vivacia's voice roared through the storm. She reached for them with wooden arms, leaning toward the small vessel as if she would tear herself loose from the ship to come to him. Her hair streamed away from her face. A wave hit her, and she took it deep enough to send green water streaming across her deck. But she rose from it, and as she came up from the trough, her hands still reached. The storm she battled threatened to sweep her away, and yet she yearned toward him, mindless of her own safety.

"I shall live!" Kennit bellowed suddenly into the storm. "I demand it." His one hand gripped his other wrist as he pointed into the storm. "I COMMAND IT!" he roared.

The king worked his first miracle.

From the depths of the very sea that opposed him, the creature rose to his command. The serpent rose at the stern of the vessel. She opened wide her jaws and added her roar to his. Etta shrank down, small, foolish creature that she was, clutching Wintrow to her breast. She groped for a knife long lost even as she wailed out her hopeless terror.

Then the sea serpent, vast beast though she was, bent her head to Kennit's will. She made deep obeisance to him as he stood in the bow, defying the storm. He turned toward her at the sailor's voices. Face white and taut, he pointed at her wordlessly. His mouth was open, but either he said nothing to the creature, or the wind blew his words away. Later, the rowers would tell the rest of the crew that however it was he commanded her, it was not for human ears to hear. She set her broad serpent's brow to the stern of the boat and pushed. Suddenly, the small boat was cutting through the water toward the *Vivacia*. Kennit, exhausted by this display of power, sank suddenly down to his seat in the bow. Etta dared not look at him. His face shone with something, an emotion that perhaps only the god-touched could feel.

Behind her, the stern of the small boat steamed and stank where the serpent's slime touched it. It would have been faithless of her to be afraid of what it did, for it acted on Kennit's command. She bent forward over Wintrow's body, holding him as tenderly as she could, as the creature shoved them through the waves. She had no mercy on the tiny vessel, but forced it through the waves that opposed them. The rowers abandoned their oars and huddled in the bottom of the boat, wordless with terror and awe.

The *Vivacia* plunged doggedly toward them. There was a moment when two oceans seemed to collide in turmoil. There was no pattern to wave nor winds. The breath of the world lashed them, threatening to snatch the clothes from their bodies, and the hair from their heads. Etta felt deafened by the onslaught, but the serpent inexorably pushed the tiny boat on.

Then they were suddenly in the same wind and the same current as Vivacia. Joyously both sea and air caught at them, and conspired with the serpent to bring them together. The wind and current that *Vivacia* opposed swept their small boat toward her reaching arms. Vivacia took a wave hard. The sailors that waited at the bow of the ship, lines ready for throwing, clung madly to her railings instead to keep from being swept away by green water.

But as Vivacia came up from the wave that had swamped her briefly, her great arms cupped and held the helpless boat. She rose from the wave with it clasped to her. Etta had never been so close to the figurehead. As she bore them up out of the deep, her voice boomed out over them. "Thank you, thank you! A thousand blessings upon you, sister of the sea. Thank you!" Silver tears of joy streamed down the liveship's carved face and fell like jewels into the water.

As the frightened sailors scrabbled toward their fellows on deck, Kennit sat roaring with joyous laughter in the bow of the boat. If there was an echo of madness in his mirth, that was the least fearsome thing about him now. For as his crewmen reached down to lay hands on him and haul him on board, the great green and gold serpent rose from the storming depths and gazed upon him. Etta felt gripped by that whirling gold stare. She looked into the depths of the creature's eyes and almost knew . . . something.

Then the creature roared one final time and sank back into the suddenly calming depths.

The small boat was going to pieces around them, the planks twisting away from their fellows as the stern gave way. Etta felt herself and Wintrow cradled in the ship's hands as Vivacia let the useless pieces of wood fall away. The ship herself lifted them to where eager hands gripped them and pulled them abroad. "Gently, gently!" she cried as they seized Wintrow from her arms. "Bring fresh water. Cut his clothes away and pour over him water and wine. Then . . . then . . ."

Vivacia suddenly cried aloud in wonder. She clasped her steaming hands together as if she prayed. "I know you!" she cried out abruptly. "I know you!"

Kennit reached down to where Etta crawled on the deck. His long-fingered hand cupped her cheek. "I will take care of it, my dear," he told her. The same hand that had commanded both sea and serpent touched her skin. Etta fell to the deck and knew no more.

.   .   .

KENNIT HAD FOLLOWED ETTA'S ADVICE ABOUT WINTROW, FOR LACK OF ANY
better. The boy, loosely wrapped in a length of linen, now slept in his
own bed. Breath whistled in and out of him. He was ghastly. His entire
body was so swollen as to be almost shapeless. The skin had blistered and
bubbled up from his body. The slime had eaten through his clothing, and
then melted skin and fabric together. In washing him, great patches of his
skin had sloughed away, leaving raw red stretches of flesh. Kennit suspected it was good that he was unconscious. Otherwise, the pain would
have been terrible.

Kennit rose stiffly. He had been sitting on the foot of the bed. Now
that the storm was over, he had time to think things through. But he
would not. Some things were not to be too carefully considered. He would
not ask Vivacia how she had known that she must abandon her post in
Deception Cove and seek him out. He would not question what the
serpent had done. He would not try to change the groveling deference the
crew was currently showing him.

There was a tap at the door and Etta entered. Her eyes went to
Wintrow and then back to Kennit. "I've a bath waiting for you," she said,
and then her words halted. She looked at him as if she did not know what
name to call him by. He had to smile at that.

"That is good. Keep watch here, with him. Do whatever you think
wise to make him easy. Keep giving him water whenever he stirs. I'll be
back soon. I can manage my bath by myself."

"I put out dry clothes for you," she managed to say. "And hot food
awaits you. Sorcor is abroad, asking to see you. I didn't know what to say to
him. The lookout on the *Marietta* saw it all. Sorcor was going to have him
flogged for lying. I told him the sailor wasn't lying. . . ." Her words ran out.

He looked at her. She had changed into a loose woolen robe. Her wet
hair was smoothed to her skull, reminding him of a seal's head. She stared
at him. Her scalded hands were clutched together in front of her. Her
breath came short and fast.

"And what else?" he prompted her gently.

She moistened her lips and held out her hand. "This was in my boot.
When I changed. I think . . . it must have come from the Others Island."

She held out her hands toward him. Cupped in them, no bigger than
a quail's egg, was a baby. The infant was curled tight in sleep, eyes closed,
lashes on his cheeks, tiny round knees drawn up to his chest. Whatever it
was carved from mimicked perfectly the fresh pink of young flesh. A tiny
serpentine tail wrapped its body.

"What does it mean?" Etta demanded, her voice quavering.

Kennit touched it with a fingertip, his weathered skin dark against it.
"I think we both know, don't we?" he asked her solemnly.

CHAPTER THIRTY-FIVE

Trehaug

"I LIKE IT HERE. IT'S LIKE LIVING IN A TREE-HOUSE CITY." SELDEN WAS sitting on the foot of the divan where she lay. He bounced thoughtfully as he spoke. Where did he get the energy? Malta wished her mother would come in and shoo him away.

"I always thought you belonged in a tree," Malta teased her brother weakly. "Why don't you go and play somewhere?" He gave her an owly stare, then smiled cautiously. He looked around the sitting room, then edged closer to her on the divan. He sat on her foot and she winced and pulled it away. She still ached all over.

Selden leaned too close to her and whispered in her face, "Malta? Promise me something?"

She leaned back from him. He'd been eating spiced meat. "What?"

He glanced around again. "When you and Reyn get married, can I live here with you in Trehaug?"

She didn't tell him how unlikely it was that she would ever marry Reyn. "Why?" she asked him.

He sat up straight, swinging his feet now. "I like it here. There are boys to play with, and I get to have my lessons with some of the Khuprus sons. I love the swinging bridges. Mother is always afraid I'll fall off them, but most of them have nets strung under them as well. I like watching the fire birds spoon in the shallows of the river." He paused, then added boldly, "I like it that not everyone here is so worried all the time." He leaned even closer and added, "And I like the old city. I sneaked into it last night, with Wilee, after everyone else was asleep. It's spooky. I loved it."

"Were you in the city when it quaked last night?"

"That was the best part!" His eyes were alight with the adventure.

"Well, don't do it again. And don't tell Mama," she warned him automatically.

"Do I look stupid?" he demanded in a superior way.

"Yes," she confirmed.

He grinned. "I'm going to go find Wilee. He promised to take me out in one of the thick boats, if we could sneak one."

"Watch out, or the river will eat it from under you."

He gave her a worldly look. "That's a myth. Oh, if there was a quake and the river ran white, then it might eat it fast. But Wilee says a thick boat will last ten days, sometimes more if the river runs regular. They last even longer if you pull them out at night, turn them upside down and piss on them."

"Ew. That is probably another myth, one told to make you look foolish when you repeat it."

"No. Wilee and I saw the men pissing on the boats two nights ago."

"Go away, dirty boy." She tugged her coverlet away from him.

He stood up. "Can I live with you, after you marry Reyn? I never want to go back to Bingtown."

"We'll see," she said firmly. Go back to Bingtown? She wondered if there even was a Bingtown. There had been no word from Grandmother since they arrived, and there wasn't likely to be. The only messages the birds carried back and forth had to do with the war. The *Kendry* that had ferried them up the river was the only liveship making the run. The others were all on patrol near the mouth of the river and around Bingtown Harbor, trying to drive off not only Chalcedean galleys but sea serpents. Lately the waters near the river mouth were infested with them.

As abruptly as a bird taking flight, Selden hopped off the divan and left the chamber. She shook her head as she looked after him. He had recovered so swiftly. More than recovered; he had suddenly become a person. Was that what parents meant when they said children grew up so fast? She felt almost sentimental about her annoying little brother. She wondered, wryly, if that meant she were growing up, too.

She leaned back on the divan and closed her eyes again. The windows of the chamber were open and the river air flowed in one and out the other. She had almost become accustomed to the smell. Someone scratched lightly at the door, then entered.

"Well. You look much better today." The healer was chronically optimistic.

"Thank you." Malta didn't open her eyes. The woman didn't wear a veil. Her face had the pebbled texture of a muffin. The skin of her hands was as rough as the pads of a dog's feet. It made Malta's flesh crawl when the woman touched her. "I feel sure that all I need is more rest," Malta added in the hopes of being left alone.

"To lie still is actually the worst thing for you right now. Your vision has returned to normal, you told me. You no longer see two of everything?"

"My vision seems fine," Malta assured her.

"You are eating well, and your food agrees with you?"

"Yes."

"Your dizziness has gone?"

"It only bothers me if I move suddenly."

"Then you should be up and about." The woman cleared her throat, a wet sound. Malta tried not to flinch. The healer snorted loudly, as if catching her breath, then went on, "You've no broken bones that we can find. You need to get up and move about, to remind your limbs of how to work. If you lie still too long, the body forgets. You may cripple yourself."

A sour reply would only make the woman more insistent. "Perhaps I shall feel up to it this afternoon."

"Sooner than that. I will send someone to walk you. It is what you need, in order to heal. I have done my part. Now you must do yours."

"Thank you," Malta said distantly. The healer was singularly unsympathetic for one of her profession. Malta would be asleep when the healer's assistant arrived. She doubted anyone would disturb her. That had been her injury's sole benefit; since then, she had been able to sleep free of dreams. Sleep was escape once more. In sleep, she could forget Reyn's distrust of her, her father's captivity or death, even the smell of Bingtown burning. She could forget that she and her family were paupers now, herself forfeit to a bargain made before she was born. She could hide from her failures.

She listened to the scuff of the healer's retreating footsteps. She tried to will herself down into sleep, but her peace had been broken too thoroughly. First, her mother had come this morning, heavy with grief and worry, but acting as if Malta were her only concern. Then Selden and then the healer. Sleep had fled.

She gave in and opened her eyes. She stared at the domed ceiling. The wickerwork reminded her of a basket. Trehaug was certainly not what she had expected. She had envisioned a grand marble mansion for the Khuprus family in a city of fine buildings and wide roads. She had expected ornate chambers decorated with dark wood and stone, lofty ballrooms and long galleries. Instead, it was just what Selden had said it was: a tree-house city. Airy little chambers balanced in the upper limbs of the great trees along the river. Swaying bridges connected them. Everything in the sunny upper reaches of the trees was built as lightly as possible. Some of the smaller chambers were little more than very large wickerwork baskets that swung like birdcages when the wind blew. Children slept in hammocks and sat in slings. Anything that could be woven of grass or sticks was. The upper reaches of the city were insubstantial, a ghost of the ancient city they plundered.

As one descended into the depths of Trehaug, that image changed. Or so Selden told her. Malta had not ventured from her chamber since she had awakened here. Sunny chambers like hers were high in the treetops, while close to the base of the trees, workshops, taverns, warehouses and shops existed in a perpetually shady twilight. In between were the more substantial rooms of the Rain Wild Traders' homes, the dining rooms, kitchens and gathering halls. These were built of plank and beam. Keffria had told her that they were palatial rooms, some spanning several trees, and as fine as any grand Bingtown mansion could have offered. Here the wealth of the Rain Wild Traders was showcased, not only in the old city's treasures but in all the luxuries that their exotic trade had bought them. Keffria had tried to lure Malta from her bed with tales of the art and beauty to be seen there. Malta had not been tempted. Having lost all, she had no wish to admire the wealth of others.

Trehaug swung and hung over the banks of the Rain Wild River, adjacent to the open channel. But the river had no true shores. Swamp, muck and shifting bogs extended back from the open river far under the trees. The corrosive waters of the river ruled the world, and flowed where they wished. A patch of ground that was solid for a week could suddenly begin to bubble and then sink away into muck. No one trusted the ground underfoot. Pilings driven into it were either eaten away or slowly toppled over. Only the far-reaching roots of the Rain Wild trees seemed able to grip some stability there. Never had Malta seen or imagined such trees. The one time she had ventured to her window and peered down, she could not see the ground. Foliage and bridges obscured the view. Her chamber perched in the forked branch of a tree. A walkway over the limb protected its bark from foot traffic. The branch was wide enough for two men to walk abreast on it, and it led to a spiraling staircase that wound down the trunk. The staircase reminded Malta of a busy street, even to the vendors who frequented the landings.

At night, watchmen patrolled, keeping the lanterns on the staircases and bridges filled and alight. Night brought a festive air, as the city bloomed in necklaces of light. The Rain Wild folk gardened in hammocks and troughs of earth suspended in the trees. Foragers had their own path- ways through the trees and over the swamplands. They harvested the exotic fruits, flowers and gamebirds of the Rain Wild jungle. Water came from the sprawling system of rain catchers, for no one could drink much of the river water and hope to live. The thick boats, hollowed out from green tree trunks, were pulled out of the river each night and hammocked in the trees. They were the temporary transportation between the "houses," supplements to the swaying bridges and pulley carts that linked the trees. The trees supported the whole city. A quake that caused the wet ground below to bubble and gape did no more than make the great trees sway gently.

Below, on the true ground, there was the ancient city, of course, but from Selden's description, it was little more than a lump in the swamp- land. The little bit of solid ground around it was devoted to the workshops for salvage and exploration of the city. No one lived there. When she had asked Selden why, he had shrugged. "You go crazy if you spend too much time in the city." Then he had cocked his head and added, "Wilee says that Reyn might be crazy already. Before he started liking you, he spent more time down there than anyone else ever had. He nearly got the ghost disease." He had glanced about. "That's what killed his father, you know," he'd added in a hoarse whisper.

"What's the ghost disease?" she had asked him, intrigued in spite of herself.

"I don't know. Not exactly. You drown in memories. That's what Wilee said. What's that mean?"

"I don't know." His newly discovered ability to ask questions was almost worse than his former long silences had been.

She stretched where she lay on the divan, then curled back into her coverlet. The ghost disease. Drowning in memories. She shook her head and closed her eyes.

Another scratch came at the door. She did not reply. She kept still and made her breathing deep and slow. She heard the door rasp open. Someone came into her room. Someone came close to the bed and looked down on her. The person just stood over her, watching her feign sleep. Malta kept her pretense and waited for the intruder to leave.

Instead, a gloved hand touched her face.

Her eyes flew open. A veiled man stood by her. He was dressed completely in dull black.

"Who are you? What do you want?" She shrank back from his touch, clutching the coverlet.

"It's me. Reyn. I had to see you." He dared to sit down on the divan's edge.

She drew her feet up to avoid any contact with him. "You know I don't want to see you."

"I know that," he admitted reluctantly. "But we don't always get what we want, do we?"

"You seem to," she responded bitterly.

He stood up with a sigh. "I have told you. And I have written it to you, in all the letters you've returned to me. I spoke in desperation that day. I would have said anything to get you to go with me. Nevertheless, I do not intend to enforce the liveship contract between our families. I will not take you as payment for a debt, Malta Haven. I would not have you against your will."

"Yet here I am," she pointed out tartly.

"Alive," he added.

"Small thanks to the men you sent after the Satrap," she pointed out acidly. "They left me to die."

"I didn't know you'd be in the coach." His voice was stiff as he offered the excuse.

"If you had trusted me enough to tell me the truth at the ball, I wouldn't have been. Nor my mother, grandmother or brother. Your distrust of me nearly killed us all. It did kill Davad Restart, who was guilty of no more than being greedy and stupid. If I had died, you would have been the one guilty of my death. Perhaps you saved my life, but it was only after you had nearly taken it from me. Because you didn't trust me." These were the words she had longed to fling at him since she had pieced that last evening together. This was the knowledge that had turned her soul to stone. She had rehearsed the words so often, yet never truly known how deep her hurt was until she uttered them aloud. She could scarcely get them past the lump in her throat. He was silent, standing over her still. She watched the impassive drapery across his face and wondered if he felt anything at all.

She heard him catch his breath. Silence. Again the ragged intake of air. Slowly he sank down to his knees. She watched without comprehension as he knelt on the floor by her bed. His voice was so choked she could scarcely understand him. The words flooded out of him. "I know that it's my fault. I knew it through all the nights when you lay here, unstirring. It ate at me like river water cuts into a dying tree. I nearly killed you. The thought of you, lying there, bleeding and alone . . . I'd give anything to undo it. I was stupid and I was wrong. I have no right to ask it, but I beg it of you. Please forgive me. Please." His voice broke on an audible sob. His hands came up to clench into fists against his veil.

Both her hands flew up to cover her mouth. In shock, she watched his shoulders shake. He was weeping. She spoke her astonished thought aloud. "I never heard a man say such words. I didn't think one could." In one shattering instant, her basic concept of men was re-ordered. She didn't have to hammer Reyn with words or break him with unflinching accusations. He could admit he was wrong. *Not like my father*, the traitor thought whispered. She refused to follow it.

"Malta?" His voice was thick with tears. He still knelt before her.

"Oh, Reyn. Please get up." It was too unsettling to see him this way. "But—"

She astonished herself. "I forgive you. It was a mistake." She had never known those words could be so easy to say. She didn't have to hold it back. She could let it go. She didn't have to save his guilt up to club him with later, when she wanted something from him. Maybe they would never do that to each other. Maybe it wouldn't be about who was wrong or right, or who controlled whom.

So what would it be about, between them?

He came to his feet shakily. He turned his back to her, lifted his veil and dragged his sleeve across his eyes like a child, before finding his handkerchief. He wiped his eyes. She heard him take a deep breath.

Quietly, she tested this new idea. "You would not stop me if I chose to return to Bingtown today?"

He shrugged, still not facing her. "I would not have to. The *Kendry* doesn't sail until tomorrow night." His effort at levity failed him. He added miserably as he turned back to her, "You could go then, if you insisted. It's the only way back to Bingtown, or what's left of it."

She sat up slowly. The question broke from her. "Have you had news of Bingtown? Of my home and grandmother?"

He shook his head as he sat down beside her. "I'm sorry. No. There are not many message birds, and all are used for news of the war." Reluctantly, he added, "There are many stories of pillaging. The New Traders rose up. Some of their slaves fight beside them. Others have crossed over to side with the Bingtown Traders. It is neighbor against neighbor in Bingtown, the ugliest kind of fighting, for they know one another's weaknesses best. In such battles, there are always some who take no side, but loot and plunder whoever is weakest. Your mother hopes that your grandmother fled to her little farm as she had intended. She would be safer there. The Old Trader estates are—"

"Stop. I don't want to hear of it, I don't want to think of it." She clapped her hands over her ears and huddled into a ball, her eyes tight shut. Home had to exist. Somewhere there had to be a place with solid walls and safe routine. Her breath came fast and hard. She recalled little of her flight from Bingtown. Everything had hurt so much, and when she had tried to see, images were doubled and tripled atop one another. The horse had been rough-paced, and Reyn had held her in front of him. They had ridden too fast, too hard. The thick smoke in the air, and the distant screams and shouts. Some of the roads had been blocked by fallen debris from burning buildings. All the docks in the harbor had been charred and smoking wreckage. Reyn had found a leaky boat. Selden had held her upright so she did not fall over into the dirty bilge while Reyn and her mother plied the worm-eaten oars to get them out to the *Kendry*. . . .

She found she was in his lap, still huddled in a ball. He sat on the bed, holding her and rocking her as he patted her back slowly. He had tucked her head under his chin. "Hush, hush, it's all done, it's all over," he kept saying. His arms were strong around her. Home was gone. This was the only safe place left, but his words were too true to comfort her. It was all done, it was all over, it was all ruined. Too late to try harder, too late to even weep over it. Too late for everything. She curled tighter into him and put her arms around him. She held him tightly.

"I don't want to think anymore. I don't want to talk anymore."

"Me, neither." Her head was against his chest. His words thrummed deep inside him.

She sniffed, then sighed heavily. She almost wiped her eyes on her sleeve, then remembered herself. She groped for her handkerchief. Instead, he pressed his into her hands. It was damp from his tears. She wiped her own eyes on it. "Where is my mother?" she asked wearily.

"With my mother. And some of our Council. They are talking about what is to be done."

"My mother?"

"Trader Vestrit of the Bingtown Traders has as much a right to speak as any other Trader. And she has some brilliant ideas. She suggested thick, greenwood buckets of Rain Wild River water might be employed as a weapon against the galleys. Load them in catapults to break apart on their decks. The damage might not be immediate, but over time their ships would start to weaken and come apart, not to mention scalding their rowers."

"Unless they knew to piss on the decks," she muttered.

Reyn gave an involuntary laugh. His arms tightened around her. "Malta Vestrit, the things you know astonish me. How did you learn that secret?"

"Selden told me. Children can spy out anything."

"That is true," he replied thoughtfully. "Children and servants are near invisible. Much of our information before the riots came from Amber's net of slaves."

She leaned her head on his shoulder. He put both his arms around her and held her. It wasn't romantic. Nothing was romantic anymore. Only tired. "Amber? The bead-maker?" she asked. "What had she to do with the slaves?"

"She talked to them. A lot. I gather that she marked her face and masqueraded as a slave at the water well, and the washing fountains and places where slaves gathered to do their work. At first, she gathered knowledge just from their gossip, but eventually she enlisted some of the slaves themselves to help her. She opened that net to the Tenira family. Grag and his father made good use of it."

"What kind of knowledge?" she asked dully. She didn't know why she cared. It all came down to one thing. War. People killing each other and destroying things.

"The latest gossip from Jamaillia. Which nobles are allied with each other, which ones have substantial interests in Chalced. It was all information that we needed, to make our case in Jamaillia. We are not a rebel province, not really. What we do is in the interest of the Satrapy. There is a group of Jamaillian nobles who would overthrow the Satrap and seize his power for themselves. They encouraged him to come to Bingtown, in the hopes of exactly what happened. Riots. Attempts on the Satrap's life." Almost reluctantly, he admitted, "Trader Restart was not a traitor. His pushiness when the Chalcedean fleet arrived actually put the traitors' plans awry, for the Satrap ended up at his home instead of in their power. But for his intervention, the assault on Bingtown would have begun much sooner."

"Why is any of that important?" she asked dully.

"It's a complicated situation. Essentially, it is Jamaillia's civil war, not ours. They've just decided to hold it in our territories. Some of the Jamaillian nobles are willing to give Bingtown over to Chalced, in return for favorable trading treaties, a chunk of what the Satrap has always claimed for himself and more power for themselves in Jamaillia. They've gone to great lengths to establish their families and claims in Bingtown. Now they've made it look like the Bingtown Traders have rebelled against the Satrapy. But it's all a mask for their own plots to overthrow an incompetent Satrap and steal the throne's power for themselves. Do you understand?"

"No. And I don't care. Reyn, I just want my father back. I want to go home. I want it all to be like it was before."

He dropped his head forward so that his forehead rested on her shoulder. "Someday," he said in a muffled voice, "you will want something I can give you. At least, so I pray to Sa."

For a time, they just sat together in silence. A scratch came at the door. Reyn jumped, but he couldn't very well dump her out of his arms. The door opened and the Rain Wild woman framed in it looked completely scandalized. Her mouth actually hung open. She took a gasp of air, then blurted, "I came to assist Malta Vestrit. The healer advised she should get up and do some walking."

"I'll see to it myself," Reyn announced calmly, as if he had a perfect right to be alone with her in her chamber holding her in his arms. Malta looked down at her hands clasped in her lap. She could not control the blush that heated her cheeks.

"I . . . that is . . ."

"You may tell the healer I've seen to it," he instructed her firmly. As the woman darted away, leaving the door ajar, he added in an undertone, "And my mother. And my brother. And anyone else you meet on the way to tattle on me." He shook his head and the fabric of his veil whispered against her hair. "I shall hear about this. For hours." His arms tightened briefly around her, then released her. "Come. At least don't make me a liar as well as a sneak. Get up and walk with me." He lifted her off his lap. She stood, and handed him her coverlet. She wore a house-robe, a modest enough garment, but not one in which a young lady should be seen by those outside her household. She lifted a hand to her hair. As she pushed it back from her forehead, her fingers grazed the scar there. She winced.

"Does it still hurt?" Reyn asked immediately.

"Not much. It still surprises me that it is there. I must look a fright. I haven't combed my hair today. . . . Reyn, they won't give me a looking-glass. Is it bad?"

He tilted his head to look at her. "You would say yes. I say no. It is livid now, and swollen, but time will fade it." He shook his veiled face. "But it will never fade from my memory that I put it there. . . ."

"Reyn. Don't," Malta begged him.

He took a breath. "You don't look a fright. You look like a tousled kitten." His gloved hand thumbed a last tear from her face.

She walked stiffly to a little table where her toiletries were. The hairbrush on it was unfamiliar. No doubt, Reyn's family had provided it, as they did the room where she slept and the food she ate and the clothes she wore. Her family had come away from Bingtown with nothing. Nothing. They had lived on charity since they arrived here.

"Let me," Reyn begged. He took the brush from her hand. She stared out the window as he drew it gently through her hair. "It's so thick. Like strands of heavy silk, and so black. How do you manage it? My mother always complained of my hair when I was a boy, yet I think long straight hair would be harder to manage than curls."

"You have curly hair?" Malta asked him idly.

"Like fraying knots, my older sister tells me. When Tillamon had to comb it for me when I was little, I swear she ripped out as much as she left on my head."

She turned to him abruptly. "Let me see you."

He went down suddenly on one knee before her, hairbrush in hand. "Malta Vestrit, will you marry me?"

It shocked her. "Do I have a choice?" she demanded.

"Of course." He didn't move from where he knelt.

She took a breath. "I can't, Reyn. Not yet."

He stood easily. Taking her by the shoulders, he turned her away from him. He drew the brush smoothly through her hair again. If she had hurt him, it didn't sound in his voice. "Then you can't see my face."

"Is that a Rain Wild custom?"

"No. It's Reyn Khuprus' custom regarding Malta Vestrit. You can see me when you say you'll marry me."

"That's ridiculous," she protested.

"No. It's crazy. Just ask my mother or my brother. They'll tell you I'm crazy."

"Too late. That was more news my little brother brought me. Reyn Khuprus is crazy from spending too much time in the city. You drowned in memories."

She had spoken the words lightly, as a jest. It shocked her when he dropped the hairbrush and stood stock-still. After a moment, he asked in hushed horror, "Do they really say that of me?"

"Reyn, I jested." She turned to face him, but he walked swiftly away from her to stare out the window.

"Drowned in memories. You can't have made that up, Malta Vestrit. It's a Rain Wild phrase. They do say that of me, don't they?"

"One little boy speaking to another . . . you know how children tell tales to impress one another, how they exaggerate—"

"How they repeat what they've heard their elders say," he finished dully.

"I thought it was just a . . . Is it truly that serious? To drown in memories?"

"Yes," he said dully. "Yes it is. When you become dangerous, they generally give you a very gentle poison. You die in your sleep. If you are still able to sleep. Sometimes, I can still sleep. Not often, and not for long, but it makes true sleep all the sweeter."

"The dragon," Malta confirmed softly.

He started as if stabbed and turned to stare at her.

"From our dream," she went on softly. How long ago that seemed.

"She threatened she would go after you, but I thought it was an idle boast." He sounded ill.

"She—" Malta started to tell how the dragon had tormented her. Then she stopped. "She hasn't bothered me since I was hurt. She's gone."

He was silent for a time. "I suppose when you were unconscious, she lost her link with you."

"Can that happen?"

"I don't know. I know very little about her. Except that no one else believes in her. They all think I'm crazy." He laughed tremulously.

She held out her hand. "Come. Let's walk. You promised me once to show me your city."

He shook his head slowly. "I'm not supposed to go there anymore. Not unless my brother or mother deems it necessary. I promised." There was deep loss in his voice.

"Why? Whatever for?"

He choked on a small laugh. "For you, my dear. I bargained away my city for you. They promised that if I stayed away from it, save by their leave, that if I surrendered all hope of ever freeing the dragon, they would forgive the liveship debt, and give me a man's allowance to spend as I wanted, and allow me to visit you whenever I wished."

If she had not shared dreams with him, she would not have understood what he had given up for her. But she did know. The city was his heart. Plumbing its secrets, walking its whispering streets, coaxing its mysteries to unfold for him was his essence. He had given up the core of his being, for her.

He continued quietly. "So, you see. The contract is already settled.

You don't have to marry me to discharge it." His gloved hands tangled desperately against each other.

"And the dragon?" Malta asked breathlessly.

"She hates me now. I suppose that if she can drown me in her memories, she will. She tries to get me to come to her. But I resist."

"How?"

He sighed. With a twinge of humor, he confessed, "When it gets really bad, I get so drunk I can't even crawl. Then I pass out."

"Oh, Reyn." She shook her head in sympathy. And she has him to herself then, Malta conjectured. To torment as she wishes, in her world, with no escape for him. She took a breath. "What if I married you as part of the contract? If I said I preferred to pay it off that way, rather than have your family forgive it? Would that free you from your bargain?"

He shook his head slowly. "It wouldn't release me from my contract." He cocked his head at her. "Would you really do that?"

She didn't know. She could not decide. He had made such a terrible bargain, just to be with her. But she could still not say, easily, that she wished to marry him. She knew so little about him. How could he have doubted her, and yet still have given his city up for her? It made no sense. Men were not at all what she had believed they were.

She held out her hand to him. "Take me for a walk." Without a word, he took her hand. He led her out of the small chamber, to take her strolling on the walkway that spiraled up the trunk of the immense tree. She held his hand and did not look down nor back.

"I FAIL TO SEE WHAT GOOD IT DOES FOR US TO KEEP HIM. IT LOOKS LIKE we've kidnapped him." The lean Rain Wild Trader flung himself irritably back in his chair.

"Trader Polsk, you are thick-witted. The advantage is obvious. If we have the Satrap, he himself can speak out for us. He can say he was not kidnapped, but rescued by us from the New Traders' assassination plot." Trader Freye, the woman who criticized Trader Polsk so roughly, sat next to him. Keffria decided they were either friends, or related.

"Have we completely convinced him that that is the truth of the matter? The last time I heard him speak, he seemed to feel he had been snatched from an affable host and spirited away. He didn't use the word kidnapped, but I don't think it was far from his tongue," Trader Polsk replied.

"We should put him in different chambers. He cannot help but feel a prisoner, held in such a place." This from Trader Kewin. His veil was sewn so thickly with pearls that it rattled when he spoke.

"He is safest where he is. We all agreed to that hours ago. Please,

Traders, let us not re-tread ground we have already packed into bricks. We need to move past why we hold him or where we hold him to what we plan to do with him." Jani Khuprus sounded both weary and annoyed. Keffria sympathized.

There were moments when Keffria looked around herself and wondered where her life had gone. Here she was, sitting in a large chair at an imposing table, flanked by the most powerful Traders of the Rain Wild folk. The plans they discussed amounted to treason against the Jamaillian Satrapy. Yet, what surrounded her was not as strange as what was missing. Everything. Husband, son, mother, wealth and home had all vanished from her life. She looked around at the lightly veiled faces and wondered why they tolerated her here. What could she contribute to their Council? She spoke up anyway.

"Trader Khuprus is right. The sooner we can take action, the more lives we will save. We must get word to Jamaillia that he is alive and well. We must emphasize that we mean no harm to him, and that we hold him only for his own safety. Furthermore, I think we need to separate that message from any other negotiations. If we mention land grants or slavery or tariffs in the same missive, they will assume we are bartering the Satrap's life for what we desire."

"And why shouldn't we?" Trader Lorek spoke up suddenly. She was a massive woman. A muscled fist smacked the table. "Answer me that, first. Why are we holding that spoiled adolescent in a fine chamber that he treats like a pig-sty and feeding him our best foods and wines when he has treated us as both loathesome and honorless? I say, bring him out here and make him look at us. Give him a dip or two in the Rain Wild River, and a month of hard work, and see if he doesn't gain a bit of respect for our ways. Then trade his life for what we want."

Silence followed this outburst. Then Trader Kewin replied to Keffria's comments. Most of the Council seemed to ignore Trader Lorek's little outbursts, Keffria noted. "To whom do we send such a message? Companion Serilla suspected that the conspiracy extends through many of the Jamaillian noble houses. They may be angered that we have preserved his life. Before we brag that we have foiled the plot, perhaps we should find out who was behind it."

Trader Polsk leaned his chair back. "Let a thick-witted old man boil it down for you. Get rid of him. Ship the kid back where he came from. Let them deal with him. They can kill him there, if they're so set on it. And each other, for all I care. Tie a note around his neck that we're done with him and we're done with Jamaillia, and we're going to do things our own way now. While we're at it, let's clean the Chalcedeans out of our bays and waterways, and make that stick this time, too."

Several Traders nodded but Jani Khuprus sighed. "Trader Polsk, you do cut to the heart of it. Many of us wish it were that simple. But it isn't.

We cannot risk war with Chalced and Jamaillia at the same time. If we must placate one, let it be Jamaillia."

Trader Kewin shook his head violently. "Let us not ally with anyone until we know who supports whom. We need to know what is going on in Jamaillia. I fear we must make the Satrap more comfortable and keep him, while we send a ship of delegates to Jamaillia, under a truce flag, to find out how things lie there."

"Would they respect a truce flag?" one demanded, while another Trader cut in with, "Past pirates and Chalcedean mercenaries, and back again? Do you know how long that trip could take? There may be nothing left of Bingtown by then."

Perhaps it was the mention of her home, but suddenly things seemed icily clear to Keffria. She knew what it was that she brought to this meeting. It was the same thing her ancestors had brought when they first came to the Cursed Shores to carve homes from hostile territory. She had herself: her courage, and her wits. It was all she had left to offer anyone. "We don't need to go to Jamaillia to discover that," she said quietly. All the veiled faces at the table turned abruptly to her. "The answers we need are in Bingtown. There are traitors there who were willing to let a boy be killed for the sake of snatching more of our land and making it over in Chalced's image. Traders, we do not need to go to Jamaillia to discover who our friends are. We need only go so far as Bingtown to find who our enemies are, both there and in Jamaillia."

Trader Lorek slammed the table again. "How are we to do that, Trader Vestrit? Ask them nicely? Or do you suggest we take a few captives and wring it out of them?"

"Neither," Keffria said quietly. She looked around the table at the veiled faces. From their rapt silence, they appeared to be listening. She took a breath. "I could flee to them and throw myself upon their sympathies." She took a breath. "Look at me. Pirates have taken my Chalcedean husband. I've been driven from my home, my daughter and son 'killed' in the kidnapping of the Satrap, to say nothing of my old friend Davad Restart. I could persuade them that my sympathies are with them. And somehow, I could get word back to you of what I discover about them."

"Too dangerous." Polsk condemned the idea quickly.

"You don't have enough to offer them," Trader Freye said quietly. "You'd need more to bargain with. Information about us or the river. Something."

Keffria thought for a moment. "A note from the Satrap, in his own hand, saying he is alive and imploring aid of his nobles. I could offer to betray him."

"That's not quite it." Freye shook her head.

Keffria suddenly knew. "My liveship," she said quietly. "I could offer them a bargain. Ask them to rescue my family ship and husband. In return, I'd use the *Vivacia* to bring them up the river to where they could attack you and recapture the Satrap."

"That would work," Jani Khuprus agreed reluctantly. "They'd be suspicious of you if you came just to gift them with a betrayal. But if you come asking a favor or seeking a bargain, they'll accept your motives."

Polsk snorted. "It falls apart too easily. What if someone has talked to your mother? How would you come by such a note from the Satrap? All know Malta was promised to Reyn. They would not believe your sudden animosity."

"I believe my mother fled the city the same day I did. And I spoke to no one after the ball; we all simply vanished. I could say that we were kidnapped along with the Satrap, that my children died from their injuries, but I was held with him. I gained his trust, he wrote the note, I escaped, but I decided to betray him because I blamed him."

Keffria paused as her inventiveness ran out. What was she thinking? It was all too thin a weaving; any fool could see through it. The other Traders would know that, and dissuade her from going. She herself knew that she could not do it. Her sister Althea could have, even her daughter Malta had the spirit and courage. But she was only a quiet mouse of a woman, sheltered and naïve. They could all see that about her. They would never let her do it. She suddenly felt foolish for even suggesting such a laughable plan.

Trader Polsk steepled his lean fingers on the table before him. "Very well. You're right. Nonetheless, I insist that Trader Vestrit take a night to think this over before she commits to it. She has been through a great ordeal. Her children would be safe here, but we would be sending her into great danger, with few resources."

"The *Kendry* sails tomorrow. Could she be ready by then?" Trader Lorek pushed.

"We still have links with slaves in some of the New Trader households. They could pass information to us. I'll get you a list of names to commit to memory," Trader Freye offered. She looked around the table. "We all accept, of course, that this plan must not leave this room."

"Of course not. I myself will speak of it only to the *Kendry*'s captain, to suggest that there may be a stowaway on his ship. One he should not ferret out. He can keep his crew clear of her."

"You will need supplies, and yet we cannot outfit you too efficiently, or your story will not ring true," Jani worried aloud.

"We should prepare her a bracelet. Gold, painted to look like cheap enamel. If she is threatened, she may be able to buy her life with it," Freye added.

Keffria listened as the plan she had suggested took shape around her. She wondered if she were the fish caught in the net, or the fisherman who had thrown it. The dread she felt was a familiar sensation; the lifting elation that accompanied it was not. What was she becoming?

"I insist we allow her at least one night to consider this well," Polsk repeated.

"I will sail with the *Kendry*," Keffria asserted quietly. "I leave my children in your care. I will tell them I am returning to Bingtown to persuade their grandmother to join us here. I beg you to tell them no more than that."

Veiled heads all around the table nodded. Jani Khuprus spoke quietly. "I only pray that we still hold Bingtown Harbor when you get there. Otherwise, this whole plan is for naught."

IT WAS A BLACK AND SILVER NIGHT. SHE SUPPOSED IT WAS BEAUTIFUL, IN ITS own way, but Malta had no time for considering beauty in her life. Not anymore. The gleaming moon above, the rush of the deadly river below, and in between fog drifting and a light breeze blowing were all things to ignore as she focused on the gentle swaying of the bridge beneath her feet.

It was sickening.

There was a rope railing, but it was slack and right at the edge of the walkway. She preferred to stay to the middle of the span as she walked along carefully. She placed each of her feet carefully, to keep from making the bridge sway any more than it already was. She kept her arms crossed tightly on her chest, hugging herself. The spaced lanterns on the railing doubled and tripled her shadow, making her recall the fuzzy visions from her injury. She felt queasy.

She heard a wild clattering of feet and Selden came racing up to her. She dropped to her hands and knees, and clutched at the planks of the bridge.

"What are you doing?" the boy demanded. "Come on, Malta, hurry up or we'll never get there. There's only three more bridges, and one trolley span."

"Trolley span?" she asked weakly.

"You sit in a little box and yank yourself along on a pulley sort of thing. It's fun. You can go really fast."

"Can you go really slow, too?"

"I don't know. I never tried that."

"We'll try it tonight," she said firmly. She took a shuddering breath and came to her feet. "Selden. I'm not used to the bridges yet. Could you go more slowly and not make them swing so much?"

"Why?"

"So your sister doesn't knock your head off," she suggested.

"You don't mean that," he informed her. "Besides, you'd never catch me. Here. Take my hand and don't think about it so much. Come on."

His hand felt dirty and damp in hers. She held it tightly and followed him, her heart in her throat.

"Why do you want to go into the city, anyway?"

"I'm curious. I'd like to see it."

"Why didn't Reyn take you?"

"He didn't have time today."

"Couldn't he make time to take you tomorrow?"

"Could we just walk and not talk?"

"If you want." He was silent for three breaths. "You don't want him to know you're doing this, do you?"

Malta hurried after him, trying to ignore the sickening sway of the bridge. Selden seemed to have the trick of timing his stride to it. She felt that that if she stumbled, she might go right over the edge. "Selden," she asked quietly, "do you want Mama to know about you and the thick boats?"

He didn't reply. This bargain didn't need to be formalized.

The only thing worse than the bridges was the trolley span. The trolley box was made of basketwork. Selden stood up in it to work it while she sat in the saggy bottom and wondered if it were going to give way any second. She gripped the edge of the basket tightly and tried not to think what would happen if the rope gave way.

The trolley span ended in the limbs of a great tree. A walkway spiraled around its trunk to the ground. By the time they reached the solid earth, her legs were like jelly, not just from nervousness but from the unaccustomed exercise. She looked around in the darkness, baffled. "This is the city?"

"Not really. Most of these are buildings the Rain Wilders put up to work in. We're on top of the old city. Come on. Follow me. I'll show you one of the ways in."

The log buildings were set cheek by jowl. Selden led her through them as if they were a garden maze. Once they crossed a wider road set with torches. She concluded that there were probably more prosaic ways of reaching the buried city. They had come by the path that the children used. Selden glanced back at her as he led her on. She caught the flash of excitement in his eyes. He led her eventually to a heavy door made of logs. It was set flat to the ground like a trap door. "Help me," he hissed.

She shook her head. "It's chained shut."

"It only looks like it is. The grown-ups don't use this way anymore, because part of the tunnel caved in. But there's room to get through, if you aren't too big. Like us."

She crouched down beside him. The door was slippery with mold. Her fingernails slid on it, filling them with dirt. But it opened, revealing a square of deeper night. With small hope she asked Selden, "Are there torches down there, or candles?"

"No. You don't need them. I'll show you. You just touch this stuff and it lights up a little bit, but only while you're touching it. It's not much, but it's enough to go by."

He clambered down into the darkness. An instant later, she saw a dim glow around his fingers. It was enough to outline his hand on the wall. "Come on. Hurry up."

He didn't say she had to shut the door and she was glad not to. She groped her way down into the darkness. It smelled of damp and stagnant water. What was she doing? What was she thinking? She gritted her teeth and set her hand beside Selden's. The result was astonishing. A sudden bar of light shot out from beneath her fingers. It ran the length of the tunnel before them before vanishing around a curve. Along the way, it arched over doorways. In some places, runes shone on it. She froze in astonishment.

For a time, Selden was silent. Then he said doubtfully, "Reyn showed you how to do that, didn't he?"

"No. I didn't do anything except touch it. It's jidzin." She cocked her head. Strains of music reached her ears from far down the hall. It was strange. She could not identify the instruments, but it was oddly familiar.

Selden's eyes were very wide. "Wilee told me that Reyn could make it do that, sometimes. I didn't believe him."

"Maybe it just happens sometimes."

"Maybe," he agreed doubtfully.

"What is that tune? Do you know it?"

He frowned at her. "What tune?"

"That music. Very far away. Don't you hear it?"

Silence held for a long time. "No. I just hear water dripping."

After a moment, she asked, "Are we going to go on?"

"Of course," he said doubtfully. He walked more slowly now, trailing his fingers along the strip of jidzin. She followed him, copying him. "Where did you want to go?" he asked after a minute.

"I want to go to where the dragon is buried. Do you know where that is?"

He turned and looked at her with a furrowed brow. "A buried dragon?"

"That's what I heard. Do you know where that is?"

"No." He scratched his cheek with dirty fingers, leaving brown stripes. "I never heard of that." He looked at his feet. "Actually, I didn't go much past the caved-in part."

"Then take me there."

They moved in silence now. Some of the doors they passed had been broken open. Malta peered in hopefully as they passed. Most led only to collapsed chambers full of earth and roots. Two had been cleared of debris, but held nothing of interest. Thick glass windows looked out on walls of earth. They went on. Sometimes the music seemed clearer, sometimes it faded. A trick of the tunnels, she decided.

They came to a place where the ceiling and one wall had given way. Earth had cascaded across the stone floor. With his free hand, Selden pointed up the pile of debris toward the ceiling. He whispered, "You have to climb up there and squeeze through. Wilee said it's tight going for a short way, and then you come out again."

She looked up at it doubtfully. "Did you fit through there?"

Selden looked down and shook his head. "I don't like small places. I don't even really like to be in here. The bridges and trolleys are more fun. Last time we were in here, there was that shake. Wilee and all of us just ran like rabbits to get out." He seemed humiliated to admit it.

"I'd run, too," she assured him.

"Let's go back now."

"I'm going to go just a bit further, just to see if I can. Will you wait here for me?"

"I suppose so."

"You could wait for me by the door if you want. Keep watch there?"

"I suppose so. You know, Malta, if we get caught down here, by ourselves, like this . . . well, it seems somewhat rude. Different from Wilee bringing me down here. Like we're spying on our hosts."

"I know what I'm doing," she assured him. "I won't be gone long."

"I hope so," he murmured as she left him.

For the first part, it was not so hard. She waded through the damp earth, keeping her hand on the light strip. Soon she had to crouch. Then the level of the debris covered the jidzin. Reluctantly she lifted her fingers from it. The light dimmed behind her. She set her teeth and groped her way forward on her hands and knees. She kept being tangled in her skirts until she got the knack of it. When she bumped her head on the ceiling, she stopped. Her hands were cold and the fabric of her skirt was thick and heavy with mud. How was she going to explain that? She pushed the worry aside. Too late, anyway. A little further, she told herself. She crouched lower and crawled on. Soon she was on her elbows and pushing herself along on her knees. The only sounds she could hear were her own breathing and distant dripping. She halted to catch her breath. The darkness pressed against her eyes. Suddenly the whole weight of the hill above seemed to be pressing down on her. This was ridiculous. She was going back.

She tried to back up. Her skirt started to crawl up around her waist, and her bare knees met the cold earth. She felt like she was wallowing on her belly in mud. She halted. "Selden?"

There was no answer. He'd probably gone back to the door as soon as she was out of sight. She set her head down on her arms and closed her eyes. Dizziness rocked her for a moment. She shouldn't have tried this. The whole idea was stupid. What had made her think she could succeed where Reyn had failed?

CHAPTER THIRTY-SIX

Dragon and Satrap

MALTA WAS GETTING COLD. THE DAMP EARTH BENEATH HER, MORE MUD than soil, had saturated her clothing. The longer she was still, the more her body ached. She had to do something, go on or go back. Both options seemed too much trouble. Maybe she could just lie here until somebody else did something about it.

As her breathing calmed, the distant music swelled. When she gave it her attention, it seemed clearer. She knew that tune. Surely, she had danced to it, a long time ago. She heard herself humming softly with it. She opened her eyes and lifted her head. Was there light ahead, or was it a trick of her mind? The pastel lights shifted when she moved her eyes. She crawled on, towards the light and the music.

With a suddenness that surprised her, she was going downhill. She lifted her head and found there was space above her now. She started to get to her hands and knees, and abruptly slid. She went down the muddy slope on her belly like an otter. She cried out and tried to put her hands over her face. It was too reminiscent of the wildly tumbling coach. But she slid to a stop without hitting any obstacles. Her outstretched hands found shallow mud, and then cold stone. The floor of the corridor. She was past the cave-in.

Malta was still afraid to stand. She crept, feeling before her, until she found the wall. She moved her hands up cautiously as she crouched and then stood. Suddenly her muddy fingers found the jidzin strip. As soon as she touched it, the corridor blazed with light. She squeezed her eyes shut then opened them slowly. She stared down the corridor with wondering eyes.

Back at the entrance, the walls had been deteriorated, the friezes faded and worn. Here the light emanated not only from the strip, but also from decorative swirls in the wall. Gleaming black tiles shone on the floor. The music was louder, and she heard a woman's peal of sudden laughter.

She looked down at her muddy and drenched clothing. She hadn't expected anything like this. She had thought the city would be deserted. If she ran into anyone in her bedraggled condition, what would she do? Malta smiled foolishly; she supposed she could always plead her head injury and pretend her mind was wandering. Considering her actions this evening, perhaps she *was* out of her mind. Her wet skirts slapped against her legs as she tiptoed down the corridor. There were doors to pass, but most of them were blessedly shut. The few open ones revealed opulent rooms, with thick rugs on the floors and startling art on the walls. She had never seen such furniture: couches that were tasseled and draped with rich fabrics, chairs she could have curled up and slept in, tables that were more like pedestals. This must be the legendary wealth of the Rain Wilds. Yet she had been told no one lived in the city. She shrugged. Perhaps that meant they did not eat or sleep here. She pressed on. At some point, she decided she was not going back the way she had come, no matter what befell her. She could not force herself through that wet, muddy tunnel again. She'd find another way out.

The music died away for a moment, then swirled back. This was another tune, but she knew it as well. She hummed with it a moment to prove she did, then a sudden chill shivered up her back. She recalled where she had heard this music before; it had been in the first dream that she had ever shared with Reyn. In the dream, she had walked with him in a silent city. Then he had brought her to a place where there was music, and light, and people talking. The music was the same; that was how she knew it.

Still, it seemed odd she knew it so well. She felt a distant grinding through her feet, and then the floor stepped sideways underneath her. She clutched at the wall desperately. It trembled under her hand. Would the quake continue? Would the whole city fall down on top of her? Her heart hammered and her head spun. The hallway was suddenly full of people. Tall elegant women with golden skin and improbable hair swept past her, chattering gaily to one another in a language she had once known. They didn't so much as glance at her. Their sleek skirts swept the floor yet were split to the waist. Golden legs flashed scandalously as they walked. Their perfumes were heavy and sweet.

She swayed, blinked and was blind. She had lost the wall. She gave a soft shriek at the sudden blackness, the smell of mold and damp and the silence. There was a pebbly, sliding sound in the distance. She tottered toward the wall, caught herself against it, and the light suddenly sprang back into being. The corridor was empty in both directions. She had imagined it all. She lifted her free hand to her forehead and touched the injury there. She should not have tried this. It was too much for her. Best to find a way out, and go back to her chamber and bed. If she met anyone, she wouldn't have to pretend that her mind was wandering. She was now seriously afraid that it was.

She stepped out resolutely, trailing her fingers on the strip. She no longer hesitated at corners or peered into rooms. She hurried through the labyrinth of corridors, turning down those that looked largest and most used. The music grew loud at one point, but then a wrong turning led her astray from it. She came at length to a broad corridor, well lit. An odd pattern that suggested winged creatures in flight decorated the walls.

The wide corridor culminated in a tall arched door of embossed metal. Malta halted and stared at it. She knew the insignia on it. It matched the one on the Khuprus coach door. It was a big chicken with a crown, looking as if it wanted to fight. For such a silly motif, it looked both haughty and threatening. She almost admired it.

From beyond the door came the sounds of a party in progress. People were talking and laughing. Music was playing merrily and she heard the lively slap of the dancers' feet against the door. She looked down at her dress once more. Well, there was no help for it. She just wanted to get out of this place and go back. She should be accustomed to humiliation by now. She set one hand to her brow as if she felt faint. She put her other hand on the great door and pushed.

She was plunged into sudden blackness, stumbling forward as the big door gave swiftly and easily at her touch. The cold and the damp rose up all around her. She trod in a deep puddle of cold water. "Help!" she cried out foolishly. But the music and the voices were stilled. The room smelled like a stagnant pond. Either she was blind, or the darkness was absolute.

"Hello?" she called again. Hands held out before her, she edged forward. But there were steps, going down, and before she could help herself, she toppled. Touch told her the steps were broad and shallow. She did not fall far. She did not stand again, but felt her way with her hands as she crawled down them. At the bottom of the steps, she crawled a short way. Then she stood and went even more slowly, feeling her way in front of her through the dark. "Hello?" she called again. Her voice bounced in the room. It must be immense.

Her groping hands suddenly encountered a rough wooden barrier.

"Hello, Malta Vestrit," the dragon said to her. "So we meet at last. I knew you'd come to me."

"DON'T SPEAK LIKE THAT ABOUT YOUR BROTHER!" JANI KHUPRUS SNAPPED. She slapped her needlework down onto the table beside her.

Bendir sighed. "I'm only telling you what other people are saying. Not what I'm saying. If someone poisons him, it won't be me." He tried for a grin.

Jani clutched at her chest. "That isn't even remotely funny. Oh, Sa, why did not we get that log cut up before he came back?"

"He planned to stay in Bingtown for several weeks, not one night. I thought I had time. That log is bigger and harder than any other wizardwood we've ever cut. Once the pigeons carried us the Bingtown news, I knew we had other things to worry about."

"I know, I know." His mother dismissed all his excuses with a flap of her hand. "Where is he now?"

"Where he is every night. He's in his room, drinking by himself. And talking to himself. Wild words about dragons and Malta. And killing himself."

"What?" She stared at him. His words destroyed the small island of evening peace in her sitting room.

"That's what Geni heard through the door; it was why she ran to tell me. He keeps saying she'll kill him at his own hands. That Malta will die, too," he added unwillingly.

"Malta? He's angry with Malta? But I thought they made up today. I heard . . ." Jani's voice faltered reluctantly.

Bendir picked up her words. "We all heard. Reyn was in her bed-chamber, holding her on his lap and fondling her. Given his other behavior lately, a common scandal like simple lust was almost a relief."

"They've been through a lot. He thought she would die, and blamed himself. It's natural for him to cling to her now." It was a feeble excuse and Jani knew it. She wondered if Keffria had heard of it yet. Would it change her plans? Why did Reyn have to behave so strangely just now, when there were so many other crises to deal with?

"Well, I certainly wish he was 'clinging' to her now, instead of ranting and raving in his room," Bendir observed coldly.

Jani Khuprus stood abruptly. "This isn't good for any of us. I can't talk sense to him tonight, if he's drunk, but we'll take the brandy away and insist he sleep. Tomorrow, I'll demand he mend his behavior. You should find some work for him."

Bendir's eyes lit. "I'd like to send him back into the city. Rewo found a mound, further back in the swamp. He thinks it might be the upper story of another building. I'd like to put Reyn on it."

"I don't think that's wise. I don't think he should get anywhere near the city."

"It's the only thing he's good at," Bendir began, then clamped his lips at his mother's glare. He led the way and Jani followed him out into the night. They were still two catwalks away from Reyn's chamber when she began to hear his voice. It was slurred. Another level, and every word of his drunken rambling was plain. It was worse than she had feared. Her heart sank. He couldn't go as his father had gone, talking only to himself. *Please, Sa, mother of all, do not be so unfair.*

Reyn's voice rose in a sudden shout. Bendir broke into a run. Jani hurried after him. The door of Reyn's chamber was suddenly flung open. Golden lamplight flooded the night. Her son lurched into view, and then halted, clutching at the doorframe. It was obvious he couldn't stand by himself. "Malta!" he bellowed into the night. "NO! Malta, no!" He staggered out, his arms flailing wildly as he reached for a railing and missed.

Bendir's shoulder hit Reyn in the chest. He strong-armed his brother back into the room and onto the floor. Reyn seemed incapable of putting up any real resistance. He thrashed his arms, but went down flat on his back, groaning loudly as the air was driven out of him. Then Reyn shut his eyes and was still. He had passed out. Jani hastily shut the door behind her. "Let's get him up onto his bed," she said with weary relief.

Then Reyn rolled his head to one side. He opened his eyes and tears flowed down his cheeks. "No!" he wailed. "Let me up. I have to get to Malta. The dragon has her. She'll take her. I have to rescue Malta."

"Don't be ridiculous," Jani snapped at her son. "It's late at night, and you're in no condition to see or be seen by anyone. Bendir is going to help you to bed and that's as far as you are going."

His older brother stood over him, then bent and grasped him by the shirtfront. He dragged him half off the floor, two steps to the bed, and dumped him mostly on it. He straightened, and brushed his hands together. "Done," he panted. "Take the brandy, and put out the lantern. Reyn, stay here and sleep it off. No more shouting." His voice brooked no nonsense.

"Malta," Reyn drawled again in misery.

"You're drunk," Bendir retorted.

"Not that drunk." Reyn tried to sit up, but Bendir pushed him back. The younger man made fists, but then suddenly turned to his mother. "The dragon has Malta. She's there for me. She's going to take her."

"Malta is going to take the dragon?" Jani frowned at his words.

"NO!" he roared in his frustration. He tried to get up, but Bendir shoved him back, more roughly this time. Reyn swung at his older brother, who easily evaded the roundhouse punch, and warned him fiercely, "Don't try that. I'll knock you silly."

"Mama!" The wail sounded ridiculous coming from a grown man. "Malta went to the dragon." He drew a deep breath, then spoke slowly and carefully. "The dragon has Malta now, instead of me." He lifted both hands and patted at his head. "The dragon is gone. I don't feel her anymore. Malta made her leave me alone."

"That's good, Reyn." Jani tried to be comforting. "The dragon is gone. All gone now. Go to sleep. In the morning, I want you to tell me all about it. I have some things to tell you, too." She ignored her elder son's disgusted snort.

Reyn took a huge breath, and sighed it out. "You aren't listening. You don't understand. I'm so tired. All I want to do is sleep. But I have to go to her. I have to take the dragon back and make Malta go. She'll die and it's all my fault."

"Reyn." Jani sat down on the edge of her son's bed. She tugged a blanket over him. "You're drunk and you're tired and you're not making sense. There is no dragon. Only an old log. Malta is not in danger. Her injury was an accident, not truly your fault. She grows stronger every day. Soon she'll be up and about again. Now go to sleep."

"Never try to reason with a drunk," Bendir suggested, as if to himself.

Reyn groaned. "Mother." He took a deep breath, as if to speak. Instead, he sighed. "I'm so tired. I haven't slept in so long. But listen. Listen. Malta went to the city, to the Rooster Crown Chamber. Go get her. That's all. Please. Please do that."

"Of course. You go to sleep now. Bendir and I will take care of it." She patted his hand and brushed his curly hair back from his pebbled brow.

Bendir made a disgusted noise. "You treat him like a baby!" He gathered up the bottles from the table and went to the door. One by one, he heaved them out into the swamp. Jani ignored his display of temper. She sat by Reyn, watching his eyes slowly droop and then close. Drowned in the memories. No. He wasn't, not her son. This was just the rambling of a drunken man. He was still himself. He saw her, he saw his brother. He didn't talk to ghosts. He was in love with a real live girl. He hadn't drowned, and he wouldn't.

Bendir came back into the chamber. He picked up the lantern from the table. "Coming?" he asked her.

She nodded, and followed her eldest son. As she shut the door, Reyn was breathing deeply and evenly.

"AND YOU WILL LEAVE HIM ALONE, FOREVER," MALTA STIPULATED BRAVELY.

The dragon laughed. *"Once I am free, little one, why should I be interested in your brief little lives? I will fly away to seek my own kind. Of course, I will leave him alone. Now. Let me show you."*

Malta stood in the black chamber. Both her hands and her aching forehead rested against the block of wood. She took a breath. "And you will go and rescue my father."

"Certainly," the dragon purred. *"I already told you I would. Now release me."*

"But how will I know you will keep your word?" Malta cried out in agony. More decisively, she added, "You have to give me something, some sort of a sign."

"I give you my word." The dragon was getting impatient.

"I need more than that." Malta pondered. There was something, if she could just remember it. Then she had it. "Tell me your name."

"No." The dragon was adamant. *"But once I am free, I will bring you*

treasure such as you have never dreamed existed. Diamonds as big as pigeon's eggs. I will fly to the south and bring you back the flowers that never fade, the blossoms that cure your kind of any ill just by breathing their scent. I will fly to the north and bring you back the ice that is harder than any metal and never melts. I will show you how to make blades from it that can cut even stone. I will fly to the east and bring you back—"

"No tales!" Malta protested. "No treasures. I ask only that you will leave Reyn alone, and that you will rescue my father. The name of the ship is *Vivacia*. You have to remember that. You must find the ship, kill the pirates and rescue him."

"Yes, yes. Just . . ."

"No. Swear it by your name. Say that by your name you swear to rescue Kyle Haven and to leave Reyn Khuprus in peace. Say that, and I'll do as you say."

She felt the blast of the dragon's anger like a slap against her whole body. *"You dare to dictate to me? I have you now, little bug. Deny me, and I'll ride your soul to the end of your days. I will rule you. I will tell you to pull the nails from your own hands, and you will do it. I will demand you smother your babies, and you will obey. I will make of you a monster that even your own folk will—"*

A little tremor shivered the chamber, breaking into the dragon's threats. Malta pressed her lips together to keep from crying out.

"You see, you anger the gods with your demands on me! Do as I tell you, or they will make the whole hill fall on you."

"And on you, also," Malta pointed out relentlessly. "I care not what you threaten me with. If you could do such things, you would have forced Reyn to obey you long ago. Say your name! Say your name or I do nothing for you. Nothing!"

The dragon was silent. Malta waited. She was so cold. She had gone beyond shivering to a bone-jolting shaking that made her head pound and her spine hurt. Her feet felt numb. She thought she was standing in a puddle but could no longer be sure. She had come to the city, she had found the dragon, but she was still going to fail. She couldn't save anybody, not her father, not the man who had given up his city for her. This was all she was, a helpless woman with no power in the world. She dropped her hands from the wood and turned away from it. She began to grope her way across the room. She hoped she was going in the right direction.

The dragon's voice rang suddenly in the stillness. *"Tintaglia. My name is Tintaglia."*

"And?" Malta halted where she stood, breathless with hope.

"And if you free me, I promise I will leave Reyn Khuprus in peace and I will rescue your father, Kyle Haven."

Malta took a deep breath. She lifted her hands and walked boldly across the chamber. When her hands rested on the wood, she bowed her head. She sighed out all resistance. "Tell me how to free you."

The dragon spoke quickly, eagerly. *"There is a great door in the south wall. The Elderlings created art here, in this chamber. They made living sculptures of my kind, from the memory stone. Old men would carve them in this chamber, safe from wind and weather. Then they would die into them and the sculptures would briefly take on their lives. The door would open, the simulacra would emerge into sunlight and fly over the city. They would live a brief time, and then their memories and false life would fade. There was a graveyard of them, back in the mountains. The Elderlings thought of it as art. We found it amusing to see ourselves copied in stone. So we tolerated it."*

"None of that means anything to me," Malta chided her. The cold was creeping up her legs. Her knees ached with it. She was tired of talking. Let her do whatever she must do and be done with it.

"There are panels in the wall that conceal the levers and cranks that open the great door. Find them, and use them. When the sun rises tomorrow and touches my cradle, I will be freed."

Malta frowned. "If it's so easy, why didn't Reyn do it?"

"He wanted to, but he was afraid. Males are timorous creatures at best. They think only to feed and breed. But you and I, young queen, we know there is more. Females must be ruthless, to shelter their young and continue the race. Chances must be taken. Males will quiver in the shadow, fearing their own deaths. We know that the only thing to be feared is the end of the race."

The words rang oddly in Malta's soul. *Almost true,* she whispered to herself. But she could not sort out the part of it that was false.

"Where are the panels?" she asked wearily. "Let us just do this."

"I don't know," the dragon admitted. *"I was never in this chamber. What I know, I know from the lives of others. You must find them."*

"How?"

"You must learn from those who knew. Come to me, and let down your walls, Malta Vestrit. Let me open the memories of the city to you, and you will know all."

"The memories of the city?"

"It was their conceit, to store their memories in the bones of their city. They brush your kind, but you cannot master them at will. I can help you find them. Let me."

All the pieces tumbled into place for her. She suddenly grasped what her part of the bargain must be. She took a deep breath. Then she leaned on the wood, pressing her hands, her arms, her breast, her cheek to it. Another breath, as if she poised for a dive. She forbade herself to fear or resist. She spoke with a dry mouth.

"Drown me in the memories."

The dragon did not wait to hear more.

The chamber sprang to life. Malta Vestrit vanished like an apparition. A hundred other lives blossomed around her. Tall people, with eyes of copper and violet and skin like honey, filled the room. They danced, they talked, they drank while stars shone above through the impossibly clear dome roof of the building. Then, in the wink of an eye, it was dawn. The early light crept in, to shine on the exotic plants that bloomed in tubs throughout the room. In one corner of the immense room, a tiered fountain leaped and fish darted in its water. It was noon and doors were opened to allow the breeze to cool the chamber. Then it was evening, and the doors were closed and the Elderfolk gathered again to talk and laugh and dance to music. Another blink and the sun returned. A door opened, and an immense block of black stone veined with silver was dragged into the room on rollers. Days passed like petals falling from apple blossoms. A group of old men moved around the stone with hammers and chisels. A dragon emerged. The old men leaned on it, faded into it. The doors opened. The dragon stirred and then strode forth to the cheers and tears of the well-wishers. It launched and flew away. Folk gathered to drink and dance and talk. Another block of stone was dragged in. Days and nights dripped by like black and white beads coming unstrung. Malta stood rooted in time and the days flowed around her. She watched and waited, and soon no longer knew that she did that. The memories filled the chamber slowly, like thick honey. She soaked in them and understood all, far more than her mind could hold. The memories had been stored here, for that had been a pleasure they cultivated, the sampling of one another's memories. But not like this, Malta wailed, not in a flood that spared no detail, glossed over no emotion. It was too much, too much. She was neither Elderling nor dragon. She was not meant to hold this much. She could not hold this much. It bled out of her; she forgot as much as she held. She groped after the one important detail she must find and hold. The panels. The levers and wheels. That was the only important memory. She let go of all else.

Her body sprawled in the cold puddle. Cold rose through her flesh and into her bones, but the months and the years turned cartwheels around her, impressing every swift second upon her burning memory. She knew enough and then she knew more. The days wheeled out both before and behind her, time moving in both directions. She saw the blocks of the walls being set in place, and she saw the workmen desperately bringing in the dragon cradles. They pulled them on ropes, trundling them along on rollers, for outside the sky had blackened and the earth was shaking and ash rained from the sky swift and thick as a black snowfall. Suddenly it all stopped. She had reached the setting of the first brick in one direction, and in the other the folk had fled or lay dying. She knew it all, and she knew nothing.

Malta. Get up.

Which one was she? Why should she matter more than any other should? They all were, in the end, interchangeable. Weren't they?

Malta Vestrit. Do you remember? Do you remember how to open the door?

Move the body. Sit up in it. Such a short, ungainly body. Such a short life it had led. How stupid she was. Blink the eyes. The chamber is dark, but it is so simple to recall the chamber as it once was, full of light. The sun shone overhead, and rainbowed down through the crystal panels. There. Now. To work. The doors.

There were two doors in the chamber. She had entered by the north door. It was too small for the dragon to pass through. The cradle had been brought in through the south door. She could recall little else of who she was or why she was here, but she recalled the opening of the door. Ordinarily, it would have been done by four strong men. She would have to do it alone. She went to the first panel beside the south door and found the catch. Her fingernails bent against it, and still the decorative door would not open. She had no tools. She pounded on it with her fist. Something snicked inside it. She tugged again at the catch. This time it reluctantly swung open. With a crash, the panel broke off its ancient hinges and fell to the floor. No matter.

Again, the chamber's memory and her touch were at odds. The well-oiled crank that should have been there was draped in cobwebs and pitted with corrosion. She found the handle and strove to turn it anyway. It would not budge. Oh. The lever. Pull the lever first. She groped for it and found it. The polished wooden handle was gone. Bare metal met her grasp. She seized it in both hands and pulled. It did not move.

When she finally braced both her feet against the wall and dragged down on it, the lever gave. It moved fractionally then suddenly surrendered to her weight. There was a terrible rending sound from within the wall as she fell to the stone floor. For a moment, she was half stunned. A groaning shivered behind the panel. She clambered to her feet again. Now. The crank. No, no, that would not work. The other lever first. The door must be released on both sides before the cranks could lift it.

She no longer cared about her torn nails and bleeding hands. She wrenched the second panel open. As she did so, damp earth cascaded into the room from the compartment. The wall was breached here. She didn't care. With her hands, she dug away around the lever until she could wrap both her hands around it. She seized it and pulled violently at it. It traveled a short way, and then stopped. This time she clambered up the decorative scrollwork on the wall, to stand atop the lever. Bouncing her weight on it moved it down another notch. Far overhead, something groaned. Malta braced her entire body and shoved down with her feet. The lever gave, then suddenly broke off under her. She fell past it, tearing her skirts on the jagged metal. Her knee smacked sharply against the stone floor and for a time, all she knew was pain.

Malta. Get up.

"I know. I will." Her own voice sounded thin and odd to her. She got to her feet and limped back to the panel. The crank handle was mounted on a spoked wheel the size of a carriage wheel. It was made of metal. Damp earth was packed solidly around it. For an eternity, she dug at it. The soil was cold and wet and abrasive. It packed under her nails and sanded into her skin.

Just try it.

Obediently, she set both hands to the handle on the wheel. Her memory told her that two men should be on this crank and two on its partner. They would all have worked in synchronicity to turn them.

But she was the only one here. She put her weight on it and dragged down. Miraculously, it turned, but not far. Far up the wall, something shifted. She left this crank and walked back to the other one. At least this one was not packed with earth. She seized the handle and turned it. It moved more smoothly than its partner, but not much farther. She walked back to the first crank. It turned a notch. She went back to the other crank, and turned it. As she turned it, she could hear something moving in the wall. There was a tiny shifting. The door itself moved fractionally. She leaned on the crank and it moved again. Odd sounds whispered through the wall and door. Ancient chains moved on pulleys, her memories whispered. Counterweights began their descent. That was how she had designed it, remember? Remember. Remember how it was designed. Remember how the whole dome was designed.

She suddenly saw the whole wall and door and their mechanisms differently. The memory of how it should have been contrasted too strongly with what her hands told her. She felt the dirt and wet earth with her hands, shutting her eyes to block out the memory of how it had been. She groped her way across the door, feeling the bulges in its structure, the cracks that crossed it. She spun suddenly. "This whole side of the structure will give way if the door is moved. Only chance has kept it intact this long."

"It will give way, the earth will fall away from it, and the light will shine in," the dragon predicted. *"Continue."*

"If you are wrong, you will be buried here, and I along with you."

"I prefer that than to continue as I am. Turn the cranks, Malta. You promised."

So potent a thing is a name. She snapped back to herself, a young woman in muddy clothes in the darkness. The proud young builder was gone, not even a memory, as dreams wisp away when the awakened one clutches at them. She took the crank in her hand and turned it another notch.

It was the last motion either crank would make. From one to the other she went, back and forth, tugging and cursing. It was as far as the ancient mechanism would move. The wall muttered uneasily to itself, but the door would not move.

"It's jammed. I can't do it. I tried. I'm sorry."

For a long instant, the dragon was silent. Then she commanded, *"Get help. Your brother . . . I see him. You dominate him easily. Fetch him, and two rods to use as levers. Go now. Now."*

There were good and sound reasons to resist this command, but Malta could not recall what they were. She could barely recall this brother the dragon spoke of. The door and the means to open it were all she clearly knew. The rods were a good idea. Shoved through the spokes of the wheel, she could use them as levers to force the cranks to turn.

She walked in light remembered from another time. She dragged her weary steps up the broad stair and out the north door. As she walked, her fingers found the jidzin strip and trailed along it. The corridor illuminated itself to guide her. A blink of her tired eyes, and it thronged with life. Nobles swept past her, their gangly pages in attendance on them. A seamstress and her two young apprentices backed, bowing, out of a door, rich fabrics draped over their arms. A nursemaid with a chubby-kneed child wailing in her arms hastened toward her and then through her. The nurse called a cheery greeting to a young man in a beribboned cap, and he whistled in reply. Malta was the unseen ghost here, not they. The city was theirs.

She stumbled suddenly on fallen stone. She lost her touch on the wall and was plunged once more into darkness. This was her time, her life, and it was dark and dank and riddled with collapsed corridors and jammed doors. This fall of earth, her groping hands told her, completely blocked the corridor. She could not go that way.

She touched the wall to get her bearings and instantly knew a better route that led to a closer exit. She turned her steps that way and hurried along. She no longer listened to the exhausted complaints of her body. She lived now in a thousand different moments; why focus on the one where she was in pain? She trotted along, her bedraggled skirts alternately slapping or clinging to her legs.

She slammed to the floor. "A quake," she said dully, aloud, after it had passed. She lay still on the stone for a time afterwards, waiting for the echo-shake that often followed. Nothing happened. There were sounds, shifting and grating sounds. None of them seemed to come from nearby. Cautiously she came to her feet. She touched the light strip. Light flickered along it, but dimly. Malta had to reach for memories of how the corridor should be before she went on.

There were screams in the distance. She ignored them as she ignored the chatter of strolling couples and the barking of a small dog that brushed past her unfelt. Ghosts and memories. She had a door to open.

She turned down a side corridor that would lead her out. The screaming was close here. A woman's voice cried out, "Please, please, the door is stuck. Get us out of here. Get us out before we die!" As Malta's hands trailed past the door, she felt the vibration of the woman's pounding. More in curiosity than in answer to the plea, she set her shoulder to the door. "Pull!" she shouted as she pushed on it. The jammed door suddenly flew open. A woman rushed out of it as soon as it did. She collided with Malta, sending them both to the floor. A pale man stood behind her. Real yellow lanternlight spilled out of the room behind them, near blinding Malta. The woman trampled Malta as she scrambled to her feet. "Get up!" she shrieked at her. "Take us out of here. The wall has cracked and mud is leaking in!"

Malta sat up and looked past her into a well-appointed chamber. The carpeted floor was being engulfed by a slow wave of mud. A crack in the wall was the source of it. Even as Malta stared at it, a little water suddenly bubbled through it. The mud began to flow faster, thinned by the water. Its passage ate at the wall. "The whole wall will give way soon," she observed with certainty.

The pale young man glanced at it over his shoulder. "You are probably right." He looked down on her. "Your masters assured us we would be safe here. That no one and nothing could find me here. What is the good of my hiding from assassins, only to be drowned in stinking mud?" Malta blinked. The Elder phantasms faded. The Satrap of Jamaillia scowled down at her. "Well, don't just lie there. Get up and take us to your masters. They will feel my wrath."

Companion Kekki had gone back into the chamber to snatch up a lantern. "She is useless," she declared to the Satrap. "Follow me. I think I know the way."

Malta lay on the floor, watching them go. This was very significant, she told herself dazedly. The Satrap of Jamaillia had been brought to Trehaug, for his own safety. She had not known that. Someone should have told her about it. Didn't he trust her? She closed her eyes to try to think about it more clearly. She thought of going to sleep.

The floor bucked under her, slapping her cheek. Down the hall from where she sprawled, Kekki and the Satrap screamed. The shrill sound did not scare Malta half so much as the deep rumbling from the chamber they had vacated. She scrabbled to her feet as the floor was still trembling. She seized the door and dragged it scraping shut. Could a door hold back a collapsing hillside?

She clutched at her head suddenly. Take control. She chose the moment and brought it to life around her. Chaos swirled past her. It might save them.

She turned and ran. Ahead of her, she saw the jouncing lantern the

Companion carried. She caught up with the Satrap and his woman. "You're going the wrong way," she informed them tersely. "Follow me." She snatched the lantern from Kekki's hand. "This way," she ordered them, and set off. They followed on her heels. Around them, phantoms shrieked thinly as they fled. Malta followed the flight of the Elderlings. If they had escaped their final cataclysm, perhaps she would as well.

CHAPTER THIRTY-SEVEN

Death of the City

THE QUAKE IN THE HOURS BEFORE THE SUMMER DAWN DID NOT WAKE Keffria. She hadn't been able to sleep. There had been a little bump in the night that she had ignored. This one was different. It started out as a sharp jolt, but it was the long shivering that followed that got her to her feet. Her Rain Wild hosts had warned her that the motion of the trees exaggerated the shifting of the earth below them. Nevertheless, she held onto the post of her bed as she hastily donned her clothes. Selden would think this was great fun, but Malta might be alarmed by it. She would go to her right away. And once there, she would force herself to tell Malta she was returning to Bingtown. She dreaded that. She had gone to see Malta yesterday evening, but found her sleeping. She hadn't had the heart to disturb her. The swelling had gone down from her head injury, but both her eyes were still deeply blackened. Knowing sleep was the best healer, Keffria had tiptoed away.

The healer had insisted that Malta be put in a sunny chamber, far up the tree from Keffria's room. Her path would take her over several bridges and then up a winding stair. She still wasn't accustomed to the gently swaying footpaths. Selden ran back and forth on them all day, but they still made Keffria nervous. She wished there was more light, but it would be a while until the sun penetrated the foliage all around her. She crossed her arms over her chest and kept to the direct middle of the path. She would not think of how the bridge would sway if there were another quake while she was crossing it. She put all such thoughts out of her mind. She realized she was walking with tiny, mincing steps and deliberately tried to normalize her stride. She was glad to reach the winding staircase that twined up the tree's trunk.

She rehearsed ways of telling Malta she was leaving her here. It would be hard. When Keffria left, Malta would be very alone, save for Selden. She had refused to see Reyn at all. She still blamed him. Keffria herself had forgiven him on the *Kendry* during their upriver journey. She believed the men who had accosted the carriage had gone far beyond their orders to seize the Satrap. The guilt and remorse of the young Rain Wilder as he kept vigil outside Malta's stateroom door had convinced Keffria that he had never intended harm to his beloved. Perhaps in time Malta would see as much, but in the meantime, Keffria would be leaving her children to depend only on one another. The doubts that had assailed her all night returned. She ventured out on the limb that led to Malta's room.

She nodded a brief greeting to a woman who had come to the door of a nearby chamber. The skin of her face was heavily pebbled. Growths wattled her throat and chin. Tillamon, Reyn's older sister, smiled brightly at her. "Quite a bump we had," Keffria observed inanely.

"I hope everyone is all right. Last month, we lost two bridges in a quake like that one," Tillamon observed cheerily.

"Oh, dear," Keffria heard herself reply. She hastened on.

She tapped at the door and waited. There was no reply. "Malta, dear, it is me," she announced and went in. The relief she felt at being off the catwalk evaporated as she stared at Malta's empty bed. "Malta?" Stupidly she went to stir the empty blankets as if they could somehow conceal her daughter. She went back to the door and leaned out it. "Malta?" she called questioningly.

Reyn's sister was still in her doorway. "Did the healer take Malta somewhere?" Keffria called to her.

Tillamon shook her head.

Keffria tried not to be frightened. "It's just so strange. She's gone. She's too ill to be out of her bed yet. And she is never an early riser, even when she feels well." She would not look at the railings by the walk. She would not wonder if a dizzy girl could stagger up from her sick bed and . . .

The woman cocked her head. "She was out walking with Reynie yesterday," she volunteered. A small smile came and went from her face. "I heard they had made up," she offered apologetically.

"But that doesn't explain why she isn't in her bed . . . oh." Keffria stared at her.

"Oh, no. I didn't mean it like that. Reynie would never . . . he's not like that." She was falling over her own words. "I had better fetch my mother," she proposed awkwardly.

There was something going on here, Keffria decided. Something she should have known about. "I think I had best go with you," she replied with a sinking heart.

It took more than tapping to waken Jani Khuprus. When she came to the door in her house-robe, her eyes were both weary and anxious. For an instant, Keffria almost pitied her. But Malta was at stake here. She met Jani's gaze squarely as she said, "Malta is not in her bed. Do you know where she might be?"

The fear that ghosted across Jani's face told Keffria all. She looked at her daughter. "Tillamon. Return to your chamber. This is only for Keffria and me."

"But, Mother," her daughter began, trailing off at the look her mother gave her. She shook her head, but turned and left. Jani's eyes came back to Keffria. The fine lines on her Rain Wild face suddenly stood out more clearly. She looked ill. She took a deep breath. "It is possible she is with Reyn somewhere. Late last night, he became . . . very worried about her. He might have gone to her. . . . This is not like Reyn, but he has not been himself, lately." She sighed. "Come with me."

Jani led the way swiftly. She had not paused to dress properly or veil herself. Even powered by anger and fear, Keffria could barely keep up with her.

As they neared Reyn's chamber, misgivings assailed Keffria. If Malta and Reyn had settled their differences, they might . . . She wanted suddenly to stop and think things through more carefully. "Jani," she began as the other woman lifted her hand to knock. But she didn't knock. She simply pushed the door of Reyn's room open.

A heavy smell of brandy and sweat hung in the air. Jani peered in, then stepped aside to allow Keffria the view. Reyn sprawled facedown on his bed. His arm hung over the side, the back of his wrist against the floor. His breathing was hoarse and heavy. He slept as one exhausted, and he slept alone.

Jani's fingers were on her lips as she pulled the door shut. Keffria held her apology in until they were well away from his chamber.

"Jani, I am so—" she began, but the other woman turned to her quickly with a twisted smile.

"We both well know that we have cause to worry with those two. Reyn has come to this passion late in his life. Malta has been distant with him since she arrived, yet I do not believe her heart is cold toward him. The sooner they come to an understanding, the easier it will be for all of us."

Keffria nodded wearily, grateful for her understanding. "But where could she be? She is too ill to be out and about alone."

"I share your concern. Let me send out some runners to see if anyone has seen her. Could she have gone off with Selden, perhaps?"

"Perhaps. The last few weeks have brought them closer. I know he has been longing to show her the city." Keffria lifted her splinted hand to her forehead. "This behavior makes me wonder if I am wise to leave them here. I thought Malta was maturing, but for her to go off like this, with no word at all. . . ."

Jani halted on the narrow walk and took Keffria's arm. Her eyes, still unveiled in the morning's haste, met Keffria's squarely. "I promise I shall care for them as my own. There is no need to foster Selden anywhere else but with us. It will do Reyn good to have the care of a young boy, before he has sons of his own." Jani smiled and the hope on her face took away much of the Rain Wild strangeness. Then an almost pleading look replaced it. "What you offered to do for us yesterday is incredibly brave. I feel selfish to urge you toward it. Yet, you are the only one so uniquely suited to spy for us."

"Spy." The word sat oddly on her tongue. "I suppose—" Keffria began, but her words were broken by the bronze tones of a great bell. "What is that?" she asked, but Jani was staring, stricken, toward the ancient city.

"It means that there has been a collapse, and folk may be trapped. That is the only time the bell is rung. All who can work, must. I have to go, Keffria." Without another word, the Rain Wild Trader turned and sprinted away, leaving Keffria gaping after her. Slowly she turned her eyes toward the buried city. She could not see much of it through the trees, but the panorama of Trehaug was spread out in levels before her. People were calling to one another, men dragging on shirts as they crossed catwalks, while women came after them carrying tools and water jugs. Keffria resolved she would find Malta and Selden. They would go together, to help wherever they could, if Malta was up to it. It might provide an opportunity for her to tell them she was returning to Bingtown as soon as the *Kendry* sailed.

MALTA HAD LOST TRACK OF HOW MANY DEAD ENDS THEY HAD DISCOVERED. It was maddening to watch the phantom inhabitants of the dead city vanish down the collapsed tunnels. The apparitions simply disappeared into the cascades of earth and stone. Each time she fetched up against a barrier of damp earth, the Satrap and his Companion became more distressed.

"You said you knew the way!" he accused her.

"I do know the way. I know all the ways. All we have to do is find one that is not blocked."

She had concluded long ago that he did not recognize her as the girl from the dance and the coach ride. He treated her as a rather stupid servant. She did not blame him. She was having a hard time holding on to that Malta, too. Her memories of the ball and the accident seemed hazier and more distant than the memories of the city around her. Her life as Malta seemed the tale of a frivolous and spoiled girl. Even now, escape and survival did not drive her as hard as her need to find her brother and return with rods so they might free the dragon. She had to find a way out. Helping them was incidental.

She passed the theatre, then abruptly turned back to the entrance to that vast chamber. The door gaped blackly in the wall. She held the wavering lantern high to see how it had fared. The once-magnificent chamber had partially collapsed. Efforts had been made to remove the

earth, but the great blocks of stone that had once supported the lofty
ceiling had thwarted the diggers. She peered hopefully and decided it was
worth a chance. "This way," she said to those following her.

Kekki wailed, "Oh, that is foolish. It has already mostly fallen down.
We need to find a way out, not go deeper into ruin."

Easier to explain than to argue. "Every theatre must have a way for
the actors to come and go. The Elderlings preferred that they remain
unseen, to better preserve the illusion of the play. Behind the stage,
which yet stands, there are apartments and a means of egress. Often have
I come and gone that way. Come. Follow me with trust and you may yet
be saved."

Kekki looked affronted. "Don't give yourself airs with me, little maid.
You forget yourself."

Malta was silent for a moment. "More than you know," she agreed in
a stranger's voice. Whose words had those been, whose diction? She did
not know and there was no time to trace a single memory. She led them
to the stage, up and across it and then down behind it. Some debris
blocked the hidden door, but most of it was wood rather than stone. No
one had been this way in a long, long time. Perhaps the Rain Wild folk
had never even discovered this door. She put the lantern down and set to
work clearing it while the Satrap and his Companion watched. She
worked the latch by tracing the sign of the actors' guild upon the light
panel. When that did not work, she kicked the door. It swung slowly into
darkness. The lintel above groaned threateningly, but held.

She prayed the corridor would be clear. She set her hand to the light
strip in the wall, and the narrow hall suddenly glowed into life. Clear and
straight, it ran off ahead of her, beckoning them to freedom. "This way,"
Malta announced. Kekki caught up the lantern, but Malta was ready to
trust to the light strip now. Her fingers rode it lightly as she walked the
hall. Echoes of someone else's anticipation rustled in her heart. That door
led to the wardrobe, those to the chambers where the dancers might
change and loosen their limbs. It had been a great theatre, the finest in
any of the Elderlings' cities. The back door, she recalled, opened onto a
wonderful verandah and a boathouse that overlooked the river. Some of
the actors and singers had kept their own small vessels stored there, for
moonlit trysts on the river.

With a shake of her head, Malta rattled it free of dreams. A door out,
she told herself. That was all she sought, a door out of the buried city.

The corridor ran on and on, past practice rooms and past the small
shops of those who supported the artists of the theatre. That had been a
costumer's shop, and this door had gone to a fine little drug den. Here was
the wigmaker, and there was the paint-and-paste artist's shop. Gone, all
gone, still and dead. This had been the beating heart of the city, for what
art is greater than art that imitates life itself? Malta hurried past them, but

inside her heart, the memories of a hundred artists mourned their own demise.

When she did see daylight ahead, it was so pale and gray, it seemed a cheat. The final stretch of the corridor was damaged. The light strip was gone, and their lantern failing. They would have to hurry now. The blocks that made up the walls had lost their plaster and frescoes. They bowed in, and gleams of water edged down them. Stains on the wall showed Malta that this corridor had been flooded, and more than once. Whenever the river was swollen with the rains, it probably filled these tunnels. It was only good fortune that the way was clear now. Even so, they waded through soft muck. Malta had long ago given up any care for her clothes, but both the Satrap and his Companion made dismayed noises as they squelched along behind her.

The verandah and boathouse that had once been the terminus of this corridor were now tumbled wreckage. There was no clear pathway. Malta ignored the protests of the others, and picked her way through, moving always toward the gray daylight ahead. Rains had washed dirt and leaves into what remained of the corridor. Some quake long ago had cleft both earth and corridor. "We're out!" Malta called back to them. She climbed over the remains of stacked boats, wriggled through the muddy cleft and suddenly stumbled out into early morning light. She drew breath after breath of the fresh air, rejoicing simply in the open space around her. She had not realized how being surrounded by dark and earth had oppressed her spirits until she stood clear of it. She stood clear, also, of all the whispering spirits. It was like wakening from a long and confusing dream. She started to rub her face, then stopped. Her hands were smeared and gritty. The few fingernails she had left were packed with mud. Her clothing clung to her in muddy rags. She discovered she had but one shoe on. Where and who had she been?

She was still blinking as the Satrap and his Companion emerged. They were a bit muddy, but not near as bedraggled as Malta. She turned to smile at them, expecting thanks. Instead, Magnadon Satrap Cosgo demanded, "Where is the city? What is the use of bringing us out of the wreckage to this forsaken spot?"

Malta gazed all around her. Trees. Sluggish gray water around the bases of the trees. She stood on a hump of tussocky ground in the middle of a swamp. She had lost all her bearings in her time underground. She oriented herself by the rising sun and looked for Trehaug. The forest blocked her view. She shrugged. "We're either upriver or downriver of it," she hazarded to herself.

"As we seem to be on a tiny island, that seems a very safe thing to say," the Satrap opined.

Malta climbed to higher ground for a better view, but it only confirmed his sour guess. It was not so much an island as a hummock in a swamp. She could not be sure which direction was the river channel and which led to swamp. The immense gray columns of the river trees extended as far as she could see in every direction.

"We'll have to go back," she concluded, her heart sinking. She did not know if she could face those ranked ghosts again.

"No!" Kekki uttered the word with a little shriek, then sat flat on the ground. She began sobbing hopelessly. "I cannot. I will not go back into the dark. I won't."

"Obviously we don't have to," the Satrap observed impatiently. "We climbed over a number of little boats getting out. Maid, go back in and find the best one. Drag it out here, and row us back to the city." He looked about in disgust, then drew a kerchief out of his pocket and spread it on the ground. He sat down on it. "I shall rest here." He shook his head. "This is a poor way for these Traders to treat their rightful leader. They will regret their careless misuse of me."

"Possibly. But not as much as we regret how we have allowed you to misuse us," Malta heard herself say. She was suddenly angry with these ungrateful wretches. She had toiled through the night to guide them out of the tunnels, and this was her thanks? To be ordered to fetch a boat and row them to Trehaug? She shook out her ragged skirts and mocked a curtsey at the Satrap. "Malta Vestrit, of the Bingtown Traders, bids Magnadon Satrap Cosgo and his Companion Kekki farewell. I am not your servant to be put to your bidding. Nor do I consider myself your subject anymore. Good-bye."

She pushed her hair back from her face and turned toward the muddy crack in the earth. She took a deep breath. She could do this. She had to do this. Once she got back to Trehaug, they could send a rescue party after the Satrap. Perhaps a time sitting marooned on this hummock of land would teach him a little humility.

"Wait!" he commanded. "Malta Vestrit? The girl from the Summer Ball?"

She looked over her shoulder. She acknowledged the connection with a nod.

"Leave me here, and I will never send my ships to rescue your father!" he informed her grandiosely.

"Your ships?" She laughed, a bit wildly. "What ships? You never intended to help me. I am surprised you can even remember that you said you would."

"Fetch the boat and row us to safety. Then you shall see how a Satrap of Jamaillia keeps his promises."

"Probably much the same way as he honors the charters of his ancestors," Malta scoffed. She turned her back and began to climb back down into the dark. Far down the corridor, she heard sounds like distant but thunderous applause. Dread rose in her. Drowned in memories. She knew what it meant now. Could she traverse the city again and remain herself? She forced herself to keep going. Once more, she scrabbled over the boats, noting in passing that they were not as dilapidated as she had thought. Some sort of hammered metal had been applied to the hulls. As she clambered over them, her hands came away powdered white where she had touched them. Far down the corridor, there was another roar of applause. She walked slowly toward it, but suddenly a cloud of dust wafted into her face. She coughed and choked for a moment. When she blinked her eyes clear of grit and looked down the corridor, she could see a mist of dust hanging in the air. She stared a moment longer, refusing to recognize what she instinctively knew. The corridor had caved in. There was no going back that way.

She swayed with weariness, then stiffened her back and stood straight. When it was all over, then she could rest. She walked back slowly to the stacked rowboats. She eyed them skeptically. The top one had broken seats. She picked at a splinter of it, then recognized the wood. Cedar. Her father called it eternity wood. She began to work the top boat loose from the others, to see if the one below it might be better.

"REYN? REYN, DEAR, WE NEED YOU. YOU HAVE TO WAKE UP NOW."

He rolled away from the gentle voice and the hands that plucked at him. "Go away," he said distinctly, and dragged the pillow over his head. Dimly he wondered why he was sleeping in his clothes and shoes.

Bendir had always been more direct. He seized his younger brother's ankles. Reyn came all the way awake as he thudded onto the floor. He was instantly furious.

"Bendir!" Mother rebuked him, but his brother was unrepentant.

"We don't have time to talk nicely. He should have come as soon as the bell rang. I don't care how lovesick he is, or how hungover."

The words penetrated both his anger and sleepiness. "The bell? A cave-in?"

"Half the damn city has fallen in," Bendir explained tersely. "While you were drunk enough to walk on your lips, we had two quakes last night. Sharp shocks. We have crews digging in and shoring up as we go, but it's taking a long time. You know the structure of the city better than anyone does. We need you."

"Malta? Is Malta all right?" Reyn asked anxiously. She had been in the dragon chamber. Had they got her out in time?

"Forget Malta!" his brother ordered him roughly. "If you want to worry about someone, the Satrap and his woman are blocked in down there, unless they're already dead. That would be a fine irony, for us to bring him up the river to protect him only to have him die in the city."

Reyn staggered upright. He was already dressed, down to his boots. He pushed his wild curls back from his face. "Let's go. You got Malta out all right, last night?"

The question was no more than a formality. His brother and mother would not be so calm if she were trapped down there.

"That was just a dream you had," Bendir said roughly.

Reyn halted where he stood. "No," he said flatly. "It wasn't. She went into the city, to the Crowned Rooster Chamber. I told you that. I know I did. I told you that you had to get her out of there. Didn't you do it?"

"She's sick in bed, not down in the city," Bendir exclaimed in annoyance.

His mother had gone pale. She set her hand to the doorframe and clutched it. Breathlessly she said, "Keffria came to me at dawn. Malta was not in her bed. She thought—" she shook her head at both of them. "She thought her daughter might be with Reyn. We came here, and of course, she was not. Then, the bell rang and . . ." Her voice trailed off. More determinedly, she added, "But how could Malta have reached the city, let alone gone into it? She has scarcely left her bed since she got here. She would not know the way, let alone how to reach the Crowned Rooster Chamber."

"Selden," Reyn said harshly. "Her little brother. He's been all over Trehaug with Wilee Crane. Sa knows I've chased Wilee out of the city a score of times. Her brother would know the way in by now, if he has been playing with Wilee. Where's Selden?"

"I don't know," his mother admitted it with dread.

Bendir broke in without apology. "There are people who are definitely buried in the city, Reyn. The Satrap and his Companion, not to mention the Vintagli family's digging crew. They had just begun excavating a chamber near the one where they found the butterfly murals. At least two other families had night crews at work down there. We don't have time to worry about those who might be down there. We need to concentrate on the ones we know are down there."

"I know Malta is down there," Reyn said bitterly. "And I know where. The Crowned Rooster Chamber. I told you that last night. I'm going after her first."

"You can't!" Bendir barked, but Jani cut him off.

"Don't argue. Reyn, come and dig. The main tunnel leads toward both the Crowned Rooster Chamber and the apartments we allotted to the Satrap. Work together and you can get access to both."

Reyn gave his brother a betrayed look. "If only you'd listened to me last night," he said accusingly.

"If only you'd been sober last night," Bendir retorted. He turned on his heel and left the room. Jani and Reyn hastened after him.

UNSTACKING THE BOATS TO FIND THE BEST ONE WAS A DIFFICULT TASK IN the tight space of the collapsed boat-house. After she had chosen the best one, getting it outside proved even more of a task. Kekki was virtually useless. When her weeping finally stilled, it was because she had fallen asleep. The Satrap made an effort, but it was like being assisted by a large child. He had no concept of physical work. She tried to keep her temper with him, even reminding herself that last year she had been just as ignorant.

He was afraid of the work. He would not grip the wood, let alone put real muscle into dragging the boat out. With an effort, Malta held her tongue. By the time they had managed to get the boat out of the cleft and onto the leaf-strewn ground outside, she was completely exhausted. The Satrap brushed his hands and beamed down on the boat as if he had brought it out himself. "Well," he declared with satisfaction. "That's done it. Fetch some oars and we're off."

Malta had sunk down to the ground and leaned back against a tree. "Don't you think," she asked, fighting to hold back the sarcasm, "that we should see if it still floats first?"

"Why shouldn't she?" He put a foot on the boat's prow possessively. "She looks fine to me."

"Wood shrinks when it's out of water. We should put it in shallow water, and let the wood swell up a bit and see how much water it ships. If you have never heard before, I'll tell you now. The water of the Rain Wild River eats wood. And flesh. If it doesn't float high and dry, we'll need to put something in the bottom to rest our feet on. Besides, I'm too exhausted to row anywhere just now, and we aren't sure where we are. If we wait until dusk, we may be able to see the lights of Trehaug through the trees. That would save us a lot of time and effort."

He stood, looking down at her, balanced between offense and consternation. "Are you refusing to obey me?"

She met his gaze unflinchingly. "Do you want to die on the river?" she asked.

He bridled at that. "Do not dare to speak to me as if you were a Companion!"

"Perish the thought," Malta agreed with him. She wondered if anyone else had ever dared to disagree with him before. With a groan, she got to her feet. "Help me," she said, and began to shove the boat toward the swamp. His help consisted in taking his foot off the prow. She ignored that. She put the boat in shallow standing water. There was no line to tie it up, but there was no current to draw it away either. She hoped it would stay there, and was suddenly too weary to worry any more about it.

She looked at the Satrap, who was still glaring at her. "If you're going to stay awake, maybe you could find some oars. And you might keep an eye on the boat so it does not float away. It's the best of the lot that was down there, and none too good at that." She wondered at her tone, and then as she lay down on the earth and closed her eyes, she identified it. That was how her grandmother had always spoken to her. She understood why, now. She ached all over, and the ground was hard. She slept.

REYN HAD NOT CONVINCED THEM; HE HAD SIMPLY GONE ON. IF HE HAD waited for them to completely clear and shore up the main passage before advancing along it, Malta would certainly be dead before he got to her. He had wormed his way past two blocking falls and finally reached a portion of the main passage that was still intact when he came to the end of the thin line he had been paying out. He set a large chunk of fallen rock atop it. He had paused to mark his sign on the wall with star-chalk. The stuff would show well in even the faintest light. They would know he had been there and gone on. He had marked his passage through the falls, indicating the best places to start the re-excavation. He had an instinct for these things.

The scene with Malta's mother had been awful. He had found her helping to barrow out rubble from the tunnel. The bandages on her damaged hand were smudged with dirt. When he asked her if she had seen Malta, the worry she had contained had broken forth on her face. "No," she said hoarsely. "Nor Selden. But, of course, they could not be down there."

"Of course not," he lied, feeling ill. "I'm sure they'll turn up. They probably went walking in Trehaug together. No doubt they are wondering where everyone else has gone." He tried to put some of his own belief in his tale, but could not find it. She read the horror in his eyes. A sob caught in her throat. He could not face her. He headed down into the buried city. He did not promise her that he would bring her children back to her. He had already lied to her once.

Despite the fresh falls, he had moved with confidence through his city. He knew the strengths and weaknesses of it as he knew his own body. He diverted the diggers from one tunnel that he was certain was a loss, and moved them to another fall that they swiftly cleared. Bendir wanted him to go from site to site, carrying a lantern and map and passing out advice. He had flatly refused. "I'm working with those who are tunneling toward the Crowned Rooster Chamber. Once we reach there and rescue Malta, I'll work wherever else you put me. But that is my priority."

There had nearly been a confrontation, but Mother had reminded

Bendir again that the trapped Satrap and his Companion were along that route as well. Bendir grudgingly nodded. Reyn picked up his supplies and set out. He carried water, chalk, line, candles and a tinderbox in a bag slung over his shoulder. Digging and prying tools clanked at his belt. He did not bother with a lantern. The other men might need light to work by, but not him.

As he hurried down the passage, he trailed the chalk along the wall just above the failed jidzin. Truly, the city was dying when he could not waken even a glow from it. Perhaps it was broken in too many pieces now to work anymore. He wondered mournfully if he had forever lost his chance to puzzle out how it had worked.

He came to the chamber where they had secured the Satrap. It had been one of the most beautiful chambers they had ever discovered, but the Satrap and his Companion had wallowed in it as if it were a sty. Cosgo truly seemed to have no idea of how to care for himself. Reyn understood the need for servants. His family had hired help who cooked, cleaned and sewed. But a servant to put the shoes on your feet? A servant to comb your hair for you? What sort of a man needed another man to do that for him?

Water was oozing slowly from beneath the door. Reyn tried to open it, but something heavy pressed against it from the other side. Probably a wall of earth and mud, he reflected grimly. Reyn pounded on the door and shouted, but got no response. He listened to the silence. He tried to feel sorry for how they had perished, but could only remember the look he had seen on the man's face as he looked down at Malta in his arms. Even the memory of it knotted the muscles in Reyn's shoulders. The mud and earth had given the Satrap a swifter death than Reyn would have worked on him, if he had ever looked at Malta like that again.

He marked the door to let the diggers know he regarded it as hopeless. Let them rescue the living in the next few days. Recovering bodies could wait. He set his chalk to the wall and walked on.

A dozen strides further and he stumbled over a body. He fell with an oath, then immediately groped his way back. Someone small, the body still warm. Alive. "Malta?" he dared to hope.

"No. It's Selden," replied a small miserable voice.

He gathered the trembling boy in close to him. His body was chilled. Reyn sat on the floor and pulled him into his lap. He chafed his arms and legs as he asked him, "Where is Malta? Close by?"

"I don't know." The boy's teeth began to chatter. Waves of shivering ran over him. "She went in. I was afraid. Then there was the quake. When she didn't come out, I made myself follow her." He peered up at Reyn in the darkness. "Are you Reyn?"

Bit by bit, Reyn pieced the story together. He gave the lad water, and lit a candle to give him courage. In the flickering light it cast, Selden looked like a little gray old man. His face was smeared with dirt, his clothes heavy with it. His hair was caked to his skull. He could not tell Reyn where he had wandered in his searching. Only that he had called and called for her, and not finding her, he had pressed on. In his heart Reyn cursed both Wilee, for showing Selden how to sneak into the city, and himself, for not seeing that the abandoned tunnels were better secured against adventurous small boys. Two parts of Selden's account struck more fear into Reyn than he could explain. Malta had come here, deliberately seeking the dragon. Why? But as ominous as that was, when Selden mentioned the music she had heard, Reyn bit his lip. How could she have heard it? She was Bingtown born. Few even of Rain Wild stock could hear those elusive notes. Those who could were kept out of the tunnels. That was why he had never told his mother or his brother that he could hear it. Those who heard the music eventually drowned in the memories. So said all who worked the city. Even his father. His father had heard the music and worked the city anyway, until the day they found him sitting in the dark, surrounded by small cubes of black stone. He had drowned in the memories of the city, losing all remembrance of his own life. When they found him, he was sitting in the darkness, stacking blocks like a great babe.

"Selden," he spoke softly. "I have to go on. I know the way to the chamber where the dragon is buried. I think Malta would have discovered the way there. Now." He took a breath. "You have to decide. You can wait here for the diggers. Perhaps Malta and I will be back before they get here. Or you can go on with me, to look for Malta. Do you understand why I can't take you back to the surface right now?"

The boy scratched the caked dirt on his face. "Because she might be dead before you got back to her." He sighed heavily. "That's the same reason I didn't go back out and look for help, back when I knew the way out. I was afraid help would be too late."

"You've a brave heart, Selden. That doesn't mean you should have let it lead you here, but it's a brave heart, none the less." He stood the boy on his feet, then stood up himself. He took Selden's hand. "Come on. Let's go find your sister."

The boy clutched the candle as if it held his life. He was game, but exhausted. For a short way, Reyn slowed his pace to the boy's. Then, despite Selden's objections, he boosted the boy to his back. Selden held the candle aloft and Reyn trailed his chalk along the wall. They pressed on against the darkness.

Even the wavering light of the candle was not kind. It showed Reyn all he had avoided knowing. His city was surrendering. The quakes of last night had pushed it beyond endurance. It would persist for a time as fragments of itself—disconnected wings and isolated chambers—but eventually all would crumble. The earth had swallowed it years ago. Now it would digest it. His dream of seeing the entire sprawling edifice un-earthed and lit again with the light of day was a dream with no future.

He strode resolutely along, humming to himself. The boy on his shoulders was silent. Had he not held the candle so unwaveringly, Reyn would have believed him asleep. His humming masked the other sounds he did not want to hear. Distant groans of overstressed timbers, dripping and trickling water, and the faint, pale echoes of ancient voices talking and laughing in a by-gone day. He had long ago learned to guard against being too aware of them. Today, as he mourned the passing of his city, its memories pressed against him, seeking to burn themselves into his mind. "Remember us, remember us," they seemed to plead. If he had not had Malta to think of, he would have given in to them. Before Malta, the city had been his life. He would not have been able to contemplate surviving its death. But he did have Malta, he thought fiercely to himself. He did have her, and he would not surrender her, not to the city, not to the dragon. If all else he loved must perish, her he would preserve.

The door to the Crowned Rooster Chamber hung ajar. No. A closer look revealed it had been forced out of its frame. He gazed briefly on the gaudy cockerel that had become his family's symbol. He slid Selden from his back to the floor. "Wait right here. This chamber is dangerous."

Selden's eyes widened. It was the first time Reyn had spoken aloud of the danger. "Will it fall down on you?" he asked anxiously.

"It crushed me a long time ago," Reyn admitted. "Stay here. Keep the candle."

If Malta were alive and conscious, she would have heard their voices. She would have called out. So. He would look for her body and hope the breath of life was in it yet. He knew she had come here. Without hope, he slapped the jidzin beside the entrance. A faint glow, lighting little more than itself, trickled like slow syrup away from his hand. He forced himself to stand patiently as it encircled the room.

The damage was immense. The domed ceiling had given way in two places, dumping wet earth in mounds onto the floor. Roots dangled down beside the hanging fragments of crystal panes. He saw no sign of Malta. Hand trailing on the light bar, he made a slow circuit of the room. When he came to the first fallen panel with its mechanisms inside it, he felt ill. Here was what he had known must exist. He had searched for it so long, only to have the random violence of the quake reveal it. When he reached the second panel, he scowled. He lit another candle for himself, to confirm what he already knew. Human hands had dug out the packed earth from around these mechanisms. A few small muddy footprints could be clearly seen within the glow of the candle. She had been here.

"Malta!" he called, but there was no reply.

In the center of the room, the immense log of wizardwood was a contained silence. He longed to know what the dragon knew, but to touch the wood would be to give himself back to her power. The leash she had had on him had been snapped. Soon the earth would collapse on her, burying her, and he would be free of her forever. She could not seize him if he did not touch the wood. She had only been able to reach Malta's mind through his.

"Malta!" he called again, far louder. His voice, which once would have rung in this chamber, was swallowed and damped by the wet earth.

"Did you find her?" Selden called anxiously from the door.

"Not yet. But I will."

Dread was in the boy's voice as he called out, "There's water coming. From under the wall. It will run down the steps soon."

Earth might press, but water devoured. With an angry roar, Reyn charged at the log of silent wood. He slammed his hands flat onto it. "Where is she?" he demanded. "Where is she?"

The dragon laughed. Her laughter boomed through his mind, slamming him with familiar pain. She was back, back in his head. He was sickened by what he had done, but knew he had had no choice.

"Where is Malta?"

"Not here." Insufferable smugness.

"I know that, damn you. Where is she? I know you are linked with her, I know that you know."

She gave him a faint waft of Malta, like waving a bit of meat above a dog's nose. He sensed her through the dragon. He felt her exhaustion, and knew the leaden ache of her sleep.

"This city cannot stand much longer. It is going to collapse. If you don't help me find her and get her out, she'll die."

"How excited you are about that! Yet it never seemed to bother you that that was my eventual fate."

"That's not true. Damn you, dragon, you know that is not true. I have agonized over your fate; I have begged and pleaded with my kind to help you. Through the years of my youth, I near worshiped you. There was not a day I did not come to you. I did not try to escape you until you turned against me."

"Yet you were never willing to surrender to me. A pity. You could have learned all the secrets of the city in a single night. As Malta did."

His heart stood still in him. "You drowned her," he said flatly. "You drowned her in the city's memories."

"She dove into them, most willingly. From the moment she entered the city, she was far more open to it than any other I have encountered. She dove and she swam. And she tried to save me. For your sake and the sake of her father."

You were the price I was to pay, Reyn. I was to leave you in peace forever in exchange for her freeing me. A pity for you that she did not succeed."

"The water is coming faster, Reyn!" The boy's shrill voice broke into the dialogue in his mind. Reyn turned to look at him. The candle illuminated his small gray face. He stood on the steps, just inside the door. The water flowed past his feet in a sheet and cascaded silently down the broad shallow stairs. It reflected the light of the boy's candle with an eerie beauty. Death gleamed in the darkness.

He smiled sickly at the little boy. "It will be all right," he lied ruthlessly. "Come here, Selden. There is a last thing for us to do, you and I. Then we'll be finished here."

He took the boy's gritty hand in his. Wherever Malta slept in the city, she slept her last sleep. The sheeting water told him all. It would all be over far more swiftly than he had ever feared.

He turned his back on the wizardwood log. He led Selden to the first panel on the wall. He fixed the candle to the wall with a bit of wax, then smiled at the boy in the darkness. "There's a great big door here. All we have to do, you and I, is open it. A lot of dirt will come down with it, as it opens. Don't be afraid. Once we get these cranks to turn, we just have to keep turning them. No matter what. Can you do that?"

"I guess so," the boy replied dubiously. He could not seem to take his eyes off the water.

"Let me try this one first. I'll let you have whichever one is easier to turn."

Reyn set his hands to the crank. He bore down on it with all his weight. It did not move. Remorselessly, he took a claw tool from his belt. He struck the main shaft of the crank mechanism several times, then tried his strength against it again. It resisted for a moment, then slowly the wheel turned, grating past some coarseness in its works. It would turn, but it would be hard work for the boy. Reyn took a pry bar from his belt and shoved it through the spokes of the crank. "You work it like this. Stick it through a spoke, brace it against this thing and then pull down. Try it."

Selden was able to move the wheel a notch. Reyn heard the thud of the counterweight inside the wall. He smiled with satisfaction. "Good. Now move the bar to the next spoke and get a fresh bight on it. That's right."

When he was content that the boy had the knack of it, he left him there and moved to the other panel. He worked quickly to clear more of the soil away from the workings. He refused to think about the results of what he was doing. He focused instead on how he would accomplish it.

"What are you doing?" The dragon's voice was soft in his mind.

He laughed aloud. "You know what I'm doing," he muttered to her. "You know every thought in my head. Don't give me doubts now."

"I don't know everything about you, Reyn Khuprus. I never foresaw that you might do this. Why?"

He roared with laughter this time. He pitied Selden. The poor boy stared at him in wonder, but feared to ask what was wrong or even to whom he spoke. "I love you. I love the city, and for me you have always been the heart of the city. I love you and so I strive to save what I can of it. What might survive."

"You believe you will die if you turn the crank. You and the boy both."

He nodded to himself. "Yes. But it will be more quickly than if we wait and let the water eat out the walls and bring them down on us."

"Can't you go back the way you came?"

"Do you seek to dissuade me from what you have begged me to do for years?" he asked her in amusement. Then he answered her question. "The way back is already gone. The Satrap's chamber was oozing water. That door is only wood. It could not hold. I suspect it is the source of the water that flows in even now. I am done, dragon, and the boy with me. However, if we collapse the ceiling, some light may break through. If it does, then you may survive us. If not, then we will all be buried together."

He waited in vain for her reply. When it came, it surprised him. She left him. There was no lingering aura of gratitude, not even a farewell. She was simply gone.

He rapped the shaft sharply with his claw tool. He set his hands to the crank. He suspected that once the counterweights in the wall started moving, the momentum might take over. Or perhaps the wheel would turn no more than a notch or two. He would not think of that. Slow death alone he might be able to face. Slow death with a young boy at his side would be torture eternal. He shoved the claw tool through the spokes of the wheel and braced it. He looked at Selden. The whites of the boy's fearful eyes gleamed in the candlelight. "Now!" he told him.

They leaned on the bars. The wheels turned grudgingly, but they turned. The door groaned warningly. Move the bar up a spoke, lean. Move the bar up a spoke, lean on it again. Reyn heard the counterweights shifting inside the wall. Surely by now something should suddenly take over the work of the task. He wondered how many barrows full of earth were pressed up against the door. It had settled solidly for years; how many, no one knew. How could he even imagine that he could open it, let alone that the earth would break in and light shine through? It was ridiculous. Move the bar up another spoke. Lean on it.

Cruelly, the light bar suddenly sprang to life, illuminating the final destruction of the city. It lit up the spreading cracks across the murals and the gleaming water on the floor. For the first and last time in his life, Reyn got a fleeting glimpse of the true beauty of the room. He stared up in awe. As he looked, something cracked sharply, not in the door, but up overhead. Crystal shards of one of the great windows of the dome fell like great icicles. They shattered to dust on the floor of the chamber. A trickling of soil followed them. Nothing more.

"Keep going, lad," Reyn encouraged Selden. In unison they moved their bars, and leaned on them. Another groaning notch.

Suddenly, on Reyn's side of the door, there was a tremendous series of pops. Instinct sent him diving toward Selden as the door suddenly burst unevenly from its track. The edge of the door bowed in, a great vertical crack that reached from the floor to the top of the door. Suddenly the sagging and splitting spread from there. Like the shell of a dropped egg, the cracks spread out across the dome above. Crystal panes and plaster frescoes fell like rotten fruit from windswept trees. There was no place to escape the bombardment as the ceiling randomly surrendered to the weight of earth atop it.

Reyn clutched the boy to him and hunched over him as if his paltry body could save him from the forces of the earth. The boy clung to him, too frightened to scream. One great intact panel of the ceiling fell with a crash. It landed against the wizardwood log and leaned there. Selden wriggled loose from his grip. "Under there. We should get under there!" Before he could clutch at him, the boy was racing across the chamber, dodging falling pieces of ceiling and heaps of debris on the floor. He scooted under the fallen ceiling piece.

"The rising water will drown us there!" Reyn roared after him. Then he was following the boy's zigzag course, to scuttle into the dubious shelter of the leaning ceiling panel. The light bar failed. They plunged into darkness as the ceiling came down with a roar.

SHE WOKE UP BECAUSE SOMEONE WAS NUDGING HER IN THE BACK. "IT'S NOT funny, Selden! That hurts!" she snapped at him.

She rolled over, fully intending to give him a good shaking. Suddenly the warmth and safety of her bedroom at home vanished. She was cold and stiff. Leaves crinkled under her cheek. The Satrap poked her again with his foot. "Get up!" he commanded her. "I see lights through the trees."

"Kick me again, and you'll see lights with your eyes shut!" she snapped at him. He actually stepped back from the threat.

It was evening. It was not quite dark enough for stars to show, but it was dark enough that the yellow gleam of lamplight showed well. Her heart lifted and sank simultaneously. They knew where to go now, but it seemed very far away. She stood slowly, easing her body to her feet. Everything hurt.

"Did you find any oars?" she asked the Satrap.

"I am not a servant," he pointed out coldly.

She folded her arms on her chest. "Neither am I," she declared. She scowled to herself. It was going to be black as a tomb back in the collapsed boat-house. How could the Satrap, rightful ruler of all Jamaillia, be such a useless, stupid man? Her wandering eyes took in Kekki. The Companion was sitting hopefully in the boat. She looked like a dog expecting an outing. The water was so shallow that the boat had sunk to the bottom under her weight. Malta barely repressed a terrible urge to laugh. She looked back at the Satrap. He was staring at her severely. Then she did laugh. "I suppose the only way I'm going to be rid of you both is to take you back to Trehaug."

"At which time, I will see you are punished appropriately for your lack of respect," the Satrap announced imperiously.

She cocked her head at him. "Is that supposed to make me eager to take you back?"

He was silent for a moment. Then he drew himself up. "If you act swiftly to obey me now, I shall take that into account when I judge you."

"Will you?" she asked him archly. Then, suddenly, she wearied of the game. She walked away from him, back to the dark cave-like opening where the remains of the building projected from the earth. There was no part of her body that did not hurt. Her feet were bruised and sore, her knees and back ached as she crouched down to re-enter the ruins. She searched in the dark, by touch. She had no means of re-lighting the lantern they had carried. She found no oars, but did manage to pull loose some pieces of wood that might serve. Like the boats, they were cedar. They would not fit the oarlocks, but she could pole with one of them, she thought. As long as she kept to the shallows of the swamps, they would do. It would be hard work, but they could get back to Trehaug. Once there, she would have to confess all her foolishness. She would not think about that, not just yet.

She frowned to herself, briefly, as she crawled out of the ruins dragging her boards. She had intended to do something. Something to do with the city, with boards like these. When she had left the city, she had had some firm, fixed purpose. She groped after it, but could only recall a dream from her afternoon's sleep. A dream of flying through darkness. She shook her head. It was most peculiar. It was not that she could not remember; the problem was that she remembered so much, she could not sort out what parts of it belonged to her. From the time she had entered the buried city, few of her actions seemed like something she would do.

When she got back to the boat, she found both the Satrap and his Companion sitting in it. "You'll have to get out," she pointed out to them patiently. "We'll have to push the boat to deeper water before you can get in. Otherwise, it won't float."

"Can't you just row us to deeper water?" Kekki asked plaintively.

"No. I can't. The boat has to be floating before we can row it." As she waited for them to disembark, Malta reflected that she had never paused to think how much she knew simply by virtue of her upbringing. There was a lot to be said, after all, for being a Trader's daughter.

It took some time in the twilight to find a place suitable to launch. Both Kekki and the Satrap seemed extremely uneasy with the rocking of the small vessel as they clambered down into it from a tree root. Malta directed one to each end and took the center. She would have to stand to pole the boat along. When she had been younger, she had had a little pram she had rowed about in the ornamental pond. This was very different from that. She wondered if she could do it. Then she lifted her eyes to the glimmering lights of Trehaug. She would make it. She knew it. She seized one end of her board and pushed the boat off.

CHAPTER THIRTY-EIGHT

Paragon's Captain

TWO DAYS HAD PASSED SINCE THE BATTLE WITH THE SERPENT. THE SHIP had almost settled back into routine. Haff had attempted to return to his duties, but after an hour in the sun, he had fainted and nearly fallen from the rigging. His attitude toward Althea was markedly more deferential. The rest of the crew seemed to be following his example. Haff had not thanked her for saving his life, but she told herself she hadn't really expected that from him. It was, after all, part of her duties. She'd be content if he accepted that there were areas in which she was his better. She wondered idly which act had actually finally gained the men's respect: threatening to throw Artu overboard or standing up to the serpent. She still hurt all over, but if it had finally secured her berth as second, then it had been worth it.

Brashen still looked terrible. The blisters on his face had broken and the skin was peeling. It made him look lined and old and weary. Or perhaps he actually felt that way. Brashen had summoned them to his cabin. Now, as Althea glanced from Lavoy to Amber to Brashen, she wondered why. His eyes were grave as he announced, "The crew seems to have finally settled into its duties. The ship is being run competently, though there is still room for everyone to sharpen up. Unfortunately, in the waters ahead, seamanship may not be as important as our ability to fight. We need to determine our expectations from the crew, in the event of encountering pirates and serpents." He frowned and leaned back in his chair. Then he nodded at the table and the chairs surrounding it. A handful of canvas scraps was on one corner of the table. There was also a bottle of brandy and four glasses. "Please. Be seated." As they took their seats, he poured a jot of brandy into each glass. When all were settled, he offered them a toast. "To our success, thus far. And to our continued success."

They drank together. Brashen leaned forward and rested his arms on the table. "Here is how I see things. The men know how to brawl. Believe it or not, that was one of the things I considered in hiring. But now they need to be taught how to battle. By that, I mean as a unified force, one that listens to commands even in the midst of danger. They need to know how to defend Paragon, as well as how to attack another ship intelligently. It can't be every man for himself. They have to trust the judgment of the officers. Haff learned the hard way that the ship's officers have reasons for their orders. I want to start training the men while that is still fresh in their minds."

Brashen's eyes roamed the table and came to rest on Lavoy. "We discussed this when you were hired. It's time to begin training. I want some drill every day. The weather has been fine, the ship fair sails himself. Let's learn while we have leisure for it. I also want to see more cohesiveness in the crew. Some of the men still treat those who were formerly slaves as beneath them. I want that changed. There should be no sense of difference from man to man. They're all crewmen, no more, nor less."

Lavoy was nodding. "I'll mix them up more. Up to now, I've let them pair up for work as they wanted. I'll start assigning work groups. They'll resist at first. There'll be a few broken heads before it's all settled."

Brashen sighed. "I know. But try not to let them disable each other in the process of getting acquainted."

Lavoy gave a mirthless laugh. "I was talking about what I might have to do to them. But I take your drift. I'll start drilling them with weapons. Wooden stuff, to start with."

"Let them know that the better fighters will get the better weapons. That may make them strive a bit harder." Brashen abruptly shifted his attention to Amber. "As long as we are speaking of weapons, I'll say this now. I want you to arm the ship. Can you devise a suitable weapon for Paragon to use to fend off serpents? A spear of some kind? And do you think he could be taught to employ it against another ship as well?"

"I suppose I could." Amber sounded surprised.

"Then do it. And create a mounting system for it, so that he can have quick access to it on his own." Brashen looked concerned. "I fear we'll have more trouble with those creatures, the deeper we go into pirate waters. I want to be ready next time."

Amber looked disapproving. "Then I suggest that, based on what I've heard from Althea, the crew has to be made to understand that serpents won't react like most animals. The men should be told to ignore them and not provoke them until they've actually begun an attack. They won't flee from a spear jab. They'll attempt revenge." She crossed her arms on her chest when Brashen frowned at her and continued, "You know it's true. And that being the case, are we wise to arm Paragon? It isn't just that he's blind. His judgment is not always . . . well-considered. He might attack a serpent that was merely curious, or even well-disposed toward us. I suggest that he should have a weapon, but not one he can seize on his own impulse. The serpents affect him strangely. From what he says, I suspect it may be mutual. He claims that the serpent we killed had been following us for days, trying to talk to him. As much as we can, I suggest we avoid the serpents. When we do encounter them, I think we should avoid making enemies of them." She shook her head. "The death of the last serpent has affected him strangely. He seems almost to mourn it."

Lavoy made a small contemptuous sound. "Make enemies of the serpents? Serpents talking to Paragon? You sound as mad as the ship. Serpents are animals. They don't think, or plan; they don't have feelings. If we hurt them bad enough, kill enough of them, they'll avoid us. I'm with the captain. Arm the ship." He shrugged at her cold stare. He cocked his head and challenged her. "Only a fool would think differently."

Amber was unruffled. "I think differently." She gave Lavoy a cool and mirthless smile. "It's not the first time I've been called a fool, and likely not the last. Still, I will tell you this. In my opinion, men deny animals have feelings and thoughts for one basic reason: so they won't feel guilty about what they do to them. But in your case, I think it's so you don't fear them quite as much."

Lavoy shook his head in disgust. "I'm not a coward. And I'm not likely to feel bad about anything I do to a serpent. Unless I'm stupid enough to be his supper." He shifted his feet, and turned his attention to Brashen. "Sir. If you're satisfied, I'd like to get back on the deck. To have us all closeted like this will make the crew jumpy."

Brashen gave him a nod. He leaned forward in his chair to make a note in the logbook in front of him. "Begin weapons drill. But emphasize quick obedience as much as skill right now. Make sure they understand they aren't to act until they're told to, especially if the enemy is a serpent. Make the best use of the men we have. Two of the former slaves have substantial weapons experience. Put them in charge of some of the drills. And Jek. She's quick and knows her way around a blade. I want any barriers that might keep them from fighting as a unit broken down." Brashen frowned for a moment. "Amber will create a weapon for the ship, and she will instruct him in it." He met the carpenter's eyes. "When he is armed will be at her discretion, unless I countermand it. I believe her observations regarding serpents and their effect on the ship have merit. Our tactic regarding serpents will be first to avoid and ignore. We fight them only if we're attacked." He paused to let his words sink in on Lavoy. His voice was firm as he added, "I think I've covered all I had for you. You can go."

A terrible look fleeted over Lavoy's face. Amber met it squarely. Brashen had done little save rephrase Amber's suggestions as an order. Another man might have accepted that, but Lavoy clearly resented it. Althea watched him thinly mask his resentment as he bowed curtly to

Brashen and headed for the door. She and Amber both stood to follow, but a curt sign from Brashen stopped them. "I've other tasks to go over with both of you. Sit down."

Lavoy halted. Glints of anger danced in his eyes. "Are these tasks I should be aware of, sir?"

Brashen eyed him coldly. "If they were, I'd have ordered you to stay. You have your tasks. Get to them."

Althea took a silent breath and held it. She thought Lavoy would challenge Brashen right then. The stare that held between the two men was edged. Lavoy moved his mouth as if he would speak, then curtly nodded instead. He turned. He did not slam the door as he left, but shut it smartly.

"Was that wise?" Amber dared to ask in the silence that followed.

Brashen gave her a cold captain's look. "Not wise perhaps, but necessary." He sighed as he leaned back in his chair. He poured himself another jot of brandy. Instructively, he addressed Amber. "He's the mate. I can't allow him to think he is my voice, nor that no opinion save his and mine count. I asked you here for your opinion. For him to disparage that is not acceptable." He allowed himself a small, tight smile. "But keep in mind that for me to do that would be entirely within my authority."

Amber frowned, but Althea instantly grasped his position. She suddenly looked at him with new eyes. He had it. Whatever that indefinable quality was that made a man capable of captaining a ship, Brashen had it. There were new lines in his brow and at the corners of his eyes. But he had also drawn that cold hard line that separated the commander from his crew. She wondered if he were lonely. Then she knew it did not matter. He was what he had to be. He could not be any other way and still command effectively. She felt a pang of loss that the line must separate him from her as well. But the surge of pride she felt in him overwhelmed any selfish regrets. This was what her father had seen in him. Brashen had justified all of Ephron Vestrit's belief.

For an instant, he looked at her without speaking, as if he could sense her thoughts. Then he gestured at the scraps of canvas on the table. "Althea. You've always had a better hand with a pen than I did. These are rough sketches. I'd like you to make clean copies of them. They're all I could chart of the pirate ports I visited with the *Springeve*. We'll look for *Vivacia* first in Divvytown, but I doubt we'll be lucky enough to catch her there. These bits of charts may come in handy. If you have any questions, I'll go over them with you. When they're finished, we need to bring Lavoy in on them as well. He doesn't read, but his memory is sharp. It's important this knowledge is shared amongst us."

The words he left unspoken chilled her. He was obviously considering what would be best for the ship and crew in case of his death. She had avoided thinking of such things. He had not. That, too, was part of command. He pushed the scraps of canvas toward her and she began to leaf through them. His next words to Amber brought her attention back to him.

"Amber. Last night, you were over the side. Paragon was holding you. I heard your voices."

"I was," Amber agreed evenly.

"Doing what?"

The carpenter looked extremely uncomfortable. "Experimenting."

Brashen sighed out through his nose. "I won't tolerate that from Lavoy. What makes you think you can adopt that attitude?" More gently, he added, "If it happens on the ship, and I think it's my business, I'll know about it. So tell me."

Amber looked down at her gloved hands. "We all discussed this before we left Bingtown. Paragon knows of the work I did on Ophelia. He supposes that if I could restore her hands, I could give him eyes again." Amber licked her lips. "I have my doubts."

Brashen's tone was dangerous. "As I do. As you were well aware. I told you before we sailed, this is no time for risky experiments in wizardwood carving. A failure that disappointed him could endanger us all."

Anger flickered over Amber's face.

"I know what you are thinking," Brashen told her. "But it isn't something that is between the two of you. It involves all of us."

She took a breath. "I haven't touched his eyes, sir. Nor told him that I would."

"Then what were you doing?"

"Erasing the scar from his chest. The seven-pointed star."

Brashen looked intrigued. "Has he told you what the star means?"

Amber shook his head. "I don't know. I only know that whatever memories it holds for him are extremely unpleasant. It was a sort of a compromise. That encounter with the serpent disturbed him. Deeply. He has thought of little else since then. I sense that he is reconsidering all he is. He's like a boy in adolescence. He has decided that nothing is the way he believed it to be, and is reconstructing his whole vision of the world." She took a deep breath as if to say something important. She seemed to reconsider it, and said instead, "It's a very intense time for him. It is not necessarily bad, what he's doing, but it's deeply introspective. For Paragon, that means sifting through some very bad memories. I sought to distract him."

"You should have asked me first. And you should not be over the side without someone watching you."

"Paragon was watching me," she pointed out. "And holding me while I did the work."

"Nevertheless." Brashen made the single word a sharp warning.

"When you are over the side, I want to be aware of it." More gently, he asked, "How is the work progressing?"

Amber kept her temper. "Slowly. The wood is very hard. I don't want to just plane it off and leave a different sort of scar. I'm more obscuring than erasing it."

"I see." Brashen stood and paced a turn around the chamber. "Do you think it's possible you could restore his eyes?"

Amber shook her head regretfully. "I'd have to rework his whole face. The wood is simply gone. Even if I just carved eyes there, there is no guarantee he could see out of them. I have no idea how the magic of wizardwood works. Nor does he. I'd be taking a great risk, and possibly damaging him more."

"I see." Brashen considered a moment longer. "Carry on with the scar, but I want you to take the same precautions I'd expect of any other hand. This includes having a partner of some kind when you are over the side. In addition to Paragon." He was silent briefly, then nodded. "That's all, then. You can go."

Althea suspected it was not easy for Amber to accede to Brashen's authority. She rose to his command, not resentfully, as Lavoy had, but stiffly, as if it offended her sense of self. Althea rose to follow her out, but Brashen's voice stopped her at the door. "A last word with you, Althea."

She turned back to him. He glanced at the door standing ajar. She shut it quietly. He took a deep breath. "A favor. I've put Amber in a bad position with Lavoy. Watch over her—no, that's not what I mean. She's as dangerous to him as he is to her. He just doesn't know that yet. Watch the situation. If it looks as if they will clash, warn me. Lavoy is bound to have resentments, but I won't permit him to take them too far."

She nodded, then spoke the words. "Yes, sir."

"One other thing." He hesitated. "You're all right? Your hands, I mean?"

"I think so." She flexed her fingers for him. She waited.

It took a time before he spoke. "I want you to know—" His voice went quiet. "I wanted to kill Artu. I still do. You know that."

She smiled crookedly. "So did I. I tried." She pondered an instant. "But it was better as it came out. I beat him. He knows it. The crew knows it. If you had jumped in, I'd still be trying to prove myself to them. But it would be worse now." She suddenly knew what he had to hear from her. "You did the right thing, Captain Trell."

His real smile broke through briefly. "I did, didn't I?" There was real satisfaction in his voice.

She crossed her arms and held them tightly against her chest to keep from going to him. "The crew respects your command. So do I."

He sat a bit straighter. He didn't thank her. It wouldn't have been appropriate. She walked quietly from the room. She didn't look back at him as she quietly closed the door between them.

AS SHE CLOSED THE DOOR, BRASHEN SHUT HIS EYES. HE'D MADE THE RIGHT decision. And they had made the right decision. They both knew it. They had agreed that it was better this way. Better. He wondered when it was going to get easier.

Then he wondered if it would ever get easier.

"THERE'S TWO OF US." PARAGON DIVULGED THE SECRET TO HER AS HE HELD her in his hands. She weighed so little. She was like a doll stuffed with millet.

"So there is," Amber agreed. "You and I." The rasp moved carefully over his chest. It reminded him of a cat's tongue. No, he corrected himself. It would have reminded Kerr Ludluck of a cat's tongue. That long-dead boy had liked cats and kittens. Paragon had never had one.

Paragon. Now there was a name for him. If only they knew. The secret he held slipped from him again. "Not you and I. Me and me. There's two of us."

"Sometimes I feel that way myself," Amber replied easily. Sometimes, when she was working, he felt like she went somewhere else.

"Who is your other me?" he demanded.

"Oh. Well. A friend I had. We used to talk a lot. Sometimes I hear myself still talking to him, and I know how he would answer."

"I'm not like that. There has always been two of me."

She returned the rasp to the tool sling. He could feel her do it, and felt the shift of her weight as she searched for something else. "I'm going to use sandpaper now. Are you ready?"

"Yes."

She went on as if she had not interrupted the conversation. "If there are two of you, I like both. Keep still now." The sandpaper worked back and forth against his chest. The friction made heat. He smiled to her words because they were true, even if she didn't know it.

"Amber? Have you always known who you were?" he asked curiously.

The sandpaper stopped. In a guarded voice, she replied, "Not always. But I always suspected." She added in her normal voice, "That's a very odd question to ask."

"You're a very odd person," he teased, and grinned.

The sandpaper moved against him slowly. "You are one spooky ship," she said quietly.

"I haven't always known who I was," he admitted. "But now I do, and that makes it all easier."

She set aside the sandpaper. He heard the clink of tools as she rummaged for something else. "I have no idea what you mean by that, but I'm happy for you." She was distracted again. "This is an oil pressed from seeds. On ordinary wood, it swells the fibers and can erase a scratch. I have no idea what it will do on wizardwood. Shall we try a little and see?"

"Why not?"

"A moment." Amber leaned back in his arms. Her feet were braced against his belly. She wore a safety line, but he knew she trusted more to him. "Althea?" Amber called up to the deck. "Have you ever used oil on wizardwood? For maintenance?"

He felt Althea stand. She had been lying flat on her belly, drawing something. She came to the railing and leaned over. "Of course. But not on painted surfaces like the figurehead."

"But he's not really painted. The color is just . . . there. All through the wood."

"Then why is the chopped part of his face gray?"

"I don't know. Paragon, do you know why?"

"Because it is." It was odd. When he tried to tell them something about himself, they didn't listen. Then they pried into things that were not their business. He tried again. "Althea. There are two of me."

"Go ahead and use the oil. It can't hurt. It will either sink in and swell the wood, or it will stay on top and we can wipe it off."

"What if it stains?"

"It shouldn't. Try a little bit and see."

"I'm not just what the Ludlucks made of me!" he burst out suddenly. "There is a me I was before, just as much a part of me. I don't have to be whom they made me. I can be who I was. Before."

A shocked silence greeted his words. Amber was still in his hands. It shocked him when she reached out and set her gloved hands on either side of his face. "Paragon," she said quietly. "Perhaps the greatest thing one can discover is that you can decide who you are. You don't have to be whom the Ludlucks made you. You don't even have to be who you were before that. You can choose. We are all creatures of our own devising." Her hands traveled over the high bones of his cheeks. When her hands came to where his beard began, she tugged it playfully, on either side. It could not have been a stronger reminder of the human elements in his makeup. Yet it was as she had just said.

"I don't have to be what you want me to be, either," he reminded them both. His hands closed around Amber. Such a trifling toy she was, a creature made mostly of water enclosed in a bag of thin skin. If humans ever grasped completely how fragile they were, they would not be so cocky. With one hand, he casually snapped her safety line.

"I want to be alone now," he told her. "I have something I want to think about." He lifted her over his head and he felt her stiffen in his hands. Her sudden realization that he could dash her down into the water brought a smile to his lips. She knew now what he had finally discovered. "I have choices to consider," he told her. He swung her over his head and held her steady until she grasped the railing. When he knew she was secure, he let go of her. Althea was there, grabbing hold of her and pulling her onto the deck. He heard Althea's low question, "Are you all right?"

"I'm fine," Amber said softly. "Just fine. And I think Paragon is going to be just fine also."

CHAPTER THIRTY-NINE

Dragon Rising

DAWN AND DAYLIGHT WERE ALWAYS TWO DIFFERENT THINGS IN THE RAIN Wilds. The rising of the sun meant little until it was high enough to clear the lush canopy of the Rain Wild forest. Reyn Khuprus watched the first thin trickling of light through a gap between mud and crystal. The wizardwood log at his back, the fallen section of thick crystal dome that had sheltered them and the mud that surrounded them now bordered his world. He half-crouched and half-leaned against the wizardwood block. The fallen arch of ceiling dome overhead had protected them from the falling debris, but the rising muck and water had found them. The fallen section had acted as a partial dam. In its shelter, the thick mud had only flowed in thigh-deep on him, with a layer of chill water on top of it. He held Selden in his arms, sharing his scant body warmth. Despite all, the boy was asleep. Exhaustion and despair had claimed him.

Reyn did not wake him now. The pale light was a false hope. It came from a small crack far overhead. Although much of the building's constructed dome and ceiling had fallen in, the thick layer of roots woven through the soil still supported the earth above them. Only one small, root-fringed crevice admitted the daylight. Even if he had been able to claw clear of the muck and debris that surrounded them, they could never reach the tiny hole to escape.

As he watched the light gain strength, he knew with despair that they would try. The boy in his arms would wake. They would dig their way out and stand on top of the wizardwood log and call for help. But no one would hear them. They would die here, and it would not be swift.

He hoped Malta's end had been faster.

Selden stirred, lifting his head from Reyn's shoulder. The shift in his weight woke new pain in Reyn's back. Selden made a questioning sound. Then he set his head back down on Reyn's shoulder. Helpless, silent sobs shook the boy. Reyn patted him with a muddy hand and said the useless, inevitable words. "Well. I suppose we should try to get out of here."

"How?" Selden asked.

"We'll have to dig this gap bigger and shove you out of it. Then you'll climb up on top of the log." He shrugged. "From there, we'll have to figure out what to do next. Call for help, I suppose."

"What about you? You're stuck in pretty deep."

Reyn tried to shift his feet. The boy was right. The flowing muck that had flooded the chamber last night was settling. From his thighs down, he was engulfed in a thick porridge of earth and water. It gripped his legs heavily. "Once I've got you up there, I'll be able to dig myself out. Then I'll join you on the log." The lie came easily.

Selden shook his head. "It won't work. Not for either of us. Look. It's melting."

He lifted one grubby hand free from its clutch around Reyn's neck and pointed.

The thin slice of sunlight shafted down through the dim chamber. Motes danced in it like dust. But these motes twisted and turned in an odd updraft of steam. There was a distinctive unpleasant scent in the air. "Smells like your hands after you've played with garter snakes," Selden observed. "But stinkier."

"Hold tight to me. I need both my hands free," Reyn replied.

It was not the hope of escape that made him dig like a dog. He only wanted to see what was happening. The thick crystal of the dome piece that sheltered them admitted light but was too dirty to see through. He wanted a clear view. He had wondered too long not to take this last chance to know. So he pulled handfuls of muck into their sheltered burrow, heedless that he buried himself deeper. He enlarged fractionally the opening they could see through, and then stared.

Sunlight rested on the upper corner of the wizardwood log nearest to him. It bubbled wetly and then melted down, like sea foam left on the beach by a retreating tide. It made no sense. Sunlight had never affected the wizardwood planks they had hauled out of the city. Liveships did not melt in the sun.

"Because liveships are dead," a voice whispered in his mind. *"But I am not. I live."*

It was not a swift process. As the sun rose higher, the shaft of light traveled over the wizardwood. It left bubbling goo in its wake. When the sun was overhead and strongest, the reaction quickened. The wood simmered like steaming porridge. The stench of reptile grew stronger.

The boy grew bored with watching the phenomenon. He was hungry, thirsty, tired and cold. So was Reyn, but somehow his own discomfort did not matter. Malta's death had numbed his instinct for self-preservation. He saw little chance for their survival. It was hard to press himself to act, but the melting of the wizardwood finally forced him. As the immense log bubbled and collapsed in on itself, the heavy crystal section of ceiling propped against it and cupped over them began to lean lower. As he and Selden were beneath it, they had to move or face immediate drowning.

He lifted the boy higher and Selden twisted in his arms, so that he was on his back as Reyn thrust him out of the closing gap. Reaching up, Selden caught the broken lip of the ceiling piece. He dragged himself out from under it. Twisting onto his belly, he wallowed through the muck and finally clambered onto the crystal section. Now it was Reyn's turn. He had to move fast, for the boy's weight on top was pushing the ceiling piece deeper into the mire. He dug with his hands and arms in the muck, like a sea turtle thrashing out a nest in the sand. He felt his feet come out of his boots. He thrust his hands into the muck to unbuckle his belt of tools and wiggle free of it. Flopping and wallowing, he crabbed out from under the curved edge of the crystal section. He had to put his face in the mud to wriggle through, but he managed it. Once he had emerged from beneath the cupping crystal, he had to turn and flounder his way back to it. Wallowing to stay on top of the muck, he struggled to haul himself out onto the smooth curved surface of the crystal. Selden helped as much as he was able, clutching at Reyn's wrists and tugging mightily. With a final heave, he flopped his way onto the ceiling fragment.

For a moment, he lay belly down and panting. Then the ceiling section gave a short lurch and began sinking beneath him. He hoped the bubble of air trapped beneath it would slow the process. He opened his eyes and lifted his head. Selden, wordless with wonder, clutched at him.

Beside them, the melting wizardwood log was not dribbling away into the muck. It was liquefying and being absorbed. Revealed now was the curled and emaciated form of a dragon embedded in it. As the wizardwood around her melted, it flowed toward her. The shaft of sunlight illuminated a miracle. Her skin absorbed the liquid, and her body swelled with it. She changed from black to deep blue. The bones and withered muscle and skin plumped with life and took on flesh. She stirred feebly in the collaps-ing remnants of her chrysalis. She twisted, and Reyn got his first glimpse of her wings. They were folded tight against her back. They looked like sticks and wet paper. She made an effort to unfurl one. It was insubstan-tial, a thin flap of transparent hide stretched over thin bone or white cartilage. She lifted her snout, snorted, and then abruptly opened one new wing. It was immense. It slapped against the melting remains of the wizardwood and the surrounding muck. Awkwardly she rolled from side to side, trying to get her feet under her. She leaned on her untried wings like crutches, splatting mud with them as she struggled to right herself. She unlimbered a long neck, lifting her head blindly toward the sunlight, and opened her mouth as if she could drink the light. Thick white lids covered her eyes. Her head swayed on her neck as she yearned toward the light.

She shifted again, to reveal a long tail bunched beneath her. The remains of the wizardwood were vanishing rapidly. The heavy mud was already lapping in to replace it. Reyn watched helplessly. She would be engulfed before she had ever flown.

Then, with a sound like wet canvas unfurling, she raised her wings. Mud smeared them. She flopped them awkwardly, and a heavy reptilian odor wafted over Reyn and the boy. Pulsing veins were outlined briefly in the stretched membrane of her wings. Then, like dye spilled in water, color flowed through them. Her wings went from transparent to translucent to a rich sparkling blue. As she waved them slowly and unevenly, Reyn could see the strength building in them. She unlidded her eyes suddenly; they glinted silver. She looked at herself. *"Blue. Not silver, as I dreamed. Blue."*

"You're beautiful," Reyn breathed.

She startled at his voice. She coiled her neck to stare intently at Reyn and Selden. Selden scuttled into the shelter of Reyn's body. "It's going to eat us!" he wailed.

"I don't think so," Reyn breathed. "But lie still. Don't move." The boy remained plastered against his side. Reyn slowly put an arm over Selden to reassure him. He kept his own eyes fixed on the dragon. Her tail uncoiled, slicing a path over the surface of the engulfing mud. She suddenly threw back her head and trumpeted. It rang in Reyn's ears as much as his mind. Triumph and defiance were in that cry. It crashed against the confines of the chamber.

She reared back abruptly on her hind legs, balancing herself against the thick portion of her serpentine tail. He saw her crouch, and clutched Selden more tightly. Wings half spread, she sprang suddenly toward the crack in the ceiling. Her head crashed against the remnants of the dome, and she fell back. But her forepaws had clutched and scrabbled briefly against the overhead crack. As she dropped, a ragged section of earth and roots came with her. The wind of her battering wings and the fall of earth buffeted Reyn and Selden. Her sprawling displacement of the mud made their island tilt toward her. Reyn clutched frantically at the smooth surface as it threatened to spill them into the mud under her great churning feet.

She gathered herself for another try. Reyn clutched Selden and tried to stay on top of the debris. She sprang again. This time her head went through the hole overhead. Her clutching forelegs seized the edge of the opening. Her huge body dangled momentarily. Her hind legs kicked and her tail lashed past them, missing them but not by much. Her wings bunched against the ceiling and held her back as she tried to crawl out. With a rending sound, more of the ceiling overhead gave way. She came down in an avalanche of ceiling bits and dirt. A slide of earth followed, collapsing in with her, including an entire tree that came to rest leaning drunkenly against the opening. The dragon landed heavily on her side in the muck.

Selden struggled against Reyn's grip on him. "If we can get to that tree, we can climb out!" he cried. He pointed at the leaning trunk and limbs that bridged a path to the surface.

"Not while she's thrashing around. We'll be trampled into the muck."

"If we stay here, she'll trample us anyway," Selden shouted. "We have to try!"

"Stay down!" Reyn ordered him, and enforced it with his weight. The boy whimpered under his chest as the crystal tilted more sharply.

She sprang again. She clawed the tree out of her way, and gained the edge of the enlarged hole. All light was blocked as she clung there, kicking and scrabbling. Reyn felt the swift brush of her tail tip. It tore the coarse fabric of his trousers and scoured the skin from his calf in passing. He roared with pain, but kept his grip on Selden. Clumps of earth, straggles of root and pieces of ceiling rained down around them as the wedged dragon fought to emerge from her tomb. Some light broke through to them. It outlined her struggling body above them. The tail swept again, and this time it slapped them both solidly. Reyn and Selden were flung from their crystal island into the mire. They splatted in the thin layer of water and then felt the swift suck of the mud. "Spread your weight!" Reyn ordered the boy. He splayed his limbs out over the mire, hoping to float atop it a little longer.

"She's going to fall and crush us," Selden wailed. He clutched at Reyn and instinctively tried to climb on top of him. Reyn stiff-armed the boy away. "Lay wide on the top, and pray!" he shouted.

More of the dome was coming down. Debris was mixed with the earth. Small trees and some coarse ferns and grasses crashed down. "She's going to make it," Reyn roared as she hitched her rib cage up over the edge. He heard her triumphant trumpet. The soar of joy in his heart surprised him. There was a final shower of earth and debris. Then sunlight flooded the ruined chamber. Her long tail lashed its way up and vanished. He heard her roar again, and felt the wind of her frantically beating wings. He did not see her rise with his eyes, but he felt it in his heart. Stillness flowed back with her passing. She was gone.

Tears streamed down his face. He stared up at the small window of blue summer sky. She might be the last of her kind, but at least she would fly before she died.

"Reyn. Reyn!" There was annoyance in Selden's voice. He turned his face toward the sound and then blinked his eyes to adjust them. The boy had pulled himself out onto a large chunk of grassy earth that had landed upright on the muck. He stood up and pointed at a dangling network of roots that hung down from the ceiling. "I think we can pile up enough stuff for me to grab hold of those roots. I could climb out and go for help." His eyes darted around the room hopefully. In addition to more hunks of crystal, there were pieces of old timber and parts of trees now atop the muck.

Careless of mud and water, Reyn rolled over on his back and considered it. The roots were not thick, but the boy didn't weigh much. "I think you're right," he conceded. "Maybe we'll come out of this alive after all." He rolled back to his belly and began to flounder his way over to the boy.

As he grasped at the coarse grass and hauled himself out of the mud and onto solid ground, Selden asked him, "Do you think maybe Malta got out, too?"

"She might have," Reyn said. He thought he lied, but as he spoke, a sudden lift in his heart told him he not only hoped, he believed it possible. With the flight of the dragon, all things seemed possible. As if in echo of his thought, he heard the far-away echoing of the dragon's trumpeting cry. He glimpsed a flash of a brighter blue against the sky.

"If my mother or brother sees or hears her, they'll know where she came from. They'll search and send help to us. We're going to live."

Selden met the older man's eyes. "Until then, let's try to get ourselves out," he proposed. "After all we've been through, I don't want to be rescued by someone else. I want to do it myself."

Reyn grinned and nodded.

TINTAGLIA BANKED OVER THE WIDE RAIN WILD RIVER VALLEY. SHE TASTED the summer air, rich with all the smells of life. She was free, free. She beat her wings strongly, flapping them harder than she must, for the simple joy of experiencing her own strength. She rose through the blue summer day, soaring up to where the air was thin and chill. The river became a sparkling silver thread in the green tapestry below her. She had in her memory the experiences of all her forebears to draw upon, but she savored for the first time her own flight. She was free now, free to create her own memory and life. She circled lazily down, considering all that lay before her.

She had a task before her, the task that she alone remained to perform. She must find the young ones, and protect and guide them in their migration up the river. She hoped that some remained alive to be guided. If not, she would truly be the last of her kind.

She tried to dismiss the humans from her mind. They were not Elderlings, who knew the ways of her kind and accorded dragons proper respect. They were humans. One could not owe anything to such beings. They were creatures of a few breaths, frantic to eat and breed before their brief span of days was done. What could one of her kind owe to something that died and rotted swifter than a tree did? Could one be in debt to a butterfly or a blade of grass?

She touched them briefly with her mind, a final time. They had not long to live. The female struggled like a beetle in a puddle, floating and flailing against moving water. Reyn Khuprus was where she had left him, mired in mud and squirming like a worm. He struggled in the self-same chamber where she had languished for so many years.

The brevity of their lives suddenly touched her. In the momentary twinkling of their existence, each of them had tried to aid her. Each had taken time from their mate quest to try to free her. Poor little bugs. It was a small cost to her, these few moments out of the vast store of years to come. She turned a lazy loop in the sweet summer air. Then with strong, steady beats of her wings, she drove herself back toward the buried city.

"I'm coming!" she called to them both. "Don't fear. I'll save you."

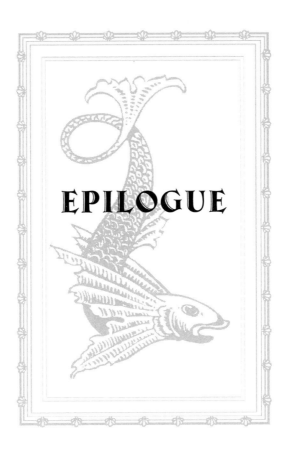

EPILOGUE

CHAPTER FORTY

The Memory of Wings

"WE KNOW WHERE WE ARE GOING, AND WHY. WHY MUST WE PUSH OUR-selves so hard, swimming so swiftly and for so much of the day?" The slender green minstrel was limp in the grasp of the tangle. He lacked even the strength to return the grip of the other serpents. He trusted them to hold him as he swayed in the moving current like seaweed. Shreever pitied him. She lapped another coil of her length around his frail body and held him more securely.

"I think," she bugled softly, "that Maulkin drives us so hard because he fears that our memories may fade again. We must reach our goal before we lose our purpose. Before we forget where we go, and why we go there."

"There is more to it than that," Sessurea added. He, too, sounded weary. But there was a lilt of pleasure in his voice. There was such com-fort in knowing the answer. "The seasons are turning. We are nearer the end of summer than the beginning. We should have been there by now."

"We should even now be wrapped in silt and memories, letting the sun bake our memories into us while we make our change," Kelaro added.

"Our cases must be hard and strong before the rains come and the chill of winter. Otherwise, we may perish before we have completed our metamorphosis," scarlet Sylic reminded them all.

The other serpents in the tangle added their voices, speaking low to one another. "The water must still be warm for the threads to form best."

"Sunlight and warmth are needed for the shell to be hard."

"It must bake through, solid and firm, before the change can begin."

Maulkin opened his great eyes. His false eyes shimmered gold with pleasure. "Sleep and rest, little ones," he told them blandly, ignoring the fact that several of the serpents were far larger than he was, and many were his equal. "Dream well and take comfort in all we know. Speak of it to one another. Sharing the memories Draquius gave us will help us to preserve them."

They trumpeted their agreements softly as they wrapped and secured one another. The tangle had grown. In the wake of Draquius' sacrifice, many of the feral serpents had shown signs of returning memory. Some still did not speak. Nevertheless, from time to time intelligence flashed briefly in their eyes, and they behaved as if they were a true part of the tangle, even to joining the others at rest. There was comfort in greater numbers. When they met other serpents now, the outsiders either avoided Maulkin's tangle or followed and gradually became a part of them. Maulkin had confided to them the hope that when they reached the river and migrated up to the cocooning grounds, even the most bestial might feel the stir of memories.

Shreever lidded her eyes and sank down to dream. That was another recovered pleasure. In her dreams, she flew again, as she recalled her forebears had done. In her dreams, she had already changed to a fine dragon, with the freedom of the three realms.

"But do not become overly confident in these memories," Maulkin abruptly added. He did not proclaim it loudly. Only she, Sessurea and a few others closest to him opened their eyes to his voice.

"What do you mean?" Shreever asked him in dread. Had not they suffered enough? Now they remembered. What was to stop them from reaching their goal?

"Nothing is quite right," Maulkin said quietly. "Nothing is as it was, nothing is exactly as it should be. We must swim fast and well, to allow ourselves time to overcome obstacles along the way. Be assured, there will be obstacles."

"What do you mean?" Sessurea asked plaintively, but Shreever thought she already knew. She kept silent and listened to the prophet's reply.

"Look around you," he bade them. "What do you see?"

Sessurea spoke for them all. "I see the Plenty. I see the remains of old structures tumbled on the seafloor. I see the Arch of Rythos in the distance. . . ."

"And is not the Arch of Rythos, in all your memories, a pleasant place to perch after an afternoon of flying about the Lack? Did not it stand tall and proud at the entrance to Rythos Harbor? Why is it scattered and broken and swallowed by the Plenty?"

No one replied. All waited for his answer.

"I do not know either," Maulkin rumbled softly when the silence had grown long. "However, I suspect that these things are what have long confused us. They are why things were almost familiar, why we could nearly recall the way, and yet could not."

"Is the fault ours alone?" Tellur demanded. Shreever had thought the slender green minstrel was asleep. His tired voice had an indignant ring to it. "The memories that Draquius bequeathed to us tell us that we should look for serpents who remember, ones in whom the memories have remained clean and strong. Not only those ones, but also guides are supposed to assist us. Where are the grown dragons that should have stood guard at the river mouths, to protect us as we swarm? Why have we seen nothing of the generation that went before us?"

Maulkin's voice went soft with pity. "Have not you grasped it, Tellur? Draquius told us what became of them. Some perished in the rain of smoke and ash. Those few who had a chance at survival were slain and their memories stolen. They are the silver ones we have encountered from time to time. They smell to us like Ones Who Remember, because at one time they were. All that is left is their stolen memories."

For a moment, all was silence. Slowly the sick realization settled into Shreever. This tangle was all that was left. They had to survive, on their own, if their species was to continue. They must puzzle out for themselves which river led to the cocooning grounds. They must defy predators to swarm up the river. Somehow, they must create their own cases, without the loving aid of grown dragons. And once encased and helpless, they would have to trust to luck to survive the winter. There would be no dragons standing watch over them. Her gaze traveled from serpent to serpent. How many of those tangled here would spread their dragon wings next spring? Would there be enough survivors to select suitable mates when the time came? How many would survive to guard the nests until the eggs hatched? When the young serpents wriggled from the beach to the sea, to begin their first cycle of migrating and feeding in the sea, there would be no grown serpents to teach them the ways of the sea. The odds against the survival of her kind suddenly seemed insurmountable. If she survived to become a dragon, she faced a long, long life of watching dragons and sea serpents vanish from the three realms. How could it be endured?

"They belonged to us," Tellur declared bluntly.

"What does?" Shreever asked distantly. The future, she thought to herself. The tomorrows belonged to us. No longer.

"The memories. The memories stored in the silver ones. They are ours, and having them makes us stronger." He suddenly broke free of the tangle with a lash of his tail. "We should take them back!"

"Tellur." Maulkin gently untangled himself from the others. He moved to flank the smaller serpent without challenging him. "We do not have time to take vengeance."

"Not vengeance! I am talking of taking what is rightfully ours, what is greater sustenance to us than the food we eat. The memories were shared amongst us. What one should have possessed was divided amongst many; nevertheless, we became wiser, and each has shared what was learned. How much more would we benefit from a greater portion of those memories? We should seek them out and take back what is ours."

Swifter than a school of herring changes direction, Maulkin wrapped him. He had glided up to the small minstrel so easily and calmly that

Tellur had never seen it coming. Maulkin's golden eyes twined about Tellur's green coat, and his great head wound up face-to-face with Tellur's small one. Maulkin opened wide his jaws, and breathed a fine mist of toxin at the minstrel. Dominated, the smaller serpent became quiescent in his coils. Tellur's eyes spun in lazy dreams.

"We have no time for that," Maulkin asserted quietly to all of them as he towed his lax companion back to the tangle. "If the opportunity to take another silver presents itself, we shall have it. That I promise you. But we cannot delay our migration to seek them. Rest well, Maulkin's tangle, for tomorrow we press on."

Tomorrow, Shreever thought to herself as the tangle writhed, coiled and re-anchored itself. There is yet another tomorrow that is ours. She lidded her eyes against silt and let herself dream of wings.

SHE WAS CRIPPLED. SHE WOULD NEVER SWIM AS EASILY AS A DRAGON RIDING an updraft. She had been kept too long in confinement and fed too restricted a diet. She could not straighten her body to its full length, stunted though that was. She was heavy and thick where she should have been sleek and muscular. Perhaps it was permanent, perhaps it was hopeless.

But without doubt she was free.

And without doubt or regret, she had slain the Abominations who had imprisoned her. Never would they torment another young serpent as they had tormented her. She wished she could kill them over and over again, endlessly, and forever take satisfaction in the act. Even as she desired it, she recognized it as yet another of the deformities they had inflicted on her. She tried to cast it out of herself.

She had seen the little two-legs taken up in a rowboat, and then followed it protectively until it was taken up by a greater vessel. The scent of the ship troubled her. It smelled like a serpent, and yet it was not. Moreover, it smelled like One Who Remembered, and yet it was a tongueless thing that answered her not. She did not want to consider how that could be. The answers could be hidden in the boy's knowledge that she had shared so briefly. She considered taking the time to follow the ship and puzzle these things out.

But a greater urgency beckoned her. After all the seasons of imprisonment, fate had freed her. She was destined to be a guide to her own kind, yet here she was, still close to the beach where she had hatched. She had not migrated with them; she had not fed with them and grown in bulk, as she should have. Yet as twisted and stunted as she might be, she still held that which was most essential to them. In her glands and toxins resided the ancient knowledge of her race. It was to be shared with them, before they swarmed up the river to begin their change. As she humped and writhed through the water, she doubted that she herself could make the arduous journey up the river. Yet she would seek out the others and share with them the stored memories.

She came briefly up into the Lack, tasting the free salt wind. On the deck of the silver vessel, men cried out at the sight of her. She dove swiftly again and made her decision. The silver ship was bound back toward the islands. Beyond the islands was the mainland, and in the mainland was the mouth of the river that led to the cocooning grounds. That was her destination. She would stay alongside the silver vessel as long as their paths lay in the same direction. There was something, perhaps, to be learned here. Besides, she was intrigued with the small thinking animals on the ship. She would study them. When at last she rejoined whatever remained of her own kind, she would have memories of her own to share as well. Let her confined life offer at least that much to her kind. She Who Remembered dove deep and tried to stretch her crippled muscles. As she returned almost to the surface, she found that position where the wake of the ship helped draw her along after it. She settled into it, and continued toward her destiny.

ABOUT THE AUTHOR

ROBIN HOBB was born in California but spent most of her formative years in Fairbanks, Alaska. She presently resides in Tacoma, Washington, with a rather large canine, four cats, and various and sundry offspring and relatives. A lifelong love of fantasy and science fiction led her to pursue her career in that area. She is the author of The Farseer Trilogy (*Assassin's Apprentice*, *Royal Assassin*,and *Assassin's Quest*). She is presently engaged in finishing the Liveship Trader's Trilogy, with *Ship of Destiny* to come in 2000.